D1079619

By Ian Rankin

The Inspector Rebus series
Knots & Crosses
Hide & Seek
Tooth & Nail
Strip Jack
The Black Book
Mortal Causes
Let It Bleed
Black & Blue
The Hanging Garden
Death Is Not The End (*novella*)
Dead Souls
Set in Darkness
The Falls
Resurrection Men
A Question of Blood
Fleshmarket Close
The Naming of the Dead

Other novels
The Flood
Watchman
Westwind

Writing as Jack Harvey
Witch Hunt
Bleeding Hearts
Blood Hunt

Short stories
A Good Hanging and Other Stories
Beggars Banquet

Non-fiction
Rebus's Scotland

Omnibus editions
Rebus: The Early Years (Knots & Crosses, Hide & Seek, Tooth & Nail)
Rebus: The St Leonard's Years (Strip Jack, The Black Book, Mortal Causes)
Rebus: The Lost Years (Let It Bleed, Black & Blue, The Hanging Garden)
Rebus: Capital Crimes (Dead Souls, Set in Darkness, The Falls)

All Ian Rankin's titles are available on audio. Also available:
Jackie Leven Said by Ian Rankin and Jackie Leven.

Born in the Kingdom of Fife in 1960, Ian Rankin graduated from the University of Edinburgh and has since been employed as grape-picker, swineherd, taxman, alcohol researcher, hi-fi journalist and punk musician. His first Rebus novel, *Knots & Crosses*, was published in 1987 and the Rebus books have now been translated into 26 languages. Ian Rankin has been elected a Hawthornden Fellow, and is a past winner of the prestigious Chandler-Fulbright Award, as well as two CWA short-story 'Daggers' and the 1997 CWA Macallan Gold Dagger for Fiction for *Black & Blue*, which was also shortlisted for the Mystery Writers of America 'Edgar' award for Best Novel. *Black & Blue*, *The Hanging Garden*, *Dead Souls* and *Mortal Causes* have been televised on ITV, starring John Hannah as Inspector Rebus. *The Falls* and *Fleshmarket Close* have also been shown on ITV, starring Ken Stott as Rebus. *Dead Souls*, the tenth novel in the series, was shortlisted for the CWA Gold Dagger Award in 1999. An Alumnus of the Year at Edinburgh University, he has also been awarded four honorary doctorates, from the University of Abertay Dundee in 1999, from the University of St Andrews in 2001, in 2003 from the University of Edinburgh and in 2005 from the Open University. In 2002 Ian Rankin was awarded an OBE for services to literature. In 2004 *Resurrection Men* won the Edgar Award for Best Novel. In 2005 *Fleshmarket Close* won the Crime Thriller of the Year award at the British Book Awards. Ian is the winner of the Crime Writers' Association Diamond Dagger 2005. In 2005 he was also awarded the Grand Prix du Littérature Policier (France), the Deutsche Krimi Prize (Germany) and the Icons of Scotland award. He lives in Edinburgh with his wife and two sons. Visit his website at www.ianrankin.net.

IAN RANKIN

The Hanging Garden
Hide & Seek

The Hanging Garden
First published in Great Britain by Orion Books Ltd in 1998

Hide & Seek
First published in Great Britain by Orion Books Ltd in 1993

This omnibus edition published in 2009
by Orion Books Ltd
Orion House, 5 Upper St. Martin's Lane,
London
WC2H 9EA

An Hachette UK company

A CIP catalogue record for this book is available
at the British Library.

ISBN 9781407221199

Printed in Great Britain by Clay Ltd, St Ives plc

The Orion Publishing Group's policy is to use papers that are
natural, renewable and recyclable products and made from wood
grown in sustainable forests. The logging and manufacturing
processes are expected to conform to the environmental
regulations of the country of origin.

www.orionbooks.co.uk

The Hanging Garden

'If all time is eternally present
All time is unredeemable.'

T.S. Eliot, 'Burnt Norton'

'I went to Scotland and found nothing
there that looks like Scotland'

Arthur Freed, Producer *Brigadoon*

They were arguing in the living-room.

'Look, if your bloody job's so precious ...'

'What do you want from me?'

'You know bloody well!'

'I'm working my arse off for the three of us!'

'Don't give me that crap.'

And then they saw her. She was holding her teddy bear, Pa Broon, by one well-chewed ear. She was peering round the doorway, thumb in her mouth. They turned to her.

'What is it, sweetie?'

'I had a bad dream.'

'Come here.' The mother crouched down, opening her arms. But the girl ran to her father, wrapped herself around his legs.

'Come on, pet, I'll take you back to bed.'

He tucked her in, started to read her a story.

'Daddy,' she said, 'what if I fall asleep and don't wake up? Like Snow White or Sleeping Beauty?'

'Nobody sleeps forever, Sammy. All it takes to wake them up is a kiss. There's nothing the witches and evil queens can do about that.'

He kissed her forehead.

'Dead people don't wake up,' she said, hugging Pa Broon. 'Not even when you kiss them.'

1

John Rebus kissed his daughter.

'Sure you don't want a lift?'

Samantha shook her head. 'I need to walk off that pizza.'

Rebus put his hands in his pockets, felt folded banknotes beneath his handkerchief. He thought of offering her some money – wasn't that what fathers did? – but she'd only laugh. She was twenty-four and independent; didn't need the gesture and certainly wouldn't take the money. She'd even tried to pay for the pizza, arguing that she'd eaten half while he'd chewed on a single slice. The remains were in a box under her arm.

'Bye, Dad.' She pecked him on the cheek.

'Next week?'

'I'll phone you. Maybe the three of us ...?' By which she meant Ned Farlowe, her boyfriend. She was walking backwards as she spoke. One final wave, and she turned away from him, head moving as she checked the evening traffic, crossing the road without looking back. But on the opposite pavement she half-turned, saw him watching her, waved her hand in acknowledgement. A young man almost collided with her. He was staring at the pavement, the thin black cord from a pair of earphones dribbling down his neck. Turn round and look at her, Rebus commanded. Isn't she incredible? But the youth kept shuffling along the pavement, oblivious to her world.

And then she'd turned a corner and was gone. Rebus could only imagine her now: making sure the pizza box was secure beneath her left arm; walking with eyes fixed firmly ahead of her; rubbing a thumb behind her right ear, which she'd recently had pierced for the third time. He knew that her nose would twitch when she thought of something funny. He knew that if she wanted to concentrate, she might tuck the corner of one jacket-lapel into her mouth. He knew that she wore a bracelet of braided leather, three silver rings, a cheap watch with black plastic strap and indigo face. He knew that the brown of her hair was its natural colour. He knew she was headed for a Guy Fawkes party, but didn't intend staying long.

He didn't know nearly enough about her, which was why he'd wanted them to meet for dinner. It had been a tortuous process: dates rejigged, last-minute cancellations. Sometimes it was her fault, more often his. Even tonight he should have been elsewhere. He ran his hands down the front of his jacket, feeling the bulge in his inside breast pocket, his own little time-bomb. Checking his watch, he saw it was nearly nine o'clock. He could drive or he could walk – he wasn't going far.

He decided to drive.

Edinburgh on firework night, leaves blown into thick lines down the pavement. One morning soon he would find himself scraping frost from his car windscreen, feeling the cold like jabs to his kidneys. The south side of the city seemed to get the first frost earlier than the north. Rebus, of course, lived and worked on the south side. After a stint in Craigmillar, he was back at St Leonard's. He could make for there now – he was still on shift after all – but he had other plans. He passed three pubs on his way to his car. Chat at the bar, cigarettes and laughter, a fug of heat and alcohol: he knew these things better than he knew his own daughter. Two out of the three bars boasted 'doormen'. They didn't seem to be called bouncers these days. They were doormen or front-of-house managers, big guys with

4

short hair and shorter fuses. One of them wore a kilt. His face was all scar tissue and scowl, the scalp shaved to abrasion. Rebus thought his name was Wattie or Wallie. He belonged to Telford. Maybe they all did. Graffiti on the wall further along: Won't Anyone Help? Three words spreading across the city.

Rebus parked around the corner from Flint Street and started walking. The street was in darkness at ground level, except for a café and amusement arcade. There was one lamppost, its bulb dead. The council had been asked by police not to replace it in a hurry – the surveillance needed all the help it could get. A few lights were shining in the tenement flats. There were three cars parked kerbside, but only one of them with people in it. Rebus opened the back door and got in.

A man sat in the driver's seat, a woman next to him. They looked cold and bored. The woman was Detective Constable Siobhan Clarke, who had worked with Rebus at St Leonard's until a recent posting to the Scottish Crime Squad. The man, a Detective Sergeant called Claverhouse, was a Crime Squad regular. They were part of a team keeping twenty-four-hour tabs on Tommy Telford and all his deeds. Their slumped shoulders and pale faces bespoke not only tedium but the sure knowledge that surveillance was futile.

It was futile because Telford owned the street. Nobody parked here without him knowing who and why. The other two cars parked just now were Range Rovers belonging to Telford's gang. Anything but a Range Rover stuck out. The Crime Squad had a specially adapted van which they usually used for surveillance, but that wouldn't work in Flint Street. Any van parked here for longer than five minutes received close and personal attention from a couple of Telford's men. They were trained to be courteous and menacing at the same time.

'Undercover bloody surveillance,' Claverhouse growled. 'Only we're not undercover and there's nothing to survey.' He tore at a Snickers wrapper with his teeth and offered the first bite to Siobhan Clarke, who shook her head.

'Shame about those flats,' she said, peering up through the windscreen. 'They'd be perfect.'

'Except Telford owns them all,' Claverhouse said through a mouthful of chocolate.

'Are they all occupied?' Rebus asked. He'd been in the car a minute and already his toes were cold.

'Some of them are empty,' Clarke said. 'Telford uses them for storage.'

'But every bugger in and out of the main door gets spotted,' Claverhouse added. 'We've had meter readers and plumbers try to wangle their way in.'

'Who was acting the plumber?' Rebus asked.

'Ormiston. Why?'

Rebus shrugged. 'Just need someone to fix a tap in my bathroom.'

Claverhouse smiled. He was tall and skinny, with huge dark bags under his eyes and thinning fair hair. Slow-moving and slow-talking, people often underestimated him. Those who did sometimes discovered that his nickname of 'Bloody' Claverhouse was merited.

Clarke checked her watch. 'Ninety minutes till the changeover.'

'You could do with the heating on,' Rebus offered. Claverhouse turned in his seat.

'That's what I keep telling her, but she won't have it.'

'Why not?' He caught Clarke's eyes in the rearview. She was smiling.

'Because,' Claverhouse said, 'it means running the

6

engine, and running the engine when we're not going anywhere is wasteful. Global warming or something.'

'It's true,' Clarke said.

Rebus winked at her reflection. It looked like she'd been accepted by Claverhouse, which meant acceptance by the whole team at Fettes. Rebus, the perennial outsider, envied her the ability to conform.

'Bloody useless anyway,' Claverhouse continued. 'The bugger knows we're here. The van was blown after twenty minutes, the plumber routine didn't even get Ormiston over the threshhold, and now here we are, the only sods on the whole street. We couldn't blend in less if we were doing panto.'

'Visible presence as a deterrent,' Rebus said.

'Aye, right, a few more nights of this and I'm sure Tommy'll be back on the straight and narrow.' Claverhouse shifted in his seat, trying to get comfortable. 'Any word of Candice?'

Sammy had asked her father the same thing. Rebus shook his head.

'You still think Tarawicz snatched her? No chance she did a runner?'

Rebus snorted.

'Just because you want it to be them doesn't mean it was. My advice: leave it to us. Forget about her. You've got that Adolf thing to keep you busy.'

'Don't remind me.'

'Did you ever track down Colquhoun?'

'Sudden holiday. His office got a doctor's line.'

'I think we did for him.'

Rebus realised one of his hands was caressing his breast pocket. 'So is Telford in the café or what?'

'Went in about an hour ago,' Clarke said. 'There's a room at the back, he uses that. He seems to like the arcade, too. Those games where you sit on a motorbike and do the circuit.'

'We need someone on the inside,' Claverhouse said. 'Either that or wire the place.'

'We couldn't even get a plumber in there,' Rebus said. 'You think someone with a fistful of radio mikes is going to fare any better?'

'Couldn't do any worse.' Claverhouse switched on the radio, seeking music.

'Please,' Clarke pleaded, 'no country and western.'

Rebus stared out at the café. It was well-lit with a net curtain covering the bottom half of its window. On the top half was written 'Big Bites For Small Change'. There was a menu taped to the window, and a sandwich board on the pavement outside, which gave the café's hours as 6.30 a.m. – 8.30 p.m. The place should have been closed for an hour.

'How are his licences?'

'He has lawyers,' Clarke said.

'First thing we tried,' Claverhouse added. 'He's applied for a late-night extension. I can't see the neighbours complaining.'

'Well,' Rebus said, 'much as I'd love to sit around here chatting …'

'End of liaison?' Clarke asked. She was keeping her humour, but Rebus could see she was tired. Disrupted sleep pattern, body chill, plus the boredom of a surveillance you know is going nowhere. It was never easy partnering Claverhouse: no great fund of stories, just constant reminding that they had to do everything 'the right way', meaning by the book.

'Do us a favour,' Claverhouse said.

'What?'

'There's a chippy across from the Odeon.'

'What do you want?'

'Just a poke of chips.'

'Siobhan?'

'Irn-Bru.'

'Oh, and John?' Claverhouse added as Rebus stepped out of the car. 'Ask them for a hot-water bottle while you're at it.'

A car turned into the street, speeding up then screeching to a halt outside the café. The back door nearest the kerb opened, but nobody got out. The car accelerated away, door still hanging open, but there was something on the pavement now, something crawling, trying to push itself upright.

'Get after them!' Rebus shouted. Claverhouse had already turned the ignition, slammed the gear-shift into first. Clarke was on the radio as the car pulled away. As Rebus crossed the street, the man got to his feet. He stood with one hand against the café window, the other held to his head. As Rebus approached, the man seemed to sense his presence, staggered away from the café into the road.

'Christ!' he yelled. 'Help me!' He fell to his knees again, both hands scrabbling at his scalp. His face was a mask of blood. Rebus crouched in front of him.

'We'll get you an ambulance,' he said. A crowd had gathered at the window of the café. The door had been pulled open, and two young men were watching, like they were onlookers at a piece of street theatre. Rebus recognised them: Kenny Houston and Pretty-Boy. 'Don't just stand there!' he yelled. Houston looked to Pretty-Boy, but Pretty-Boy wasn't moving. Rebus took out his mobile, called in the emergency, his eyes fixing on Pretty-Boy: black wavy hair, eyeliner. Black leather jacket, black polo-neck, black jeans. Stones: 'Paint it Black'. But the face chalk-white, like it had been powdered. Rebus walked up to the door. Behind him, the man was beginning to wail, a roar of pain echoing into the night sky.

'We don't know him,' Pretty-Boy said.

'I didn't ask if you knew him, I asked for help.'

Pretty-Boy didn't blink. 'The magic word.'

Rebus got right up into his face. Pretty-Boy smiled and nodded towards Houston, who went to fetch towels.

Most of the customers had returned to their tables. One was studying the bloody palmprint on the window. Rebus saw another group of people, watching from the doorway of a room to the back of the café. At their centre stood Tommy Telford: tall, shoulders straight, legs apart. He looked almost soldierly.

'I thought you took care of your lads, Tommy!' Rebus called to him. Telford looked straight through him, then turned back into the room. The door closed. More screams from outside. Rebus grabbed the dishtowels from Houston and ran. The bleeder was on his feet again, weaving like a boxer in defeat.

'Take your hands down for a sec.' The man lifted both hands from his matted hair, and Rebus saw a section of scalp rise with them, like it was attached to the skull by a hinge. A thin jet of blood hit Rebus in the face. He turned away and felt it against his ear, his neck. Blindly he stuck the towel on to the man's head.

'Hold this.' Rebus grabbing the hands, forcing them on to the towel. Headlights: the unmarked police car. Claverhouse had his window down.

'Lost them in Causewayside. Stolen car, I'll bet. They'll be hoofing it.'

'We need to get this one to Emergency.' Rebus pulled open the back door. Clarke had found a box of paper hankies and was pulling out a wad.

'I think he's beyond Kleenex,' Rebus said as she handed them over.

'They're for you,' she said.

2

It was a three-minute drive to the Royal Infirmary.
Accident & Emergency was gearing up for firework
casualties. Rebus went to the toilets, stripped, and rinsed
himself off as best he could. His shirt was damp and cold to
the touch. A line of blood had dried down the front of his
chest. He turned to look in the mirror, saw more blood on
his back. He had wet a clump of blue paper towels. There
was a change of clothes in his car, but his car was back near
Flint Street. The door of the toilets opened and Claverhouse came in.

'Best I could do,' he said, holding out a black t-shirt.
There was a garish print on the front, a zombie with
demon's eyes, wielding a scythe. 'Belongs to one of the
junior doctors, made me promise to get it back to him.'

Rebus dried himself off with another wad of towels. He
asked Claverhouse how he looked.

'There's still some on your brow.' Claverhouse wiped
the bits Rebus had missed.

'How is he?' Rebus asked.

'They reckon he'll be okay, if he doesn't get an infection
on the brain.'

'What do you think?'

'Message to Tommy from Big Ger.'

'Is he one of Tommy's men?'

'He's not saying.'

'So what's his story?'

'Fell down a flight of steps, cracked his head at the bottom.'

'And the drop-off?'

'Says he can't remember.' Claverhouse paused. 'Eh, John ...?'

'What?'

'One of the nurses wanted me to ask you something.'

His tone told Rebus all he needed to know. 'AIDS test?'

'They just wondered.'

Rebus thought about it. Blood in his eyes, his ears, running down his neck. He looked himself over: no scratches or cuts. 'Let's wait and see,' he said.

'Maybe we should pull the surveillance,' Claverhouse said, 'leave them to get on with it.'

'And have a fleet of ambulances standing by to pick up the bodies?'

Claverhouse snorted. 'Is this sort of thing Big Ger's style?'

'Very much so,' Rebus said, reaching for his jacket.

'But not that nightclub stabbing?'

'No.'

Claverhouse started laughing, but there was no humour to the sound. He rubbed his eyes. 'Never got those chips, did we? Christ, I could use a drink.'

Rebus reached into his jacket for the quarter-bottle of Bell's.

Claverhouse didn't seem surprised as he broke the seal. He took a gulp, chased it down with another, and handed the bottle back. 'Just what the doctor ordered.'

Rebus started screwing the top back on.

'Not having one?'

'I'm on the wagon.' Rebus rubbed a thumb over the label.

'Since when?'

'The summer.'

'So why carry a bottle around?'

Rebus looked at it. 'Because that's not what it is.'

Claverhouse looked puzzled. 'Then what is it?'

'A bomb.' Rebus tucked the bottle back into his pocket. 'A little suicide bomb.'

They walked back to A&E. Siobhan Clarke was waiting for them outside a closed door.

'They've had to sedate him,' she said. 'He was up on his feet again, reeling all over the place.' She pointed to marks on the floor — airbrushed blood, smudged by footprints.

'Do we have a name?'

'He's not offered one. Nothing in his pockets to identify him. Over two hundred in cash, so we can rule out a mugging. What do you reckon for a weapon? Hammer?'

Rebus shrugged. 'A hammer would dent the skull. That flap looked too neat. I think they went for him with a cleaver.'

'Or a machete,' Claverhouse added. 'Something like that.'

Clarke stared at him. 'I smell whisky.'

Claverhouse put a finger to his lips.

'Anything else?' Rebus asked. It was Clarke's turn to shrug.

'Just one observation.'

'What's that?'

'I like the t-shirt.'

Claverhouse put money in the machine, got out three coffees. He'd called his office, told them the surveillance was suspended. Orders now were to stay at the hospital, see if the victim would say anything. The very least they wanted was an ID. Claverhouse handed a coffee to Rebus.

'White, no sugar.'

Rebus took the coffee with one hand. In the other he

held a polythene laundry-bag, inside which was his shirt. He'd have a go at cleaning it. It was a good shirt.

'You know, John,' Claverhouse said, 'there's no point you hanging around.'

Rebus knew. His flat was a short walk away across The Meadows. His large, empty flat. There were students through the wall. They played music a lot, stuff he didn't recognise.

'You know Telford's gang,' Rebus said. 'Didn't you recognise the face?'

Claverhouse shrugged. 'I thought he looked a bit like Danny Simpson.'

'But you're not sure?'

'If it's Danny, a name's about all we can hope to get out of him. Telford picks his boys with care.'

Clarke came towards them along the corridor. She took the coffee from Claverhouse.

'It's Danny Simpson,' she confirmed. 'I just got another look, now the blood's been cleaned off.' She took a swallow of coffee, frowned. 'Where's the sugar?'

'You're sweet enough already,' Claverhouse told her.

'Why did they pick on Simpson?' Rebus asked.

'Wrong place, wrong time?' Claverhouse suggested.

'Plus he's pretty low down the pecking order,' Clarke added, 'making it a gentle hint.'

Rebus looked at her. Short dark hair, shrewd face with a gleam to the eyes. He knew she worked well with suspects, kept them calm, listened carefully. Good on the street, too: fast on her feet as well as in her head.

'Like I say, John,' Claverhouse said, finishing his coffee, 'any time you want to head off ...'

Rebus looked up and down the empty corridor. 'Am I in the way or something?'

'It's not that. But your job's *liaison* – period. I know the way you work: you get attached to cases, maybe even over-attached. Look at Candice. I'm just saying …'

'You're saying, don't butt in?' Colour rose to Rebus's cheeks: *Look at Candice*.

'I'm saying it's our case, not yours. That's all.'

Rebus's eyes narrowed. 'I don't get it.'

Clarke stepped in. 'John, I think all he means is –'

'Whoah! It's okay, Siobhan. Let the man speak for himself.'

Claverhouse sighed, screwed up his empty cup and looked around for a bin. 'John, investigating Telford means keeping half an eye on Big Ger Cafferty and his crew.'

'And?'

Claverhouse stared at him. 'Okay, you want it spelling out? You went to Barlinnie yesterday – news travels in our business. You met Cafferty. The two of you had a chinwag.'

'He asked me to go,' Rebus lied.

Claverhouse held up his hands. 'Fact is, as you've just said, he asked you and you went.' Claverhouse shrugged.

'Are you saying I'm in his pocket?' Rebus's voice had risen.

'Boys, boys,' Clarke said.

The doors at the end of the corridor had swung open. A young man in dark business suit, briefcase swinging, was coming towards the drinks machine. He was humming some tune. He stopped humming as he reached them, put down his case and searched his pockets for change. He smiled when he looked at them.

'Good evening.'

Early-thirties, black hair slicked back from his forehead. One kiss-curl looped down between his eyebrows.

'Anyone got change of a pound?'

They looked in their pockets, couldn't find enough coins.

'Never mind.' Though the machine was flashing EXACT

MONEY ONLY he stuck in the pound coin and selected tea, black, no sugar. He stooped down to retrieve the cup, but didn't seem in a hurry to leave.

'You're police officers,' he said. His voice was a drawl, slightly nasal: Scottish upper-class. He smiled. 'I don't think I know any of you professionally, but one can always tell.'

'And you're a lawyer,' Rebus guessed. The man bowed his head in acknowledgement. 'Here to represent the interests of a certain Mr Thomas Telford.'

'I'm Daniel Simpson's legal advisor.'

'Which adds up to the same thing.'

'I believe Daniel's just been admitted.' The man blew on his tea, sipped it.

'Who told you he was here?'

'Again, I don't believe that's any of your business, Detective …?'

'DI Rebus.'

The man transferred his cup to his left hand so he could hold out his right. 'Charles Groal.' He glanced at Rebus's t-shirt. 'Is that what you call "plain clothes", Inspector?'

Claverhouse and Clarke introduced themselves in turn. Groal made great show of handing out business cards.

'I take it,' he said, 'you're loitering here in the hope of interviewing my client?'

'That's right,' Claverhouse said.

'Might I ask why, DS Claverhouse? Or should I address that question to your superior?'

'He's not my –' Claverhouse caught Rebus's look.

Groal raised an eyebrow. 'Not your superior? And yet he manifestly is, being an Inspector to your Sergeant.' He looked towards the ceiling, tapped a finger against his cup. 'You're not strictly colleagues,' he said at last, bringing his gaze back down to focus on Claverhouse.

16

'DS Claverhouse and myself are attached to the Scottish Crime Squad,' Clarke said.

'And Inspector Rebus isn't,' Groal observed. 'Fascinating.'

'I'm at St Leonard's.'

'Then this is quite rightly part of your division. But as for the Crime Squad …'

'We just want to know what happened,' Rebus went on.

'A fall of some kind, wasn't it? How is he, by the way?'

'Nice of you to show concern,' Claverhouse muttered.

'He's unconscious,' Clarke said.

'And likely to be in an operating theatre fairly soon. Or will they want to X-ray him first? I'm not very up on the procedures.'

'You could always ask a nurse,' Claverhouse said.

'DS Claverhouse, I detect a certain hostility.'

'Just his normal tone,' Rebus said. 'Look, you're here to make sure Danny Simpson keeps his trap shut. We're here to listen to whatever bunch of shite the two of you eventually concoct for our delectation. I think that's a pretty fair summary, don't you?'

Groal cocked his head slightly to one side. 'I've heard about you, Inspector. Occasionally stories can become exaggerated but not, I'm pleased to say, in your case.'

'He's a living legend,' Clarke offered. Rebus snorted and headed back into A&E.

There was a woolly-suit in there, seated on a chair, his cap on his lap and a paperback book resting on the cap. Rebus had seen him half an hour before. The constable was sitting outside a room with its door closed tight. Quiet voices came from the other side. The woolly-suit was called Redpath and he worked out of St Leonard's. He'd been in the force a bit under a year. Graduate recruit. They called him 'The Professor'. He was tall and spotty and had a shy look about him. He closed the book as Rebus approached, but kept a finger in his page.

'Science fiction,' he explained. 'Always thought I'd grow out of it.'

'There are a lot of things we don't grow out of, son. What's it about?'

'The usual: threats to the stability of the time continuum, parallel universes.' Redpath looked up. 'What do you think of parallel universes, sir?'

Rebus nodded towards the door. 'Who's in there?'

'Hit and run.'

'Bad?' The Professor shrugged. 'Where did it happen?'

'Top of Minto Street.'

'Did you get the car?'

Redpath shook his head. 'Waiting to see if she can tell us anything. What about you, sir?'

'Similar story, son. Parallel universe, you could call it.'

Siobhan Clarke appeared, nursing a fresh cup of coffee. She nodded a greeting towards Redpath, who stood up: a courtesy which gained him a sly smile.

'Telford doesn't want Danny talking,' she said to Rebus.

'Obviously.'

'And meantime he'll want to even the score.'

'Definitely.'

She caught Rebus's eyes. 'I thought he was a bit out of order back there.' Meaning Claverhouse, but not wanting to name names in front of a uniform.

Rebus nodded. 'Thanks.' Meaning: you did right not to say as much at the time. Claverhouse and Clarke were partners now. It wouldn't do for her to upset him.

A door slid open and a doctor appeared. She was young, and looked exhausted. Behind her in the room, Rebus could see a bed, a figure on the bed, staff milling around the various machines. Then the door slid closed.

'We're going to do a brain scan,' the doctor was telling Redpath. 'Have you contacted her family?'

'I don't have a name.'

'Her effects are inside.' The doctor slid open the door again and walked in. There was clothing folded on a chair, a bag beneath it. As the doctor pulled out the bag, Rebus saw something. A flat white cardboard box.

A white cardboard pizza box. Clothes: black denims, black bra, red satin shirt. A black duffel-coat.

'John?'

And black shoes with two-inch heels, square-toed, new-looking except for the scuff marks, like they'd been dragged along the road.

He was in the room now. They had a mask over her face, feeding her oxygen. Her forehead was cut and bruised, the hair pushed away from it. Her fingers were blistered, the palms scraped raw. The bed she lay on wasn't really a bed but a wide steel trolley.

'Excuse me, sir, you shouldn't be in here.'

'What's wrong?'

'It's this gentleman –'

'John? John, what is it?'

Her earrings had been removed. Three tiny pin-pricks, one of them redder than its neighbours. The face above the sheet: puffy blackened eyes, a broken nose, abrasions on both cheeks. Split lip, a graze on the chin, eyelids which didn't even flutter. He saw a hit and run victim. And beneath it all, he saw his daughter.

And he screamed.

Clarke and Redpath had to drag him out, helped by Claverhouse who'd heard the noise.

'Leave the door open! I'll kill you if you close that door!'

They tried to sit him down. Redpath rescued his book

from the chair. Rebus tore it from him and threw it down the hall.

'How could you read a fucking book?' he spat. 'That's Sammy in there! And you're out here reading a book!'

Clarke's cup of coffee had been kicked over, the floor slippy, Redpath going down as Rebus pushed at him.

'Can you jam that door open?' Claverhouse was asking the doctor. 'And what about a sedative?'

Rebus was clawing his hands through his hair, bawling dry-eyed, his voice hoarse and uncomprehending. Staring down at himself, he saw the ludicrous t-shirt and knew that's what he'd take away from this night: the image of an Iron Maiden t-shirt and its grinning bright-eyed demon. He hauled off his jacket and started tearing at the shirt.

She was behind that door, he thought, and I was out here chatting as casual as you like. She'd been in there all the time he'd been here. Two things clicked: a hit and run; the car speeding away from Flint Street.

He grabbed at Redpath. 'Top of Minto Street. You're sure?'

'What?'

'Sammy ... top of Minto Street?'

Redpath nodded. Clarke knew straight away what Rebus was thinking.

'I don't think so, John. They were headed the opposite way.'

'Could have doubled back.'

Claverhouse had caught some of the exchange. 'I just got off the phone. The guys who did Danny Simpson, we picked up the car. White Escort abandoned in Argyle Place.'

Rebus looked at Redpath. 'White Escort?'

Redpath was shaking his head. 'Witnesses say dark-coloured.'

Rebus turned to the wall, stood there with his palms

pressed to it. Staring at the paintwork, it was like he could see *inside* the paint.

Claverhouse put a hand on his shoulder. 'John, I'm sure she's going to be fine. The doctor's gone to fetch you a couple of tablets, but meantime what about one of these?'

Claverhouse with Rebus's jacket folded in the crook of his arm, the quarter-bottle in his hand.

The little suicide bomb.

He took the bottle from Claverhouse. Unscrewed its top, his eyes on the open doorway. Lifted the bottle to his lips.

Drank.

Book Two

'In the Hanging Garden/No one sleeps'

*A seaside holiday: caravan park, long walks and sandcastles.
He sat in a deck-chair, trying to read. Cold wind blowing,
despite the sun. Rhona rubbed suntan lotion on Sammy, said
you couldn't be too careful. Told him to keep an eye open, she
was going back to the caravan for her book. Sammy was
burying her father's feet in the sand.*

*He was trying to read, but thinking about work. Every day
of the holiday, he sneaked off to a phone-box and called the
station. They kept telling him to go and enjoy himself, forget
about everything. He was halfway through a spy thriller. The
plot had already lost him.*

*Rhona was doing her best. She'd wanted somewhere foreign,
a bit of glamour and heat to go with the sunshine. Finances,
however, were on his side. So here they were on the Fife coast,
where he'd first met her. Was he hoping for something? Some
memory rekindled? He'd come here with his own parents,
played with Mickey, met other kids, then lost them again at the
end of the fortnight.*

*He tried the spy novel again, but case-work got in the way.
And then a shadow fell over him.*

'Where is she?'

*'What?' He looked down. His feet were buried in sand, but
Sammy wasn't there. How long had she been gone? He stood
up, scanned the seashore. A few tentative bathers, going in no
further than their knees.*

'Christ, John, where is she?'

He turned round, looked at the sand dunes in the distance.

'The dunes …?'

They warned her. There were hollows in the dunes where the sand was eroding. Small dens had been created – a magnet for kids. Only they were prone to collapse. Earlier in the season, a ten-year-old boy had been dug out by frantic parents. He hadn't quite choked on the sand …

They were running now. The dunes, the grass, no sign of her.

'Sammy!'

'Maybe she went into the water.'

'You were supposed to be keeping an eye on her!'

'I'm sorry. I …'

'Sammy!'

A small shape in one of the dens. Hopping on its hands and knees. Rhona reached in, pulled her out, hugged her.

'Sweetie, we told you not to!'

'I was a rabbit.'

Rebus looked at the fragile roof: sand meshed with the roots of plants and grasses. Punched it with a fist. The roof collapsed. Rhona was looking at him.

End of holiday.

3

John Rebus kissed his daughter.

'See you later,' he said, watching her as she left the coffee shop. Espresso and a slice of caramel shortbread – that's all she'd had time for – but they'd fixed another date for dinner. Nothing fancy, just a pizza.

It was October 30th. By mid-November, if Nature were feeling bloody, it would be winter. Rebus had been taught at school that there were four distinct seasons, had painted pictures of them in bright and sombre colours, but his native country seemed not to know this. Winters were long, outstaying their welcome. The warm weather came suddenly, people stripping to t-shirts as the first buds appeared, so that spring and summer seemed entwined into a single season. And no sooner had the leaves started turning brown than the first frost came again.

Sammy waved at him through the cafe window then was gone. She seemed to have grown up all right. He'd always been on the lookout for evidence of instability, hints of childhood traumas or a genetic predisposition towards self-destruction. Maybe he should phone Rhona some day and thank her, thank her for bringing Samantha up on her own. It couldn't have been easy: that was what people always said. He knew it would be nice if he could feel some responsibility for the success, but he wasn't *that* hypocritical. The truth was, while she'd been growing up, he'd been elsewhere. It was the same with his marriage: even when in the same room as his wife, even out at the pictures or around the table at a dinner party ... the best part of him had been elsewhere, fixed on some case or other, some question that needed answering before he could rest.

Rebus lifted his coat from the back of his chair. Nothing left for it but to go back to the office. Sammy was headed back to her own office; she worked with ex-convicts. She had refused his offer of a lift. Now that it was out in the open, she'd wanted to talk about her man, Ned Farlowe. Rebus had tried to look interested, but found that his mind was half on Joseph Lintz – in other words, same problem as always. When he'd been given the Lintz case, he'd been told he was well-suited to it: his Army background for one thing; and his seeming affinity for historical cases – by which Farmer Watson, Rebus's chief superintendent, had meant Bible John – for another.

'With respect, sir,' Rebus had said, 'that sounds like a load of balls. Two reasons for me getting lumbered with this: one, no other bugger will touch it with a barge-pole; two, it'll keep me out of the way for a while.'

'Your remit,' the Farmer had said, unwilling to let Rebus rile him, 'is to sift through what there is, see if any of it amounts to evidence. You can interview Mr Lintz if it'll help. Do whatever you think necessary, and if you find enough to warrant a charge ...'

'I won't. You know I won't.' Rebus sighed. 'Sir, we've been through this before. It's the whole reason the War Crimes section was shut down. That case a few years back – lot of hoo-haa about bugger all.' He was shaking his head. 'Who wants it all dragged up, apart from the papers?'

'I'm taking you off the Mr Taystee case. Let Bill Pryde handle that.'

So it was settled: Lintz belonged to Rebus.

It had started with a news story, with documents handed over to a Sunday broadsheet. The documents had come from the Holocaust Investigation Bureau based in Tel Aviv.

They had passed on to the newspaper the name of Joseph Lintz, who had, they said, been living quietly in Scotland under an alias since the end of the war, and who was, in fact, Josef Linzstek, a native of Alsace. In June 1944, Lieutenant Linzstek had led the 3rd Company of an SS regiment, part of the 2nd Panzer Division, into the town of Villefranche d'Albarede in the Corrèze region of France. 3rd Company had rounded up everyone in the town – men, women, children. The sick were carried from their beds, the elderly pulled from their armchairs, babies hoisted from their cots.

A teenage girl – an evacuee from Lorraine – had seen what the Germans were capable of. She climbed into the attic of her house and hid there, watching from a small window in the roof-tiles. Everyone was marched into the village square. The teenager saw her schoolfriends find their families. She hadn't been in school that day: a throat infection. She wondered if anyone would tell the Germans ...

There was a commotion as the mayor and other dignitaries remonstrated with the officer in charge. While machine guns were aimed at the crowd, these men – among them the priest, lawyer, and doctor – were set upon with rifle butts. Then ropes were produced, and strung over half a dozen of the trees which lined the square. The men were hauled to their feet, their heads pushed through the nooses. An order was given, a hand raised then dropped, and soldiers pulled on each rope, until six men were hanging from the trees, bodies writhing, legs kicking uselessly, the movements slowing by degrees.

As the teenager remembered it, it took an age for them to die. Stunned silence in the square, as if the whole village knew now, knew that this was no mere check of identity papers. More orders were barked. The men, separated from

the women and children, were marched off to Prudhomme's barn, everyone else shepherded into the church.
The square grew empty, except for a dozen or so soldiers,
rifles slung over their shoulders. They chatted, kicked up
dust and stones, shared jokes and cigarettes. One of them
went into the bar and switched the radio on. Jazz music
filled the air, competing with the rustle of leaves as a breeze
twisted the corpses in the trees.

'It was strange,' the girl later said. 'I stopped seeing them
as dead bodies. It was as if they'd become something else,
parts of the trees themselves.'

Then the explosion, smoke and dust billowing from the
church. A moment's silence, as though a vacuum had been
created in the world, then screams, followed immediately
by machine-gun fire. And when it finally stopped, she could
still hear it. Because it wasn't just inside the church: it was
in the distance, too.

Prudhomme's barn.

When she was finally found – by people from surrounding villages – she was naked except for a shawl she had
found in a trunk. The shawl had belonged to her
grandmother, dead the previous year. But she was not alone
in escaping the massacre. When the soldiers had opened fire
in Prudhomme's barn, they'd aimed low. The first row of
men to fall had been wounded in the lower body, and the
bodies which fell on them shielded them from further fire.
When straw was strewn over the mound and set alight,
they'd waited as long as they could before starting to claw
their way out from beneath, expecting at any moment to be
shot. Four of them made it, two with their hair and clothes
on fire, one dying later from his wounds.

Three men, one teenage girl: the only survivors.

The death toll was never finalised. No one knew how
many visitors had been in Villefranche that day, how many
refugees could be added to the count. A list was compiled

of over seven hundred names, people who had most likely been killed.

Rebus sat at his desk and rubbed his eyes with his knuckles. The teenage girl was still alive, a pensioner now. The male survivors were all dead. But they'd been alive for the Bordeaux trial in 1953. He had summaries of their evidence. The summaries were in French. A lot of the material sitting on his desk was French, and Rebus didn't speak French. That was why he'd gone to the Modern Languages department at the university and found someone who could. Her name was Kirstin Mede, and she lectured in French, but also had a working knowledge of German, which was handy: the documents which weren't in French were in German. He had a one-page English summary of the trial proceedings, passed on from the Nazi hunters. The trial had opened in February 1953 and lasted just under a month. Of seventy-five men identified as having been part of the German force at Villefranche, only fifteen were present – six Germans and nine French Alsatians. Not one of them was an officer. One German received the death sentence, the others jail terms of between four and twelve years, but they were all released as soon as the trial finished. Alsace hadn't been enjoying the trial, and in a bid to unite the nation, the government had passed an amnesty. The Germans, meantime, were said to have already served their sentences.

The survivors of Villefranche had been horrified.

Even more extraordinary to Rebus's mind, the British had apprehended a couple of German officers involved in the massacre, but had refused to hand them over to the French authorities, returning them to Germany instead, where they lived long and prosperous lives. If Linzstek had been captured then, there would have been none of the present commotion.

Politics: it was all down to politics. Rebus looked up and

Kirstin Mede was standing there. She was tall, deftly constructed, and immaculately dressed. She wore make-up the way women usually did only in fashion adverts. Today she was wearing a check two-piece, the skirt just touching her knees, and long gold-coloured earrings. She had already opened her briefcase and was pulling out a sheaf of papers.

'Latest translations,' she said.

'Thanks.'

Rebus looked down at a note he'd made to himself: 'Corrèze trip necessary??' Well, the Farmer had said he could have whatever he wanted. He looked up at Kirstin Mede and wondered if the budget would stretch to a tour guide. She was sitting opposite him, putting on half-moon reading glasses.

'Can I get you a coffee?' he asked.

'I'm a bit pushed today. I just wanted you to see these.' She laid two sheets of paper on his desk so that they faced him. One sheet was the photocopy of a typed report, in German. The second sheet was her translation. Rebus looked at the German.

'– *Der Beginn der Vergeltungsmassnahmen hat ein merkbares Aufatmen hervorgerufen und die Stimmung sehr günstig beeinflusst.*'

'The beginning of reprisals,' he read, 'has brought about a marked improvement in morale, with the men now noticeably more relaxed.'

'It's supposed to be from Linzstek to his commander,' she explained.

'But no signature?'

'Just the typed name, underlined.'

'So it doesn't help us identify Linzstek.'

'No, but remember what we were talking about? It gives a reason for the assault.'

'A touch of R&R for the lads?'

Her look froze him. 'Sorry,' he said, raising his hands.

32

'Far too glib. And you're right, it's almost like the Lieutenant is trying to justify the whole thing in print.'

'For posterity?'

'Maybe. After all, they'd just started being the losing side.' He looked at the other papers. 'Anything else?'

'Some further reports, nothing too exciting. And some of the eyewitness testimony.' She looked at him with pale grey eyes. 'It gets to you after a while, doesn't it?'

Rebus looked at her and nodded.

The female survivor of the massacre lived in Juillac, and had been questioned recently by local police about the man in charge of the German troops. Her story hadn't changed from the one she'd told at the trial: she'd seen his face only for a few seconds, and looking down from the attic of a three-storey house. She'd been shown a recent photo of Joseph Lintz, and had shrugged.

'Maybe,' she'd said. 'Yes, maybe.'

Which would, Rebus knew, be turfed out by the Procurator-Fiscal, who knew damned well what any defence lawyer with half a brain would do with it.

'How's the case coming?' Kirstin Mede asked. Maybe she'd seen some look cross his face.

'Slowly. The problem is all this stuff.' He waved towards the strewn desk. 'On the one hand I've got all this, and on the other I've got a wee old man from the New Town. The two don't seem to go together.'

'Have you met him?'

'Once or twice.'

'What's he like?'

What was Joseph Lintz like? He was cultured, a linguist. He'd even been a Professor at the university, back in the early 70s. Only for a year or two. His own explanation: 'I was filling a vacuum until they could find someone of greater standing'. He'd been Professor of German. He'd lived in Scotland since 1945 or '46 – he was vague about

33

exact dates, blaming his memory. His early life was vague, too. He said papers had been destroyed. The Allies had had to create a duplicate set for him. There was only Lintz's word that these new papers were anything but an official record of lies he'd told and which had been believed. Lintz's story – birth in Alsace; parents and relatives all dead; forced enlistment in the SS. Rebus liked the touch about joining the SS. It was the sort of admission that would make officials decide: he's been honest about his involvement with that, so he's probably being honest about the other details. There was no actual record of a Joseph Lintz serving with any SS regiment, but then the SS had destroyed a lot of their own records once they'd seen the way the war was headed. Lintz's war record was vague, too. He mentioned shell-shock to explain the gaps in his memory. But he was vehement that he had never been called Linzstek and had never served in the Corrèze region of France.

'I was in the east,' he would say. 'That's where the Allies found me, in the east.'

The problem was that there was no convincing explanation as to how Lintz had found himself in the United Kingdom. He said he'd asked if he could go there and start a new life. He didn't want to return to Alsace, wanted to be as far away from the Germans as possible. He wanted water between him and them. Again, there was no documentation to back this up, and meantime the Holocaust investigators had come up with their own 'evidence', which pointed to Lintz's involvement in the 'Rat Line'.

'Have you ever heard of something called the Rat Line?' Rebus had asked at their first meeting.

'Of course,' Joseph Lintz had said. 'But I never had anything to do with it.'

Lintz: in the drawing-room of his Heriot Row home. An elegant four-storey Georgian edifice. A huge house for a man who'd never married. Rebus had said as much. Lintz had merely shrugged, as was his privilege. Where had the money come from?

'I've worked hard, Inspector.'

Maybe so, but Lintz had purchased the house in the late-1950s on a lecturer's salary. A colleague from the time had told Rebus everyone in the department suspected Lintz of having a private income. Lintz denied this.

'Houses were cheaper back then, Inspector. The fashion was for country properties and bungalows.'

Joseph Lintz: barely five foot tall, bespectacled. Parchment hands with liver spots. One wrist sported a pre-war Ingersoll watch. Glass-fronted bookcases lining his drawing-room. Charcoal-coloured suits. An elegant way about him, almost feminine: the way he lifted a cup to his lips; the way he flicked specks from his trousers.

'I don't blame the Jews,' he'd said. 'They'd implicate everyone if they could. They want the whole world feeling guilty. Maybe they're right.'

'In what way, sir?'

'Don't we all have little secrets, things we're ashamed of?' Lintz had smiled. 'You're playing their game, and you don't even know it.'

Rebus had pressed on. 'The two names are very similar, aren't they? Lintz, Linzstek.'

'Naturally, or they'd have absolutely no grounds for their accusations. Think, Inspector: wouldn't I have changed my name more radically? Do you credit me with a modicum of intelligence?'

'More than a modicum.' Framed diplomas on the walls, honorary degrees, photos taken with university chancellors, politicians. When the Farmer had learned a little more about Joseph Lintz, he'd cautioned Rebus to 'ca' canny'. Lintz was a patron of the arts – opera, museums, galleries – and a great giver to charities. He was a man with *friends*.

But also a solitary man, someone who was happiest when tending graves in Warriston Cemetery. Dark bags under his eyes, pushing down upon the angular cheeks. Did he sleep well?

'Like a lamb, Inspector.' Another smile. 'Of the sacrificial kind. You know, I don't blame you, you're only doing your job.'

'You seem to have no end of forgiveness, Mr Lintz.'

A careful shrug. 'Do you know Blake's words, Inspector? "And through all eternity/ I forgive you, you forgive me." I'm not so sure I can forgive the media.' This last word voiced with a distaste which manifested itself as a twist of facial muscles.

'Is that why you've set your lawyer on them?'

' "Set" makes me sound like a hunter, Inspector. This is a *newspaper*, with a team of expensive lawyers at its beck and call. Can an individual hope to win against such odds?'

'Then why bother trying?'

Lintz thumped both arms of his chair with clenched fists. 'For the principle, man!' Such outbursts were rare and short-lived, but Rebus had experienced enough of them to know that Lintz had a temper ...

'Hello?' Kirstin Mede said, angling her head to catch his gaze.

'What?'

She smiled. 'You were miles away.'

'Just across town,' he replied.

She pointed to the papers. 'I'll leave these here, okay? If you've any questions ...'

'Great, thanks.' Rebus got to his feet.

'It's okay, I know my way out.'

But Rebus was insistent. 'Sorry, I'm a bit ...' He waved his hands around his head.

'As I said, it gets to you after a while.'

As they walked back through the CID office, Rebus

could feel eyes following them. Bill Pryde came up, preening, wanting to be introduced. He had curly fair hair and thick blond eyelashes, his nose large and freckled, mouth small and topped with a ginger moustache – a fashion accessory he could well afford to lose.

'A pleasure,' he said, taking Kirstin Mede's hand. Then, to Rebus: 'Makes me wish we'd swopped.'

Pryde was working on the Mr Taystee case: an ice-cream man found dead in his van. Engine left running in a lock-up, looking initially like suicide.

Rebus steered Kirstin Mede past Pryde, kept them moving. He wanted to ask her out. He knew she wasn't married, but thought there might be a boyfriend in the frame. Rebus was thinking: what would she like to eat – French or Italian? She spoke both those languages. Maybe stick to something neutral: Indian or Chinese. Maybe she was vegetarian. Maybe she didn't like restaurants. A drink then? But Rebus didn't drink these days.

'... So what do you think?'

Rebus started. Kirstin Mede had asked him something. 'Sorry?'

She laughed, realising he hadn't been listening. He began to apologise, but she shook it off. 'I know,' she said, 'you're a bit ...' And she waved her hands around her head. He smiled. They'd stopped walking. They were facing one another. Her briefcase was tucked under one arm. It was the moment to ask her for a date, any kind of date – let *her* choose.

'What's that?' she said suddenly. It was a shriek, Rebus had heard it, too. It had come from behind the door nearest them, the door to the women's toilets. They heard it again. This time it was followed by some words they understood.

'Help me, somebody!'

Rebus pushed open the door and ran in. A WPC was pushing at a cubicle door, trying to force it with her shoulder. From behind the door, Rebus could hear choking noises.

'What is it?' he said.

'Picked her up twenty minutes ago, she said she needed the loo.' The policewoman's cheeks wore a flush of anger and embarrassment.

Rebus grabbed the top of the door and hauled himself up, peering over and down on to a figure seated on the pan. The woman there was young, heavily made-up. She sat with her back against the cistern, so that she was staring up at him, but glassily. And her hands were busy. They were busy pulling a streamer of toilet-paper from the roll, stuffing it into her mouth.

'She's gagging,' Rebus said, sliding back down. 'Stand back'. He shouldered the door, tried again. Stood back and hit the lock with the heel of his shoe. The door flew open, catching the seated woman on the knees. He pushed his way in. Her face was turning purple.

'Grab her hands,' he told the WPC. Then he started pulling the stream of white paper from her mouth, feeling like nothing so much as a cheap stage-show magician. There seemed to be half a roll in there, and as Rebus caught the WPC's eye, both of them let out a near-involuntary laugh. The woman had stopped struggling. Her hair was mousy-brown, lank and greasy. She wore a black skiing jacket and a tight black skirt. Her bare legs were mottled pink, bruising at one knee where the door had connected. Her bright red lipstick was coming off on Rebus's fingers. She had been crying, was crying still. Rebus, feeling guilty about the sudden laughter, crouched down so that he could look into her makeup-streaked eyes. She blinked, then held his gaze, coughing as the last of the paper was extracted.

'She's foreign,' the policewoman was explaining. 'Doesn't seem to speak English.'

'So how come she told you she needed the toilet?'

'There are ways, aren't there?'

'Where did you find her?'

'Down the Pleasance, brazen as you like.'

'That's a new patch on me.'

'Me, too.'

'Nobody with her?'

'Not that I saw.'

Rebus took the woman's hands. He was still crouching in front of her, aware of her knees brushing his chest.

'Are you all right?' She just blinked. He made his face show polite concern. 'Okay now?'

She nodded slightly. 'Okay,' she said, her voice husky. Rebus felt her fingers. They were cold. He was thinking: junkie? A lot of the working girls were. But he'd never come across one who couldn't speak English. Then he turned her hands, saw her wrists. Recent zigzag scar tissue. She didn't resist as he pushed up one sleeve of her jacket. The arm was a mass of similar inflictions.

'She's a cutter.'

The woman was talking now, babbling incoherently. Kirstin Mede, who had been standing back from proceedings, stepped forward. Rebus looked to her.

'It's not anything I understand ... not quite. Eastern European.'

'Try her with something.'

So Mede asked a question in French, repeating it in three or four other languages. The woman seemed to understand what they were trying to do.

'There's probably someone at the uni who could help,' Mede said.

Rebus started to stand up. The woman grabbed him by the knees, pulled him to her so that he nearly lost his balance. Her grip was tight, her face resting against his legs. She was still crying and babbling.

'I think she likes you, sir,' the policewoman said. They

wrested her hands free, and Rebus stepped back, but she was after him at once, throwing herself forwards, like she was begging, her voice rising. There was an audience now, half a dozen officers in the doorway. Every time Rebus moved, she came after him on all fours. Rebus looked to where his exit was blocked by bodies. The cheap magician had become straight man in a comedy routine. The WPC grabbed her, pulled her back on to her feet, one arm twisted behind her back.

'Come on,' she said through gritted teeth. 'Back to the cell. Show's over, folks.'

There was scattered applause as the prisoner was marched away. She looked back once, seeking Rebus, her eyes pleading. For what, he did not know. He turned towards Kirstin Mede instead.

'Fancy a curry some time?'

She looked at him like he was mad.

'Two things: one, she's a Bosnian Muslim. Two, she wants to see you again.'

Rebus stared at the man from the Slavic Studies department, who'd come here at Kirstin Mede's request. They were talking in the corridor at St Leonard's.

'Bosnian?'

Dr Colquhoun nodded. He was short and almost spherical, with long black hair which was swept back either side of a bald dome. His puffy face was pockmarked, his brown suit worn and stained. He wore suede Hush Puppies – same colour as the suit. *This*, Rebus couldn't help feeling, was how dons were supposed to look. Colquhoun was a mass of nervous twitches, and had yet to make eye contact with Rebus.

'I'm not an expert on Bosnia,' he went on, 'but she says she's from Sarajevo.'

'Does she say how she ended up in Edinburgh?'

'I didn't ask.'

'Would you mind asking her now?' Rebus gestured back along the corridor. The two men walked together, Colquhoun's eyes on the floor.

'Sarajevo was hit hard in the war,' he said. 'She's twenty-two, by the way, she told me that.'

She'd looked older. Maybe she was; maybe she was lying. But as the door to the Interview Room opened and Rebus saw her again, he was struck by how unformed her face was, and he revised her age downwards. She stood up abruptly as he came in, looked like she might rush forward to him, but he held up a hand in warning, and pointed to the chair. She sat down again, hands cradling the mug of sweetened black tea. She never took her eyes off him.

'She's a big fan,' the WPC said. The policewoman – same one as the toilet incident – was called Ellen Sharpe. She was sitting on the room's other chair. There wasn't much space in the Interview Room: a table and two chairs just about filled it. On the table were twin video recorders and a twin cassette-machine. The video camera pointed down from one wall. Rebus gestured for Sharpe to give her seat to Colquhoun.

'Did she give you a name?' he asked the academic.

'She told me Candice,' Colquhoun said.

'You don't believe her?'

'It's not exactly ethnic, Inspector.' Candice said something. 'She's calling you her protector.'

'And what am I protecting her from?'

The dialogue between Colquhoun and Candice was gruff, guttural.

'She says firstly you protected her from herself. And now she says you have to continue.'

'Continue protecting her?'

'She says you own her now.'

Rebus looked at the academic, whose eyes were on

Candice's arms. She had removed her skiing jacket. Underneath she wore a ribbed, short-sleeved shirt through which her small breasts were visible. She had folded her bare arms, but the scratches and slashes were all too apparent.

'Ask her if those are self-inflicted.'

Colquhoun struggled with the translation. 'I'm more used to literature and film than ... um ...'

'What does she say?'

'She says she did them herself.'

Rebus looked at her for confirmation, and she nodded slowly, looking slightly ashamed.

'Who put her on the street?'

'You mean ...?'

'Who's running her? Who's her manager?'

Another short dialogue.

'She says she doesn't understand.'

'Does she deny working as a prostitute?'

'She says she doesn't understand.'

Rebus turned to WPC Sharpe. 'Well?'

'A couple of cars stopped. She leaned in the window to talk with the drivers. They drove off again. Didn't like the look of the goods, I suppose.'

'If she can't speak English, how did she manage to "talk" to the drivers?'

'There are ways.'

Rebus looked at Candice. He began to speak to her, very softly. 'Straight fuck, fifteen, twenty for a blow job. Unprotected is an extra fiver.' He paused. 'How much is anal, Candice?'

Colour flooded her cheeks. Rebus smiled.

'Maybe not university tuition, Dr Colquhoun, but someone's taught her a few words of English. Just enough to get her working. Ask her again how she got here.'

Colquhoun mopped his face first. Candice spoke with her head lowered.

'She says she left Sarajevo as a refugee. Went to Amsterdam, then came to Britain. The first thing she remembers is a place with lots of bridges.'

'Bridges?'

'She stayed there for some time.' Colquhoun seemed shaken by the story. He handed her a handkerchief so she could wipe her eyes. She rewarded him with a smile. Then she looked at Rebus.

'Burger chips, yes?'

'Are you hungry?' Rebus rubbed his stomach. She nodded and smiled. He turned to Sharpe. 'See what the canteen can come up with, will you?'

The WPC gave him a hard stare, not wanting to leave. 'Would you like anything, Dr Colquhoun?'

He shook his head. Rebus asked for another coffee. As Sharpe left, Rebus crouched down by the table and looked at Candice. 'Ask her how she got to Edinburgh.'

Colquhoun asked, then listened to what sounded like a long tale. He scratched some notes on a folded sheet of paper.

'The city with the bridges, she says she didn't see much of it. She was kept inside. Sometimes she was driven to some rendezvous ... You'll have to forgive me, Inspector. I may be a linguist, but I'm no expert on colloquialisms.'

'You're doing fine, sir.'

'Well, she was used as a prostitute, that much I can infer. And one day they put her in the back of a car, and she thought she was going to another hotel or office.'

'Office?'

'From her descriptions, I'd say some of her ... work ... was done in offices. Also private apartments and houses. But mostly hotel rooms.'

'Where was she kept?'

'In a house. She had a bedroom, they kept it locked.'
Colquhoun pinched the bridge of his nose. 'They put her
in the car one day, and next thing she knew she was in
Edinburgh.'

'How long was the trip?'

'She's not sure. She slept part of the way.'

'Tell her everything's going to be all right.' Rebus
paused. 'And ask her who she works for now.'

The fear returned to Candice's face. She stammered,
shaking her head. Her voice sounded more guttural than
ever. Colquhoun looked like he was having trouble with the
translation.

'She can't tell you,' he said.

'Tell her she's safe.' Colquhoun did so. 'Tell her again,'
Rebus said. He made sure she was looking at him while
Colquhoun spoke. His face was set, a face she could trust.
She reached a hand out to him. He took it, squeezed.

'Ask her again who she works for.'

'She can't tell you, Inspector. They'd kill her. She's
heard stories.'

Rebus decided to try the name he'd been thinking of, the
man who ran half the city's working girls.

'Cafferty,' he said, watching for a reaction. There was
none. 'Big Ger. Big Ger Cafferty.' Her face remained
blank. Rebus squeezed her hand again. There was another
name ... one he'd been hearing recently.

'Telford,' he said. 'Tommy Telford.'

Candice pulled her hand away and broke into hysterics,
just as WPC Sharpe pushed open the door.

Rebus walked Dr Colquhoun out of the station, recalling
that just such a walk had got him into this in the first place.

'Thanks again, sir. If I need you, I hope you won't mind
if I call?'

'If you must, you must,' Colquhoun said grudgingly.

'Not too many Slavic specialists around,' Rebus said. He had Colquhoun's business card in his hand, a home phone number written on its back. 'Well,' Rebus put out his free hand, 'thanks again.' As they shook, Rebus thought of something.

'Were you at the university when Joseph Lintz was Professor of German?'

The question surprised Colquhoun. 'Yes,' he said at last.

'Did you know him?'

'Our departments weren't that close. I met him at a few social functions, the occasional lecture.'

'What did you think of him?'

Colquhoun blinked. He still wasn't looking at Rebus. 'They're saying he was a Nazi.'

'Yes, but back then ...?'

'As I say, we weren't close. Are you investigating him?'

'Just curious, sir. Thanks for your time.'

Back in the station, Rebus found Ellen Sharpe outside the Interview Room door.

'So what do we do with her?' she asked.

'Keep her here.'

'You mean charge her?'

Rebus shook his head. 'Let's call it protective custody.'

'Does *she* know that?'

'Who's she going to complain to? There's only one bugger in the whole city can make out what she's saying, and I've just packed him off home.'

'What if her man comes to get her?'

'Think he will?'

She thought about it. 'Probably not.'

'No, because as far as he's concerned, all he has to do is wait, and we'll release her eventually. Meantime, she doesn't speak English, so what can she give us? And she's here illegally no doubt, so if she talks, all *we'd* probably do is kick her out of the country. Telford's clever ... I hadn't

45

realised it, but he is. Using illegal aliens as prossies. It's sweet.'

'How long do we keep her?'

Rebus shrugged.

'And what do I tell my boss?'

'Direct all enquiries to DI Rebus,' he said, going to open the door.

'I thought it was exemplary, sir.'

He stopped. 'What?'

'Your knowledge of the charge-scale for prostitutes.'

'Just doing my job,' he said, smiling.

'One last question, sir ... ?'

'Yes, Sharpe?'

'Why? What's the big deal?'

Rebus considered this, twitched his nose. 'Good question,' he said finally, opening the door and going in.

And he knew. He knew straight away. She looked like Sammy. Wipe away the make-up and the tears, get some sensible clothes on her, and she was the spitting image.

And she was scared.

And maybe he could help her.

'What can I call you, Candice? What's your real name?'

She took hold of his hand, put her face to it. He pointed to himself.

'John,' he said.

'Don.'

'John.'

'Shaun.'

'John.' He was smiling; so was she. 'John.'

'John.'

He nodded. 'That's it. And you?' He pointed at her now. 'Who are you?'

She paused. 'Candice,' she said, as a little light died behind her eyes.

4

Rebus didn't know Tommy Telford by sight, but he knew where to find him.

Flint Street was a passageway between Clerk Street and Buccleuch Street, near the university. The shops had mostly closed down, but the games arcade always did good business, and from Flint Street Telford leased gaming machines to pubs and clubs across the city. Flint Street was the centre of his eastern empire.

The franchise had until recently belonged to a man called Davie Donaldson, but he'd suddenly retired on 'health grounds'. Maybe he'd been right at that: if Tommy Telford wanted something from you and you weren't forthcoming, predictions of your future health could suddenly change. Donaldson was now in hiding somewhere: hiding not from Telford but from Big Ger Cafferty, for whom he had been holding the franchise 'in trust' while Cafferty bided his time in Barlinnie jail. There were some who said Cafferty ran Edinburgh as effectively from inside as he ever had done outside, but the reality was that gangsters, like Nature, abhorred a vacuum, and now Tommy Telford was in town.

Telford was a product of Ferguslie Park in Paisley. At eleven he'd joined the local gang; at twelve a couple of woolly-suits had visited him to ask about a spate of tyre slashings. They'd found him surrounded by other gang members, nearly all of them older than him, but he was at the centre, no doubt about it.

His gang had grown with him, taking over a sizeable chunk of Paisley, selling drugs and running prostitutes, doing a bit of extortion. These days he had shares in casinos and video shops, restaurants and a haulage firm, plus a property portfolio which made him landlord to several hundred people. He'd tried to make his mark in Glasgow, but had found it sealed down tight, so had gone exploring elsewhere. There were stories he'd become friendly with some big villain in Newcastle. Nobody could remember anything like it since the days when London's Krays had rented their muscle from 'Big Arthur' in Glasgow.

He'd arrived in Edinburgh a year ago, moving softly at first, buying a casino and hotel. Then suddenly he was inescapably *there*, like the shadow from a raincloud. With the chasing out of Davie Donaldson he'd given Cafferty a calculated punch to the gut. Cafferty could either fight or give up. Everyone was waiting for it to get messy ...

The games arcade called itself Fascination Street. The machines were all flashing insistence, in stark contrast to the dead facial stares of the players. Then there were shoot-'em-ups with huge video screens and digital imprecations. 'Think you're tough enough, punk?' one of them challenged as Rebus walked past. They had names like Harbinger and NecroCop, this latter reminding Rebus of how old he felt. He looked at the faces around him, saw a few he recognised, kids who'd been pulled into St Leonard's. They'd be on the fringes of Telford's gang, awaiting the call-up, hanging around like foster children, hoping The Family would take them. Most of them came from families who weren't families, latchkey kids grown old before their time.

One of the staff came in from the café.

'Who ordered the bacon sarnie?'

Rebus smiled as the faces turned to him. Bacon meant

pig meant him. A moment's examination was all he warranted. There were more pressing demands on their attention. At the far end of the arcade were the really big machines: half-size motorbikes you sat astride as you negotiated the circuit on the screen in front of you. A small appreciative coterie stood around one bike, on which sat a young man dressed in a leather jacket. Not a market-stall jacket, something altogether more special. Quality goods. Shiny sharp-toed boots. Tight black denims. White polo neck. Surrounded by fawning courtiers. Steely Dan: 'Kid Charlemagne'. Rebus found a space for himself in the midst of the glaring onlookers.

'No takers for that bacon sarnie?' he asked.

'Who are you?' the man on the machine demanded.

'DI Rebus.'

'Cafferty's man.' Said with conviction.

'What?'

'I hear you and him go back.'

'I put him inside.'

'Not every cop gets visiting rights though.' Rebus realised that though Telford's gaze was fixed on the screen, he was watching Rebus in its reflection. Watching him, talking to him, yet still managing to control the bike through hairpin bends.

'So is there some problem, Inspector?'

'Yes, there's a problem. We picked up one of your girls.'

'My what?'

'She calls herself Candice. That's about as much as we know. But foreign lassies are a new one on me. And you're fairly new around here, too.'

'I'm not getting your drift, Inspector. I supply goods and services to the entertainment sector. Are you accusing me of being a pimp?'

Rebus stuck out a foot and pushed the bike sideways. On

the screen, it spun and hit a crash barrier. A moment later, the screen changed. Back to the start of the race.

'See, Inspector,' Telford said, still not turning round. 'That's the beauty of games. You can always start again after an accident. Not so easy in real life.'

'What if I cut the power? Game over.'

Slowly, Telford swivelled from the hips. Now he was looking at Rebus. Close up, he looked so young. Most of the gangsters Rebus had known, they'd had a worn look, undernourished but overfed. Telford had the look of some new strain of bacteria, not yet tested or understood.

'So what is it, Rebus? Some message from Cafferty?'

'Candice,' Rebus said quietly, the slight tremor in his voice betraying his anger. With a couple of drinks in him, he'd have had Telford on the floor by now. 'From tonight, she's off the game, understood?'

'I don't know any Candice.'

'Understood?'

'Hang on, let's see if I've got this. You want me to agree with you that a woman I've never met should stop touting her hole?'

Smiles from the spectators. Telford turned back to his game. 'Where's this woman from anyway?' he asked, almost casually.

'We're not sure,' Rebus lied. He didn't want Telford knowing any more than was necessary.

'Must have been a great little chat the two of you had.'

'She's scared shitless.'

'Me, too, Rebus. I'm scared you're going to bore me to death. This Candice, did she give you a taste of the goods? I'm betting it's not every scrubber would get you this het up.'

Laughter, Rebus its brunt.

'She's off the game, Telford. Don't think about touching her.'

'Not with a bargepole, pal. Myself, I'm a clean-living sort of individual. I say my prayers last thing at night.'

'And kiss your cuddly bear?'

Telford looked at him again. 'Don't believe all the stories, Inspector. Here, grab a bacon sarnie on your way out, I think there's one going spare.' Rebus stood his ground a few moments longer, then turned away. 'And tell the mugs out front I said hello.'

Rebus walked back through the arcade and out into the night, heading for Nicolson Street. He was wondering what he was going to do with Candice. Simple answer: let her go, and hope she had the sense to keep moving. As he made to pass a parked car, its window slid down.

'Fucking well get in,' a voice ordered from the passenger seat. Rebus stopped, looked at the man who'd spoken, recognised the face.

'Ormiston,' he said, opening the back door of the Orion. 'Now I know what he meant.'

'Who?'

'Tommy Telford. I'm to tell you he said hello.'

The driver stared at Ormiston. 'Rumbled again.' He didn't sound surprised. Rebus recognised the voice.

'Hello, Claverhouse.'

DS Claverhouse, DC Ormiston: Scottish Crime Squad, Fettes's finest. On surveillance. Claverhouse: as thin as 'twa ply o' reek', as Rebus's father would have said. Ormiston: freckle-faced and with Mick McManus's hair – slick, pudding-bowl cut, unfeasibly black.

'You were blown before I walked in there, if that's any consolation.'

'What the fuck were you doing?'

'Paying my respects. What about you?'

'Wasting our time,' Ormiston muttered.

The Crime Squad were out for Telford: good news for Rebus.

'I've got someone,' he said. 'She works for Telford. She's frightened. You could help her.'

'The frightened ones don't talk.'

'This one might.'

Claverhouse stared at him. 'And all we'd have to do is …?'

'Get her out of here, set her up somewhere.'

'Witness relocation?'

'If it comes to that.'

'What does she know?'

'I'm not sure. Her English isn't great.'

Claverhouse knew when he was being sold something. 'Tell us,' he said.

Rebus told them. They tried not to look interested.

'We'll talk to her,' Claverhouse said.

Rebus nodded. 'So how long has this been going on?'

'Ever since Telford and Cafferty squared off.'

'And whose side are we on?'

'We're the UN, same as always,' Claverhouse said. He spoke slowly, measuring each word and phrase. A careful man, DS Claverhouse. 'Meantime, you go charging in like some bloody mercenary.'

'I've never been a great one for tactics. Besides, I wanted to see the bastard close up.'

'And?'

'He looks like a kid.'

'And he's as clean as a whistle,' Claverhouse said. 'He's got a dozen lieutenants who'd take the fall for him.'

At the word 'lieutenants', Rebus's mind flashed to Joseph Lintz. Some men gave orders, some carried them out: which group was the more culpable?

'Tell me something,' he said, 'the teddy bear story … is it true?'

Claverhouse nodded. 'In the passenger seat of his Range

Rover. A fucking huge yellow thing, sort they raffle in the pub Sunday lunchtime.'

'So what's the story?'

Ormiston turned in his seat. 'Ever hear of Teddy Willocks? Glasgow hardman. Carpentry nails and a claw-hammer.'

Rebus nodded. 'You welched on someone, Willocks came to see you with the carpentry bag.'

'But then,' Claverhouse took over, 'Teddy got on the wrong side of some Geordie bastard. Telford was young, making a name for himself, and he very badly wanted an in with this Geordie, so he took care of Teddy.'

'And that's why he carries a teddy around with him,' Ormiston said. 'A reminder to everyone.'

Rebus was thinking. Geordie meant someone from Newcastle. Newcastle, with its bridges over the Tyne ...

'Newcastle,' he said softly, leaning forward in his seat.

'What about it?'

'Maybe Candice was there. Her city of bridges. She might link Telford to this Geordie gangster.'

Ormiston and Claverhouse looked at one another.

'She'll need a safe place to stay,' Rebus told them. 'Money, somewhere to go afterwards.'

'A first-class flight home if she helps us nail Telford.'

'I'm not sure she'll want to go home.'

'That's for later,' Claverhouse said. 'First thing is to talk to her.'

'You'll need a translator.'

Claverhouse looked at him. 'And of course you know just the man ... ?'

She was asleep in her cell, curled under the blanket, only her hair visible. The Mothers of Invention: 'Lonely Little Girl'. The cell was in the women's block. Painted pink and blue, a slab to sleep on, graffiti scratched into the walls.

'Candice,' Rebus said quietly, squeezing her shoulder. She started awake, as if he'd administered an electric shock. 'It's okay, it's me, John.'

She looked round blindly, focused on him slowly. 'John,' she said. Then she smiled.

Claverhouse was off making phone calls, squaring things. Ormiston stood in the doorway, appraising Candice. Not that Ormiston was known to be choosy. Rebus had tried Colquhoun at home, but there'd been no answer. So now Rebus was gesturing, letting her know they wanted to take her somewhere.

'A hotel,' he said.

She didn't like that word. She looked from him to Ormiston and back again.

'It's okay,' Rebus said. 'It's just a place for you to sleep, that's all, somewhere safe. No Telford, nothing like that.'

She seemed to soften, came off the bed and stood in front of him. Her eyes seemed to say, I'll trust you, and if you let me down I won't be surprised.

Claverhouse came back. 'All fixed,' he said, his examination falling on Candice. 'She doesn't speak any English?'

'Not as practised in polite society.'

'In that case,' Ormiston said, 'she should be fine with us.'

Three men and a young woman in a dark blue Ford Orion, heading south out of the city. It was late now, past midnight, black taxis cruising. Students were spilling from pubs.

'They get younger every year.' Claverhouse was never short of a cliché.

'And more of them end up joining the force,' Rebus commented.

Claverhouse smiled. 'I meant prossies, not students. We pulled one in last week, said she was fifteen. Turned out she was twelve, on the run. All grown up about it.'

Rebus tried to remember Sammy at twelve. He saw her

scared, in the clutches of a madman with a grievance against Rebus. She'd had lots of nightmares afterwards, till her mother had taken her to London. Rhona had phoned Rebus a few years later. She just wanted to let him know he'd robbed Sammy of her childhood.

'I phoned ahead,' Claverhouse said. 'Don't worry, we've used this place before. It's perfect.'

'She'll need some clothes,' Rebus said.

'Siobhan can fetch her some in the morning.'

'How is Siobhan?'

'Seems fine. Hasn't half cut into the jokes and the language though.'

'Ach, she can take a joke,' Ormiston said. 'Likes a drink, too.'

This last was news to Rebus. He wondered how much Siobhan Clarke would change in order to blend with her new surroundings.

'It's just off the bypass,' Claverhouse said, meaning their destination. 'Not far now.'

The city ended suddenly. Green belt, plus the Pentland Hills. The bypass was quiet, Ormiston doing the ton between exits. They came off at Colinton and signalled into the hotel. It was a motorist's stop, one of a nationwide chain: same prices, same rooms. The cars which crowded the parking area were salesmen's specials, cigarette packets littering the passenger seats. The reps would be sleeping, or lying in a daze with the TV remote to hand.

Candice seemed reluctant to get out of the car, until she saw that Rebus was coming, too.

'You light up her life,' Ormiston offered.

At reception, they signed her in as one half of a couple – Mrs Angus Campbell. The two Crime Squad cops had the routine off pat. Rebus watched the hotel clerk, but a wink from Claverhouse told him the man was okay.

'Make it the first floor, Malcolm,' Ormiston said. 'Don't want anyone peeking in the windows.'

Room number 20. 'Will someone be with her?' Rebus asked as they climbed the stairs.

'Right there in the room,' Claverhouse said. 'The landing's too obvious, and we'd freeze our bums off in the car. Did you give me Colquhoun's number?'

'Ormiston has it.'

Ormiston was unlocking the door. 'Who's on first watch?'

Claverhouse shrugged. Candice was looking towards Rebus, seeming to sense what was being discussed. She snatched at his arm, jabbering in her native tongue, looking first to Claverhouse and then to Ormiston, all the time waving Rebus's arm.

'It's okay, Candice, really. They'll take care of you.'

She kept shaking her head, holding him with one hand and pointing at him with the other, prodding his chest to make her meaning clear.

'What do you say, John?' Claverhouse asked. 'A happy witness is a willing witness.'

'What time's Siobhan expected?'

'I'll hurry her up.'

Rebus looked at Candice again, sighed, nodded. 'Okay.' He pointed to himself, then to the room. 'Just for a little while, okay?'

Candice seemed satisfied with this, and went inside. Ormiston handed Rebus the key.

'I don't want you young things waking the neighbours now ...'

Rebus closed the door on his face.

The room was exactly as expected. Rebus filled the kettle and switched it on, dumped a tea-bag into a cup. Candice pointed to the bathroom, made turning motions with her hands.

'A bath?' He gestured with his arm. 'Go ahead.'

The curtain over the window was closed. He parted it and looked out. A grassy slope, occasional lights from the bypass. He made sure the curtains were closed tight, then tried adjusting the heating. The room was stifling. There didn't seem to be a thermostat, so he went back to the window and opened it a fraction. Cold night air, and the swish of nearby traffic. He opened the pack of custard creams, two small biscuits. Suddenly he felt ravenous. He'd seen a snack machine in the lobby. Plenty of change in his pockets. He made the tea, added milk, sat down on the sofa. For want of any other distractions, he turned the TV on. The tea was fine. The tea was absolutely fine, no complaints there. He picked up the phone and called Jack Morton.

'Did I wake you?'

'Not really. How's it going?'

'I wanted a drink today.'

'So what's new?'

Rebus could hear his friend making himself comfortable. Jack had helped Rebus get off the booze. Jack had said he could phone any time he liked.

'I had to talk to this scumbag, Tommy Telford.'

'I know the name.'

Rebus lit a cigarette. 'I think a drink would have helped.'

'Before or after?'

'Both.' Rebus smiled. 'Guess where I am now?'

Jack couldn't, so Rebus told him the story.

'What's your angle?' Jack asked.

'I don't know.' Rebus thought about it. 'She seems to need me. It's been a long time since anyone's felt like that.' As he said the words, he feared they didn't tell the whole story. He remembered another argument with Rhona, her screaming that he'd exploited every relationship he'd ever had.

'Do you still want that drink?' Jack was asking.

'I'm a long way from one.' Rebus stubbed out his cigarette. 'Sweet dreams, Jack.'

He was on his second cup of tea when she came back in, wearing the same clothes, her hair wet and hanging in rat's-tails.

'Better?' he asked, making the thumbs-up sign. She nodded, smiling. 'Do you want some tea?' He pointed to the kettle. She nodded again, so he made her a cup. Then he suggested a trip to the snack machine. Their haul included crisps, nuts, chocolate, and a couple of cans of Coke. Another cup of tea finished off the tiny cartons of milk. Rebus lay along the sofa, shoes off, watching soundless television. Candice lay on the bed, fully-clothed, sliding the occasional crisp from its packet, flicking channels. She seemed to have forgotten he was there. He took this as a compliment.

He must have fallen asleep. The touch of her fingers on his knee brought him awake. She was standing in front of him, wearing the t-shirt and nothing else. She stared at him, fingers still resting on his knee. He smiled, shook his head, led her back to bed. Made her lie down. She lay on her back, arms stretched. He shook his head again and pulled the duvet over her.

'That's not you any more,' he told her. 'Goodnight, Candice.'

Rebus retreated to the sofa, lay down again, and wished she would stop saying his name.

The Doors: 'Wishful Sinful' ...

A tapping at the door brought him awake. Still dark outside. He'd forgotten to close the window, and the room was cold. The TV was still playing, but Candice was asleep, duvet kicked off, chocolate wrappers strewn around her bare legs and thighs. Rebus covered her up, then tiptoed to the door, peered through the spyhole, and opened up.

'For this relief, much thanks,' he whispered to Siobhan Clarke.

She was carrying a bulging polythene bag. 'Thank God for the twenty-four-hour shop.' They went inside. Clarke looked at the sleeping woman, then went over to the sofa and started unpacking the bag.

'For you,' she whispered, 'a couple of sandwiches.'

'God bless the child.'

'For sleeping beauty, some of my clothes. They'll do till the shops open.'

Rebus was already biting into the first sandwich. Cheese salad on white bread had never tasted finer.

'How am I getting home?' he asked.

'I called you a cab.' She checked her watch. 'It'll be here in two minutes.'

'What would I do without you?'

'It's a toss-up: either freeze to death or starve.' She closed the window. 'Now go on, get out of here.'

He looked at Candice one last time, almost wanting to wake her to let her know he wasn't leaving for good. But she was sleeping so soundly, and Siobhan could take care of everything.

So he tucked the second sandwich into his pocket, tossed the room-key on to the sofa, and left.

Four-thirty. The taxi was idling outside. Rebus felt hungover. He went through a mental list of all the places he could get a drink at this time of night. He didn't know how many days it had been since he'd had a drink. He wasn't counting.

He gave his address to the cabbie, and settled back, thinking again of Candice, so soundly asleep, and protected for now. And of Sammy, too old now to need anything from her father. She'd be asleep too, snuggling into Ned Farlowe. Sleep was innocence. Even the city looked innocent in sleep. He looked at the city sometimes and saw a beauty his cynicism couldn't touch. Someone in a bar – recently? years back? – had challenged him to define romance. How could he do that? He'd seen too much of love's obverse: people killed for passion and from lack of it. So that now when he saw beauty, he could do little but respond to it with the realisation that it would fade or be brutalised. He saw lovers in Princes Street Gardens and imagined them further down the road, at the crossroads where betrayal and conflict met. He saw valentines in the shops and imagined puncture wounds, real hearts bleeding.

Not that he'd voiced any of this to his public bar inquisitor.

'Define romance,' had been the challenge. And Rebus's response? He'd picked up a fresh pint of beer and kissed the glass.

He slept till nine, showered and made some coffee. Then he phoned the hotel, and Siobhan assured him all was well.

'She was a bit startled when she woke up and saw me instead of you. Kept saying your name. I told her she'd see you again.'

'So what's the plan?'

'Shopping – one quick swoop on The Gyle. After that, Fettes. Dr Colquhoun's coming in at noon for an hour. We'll see what we get.'

Rebus was at his window, looking down on a damp Arden Street. 'Take care of her, Siobhan.'

'No problem.'

Rebus knew there'd be no problem, not with Siobhan. This was her first real action with the Crime Squad, she'd be doing her damnedest to make it a success. He was in the kitchen when the phone rang.

'Is that Inspector Rebus?'

'Who's speaking?' A voice he didn't recognise.

'Inspector, my name is David Levy. We've never met. I

apologise for calling you at home. I was given this number by Matthew Vanderhyde.'

Old man Vanderhyde: Rebus hadn't seen him in a while. 'Yes?'

'I must say, I was astonished when it transpired he knew you.' The voice was tinged with a dry humour. 'But by now nothing about Matthew should surprise me. I went to him because he knows Edinburgh.'

'Yes?'

Laughter on the line. 'I'm sorry, Inspector. I can't blame you for being suspicious when I've made such a mess of the introductions. I am a historian by profession. I've been contacted by Solomon Mayerlink to see if I might offer assistance.'

Mayerlink ... Rebus knew the name. Placed it: Mayerlink ran the Holocaust Investigation Bureau.

'And exactly what "assistance" does Mr Mayerlink think I need?'

'Perhaps we could discuss it in person, Inspector. I'm staying in a hotel on Charlotte Square.'

'The Roxburghe?'

'Could we meet there? This morning, ideally.'

Rebus looked at his watch. 'An hour?' he suggested.

'Perfect. Goodbye, Inspector.'

Rebus called into the office, told them where he'd be.

5

They sat in the Roxburghe's lounge, Levy pouring coffee. An elderly couple in the far corner, beside the window, pored over sections of newspaper. David Levy was elderly, too. He wore black-rimmed glasses and had a small silver beard. His hair was a silver halo around a scalp the colour of tanned leather. His eyes seemed constantly moist, as if he'd just chewed on an onion. He sported a dun-coloured safari suit with blue shirt and tie beneath. His walking-stick rested against his chair. Now retired, he'd worked in Oxford, New York State, Tel Aviv itself, and several other locations around the globe.

'I never came into contact with Joseph Lintz, however. No reason why I should, our interests being different.'

'So why does Mr Mayerlink think you can help me?'

Levy put the coffee pot back on its tray. 'Milk? Sugar?' Rebus shook his head to both, then repeated his question.

'Well, Inspector,' Levy said, tipping two spoonfuls of sugar into his own cup, 'it's more a matter of moral support.'

'Moral support?'

'You see, many people before you have been in the same position in which you now find yourself. I'm talking about objective people, professionals with no axe to grind, and no real stake in the investigation.'

Rebus bristled. 'If you're suggesting I'm not doing my job ...'

A pained look crossed Levy's face. 'Please, Inspector,

I'm not making a very good job of this, am I? What I mean is that there will be times when you will doubt the validity of what you are doing. You'll doubt its worth.' His eyes gleamed. 'Perhaps you've already had doubts?'

Rebus said nothing. He had a drawerful of doubts, especially now that he had a real, living, breathing case – Candice. Candice, who might lead to Tommy Telford.

'You could say I'm here as your conscience, Inspector.' Levy winced again. 'No, I didn't put that right, either. You already have a conscience, that's not under debate.' He sighed. 'The question you've no doubt been pondering is the same one I've asked myself on occasions: can time wash away responsibility? For me, the answer would have to be no. The thing is this, Inspector.' Levy leaned forward. 'You are not investigating the crimes of an old man, but those of a young man who now happens to be old. Focus your mind on that. There have been investigations before, half-hearted affairs. Governments wait for these men to die rather than have to try them. But each investigation is an act of remembrance, and remembrance is never wasted. Remembrance is the only way we learn.'

'Like we've learned with Bosnia?'

'You're right, Inspector, as a species we've always been slow to take in lessons. Sometimes they have to be hammered home.'

'And you think I'm your carpenter? Were there Jews in Villefranche?' Rebus couldn't remember reading of any.

'Does it matter?'

'I'm just wondering, why the interest?'

'To be honest, Inspector, there is a slight ulterior motive.' Levy sipped coffee, considering his words. 'The Rat Line. We'd like to show that it existed, that it operated to save Nazis from possible tormentors.' He paused. 'That it worked with the tacit approval – the *more* than tacit approval – of several western governments and even the Vatican. It's a question of general complicity.'

'What you want is for everyone to feel guilty?'

'We want recognition, Inspector. We want the truth. Isn't that what you want? Matthew Vanderhyde would have me believe it is your guiding principle.'

'He doesn't know me very well.'

'I wouldn't be so sure of that. Meantime, there are people out there who want the truth to stay hidden.'

'The truth being …?'

'That known war criminals were brought back to Britain – and elsewhere – and offered new lives, new identities.'

'In exchange for what?'

'The Cold War was starting, Inspector. You know the old saying: My enemy's enemy is my friend. These murderers were protected by the secret services. Military Intelligence offered them jobs. There are people who would rather this did not become general knowledge.'

'So?'

'So a trial, an open trial, would expose them.'

'You're warning me about spooks?'

Levy put his hands together, almost in an attitude of prayer. 'Look, I'm not sure this has been a completely satisfactory meeting, and for that I apologise. I'll be staying here for a few days, maybe longer if necessary. Could we try this again?'

'I don't know.'

'Well, think about it, won't you?' Levy extended his right hand. Rebus took it. 'I'll be right here, Inspector. Thank you for seeing me.'

'Take care, Mr Levy.'

'*Shalom*, Inspector.'

At his desk, Rebus could still feel Levy's handshake. Surrounded by the Villefranche files, he felt like the curator of some museum visited only by specialists and cranks. Evil had been done in Villefranche, but had Joseph Lintz been responsible? And even if he had, had he perhaps atoned during the past half-century? Rebus phoned the Procurator-Fiscal's office to let them know how little progress he was making. They thanked him for calling. Then he went to see the Farmer.

'Come in, John, what can I do for you?'

'Sir, did you know the Crime Squad had set up a surveillance on our patch?'

'You mean Flint Street?'

'So you know about it?'

'They keep me informed.'

'Who's acting as liaison?'

The Farmer frowned. 'As I say, John, they keep me informed.'

'So there's no liaison at street level?' The Farmer stayed silent. 'By rights there should be, sir.'

'What are you getting at, John?'

'I want the job.'

The Farmer stared at his desk. 'You're busy on Villefranche.'

'I want the job, sir.'

'John, liaison means diplomacy. It's never been your strongest suit.'

So Rebus explained about Candice, and how he was already tied into the case. 'And since I'm already in, sir,' he concluded, 'I might as well act as liaison.'

'What about Villefranche?'

'That remains a priority, sir.'

The Farmer looked into his eyes. Rebus didn't blink. 'All right then,' he said at last.

'You'll let Fettes know?'

'I'll let them know.'

'Thank you, sir.' Rebus turned to leave.

'John ...?' The Farmer was standing behind his desk. 'You know what I'm going to say.'

'You're going to tell me not to tread on too many toes, not to go off on my own little crusade, to keep in regular contact with you, and not betray your trust in me. Does that just about do it, sir?'

The Farmer shook his head, smiling. 'Bugger off,' he said.

Rebus buggered off.

When he walked into the room, Candice rose so quickly from her chair that it fell to the floor. She came forward and gave him a hug, while Rebus looked at the faces around them – Ormiston, Claverhouse, Dr Colquhoun, and a WPC.

They were in an Interview Room at Fettes, Lothian and Borders Police HQ. Colquhoun was wearing the same suit as the previous day and the same nervous look. Ormiston was picking up Candice's chair. He'd been standing against one wall. Claverhouse was seated at the table beside Colquhoun, a pad of paper in front of him, pen poised above it.

'She says she's happy to see you,' Colquhoun translated.

'I'd never have guessed.' Candice was wearing new clothes: denims too long for her and turned up four inches at the ankle; a black woollen v-neck jumper. Her skiing jacket was hanging over the back of her chair.

'Get her to sit down again, will you?' Claverhouse said. 'We're pushed for time.'

There was no chair for Rebus, so he stood next to Ormiston and the WPC. Candice went back to the story she'd been telling, but glanced regularly towards him. He noticed that beside Claverhouse's pad of paper sat a brown folder and an A4-sized envelope. On top of the envelope sat a black and white surveillance shot of Tommy Telford.

'This man,' Claverhouse asked, tapping the photo, 'she knows him?'

Colquhoun asked, then listened to her answer. 'She ...' He cleared his throat. 'She hasn't had any direct dealings with him.' Her two-minute commentary reduced to this. Claverhouse dipped into the envelope, spread more photos before her. Candice tapped one of them.

'Pretty-Boy,' Claverhouse said. He picked up the photo of Telford again. 'But she's had dealings with this man, too?'

'She's ...' Colquhoun mopped his face. 'She's saying something about Japanese people ... Oriental businessmen.'

Rebus shared a look with Ormiston, who shrugged.

'Where was this?' Claverhouse asked.

'In a car ... more than one car. You know, a sort of convoy.'

'She was in one of the cars?'

'Yes.'

'Where did they go?'

'They headed out of town, stopping once or twice.'

'Juniper Green,' Candice said, quite clearly.

'Juniper Green,' Colquhoun repeated.

'They stopped there?'

'No, they stopped before that.'

'To do what?'

Colquhoun spoke with Candice again. 'She doesn't know. She thinks one of the drivers went into a shop for some cigarettes. The others all seemed to be looking at a building, as if they were interested in it, but not saying anything.'

'What building?'

'She doesn't know.'

Claverhouse looked exasperated. She wasn't giving him much of anything, and Rebus knew that if there was nothing she could trade, Crime Squad would dump her straight back on the street. Colquhoun was all wrong for this job, completely out of his depth.

'Where did they go after Juniper Green?'

'Just drove around the countryside. For two or three hours, she thinks. They would stop sometimes and get out, but just to look at the scenery. Lots of hills and ...' Colquhoun checked something. 'Hills and flags.'

'Flags? Flying from buildings?'

'No, stuck into the ground.'

Claverhouse gave Ormiston a look of hopelessness.

'Golf courses,' Rebus said. 'Try describing a golf course to her, Dr Colquhoun.'

Colquhoun did so, and she nodded agreement, beaming at Rebus. Claverhouse was looking at him, too.

'Just a guess,' Rebus said with a shrug. 'Japanese businessmen, it's what they like about Scotland.'

Claverhouse turned back to Candice. 'Ask her if she ... accommodated any of these men.'

Colquhoun cleared his throat again, colour flooding his cheeks as he spoke. Candice looked down at the table, moved her head in the affirmative, started to speak.

'She says that's why she was there. She was fooled at first. She thought maybe they just wanted a pretty woman to look at. They had a nice lunch ... the beautiful drive ... But then they came back into town, dropped the Japanese off at a hotel, and she was taken up to one of the hotel rooms. Three of them ... she, as you put it yourself, DS Claverhouse, she "accommodated" three of them.'

'Does she remember the name of the hotel?'

She didn't.

'Where did they have lunch?'

'A restaurant next to flags and ...' Colquhoun corrected himself. 'Next to a golf course.'

'How long ago was this?'

'Two or three weeks.'

68

'And how many of them were there?'

Colquhoun checked. 'The three Japanese, and maybe four other men.'

'Ask her how long she's been in Edinburgh,' Rebus asked.

Colquhoun did so. 'She thinks maybe a month.'

'A month working the street ... funny we haven't picked her up.'

'She was put there as a punishment.'

'For what?' Claverhouse asked. Rebus had the answer.

'For making herself ugly.' He turned to Candice. 'Ask her why she cuts herself.'

Candice looked at him and shrugged.

'What's your point?' Ormiston asked.

'She thinks the scars will deter punters. Which means she doesn't like the life she's been leading.'

'And helping us is her only sure ticket out?'

'Something like that.'

So Colquhoun asked her again, then said: 'They don't like that she does it. That's why she does it.'

'Tell her if she helps us, she won't ever have to do anything like that again.'

Colquhoun translated, glancing at his watch.

'Does the name Newcastle mean anything to her?' Claverhouse asked.

Colquhoun tried the name. 'I've explained to her that it's a town in England, built on a river.'

'Don't forget the bridges,' Rebus said.

Colquhoun added a few words, but Candice only shrugged. She looked upset that she was failing them. Rebus gave her another smile.

'What about the man she worked for?' Claverhouse asked. 'The one before she came to Edinburgh.'

She seemed to have plenty to say about this, and kept touching her face with her fingers while she talked.

Colquhoun nodded, made her stop from time to time so he could translate.

'A big man ... fat. He was the boss. Something about his skin ... a birthmark maybe, certainly something distinctive. And glasses, like sunglasses but not quite.'

Rebus saw Claverhouse and Ormiston exchange another look. It was all too vague to be much use. Colquhoun checked his watch again. 'And cars, a lot of cars. This man crashed them.'

'Maybe he got a scar on his face,' Ormiston offered.

'Glasses and a scar aren't going to get us very far,' Claverhouse added.

'Gentlemen,' Colquhoun said, while Candice looked towards Rebus, 'I'm afraid I'm going to have to leave.'

'Any chance of coming back in later, sir?' Claverhouse asked.

'You mean today?'

'I thought maybe this evening ...?'

'Look, I do have other commitments.'

'We appreciate that, sir. Meantime, DC Ormiston will run you back into town.'

'My pleasure,' Ormiston said, all charm. They needed Colquhoun, after all. They had to keep him sweet.

'One thing,' Colquhoun said. 'There's a refugee family in Fife. From Sarajevo. They'd probably take her in. I could ask.'

'Thank you, sir,' Claverhouse said. 'Maybe later on, eh?'

Colquhoun seemed disappointed as Ormiston led him away.

Rebus walked over to Claverhouse, who was shuffling his photos together.

'Bit of an oddball,' Claverhouse commented.

'Not used to the real world.'

'Not much help either.'

Rebus looked towards Candice. 'Mind if I take her out?'

'What?'

'Just for an hour.' Claverhouse stared at him. 'She's been cooped up here, and only her hotel room to look forward to. I'll drop her back there in an hour, hour and a half.'

'Bring her back in one piece, preferably with a smile on her face.'

Rebus motioned for Candice to join him.

'Japanese and golf courses,' Claverhouse mused. 'What do you think?'

'Telford's a businessman, we know that. Businessmen do deals with other businessmen.'

'He runs bouncers and slot machines: what's the Japanese connection?'

Rebus shrugged. 'I leave the hard questions to the likes of you.' He opened the door.

'And, John?' Claverhouse warned, nodding towards Candice. 'She's Crime Squad property, okay? And remember, *you* came to *us*.'

'No bother, Claverhouse. And by the way, I'm your B Division liaison.'

'Since when?'

'With immediate effect. If you don't believe me, ask your boss. This might be your case, but Telford works out of *my* territory.'

He took Candice by the arm and marched her from the room.

He stopped the car on the corner of Flint Street.

'It's okay, Candice,' he said, seeing her agitation. 'We're staying in the car. Everything's all right.' Her eyes were darting around, looking for faces she didn't want to see. Rebus started the car again and drove off. 'Look,' he told her, 'we're leaving.' Knowing she couldn't understand. 'I'm guessing this is where you started from that day.' He looked at her. 'The day you went to Juniper Green. The

Japanese would be staying in a central hotel, somewhere pricey. You picked them up, then headed east. Along Dalry Road maybe?' He was speaking for his own benefit. 'Christ, I don't know. Look, Candice, anything you see, anything that looks familiar, just let me know, okay?'

'Okay.'

Had she understood? No, she was smiling. All she'd heard was that final word. All she knew was that they were heading away from Flint Street. He took her down on to Princes Street first.

'Was it a hotel here, Candice? The Japanese? Was it here?' She gazed from the window with a blank look.

He headed up Lothian Road. 'Usher Hall,' he said. 'Sheraton ... Any of it ring a bell?' Nothing did. Out along the Western Approach Road, Slateford Road, and on to Lanark Road. Most of the lights were against them, giving her plenty of time to study the buildings. Each newsagent's they passed, Rebus pointed it out, just in case the convoy had paused there to buy cigarettes. Soon they were out of town and entering Juniper Green.

'Juniper Green!' she said, pointing at the signpost, delighted to have something to show him. Rebus attempted a smile. There were plenty of golf courses around the city. He couldn't hope to take her to every one of them, not in a week never mind an hour. He stopped for a few moments by the side of a field. Candice got out, so he followed, lit a cigarette. There were two stone gateposts next to the road, but no sign of a gate between them, or any sort of path behind them. Once there might have been a track, and a house at the end of it. Atop one of the pillars sat the badly worn representation of a bull. Candice pointed towards the ground behind the other pillar, where another lump of carved stone lay, half-covered by weeds and grass.

'Looks like a serpent,' Rebus said. 'Maybe a dragon.' He looked at her. 'It'll all mean something to somebody.' She looked back at him blankly. He saw Sammy's features, reminded himself that he wanted to help her. He was in danger of letting that slip, of focusing on how she might help them get to Telford.

Back in the car, he branched off towards Livingston, intending to head for Ratho and from there back into town. Then he noticed that Candice had turned to look out of the back window.

'What is it?'

She came out with a stream of words, her tone uncertain. Rebus turned the car anyway, and drove slowly back the way they'd just come. He stopped at the side of the road, opposite a low dry-stone wall, beyond which lay the undulations of a golf course.

'Recognise it?' She mumbled more words. Rebus pointed. 'Here? Yes?'

She turned to him, said something which sounded apologetic.

'It's okay,' he told her. 'Let's take a closer look anyway.' He drove to where a vast iron double-gate stood open. A sign to one side read POYNTINGHAME GOLF AND COUNTRY CLUB. Beneath it: 'Bar Lunches and A La Carte, Visitors Welcome'. As Rebus drove through the gates, Candice started nodding again, and when an oversized Georgian house came into view she almost bounced in her seat, slapping her hands against her thighs.

'I think I get the picture,' Rebus said.

He parked outside the main entrance, squeezing between a Volvo estate and a low-slung Toyota. Out on the course, three men were finishing their round. As the final putt went in, hands went to wallets and money changed hands.

Two things Rebus knew about golf: one, to some people it was a religion; two, a lot of players liked a bet. They'd bet on final tally, each hole, even every shot if they could.

And didn't the Japanese have a passion for gambling?

He took Candice's arm as he escorted her into the main building. Piano music from the bar. Panatella smoke and oak-panelling. Huge portraits of self-important unknowns. A few old wooden putters, framed behind glass. A poster advertised a Halloween dinner-dance for that evening. Rebus walked up to reception, explained who he was and what he wanted. The receptionist made a phone call, then led them to the Chief Executive's office.

Hugh Malahide, bald and thin, mid-forties, already had a slight stammer, which intensified when Rebus asked his first question. By throwing it back at the questioner, he seemed to be playing for time.

'Have we had any Japanese visitors recently? Well, we do get a few golfers.'

'These men came to lunch. Maybe a fortnight, three weeks back. There were three of them, plus three or four Scottish men. Probably driving Range Rovers. The table may have been reserved in the name of Telford.'

'Telford?'

'Thomas Telford.'

'Ah, yes ...' Malahide wasn't enjoying this at all.

'You know Mr Telford?'

'In a manner of speaking.'

Rebus leaned forward in his chair. 'Go on.'

'Well, he's ... look, the reason I seem so reticent is because we don't want this made common knowledge.'

'I understand, sir.'

'Mr Telford is acting as go-between.'

'Go-between?'

'In the negotiations.'

Rebus saw what Malahide was getting at. 'The Japanese want to buy Poyntinghame?'

'You understand, Inspector, I'm just the manager here. I mean, I run the day-to-day business.'

'But you're the Chief Executive.'

'With no personal share in the club. The actual owners were set against selling at first. But an offer has been made, and I believe it's a very good one. And the potential buyers ... well, they're persistent.'

'Have there been any threats, Mr Malahide?'

He looked horrified. 'What sort of threats?'

'Forget it.'

'The negotiations haven't been *hostile*, if that's what you mean.'

'So these Japanese, the ones who had lunch here ... ?'

'They were representing the consortium.'

'The consortium being ... ?'

'I don't know. The Japanese are always very secretive. Some big company or corporation, I'd guess.'

'Any idea why they want Poyntinghame?'

'I've wondered that myself.'

'And?'

'Everyone knows the Japanese love golf. It might be a prestige thing. Or it could be that they're opening a plant of some kind in Livingston.'

'And Poyntinghame would become the factory social club?'

Malahide shivered at the thought. Rebus got to his feet.

'You've been very helpful, sir. Anything else you can tell me?'

'Look, this has been off the record, Inspector.'

'I've no problem with that. I don't suppose you've got any names?'

'Names?'

'Of the diners that day.'

Malahide shook his head. 'I'm sorry, not even credit card details. Mr Telford paid cash as usual.'

'Did he leave a big tip?'

'Inspector,' smiling, 'some secrets are sacrosanct.'

'Let's keep this conversation that way, too, sir, all right?'

Malahide looked at Candice. 'She's a prostitute, isn't she? I thought as much the day they were here.' There was revulsion in his voice. 'Tarty little thing, aren't you?'

Candice stared at him, looked to Rebus for help, said a few words neither man understood.

'What's she saying?' Malahide asked.

'She says she once had a punter who looked just like you. He dressed in plus-fours and made her whack him with a mashie-niblick.'

Malahide showed them out.

6

Rebus telephoned Claverhouse from Candice's room.

'Could be something or nothing,' Claverhouse said, but Rebus could tell he was interested, which was good: the longer he stayed interested, the longer he'd want to hang on to Candice. Ormiston was on his way to the hotel to resume babysitting duties.

'What I want to know is, how the hell did Telford land something like this?'

'Good question,' Claverhouse said.

'It's way out of his previous sphere, isn't it?'

'As far as we know.'

'A chauffeur service for Jap companies ...'

'Maybe he's after the contract to supply their gaming machines.'

Rebus shook his head. 'I still don't get it.'

'Not your problem, John, remember that.'

'I suppose so.' There was a knock at the door. 'Sounds like Ormiston.'

'I doubt it. He's just left.'

Rebus stared at the door. 'Claverhouse, wait on the line.'

He left the receiver on the bedside table. The knock was repeated. Rebus motioned for Candice, who'd been flicking through a magazine on the sofa, to move into the bathroom. Then he crept up to the door and put his eye to the spyhole. A woman: the day-shift receptionist. He unlocked the door.

'Yes?'

'Letter for your wife.'

He stared at the small white envelope which she was trying to hand him.

'Letter,' she repeated.

There was no name or address on the envelope, no stamp. Rebus took it and held it to the light. A single sheet of paper inside, and something flat and square, like a photograph.

'A man handed it in at reception.'

'How long ago?'

'Two, three minutes.'

'What did he look like?'

She shrugged. 'Tallish, short brown hair. He was wearing a suit, took the letter out of a briefcase.'

'How do you know who it's for?'

'He said it was for the foreign woman. He described her to a T.'

Rebus was staring at the envelope. 'Okay, thanks,' he mumbled. He closed the door, went back to the telephone.

'What is it?' Claverhouse asked.

'Someone's just dropped off a letter for Candice.' Rebus tore open the envelope, holding the receiver between shoulder and chin. There was a Polaroid photo and a single sheet, handwritten in small capitals. Foreign words.

'What does it say?' Claverhouse asked.

'I don't know.' Rebus tried a couple of words aloud. Candice had emerged from the bathroom. She snatched the paper from him and read it quickly, then fled back into the bathroom.

'It means something to Candice,' Rebus said. 'There's a photo, too.' He looked at it. 'She's on her knees gamming some fat bloke.'

'Description?'

'The camera's not exactly interested in his face. Claverhouse, we've got to get her away from here.'

'Hang on till Ormiston arrives. They might be trying to panic you. If they want to snatch her, one cop in a car isn't going to cause much of a problem. Two cops just might.'

'How did they know?'

'We'll think about that later.'

Rebus was staring at the bathroom door, remembering the locked cubicle at St Leonard's. 'I've got to go.'

'Be careful.'

Rebus put down the receiver.

'Candice?' He tried the door. It was locked. 'Candice?' He stood back and kicked. The door wasn't as strong as the one in St Leonard's; he nearly took it off its hinges. She was seated on the toilet, a plastic safety razor in her hand, slashing it across her arms. There was blood on her t-shirt, blood spraying the white tiled floor. She started screaming at him, the words collapsing into monosyllables. Rebus grabbed the razor, nicked his thumb in the process. He pulled her off the toilet, flushed the razor, and started wrapping towels around her arms. The note was lying in the bath. He waved it in her face.

'They're trying to scare you, that's all.' Not even half-believing it himself. If Telford could find her this quickly, if he had the means of writing to her in her own language, then he was much stronger, much cleverer than Rebus had suspected.

'It's going to be okay,' he went on. 'I promise. It's all okay. We'll look after you. We'll get you out of here, take you somewhere he can't get to you. I promise, Candice. Look, this is me talking.'

But she was bawling, tears dripping from her cheeks, head shaking from side to side. For a time, she'd actually believed in knights on white chargers. Now, she was realising how stupid she'd been ...

The coast seemed to be clear.

Rebus took her in his car, Ormiston tucked in behind. No other way to play it. It was a trade-off: a speedy exit versus hanging around for a cavalry escort. And the way Candice was bleeding, they couldn't afford to wait. The drive to the hospital was nerve-tingling, then there was the wait while her wounds were checked and some of them sewn up. Rebus and Ormiston waited in A&E, drinking coffee from beakers, asking one another questions they couldn't answer.

'How did he know?'

'Who did he get to write the note?'

'Why give us a warning? Why not just grab her?'

'What does the note say?'

It struck Rebus that they were near the university. He took Dr Colquhoun's card from his pocket and phoned his office. Colquhoun was in. Rebus read the message out to him, spelling some of the words.

'They sound like addresses,' Colquhoun said. 'Untranslatable.'

'Addresses? Are any towns named?'

'I don't think so.'

'Sir, we'll be taking her to Fettes if she's well enough ... any chance you could meet us there? It's important.'

'Everything with you chaps is important.'

'Yes, sir, but this is *important*. Candice's life may be in danger.'

Colquhoun took time answering. 'I suppose in that case ...'

'I'll send a car for you.'

After an hour, she was well enough to leave. 'The cuts weren't too deep,' the doctor said. 'Not life-threatening.'

'They weren't meant to be.' Rebus turned to Ormiston. 'She thinks she's going back to Telford, that's why she did it. She *knows* she's going back to him.'

Candice looked as though all the blood had been drained

from her. Her face seemed more skeletal than before, and her eyes darker. Rebus tried to recall what her smile looked like. He doubted he'd be seeing one for a while. She kept her arms folded protectively in front of her, and wouldn't meet his eyes. Rebus had seen suspects act that way in custody: people for whom the world had become a trap.

At Fettes, Claverhouse and Colquhoun were already waiting. Rebus handed over the note and photo.

'As I said, Inspector,' Colquhoun stated, 'addresses.'

'Ask her what they mean,' Claverhouse demanded. They were in the same room as before. Candice knew her place, and was already seated, her arms still folded, showing cream-coloured bandages and pink plasters. Colquhoun asked, but it was as though he'd ceased to exist. Candice stared at the wall in front of her, unblinking, her only motion a slight rocking to and fro.

'Ask her again,' Claverhouse said. But Rebus interrupted before Colquhoun could start.

'Ask her if people she knows live there, people who are important to her.'

As Colquhoun formed the question, the rocking grew slightly in intensity. There were fresh tears in her eyes.

'Her mother and father? Brothers and sisters?'

Colquhoun translated. Candice tried to stop her mouth trembling.

'Maybe she left a kid behind ...'

As Colquhoun asked, Candice flew from her chair, shouting and screaming. Ormiston tried to grab her, but she kicked out at him. When she'd calmed, she subsided in a corner of the room, arms over her head.

'She's not going to tell us anything,' Colquhoun translated. 'She was stupid to believe us. She just wants to go now. There's nothing she can help us with.'

Rebus and Claverhouse shared a look.

'We can't hold her, John, not if she wants to leave. It's

been dodgy enough keeping her away from a lawyer. Once she starts asking to go ...' He shrugged.

'Come on, man,' Rebus hissed, 'she's shit-scared, and with good reason. And now you've got all you're going to get out of her, you're just going to hand her back to Telford?'

'Look, it's not a question of –'

'He'll kill her, you know he will.'

'If he was going to kill her, she'd be dead.' Claverhouse paused. 'He's cleverer than that. He knows damned well all he had to do was give her a fright. He *knows* her. It sticks in my craw, too, but what can we do?'

'Just keep her a few days, see if we can't ...'

'Can't what? You want to hand her over to Immigration?'

'It's an idea. Get her the hell away from here.'

Claverhouse pondered this, then turned to Colquhoun. 'Ask her if she wants to go back to Sarajevo.'

Colquhoun asked. She slurred some answer, choking back tears.

'She says if she goes back, they'll kill everyone.'

Silence in the room. They were all looking at her. Four men, men with jobs, family ties, men with lives of their own. In the scheme of things, they seldom realised how well off they were. And now they realised something else: how helpless they were.

'Tell her,' Claverhouse said quietly, 'she's free to walk out of here at any time, if that's what she really wants. If she stays, we'll do our damnedest to help her ...'

So Colquhoun spoke to her, and she listened, and when he'd finished she pushed herself back on to her feet and looked at them. Then she wiped her nose on her bandages, pushed the hair out of her eyes, and walked to the door.

'Don't go, Candice,' Rebus said.

She half-turned towards him. 'Okay,' she said.

Then she opened the door and was gone.

Rebus grabbed Claverhouse's arm. 'We've got to pull Telford in, warn him not to touch her.'

'You think he needs telling?'

'You think he'd listen?' Ormiston added.

'I can't believe this. He scared her half to death, and as a result we let her walk? I really can't get my head round this.'

'She could always have gone to Fife,' Colquhoun said. With Candice out of the room, he seemed to have perked up a bit.

'Bit late now,' Ormiston said.

'He beat us this time, that's all,' Claverhouse said, his eyes on Rebus. 'But we'll take him down, don't worry.' He managed a thin, humourless smile. 'Don't think we're giving up, John. It's not our style. Early days yet, pal. Early days ...'

She was waiting for him out in the car park, standing by the passenger-door of his battered Saab 900.

'Okay?' she said.

'Okay,' he agreed, smiling with relief as he unlocked the car. He could think of only one place to take her. As he drove through The Meadows, she nodded, recognising the tree-lined playing fields.

'You've been here before?'

She said a few words, nodded again as Rebus turned into Arden Street. He parked the car and turned to her.

'You've been *here*?'

She pointed upwards, fingers curled into the shape of binoculars.

'With Telford?'

'Telford,' she said. She made a show of writing something down, and Rebus took out his notebook and pen, handed them over. She drew a teddy bear.

'You came in Telford's car?' Rebus interpreted. 'And he

watched one of the flats up there?' He pointed to his own flat.

'Yes, yes.'

'When was this?' She didn't understand the question. 'I need a phrasebook,' he muttered. Then he opened his door, got out and looked around. The cars around him were all empty. No Range Rovers. He signalled for Candice to get out and follow him.

She seemed to like his living-room, went straight to the record collection but couldn't find anything she recognised. Rebus went into the kitchen to make coffee and to think. He couldn't keep her here, not if Telford knew about the place. Telford ... why had he been watching Rebus's flat? The answer was obvious: he knew the detective was linked to Cafferty, and therefore a potential threat. He thought Rebus was in Cafferty's pocket. Know your enemy: it was another rule Telford had learned.

Rebus phoned a contact from the *Scotland on Sunday* business section.

'Japanese companies,' Rebus said. 'Rumours pertaining to.'

'Can you narrow that down?'

'New sites around Edinburgh, maybe Livingston.'

Rebus could hear the reporter shuffling papers on his desk. 'There's a whisper going round about a microprocessor plant.'

'In Livingston?'

'That's one possibility.'

'Anything else?'

'Nope. Why the interest?'

'Cheers, Tony.' Rebus put down the receiver, looked across at Candice. He couldn't think where else to take her. Hotels weren't safe. One place came to mind, but it would be risky ... Well, not so very risky. He made the call.

'Sammy?' he said. 'Any chance you could do me a favour ... ?'

Sammy lived in a 'colonies' flat in Shandon. Parking was almost impossible on the narrow street outside. Rebus got as close as he could.

Sammy was waiting for them in the narrow hallway, and led them into the cramped living-room. There was a guitar on a wicker chair and Candice lifted it, setting herself on the chair and strumming a chord.

'Sammy,' Rebus said, 'this is Candice.'

'Hello there,' Sammy said. 'Happy Halloween.' Candice was putting chords together now. 'Hey, that's Oasis.'

Candice looked up, smiled. 'Oasis,' she echoed.

'I've got the CD somewhere ...' Sammy examined a tower of CDs next to the hi-fi. 'Here it is. Shall I put it on?'

'Yes, yes.'

Sammy switched the hi-fi on, told Candice she was going to make some coffee, and beckoned for Rebus to follow her into the kitchen.

'So who is she?' The kitchen was tiny. Rebus stayed in the doorway.

'She's a prostitute. Against her will. I don't want her pimp getting her.'

'Where's she from again?'

'Sarajevo.'

'And she doesn't have much English?'

'How's your Serbo-Croat?'

'Rusty.'

Rebus looked around. 'Where's your boyfriend?'

'Out working.'

'On the book?' Rebus didn't like Ned Farlowe. Partly it was that name: 'Neds' were what the *Sunday Post* called hooligans. They robbed old ladies of their pension books and walking-frames. Those were the Neds of this world. And Farlowe meant Chris Farlowe: 'Out of Time', a number one that should have belonged to the Stones. Farlowe was researching a history of organised crime in Scotland.

'Sod's law,' Sammy said. 'He needs money to buy the time to write the thing.'

'So what's he doing?'

'Just some freelance stuff. How long am I babysitting?'

'A couple of days at most. Just till I find somewhere else.'

'What will he do if he finds her?'

'I'm not that keen to find out.'

Sammy finished rinsing the mugs. 'She looks like me, doesn't she?'

'Yes, she does.'

'I've got some time off coming. Maybe I'll phone in, see if I can stay here with her. What's her real name?'

'She hasn't told me.'

'Has she any clothes?'

'At a hotel. I'll get a patrol car to bring them.'

'She's really in danger?'

'She might be.'

Sammy looked at him. 'But I'm not?'

'No,' her father said. 'Because it'll be our secret.'

'And what do I tell Ned?'

'Keep it short, just say you're doing your dad a favour.'

'You think a journalist's going to be content with that?'

'If he loves you.'

The kettle boiled, clicked off. Sammy poured water into three mugs. Through in the living-room, Candice's interest had shifted to a pile of American comic books.

Rebus drank his coffee, then left them to their music and their comics. Instead of going home, he made for Young Street and the Ox, ordering a mug of instant. Fifty pee.

86

Pretty good deal, when you thought about it. Fifty pence for … what, half a pint? A pound a pint? Cheap at twice the price. Well, one-point-seven times the price, which would take it to the price of a beer … give or take.

Not that Rebus was counting.

The back room was quiet, just somebody scribbling away at the table nearest the fire. He was a regular, a journalist of some kind. Rebus thought of Ned Farlowe, who would want to know about Candice, but if anyone could keep him at bay, Sammy could. Rebus took out his mobile, phoned Colquhoun's office.

'Sorry to bother you again,' he said.

'What is it now?' The lecturer sounded thoroughly exasperated.

'Those refugees you mentioned. Any chance you could have a word with them?'

'Well, I …' Colquhoun cleared his throat. 'Yes, I suppose I could talk to them. Does that mean …?'

'Candice is safe.'

'I don't have their number here.' Colquhoun sounded fuddled again. 'Can it wait till I go home?'

'Phone me when you've talked to them. And thanks.'

Rebus rang off, finished his coffee, and called Siobhan Clarke at home.

'I need a favour,' he said, feeling like a broken record.

'How much trouble will it get me in?'

'Almost none.'

'Can I have that in writing?'

'Think I'm stupid?' Rebus smiled. 'I want to see the files on Telford.'

'Why not just ask Claverhouse?'

'I'd rather ask you.'

'It's a lot of stuff. Do you want photocopies?'

'Whatever.'

'I'll see what I can do.' Voices were raised in the front bar. 'You're not in the Ox, are you?'

'As it happens, yes.'

'Drinking?'

'A mug of coffee.'

She laughed in disbelief and told him to take care. Rebus ended the call and stared at his mug. People like Siobhan Clarke, they could drive a man to drink.

7

It was 7 a.m. when the buzzer sounded, telling him there was someone at his tenement's main door. He staggered along the hall to the intercom, and asked who the bloody hell it was.

'The croissant man,' a rough English voice replied.

'The what?'

'Come on, dick-brain, wakey-wakey. Memory's not so hot these days, eh?'

A name tilted into Rebus's head. 'Abernethy?'

'Now open up, it's perishing down here.'

Rebus pushed the buzzer to let Abernethy in, then jogged back to the bedroom to put on some clothes. His mind felt numb. Abernethy was a DI in Special Branch, London. The last time he'd been in Edinburgh had been to chase terrorists. Rebus wondered what the hell he was doing here now.

When the doorbell sounded, Rebus tucked in his shirt and walked back down the hall. True to his word, Abernethy was carrying a bag of croissants. He hadn't changed much: same faded denims and black leather bomber, same cropped brown hair spiked with gel. His face was heavy, pockmarked, and his eyes an unnerving, psychopath's blue.

'How've you been, mate?' Abernethy slapped Rebus's shoulder and marched past him into the kitchen. 'Get the kettle on then.' Like they did this every day of the week. Like they didn't live four hundred miles apart.

'Abernethy, what the hell are you doing here?'

'Feeding you, of course, same thing the English have always done for the Jocks. Got any butter?'

'Try the butter-dish.'

'Plates?'

Rebus pointed to a cupboard.

'Bet you drink instant: am I right?'

'Abernethy …'

'Let's get this ready first, then talk, okay?'

'The kettle boils quicker if you switch it on at the plug.'

'Right.'

'And I think there's some jam.'

'Any honey?'

'Do I look like a bee?'

Abernethy smirked. 'Old Georgie Flight sends his love, by the way. Word is, he'll be retiring soon.'

George Flight: another ghost from Rebus's past. Abernethy had unscrewed the top from the coffee jar and was sniffing the granules.

'How fresh is this?' He wrinkled his nose. 'No class, John.'

'Unlike you, you mean? When did you get here?'

'Hit town half an hour ago.'

'From London?'

'Stopped a couple of hours in a lay-by, got my head down. That A1 is murder though. North of Newcastle, it's like coming into a third-world country.'

'Did you drive four hundred miles just to insult me?'

They took everything through to the table in the living-room, Rebus shoving aside books and notepads, stuff about the Second World War.

'So,' he said, as they sat down, 'I'm assuming this isn't a social call?'

'Actually it is, in a way. I could have just telephoned, but I suddenly thought: wonder how the old devil's getting on?

Next thing I knew, I was in the car and heading for the North Circular.'

'I'm touched.'

'I've always tried to keep track of what you're up to.'

'Why?'

'Because last time we met ... well, you're different, aren't you?'

'Am I?'

'I mean, you're not a team player. You're a loner, bit like me. Loners can be useful.'

'Useful?'

'For undercover, jobs that are a bit out of the ordinary.'

'You think I'm Special Branch material?'

'Ever fancied moving to London? It's where the action is.'

'I get action enough up here.'

Abernethy looked out of the window. 'You couldn't wake this place with a fifty-megaton warhead.'

'Look, Abernethy, not that I'm not enjoying your company or anything, but why *are* you here?'

Abernethy brushed crumbs from his hands. 'So much for the social niceties.' He took a gulp of coffee, squirmed at its awfulness. 'War Crimes,' he said. Rebus stopped chewing. 'There's a new list of names. You know that, because you've got one of them living on your doorstep.'

'So?'

'So I'm heading up the London HQ. We've established a temporary War Crimes Unit. My job's to collate gen on the various investigations, create a central register.'

'You want to know what I know?'

'That's about it.'

'And you drove through the night to find out? There's got to be more to it.'

Abernethy laughed. 'Why's that?'

'There just has. A collator's job is for someone good at office work. That's not you, you're only happy in the field.'

'What about you? I'd never have taken you for a historian.' Abernethy tapped one of the books on the table.

'It's a penance.'

'What makes you think it's any different with me? So, what's the score with Herr Lintz?'

'There's no score. So far all the darts have missed the board. How many cases are there?'

'Twenty-seven originally, but eight of those are deceased.'

'Any progress?'

Abernethy shook his head. 'We got one to court, trial collapsed first day. Can't prosecute if they're ga-ga.'

'Well, for your information, here's where the Lintz case stands. I can't prove he was and is Josef Linzstek. I can't disprove his story of his participation in the war, or how he came to Britain.' Rebus shrugged.

'Same tale I've been hearing up and down the country.'

'What did you expect?' Rebus was picking at a croissant.

'Shame about this coffee,' Abernethy said. 'Any decent caffs in the neighbourhood?'

So they went to a café, where Abernethy ordered a double espresso, Rebus a decaf. There was a story on the front of the *Record* about a fatal stabbing outside a nightclub. The man reading the paper folded it up when he'd finished his breakfast and took it away with him.

'Any chance you'll be talking to Lintz today?' Abernethy asked suddenly.

'Why?'

'Thought I might tag along. It's not often you get to meet someone who might have killed seven hundred Frenchies.'

'Morbid attraction?'

'We're all a bit that way inclined, aren't we?'

'I've nothing new to ask him,' Rebus said, 'and he's already been muttering to his lawyer about harassment.'

'He's well-connected?'

Rebus stared across the table. 'You've done your reading.'

'Abernethy the Conscientious Cop.'

'Well, you're right. He has friends in high places, only a lot of them have been hiding behind the curtains since this all started.'

'Sounds like you think he's innocent.'

'Until proven guilty.'

Abernethy smiled, lifted his cup. 'There's a Jewish historian been going around. Has he contacted you?'

'What's his name?'

Another smile. 'How many Jewish historians have you been in touch with? His name's David Levy.'

'You say he's been going around?'

'A week here, a week there, asking how the cases are going.'

'He's in Edinburgh just now.'

Abernethy blew on his coffee. 'So you've spoken with him?'

'Yes, as it happens.'

'And?'

'And what?'

'Did he try his "Rat Line" story?'

'Again, why the interest?'

'He's tried it with everyone else.'

'What if he has?'

'Jesus, do you always answer a question with a question? Look, as collator, this guy Levy's name has popped up on my computer screen more than once. That's why I'm interested.'

'Abernethy the Conscientious Cop.'

'That's right. So shall we go see Lintz?'

'Well, seeing you've come all this way ...'

On the way back to the flat, Rebus stopped at a newsagent's and bought the *Record*. The stabbing had taken place outside Megan's Nightclub, a new establishment in Portobello. The fatality had been a 'doorman', William Tennant, aged 25. The story had made the front page because a Premier League footballer had been on the periphery of the incident. A friend who'd been with him had received minor cuts. The attacker had fled on a motorbike. The footballer had offered no comment to reporters. Rebus knew him. He lived in Linlithgow and a year or so back had been caught speeding in Edinburgh, with – in his own words – a 'wee bitty Charlie', meaning cocaine, on his person.

'Anything interesting?' Abernethy asked.

'Someone killed a bouncer. Quiet little backwater, eh?'

'A story like that, in London it wouldn't rate a column inch.'

'How long are you staying here?'

'I'll be off today, want to drop in on Carlisle. They're supposed to have another old Nazi. After that, it's Blackpool and Wolverhampton before home.'

'A sucker for punishment.'

Rebus drove them the tourist route: down The Mound and across Princes Street. He double parked in Heriot Row, but Joseph Lintz wasn't home.

'Never mind,' he said. 'I know where he'll probably be.' He took them down Inverleith Row and turned right into Warriston Gardens, stopping at the cemetery gates.

'What is he, a gravedigger?' Abernethy got out of the car and zipped his jacket.

'He plants flowers.'

'Flowers? What for?'

'I'm not sure.'

A cemetery should have been about death, but Warriston

didn't feel that way to Rebus. Much of it resembled a rambling park into which some statuary had been dropped. The newer section, with stone driveway, soon gave way to an earthen path between fading inscriptions. There were obelisks and Celtic crosses, lots of trees and birds, and the electric movements of squirrels. A tunnel beneath a walkway took you to the oldest part of the cemetery, but between tunnel and driveway sat the heart of the place, with its roll-call of Edinburgh's past. Names like Ovenstone, Cleugh, and Flockhart, and professions such as actuary, silk merchant, ironmonger. There were people who'd died in India, and some who'd died in infancy. A sign at the gate informed visitors that the place had been the subject of a compulsory purchase by the City of Edinburgh, because previous private owners had let it fall into neglect. But that same neglect was at least part of its charm. People walked their dogs here, or came to practise photography, or just mused among the tombstones. Gays came looking for company, others for solitude.

After dark, of course, the place had another reputation entirely. A Leith prostitute – a woman Rebus had known and liked – had been found murdered here earlier in the year. Rebus wondered if Joseph Lintz knew about that …

'Mr Lintz?'

He was trimming the grass around a headstone, doing so with a half-sized pair of garden shears. There was a sheen of sweat on his face as he forced himself upright.

'Ah, Inspector Rebus. You have brought a colleague?'

'This is DI Abernethy.'

Abernethy was examining the headstone, which belonged to a teacher called Cosmo Merriman.

'They let you do this?' he asked, his eyes finally finding Lintz's.

'No one has tried to stop me.'

'Inspector Rebus tells me you plant flowers, too.'

'People assume I am a relative.'

'But you're not, are you?'

'Only in so far as we are the family of man, Inspector Abernethy.'

'You're a Christian then?'

'Yes, I am.'

'Born and bred?'

Lintz took out a handkerchief and wiped his nose. 'You're wondering if a Christian could commit an atrocity like Villefranche. It's perhaps not in my interest to say this, but I think it entirely possible. I've been explaining this to Inspector Rebus.'

Rebus nodded. 'We've had a couple of talks.'

'Religious belief is no defence, you see. Look at Bosnia, plenty of Catholics involved in the fighting, plenty of good Muslims, too. "Good" in that they are believers. And what they believe is that their faith gives them the right to kill.'

Bosnia: Rebus saw a sharp image of Candice escaping the terror, only to end up more terrified still, and more trapped than ever.

Lintz was stuffing the large white handkerchief into the pocket of his baggy brown cord trousers. In the outfit – green rubber overshoes, green woollen jersey, tweed jacket – he did look like a gardener. Little wonder he attracted so little attention in the cemetery. He blended in. Rebus wondered how artful it was, how deeply he'd learned the skill of invisibility.

'You look impatient, Inspector Abernethy. You're not a man for theories, am I right?'

'I wouldn't know about that, sir.'

'In that case, you must not know very much. Now Inspector Rebus, he listens to what I have to say. More than that, he looks *interested*. Whether he is or not, I can't judge, but his performance – if performance it be – is exemplary.' Lintz always spoke like this, like he'd been rehearsing each line. 'Last time he visited my home, we discussed human duality. Would you have any opinion on *that*, Inspector Abernethy?'

The look on Abernethy's face was cold. 'No, sir.'

Lintz shrugged: case against the Londoner proven. 'Atrocities, Inspector, occur by an effort of the collective will.' Spelling it out; sounding like the lecturer he had once been. 'Because sometimes all it takes to turn us into devils is the fear of being an outsider.'

Abernethy sniffed, hands in pockets. 'Sounds like you're justifying war crimes, sir. Sounds to me like you might even have been there yourself.'

'Do I need to be a spaceman to imagine Mars?' He turned to Rebus, gave him the fraction of a smile.

'Well, maybe I'm just a bit too simple, sir,' Abernethy said. 'I'm also a bit parky. Let's walk back to the car and carry on our discussion there, all right?'

While Lintz packed his few small tools into a canvas bag, Rebus looked around, saw movement in the distance, between headstones. The crouched figure of a man. Split-second glimpse of a face he recognised.

'What is it?' Abernethy asked.

Rebus shook his head. 'Nothing.'

The three men walked in silence back to the Saab. Rebus opened the back door for Lintz. To his surprise, Abernethy got into the back, too. Rebus took the driver's seat, felt warmth returning slowly to his toes. Abernethy had his arm along the back of the seat, his body twisted towards Lintz.

'Now, Herr Lintz, my role in all this is quite straightforward. I'm collating all the information on this latest outbreak of alleged old Nazis. You understand that with allegations such as these, very serious allegations, we have a duty to investigate?'

'Spurious allegations rather than "serious" ones.'

'In which case you've nothing to worry about.'

'Except my reputation.'

'When you're exonerated, we'll take care of that.'

Rebus was listening closely. None of this sounded like Abernethy. The hostile graveside tone had been replaced by something much more ambiguous.

'And meantime?' Lintz seemed to be picking up whatever the Londoner was saying between the lines. Rebus felt deliberately excluded from the conversation, which was why Abernethy had got into the back seat in the first place. He'd placed a physical barrier between himself and the officer investigating Joseph Lintz. There was something going on.

'Meantime,' Abernethy said, 'co-operate as fully as you can with my colleague. The sooner he's able to reach his conclusions, the sooner this will all be over.'

'The problem with conclusions is that they should be conclusive, and I have so little proof. This was wartime, Inspector Abernethy, a lot of records destroyed ...'

'Without proof either way, there's no case to answer.'

Lintz was nodding. 'I see,' he said.

Abernethy hadn't voiced anything Rebus himself didn't feel; the problem was, he'd voiced it to the suspect.

'It would help if your memory improved,' Rebus felt obliged to add.

'Well, Mr Lintz,' Abernethy was saying, 'thanks for your time.' His hand was on the elderly man's shoulder: protective, comforting. 'Can we drop you somewhere?'

'I'll stay here a little longer,' Lintz said, opening the door and easing himself out. Abernethy handed the bag of tools to him.

'Take care now,' he said.

Lintz nodded, gave a small bow to Rebus, and shuffled back towards the gate. Abernethy climbed into the passenger seat.

'Rum little bugger, isn't he?'

'You as good as told him he was off the hook.'

'Bollocks,' Abernethy said. 'I told him where he stands, let him know the score. That's all.' He saw the look on Rebus's face. 'Come on, do you really want to see him in court? An old professor who keeps cemeteries tidy?'

'It doesn't make it any easier if you sound like you're on his side.'

'Even supposing he *did* order that massacre – you think a trial and a couple of years in clink till he snuffs it is the answer? Better to just give them all a bloody good scare, stuff the trial, and save the taxpayer millions.'

'That's not our job,' Rebus said, starting the engine.

He took Abernethy back to Arden Street. They shook hands, Abernethy trying to sound like he wanted to stay a little longer.

'One of these days,' he said. And then he was gone. As his Sierra drew away, another car pulled into the space he'd just vacated. Siobhan Clarke got out, bringing with her a supermarket carrier-bag.

'For you,' she said. 'And I think I'm owed a coffee.'

She wasn't as fussy as Abernethy, accepted the mug of instant with thanks and ate a spare croissant. There was a message on the answering machine, Dr Colquhoun telling him the refugee family could take Candice tomorrow. Rebus jotted down the details, then turned his attention to the contents of Siobhan's carrier-bag. Maybe two hundred sheets of paper, photocopies.

'Don't get them out of order,' she warned. 'I didn't have time to staple them.'

'Fast work.'

'I went back into the office last night. Thought I'd get it done while no one was about. I can summarise, if you like.'

'Just tell me who the main players are.'

She came to the table and pulled a chair over beside him,

found a sequence of surveillance shots. Put names to the faces.

'Brian Summers,' she said, 'better known as "Pretty-Boy". He runs most of the working girls.' Pale, angular face, thick black lashes, a pouting mouth. Candice's pimp.

'He's not very pretty.'

Clarke found another picture. 'Kenny Houston.'

'From Pretty-Boy to Plug-Ugly.'

'I'm sure his mother loves him.' Prominent teeth, jaundiced skin.

'What does he do?'

'He runs the doormen. Kenny, Pretty-Boy and Tommy Telford grew up on the same street. They're at the heart of The Family.' She sifted through more photos. 'Malky Jordan ... he keeps the drugs flowing. Sean Haddow ... bit of a brainbox, runs the finances. Ally Cornwell ... he's muscle. Deek McGrain ... There's no religious divide in The Family, Prods and Papes working together.'

'A model society.'

'No women though. Telford's philosophy: relationships get in the way.'

Rebus picked up a sheaf of paper. 'So what have we got?'

'Everything but the evidence.'

'And surveillance is supposed to provide that?'

She smiled over the top of her mug. 'You don't agree?'

'It's not my problem.'

'And yet you're interested.' She paused. 'Candice?'

'I don't like what happened to her.'

'Well, just remember: you didn't get this stuff from me.'

'Thanks, Siobhan.' He paused. 'Everything going all right?'

'Fine. I like Crime Squad.'

'Bit livelier than St Leonard's.'

'I miss Brian.' Meaning her one-time partner, now out of the force.

'You ever see him?'

'No, do you?'

Rebus shook his head, got up to show her out.

He spent about an hour sifting through the paperwork, learning more about The Family and its convoluted workings. Nothing about Newcastle. Nothing about Japan. The core of The Family – eight or nine of them – had been at school together. Three of them were still based in Paisley, taking care of the established business. The rest were now in Edinburgh, and busy prying the city away from Big Ger Cafferty.

He went through lists of nightclubs and bars in which Telford had an interest. There were incident reports attached: arrests in the vicinity. Drunken brawls, swings taken at bouncers, cars and property damaged. Something caught Rebus's eye: mention of a hot-dog van, parked outside a couple of the clubs. The owner questioned: possible witness. But he'd never seen anything worth the recall. Name: Gavin Tay.

Mr Taystee.

Recent dodgy suicide. Rebus gave Bill Pryde a bell, asked how that investigation was going.

'Dead end street, pal,' Pryde said, not sounding too concerned. Pryde: too long the same rank, and not going anywhere. Beginning the long descent into retirement.

'Did you know he ran a hot-dog stall on the side?'

'Might explain where he got the cash from.'

Gavin Tay was an ex-con. He'd been in the ice-cream business a little over a year. Successful, too: new Merc parked outside his house. His financial records hadn't hinted at money to spare. His widow couldn't account for the Merc. And now: evidence of a job on the side, selling food and drink to punters stumbling out of nightclubs.

Tommy Telford's nightclubs.

Gavin Tay: previous convictions for assault and reset. A

persistent offender who'd finally gone straight ... The room began to feel stuffy, Rebus's head clotted and aching. He decided to get out.

Walked through The Meadows and down George IV Bridge, took the Playfair Steps down to Princes Street. A group was sitting on the stone steps of the Scottish Academy: unshaven, dyed hair, torn clothes. The city's dispossessed, trying their best not to be ignored. Rebus knew he had things in common with them. In the course of his life, he'd failed to fit several niches: husband, father, lover. He hadn't fit in with the Army's ideas of what he should be, and wasn't exactly 'one of the lads' in the police. When one of the group held out a hand, Rebus offered a fiver, before crossing Princes Street and heading for the Oxford Bar.

He settled into a corner with a mug of coffee, got out his mobile, and called Sammy's flat. She was home, all was well with Candice. Rebus told her he had a place for Candice, she could move out tomorrow.

'That's fine,' Sammy said. 'Hold on a second.' There was a rustling sound as the receiver was passed along.

'Hello, John, how are you?'

Rebus smiled. 'Hello, Candice. That's very good.'

'Thank you. Sammy is ... uh ... I am teaching how to ...' She broke into laughter, handed the receiver back.

'I'm teaching her English,' Sammy said.

'I can tell.'

'We started with some Oasis lyrics, just went from there.'

'I'll try to come round later. What did Ned say?'

'He was so shattered when he came home, I think he barely noticed.'

'Is he there? I'd like to talk to him.'

'He's out working.'

'What did you say he was doing again?'

'I didn't.'

'Right. Thanks again, Sammy. See you later.'

He took a swig of coffee, washed it around his mouth. Abernethy: he couldn't just let it go. He swallowed the coffee and called the Roxburghe, asked for David Levy's room.

'Levy speaking.'

'It's John Rebus.'

'Inspector, how good to hear from you. Is there something I can do?'

'I'd like to talk to you.'

'Are you in your office?'

Rebus looked around. 'In a manner of speaking. It's a two-minute walk from your hotel. Turn right out of the door, cross George Street, and walk down to Young Street. Far end, the Oxford Bar. I'm in the back room.'

When Levy arrived, Rebus bought him a half of eighty-bob. Levy eased himself into a chair, hanging his walking-stick on the back of it. 'So what can I do for you?'

'I'm not the only policeman you've spoken to.'

'No, you're not.'

'Someone from Special Branch in London came to see me today.'

'And he told you I'd been travelling around?'

'Yes.'

'Did he warn you against speaking to me?'

'Not in so many words.'

Levy took off his glasses, began polishing them. 'I told you, there are people who'd rather this was all relegated to history. This man, he came all the way from London just to tell you about me?'

'He wanted to see Joseph Lintz.'

'Ah.' Levy was thoughtful. 'Your interpretation, Inspector?'

'I was hoping for yours.'

'My utterly subjective interpretation?' Rebus nodded. 'He wants to be sure of Lintz. This man works for Special Branch, and as everyone knows Special Branch is the public arm of the secret services.'

'He wanted to be confident I wasn't going to get anything out of Lintz?'

Levy nodded, staring at the smoke from Rebus's cigarette. This case was like that: one minute you could see it, the next you couldn't. Like smoke.

'I have a little book with me,' Levy said, reaching into his pocket. 'I'd like you to read it. It's in English, translated from the Hebrew. It's about the Rat Line.'

Rebus took the book. 'Does it prove anything?'

'That depends on your terms.'

'Concrete proof.'

'Concrete proof exists, Inspector.'

'In this book?'

Levy shook his head. 'Under lock and key in Whitehall, kept from scrutiny by the Hundred Year Rule.'

'So there's no way to prove anything.'

'There's one way ...'

'What?'

'If someone talks. If we can get just *one* of them to talk ...'

'That's what this is all about: wearing down their resistance? Looking for the weakest link?'

Levy smiled again. 'We have learned patience, Inspector.' He finished his drink. 'I'm so grateful you called. This has been a much more satisfactory meeting.'

'Will you send your bosses a progress report?'

Levy chose to ignore this. 'We'll talk again, when you've read the book.' He stood up. 'The Special Branch officer ... I've forgotten his name?'

'I didn't give it.'

Levy waited a moment, then said, 'Ah, that explains it

then. Is he still in Edinburgh?' He watched Rebus shake his head. 'Then he's probably on his way to Carlisle, yes?'

Rebus sipped coffee, offered no comment.

'My thanks again, Inspector,' Levy said, undeterred. 'Thanks for dropping by.'

Levy took a final look around. 'Your office,' he said, shaking his head.

8

The Rat Line was an 'underground railway', delivering
Nazis – sometimes with the help of the Vatican – from their
Soviet persecutors. The end of the Second World War
meant the start of the Cold War. Intelligence was necessary,
as were intelligent, ruthless individuals who could provide a
certain level of expertise. It was said that Klaus Barbie, the
'Butcher of Lyons', had been offered a job with British
Intelligence. It was rumoured that high-profile Nazis had
been spirited away to America. It wasn't until 1987 that the
United Nations released its full list of fugitive Nazi and
Japanese war criminals, forty thousand of them.

Why so late in releasing the list? Rebus thought he could
understand. Modern politics had decreed that Germany
and Japan were part of the global brotherhood of capital-
ism. In whose interests would it be to reopen old wounds?
And besides, how many atrocities had the Allies themselves
hidden? Who fought a war with clean hands? Rebus, who'd
grown to adulthood in the Army, could comprehend this.
He'd done things ... He'd served time in Northern Ireland,
seen trust disfigured, hatred replace fear.

Part of him could well believe in the existence of a Rat
Line.

The book Levy had given him went into the mechanics
of how such an operation might have worked. Rebus
wondered: was it really possible to disappear completely, to
change identity? And again, the recurring question: did any
of it matter? There did exist sources of identification, and

there *had* been court cases – Eichmann, Barbie, Demjanjuk – with others ongoing. He read about war criminals who, rather than being tried or extradited, were allowed to return home, running businesses, growing rich, dying of old age. But he also read of criminals who served their sentences and became 'good people', people who *had* changed. These men said war itself was the real culprit. Rebus recalled one of his first conversations with Joseph Lintz, in the drawing-room of Lintz's home. The old man's voice was hoarse, a scarf around his throat.

'At my age, Inspector, a simple throat infection can feel like death.'

There didn't seem to be many photographs around. Lintz had explained that a lot had gone missing during the war.

'Along with other mementoes. I do have these photos though.'

He'd shown Rebus half a dozen framed shots, dating back to the 1930s. As he'd explained who the subjects were, Rebus had suddenly thought: what if he's making it up? What if these are just a bunch of old photos he picked up somewhere and had framed? And the names, the identities he now gave to the faces – had he invented them? He'd seen in that instant, for the first time, how easy it might be to construct another life.

And then, later in their conversation that day, Lintz, sipping honeyed tea, had started discussing Villefranche.

'I've been thinking a lot about it, Inspector, as you might imagine. This Lieutenant Linzstek, he was in charge on the day?'

'Yes.'

'But presumably under orders from above. A lieutenant is not so very far up the pecking order.'

'Perhaps.'

'You see, if a soldier is under orders … then they must carry out those orders, no?'

'Even if the order is insane?'

'Nevertheless, I'd say the person was at the very least *coerced* into committing the crime, and a crime that very many of us would have carried out under similar circumstances. Can't you see the hypocrisy of trying someone, when you'd probably have done the same thing yourself? One soldier standing out from the crowd … saying no to the massacre: would you have made that stand yourself?'

'I hope so.' Rebus thinking back to Ulster and the 'Mean Machine' …

Levy's book didn't prove anything. All Rebus knew was that Josef Linzstek's name was on a list as having used the Rat Line, posing as a Pole. But where had the list originated? In Israel. Again, it was highly speculative. It wasn't *proof*.

And if Rebus's instincts told him Lintz and Linzstek were one and the same, they were still failing to tell him whether it mattered.

He dropped the book back to the Roxburghe, asked the receptionist to see that Mr Levy got it.

'I think he's in his room, if you'd like to …'

Rebus shook his head. He hadn't left any message with the book, knowing Levy might interpret this as a message in itself. He went home for his car, drove down to Haymarket and along to Shandon. As usual, parking near Sammy's flat was a problem. Everyone was home from work and tucked in front of their televisions. He climbed the stone steps, wondering how treacherous they'd get when the frosts came, and rang the bell. Sammy herself led him into the living room, where Candice was watching a game show.

'Hello, John,' she said. 'Are you my wonderwall?'

'I'm nobody's wonderwall, Candice.' He turned to Sammy. 'Everything all right?'

'Just fine.'

At that moment, Ned Farlowe walked in from the kitchen. He was eating soup from a bowl, dunking a folded slice of brown bread into it.

'Mind if I have a word?' Rebus said.

Farlowe shook his head, then jerked it in the direction of the kitchen.

'Can I eat while we talk? I'm starving.' He sat down at the foldaway table, got another slice of bread from the packet and spread margarine on it. Sammy put her head round the doorway, saw the look on her father's face, and made a tactical retreat. The kitchen was about seven foot square and too full of pots and appliances. Swinging a cat, you could have done a lot of damage.

'I saw you today,' Rebus said, 'skulking in Warriston Cemetery. Coincidence?'

'What do you think?'

'I'm asking you.' Rebus leaned his back against the sink unit, folded his arms.

'I'm watching Lintz.'

'Why?'

'Because I'm being paid to.'

'By a newspaper?'

'Lintz's lawyer has interim interdicts flying around. Nobody can afford to be seen near him.'

'But they still want him watched?'

'If there's a court case coming, they want to know as much as possible, stands to reason.'

By court case, Farlowe didn't mean any trial of Lintz, but rather of the newspapers themselves, for libel.

'If he catches you ...'

'He doesn't know me from Adam. Besides, there'd

always be somebody to take my place. Now do I get to ask a question?'

'Let me say something first. You know I'm investigating Lintz?' Farlowe nodded. 'That means we're too close. If you find out anything, people might think it came from me.'

'I haven't told Sammy what I'm doing, *specifically* so there's no conflict of interests.'

'I'm just saying others might not believe it.'

'A few more days, I'll have enough money to fund the book for another month.' Farlowe had finished his soup. He carried the empty bowl over to the sink, stood next to Rebus.

'I don't want this to be a problem, but the bottom line is: what can you do about it?'

Rebus stared at him. His instinct was to stuff Farlowe's head into the sink, but how would that look with Sammy?

'Now,' Farlowe said, 'do I get to ask my question?'

'What is it?'

'Who's Candice?'

'A friend of mine.'

'So what's wrong with *your* flat?'

Rebus realised he was no longer dealing with his daughter's boyfriend. He was confronted with a journalist, someone with a nose for a story.

'Tell you what,' said Rebus, 'say I didn't see you in the cemetery. Say we didn't just have this little chat.'

'And I don't ask about Candice?' Rebus stayed quiet. Farlowe considered the deal. 'Say I get to ask you a few questions for my book.'

'What sort of questions?'

'About Cafferty.'

Rebus shook his head. 'I could talk about Tommy Telford though.'

'When?'

'When we've got him behind bars.'

Farlowe smiled. 'I could be on the pension by then.' He waited, saw Rebus was going to give him nothing.

'She's only here till tomorrow anyway,' Rebus said.

'Where's she off to?'

Rebus just winked. Left the kitchen, returned to the living-room. Talked to Sammy while Candice's game show reached its climax. Whenever she heard audience laughter, she joined in. Rebus made arrangements for the following day, then left. There was no sign of Farlowe. He'd either hidden himself in the bedroom or else gone back out. It took Rebus a few moments to remember where he'd parked his car. He drove home carefully; stopped for all the lights.

The parking spaces were all taken in Arden Street. He left the Saab on a yellow line. As he approached his tenement door, he heard a car door open and spun towards the sound.

It was Claverhouse. He was on his own. 'Mind if I come in?'

Rebus thought of a dozen reasons for saying yes. But he shrugged and made for the door. 'Any news of the stabbing at Megan's?' he asked.

'How did you know we'd be interested?'

'A bouncer gets stabbed, the attacker flees on a waiting motorbike. It was premeditated. And the majority of the bouncers work for Tommy Telford.'

They were climbing the stairs. Rebus's flat was on the second floor.

'Well, you're right,' Claverhouse said. 'Billy Tennant worked for Telford. He controlled the traffic in and out of Megan's.'

'Traffic as in dope?'

'The footballer's friend, the one who got wounded, he's a known dealer. Works out of Paisley.'

'Therefore connected to Telford, too.'

'We're speculating he was the target, Tennant just got in the way.'

'Leaving only one question: who was behind it?'

'Come on, John. It was Cafferty, obviously.'

'Not Cafferty's style,' Rebus said, unlocking his door.

'Maybe he's learned a thing or two from the Young Pretender.'

'Make yourself at home,' Rebus said, walking down the hall. The breakfast things were still on the dining table. Siobhan's bag of goodies was down the side of a chair.

'A guest.' Claverhouse had noticed the two mugs, two plates. He looked around. 'She's not here now though?'

'She wasn't here for breakfast either.'

'Because she's at your daughter's.'

Rebus froze.

'I went to settle up with the hotel. They said a police car had come and taken all her things away. So then I asked around, and the driver gave me Samantha's address as the drop-off.' Claverhouse sat down on the sofa, crossed one leg over the other. 'So what's the game, John, and how come you've seen fit to leave me on the bench?' He sounded calm now, but Rebus could tell there'd been a storm.

'Do you want a drink?'

'I want an answer.'

'When she walked out … she waited beside my car. I couldn't think where to take her, so I brought her here. But she recognised the street. Telford had been watching my flat.'

Claverhouse looked interested. 'Why?'

'Maybe because I know Cafferty. I couldn't let Candice stay here, so I took her to Sammy's.'

'Is she still there?' Rebus nodded. 'So what happens now?'

'There's a place she can go, the refugee family.'

'For how long?'

'What do you mean?'

Claverhouse sighed. 'John, she's … the only life she's known here is prostitution.'

Rebus went over to the hi-fi for something to do, looked through his tapes. He needed to do *some*thing.

'What's she going to do for money? Are you going to provide? What does that make you?'

Rebus dropped a CD, turned on his heels. 'Nothing like that,' he spat.

Claverhouse had his hands up, palms showing. 'Come on, John, you know yourself there's –'

'I don't know anything.'

'John …'

'Look, get out, will you?' It wasn't just that it had been a long day, more that it felt like the day would never end. He could feel the evening stretch to infinity, no rest available to him. In his head, bodies were swaying gently from trees while smoke engulfed a church. Telford was on his arcade motorbike, cannoning off spectators. Abernethy was touching an old man's shoulder. Soldiers were rifle-butting civilians. And John Rebus … John Rebus was in every frame, trying hard to remain an onlooker.

He put Van Morrison on the hi-fi: *Hardnose the Highway*. He'd played this music on East Neuk beaches and tenement stakeouts. It always seemed to heal him, or at least patch the wounds. When he turned back into the room, Claverhouse was gone. He looked out of his window. Two kids lived in the second-floor flat across from his. He'd watched them often from this window, and they never once saw him, for the simple reason that they never so much as glanced outside. Their world was complete and all-absorbing, anything outside their window an irrelevance. They were in bed now, their mother closing the shutters. Quiet city. Abernethy was right about that. There were large chunks of Edinburgh where you could live your whole life and never encounter a spot of bother. Yet the murder rate in Scotland was double that of its southern neighbour, and half those murders took place in the two main cities.

Not that the statistics mattered. A death was a death. Something unique had disappeared from the world. One murder or several hundred ... they all meant something to the survivors. Rebus thought of Villefranche's sole existing survivor. He hadn't met her, probably never would. Another reason it was hard to get passionate about a historical case. In a contemporary one, you had many of the facts to hand, and could talk to witnesses. You could gather forensic evidence, question people's stories. You could measure guilt and grief. You became part of the whole story. This was what interested Rebus. The people interested him; their stories fascinated him. When part of their lives, he could forget his own.

He noticed the answering-machine was flashing: one message.

'Oh, hello there. I'm ... um, I don't know how to put this ...' Placed the voice: Kirstin Mede. She sighed. 'Look, I can't do this any more. So please don't ... I'm sorry, I just can't. There are other people who can help you. I'm sure one of them ...'

End of message. Rebus stared down at the machine. He didn't blame her. *I can't do this any more.* That makes two of us, Rebus thought. The only thing was, *he* had to keep going. He sat down at his table and pulled the Villefranche paperwork towards him: lists of names and occupations, ages and dates of birth. Picat, Mesplede, Rousseau, Deschamps. Wine merchant, china painter, cartwright, housemaid. What did any of it mean to a middle-aged Scot? He pushed it aside and lifted Siobhan's paperwork on to the table.

Off with Van the Man; on with side one of *Wish You*

Were Here. Scratched to hell. He remembered it had come in a black polythene wrapper. When opened, there'd been this smell, which afterwards he'd learned was supposed to be burning flesh ...

'I need a drink,' he said to himself, sitting forward in his chair. 'I want a drink. A few beers, maybe with whiskies attached.' Something to smooth the edges ...

He looked at his watch; not even near to closing time. Not that it mattered much in Edinburgh, the land that closing time forgot. Could he make it to the Ox before they shut up shop? Yes, too easily. It was nicer to have a challenge. Wait an hour or so and then repeat the debate.

Or call Jack Morton.

Or go out, right now.

The telephone rang. He picked it up.

'Hello?'

'John?' Making it sound like 'Sean'.

'Hello, Candice. What's up?'

'Up?'

'Is there a problem?'

'Problem, no. I just wanting ... I say to you, see you tomorrow.'

He smiled. 'Yes, see you tomorrow. You speak very good English.'

'I was chained to a razor blade.'

'What?'

'Line from song.'

'Oh, right. But you're not chained to it now?'

She didn't seem to understand. 'I'm ... uh ...'

'It's okay, Candice. See you tomorrow.'

'Yes, see you.'

Rebus put down the receiver. Chained to a razor blade ... Suddenly he didn't want a drink any more.

9

He picked Candice up the next afternoon. She had two carrier bags, her worldly belongings. She gave Sammy as much of a hug as her bandaged arms would allow.

'See you again, Candice,' Sammy said.

'Yes, see you. Thanks ...' Lost for an ending to the sentence, Candice opened her arms wide, bags swinging.

They stopped off at McDonald's (her choice) for something to eat. Zappa and the Mothers: 'Cruising for Burgers'. The day was bright and crisp, just right for crossing the Forth Bridge. Rebus took it slowly, so Candice could take in the view. He was heading towards Fife's East Neuk, a cluster of fishing villages popular with artists and holidaymakers. Out of season, Anstruther seemed practically deserted. Though Rebus had an address, he stopped to ask directions. Finally, he parked in front of a small terraced house. Candice stared at the red door until he gestured for her to follow him. He hadn't been able to make her understand what they were doing here. Hoped Mr and Mrs Drinic would make a better job of it.

The door was opened by a woman in her early forties. She had long black hair, and peered at him over half-moon glasses. Then her attention shifted to Candice, and she said something in a language both women understood. Candice replied, looking a little shy, not sure what was going on.

'Come in, please,' Mrs Drinic said. 'My husband is in the kitchen.'

They sat around the kitchen table. Mr Drinic was heavily

built, with a thick brown moustache and wavy brown and silver hair. A pot of tea was produced, and Mrs Drinic drew her chair beside Candice's and began talking again.

'She's explaining to the girl,' Mr Drinic said.

Rebus nodded, sipped the strong tea, listened to a conversation he could not understand. Candice, cautious at first, grew more animated as she told her story, and Mrs Drinic was a skilled listener, sympathising, showing shared horror and exasperation.

'She was taken to Amsterdam, told there would be a job there for her,' Mr Drinic explained. 'I know this has happened to other young women.'

'I think she left a child behind.'

'A son, yes. She's telling my wife about him.'

'What about you?' Rebus asked. 'How did you end up here?'

'I was an architect in Sarajevo. No easy decision, leaving your whole life behind.' He paused. 'We went to Belgrade first. A refugee bus brought us to Scotland.' He shrugged. 'That was nearly five years ago. Now I am a carpenter.' A smile. 'Distance no object.'

Rebus looked at Candice, who had started crying, Mrs Drinic comforting her.

'We will look after her,' Mrs Drinic said, staring at her husband.

Later, at the door, Rebus tried to give them some money, but they wouldn't take it.

'Is it all right if I come and see her sometime?'

'But of course.'

He stood in front of Candice.

'Her real name is Karina,' Mrs Drinic said quietly.

'Karina.' Rebus tried out the word. She smiled, her eyes softer than Rebus remembered them, as if some transformation were beginning. She bent forward.

'Kiss the girl,' she said.

A peck on both cheeks. Her eyes filling with tears again. Rebus nodded, to let her know he understood everything.

At his car, he waved once, and she blew him another kiss. Then he drove around the corner and stopped, gripping the steering-wheel hard. He wondered if she'd cope. If she'd learn to forget. He thought again of his ex-wife's words. What would she think of him now? Had he exploited Karina? No, but he wondered if that was only because she hadn't been able to give him anything on Telford. He felt he had somehow failed to do the right thing. So far, the only choice she'd had to make was when she'd waited for him by his car rather than going back to Telford. Before then and after, all the decisions had been taken for her. In a sense, she was still as trapped as ever, because the locks and chains were in her mind; they were what she expected from life. It would take time for her to change, to begin trusting the world again. The Drinics would help her.

Heading south down the coast, thinking about families, he decided to visit his brother.

Mickey lived on an estate in Kirkcaldy, his red BMW parked in the driveway. He was just home from work and suitably surprised to see Rebus.

'Chrissie and the kids are at her mum's,' he said. 'I was going to grab a curry for dinner. How about a beer?'

'Maybe just a coffee,' Rebus said. He sat in the lounge until Mickey returned, toting a couple of old shoe-boxes.

'Look what I dug out of the attic last weekend. Thought you might like a look. Milk and sugar?'

'A spot of milk.'

While Mickey went to the kitchen to fetch the coffee, Rebus examined the boxes. They were filled with packets of photographs. The packets had dates on them, some with questionmarks. Rebus opened one at random. Holiday snaps. A fancy dress parade. A picnic. Rebus didn't have any pictures of his parents, and the photos startled him. His mother had thicker legs than he remembered, but a tidy body, too. His father used the same grin in every shot, a grin Rebus shared with Mickey. Digging further into the box, he found one of himself with Rhona and Sammy. They were on a beach somewhere, the wind playing havoc. Peter Gabriel: 'Family Snapshot'. Rebus couldn't place it at all. Mickey came back through with a mug of coffee and a bottle of beer.

'There are some,' he said, 'I don't know who the people are. Relatives maybe? Grandma and Grandad?'

'I'm not sure I'd be much help.'

Mickey handed over a menu. 'Here,' he said, 'best Indian in town. Pick what you want.'

So Rebus chose, and Mickey phoned the order in. Twenty minutes till delivery. Rebus was on to another packet. These photos were older still, the 1940s. His father in uniform. The soldiers wore hats like McDonald's counter staff. They also wore long khaki shorts. 'Malaya' written on the backs of some, 'India' on the others.

'Remember, the old man got himself wounded in Malaya?' Mickey said.

'No, he didn't.'

'He showed us the wound. It was in his knee.'

Rebus was shaking his head. 'Uncle Jimmy told me it was a cut Dad got playing football. He kept picking the scab off, ended with a scar.'

'He told us it was a war wound.'

'He was fibbing.'

Mickey had started on the other box. 'Here, look at these …' Handing over an inch-thick collection of post-cards and photographs, secured with an elastic band. Rebus pulled the band off, turned the cards over, saw his own writing. The photos were of him, too: posed snaps, badly taken.

'Where did you get these?'

'You always used to send me a card or a photo, don't you remember?'

They were all from Rebus's own Army days. 'I'd forgotten,' he said.

'Once a fortnight, usually. A letter to Dad, a card for me.'

Rebus sat back in his chair and started to go through them. Judging by the postmarks, they were in chronological sequence. Training, then service in Germany and Ulster, more exercises in Cyprus, Malta, Finland, and the desert of Saudi Arabia. The tone of each postcard was breezy, so that Rebus failed to recognise his own voice. The cards from Belfast consisted of almost nothing but jokes, yet Rebus remembered that as one of the most nightmarish periods of his life.

'I used to love getting them,' Mickey said, smiling. 'I'll tell you, you almost had me joining up.'

Rebus was still thinking of Belfast: the closed barracks, the whole compound a fortress. After a shift out on the streets, there was no way to let off steam. Booze, gambling and fights – all taking place within the same four walls. All culminating in the Mean Machine ... And here were these postcards, here was the image of Rebus's past life that Mickey had lived with these past twenty-odd years.

And it was all a lie.

Or was it? Where did the reality lie, other than in Rebus's own head? The postcards were fake documents, but they were also the only ones in existence. There was nothing to contradict them, nothing except Rebus's word. It was the same with the Rat Line, the same with Joseph Lintz's story. Rebus looked at his brother and knew he could break the spell right now. All he had to do was tell him the truth.

'What's the matter?' Mickey asked.

'Nothing.'

'Ready for that beer yet? The food'll be here any second.'

Rebus stared at the cooling mug of coffee. 'More than ready,' he said, putting the rubber band back around his past. 'But I'll stick to this.' He lifted the mug, toasted his brother.

10

Next morning, Rebus went to St Leonard's, telephoned the NCIS centre at Prestwick and asked if they had anything connecting British criminals to European prostitution. His reasoning: *someone* had brought Candice – she was still Candice to him – from Amsterdam to Britain, and he didn't think it was Telford. Whoever it was, Rebus would get to them somehow. He wanted to show Candice her chains could be broken.

He got NCIS to fax him what information they had. Most of it concerned the 'Tippelzone', a licensed car park where drivers went for sex. It was worked by foreign prostitutes mainly, most of them lacking work permits, many smuggled in from Eastern Europe. The main gangs seemed to be from former Yugoslavia. NCIS had no names for any of these kidnappers-cum-pimps. There was nothing about prostitutes making the trip from Amsterdam to Britain.

Rebus went into the car park to smoke his second cigarette of the day. There were a couple of other smokers out there, a small brotherhood of social pariahs. Back in the office, the Farmer wanted to know if there was any progress on Lintz.

'Maybe if I brought him in and slapped him around a bit,' Rebus suggested.

'Be serious, will you?' the Farmer growled, stalking back to his office.

Rebus sat down at his desk and pulled forward a file.

'Your problem, Inspector,' Lintz had said to him once, 'is that you're afraid of being taken seriously. You want to give people what you think they expect. I mention the Ishtar gate, and you talk of some Hollywood movie. At first I thought this was meant to rouse me to some indiscretion, but now it seems more a game you are playing against *yourself*.'

Rebus: seated in his usual chair in Lintz's drawing-room. The view from the window was of Queen Street Gardens. They were kept locked: you had to pay for a key.

'Do educated people frighten you?'

Rebus looked at the old man. 'No.'

'Are you sure? Don't you perhaps wish you were more like them?' Lintz grinned, showing small, discoloured teeth. 'Intellectuals like to see themselves as history's victims, prejudiced against, arrested for their beliefs, even tortured and murdered. But Karadzic thinks himself an intellectual. The Nazi hierarchy had its thinkers and philosophers. And even in Babylon ...' Lintz got up, poured himself more tea. Rebus declined a refill.

'Even in Babylon, Inspector,' Lintz continued, getting comfortable again, 'with its opulence and its artistry, with its enlightened king ... do you know what they did? Nebuchadnezzar held the Jews captive for seventy years. This splendid, awe-inspiring civilisation ... Do you begin to see the madness, Inspector, the flaws that run so deep in us?'

'Maybe I need glasses.'

Lintz threw his cup across the room. 'You need to listen and to learn! You need to understand!'

The cup and saucer lay on the carpet, still intact. Tea was soaking into the elaborate design, where it would become all but invisible ...

He parked on Buccleuch Place. The Slavic Studies

department was housed in one of the tenements. He tried the secretary's office first, asked if Dr Colquhoun was around.

'I haven't seen him today.'

When Rebus explained what he wanted, the secretary tried a couple of numbers but didn't find anyone. Then she suggested he take a look in their library, which was one floor up and kept locked. She handed him a key.

The room was about sixteen feet by twelve, and smelled stuffy. The shutters across the windows were closed, giving the place no natural light. A No Smoking sign sat on one of four desks. On another sat an ashtray with three butts in it. One entire wall was shelved, filled with books, pamphlets, magazines. There were boxes of press cuttings, and maps on the walls showing Yugoslavia's changing demarcation lines. Rebus lifted down the most recent box of cuttings.

Like a lot of people he knew, Rebus didn't know much about the war in ex-Yugoslavia. He'd seen some of the news reports, been shocked by the pictures, then had got on with his life. But if the cuttings were to be believed, the whole region was being run by war criminals. The Implementation Force seemed to have done its damnedest to avoid confrontation. There had been a few arrests recently, but nothing substantial: out of a meagre seventy-four suspects charged, only *seven* had been apprehended.

He found nothing about slave traders, so thanked the secretary and gave her back her key, then crawled through the city traffic. When the call came on his mobile, he nearly went off the road.

Candice had disappeared.

Mrs Drinic was distraught. They'd had dinner last night, breakfast this morning, and Karina had seemed fine.

'There was a lot she said she couldn't tell us,' Mr Drinic

said, standing behind his seated wife, hands stroking her shoulders. 'She said she wanted to forget.'

And then she'd gone out for a walk down to the harbour, and hadn't returned. Lost maybe, though the village was small. Mr Drinic had been working; his wife had gone out, asking people if they'd seen her.

'And Mrs Muir's son,' she said, 'he told me she'd been taken away in a car.'

'Where was this?' Rebus asked.

'Just a couple of streets away,' Mr Drinic said.

'Show me.'

Outside his home on Seaford Road, Eddie Muir, aged eleven, told Rebus what he'd seen. A car stopping beside a woman. A bit of chat, though he couldn't hear it. The door opening, the woman getting in.

'Which door, Eddie?'

'One of the back ones. Had to be, there were two of them in the car already.'

'Men?'

Eddie nodded.

'And the woman got in by herself? I mean, they didn't grab her or anything?'

Eddie shook his head. He was straddling his bike, keen to be going. One foot kept testing a pedal.

'Can you describe the car?'

'Big, a bit flash. Not from round here.'

'And the men?'

'Didn't really get a good look. Driver was wearing a Pars shirt.'

Meaning a football shirt, Dunfermline Athletic. Which would mean he was from Fife. Rebus frowned. A pick-up? Could that be it? Candice back to her old ways so soon? Not likely, not in a place like this, on a street like this. It was no chance encounter. Mrs Drinic was right: she'd been snatched. Which meant someone had known where to find her. Had Rebus been followed yesterday? If he had, they'd been invisible. Some device on his car? It seemed unlikely, but he checked wheel-arches and the underbody: nothing. Mrs Drinic had calmed a little, her husband having administered medicinal vodka. Rebus could use a shot himself, but turned down the offer.

'Did she make any phone calls?' he asked. Drinic shook his head. 'What about strangers hanging around the street?'

'I would have noticed. After Sarajevo, it's hard to feel safe, Inspector.' He opened his arms. 'And here's the proof – nowhere's safe.'

'Did you tell anyone about Karina?'

'Who would we tell?'

Who knew? That was the question. Rebus did. And Claverhouse and Ormiston knew about the place, because Colquhoun had mentioned it.

Colquhoun knew. The nervy old Slavic Studies specialist knew ... On the way back to Edinburgh, Rebus tried phoning him at office and home: no reply. He'd told the Drinics to let him know if Candice came back, but he didn't think she'd be coming back. He remembered the look she'd given him early on when he'd asked her to trust him. *I won't be surprised if you let me down.* Like she'd known back then that he'd fail. And she'd given him a second chance, waiting for him beside his car. And he'd let her down. He got back on his mobile and called Jack Morton.

'Jack,' he said, 'for Christ's sake, talk me out of having a drink.'

He tried Colquhoun's home address and the Slavic Studies office: both locked up tight. Then he drove to Flint Street and looked for Tommy Telford in the arcade. But Telford wasn't there. He was in the café's back office, surrounded as usual by his men.

'I want to talk to you,' Rebus said.

'So talk.'

'Without the audience.' Rebus pointed to Pretty-Boy. 'That one can stay.'

Telford took his time, but finally nodded, and the room began to empty. Pretty-Boy stood against a wall, hands behind his back. Telford had his feet up on his desk, leaning back in his chair. They were relaxed, confident. Rebus knew what *he* looked like: a caged bear.

'I want to know where she is.'

'Who?'

'Candice.'

Telford smiled. 'Still on about her, Inspector? How should I know where she is?'

'Because a couple of your boys grabbed her.' But as he spoke, Rebus realised he was making a mistake. Telford's gang was a *family*: they'd grown up together in Paisley. Not many Dunfermline supporters that distant from Fife. He stared at Pretty-Boy, who ran Telford's prostitutes. Candice had arrived in Edinburgh from a city of bridges, maybe Newcastle. Telford had Newcastle connections. And the Newcastle United strip – vertical black and white lines – was damned close to Dunfermline's. Probably only a kid in Fife could make the mistake.

A Newcastle strip. A Newcastle car.

Telford was talking, but Rebus wasn't listening. He walked straight out of the office and back to the Saab. Drove to Fettes – the Crime Squad offices – and started looking. He found a contact number for a DS Miriam Kenworthy. Tried the number but she wasn't there.

'Fuck it,' he told himself, getting back into his car.

The A1 was hardly the country's fastest road – Abernethy was right about that. Still, without the daytime traffic Rebus made decent time on his way south. It was late evening when he arrived in Newcastle, pubs emptying, queues forming outside clubs, a few United shirts on display, looking like prison bars. He didn't know the city. Drove around it in circles, passing the same signs and landmarks, heading further out, just cruising.

Looking for Candice. Or for girls who might know her.

After a couple of hours, he gave up, headed back into the centre. He'd had the idea of sleeping in his car, but when he found a hotel with an empty room, the thought of en-suite facilities suddenly seemed too good to miss.

He made sure there was no mini-bar.

A long soak with his eyes closed, mind and body still racing from the drive. He sat in a chair by his window and listened to the night: taxis and yells, delivery lorries. He couldn't sleep. He lay on the bed, watching soundless TV, remembering Candice in the hotel room, asleep under sweet wrappers. Deacon Blue: 'Chocolate Girl.'

He woke up to breakfast TV. Checked out of the hotel and had breakfast in a café, then called Miriam Kenworthy's office, relieved to find she was an early starter.

'Come right round,' she said, sounding bemused. 'You're only a couple of minutes away.'

She was younger than her telephone voice, face softer than her attitude. It was a milkmaid's face, rounded, the cheeks pink and plump. She studied him, swivelling slightly in her chair as he told her the story.

'Tarawicz,' she said when he'd finished. 'Jake Tarawicz. Real name Joachim, probably.' Kenworthy smiled. 'Some of us around here call him Mr Pink Eyes. He's had dealings – meetings anyway – with this guy Telford.' She opened the brown folder in front of her. 'Mr Pink Eyes has a lot of European connections. You know Chechnia?'

'In Russia?'

'It's Russia's Sicily, if you know what I mean.'

'Is that where Tarawicz comes from?'

'It's one theory. The other is that he's Serbian. Might explain why he set up the convoy.'

'What convoy?'

'Running aid lorries to former Yugoslavia. A real humanitarian, our Mr Pink.'

'But also a way of smuggling people out?'

Kenworthy looked at him. 'You've been doing your homework.'

'Call it an educated guess.'

'Well, it gets him noticed. He got a papal blessing six months ago. Married to an Englishwoman – not for love. She was one of his girls.'

'But it gives him residency here.'

She nodded. 'He hasn't been around that long, five or six years ...'

Like Telford, Rebus thought.

'But he's built himself a rep, muscled in where there used to be Asians, Turks ... Story is, he started with a nice line in stolen icons. A ton of stuff has been lifted out of the Soviet bloc. And when that operation started drying, he moved into prossies. Cheap girls, and he could keep them docile with a bit of crack. The crack comes up from London – the Yardies control that particular scene. Mr Pink spreads their goods around the north-east. He also deals heroin for the Turks and sells some girls to Triad brothels.' She looked at Rebus, saw she had his attention. 'No racial barriers when it comes to business.'

'So I see.'

'Probably also sells drugs to your friend Telford, who distributes them through his nightclubs.'

' "Probably"?'

'We've no hard proof. There was even a story going around that Pink wasn't selling to Telford, he was *buying*.'

Rebus blinked. 'Telford's not that big.'

She shrugged.

'Where would he get the stuff?'

'It was a story, that's all.'

But it had Rebus thinking, because it might help explain the relationship between Tarawicz and Telford ...

'What does Tarawicz get out of it?' he asked, making his thoughts flesh.

'You mean apart from money? Well, Telford trains a good bouncer. Jock bouncers get respect down here. Then, of course, Telford has shares in a couple of casinos.'

'A way for Tarawicz to launder his cash?' Rebus thought about this. 'Is there anything Tarawicz *doesn't* have a finger in?'

'Plenty. He likes businesses which are fluid. And he's still a relative newcomer.'

Eagles: 'New Kid in Town'.

'We think he's been dealing arms: a lot of stuff crossing into Western Europe. The Chechens seem to have weaponry to spare.' She sniffed, gathered her thoughts.

'Sounds like he's one step ahead of Tommy Telford.' Which would explain why Telford was so keen to do business with him. He was on a learning curve, learning how to fit into the bigger picture. Yardies and Asians, Turks and Chechens, and all the others. Rebus saw them as spokes on a huge wheel which was trundling mercilessly across the world, breaking bones as it went.

'Why "Mr Pink Eyes"?' he asked.

She'd been awaiting the question, slid a colour photo towards him.

It was the close-up of a face, the skin pink and blistered, white lesions running through it. The face was puffy, bloated, and in its midst sat eyes hidden by blue-tinted glasses. There were no eyebrows. The hair above the jutting forehead was thin and yellow. The man looked like some monstrous shaved pig.

'What happened to him?' he asked.

'We don't know. That's the way he looked when he arrived.'

Rebus remembered the description Candice had given: sunglasses, looks like a car-crash victim. Dead ringer.

'I want to talk to him,' Rebus said.

But first, Kenworthy gave him a guided tour. They took her car, and she showed him where the street girls worked. It was mid-morning, no action to speak of. He gave her a description of Candice, and she promised she'd put the word out. They spoke with the few women they met. They all seemed to know Kenworthy, weren't hostile towards her.

'They're the same as you or me,' she told him, driving away. 'Working to feed their kids.'

'Or their habit.'

'That too, of course.'

'In Amsterdam, they've got a union.'

'Doesn't help the poor sods who're shipped there.' Kenworthy signalled at a junction. 'You're sure he has her?'

'I don't think Telford does. Someone knew addresses back in Sarajevo, addresses that were important to her. Someone shipped her out of there.'

'Sounds like Mr Pink all right.'

'And he's the only one who can send her back.'

She looked at him. 'Why would he do a thing like that?'

Just as Rebus was thinking their surroundings couldn't get any grimmer — all industrial decay, gutted buildings and pot-holes — Kenworthy signalled to turn in at the gates of a scrapyard.

'You're kidding?' he said.

Three Alsatians, tethered by thirty-foot chains, barked and bounded towards the car. Kenworthy ignored them, kept driving. It was like being in a ravine. Either side of them stood precarious canyon walls of car wrecks.

'Hear that?'

Rebus heard it: the sound of a collision. The car entered a wide clearing, and he saw a yellow crane, dangling a huge grab from its arm, pluck up the car it had dropped and lift it high, before dropping it again on to the carcass of another. A few men were standing at a safe distance, smoking cigarettes and looking bored. The grab dropped on to the roof of the top car, denting it badly. Glass shimmered on the oily ground, diamonds against black velvet.

Jake Tarawicz – Mr Pink Eyes – was in the crane, laughing and roaring as he picked up the car again, worrying it the way a cat might play with a mouse without noticing it was dead. If he'd seen the new additions to his audience, it didn't show. Kenworthy hadn't got out of her car immediately. First, she'd fixed on a face from her repertoire. When finally she was ready, she nodded to Rebus and they opened their doors simultaneously.

As Rebus stood upright, he saw that the grab had dropped the car and was swinging towards them. Kenworthy folded her arms and stood her ground. Rebus was reminded of those arcade games where you had to pick up a prize. He could see Tarawicz in the cab, manipulating the controls like a kid with a toy. He remembered Tommy Telford on his arcade bike, and saw at once something the two men had in common: neither had ever really grown up.

The motorised hum stopped suddenly, and Tarawicz dropped from the cab. He was wearing a cream suit and emerald shirt, open at the neck. He'd borrowed a pair of green wellies from somewhere, so as to keep his trousers clean. As he walked towards the two detectives, his men stepped into line behind him.

'Miriam,' he said, 'always a pleasure.' He paused. 'Or so

the rumour goes.' A couple of his men grinned. Rebus recognised one face: 'The Crab', that's what he'd been called in central Scotland. His grip could crush bones. Rebus hadn't seen him in a long time, and had never seen him so smartly groomed and dressed.

'All right, Crab?' Rebus said.

This seemed to disconcert Tarawicz, who half-turned towards his minion. The Crab stayed quiet, but colour had risen to his neck.

Up close, it was hard not to stare at Mr Pink Eyes's face. His eyes demanded that you meet them, but you really wanted to study the flesh in which they sat.

He was looking at Rebus now.

'Have we met?'

'No.'

'This is Detective Inspector Rebus,' Kenworthy explained. 'He's come all the way from Scotland to see you.'

'I'm flattered.' Tarawicz's grin showed small sharp teeth with gaps between them.

'I think you know why I'm here,' Rebus said.

Tarawicz made a show of astonishment. 'Do I?'

'Telford needed your help. He needed a home address for Candice, a note to her in Serbo-Croat ...'

'Is this some sort of riddle?'

'And now you've taken her back.'

'Have I?'

Rebus took a half-step forward. Tarawicz's men fanned out either side of their boss. There was a sheen on Tarawicz's face which could have been sweat or some medical cream.

'She wanted out,' Rebus told him. 'I promised I'd help her. I never break a promise.'

'She wanted out? She told you that?' Tarawicz's voice was teasing.

One of the men behind cleared his throat. Rebus had been wondering about this man, so much smaller and more reticent than the others, better dressed and with sad drooping eyes and sallow skin. Now he knew: lawyer. And the cough was his way of warning Tarawicz that he was saying too much.

'I'm going to take Tommy Telford down,' Rebus said quietly. 'That's my promise to you. Once he's in custody, who knows what he'll say?'

'I'm sure Mr Telford can look after himself, Inspector. Which is more than can be said for Candice.' The lawyer coughed again.

'I want her kept off the streets,' Rebus said.

Tarawicz stared at him, tiny black pupils like spots of absolute darkness.

'Can Thomas Telford go about his daily business unfettered?' he said at last. Behind him, the lawyer almost choked.

'You know I can't promise that,' Rebus said. 'It's not me he has to worry about.'

'Take a message to your friend,' Tarawicz said. 'And afterwards, stop being his friend.'

Rebus realised then: Tarawicz was talking about *Cafferty*. Telford had told him that Rebus was Cafferty's man.

'I think I can do that,' Rebus said quietly.

'Then do it.' Tarawicz turned away.

'And Candice?'

'I'll see what I can do.' He stopped, slid his hands into his jacket pockets. 'Hey, Miriam,' he said, his back still to them, 'I like you better in that red two-piece.'

Laughing, he walked away.

'Get in the car,' Kenworthy said through gritted teeth. Rebus got into the car. She looked nervous, dropped her keys, bent to retrieve them.

'What's wrong?'

'Nothing's wrong,' she snapped.

'The red two-piece?'

She glared at him. 'I don't have a red two-piece.' She did a three point-turn, hitting brakes and accelerator with a little more force than necessary.

'I don't get it.'

'Last week,' she said, 'I bought some red underwear … bra and pants.' She revved the engine. 'Part of his little game.'

'So how does he know?'

'That's what I'm wondering.' She shot past the dogs and out of the gate. Rebus thought of Tommy Telford, and how he'd been watching Rebus's flat.

'Surveillance isn't always one-way,' he said, knowing now who'd taught Telford the skill. A little later he asked about the scrapyard.

'He owns it. He's got a compacter, but before the cars get squashed he likes to play with them. And if you cross him, he welds your seatbelt shut.' She looked at him. 'You become part of his game.'

Never get personally involved: it was *the* golden rule. And practically every case he worked, Rebus broke it. He sometimes felt that the reason he became so involved in his cases was that he had no life of his own. He could only live *through* other people.

Why had he become so involved with Candice? Was it down to her physical resemblance to Sammy? Or was it that she had seemed to need *him*? The way she'd clung to his leg that first day … Had he wanted – just for a little while – to be someone's knight in shining armour, the real thing, not some mockery?

John Rebus: complete bloody sham.

He phoned Claverhouse from his car, filled him in. Claverhouse told him not to worry.

'Thanks for that,' Rebus said. 'I feel a whole lot better now. Listen, who's Telford's supplier?'

'For what? Dope?'

'Yes.'

'That's the real joker in the pack. I mean, he does business with Newcastle, but we can't be certain who's dealing and who's buying.'

'What if Telford's selling?'

'Then he's got a line from the continent.'

'What do Drugs Squad say?'

'They say not. If he's landing the stuff from a boat, it means transporting it from the coast. Much more likely he's buying from Newcastle. Tarawicz has the contacts in Europe.'

'Makes you wonder why he needs Tommy Telford at all ...'

'John, do yourself a favour, switch off for five minutes.'

'Colquhoun seems to be keeping his head down ...'

'Did you hear me?'

'I'll talk to you soon.'

'Are you heading back?'

'In a manner of speaking.' Rebus cut the call and drove.

11

'Strawman,' said Morris Gerald Cafferty, as he was escorted into the room by two prison guards.

Earlier in the year, Rebus had promised Cafferty he would put a Glasgow gangster, Uncle Joe Toal, behind bars. It hadn't worked, despite Rebus's best efforts. Toal, pleading old age and illness, was still a free man, like a war criminal excused for senility. Ever since then, Cafferty had felt Rebus owed him.

Cafferty sat down, rolled his neck a few times, loosening it.

'So?' he asked.

Rebus nodded for the guards to leave, waited in silence until they'd gone. Then he slipped a quarter-bottle of Bell's from his pocket.

'Keep it,' Cafferty told him. 'From the look of you, I'd say your need was greater than mine.'

Rebus put the bottle back in his pocket. 'I've brought a message from Newcastle.'

Cafferty folded his arms. 'Jake Tarawicz?'

Rebus nodded. 'He wants you to lay off Tommy Telford.'

'What does he mean?'

'Come on, Cafferty. That bouncer who got stabbed, the dealer wounded ... There's war breaking out.'

Cafferty stared at the detective. 'Not my doing.'

Rebus snorted, but looking into Cafferty's eyes, he found himself almost believing.

'So who was it?' he asked quietly.

'How do I know?'

'Nevertheless, war is breaking out.'

'That's as may be. What's in it for Tarawicz?'

'He does business with Tommy.'

'And to protect that, he needs to have *me* warned off by a cop?' Cafferty was shaking his head. 'You really buy that?'

'I don't know,' Rebus said.

'One way to finish this.' Cafferty paused. 'Take Telford out of the game.' He saw the look on Rebus's face. 'I don't mean top him, I mean put him away. That should be *your* job, Strawman.'

'I only came to deliver a message.'

'And what's in it for you? Something in Newcastle?'

'Maybe.'

'Are you Tarawicz's man now?'

'You know me better than that.'

'Do I?' Cafferty sat back in his chair, stretched out his legs. 'I wonder about that sometimes. I mean, it doesn't keep me awake at night, but I wonder all the same.'

Rebus leaned on the table. 'You must have a bit salted away. Why can't you just be content with that?'

Cafferty laughed. The air felt charged; there might have been only the two of them left in the world. 'You want me to retire?'

'A good boxer knows when to stop.'

'Then neither of us would be much cop in the ring, would we? Got any plans to retire, Strawman?'

Despite himself, Rebus smiled.

'Thought not. Do I have to say something for you to take back to Tarawicz?'

Rebus shook his head. 'That wasn't the deal.'

'Well, if he does come asking, tell him to get some life insurance, the kind with death benefits.'

Rebus looked at Cafferty. Prison might have softened him, but only physically.

'I'd be a happy man if someone took Telford out of the game,' Cafferty went on. 'Know what I mean, Strawman? It'd be worth a lot to me.'

Rebus stood up. 'No deal,' he said. 'Personally, I'd be happy if you wiped one another out. I'd be jumping for joy at ring-side.'

'Know what happens at ring-side?' Cafferty rubbed at his temples. 'You tend to get spattered with blood.'

'As long as it's someone else's.'

The laughter came from deep within Cafferty's chest. 'You're not a spectator, Strawman. It's not in your nature.'

'And you're some kind of psychologist?'

'Maybe not,' said Cafferty. 'But I know what gets people excited.'

Book Three

'Cover my face as the animals cry.'

Running through the hospital, stopping nurses to ask directions. Sweat dripping off him, tie hanging loose around his neck. Taking right turns, left turns, looking for signs. Whose fault? He kept asking himself that. A message which failed to reach him. Because he was on a surveillance. Because he wasn't in radio contact. Because the station didn't know how important the message was.

Now running, a stitch in his side. He'd run all the way from the car. Up two flights of stairs, down corridors. The place was quiet. Middle of the night.

'Maternity!' he called to a man pushing a trolley. The man pointed to a set of doors. He pushed through them. Three nurses in a glass cubicle. One of them came out.

'Can I help?'

'I'm John Rebus. My wife …'

She gave him a hard look. 'Third bed along.' Pointing … Third bed along, curtains closed around it. He pulled the curtains open. Rhona lay on her side, face still flushed, hair sticking to her brow. And beside her, nuzzling into her, a tiny perfection with wisps of brown hair and black, unfocused eyes.

He touched the nose, ran a finger round the curves of an ear. The face twitched. He bent past it to kiss his wife.

'Rhona … I'm really sorry. They didn't get the message to me until ten minutes ago. How did it … ? I mean … he's beautiful.'

'He's a she,' his wife said, turning away from him.

12

Rebus was sitting in his boss's office. It was nine-fifteen and he had slept for probably forty-five minutes the previous night. There'd been the hospital vigil and Sammy's operation: something about a blood clot. She was still unconscious, still 'critical'. He'd called Rhona in London. She'd told him she'd catch the first train she could. He'd given her his mobile number, so she could let him know when she arrived. She'd started to ask ... her voice had cracked. She'd put down the receiver. He'd tried to find some feeling for her. Richard and Linda Thompson: 'Withered and Died'.

He'd called Mickey, who said he'd drop by the hospital some time today. And that was it for the family. There were other people he could call, people like Patience, who had been his lover for a time, and Sammy's landlady until far more recently. But he didn't. He knew in the morning he'd call the office where Sammy worked. He wrote it in his notebook so he wouldn't forget. And then he'd called Sammy's flat and given Ned Farlowe the news.

Farlowe had asked a question nobody else had: 'How about you? Are you all right?'

Rebus had looked around the hospital corridor. 'Not exactly.'

'I'll be right there.'

So they'd spent a couple of hours in one another's company, not really saying very much at first. Farlowe smoked, and Rebus helped him empty the pack. He couldn't reciprocate with whisky – there was nothing in the bottle – but he'd bought the young man several cups of coffee, since Farlowe had spent nearly all his money on the taxi from Shandon …

'Wakey-wakey, John.'

Rebus's boss was shaking him gently. Rebus blinked, straightened in his chair.

'Sorry, sir.'

Chief Superintendent Watson went around the desk and sat down. 'Hellish sorry to hear about Sammy. I don't really know what to say, except that she's in my prayers.'

'Thank you, sir.'

'Do you want some coffee?' The Farmer's coffee had a reputation throughout the station, but Rebus accepted a mug gladly. 'How is she anyway?'

'Still unconscious.'

'No sign of the car?'

'Not the last I heard.'

'Who's handling it?'

'Bill Pryde started the ball rolling last night. I don't know who's taken it from him.'

'I'll find out.' The Farmer made an internal call, Rebus watching him over the rim of his mug. The Farmer was a big man, imposing behind a desk. His cheeks were a mass of tiny red veins and his thin hair lay across the dome of his head like the lines of a well-furrowed field. There were photos on his desk: grandchildren. The photos had been taken in a garden. There was a swing in the background. One of the children was holding a teddy bear. Rebus felt his throat start to ache, tried to choke it back.

The Farmer put down the receiver. 'Bill's still on it,' he said. 'Felt if he worked straight through we might get a quicker result.'

'That's good of him.'

'Look, we'll let you know the minute we get something, but meantime you'll probably want to go home ...'

'No, sir.'

'Or to the hospital.'

Rebus nodded slowly. Yes, the hospital. But not right this minute. He had to talk to Bill Pryde first.

'And meantime, I'll reassign your cases.' The Farmer started writing. 'There's this War Crimes thing, and your liaison on Telford. Are you working on anything else?'

'Sir, I'd prefer it if you ... I mean, I want to keep working.'

The Farmer looked at him, then leaned back in his chair, pen balanced between his fingers.

'Why?'

Rebus shrugged. 'I want to keep busy.' Yes, there was that. And he didn't want anyone else taking his work. It was *his*. He owned it; it owned him.

'Look, John, you're going to want some time off, right?'

'I can handle things, sir.' His gaze met the Farmer's. 'Please.'

Across the hall in the CID room he nodded as everyone came up to say how sorry they were. One person stayed at their desk – Bill Pryde knew Rebus was coming to see him.

'Morning, Bill.'

Pryde nodded. They'd met in the wee small hours at the Infirmary. Ned Farlowe had been napping in a chair, so they'd stepped into the corridor to talk. Pryde looked tireder now. He had loosened the top button of his dark green shirt. His brown suit looked lived-in.

'Thanks for sticking with it,' Rebus said, drawing over a chair. Thinking: *I'd rather have had someone else, someone sharper ...*

'No problem.'

'Any news?'

'A couple of good eyewitnesses. They were waiting to cross at the lights.'

'What's their story?'

Pryde considered his reply. He knew he was dealing with a father as well as a cop. 'She was crossing the road. Looked like she was heading down Minto Street, maybe making for the bus stop.'

Rebus shook his head. 'She was walking, Bill. Going to a friend's in Gilmour Road.'

She'd said as much over the pizza, apologising that she couldn't stay longer. Just one more coffee at the end of the meal ... one more coffee and she wouldn't have been there at that moment. Or if she'd accepted his offer of a lift ... When you thought about life, you thought of it as chunks of time, but really all it was was a series of connected moments, any one of which could change you completely.

'The car was heading south out of town,' Pryde went on. 'Looks like he ran a red light. Motorist sitting behind him seemed to think so.'

'Reckon he was drunk?'

Pryde nodded. 'Way he was driving. I mean, could be he just lost control, but in that case why didn't he stop?'

'Description?'

Pryde shook his head. 'We've got a dark car, a bit sporty. Nobody caught the licence plate.'

'It's a busy enough street, must've been other cars around.'

'A couple of people have called in.' Pryde flicked through his notes. 'Nothing helpful, but I'm going to interview them, see if I can jog a memory or two.'

'Could the car have been nicked? Maybe that's why he was in a hurry.'

'I can check.'

'I'll help you.'

Pryde considered this. 'You sure?'

'Try and stop me, Bill.'

'No skid marks,' Pryde said, 'no sign that he tried braking, either before or after.'

They were standing at the junction of Minto Street and Newington Road. The cross-streets were Salisbury Place and Salisbury Road. Cars, vans and buses queued at the traffic lights as pedestrians crossed the road.

It could have been any one of you, Rebus thought. Any one of them could have taken Sammy's place ...

'She was about here,' Pryde went on, pointing to a spot where, just past the lights, a bus lane started. The carriageway was wide, a four-lane road. She hadn't crossed at the lights. She'd been lazy, carrying on down Minto Street a few strides, then crossing in a diagonal. When she'd been a child, they'd taught her about crossing the road. Green Cross Code, all of that. Drummed it into her. Rebus looked around. At the top of Minto Street were some private houses and Bed & Breakfasts. On one corner stood a bank, on another a branch of Remnant Kings, with a takeaway next door.

'The takeaway would have been open,' Rebus said, pointing. On the third corner stood a Spar. 'That place, too. Where did you say she was?'

'The bus lane.' She'd crossed three lanes, been only a yard or two from safety. 'Witnesses say she was nearly at the kerb when he hit her. I think he was drunk, lost it for a second.' Pryde nodded towards the bank. There were two phone boxes in front of it. 'Witness called from there.' The wall behind the phone boxes had a poster glued to it. Grinning maniac behind a steering-wheel, and some writing: 'So many pedestrians, so little time'. A computer game ...

'It would have been so easy to avoid her,' Rebus said quietly.

'Sure you're okay? There's a café up the road.'

'I'm fine, Bill.' He looked around, took a deep breath. 'Looks like offices behind the Spar, doubtful anyone would have been there. But there are flats above Remnant Kings and the bank.'

'Want to talk to them?'

'And the Spar and the kebab shop. You take the B&Bs and the houses, meet back here in half an hour.'

Rebus talked to everyone he could find. In the Spar, there was a new shift on, but he got home phone numbers from the manager and called up the workers from the previous night. They hadn't seen or heard anything. First they'd known had been the flashing lights of the ambulance. The kebab shop was closed, but when Rebus banged on the door a woman came through from the back, wiping her hands on a tea-towel. He pressed his warrant card to the glass door, and she let him in. The shop had been busy last night. She didn't see the accident – she called it that, 'the accident'. And that's what it was: the word really hadn't sunk in until she said it. Elvis Costello: 'Accidents Will Happen'. Was the next line really 'It's only hit and run'?

'No,' the woman said, 'the first thing that caught my attention was the crowd. I mean, only three or four people, but I could see they were standing around something. And then the ambulance came. Will she be all right?'

The look in her eyes was one Rebus had encountered before. It almost wanted the victim dead, because then there was a story to be told.

'She's in hospital,' he said, unable to look at the woman any longer.

'Yes, but the paper said she's in a coma.'

'What paper?'

She brought him the first edition of the day's *Evening News*. There was a paragraph on one of the inside pages – 'Hit and Run Coma Victim'.

It wasn't a coma. She was unconscious, that was all. But Rebus was thankful for the story. Maybe someone would read it and come forward. Maybe guilt would begin to press down on the driver. Maybe there'd been a passenger ... It was hard to keep secrets, usually you told *some*one.

He tried Remnant Kings, but of course they had been closed last night, so he climbed to the flats above. There was no one home at the first flat. He wrote a brief message on the back of a business card and pushed it through the letterbox, then jotted down the surname on the door. If they didn't call him, he'd call them. A young man answered the second door. He was just out of his teens and pushed a thick lock of black hair away from his eyes. He wore Buddy Holly glasses and had acne scars around his mouth. Rebus introduced himself. The hand went to the hair again, a backward glance into the flat.

'Do you live here?' Rebus asked.

'Mm, yeah. Like, I'm not the owner. We rent it.'

There were no names on the door. 'Anyone else in at the moment?'

'Nope.'

'Are you all students?'

The young man nodded. Rebus asked his name.

'Rob. Robert Renton. What's this about?'

'There was an accident last night, Rob. A hit and run.' So many times he'd been in this situation, passing on the bland news of another changed life. It was a whole hour since he'd telephoned the hospital. In the end, they'd taken his mobile number, said it might be easier if they phoned him whenever there was news. They meant easier for them, not him.

'Oh, yes,' Renton was saying, 'I saw it.'

Rebus blinked. 'You saw it?'

Renton was nodding, hair bobbing in front of his eyes. 'From the window. I was up changing a CD, and –'

'Is it okay if I come in for a minute? I want to see what kind of view you had.'

Renton puffed out his cheeks, exhaled. 'Well, I suppose ...'

And Rebus was in.

The living-room was fairly tidy. Renton went ahead of him, crossed to where a hi-fi rack sat between two windows. 'I was putting on a new CD, and I looked out of the window. You can see the bus stop, and I wondered if I might catch Jane coming off a bus.' He paused. 'Jane's Eric's girlfriend.'

The words washed over Rebus. He was looking down on the street, where Sammy had been walking. 'Tell me what you saw.'

'This girl was crossing the road. She was nice-looking ... I thought so anyway. Then this car came through the lights, swerved and sent her flying.'

Rebus closed his eyes for a second.

'She must have gone ten feet in the air, hit that hedge, bounced back on to the pavement. She didn't move after that.'

Rebus opened his eyes. He was at the window, Renton standing just behind his left shoulder. Down on the street, people were crossing the road, walking over the spot where Sammy had been hit, the spot where she'd landed. Flicking ash on to the pavement where she'd lain.

'I don't suppose you saw the driver?'

'Not from this angle.'

'Any passengers?'

'Couldn't tell.'

He wears glasses, Rebus thought. How reliable is he?

'When you saw it happen, you didn't go down?'

'I'm not a medical student or anything.' He nodded towards an easel in the corner, and Rebus noticed a shelf of paints and brushes. 'Someone ran to the phone box, so I knew help was coming.'

Rebus nodded. 'Anyone else see it?'

'They were in the kitchen.' Renton paused. 'I know what you're thinking.' Rebus doubted it. 'You're thinking I wear specs, so maybe I didn't see it right. But he definitely swerved. You know ... deliberately. I mean, like he was aiming for her.' He nodded to himself.

'*Aiming* for her?'

Renton made a movement with his hand, imitating a car gliding off one course and on to another. 'He steered straight for her.'

'The car didn't lose control?'

'That would have been jerkier, wouldn't it?'

'What colour was the car?'

'Dark green.'

'And the make?'

Renton shrugged. 'I'm hopeless with cars. Tell you what though ...'

'What?'

Renton took off his glasses, started polishing them. 'Why don't I try sketching it for you?'

He moved the easel over to the window and got to work. Rebus went into the hall and called the hospital. The person he got through to didn't sound too surprised.

'No change, I'm afraid. She's got a couple of visitors with her.'

Mickey and Rhona. Rebus terminated the call, made another to Pryde's mobile.

'I'm in one of the flats over Remnant Kings. I've got an eyewitness.'

'Yes?'

'He saw the whole thing. And he's an art student.'

'Yes?'

'Come on, Bill. Do you want me to draw it for you?'
There was silence for a moment, then Pryde said 'Ah'.

13

Rebus held the mobile to his ear as he walked through the hospital.

'Joe Herdman's put together a list,' Bill Pryde was saying. 'Rover 600 series, the newer Ford Mondeos, Toyota Celica, plus a couple of Nissans. Rank outsider is the BMW 5-series.'

'It narrows things down a bit, I suppose.'

'Joe says the Rover, Mondeo and Celica are favourites. He's given me a few more details – chrome around the number-plates, stuff like that. I'm going to call our artist friend, see if anything clicks.'

A nurse was glaring at Rebus as he walked towards her.

'Let me know what he says. Talk to you later, Bill.' Rebus slipped the phone back into his pocket.

'You're not supposed to use those things in here,' the nurse snapped.

'Look, I'm in a bit of a hurry …'

'They can interfere with the machines.'

Rebus pulled up, colour leaving his face. 'I forgot,' he said. He put a shaking hand to his forehead.

'Are you all right?'

'Fine, fine. Look, I won't do it again, okay?' He started to move off. 'You can rely on that.'

Rebus took a photocopy of Renton's drawing from his pocket. Joe Herdman was a desk sergeant who knew everything about cars. He'd been useful before, turning a vague description into something more concrete. Rebus looked at the drawing as he walked. All the details were there: buildings in the background, the hedge, the onlookers. And Sammy, caught at the point of impact. She'd half-turned, was stretching out her hands as if she could push the car to a stop. But Renton had drawn fine lines issuing from the back of the car, representing the air being pushed, representing speed. Where there should have been a face, he had left a blank oval. The back half of the car was very clearly defined, the front a blur of disappearing perspective. Renton said he'd left out anything he couldn't be sure of. He promised he hadn't let his imagination fill in the blanks.

It was the face, or the lack of it … it disturbed Rebus more than anything else in the picture. He drew himself into the scene, wondered what he'd have done. Would he have concentrated on the car, caught its licence plate? Or would his attention have been focused on Sammy? Which would have prevailed: cop instincts or fatherhood? Someone at the station had said, 'Don't worry, we'll get him.' Not, 'Don't worry, she'll be all right.' Which brought it all down to two things: him – meaning the driver – and retribution, rather than her – the victim – and recovery.

'I'd just have been another witness,' Rebus said quietly. Then he folded the drawing and put it away.

Sammy had a room to herself, all tubes and machinery, the way he'd seen it in films and on TV. Only here the room was dingier, paint flaking from the walls and around the window-frames. The chairs had metal legs and rubber feet and moulded plastic seats. A woman rose as he came in. They embraced. He kissed the side of her forehead.

Aiming for her. Didn't anyone say that?

'Hello, Rhona.'

'Hello, John.'

She looked tired, of course, but her hair was stylishly cut and dyed the colour of a dull golden harvest. Her clothes were smart and she wore jewellery. He studied her eyes. Their colour was wrong. Coloured contacts. Not even her eyes were going to betray her past.

'Christ, Rhona, I'm sorry.'

He was whispering, not wanting to disturb Sammy. Which was ludicrous, because right now all he wanted in the world was for her to wake up.

'How is she?' he asked.

'Much the same.'

Mickey stood up. There were three chairs arranged in a sort of semi-circle. Mickey and Rhona had been sitting with an empty chair between them. As Rhona broke from Rebus's embrace, his brother took her place.

'This is so fucking awful,' Mickey said, his voice low. He looked the same as ever: a party animal who'd stopped getting the invites.

Niceties dispensed with, Rebus went to Sammy's bedside. Her face was still bruised, and now he could place the probable cause of each abrasion: hedge, wall, pavement. One leg was broken, both arms heavily bandaged. A teddy bear, missing one ear, lay by her head. Rebus smiled.

'You brought Pa Broon.'

'Yes.'

'Do they know yet if there's any ... ?' His eyes were on Sammy as he spoke.

'What?' Rhona wanted him to spell it out. No hiding place.

'Brain damage,' he said.

'Nobody's told us anything,' she said, sounding snubbed.

Aiming for her. Didn't anyone say that? No, none of the other onlookers had even hinted as much, but then they hadn't had Renton's grandstand view.

'Has nobody been in?'

'Not since I got here.'

'And I was here before Rhona,' Mickey added. 'Haven't seen a soul.'

It was enough. Rebus strode from the room. A doctor and two nurses were standing chatting at the end of the corridor. One of the nurses was leaning against a wall.

'What's going on?' Rebus exploded. 'Nobody's been near my daughter all morning!'

The doctor was young, male. Blond hair cut short with a parting.

'We're doing everything we can.'

'What does that mean?'

'I can appreciate that you're —'

'Fuck you, pal. Why hasn't the big man been to look at her? Why's she just lying there like a —' Rebus choked back the words.

'Your daughter was seen by two specialists this morning,' the doctor said quietly. 'We're waiting for some test results to determine whether to operate again. There's some brain swelling. The tests take a little time to process, there's nothing we can do about it.'

Rebus felt cheated: still angry, but nothing to feel angry *about*, not here. He nodded, turned away.

Back in the room, he explained the situation to Rhona. A suitcase and large holdall were sitting behind one of the machines.

'Listen,' he told her, 'it'd make sense if you stayed at the flat. It's only ten minutes away, and I could let you have the car.'

She was shaking her head. 'We're booked into the Sheraton.'

'The flat's nearer, and I tend not to charge ...' *We?* Rebus looked at Mickey, whose eyes were on the bed. Then the door opened and a man came in. Short, thickly built, breathing hard. He was rubbing his hands to let everyone know he'd been to the toilet. Loose folds of flesh furrowed his brow and bulged from his shirt collar. His hair was thick and black, like an oil-slick. He stopped when he saw Rebus.

'John,' Rhona said, 'this is a friend of mine, Jackie.'

'Jackie Platt,' the man said, reaching out a plump hand.

'When Jackie heard, he insisted on driving me up.'

Platt shrugged, his head almost disappearing into his shoulders. 'Couldn't have her training it up on her ownio.'

'Hell of a drive,' Mickey said, his tone hinting at repetition.

'Could have done without the roadworks,' Jackie Platt agreed. Rebus's eyes caught Rhona's; she looked away quickly, dodging reproach.

To Rebus, this bulk didn't belong. It was as if a character had wandered on to the wrong set. Platt hadn't been in the script.

'She looks so peaceful, don't she?' the Londoner was saying, making for the bed. He touched her arm, Sammy's bandaged arm, grazing it with the back of his hand. Rebus's fingernails dug into his palms.

Then Platt yawned. 'You know, Rhona, it might not be good manners, but I think I'm about to crash. See you back at the hotel?' She nodded, relieved. Platt picked up the suitcase. As he passed her, his hand went into his trouser pocket, came out with a fold of banknotes.

'Get a cab back, all right?'

'All right, Jackie. See you later.'

'Cheers, pet.' And he squeezed her hand. 'Take care, Mickey. All the best, John.' A huge, face-creasing wink, then he was gone. They waited in silence for a few seconds. Rhona held up her free hand, the one without the wad of notes.

'Not a word, okay?'

'Furthest thing from my mind,' Rebus said, sitting down. ' "Think I'm about to crash". Tactful or what?'

'Come on, Johnny,' Mickey said. Johnny: only Mickey could do that, using the name so that the years fell from both of them. Rebus looked at his brother and smiled. Mickey was a therapist by profession; he knew the things to say.

'Why the cases?' Rebus asked Rhona.

'What?'

'You're going to a hotel, why not leave them in his car?'

'I thought about staying here. They said I could if I wanted to. Only then I saw her … and I changed my mind.' Tears started down her face, smudging already-smudged mascara. Mickey had a handkerchief ready.

'John, what if she … ? Oh, Jesus Christ, why did this have to happen?' She was wailing now. Rebus went over to her chair, crouched in front of it, his hands resting on hers. 'She's all we've got, John. She's all we ever had.'

'She's still here, Rhona. She's right here.'

'But why her? Why Samantha?'

'I'll ask him when I find him, Rhona.' He kissed her hair, his eyes on Mickey. 'And believe me, I'm going to find him.'

Later, when Ned Farlowe visited, Rebus took him outside. There was drizzle falling, but the air felt good.

'One of the eye-witnesses,' Rebus said, 'thinks it was deliberate.'

'I don't understand.'

'He thinks the driver meant to hit Sammy.'

'I still don't get it.'

'Look, there are two scenarios. One, he was intent on hitting a pedestrian, and anyone would have done. Two, Sammy was his target. He'd been following her, saw his chance when she crossed the road, only the lights were against him so he had to jump them. Then she was so close to the kerb he had to switch lanes.'

'But why?'

Rebus stared at him. 'This is Sammy's dad and her lover, right? For the purposes of what follows, I want you to stop being a reporter.'

Farlowe stared back, nodded slowly.

'I've had a few run-ins with Tommy Telford,' Rebus said. He was seeing teddy bears: Pa Broon, and the one Telford kept in his car. 'This might have been a message for me.' Telford or Tarawicz: flip a coin. 'Or for you, if you've been asking questions about Telford.'

'You think my book ...'

'I'm keeping an open mind. I've been working the Lintz case ... and so have you.'

'Someone warning us off Lintz?'

Rebus thought of Abernethy, shrugged. 'Then there's Sammy's job, working with ex-cons. Maybe one of them had a grudge.'

'Jesus.'

'She hadn't mentioned anyone following her? Nobody odd in the area?' Same question he'd put to the Drinics, only different victim ...

Farlowe shook his head. 'Look,' he said, 'until five minutes ago I thought this was an accident. Now you're saying it was attempted murder. Are you *sure*?'

'I'm trusting a witness.' But he knew what Bill Pryde thought: a drunk driver, a crazy man. And a grandstand spectator who wore glasses and had read it wrong. He took out the drawing again.

'What's that?'

Rebus handed it over. 'This is what someone saw last night.'

'What kind of car is it?'

'Rover 600, Ford Mondeo, something like that. Dark green. Ring any bells?'

Ned Farlowe shook his head, then looked at Rebus. 'Let me help. I can ask around.'

'One kid in a coma's enough.'

The rest of the office had packed up and gone home. Now there were only Rebus and Sammy's boss, a woman called Mae Crumley. The light from half a dozen desk-lamps illuminated the haphazard office, which was on the top floor of an old four-storey building off Palmerston Place. Rebus knew Palmerston Place: there was a church there where the AA held meetings. He'd been to a couple. He could still taste whisky at the back of his throat. Not that he'd had any so far today, not in daylight hours. But then he hadn't phoned Jack Morton either.

The address might have been posher than Rebus was expecting, but the accommodation was cramped. The office was in the eaves of the building, so that you couldn't stand up in half the available space, which hadn't stopped desks being sited in the most awkward corners.

'Which is hers?' Rebus asked. Mae Crumley pointed to the desk next to her own. There was a computer there somewhere, but only its screen was showing. Loose sheets of paper, books and pamphlets and reports, the whole lot spilled on to the chair and from there down on to the floor.

'She works too hard,' Crumley said. 'We all do.'

Rebus sipped the coffee she'd made him. Cafe Hag.

'When Sammy came here,' she went on, 'the first thing she said was that her father was CID. She never tried to hide it.'

'And you'd no qualms about taking her on?'

'None at all.' Crumley folded her arms. They were big arms; she was a big woman. Her hair was a fiery red, long and frizzy and tied back with a black ribbon. She wore an oatmeal linen shirt with a denim jacket over the top of it. Her eyebrows had been plucked into thin arches over pale grey eyes. Her desk was relatively tidy, but only, as she'd explained to Rebus, because she tended to stay later than anyone else.

'What about her clients?' Rebus asked. 'Could any of them have held a grudge?'

'Against her or against you?'

'Against me *through* her.'

Crumley considered this. 'To the extent that they'd run her over just to make a point? I very much doubt it.'

'I'd be interested to see her client list.'

She shook her head. 'Look ... you shouldn't be doing this. It's too personal, you know that. I mean, who am I talking to here: Sammy's father, or a copper?'

'You think I've a score to settle?'

'Well haven't you?'

Rebus put down the coffee mug. 'Maybe.'

'And that's why you shouldn't be doing this.' She sighed. 'Number one on my wish list: Sammy back on her feet and back here. But what about if meantime I do a bit of poking around? I stand a better chance of getting them to talk than you do.'

Rebus nodded. 'I'd appreciate that.' He got to his feet. 'Thanks for the coffee.'

Outside, he checked the list the Juice Church had given him. He kept it in his pocket, didn't refer to it often. There was a meeting at Palmerston Place in about an hour and a half. No good. He knew he'd spend the time beforehand in a pub. Jack Morton had introduced him to Al-Anon, but Rebus hadn't really taken to it, though the stories had affected him.

'See,' one man had told the group, 'I had problems at work, problems with my wife, my kids. I had money problems and health problems and everything else. Practically the only problem I didn't have was with the drink. And that's because I was a drunk.'

Rebus lit himself a cigarette and drove home.

He sat in his chair and thought about Rhona. They'd shared so much over so many years … and then it had all stopped. He'd chosen his job over his marriage, and that could not be forgiven. Last time he'd seen her had been in London, wearing her new life like armour. Nobody had warned him about Jackie Platt. His phone rang, and he snatched it from the floor.

'Rebus.'

'It's Bill.' Pryde sounded halfway to excited, which was as far as he ever ventured.

'What have you got?'

'Dark green Rover 600 – I think the owner called it "Sherwood Green" – stolen yesterday evening about an hour before the collision.'

'Where from?'

'Metered parking on George Street.'

'What do you reckon?'

'My advice is, keep an open mind. Having said that, at least now we've got a licence plate. Owner reported it at six-forty last night. It hasn't turned up anywhere, so I've upped the alert status.'

'Give me the reg.' Pryde read out the letters and numbers. Rebus thanked him and put down the phone. He was thinking of Danny Simpson, dumped outside Fascination Street around the time Sammy was being hit. Coincidence? Or a double message, Telford and Rebus. Which put Big Ger Cafferty in the frame. He called the hospital, was told there was no change. Farlowe was in visiting. The nurse said he had his laptop with him.

Rebus recalled Sammy growing up – a series of isolated images. He hadn't been there for her. He saw her in a series of fast jerky impressions, as if the film had been spliced. He tried not to think about the hell she had gone through at the hands of Gordon Reeve …

He saw good people doing bad things and bad people doing good, and he tried dividing the two into groups. He saw Candice and Tommy Telford and Mr Pink Eyes. And encompassing it all, he saw Edinburgh. He saw the mass of the people just getting on with their lives, and he saluted them. They *knew* things and felt things, things he'd never feel. He used to think he knew things. As a kid, he'd known *everything*. Now he knew differently. The only thing you could be sure of was the inside of your head, and even that could deceive you. I don't even know myself, he thought. So how could he ever hope to know Sammy? And with each year, he understood less.

He thought of the Oxford Bar. Even on the wagon, he'd stayed a regular, drinking cola and mugs of coffee. A pub like the Ox was about so much more than just the hooch. It was therapy and refuge, entertainment and art. He checked his watch, thinking he could head down there now. Just a couple of whiskies and a beer, something to make him feel good about himself until the morning.

The phone rang again. He picked it up.

'Evening, John.'

Rebus smiled, leaned back in his chair. 'Jack, you must be a bloody mind reader ...'

14

Mid-morning, Rebus walked through the cemetery. He'd been to the hospital to check on Sammy – no change. Now, he felt he had time to kill …

'A bit cooler today, Inspector.' Joseph Lintz rose from his knees and pushed his glasses back up to the bridge of his nose. There were damp patches on his trousers from where he'd been kneeling. He dropped his trowel on to a white polythene bag. Beside the bag stood pots of small green plants.

'Won't the frost get them?' Rebus asked. Lintz shrugged.

'It gets all of us, but we're allowed to bloom for a while.'

Rebus turned away. Today, he wasn't in the mood for games. Warriston Cemetery was vast. In the past, it had been a history lesson to Rebus – headstones telling the story of nineteenth-century Edinburgh – but now he found it a jarring reminder of mortality. They were the only living souls in the place. Lintz had pulled out a handkerchief.

'More questions?' he asked.

'Not exactly.'

'What then?'

'Truth is, Mr Lintz, I've got other things on my mind.'

The old man looked at him. 'Maybe all this archaeology is beginning to bore you, Inspector?'

'I still don't get it, planting things before the first frost?'

'Well, I can't plant very much afterwards, can I? And at my age … any day now I could be lying in the ground. I like to think there might be a few flowers surviving above me.' He'd lived in Scotand the best part of half a century, but there was still something lurking beneath the local accent, peculiarities of phrasing and tone that would be with Joseph Lintz until he died, reminders of his far less recent history.

'So,' he said now, 'no questions today?' Rebus shook his head. 'You're right, Inspector, you do seem preoccupied. Is it something I can help with?'

'In what way?'

'I don't really know. But you've come here, questions or no. I take it there's a reason?'

A dog was bounding through the long grass, crunching on the fallen leaves, nose brushing the ground. It was a yellow labrador, short-haired and overweight. Lintz turned towards it and almost growled. Dogs were the enemy.

'I was just wondering,' Rebus was saying, 'what you're capable of.' Lintz looked puzzled. The dog began to paw at the ground. Lintz reached down, picked up a stone, and hurled it. It didn't reach the dog. The labrador's owner was rounding the corner. He was young, crop-haired and skinny.

'That thing should be kept on its lead!' Lintz roared.

'*Jawohl*!' the owner snapped back, clicking his heels. He was laughing as he passed them.

'I am a famous man now,' Lintz reflected, back to his old self after the outburst. 'Thanks to the newspapers.' He looked up at the sky, blinked. 'People send me hate by the Royal Mail. A car was parked outside my home the other night ... they put a brick through the windscreen. It wasn't my car, but they didn't know that. Now my neighbours keep clear of that spot, just in case.'

He spoke like the old man he was, a little tired, a little defeated.

'This is the worst year of my life.' He stared down at the border he'd been tending. The earth, newly turned, looked dark and rich, like crumbs of chocolate cake. A few worms and wood lice had been disturbed and were still looking for their old homes. 'And it's going to get worse, isn't it?'

Rebus shrugged. His feet were cold, the damp seeping in through his shoes. He was standing on the rough roadway, Lintz six inches above him on the grass. And still Lintz didn't reach his height. A little old man: that's what he was. And Rebus could study him, talk with him, go to his home and see what few photographs remained – according to Lintz – from the old days.

'What did you mean back there?' he said. 'What was it you said? Something about what I was capable of?'

Rebus stared at him. 'It's okay, the dog just showed me.'

'Showed you what?'

'What you're like with the enemy.'

Lintz smiled. 'I don't like dogs, it's true. Don't read too much into it, Inspector. That's the journalists' job.'

'Your life would be easier without dogs, wouldn't it?'

Lintz shrugged. 'Of course.'

'And easier without me, too?'

Lintz frowned. 'If it weren't you, it would be someone else, a boor like your Inspector Abernethy.'

'What do you think he was telling you?'

Lintz blinked. 'I'm not sure. Someone else came to see me. A man called Levy. I refused to talk to him – one privilege still open to me.'

Rebus shuffled his feet, trying to get some warmth into them. 'I have a daughter, did I ever tell you that?'

Lintz looked baffled. 'You might have mentioned it.'

'You know I have a daughter?'

'Yes … I mean, I think I knew before today.'

'Well, Mr Lintz, the night before last, someone tried to kill her, or at least do her some serious damage. She's in hospital, still unconscious. And *that* bothers me.'

'I'm so sorry. How did it … ? I mean, how do you … ?'

'I think maybe someone was trying to send me a message.'

Lintz's eyes widened. 'And you believe *me* capable of such a thing? My God, I thought we had come to understand one another, at least a little.'

Rebus was wondering. He was wondering how easy it would be to put on an act, when you'd spent half a century practising. He was wondering how easy it would be to steel yourself to killing an innocent ... or at least ordering their death. All it took was an order. A few words to someone else who would carry out your bidding. Maybe Lintz had it in him. Maybe it wouldn't be any more difficult than it had been for Josef Linzstek.

'Something you should know,' Rebus said. 'Threats don't scare me off. Quite the opposite.'

'It's good that you are so strong.' Rebus looked for meaning behind the words. 'I'm on my way home. Can I offer you some tea?'

Rebus drove, and then sat in the drawing-room while Lintz busied himself in the kitchen. Started flicking through a pile of books on a desk.

'Ancient History, Inspector,' Lintz said, bringing in the tray – he always refused offers of help. 'Another hobby of mine. I'm fascinated by that intersection at which history and fiction meet.' The books were all about Babylonia. 'Babylon is an historical fact, you see, but what about the Tower of Babel?'

'A song by Elton John?' Rebus offered.

'Always making jokes.' Lintz looked up. 'What is it you're afraid of?'

Rebus took one of the cups. 'I've heard of the Gardens of Babylon,' he admitted, putting the book down. 'What other hobbies do you have?'

'Astrology, hauntings, the unknown.'

'Have you ever been haunted?'

Lintz seemed amused. 'No.'

'Would you like to be?'

'By seven hundred French villagers? No, Inspector, I wouldn't like that at all. It was astrology that first brought me to the Chaldeans. They came from Babylonia. Have you ever heard of Babylonian numbers ...?'

Lintz had a way of turning conversations in directions *he* wanted them to take. Rebus wasn't going to be deflected this time. He waited till Lintz had the cup to his lips.

'Did you try to kill my daughter?'

Lintz paused, then sipped, swallowed.

'No, Inspector,' he said quietly.

Which left Telford, Tarawicz and Cafferty. Rebus thought of Telford, surrounded by his Family but wanting to play with the big boys. How different was a gang war from any other kind? You had soldiers, and orders given to them. They had to prove themselves, or lose face, show themselves cowards. Shoot a civilian, run down a pedestrian. Rebus realised that he didn't want the driver as such – he wanted the person who'd *driven* them to do it. Lintz's defence of Linzstek was that the young lieutenant had been under orders, that war itself was the real culprit, as though humans had no say in the matter ...

'Inspector,' the old man was saying, 'do *you* think I'm Linzstek?'

Rebus nodded. 'I know you are.'

A wry smile. 'Then arrest me.'

'Here comes the blue-nose,' Father Conor Leary said. 'Out to steal Ireland's God-given Guinness.' He paused, eyes narrowing. 'Or are you still on that abstention kick?'

'I'm trying,' Rebus said.

'Well, I won't tempt you then.' Leary smiled. 'But you know me, John. I'm not one to judge, but a wee drop never harmed a soul.'

'Problem is, you put lots of wee drops together and you get a bloody big fall.'

Father Leary laughed. 'But aren't we all the fallen? Come away in.'

Father Leary was priest of Our Lady of Perpetual Help. Years back, someone had defaced the board outside to turn 'Help' into 'Hell'. The board had been corrected many times, but Rebus always thought of the place as 'Perpetual Hell': it was what the followers of Knox and Calvin would have believed. Father Leary took him through to the kitchen.

'Here, man, sit yourself down. I haven't seen you in so long, I thought you'd renounced me.' He went to the fridge and lifted out a can of Guinness.

'Are you operating a pharmacy on the side?' Rebus asked. Father Leary looked at him. Rebus nodded towards the fridge. 'The shelves of medicine.'

Father Leary rolled his eyes. 'At my age, you go to the doctor with angina and they dose you for every conceivable ailment. They think it makes old folk feel better.' He brought a glass to the table, placed it next to his can. Rebus felt a hand fall on his shoulder.

'I'm hellish sorry about Sammy.'

'How did you hear?'

'Her name was in one of the rags this morning.' Father Leary sat down. 'Hit and run, they said.'

'Hit and run,' Rebus echoed.

Father Leary shook his head wearily, one hand rubbing slowly over his chest. He was probably in his late-sixties, though he'd never said. Well-built, with a thatch of silver hair. Tufts of grey sprouted from his ears, nose and dog-collar. His hand seemed to smother the can of Guinness. But when he poured, he poured gently, almost with reverence.

'It's a terrible thing,' he said quietly. 'Coma, is it?'

'Not until the doctors say so.' Rebus cleared his throat. 'It's only been a day and a half.'

'You know what we believers say,' Father Leary went on. 'When something like this happens, it's a test for all of us. It's a way of making us stronger.' The head on his Guinness was perfect. He took a swallow, licked his lips thoughtfully. 'That's what we *say*; it may not be what we think.' He looked into his drink.

'It didn't make me strong. I went back to the whisky.'

'I can understand that.'

'Until a friend reminded me it was the lazy way out, the cowardly way.'

'And who's to say he's not right?'

' "Faint-Heart and the Sermon",' Rebus said with a smile.

'What's that?'

'A song. But maybe it's us, too.'

'Get away, we're just two old boys having a natter. So how are you holding up, John?'

'I don't know.' He paused. 'I don't think it was an accident. And the man I think is behind it ... Sammy isn't the first woman he's tried to destroy.' Rebus looked into the priest's eyes. 'I want to kill him.'

'But so far you haven't?'

'I haven't even talked to him.'

'Because you're worried what you might do?'

'Or not do.' Rebus's mobile sounded. He gave a look of apology and switched it on.

'John, it's Bill.'

'Yes, Bill?'

'Green Rover 600.'

'Yes?'

'We've got it.'

The car had been parked illegally on the street outside

Piershill Cemetery. There was a parking ticket on its windscreen, dated the previous afternoon. If anyone had checked, they'd have found the driver's-side door unlocked. Maybe someone had: the car was empty, no coins, no map-books or cassettes. The fascia had been removed from the radio/cassette. There were no keys in the ignition. A car transporter had arrived, and the Rover was being winched aboard.

'I called in a favour at Howdenhall,' Bill Pryde was saying, 'they've promised to fingerprint it today.'

Rebus was studying the front passenger side. No dents, nothing to suggest this car had been used as a battering-ram against his daughter.

'I think maybe we need your permission, John.'

'What for?'

'Someone should go to the Infirmary and print Sammy.'

Rebus stared at the front of the car, then got out the drawing. Yes, she'd put out a hand. Her prints might be there, invisible to him.

'Sure,' he said. 'No problem. You think this is it?'

'I'll tell you once we print it.'

'You steal a car,' Rebus said, 'then you hit someone with it, and leave it a couple of miles away.' He looked around. 'Ever been on this street before?' Pryde shook his head. 'Me neither.'

'Someone local?'

'I'm wondering why they stole it in the first place.'

'Stick false plates on and sell it,' Pryde suggested. 'Spot of joy-riding maybe.'

'Joy-riders don't leave cars looking like this.'

'No, but they'd had a fright. They'd just knocked someone down.'

'And they drove all the way over here before deciding to dump it?'

'Maybe it was stolen for a job, turn over a petrol station.

Then they hit Sammy and decide to jump ship. Maybe the job was this side of town.'

'Or Sammy *was* the job.'

Pryde put a hand on his shoulder. 'Let's see what the boffins turn up, eh?'

Rebus looked at him. 'You don't go for it?'

'Look, it's a feeling you've got, and that's fair enough, but right now all you've got is that student's word for it. There were other witnesses, John, and I asked them all again, and they told me the same thing: it looked like the driver lost control, that's all.'

There was an edge of irritation to Pryde's voice. Rebus knew why: long hours.

'Will Howdenhall let you know tonight?'

'They promised. And I'll phone you straight away, okay?'

'On my mobile,' Rebus said. 'I'm going to be on the move.' He looked around. 'There was something about Piershill Cemetery recently, wasn't there?'

'Kids,' Pryde said, nodding. 'They pushed over a load of gravestones.'

Rebus remembered now. 'Just the Jewish headstones, wasn't it?'

'I think so.'

And there, sprayed on the wall near the gates, the same piece of graffiti: Won't Anyone Help?

It was late evening, and Rebus was driving. Not the M90 into Fife: tonight, he was on the M8, heading west, heading for Glasgow. He'd spent half an hour at the hospital, followed by an hour and a half with Rhona and Jackie Platt, their guest for dinner at the Sheraton. He'd worn a fresh suit and shirt. He hadn't smoked. He'd drunk a bottle of Highland Spring.

They were planning yet more tests on Sammy. The

neurologist had taken them into his office and talked them through the procedures. There would probably be another operation at the end of it. Rebus could barely remember what the man had said. Rhona had asked for the occasional explanation, but these seemed no more lucid than what had gone before.

Dinner had been a subdued affair. Jackie Platt, it turned out, sold second-hand cars.

'See, John, where I really score is the obituaries. Check the local paper, hare round there and see if they've left a car behind. Quick cash offer.'

'Sammy doesn't drive, sorry,' Rebus had said, causing Rhona to drop her cutlery on to her plate.

At the end of the meal, she'd seen him out to his car, gripped one of his arms hard.

'Get the bastard, John. I want to look him in the face. Just get the bastard who did this to us.' Her eyes were blazing.

He nodded. Stones: 'Just Wanna See His Face'. Rebus wanted it, too.

The M8, which could be a nightmare at rush-hour, was a quiet drive in the evenings. Rebus knew he was making good time, and that he would soon see the outline of the Easterhouse estate against the sky. When his phone sounded, he didn't hear it at first: blame Wishbone Ash. As *Argus* finished, he picked up.

'Rebus.'

'John, it's Bill.'

'What've you got?'

'Forensics were good as gold. There are prints all over the car, interior and exterior. Several sets.' He paused, and Rebus thought the connection had gone. 'One good palm and finger set on the front of the bonnet ...'

'Sammy's?'

'For definite.'

'So we've got our car.'

'The owner's given us a set so we can eliminate him. When we've done that …'

'We're still not home and dry, Bill. The car sat unlocked outside that cemetery, we don't know someone didn't clean it out.'

'Owner says the radio/cassette fascia was there when he left it. Also half a dozen tapes, a packet of Paracetamol, receipts for petrol and a road map. So someone cleaned it out, whether it's the bastard we want or just some scavenger.'

'At least we know it's the car.'

'I'll check again with Howdenhall tomorrow, collect any other prints and start trying to match them. Plus I'll ask around Piershill, see if anyone saw someone dumping it.'

'Meantime get some sleep, eh?'

'Try and stop me. What about you?'

'Me?' Two cups of espresso after dinner. And with the knowledge of what lay ahead. 'I'll get my head down soon enough, Bill. Talk to you tomorrow.'

On the outskirts of Glasgow, headed for Barlinnie Prison.

He'd phoned ahead, made sure they were expecting him. It was way outside any visiting hours, but Rebus had made up a story about a murder inquiry. 'Follow-up questions,' was what he'd said.

'At this time of night?'

'Lothian and Borders Police, pal. Motto: Justice Never Sleeps.'

Morris Gerald Cafferty probably didn't sleep much either. Rebus imagined him lying awake at night, hands under his head, staring into the darkness.

Scheming.

Running things through his mind: how to keep his

empire from falling, how best to combat threats like Tommy Telford. Rebus knew that Cafferty employed a lawyer – a middle-aged pinstripe from the New Town – to carry messages back to his gang in Edinburgh. He thought of Charles Groal, Telford's lawyer. Groal was young and sharp, like his paymaster.

'Strawman.'

He was waiting in the Interview Room, arms folded, chair set well away from the table. And of course his opening gambit was his nickname for Rebus.

'A lovely surprise, two visits in a week. Don't tell me you've another message from the Pole?'

Rebus sat down opposite Cafferty. 'Tarawicz isn't Polish.' He glanced towards the guard who stood by the door, lowered his voice. 'Another of Telford's boys got a doing.'

'How clumsy.'

'He was all but scalped. Are you looking for war?'

Cafferty drew his chair in to the table, leaned across towards Rebus. 'I've never backed down from a fight.'

'My daughter got hurt. Funny that, so soon after we'd had our little chat.'

'Hurt how?'

'Hit and run.'

Cafferty was thoughtful. 'I don't pick on civilians.'

Yes, Rebus thought, but she wasn't a civilian, because *he* had lured her on to the battlefield.

'Convince me,' Rebus said.

'Why should I bother?'

'The conversation we had … What you asked me to do.'

'Telford?' A whisper. Cafferty sat back for a moment to consider. When he leaned forward again, his eyes bored into Rebus's. 'There's something you've forgotten. I lost a son, remember. Think I could do that to another father? I'd do a lot of things, Rebus, but not that, never that.'

Rebus held the stare. 'All right,' he said.

'You want me to find who did it?'

Rebus nodded slowly.

'That's your price?'

Rhona's words: *I want to look him in the face.* Rebus shook his head. 'I want them *delivered* to me. I want you to do that, whatever it takes.'

Cafferty placed his hands on his knees, seemed to take his time positioning them just so. 'You know it's probably Telford?'

'Yes. If it's not you.'

'You'll be going after him then?'

'Any way I can.'

Cafferty smiled. 'But your ways aren't my ways.'

'You might get to him first. I want him *alive.*'

'And meantime, you're my man?'

Rebus stared at him. 'I'm your man,' he said.

15

Rebus got a phone call early the next morning from Leith CID, telling him Joseph Lintz was dead. The bad news was, it looked like murder: the body found hanging from a tree in Warriston Cemetery.

By the time Rebus appeared at the scene, they were cordoning it off, the doctor having concluded that most suicides wouldn't have bothered administering a violent blow to their own head before commencing with operations.

The corpse of Joseph Lintz was being zipped into a body bag. Rebus got a look at the face. He'd seen elderly corpses before, and mostly they'd looked wonderfully at peace, their faces shiny and child-like. But Joseph Lintz looked like he'd suffered. He didn't look to be at rest at all.

'You'll have come to thank us, no doubt,' a man said, walking towards Rebus. His shoulders were hunched inside a navy raincoat and he walked with head bowed, hands in pockets. His hair was thick and silver and wiry, his skin an almost jaundiced yellow – the remains of an autumn holiday tan.

'Hiya, Bobby,' Rebus said.

Bobby Hogan was Leith CID.

'To get back to my initial observation, John ...'

'What am I supposed to be thanking you for?'

Hogan nodded towards the body bag. 'Taking Mr Lintz off your hands. 'Don't tell me you were *enjoying* digging into all that?'

'Not exactly.'

'Any idea who might have wanted him dead?'

Rebus puffed out his cheeks. 'Where do you want me to start?'

'I mean, I'm right to rule out the usual, aren't I?' Hogan held up three fingers. 'It wasn't suicide, muggers aren't quite this creative, and it surely wasn't an accident.'

'Someone was making a point, no doubt about it.'

'But what sort of point?'

Scene of Crime officers were busying themselves, filling the *locus* with noise and movement. Rebus gestured for Hogan to walk with him. They were deep in the cemetery, the part Lintz had loved so much. As they walked, the place grew wilder, more overgrown.

'I was here with him yesterday morning,' Rebus said. 'I don't know if he had a routine exactly, but he came here most days.'

'We found a bag of gardening tools.'

'He planted flowers.'

'So if someone knew he'd be coming, they could have been waiting?'

Rebus nodded. 'An assassination.'

Hogan was thoughtful. 'Why hang him?'

'It's what happened at Villefranche. The town elders were strung up in the square.'

'Jesus.' Hogan stopped walking. 'I know you've got other stuff on the go, but can you help out on this, John?'

'Any way I can.'

'A list of possibles would do for a start.'

'How about an old woman living in France, and a Jewish historian who walks with a stick?'

'Is that all you've got?'

'Well, there's always me. Yesterday I as good as accused him of trying to kill my daughter.' Hogan stared at him. 'I don't think he did it.' Rebus paused, thinking of Sammy:

he'd called the hospital first thing. She was still unconscious; they still weren't using the word 'coma'. 'One more
thing,' he said. 'Special Branch, a guy called Abernethy. He
was here talking to Lintz.'

'What's the connection?'

'Abernethy's co-ordinating the various war crimes investigations. He's street-tough, not your typical desk-jockey.'

'A strange choice for the job?' Rebus nodded. 'Which
hardly makes him a suspect.'

'I'm doing my best, Bobby. We could check Lintz's
house, see if we can turn up any of the hate mail he claimed
he'd been getting.'

' "Claimed"?'

Rebus shrugged. 'You were never sure where you were
with Lintz. Do you have any idea what happened?'

'From what you've told me, I'd guess he came down here
as usual to do his gardening stint – he's certainly dressed
for it. Someone was waiting. They smacked him over the
head, stuck his neck in a noose, and hauled him up into the
tree. The rope was tied around a headstone.'

'Did the hanging kill him?'

'Doctor says yes. Haemorrhages in the eyes. What do
you call them?'

'Tardieu spots.'

'That's it. The blow to the head was just to knock him
out. Something else – bruising and cuts on the face. Looks
like someone kicked him when he was down.'

'Knock him cold, thump him in the face, then string him
up.'

'Big-time grudge.'

Rebus looked around. 'Someone with a flair for theatre.'

'And not afraid to take risks. This place might never get
exactly crowded, but it's a public space and that tree's in
open view. Anyone could have walked past.'

'What time are we talking about?'

180

'Eight, eight-thirty. I'm guessing Mr Lintz would have wanted to do his digging in daylight.'

'Could have been earlier,' Rebus suggested. 'A pre-arranged meeting.'

'Then why the tools?'

'Because by the time it got light, the meeting would be over.'

Hogan looked doubtful.

'And if it *was* a meeting,' Rebus said, 'there might be some record of it at Lintz's home.'

Hogan looked at him, nodded. 'My car or yours?'

'Better get his keys first.'

They started back up the slope.

'Searching through a dead man's pockets,' Hogan said to himself. 'Why is that never mentioned during recruitment?'

'I was here yesterday,' Rebus said. 'He invited me back for tea.'

'No family?'

'None.'

Hogan looked around the hallway. 'Big place. What happens to the money when it's sold?'

Rebus looked at him. 'We could split it two ways.'

'Or we could just move ourselves in. Basement and ground for me, you can have first and second.'

Hogan smiled, tried one of the doors off the hall. It opened on to an office. 'This could be my bedroom,' he said, going in.

'When I came here before, he always took me upstairs.'

'On you go. We'll take a floor each, then swop.'

Rebus headed up the staircase, running his hand over the varnished banister: not a speck of dust. Cleaning ladies could be invaluable informants.

'If you find a chequebook,' he called down to Hogan, 'look for regular payments to a Mrs Mop.'

Four doors led off the first-floor landing. Two were bedrooms, one a bathroom. The last door led into the huge drawing-room, where Rebus had asked his questions and listened to the stories and philosophy that Lintz had used in place of answers.

'Do you think guilt has a genetic component, Inspector?' he'd asked one time. 'Or are we taught it?'

'Does it matter, so long as it's there?' Rebus had said, and Lintz had nodded and smiled, as if the pupil had given some satisfactory answer.

The room was big, not too much furniture. Huge sash windows – recently cleaned – looked down on to the street. There were framed prints and paintings on the walls. They could have been priceless originals or junk-store stuff – Rebus was no expert. He liked one painting. It showed a ragged white-haired man seated on a rock, surrounded by a barren plain. He had a book open on his lap, but was staring skywards in horror or awe as a shining light appeared there, picking him out. It had a Biblical look, but Rebus couldn't quite place it. He knew the look on the man's face though. He'd seen it before when some suspect's carefully crafted alibi had suddenly come tumbling down.

Over the marble fireplace was a large gilt-framed mirror. Rebus studied himself in it. Behind him he could see the room. He knew he didn't fit here.

One bedroom was for guests, the other was Lintz's. A faint smell of embrocation, half a dozen medicine bottles on the bedside table. Books, too, a pile of them. The bed had been made, a dressing-gown draped across it. Lintz was a creature of habit; he'd been in no special hurry this morning.

The next floor up, Rebus found two further bedrooms and a toilet. There was a slight smell of damp in one room, and the ceiling was discoloured. Rebus didn't suppose Lintz got many visitors; no impetus to redecorate. Out on the landing again, he saw that one of the stair-rails was missing. It had been propped against the wall, awaiting repair. A house this size, things would always be going wrong.

He went back downstairs. Hogan was in the basement. The kitchen had a door on to a back garden – stone patio, lawn covered in rotting leaves, an ivy-covered wall giving privacy.

'Look what I found,' Hogan said, coming back from the utility room. He was holding a length of rope, frayed at one end where it had been cut.

'You think it'll match with the noose? That would mean the killer got it from here.'

'Meaning Lintz knew them.'

'Anything in the office?'

'It's going to take a bit of time. There's an address book, lots of entries, but most of them seem to go back a while.'

'How can you tell?'

'Old STD codes.'

'Computer?'

'Not even a typewriter. He used carbons. Lots of letters to his solicitor.'

'Trying to shut the media up?'

'You get a couple of mentions, too. Anything upstairs?'

'Go take a look. I'll check the office.'

Rebus climbed upstairs and stood in the office doorway, looking around. Then he sat down at the desk and imagined the room was his. What did he do here? He conducted his daily business. There were two filing-cabinets, but to get to them he'd have to stand up from the desk. And he was an old man. Say the cabinets were for dead correspondence. More recent stuff would be closer to hand.

He tried the drawers. Found the address book Hogan had mentioned. A few letters. A small snuff-box, its contents turned solid. Lintz hadn't even allowed himself that small vice. In a bottom drawer were some files. Rebus lifted out the one marked 'General/Household'. It comprised bills and guarantees. A large brown envelope was marked BT. Rebus opened it and took out the phone bills. They went back to the beginning of the year. The most recent bill was at the front. Rebus was disappointed to find that it wasn't itemised. Then he noticed that all the other statements *were*. Lintz had been meticulous, placing names beside calls made, double-checking British Telecom's totals at the foot of each page. The whole year was like that ... right up until recently. Frowning, Rebus realised that the penultimate statement was missing. Had Lintz mislaid it? Rebus couldn't see him mislaying anything. A missing bill would have hinted at chaos in his ordered world. No, it had to be somewhere.

But Rebus was damned if he could find it.

Lintz's correspondence was all business, either to lawyers or else to do with local charities and committees. He'd been resigning from his committees. Rebus wondered if pressure had been applied. Edinburgh could be cruel and cold that way.

'Well?' Hogan said, sticking his head round the door.

'I'm just wondering ...'

'What?'

'Whether to add on a conservatory and knock through from the kitchen.'

'We'd lose some garden space,' Hogan said. He came in, rested against the desk. 'Anything?'

'A missing phone bill, and a sudden change from being itemised.'

'Worth a call,' Hogan admitted. 'I found a chequebook in his bedroom. Stubs show payments of £60 a month to E. Forgan.'

'Where in the bedroom?'

'Marking his place in a book.' Hogan reached into the desk's top drawer, lifted out the address book.

Rebus got up. 'Pretty rich street this. Wonder how many of them do their own dusting.'

Hogan shut the book. 'No listing for an E. Forgan. Think the neighbours will know?'

'Edinburgh neighbours know *everything*. It's just that they most often keep it to themselves.'

16

Joseph Lintz's neighbours: an artist and her husband on one side; a retired advocate and his wife on the other. The artist used a cleaning lady called Ella Forgan. Mrs Forgan lived in East Claremont Street. The artist gave them a telephone number.

Conclusions drawn from the two interviews: shock and horror that Lintz was dead; praise for the quiet, considerate neighbour. A Christmas card every year, and an invitation to drinks one Sunday afternoon each July. Hard to tell when he'd been at home and when he'd been out. He went off on holiday without telling anyone except Mrs Forgan. Visitors to his home had been few – or few had been noticed, which wasn't quite the same thing.

'Men? Women?' Rebus had asked. 'Or a mixture?'

'A mixture, I'd say,' the artist had replied, measuring her words. 'Really, we knew very little about him, to say we've been neighbours these past twenty-odd years ...'

Ah, and that was Edinburgh for you, too, at least in this price bracket. Wealth was a very private thing in the city. It wasn't brash and colourful. It stayed behind its thick stone walls and was at peace.

Rebus and Hogan held a doorstep conference.

'I'll call the cleaning lady, see if I can meet her, preferably here.' Hogan looked back at Lintz's front door.

'I'd love to know where he got the money to buy this place,' Rebus said.

'That could take some excavating.'

Rebus nodded. 'Solicitor would be the place to start. What about the address book? Worth tracking down some of these elusive friends?'

'I suppose so.' Hogan looked dispirited at the prospect.

'I'll follow up on the phone bills,' Rebus said. 'If that'll help.'

Hogan was nodding. 'And remember to get me copies of your files. Are you busy otherwise?'

'Bobby, if time was money, I'd be in hock to every lender in town.'

Mae Crumley reached Rebus on his mobile.

'I thought you'd forgotten me,' he told Sammy's boss.

'Just being methodical, Inspector. I'm sure you'd want no less.' Rebus stopped at traffic lights. 'I've been in to see Sammy. Is there any news?'

'Nothing much. So you've talked to her clients?'

'Yes, and they all seemed genuinely upset and surprised. Sorry to disappoint you.'

'What makes you think I'm disappointed?'

'Sammy has a good rapport with all her clients. None of them would have wanted her hurt.'

'What about the ones who didn't want to be her clients?'

Crumley hesitated. 'There was one man ... When he was told Sammy had a police inspector for a father, he'd have nothing to do with her.'

'What's his name?'

'It couldn't have been him though.'

'Why not?'

'Because he killed himself. His name was Gavin Tay. He used to drive an ice-cream van ...'

Rebus thanked her for her call, and put down the phone. If someone had tried to kill Sammy on purpose, the question was: why? Rebus had been investigating Lintz; Ned Farlowe had been following him. Rebus had twice confronted Telford; Ned was writing a book about organised crime. Then there was Candice ... Could she have *told* Sammy something, something which might have threatened Telford, or even Mr Pink Eyes? Rebus just didn't know. He knew the most likely culprit – the most vicious – was Tommy Telford. He remembered their first meeting, and the young gangster's words to him: *That's the beauty of games. You can always start again after an accident. Not so easy in real life.* At the time it had sounded like bravado, a performance for the troops. But now it sounded like a plain threat.

And now there was Mr Taystee, connecting Sammy to Telford. Mr Taystee had worked Telford's clubs; Mr Taystee had rejected Sammy. Rebus knew he'd have to talk to the widow.

There was just the one problem. Mr Pink Eyes had intimated that if Telford wasn't left alone, Candice would suffer. He kept seeing images of Candice: torn from home and homeland; used and abused; abusing herself in the hope of respite; clinging to a stranger's legs ... He recalled Levy's words: *Can time wash away responsibility?* Justice was a fine and noble thing, but revenge ... revenge was an *emotion*, and so much stronger than an abstract like justice. He wondered if Sammy would want revenge. Probably not. She'd want him to help Candice, which meant yielding to Telford. Rebus didn't think he could do that.

And now there was Lintz's murder, unconnected but resonant.

'I've never felt comfortable with the past, Inspector,' Lintz had said once. Funny, Rebus felt the same way about the present.

Joanne Tay lived in Colinton: a newish three-bedroomed semi with the Merc still parked in the drive.

'It's too big for me,' she explained to Rebus. 'I'll have to sell it.'

He wasn't sure if she meant the house or the car. Having declined her offer of tea, he sat in the busy living-room, ornaments on every flat surface. Joanne Tay was still in mourning: black skirt and blouse, dark grooves beneath her eyes. He'd interviewed her back at the start of the inquiry.

'I still don't know why he did it,' she said now, reluctant to see her husband's death as anything other than suicide.

But the pathology and forensic tests had cast this into doubt.

'Have you ever heard,' Rebus asked, 'of a man called Tommy Telford?'

'He runs a nightclub, doesn't he? Gavin took me there once.'

'So Gavin knew him?'

'Seemed to.'

Yes: because no way was Mr Taystee setting up his hot-dog pitch outside Telford's premises without Telford's okay. And Telford's okay almost certainly meant payment of some kind. A percentage maybe ... or a favour.

'The week before Gavin died,' Rebus went on, 'you said he'd been busy?'

'Working all hours.'

'Days as well as nights?' She nodded. 'The weather was lousy that week.'

'I know. I told him: you'll never get them buying ice-cream, a day like this. Pelting down outside. But still he went out.'

Rebus shifted in his chair. 'Did he ever mention SWEEP, Mrs Tay?'

'He had some woman would visit him ... red hair.'

'Mae Crumley?'

She nodded, eyes staring at the coal-effect fire. She asked him again if he wanted some tea. Rebus shook his head and made to leave. Did pretty well: knocked over just the two ornaments on his way to the door.

*

The hospital was quiet. When he pushed open the door to Sammy's room, he saw that another bed had been added, a middle-aged woman sleeping in it. Her hands lay on the bedcovers, a white identity tag around one wrist. She was hooked up to a machine, and her head was bandaged.

Two women were sitting by Sammy's bed. Rhona, and Patience Aitken. Rebus hadn't seen Patience in a while. The women were sitting close together. Their whispered conversation stopped as he came in. He lifted a chair and placed it beside Patience's. She leaned over and squeezed his hand.

'Hello, John.'

He smiled at her, spoke to Rhona. 'How is she?'

'The specialist says those last tests were very positive.'

'What does that mean?'

'It means there's brain activity. She's not in deep coma.'

'Is that his version?'

'He thinks she'll come out of it, John.' Her eyes were bloodshot. He noticed a handkerchief gripped in one hand.

'That's good,' he said. 'Which doctor was it?'

'Dr Stafford. He's just back from holiday.'

'I can't keep track of them all.' Rebus rubbed his forehead.

'Look,' Patience said, checking her watch, 'I really should be going. I'm sure the two of you ...'

'Stay as long as you like,' Rebus told her.

'I'm already late for an appointment, actually.' She got to her feet. 'Nice to meet you, Rhona.'

'Thanks, Patience.' The two women shook hands a little awkwardly, then Rhona got up and they hugged, and the awkwardness vanished. 'Thanks for coming.'

Patience turned to Rebus. She looked radiant, he decided. Light really seemed to emanate from her skin. She was wearing her usual perfume, and had had her hair restyled.

'Thanks for looking in,' he said.

'She's going to be fine, John.' She took his hands in hers, leaned towards him. A peck on the cheek, a kiss between friends. Rebus saw Rhona watching them.

'John,' she said, 'see Patience out, will you?'

'No, that's all –'

'Of course, yes,' Rebus said.

They left the room together. Walked the first few steps in silence. Patience spoke first.

'She's great, isn't she?'

'Rhona?'

'Yes.'

Rebus was thoughtful. 'She's terrific. Have you met her paramour?'

'He's gone back to London. I've … I asked Rhona if she wanted to come stay with me. Hotels can be …'

Rebus smiled tiredly. 'Good idea. Then all you'd have to do is invite my brother over and you'd have the whole set.'

Her face cracked into an embarrassed grin. 'I suppose it must look a bit like I'm collecting you all.'

'The perfect hand of Unhappy Families.'

She turned to him. They were at the main doors of the hospital. She touched his shoulder. 'John, I'm really sorry about Sammy. Anything I can do, you've only got to ask.'

'Thanks, Patience.'

'But asking for things has never been your strong point, has it? You just sit in silence and hope they come to you.' She sighed. 'I can't believe I'm saying this, but I miss you. I think that's why I took in Sammy. If I couldn't be close to you, at least I could be close to someone who was. Does that make any sense? Is this where you say something about not deserving me?'

'You've seen the script.' He pulled back a little from her, just so he could look at her face. 'I miss you, too.'

All the nights slumped at the bar, or in his chair at home,

the long midnight drives so he could keep his restlessness alive. He'd have the TV and the hi-fi on at the same time, and the flat would still feel empty. Books he tried reading, finding he was ten pages in and couldn't remember anything. Gazing from his window at the darkened flats across the street, imagining lives at rest.

All because he didn't have *her*.

They embraced in silence for a while. 'You're going to be late,' he said.

'God, John, what are we going to do?'

'See one another?'

'That sounds like a start.'

'Tonight? Mario's at eight?' She nodded and they kissed again. He squeezed her hand. Her head was turned to look at him as she pushed open the doors.

Emerson, Lake and Palmer: 'Still … You Turn Me On.'

Rebus felt a little giddy as he walked back to Sammy's room. Only it wasn't any more, wasn't 'Sammy's room'. Now there was another patient there. They'd said there was always that possibility – shortage of space, cutbacks. The woman was still asleep or unconscious, breathing noisily. Rebus ignored her and sat where Patience had been sitting.

'I've got a message for you,' Rhona said. 'From Dr Morrison.'

'Who's he when he's at home?'

'I've no idea. All he said was, could he have his t-shirt back?'

The ghoul with the scythe … Rebus picked up Pa Broon, turned the bear in his hands. They sat in silence for a while, until Rhona shifted in her chair. 'Patience is really nice.'

'Did the two of you have a good chat?' She nodded. 'And you told her what a perfect husband I'd been?'

'You must be crazy, walking out on her.'

'Sanity's never exactly been my strong point.'

'But you used to know a good thing when you saw it.'

'Trouble is, that's never what I see when I look in the mirror.'

'What do you see?'

He looked at her. 'Sometimes I don't see anything at all.'

Later, they took a coffee-break, went to the machine.

'I lost her, you know,' Rhona said.

'What?'

'Sammy, I lost her. She came back here. She came back to you.'

'We hardly see one another, Rhona.'

'But she's *here*. Don't you get it? It's you she wants, not me.' She turned away from him, fumbled for her handkerchief. He stood close behind her, then couldn't think of anything to say. He was all out of words; every line of sympathy rang hollow to him, just another cliché. He touched the back of her neck, rubbed it. She lowered her head a little, didn't resist. Massage: there'd been a lot of massage early on in their relationship. By the end, he hadn't even given her time for a handshake.

'I don't know why she came back, Rhona,' he said at last. 'But I don't think she was running away, and I don't think it had much to do with seeing me.'

A couple of nurses ran past, urgency in their movements.

'I'd better get back,' Rhona said, rubbing a hand over her face, pulling it into something resembling composure.

Rebus went with her to the room, then said he had to be going. He bent down to kiss Sammy, feeling the breath from her nostrils against his cheek.

'Wake up, Sammy,' he cajoled. 'You can't stay in bed all your life. Time to get up.'

When there was no movement, no response, he turned and left the room.

17

David Levy was no longer in Edinburgh. At least, he wasn't at the Roxburghe Hotel. Rebus could think of only one way of contacting him. Seated at his desk, he called the Holocaust Investigation Bureau in Tel Aviv and asked to speak with Solomon Mayerlink. Mayerlink wasn't available, but Rebus identified himself and said he needed to contact him as a matter of urgency. He got a home telephone number.

'Is there news on Linzstek, Inspector?' Mayerlink's voice was a harsh rasp.

'Of a kind, yes. He's dead.'

Silence on the line, then a slow release of breath. 'That's a pity.'

'It is?'

'People die, a little bit of history dies with them. We would have preferred to see him in court, Inspector. Dead, he's worthless.' Mayerlink paused. 'I take it this ends your inquiry?'

'It changes the nature of the investigation. He was murdered.'

Static on the line; an eight-beat pause. 'How did it happen?'

'He was hung from a tree.'

There was a longer silence on the line. 'I see,' Mayerlink said at last. There was a slight echo on his voice. 'You think the allegations led to his murder?'

'What would you say?'

'I'm not a detective.'

But Rebus knew Mayerlink was lying: detection was *exactly* the role he'd chosen in life. A detective of history.

'I need to talk to David Levy,' Rebus said. 'Do you have his address and phone number?'

'He came to see you?'

'You know he did.'

'It's not that simple with David. He doesn't work for the Bureau. He's self-motivated. I ask him for help occasionally. Sometimes he helps, sometimes he doesn't.'

'But you do have some way of contacting him?'

It took Mayerlink a full minute to come up with the details. An address in Sussex, plus telephone number.

'Is David your number one suspect, Inspector?'

'Why do you ask?'

'I could tell you you're barking up the wrong tree.'

'The same tree Joseph Lintz swung from?'

'Can you really see David Levy as a murderer, Inspector?'

Safari suit, walking stick. 'It takes all sorts,' Rebus said, putting down the phone.

He tried Levy's number. It rang and rang. He gave it a couple of minutes, drank a coffee, tried again. Still no answer. He called British Telecom instead, explained what he needed, was finally put through to the right person.

'My name's Justine Graham, Inspector. How can I help?'

Rebus gave her Lintz's details. 'He used to get itemised bills, then he switched.'

He heard her fingers hammer a keyboard. 'That's right,' she told him. 'The customer asked for itemised billing to be discontinued.'

'Did he say why?'

'No record of that. You don't need to give an excuse, you know.'

'When was this?'

'A couple of months back. The customer had requested monthly billing several years previously.'

Monthly billing: because he was meticulous, kept his accounts by the month. A couple of months back – September – the Lintz/Linzstek story had blown up in the media. And, suddenly, he hadn't wanted his phone calls to be a matter of record.

'Do you have records of his calls, even the *un*itemised ones?'

'Yes, we should have that information.'

'I'd like to see a list. Everything from the first unitemised call through to this morning.'

'Is that when he died – this morning?'

'Yes.'

She was thoughtful. 'Well, I'll need to check.'

'Please do. But remember, Ms Graham, this is a murder inquiry.'

'Yes, of course.'

'And your information could be absolutely crucial.'

'I'm quite aware of –'

'So if I could have that by the end of today …?'

She hesitated. 'I'm not sure I can promise that.'

'And one last thing. The bill for September is missing. I'd like a copy of it. Let me give you the fax number here, speed things up.'

Rebus congratulated himself with another cup of coffee and a cigarette in the car park. She might or might not deliver later in the day, but he was confident she'd be trying her best. Wasn't that all you could ask of anybody?

Another call: Special Branch in London. He asked for Abernethy.

'I'll just put you through.'

Someone picked up: a grunt in place of an acknowledgement.

'Abernethy?' Rebus asked. He heard liquid being swallowed. The voice became clearer.

'He's not here. Can I help?'

'I really need to speak to him.'

'I could have him paged, if it's urgent.'

'My name's DI Rebus, Lothian and Borders Police.'

'Oh, right. Have you lost him or something?'

Rebus's expression turned quizzical. His voice carried a false note of humour. 'You know what Abernethy's like.'

A snort. 'Don't I just.'

'So any help appreciated.'

'Yeah, right. Look, give me your number. I'll get him to call you.'

Have you lost him or something? 'You've no idea where he is then?'

'It's your city, chum. Take your best shot.'

He's up here, Rebus thought. *He's right here*.

'I bet the office is quiet without him.'

Laughter on the line, then the sounds of a cigarette being lit. A long exhalation. 'It's like being on holiday. Keep him as long as you like.'

'So how long have you been without him?'

A pause. As the silence lengthened, Rebus could feel the change of atmosphere.

'What did you say your name was?'

'DI Rebus. I was only asking when he left London.'

'This morning, soon as he heard. So what have I won: the hatchback or the hostess trolley?'

Rebus's turn to laugh. 'Sorry, I'm just nosy.'

'I'll be sure to tell him that.' A single click, then the sound of an open line.

Later that afternoon, Rebus chased up British Telecom, then tried Levy's house again. This time he got through to a woman.

'Hello, Mrs Levy? My name's John Rebus. I was wondering if I could have a word with your husband?'

'You mean my father.'

'I'm sorry. Is your father there?'

'No, he's not.'

'Any idea when ... ?'

'Absolutely none.' She sounded peeved. 'I'm just his cook and cleaner. Like I don't have a life of my own.' She caught herself. 'Sorry, Mr ... ?'

'Rebus.'

'It's just that he never says how long he's going to be away.'

'He's away just now?'

'Has been for the best part of a fortnight. He rings two or three times a week, asks if there've been any calls or letters. If I'm lucky, he *might* remember to ask how *I'm* doing.'

'And how are you doing?'

A smile in her voice. 'I know, I know. I sound like I'm his mother or something.'

'Well, you know, fathers ...' Rebus stared into the middle distance ... 'if you don't tell them anything's wrong, they're happy to assume the best and hold their peace.'

'You speak from experience?'

'Too much experience.'

She was thoughtful. 'Is it something important?'

'Very.'

'Well, give me your name and number, and next time he calls I'll have him phone you.'

'Thanks.' Rebus reeled off two numbers: home and mobile.

'Got that,' she said. 'Any other message?'

'No, just have him call me.' Rebus thought for a moment. 'Has he had any other calls?'

'You mean, people trying to reach him? Why do you ask?'

'I just … no real reason.' He didn't want to say he was a policeman; didn't want her spooked. 'No reason,' he repeated.

As he came off the phone, someone handed him another coffee. 'That receiver must be red hot.'

He touched it with the tips of his fingers. It was pretty warm. Then it rang and he picked it up again.

'DI Rebus,' he said.

'John, it's Siobhan.'

'Hiya, how's tricks?'

'John, you remember that guy?' Her tone was warning him of something.

'What guy?' The humour was gone from his voice.

'Danny Simpson.' He of the flappy skull; Telford's lackey.

'What about him?'

'I've just found out he's HIV positive. His GP let the hospital know.'

Blood in Rebus's eyes, his ears, dribbling down his neck …

'Poor guy,' he said quietly.

'He should have said something at the time.'

'When?'

'When we got him to the hospital.'

'Well, he had other things on his mind, and some of them were in danger of falling off.'

'Christ, John, be serious for a minute!' Her voice was loud enough to have people glance up from their desks. 'You need to get a blood test.'

'Fine, no problem. How is he, by the way?'

'Back home but poorly. And sticking to his story.'

'Do I detect the influence of Telford's lawyer?'

'Charles Groal? That one's so slimy, he's practically primordial.'

'Saves you the cost of a valentine.'

'Look, just phone the hospital. Talk to a Dr Jones. She'll fix an appointment. They can do a test right away. Not that it'll be the last word – there's a three-month incubation.'

'Thanks, Siobhan.'

Rebus put down the receiver, drummed his fingers against it. Wouldn't *that* be a nice irony? Rebus out to get Telford, does the Good Samaritan bit for one of his men, gets AIDS and dies. Rebus stared at the ceiling.

Nice one, Big Man.

The phone rang again. Rebus snatched it up.

'Switchboard,' he said.

'Is that you, John?' Patience Aitken.

'The one and only.'

'Just wanted to check we're still on for tonight.'

'To be honest, Patience, I'm not sure I'll be at my most sparkling.'

'You want to cancel?'

'Absolutely not. But I have something to take care of. At the hospital.'

'Yes, of course.'

'No, I don't think you understand. It's not Sammy this time, it's me.'

'What's wrong?'

So he told her.

She went with him. Same hospital Sammy was in, different department. Last thing he wanted was to bump into Rhona, have to explain everything to her. Possibly HIV-infected: chances were, she'd red-card him from the bedside.

The waiting room was white, clean. Lots of information on the walls. Leaflets on every table, as if paperwork was the real virus.

'I must say, it's very pleasant for a leper colony.'

Patience didn't say anything. They were alone in the room. Someone on reception had dealt with him first, then a nurse had come out and taken some details. Now another door opened.

'Mr Rebus?'

A tall thin woman in a white coat, standing in the doorway: Dr Jones, he presumed. Patience took his arm as they walked towards her. Halfway across the floor, Rebus turned on his heels and bolted.

Patience caught up with him outside, asked what was wrong.

'I don't want to know,' he told her.

'But, John ...'

'Come on, Patience. All I got was a bit of blood splashed on me.'

She didn't look convinced. 'You need to take the test.'

He looked back towards the building. 'Fine.' Started walking away. 'But some other time, eh?'

It was one in the morning when he drove back into Arden Street. No dinner date with Patience: instead, they'd visited the hospital, sat with Rhona. He'd made a silent pact with the Big Man: bring her back and I'll keep off the booze. He'd driven Patience home. Her last words to him: 'Take that test. Get it over and done with.'

As he locked his car, a figure appeared from nowhere.

'Mr Rebus, long time no see.'

Rebus recognised the face. Pointy chin, misshapen teeth, the breathing a series of small gasps. The Weasel: one of Cafferty's men. He was dressed like a down-and-out, perfect camouflage for his role in life. He was Cafferty's eyes and ears on the street.

'We need to talk, Mr Rebus.' His hands were deep in the

pockets of a tweed coat meant for someone eight inches taller. He glanced towards the tenement door.

'Not in my flat,' Rebus stated. Some things were sacrosanct.

'Cold out here.'

Rebus just shook his head, and the Weasel sniffed hard.

'You think it was a hit?' he said.

'Yes,' Rebus answered.

'She was meant to die?'

'I don't know.'

'A pro wouldn't fuck up.'

'Then it was a warning.'

'We could do with seeing your notes.'

'Can't do that.'

The Weasel shrugged. 'Thought you wanted Mr Cafferty's help?'

'I can't give you the notes. What about if I summarise?'

'It'd be a start.'

'Rover 600, stolen from George Street that afternoon. Abandoned on a street by Piershill Cemetery. Radio and some tapes lifted – not necessarily by the same person.'

'Scavengers.'

'Could be.'

The Weasel was thoughtful. 'A warning ... That would mean a professional driver.'

'Yes,' Rebus said.

'And not one of ours ... Doesn't leave too many candidates. Rover 600 ... what colour?'

'Sherwood Green.'

'Parked on George Street?'

Rebus nodded.

'Thanks for that.' The Weasel made to turn away, then paused. 'Nice doing business with you again, Mr Rebus.'

Rebus was about to say something, then remembered he needed the Weasel more than the Weasel needed him. He wondered how much crap he'd take from Cafferty ... how long he'd have to take it. All his life? Had he made a contract with the devil?

For Sammy, he'd have done much, much worse ...

In his flat, he stuck on the CD of *Rock 'n' Roll Circus*, skipping to the actual Stones tracks. His answering machine was flashing. Three messages. The first: Hogan.

'Hello, John. Just thought I'd check, see if there's been any word from BT.'

Not by the time Rebus had left the office. Message two: Abernethy.

'Me again, bad penny and all that. Heard you've been trying to catch me. I'll call you tomorrow. Cheers.'

Rebus stared at the machine, willing Abernethy to say more, to give some hint of a location. But the machine was on to the final message. Bill Pryde.

'John, tried you at the office, left a message. But I thought you'd want to know, we've had final word on those prints. If you want to try me at home, I'm on ...'

Rebus took down the number. Two in the morning, but Bill would understand.

After a minute or so, a woman picked up. She sounded groggy.

'Sorry,' Rebus said. 'Is Bill there?'

'I'll get him.'

He heard background dialogue, then the receiver being hoisted.

'So what's this about prints?' he asked.

'Christ, John, when I said you could call, I didn't mean the middle of the night!'

'It's important.'

'Yes, I know. How's she doing anyway?'

'Still out cold.'

Pryde yawned. 'Well, most of the prints inside the car

belong to the owner and his wife. But we found one other set. Problem is, looks like they belong to a kid.'

'What makes you so sure?'

'The size.'

'Plenty of adults around with small hands.'

'I suppose so …'

'You sound sceptical.'

'More likely to be one of two scenarios. One, Sammy was hit by a joyrider. I know what you think, but it does happen. Two, the prints belong to whoever rifled the car after it was left at the cemetery.'

'The kid who took the cassette player and tapes?'

'Exactly.'

'No other prints? Not even partials?'

'The car was clean, John.'

'Exterior?'

'Same three sets on the doors, plus Sammy's on the bonnet.' Pryde yawned again. 'So what about your grudge theory?'

'Still holds. A pro would be wearing gloves.'

'That's what I was thinking. Not too many pros out there though.'

'No.' Rebus was thinking of the Weasel: *I'm dealing with slime to catch a slug.* Nothing he hadn't done before, only this time there were personal reasons.

And he didn't think there'd be a trial.

18

Breakfast was on Hogan: bacon rolls in a brown paper bag. They ate them in the CID room at St Leonard's. A Murder Room had been established in Leith, and that's where Hogan should have been.

Only he wanted Rebus's files, and he knew better than to trust Rebus to deliver them.

'Thought I'd save you the hassle,' was what he said.

'You're a gentleman,' Rebus answered, examining the interior of his roll. 'Tell me, are pigs an endangered species?'

'I lifted half a slice from you.' Hogan pulled a string of fat from his mouth, tossed it into a bin. 'Thought I was doing you a favour: cholesterol and all that.'

Rebus put the roll to one side, took a swig from the can of Irn-Bru – Hogan's idea of a morning beverage – and swallowed. What was sugar consumption compared to HIV? 'What did you get from the cleaning lady?'

'Grief. Soon as she heard her employer was dead, the taps were on.' Hogan brushed flour from his fingers: mealtime over. 'She never met any of his friends, never had occasion to answer his telephone, hadn't noticed any change in him recently, and doesn't think he was a mass murderer. Quote: "If he'd killed that many people, I'd have known".'

'What is she, psychic or something?'

Hogan shrugged. 'About all I got from her was a glowing character reference and the fact that as she was paid in advance, she owes his estate a partial refund.'

'There's your motive.'

Hogan smiled. 'Speaking of motives ...'

'You've got something?'

'Lintz's lawyer has come up with a letter from the deceased's bank.' He handed Rebus a photocopy. 'Seems our man made a cash withdrawal of five grand ten days ago.'

'*Cash?*'

'We found ten quid on his person, and about another thirty bar in the house. No five grand. I'm beginning to think blackmail.'

Rebus nodded. 'What about his address book?'

'Slow work. A lot of old numbers, people who've moved on or died. Plus a few charities, museums ... an art gallery or two.' Hogan paused. 'What about you?'

Rebus opened his drawer, pulled out the fax sheets. 'Waiting for me this morning. The calls Lintz wanted kept secret.'

Hogan looked down the list. 'Calls plural, or one in particular?'

'I've just started going through them. Best guess: there'll be callers he spoke to regularly. Those numbers will show up on the other statements. We're looking for anomalies, one-offs.'

'Makes sense.' Hogan looked at his watch. 'Anything else I should know?'

'Two things. Remember I told you about the Special Branch interest?'

'Abernethy?'

Rebus nodded. 'I tried calling him yesterday.'

'And?'

'According to his office, he was on his way up here. He'd already heard the news.'

'So I've got Abernethy sniffing around, and you don't trust him? Terrific. What's the other thing?'

'David Levy. I spoke with his daughter. She doesn't know where he is. He could be anywhere.'

'With a grudge against Lintz?'

'It's possible.'

'What's his phone number?'

Rebus patted the topmost file on his desk. 'Ready for you to take away.'

Hogan studied the foot-high pile, looking glum.

'I whittled it down to what's absolutely necessary,' Rebus told him.

'There's a month's reading there.'

Rebus shrugged. 'My case is your case, Bobby.'

With Hogan gone, Rebus went back to the British Telecom list. It was as detailed as he could have wished for. Lots of calls to Lintz's solicitor, a few to one of the city's taxi firms. Rebus tried a couple of numbers, found himself connected to charity offices: Lintz would have been phoning to tender his resignation. There were a few calls that stood out from the crowd: the Roxburghe Hotel – duration four minutes; Edinburgh University – twenty-six minutes. The Roxburghe had to mean Levy. Rebus knew Levy had talked to Lintz – Lintz himself had admitted it. Talking to him – being confronted by him – was one thing; calling him at his hotel quite another.

The number for Edinburgh University connected Rebus to the main switchboard. He asked to be put through to Lintz's old department. The secretary was very helpful. She'd been in the job over twenty years, was due to retire. Yes, she remembered Professor Lintz, but he hadn't contacted the department recently.

'Every call that comes through here, I know about it.'

'He might have got straight through to a tutor though?' Rebus suggested.

'No one's mentioned speaking to him. There's nobody here from the Professor's day.'

'He doesn't keep in touch with the department?'

'I haven't spoken to him in years, Inspector. Too many years for me to remember ...'

So who had he been talking to for over twenty minutes? Rebus thanked the secretary and put down the phone. He went through the other numbers: a couple of restaurants, a wine shop, and the local radio station. Rebus told the receptionist what he was after, and she said she'd do her best. Then he went back to the restaurants, asked them to check if Lintz had been making a reservation.

Within half an hour, the calls started coming in. First restaurant: a booking for dinner, just the one cover. The radio station: they'd asked Lintz to appear on a programme. He'd said he'd consider it, then had called back to decline. Second restaurant: a lunch reservation, two covers.

'Two?'

'Mr Lintz and one other.'

'Any idea who the "other" might have been?'

'Another gentleman, quite elderly, I think ... I'm sorry, I don't really remember.'

'Did he walk with a stick?'

'I wish I could help, but it's a madhouse here at lunchtime.'

'You remember Lintz though?'

'Mr Lintz is a regular ... was a regular.'

'Did he usually eat alone, or with company?'

'Mostly alone. He didn't seem to mind. He'd bring a book with him.'

'Do you happen to recall any of his other guests?'

'I remember a young woman ... his daughter maybe? Or granddaughter?'

'So when you say "young" ...?'

'Younger than him.' A pause. 'Maybe much younger.'

'When was this?'

'I really don't remember.' The voice impatient now.

'I appreciate your help, sir. Just one more minute of your time ... This woman, did he bring her more than once?'

'I'm sorry, Inspector. The kitchen needs me.'

'Well, if you think of anything else ...'

'Of course. Goodbye.'

Rebus put the phone down, made some notes. Just one number left. He waited for an answer.

'Yeah?' The voice grudging.

'Who's this?'

'This is Malky. Who the fuck are you?'

A voice in the background: 'Tommy says that new machine's fucked.' Rebus put the phone down. His hand was shaking. *That new machine* ... Tommy Telford on his arcade motorbike. He remembered The Family mugshots: Malky Jordan. Tiny nose and eyes in a balloon of a face. *Joseph Lintz talking to one of Telford's men? Phoning Telford's office??* Rebus found the number of Hogan's mobile.

'Bobby,' he said. 'If you're driving, better slow down right now ...'

Hogan's notion: five in cash was just Telford's style. Blackmail? But where was the connection? Something else ...?

Hogan's play: he'd talk to Telford.

Rebus's notion: five was a bit steep for a hit-man. All the same, he wondered about Lintz ... paying five thou' to Telford to set up the 'accident'. Motive: give Rebus a fright, scare him off? It put Lintz back in the frame, potentially.

Rebus had fixed up another meeting, one he didn't want

anyone knowing about. Haymarket Station was nice and anonymous. The bench on platform one. Ned Farlowe was already waiting. He looked tired: worry over Sammy. They talked about her for a couple of minutes. Then Rebus got down to business.

'You know Lintz has been murdered?'

'I didn't think this was a social call.'

'We're looking at a blackmail angle.'

Farlowe looked interested. 'And he didn't pay up?'

Oh, he paid up all right, Rebus thought. He paid up, and someone still took him out of the game.

'Look, Ned, this is *all* off the record. By rights I should take you in for questioning.'

'Because I followed him for a few days?'

'Yes.'

'And that makes me a suspect?'

'It makes you a possible witness.'

Farlowe thought about it. 'One evening. Lintz left his house, walked down the road, made a call from a phone-box, then went straight back home.'

Not wanting to use his home phone ... afraid it was bugged? Afraid of the number being traced? Telephone bugging: a favourite ploy of Special Branch.

'And something else,' Farlowe was saying. 'He met this woman on his doorstep. Like she was waiting for him. They had a few words. I think she was crying when she left.'

'What did she look like?'

'Tall, short dark hair, well-dressed. She had a briefcase with her.'

'Wearing?'

Farlowe shrugged. 'Skirt and jacket ... matching. Black and white check. You know ... elegant.'

He was describing Kirstin Mede. Her phone message to Rebus: *I can't do this any more ...*

'There's something I want to ask you,' Farlowe was saying. 'That girl Candice.'

'What about her?'

'You asked me if anything unusual had happened just before Sammy got hit.'

'Yes?'

'Well, *she* happened, didn't she?' Farlowe's eyes narrowed. 'Does she have anything to do with it?'

Rebus looked at Farlowe, who started nodding.

'Thanks for the confirmation. Who was she?'

'One of Telford's girls.'

Farlowe leaped to his feet, paced the platform. Rebus waited for him to sit down again. When he did, there could be no doubting the fury in his eyes.

'You hid one of Telford's girls with your own *daughter*?'

'I didn't have much choice. Telford knows where I live. I ...'

'You were using us!' He paused. 'Telford did this, didn't he?'

'I don't know,' Rebus said. Farlowe leaped to his feet again. 'Look, Ned, I don't want you –'

'Quite frankly, *Inspector*, I don't think you're in any position to give advice.' He started walking, and though Rebus called after him, he never once looked back.

As Rebus walked into the Crime Squad office, a paper plane glided past and crashed into the wall. Ormiston had his feet up on the desk. Country and western music was playing softly in the background, its source a tape player on the window ledge behind Claverhouse's desk. Siobhan Clarke had pulled a chair over beside him. They were poring over some report.

'Not exactly the "A-Team" in here, is it?' Rebus retrieved the plane, straightened its crumpled nose, and sent it back to Ormiston, who asked what he was doing there.

'Liaising,' Rebus told him. 'My boss wants a progress report.'

Ormiston glanced towards Claverhouse, who was tipping himself back in his chair, hands behind his head.

'Want to take a guess at the headway we've made?'

Rebus sat down opposite Claverhouse, nodded a greeting to Siobhan.

'How's Sammy?' she asked.

'Just the same,' Rebus answered. Claverhouse looked abashed, and Rebus suddenly realised that he could use Sammy as a lever, play on people's sympathy. Why not? Hadn't he used her in the past? Wasn't Ned Farlowe on the nail there?

'We've pulled the surveillance,' Claverhouse said.

'Why?'

Ormiston snorted, but it was Claverhouse who answered.

'High maintenance, low returns.'

'Orders from above?'

'It isn't as if we were close to getting a result.'

'So we just let him get on with getting on?'

Claverhouse shrugged. Rebus wondered if news would get back to Newcastle. Jake Tarawicz would be happy. He'd think Rebus was fulfilling his part of the bargain. Candice would be safe. Maybe.

'Any news on that nightclub killing?'

'Nothing to link it to your chum Cafferty.'

'He's *not* my chum.'

'Whatever you say. Stick the kettle on, Ormie.' Ormiston glanced towards Clarke, then rose grudgingly from his chair. Rebus had thought the tension in the office was all to do with Telford. Not a bit of it. Claverhouse and Clarke close together, *involved*. Ormiston off on his own, a kid making paper planes, seeking attention. An old Status Quo song: 'Paper Plane'. But the status quo here had been disturbed: Clarke had usurped Ormiston. The office junior was absolved from making the tea.

Rebus could see why Ormiston was pissed off.

'I hear Herr Lintz was a bit of a swinger,' Claverhouse said.

'Now there's a joke I haven't heard before.' Rebus's pager sounded. The display gave him a number to call.

He used Claverhouse's phone. It sounded like he was connected to a pay-phone. Street sounds, heavy traffic close by.

'Mr Rebus?' Placed the voice at once: the Weasel.

'What is it?'

'A couple of questions. The tape player from the car, any idea of the make?'

'Sony.'

'The front bit detachable?'

'That's right.'

'So all they got was the front bit?'

'Yes.' Claverhouse and Clarke, back at their report, pretending they weren't listening.

'What about the tapes? You said some tapes got stolen?'

'Opera – *The Marriage of Figaro* and Verdi's *Macbeth*.' Rebus squeezed his eyes shut, thinking. 'And another tape with film music on it, famous themes. Plus Roy Orbison's *Greatest Hits*.' This last the wife's. Rebus knew what the Weasel was thinking: whoever took the stuff, they'd try flogging it round the pubs or at a car boot sale. Car boot sales were clearing houses for knock-off. But getting whoever had lifted the stuff from the unlocked car wasn't going to nail the driver ... Unless the kid – the one who'd lifted the stuff, whose prints were on the car – had *seen* something: been hanging around on the street, watched the car screeching to a stop, a man getting out and hoofing it ...

An eye witness, someone who could describe the driver.

'The only prints we got were small, maybe a kid's.'

'That's interesting.'

'Anything else I can do,' Rebus said, 'just let me know.'
The Weasel hung up.

'Sony's a good make,' Claverhouse said, fishing.

'Some stuff lifted from a car,' Rebus told him. 'It might
have turned up.'

Ormiston had made the tea. Rebus went to fetch himself
a chair, saw someone walk past the open doorway. He
dropped the chair and ran into the corridor, grabbed at an
arm.

Abernethy spun quickly, saw who it was and relaxed.

'Nice one, son,' he said. 'You almost had knuckles for
teeth.' He was working on a piece of chewing gum.

'What are you doing here?'

'Visiting.' Abernethy looked back at the open door,
walked towards it. 'What about you?'

'Working.'

Abernethy read the sign on the door. 'Crime Squad,' he
said, sounding amused, taking in the office and the people
in it. Hands in pockets, he sauntered in, Rebus following.

'Abernethy, Special Branch,' the Londoner said by way
of introduction. 'That music's a good idea: play it at
interrogations, sap the suspect's will to live.' He was
smiling, surveying the premises like he was thinking of
moving in. The mug meant for Rebus was on the corner of
the desk. Abernethy picked it up and slurped, made a face,
started chewing again. The three Crime Squad officers
were like a frozen tableau. Suddenly they looked like a unit:
it had taken Abernethy to do that.

Had taken him all of ten seconds.

'What you working on?' No one answered. 'Must've got
the sign on the door wrong,' Abernethy said. 'Should be
Mime Squad.'

'Is there something we can do for you?' Claverhouse asked, his voice level, hostility in his eyes.

'I don't know. It was John pulled me in here.'

'And I'm pulling you out again,' Rebus said, taking his arm. Abernethy shrugged free, bunched his fists. 'A word in the corridor ... please.'

Abernethy smiled. 'Manners maketh the man, John.'

'What does that maketh you?'

Abernethy turned his head slowly, looked at Siobhan Clarke who'd just spoken.

'I'm just a regular guy with a heart of gold and twelve big inches of ability.' He grinned at her.

'To go with your twelve big points of IQ,' she said, going back to the report. Ormiston and Claverhouse weren't trying too hard to conceal their laughter as Abernethy stormed out of the room. Rebus hung back long enough to watch Ormiston pat Clarke on the back, then headed off after the Special Branch man.

'What a bitch,' Abernethy said. He was making for the exit.

'She's a friend of mine.'

'And they say you can choose your friends ...' Abernethy shook his head.

'What brings you back?'

'You have to ask?'

'Lintz is dead. Case closed as far as you're concerned.'

They emerged from the building.

'So?'

'So,' Rebus persisted, 'why come all the way back here? What is there that couldn't be done with a phone or fax?'

Abernethy stopped, turned to face him. 'Loose ends.'

'What loose ends?'

'There aren't any.' Abernethy gave a cheerless smile and took a key from his pocket. As they approached his car, he used the remote to unlock it and disable the alarm.

'What's going on, Abernethy?'

'Nothing to worry your pretty little head about.' He opened the driver's-side door.

'Are you glad he's dead?'

'What?'

'Lintz. How do you feel about him being murdered?'

'I've no feelings either way. He's dead, which means I can cross him off my list.'

'That last time you came up here, you were warning him.'

'Not true.'

'Was his phone bugged?' Abernethy just snorted. 'Did you know he might be killed?'

Abernethy turned on Rebus. 'What's it to you? I'll tell you: nothing. Leith CID are on the murder, and you're out of it. End of story.'

'Is it the Rat Line? Too embarrassing if it all came to light?'

'Christ, what *is* it with you? Just give it a rest.' Abernethy got into the car, closed the door. Rebus didn't move. The engine turned and caught, Abernethy's window slid down. Rebus was ready.

'They sent you four hundred miles just to check there were no loose ends.'

'So?'

'So there's rather a large loose end, isn't there?' Rebus paused. 'Unless you know who Lintz's killer was.'

'I leave that sort of thing to you guys.'

'Heading down to Leith?'

'I have to talk to Hogan.' Abernethy stared at Rebus. 'You're a hard bastard, aren't you? Maybe even a bit selfish.'

'How's that?'

'If I'd a daughter in hospital, police work would be the last thing on my mind.'

As Rebus lunged towards the open window, Abernethy gunned the car. Footsteps behind: Siobhan Clarke.

'Good riddance,' she said, watching the car speed off. A finger appeared from Abernethy's window. She gave a two-fingered reply. 'I didn't want to say anything in the office ...' she began.

'I took the test yesterday,' Rebus lied.

'It'll be negative.'

'Are you positive?'

She smiled a little longer than the joke merited. 'Ormiston chucked your tea away, said he was going to disinfect the mug.'

'Abernethy has that effect on people.' He looked at her. 'Remember, Ormiston and Claverhouse go back years.'

'I know. I think Claverhouse has a crush on me. It'll pass, but until it does ...'

'Tread carefully.' They started walking back towards the main entrance. 'And don't let him tempt you into the broom cupboard.'

19

Rebus went back to St Leonard's, saw that the office was coping quite well without him, and headed over to the hospital with Dr Morrison's Iron Maiden t-shirt in a plastic bag. A third bed had been moved into Sammy's room. An elderly woman lay in it. Though awake, she stared fixedly at the ceiling. Rhona was at Sammy's bedside, reading a book.

Rebus stroked his daughter's hair. 'How is she?'

'No change.'

'Any more tests planned?'

'Not that I know of.'

'That's it then? She just stays like this?'

He lifted a chair over, sat down. It had turned into a sort of ritual now, this bedside vigil. It felt almost ... the word he wanted to use was 'comfortable'. He squeezed Rhona's hand, sat there for twenty minutes, saying almost nothing, then went to find Kirstin Mede.

She was in her office at the French Department, marking scripts. She sat at a big desk in front of the window, but moved from this to a coffee-table with half a dozen chairs arranged around it.

'Sit down,' she said. Rebus sat down.

'I got your message,' he told her.

'Hardly matters now, does it? The man's dead.'

'I know you spoke with him, Kirstin.'

She glanced towards him. 'I'm sorry?'

'You waited for him outside his house. Did the two of you have a nice chat?'

Colour had risen to her cheeks. She crossed her legs, tugged the hem of her skirt towards her knee. 'Yes,' she said at last, 'I went to his house.'

'Why?'

'Because I wanted to see him close up.' Her eyes were on his now, challenging him. 'I thought maybe I could tell from his face ... the look in his eyes. Maybe something in his tone of voice.'

'And could you?'

She shook her head. 'Not a damned thing. No window to the soul.'

'What did you say to him?'

'I told him who I was.'

'Any reaction?'

'Yes.' She folded her arms. 'His words: "My dear lady, will you kindly piss off".'

'And did you?'

'Yes. Because I knew then. Not whether he was Linzstek or not, but something else.'

'What?'

'That he was at the end of his tether.' She was nodding. 'Absolutely at breaking point.' She looked at Rebus again. 'And capable of anything.'

The problem with the Flint Street surveillance was that it had been so open. A hidden operation – deep cover – that's what was needed. Rebus had decided to scout out the territory.

The tenement flats across the road from Telford's café and arcade were served by a single main door. It was locked, so Rebus chose a buzzer at random – marked HETHERINGTON. Waited, pushed again. An elderly voice came on the intercom.

'Who is it, please?'

'Mrs Hetherington? Detective Inspector Rebus, I'm your Community CID officer. Can I talk to you about home security? There've been a few break-ins around here, especially with elderly victims.'

'Gracious, you'd better come up.'

'Which floor?'

'The first.' The door buzzed, and Rebus pushed it open.

Mrs Hetherington was waiting for him in her doorway. She was tiny and frail-looking, but her eyes were lively and her movements assured. The flat was small, well-maintained. The sitting-room was heated by a two-bar electric fire. Rebus wandered over to the window, found himself looking down on to the arcade. Perfect location for a surveillance. He pretended to check her windows.

'These seem fine,' he said. 'Are they always locked?'

'I open them a bit in the summer,' Mrs Hetherington said, 'and when they need washing. But I always lock them again afterwards.'

'One thing I should warn you about, and that's bogus officials. People coming to your door, telling you they're so-and-so. Always ask to see some ID, and don't open up until you're satisfied.'

'How can I see it without opening the door?'

'Ask them to push it through the letterbox.'

'I didn't see *your* identification, did I?'

Rebus smiled. 'No, you didn't.' He took it out and showed her. 'Sometimes the fake stuff can look pretty convincing. If you're unsure, keep the door locked and call the police.' He looked around. 'You have a phone?'

'In the bedroom.'

'Any windows in there?'

'Yes.'

'Can I take a look?'

The bedroom window also looked out on to Flint Street.

Rebus noticed travel brochures on the dressing-table, a small suitcase standing near the door.

'Off on holiday, eh?' With the flat empty, maybe he could move the surveillance in.

'Just a long weekend,' she said.

'Somewhere nice?'

'Holland. Wrong time of year for the bulb-fields, but I've always wanted to go. It's a nuisance flying from Inverness, but so much cheaper. Since my husband died ... well, I've done a bit of travelling.'

'Any chance of taking me with you?' Rebus smiled. 'This window's fine, too. I'll just check your door, see if it could do with more locks.' They went into the narrow hall.

'You know,' she said, 'we've always been very lucky here, no break-ins or anything like that.'

Hardly surprising with Tommy Telford as proprietor.

'And with the panic button, of course ...'

Rebus looked at the wall next to the front door. A large red button. He'd assumed it was for the stairhead lights or something.

'Anyone who calls, anyone at all, I'm supposed to press it.'

Rebus opened the door. 'And do you?'

Two very large men were standing right outside.

'Oh, yes,' Mrs Hetherington said. 'I always do.'

For thugs, they were very polite. Rebus showed them his warrant card and explained the nature of his visit. He asked them who they were, and they told him they were 'representatives of the building's owner'. He knew the faces though: Kenny Houston, Ally Cornwell. Houston – the ugly one – ran Telford's doormen; Cornwell, with his wrestler's bulk, was general muscle. The little charade was carried out with humour and good nature on both sides. They accompanied him downstairs. Across the street,

Tommy Telford was standing in the café doorway, wagging his finger. A pedestrian crossed Rebus's line of vision. Too late, Rebus saw who it was. Had his mouth open to shout something, then saw Telford hang his head, hands going to his face. Screeching.

Rebus ran across the road, pulled the pedestrian round: Ned Farlowe. A bottle dropped from Farlowe's hand. Telford's men were closing in. Rebus held tight to Farlowe.

'I'm placing this man under arrest,' he said. 'He's *mine*, understood?'

A dozen faces glaring at him. And Tommy Telford down on his knees.

'Get your boss to the hospital,' Rebus said. 'I'm taking this one to St Leonard's ...'

Ned Farlowe sat on the ledge in one of the cells. The walls were blue, smeared brown near the toilet-pan. Farlowe was looking pleased with himself.

'Acid?' Rebus said, pacing the cell. '*Acid*? All this research must have gone to your head.'

'It's what he deserved.'

Rebus glared at him. 'You don't know what you've done.'

'I know *exactly* what I've done.'

'He'll kill you.'

Farlowe shrugged. 'Am I under arrest?'

'You'd better believe it, son. I want you kept out of harm's way. If I hadn't been there ...' But he didn't want to think about that. He looked at Farlowe. Looked at Sammy's lover, who'd just staged a full-frontal assault on Telford, the kind of assault Rebus knew wouldn't work.

Now Rebus would have to redouble his efforts. Because otherwise, Ned Farlowe was a dead man ... and when Sammy came round, he didn't want news like that to be waiting for her.

*

He drove back towards Flint Street, parked at a distance from it, and headed there on foot. Telford had the place sewn up, no doubt about it. Letting his flats to old folk might have been a charitable act but he'd made damned sure it served its purpose. Rebus wondered if, given the same circumstances, Cafferty would have been clever enough to think of panic-buttons. He suspected not. Cafferty wasn't thick, but most of what he did he did by instinct. Rebus wondered if Tommy Telford had ever made a rash move in his life.

He was staking out Flint Street because he needed an *in*, needed to find the weak link in the chain around Telford. After ten minutes of windchill, he thought of a better idea. On his mobile, he called one of the city's taxi firms. Identified himself and asked if Henry Wilson was on shift. He was. Rebus told the switchboard to put a call out to Henry. It was as simple as that.

Ten minutes later, Wilson turned up. He drank in the Ox occasionally, which was his problem really. Drunk in charge of a taxi-cab. Luckily Rebus had been around to smooth things over, as a result of which Wilson owed him a lifetime of favours. He was tall, heavily built, with short black hair and a long black beard. Ruddy-faced, and he always wore check shirts. Rebus thought of him as 'The Lumberjack'.

'Need a lift?' Wilson said, as Rebus got into the front passenger-seat.

'First thing I need is a blast of the heater.' Wilson obliged. 'Second thing I need is to use your taxi as cover.'

'You mean, sit here?'

'That's what I mean.'

'With the meter running?'

'You've got an engine problem, Henry. Your cab's out of the game for the rest of the afternoon.'

'I'm saving up for Christmas,' Wilson complained.

Rebus stared him out. The big man sighed and lifted a newspaper from the side of his seat. 'Help me pick a few winners then,' he said, turning to the racing pages.

They sat for over an hour at the end of Flint Street, and Rebus stayed in the front of the cab. His reasoning: a cab parked with a passenger in the back looked suspicious. A cab parked with two guys in the front, and you'd just think they were on their break, or at shift's end – two cabbies sharing stories and a flask of tea.

Rebus took one sip from the plastic cup and winced. Half a bag of sugar in the flask.

'I've always had a sweet tooth,' Wilson explained. He had a packet of crisps open on his lap: pickled onion flavour.

Finally, Rebus saw two Range Rovers being driven into Flint Street. Sean Haddow – Telford's money man – was driving the lead car. He got out and went into the arcade. On the passenger seat, Rebus could see a huge yellow teddy bear. Haddow was coming out again, bringing Telford with him. Telford: back from the hospital already, hands bandaged, gauze patches on his face like he'd had a particularly ropey shave. But not about to let a little thing like an acid attack get in the way of business. Haddow held the back door open, and Telford got in.

'This is us, Henry,' Rebus said. 'You're going to be following those two Range Rovers. Stay back as far as you like. Those things are so high off the ground, we'll be able to see them over anything smaller than a double-decker.'

Both Range Rovers headed out of Flint Street. The second car carried three of Telford's 'soldiers'. Rebus recognised Pretty-Boy. The other two were younger recruits, well-dressed with groomed hair. One hundred percent business.

The convoy headed for the city centre, stopped outside a

hotel. Telford had a word with his men, but entered the building alone. The cars stayed where they were.

'Are you going in?' Wilson asked.

'I think I'd be noticed,' Rebus said. The drivers of both Range Rovers had got out and were enjoying a smoke, but keeping a keen eye on people entering and leaving the hotel. A couple of prospects looked into the cab, but Wilson shook his head.

'I could be making a mint here,' he muttered. Rebus offered him a Polo. Wilson accepted with a snort.

'Brilliant,' Rebus said. Wilson looked back towards the hotel. A parking warden was talking to Haddow and Pretty-Boy. She had her notebook out. They were tapping their watches, attempting charm. Double yellow lines kerbside: no parking any time.

Haddow and Pretty-Boy held up their hands in surrender, had a quick confab, then it was back into the Range Rovers. Pretty-Boy made circling motions with one hand, letting his passengers know they were going to circle the block. The warden stood her ground till they'd moved off. Haddow was on his mobile: doubtless letting his boss know the score.

Interesting: they hadn't tried to strongarm the warden, or bribe her, nothing like that. Law-abiding citizens. Telford's rules, no doubt. Again, Rebus couldn't see any of Cafferty's men giving in so quickly.

'You going in then?' Wilson asked.

'Not much point, Henry. Telford will already be in a bedroom or somebody's suite. If he's doing business, it'll be behind closed doors.'

'So that was Tommy Telford?'

'You've heard of him?'

'I'm a taxi driver, we hear things. He's after Big Ger's cab business.' Wilson paused. 'Not that Big Ger *has* a cab business, you understand.'

'Any idea how Telford plans to wrest it away from Cafferty?'

'Scare off the drivers, or get them to switch sides.'

'What about your company, Henry?'

'Honest, legal and decent, Mr Rebus.'

'No approach by Telford?'

'Not yet.'

'Here they come again.' They watched as the two Range Rovers turned back into the street. There was no sign of the warden. A couple of minutes later, Telford emerged from the hotel, bringing with him a Japanese man with spiky hair and a shiny aquamarine suit. He carried a briefcase but didn't look like a businessman. Maybe it was the sunglasses, worn in late-afternoon twilight; maybe it was the cigarette slouching from the corner of the downturned mouth. Both men got into the back of the lead car. The Japanese leaned forward and ruffled the teddy bear's ears, making some joke. Telford didn't look amused.

'Do we follow them?' Wilson asked. He saw the look on Rebus's face, turned the key in the ignition.

They were heading west out of town. Rebus already had an inkling of their ultimate destination, but he wanted to know what route they'd take. Turned out it was much the same route he'd taken with Candice. She hadn't recognised anything until Juniper Green, but it wasn't as if there were many landmarks. On Slateford Road the back car signalled that it was pulling over.

'What do I do?' Wilson asked.

'Keep going. Make the first left you can, and turn the cab round. We'll wait for them to go past us.'

Haddow had gone into a newspaper shop. Same story as with Candice. Strange, during what was a business trip, that Telford would allow a stop. And what about the building which, according to Candice, he'd seemed so interested in? There it was: an anonymous brick edifice. A warehouse maybe? Rebus could think of reasons why a warehouse might be of interest to Tommy Telford. Haddow stayed in the shop three minutes – Rebus timed him. No one else came out, so it wasn't as if he'd had to queue. Back into the car, and the little convoy set off again. They were heading for Juniper Green, and after that Poyntinghame Country Club. Little point in tagging along: the further they got out of town, the more conspicuous the cab would be. Rebus told Henry to turn around.

He got the cabbie to drop him off at the Oxford Bar. Wilson slid down his window as he was about to move off.

'Are we square now?' he called.

'Till next time, Henry.' Rebus pushed open the door and walked into the pub.

Perched on a stool, daytime TV and Margaret the barmaid for company, Rebus ordered a mug of coffee and a corned beef and beetroot roll. For his main course Margaret suggested a bridie.

'Excellent choice,' Rebus agreed. He was thinking about the Japanese businessman. Who hadn't really looked like a businessman at all. He'd been all sharp edges, chiselled face. Fortified, Rebus walked from the Ox back to the hotel, and kept watch on it from an overpriced bar across the street. He passed the time making calls on his mobile. By the time the battery died, he'd spoken with Hogan, Bill Pryde, Siobhan Clarke, Rhona and Patience, and had been about to call Torphichen cop-shop, see if anyone there could identify the building on Slateford Road. Two hours crawled by. He broke his 'personal best' for slow drinking: two Cokes. The bar wasn't exactly crowded; no one seemed to mind. The music was on a tape-loop. 'Psycho Killer' was coming round for the third time when the Range Rovers stopped outside the hotel. Telford and the Jap shook hands, made slight bows. Telford and his men drove off.

Rebus left the bar, crossed the road, and entered the

hotel. The lift doors were closing on Mr Aquamarine. Rebus walked up to reception, showed his ID.

'The guest who just came in, I need his name.'

The receptionist had to check. 'Mr Matsumoto.'

'First name?'

'Takeshi.'

'When did he arrive?'

She checked the register again. 'Yesterday.'

'How long's he staying?'

'Three more days. Look, I should call my supervisor ...'

Rebus shook his head. 'That's all I needed to know, thanks. Mind if I sit in the lounge for a while?'

She shook her head, so Rebus wandered into the residents' lounge. He settled on a sofa – perfect view of the reception area through the glass double-doors – and picked up a newspaper. Matsumoto was in town on Poyntinghame business, but Rebus had a whiff of something altogether less savoury. Hugh Malahide's story had been that a corporation wanted to buy the club, but Matsumoto didn't look like he worked in any above-board business. When he finally emerged into reception, he'd changed into a white suit, black open-necked shirt, and Burberry trenchcoat, topped off with a woollen tartan scarf. He had a cigarette in his mouth, but didn't light it until he was outside the hotel. With the collar of his coat turned up, he started walking. Rebus followed him for the best part of a mile, and kept checking that no one was following *him*. It was possible, after all, that Telford would want to keep tabs on Matsumoto. But if there was surveillance, it was exceptional. Matsumoto wasn't playing the tourist, wasn't dawdling. He kept his head down, protecting his face from the wind, and seemed to have some destination in mind.

When he disappeared into a building, Rebus paused, studying the glass door behind which stood a flight of red-carpeted stairs. He knew where he was, didn't need the sign above the door to tell him. He was outside the Morvena Casino. The place used to be owned by a local villain called Topper Hamilton and managed by a man called Mandelson. But Hamilton was in retirement, and Mandelson had scarpered. The new owner was still an unknown quantity – or had been till now. Rebus guessed he wouldn't be far wrong if he placed Tommy Telford and his Japanese friends in the frame. He looked around, checking the parked cars: no Range Rovers.

'What the hell,' he said to himself, pushing open the door and starting to climb the stairs.

In the upstairs foyer he was eyeballed by security: two of them looking uncomfortable in their black suits and bowties, white shirts. One skinny – he'd be all about speed and manoeuvres; one a real heavyweight – slow muscle to back up the fast moves. Rebus seemed to pass whatever test they'd just given him. He bought a twenty's worth of chips and walked into the gaming room.

At one time, it would have been the drawing-room of a Georgian house. There were two huge bay windows, and ornate cornicing connected the twenty-foot-high cream walls to the pastel-pink ceiling. Now it was home to gaming tables: blackjack, dice, roulette. Hostesses moved between the tables, taking orders for drinks. There was very little noise: the gamblers took their work seriously. Rebus wouldn't have called the place busy, but what clientele there was comprised a veritable United Nations. Matsumoto's coat had disappeared into the cloakroom, and he was seated at the roulette table. Rebus sat down beside two men at the blackjack table, nodded a greeting. The dealer – young, but obviously sure of himself – smiled. Rebus won with his first hand. Lost with his second and third. Won again with his fourth. There was a voice just behind his right ear.

'Something to drink, sir?'

The hostess had bent forward to speak to him, showing plenty of cleavage.

'Coke,' he told her. 'Ice and lemon.' He pretended to watch her move away. Really, he was scoping the room. He'd sat in on the game quickly: walking around the room would have attracted everyone's interest, and he couldn't be sure if there'd be anyone here who'd know him.

He needn't have worried. The only person he recognised was Matsumoto, rubbing his hands as the croupier pushed chips towards him. Rebus stuck on eighteen. The dealer got twenty. Rebus had never been a great gambler. He'd tried the football pools, sometimes the horses, and now occasionally the lottery. But fruit machines didn't interest him; the poker sessions organised in the office didn't interest him. He had other ways of losing money.

Matsumoto lost and gave what sounded like a curse, a little bit louder than the room liked. The skinny security ape put his head around the door, but Matsumoto ignored him, and when Mr Skinny saw who was making the noise, he retreated fast. Matsumoto laughed: he might not have much English, but he knew he had power in this place. He told everyone something in a stream of Japanese, nodding, trying for eye contact. Then a hostess brought him a big tumbler of whisky and ice. He handed her a couple of chips as a tip. The croupier was telling everyone to place their bets. Matsumoto quietened down and went back to work.

Rebus's drink was a while coming, Coke the unlikely beverage of the high roller. He'd won a couple of hands, felt a bit better. Stood up to accept the drink. The table knew to leave him out of the next deal.

'Where are you from?' he asked the hostess. 'I can't place your accent.'

'I am from Ukraine.'

'You speak good English.'

'Thank you.' She turned away. Conversation was not house policy, it kept the punters away from their games. Ukraine: Rebus wondered if she was another of Tarawicz's imports. Like Candice ... A few things seemed clear to him. Matsumoto was comfortable here, therefore known. And the staff were wary of him, therefore he had clout, had Telford behind him. Telford wanted him kept sweet. It wasn't much return for all Rebus's work, but it was something.

Then someone walked in. Someone Rebus knew. Dr Colquhoun. He saw Rebus immediately and fear jumped into his face. Colquhoun: with his sick line to the university; his enforced holiday; no forwarding address. Colquhoun: who'd known Rebus was taking Candice to the Drinics.

Rebus watched him back towards the doors. Watched him turn and run.

Options: go after him, or stay with Matsumoto? Which was the more important to him now, Candice or Telford? Rebus stayed. But now Colquhoun was back in town, he'd track him down.

For definite.

After an hour and a quarter's play, he was considering cashing a cheque for more chips. Twenty quid down in a little over an hour, and Candice fighting for some space in his crowded head. He took a break, moved to a row of fruit machines, but the lights and buttons defeated him. He wasted three nudges and ran out of time on some accumulator. Another two quid gone – this time in a couple of minutes. Little wonder clubs and pubs wanted slot machines. Tommy Telford was in the right business. His hostess came to see him again, asked if he wanted another drink.

'I'm fine,' he said. 'Not much action tonight.'

'It's early,' she told him. 'Wait till after midnight ...'

No way was he sticking around that long. But Matsu-moto surprised him, threw up his hands and came out with another rush of Japanese, nodding and grinning, gathering up his chips. He cashed them and left the casino. Rebus waited all of thirty seconds, then followed. He said a breezy goodnight to the security men, felt their eyes on him all the way back down the stairs.

Matsumoto was buttoning his coat, wrapping the scarf tight around his neck. He was headed back in the direction of the hotel. Rebus, suddenly bone-tired, stopped in his tracks. He was thinking of Sammy and Lintz and the Weasel, thinking of all the time he seemed to be wasting.

'Fuck this for a game of soldiers.'

Turned on his heels and went to collect his car. Ten Years After: 'Goin' Home'.

It was a twenty-minute walk to Flint Street, a lot of it uphill and with the wind doing nobody any favours. The city was quiet: people huddled at bus stops; students munching on baked potatoes, chips with curry sauce. A few souls marching home with the concentrated tread of the sozzled. Rebus stopped, frowned, looked around. This was where he'd left the Saab. He was positive ... no, not 'positive' – the word had taken on malign overtones. He was *sure*, yes, sure he'd left the Saab right here. Where now a black Ford Sierra was parked, and behind that a Mini. But no sign of Rebus's car.

'Aw, Christ,' he exploded. There were no signs of glass by the roadside, which meant they hadn't taken a brick to one of his windows. Oh, there'd be jokes in the office about this though, whether he got the car back or not. A taxi came along and he flagged it down, then remembered he'd no cash, so waved it off again.

His flat in Arden Street wasn't that far off, but had he been a camel, he'd have been keeping well clear of any straw.

20

He was asleep in his chair by the living-room window, duvet pulled up to his neck, when the buzzer sounded. He couldn't remember setting the alarm. Consciousness brought the dawning realisation that it was his door. He staggered to his feet, found his trousers and put them on.

'All right, all right,' he called, heading for the hall. 'Keep your hair on.'

He opened the door and saw Bill Pryde.

'Jesus, Bill, is this some sort of twisted revenge?' Rebus looked at his watch: two-fifteen.

'Afraid not, John,' Pryde said. His face and voice told Rebus something bad had happened.

Something very bad indeed.

'I've been off the booze for weeks.'

'Sure about that?'

'Definite.' Rebus's eyes burned into those of DCI Gill Templer. They were in her office at St Leonard's. Pryde was there, too. His jacket was off and his sleeves rolled up. Gill Templer looked bleary from interrupted sleep. Rebus was pacing what floor there was, unable to stay seated.

'I've had nothing to drink all day but coffee and Coke.'

'Really?'

Rebus ran his hands through his hair. He felt groggy, and his head was throbbing. But he couldn't ask for Paracetamol and water: they'd assume hangover.

'Come on, Gill,' he said, 'I'm being shafted here.'

'Who authorised your surveillance?'

'Nobody. I did it in my own time.'

'How do you work that out?'

'The Chief Super said I could take a bit of time off.'

'He meant so you could visit your daughter.' She paused. 'Is that what this was all about?'

'Maybe.'

'This Mr ...' she checked her notes '... Matsumoto, he was connected to Thomas Telford. And your theory is that Telford was behind the attack on your daughter?'

Rebus thumped the wall with his fists. 'It's a set-up, oldest trick in the book. I've yet to see one perfected. There's got to be something at the scene ... something out of kilter.' He turned to his colleagues. 'You've got to let me go there, take a look around.'

Templer looked to Bill Pryde. Pryde folded his arms, shrugged assent. But it was Templer's play, she was the senior officer here. She tapped her pen against her teeth, then dropped it on to the desk.

'Will you submit to a blood test?'

Rebus swallowed. 'Why not?' he said at last.

'Come on then,' she said, getting to her feet.

The story was: Matsumoto had been on his way back to his hotel. Crossing the road, he'd been hit by a car travelling at speed. The driver hadn't stopped, not right away. But the car had travelled only another couple of hundred yards before mounting the pavement with its front wheels. It had been abandoned there, driver's door open.

A Saab 900, its identity known to half the Lothian and Borders force.

The interior reeked of whisky, the screw-top from a bottle lying on the passenger seat. No sign of the bottle, no sign of the driver. Just the car, and two hundred yards further back, the body of the Japanese businessman, growing cold by the roadside.

Nobody had seen anything. Nobody had heard anything. Rebus could believe it: never one of the city centre's busier routes, at this hour the place was dead.

'When I followed him from his hotel, he didn't come this way,' Rebus told Templer. She stood with shoulders hunched, hands deep in her coat pockets, keeping out the cold.

'So?' she asked.

'Long way round for a short-cut.'

'Maybe he wanted to see the sights,' Pryde suggested.

'What time's this supposed to have happened?' Rebus asked.

Templer hesitated. 'There's a margin of error.'

'Look, Gill, I know this is awkward. You shouldn't have brought me here, you shouldn't answer my questions. I'm the number one suspect, after all.' Rebus knew how much she had to lose. Over two hundred male Chief Inspectors in Scotland; only *five* women. Bad odds, and a lot of people waiting for her to fail. He held up his hands. 'Look, if I was blind drunk and I hit somebody, think I'd leave the car at the scene?'

'You might not know you'd hit anyone. You hear a thunk, lose control and mount the kerb, and some survival instinct tells you it's time to get out and walk.'

'Only I hadn't been drinking. I left the car near Flint Street, and that's where they took it from. Any signs it was broken into?'

She didn't say anything.

'I'll guess not,' Rebus went on. 'Because professionals don't leave marks. But to get it started, they must have wired it or got into the steering column. That's what you should be looking for.'

The car had been towed. First thing in the morning, forensics would be all over it.

Rebus laughed, shaking his head. 'It's nice though, isn't it? First they make Sammy look like a hit and run, and now they try to pin me for the same thing.'

'Who's "they"?'

'Telford and his men.'

'I thought you said they were doing business with Matsumoto?'

'They're all gangsters, Gill. Gangsters fall out.'

'What about Cafferty?'

Rebus frowned. 'What about him?'

'He's got an old grudge against you. This way, he stitches you up *and* annoys Telford.'

'So you do think I'm being stitched up?'

'I'm giving you the benefit of the doubt.' She paused. 'Not everyone will. What was Matsumoto's business with Telford?'

'Something to do with a country club – on the surface at least. Some Japanese were buying it, and Telford was clearing the way.' He shivered: should have worn a coat over his jacket. He rubbed his arm where the blood sample had been taken to test his alcohol level. 'Of course, a check of the deceased's hotel room might throw up something.'

'We've already been there,' Pryde said. 'Nothing out of the ordinary.'

'Which deadbeat did you send?'

'I went myself,' Gill Templer said, voice as icy as the wind. Rebus bowed his head in apology. She had a point though: Matsumoto and Telford had been doing business. There had been nothing about their farewell to one another to suggest a break-up, and Matsumoto had seemed happy and confident at the casino. What had Telford to gain by bumping him off?

Apart from maybe getting Rebus off his back.

Templer had mentioned Cafferty: was Big Ger capable of such a move? What did *he* stand to gain? Apart from settling a long-held grudge against Rebus, giving Telford a headache, and maybe gaining Poyntinghame and the Japanese deal for himself.

Balance the two – Telford against Cafferty. Cafferty's side tipped, went clunk as it hit the ground.

'Let's get back to the station,' Templer said. 'I'm reaching the early stages of frostbite.'

'Can I go home then?'

'We're not done with you yet, John,' she said, getting into the car. 'Not by a long chalk.'

But eventually they had to let him go. He wasn't being charged, not yet. There was work still to be done. He knew they could make a case against him if they wanted to, knew it only too well. *He'd* followed Matsumoto out of the club. *He* was the one with the grudge against Telford. *He* was the one who'd see poetic justice in sending Telford a message by driving over one of his associates.

He, John Rebus, was firmly in the frame. It was tightly constructed and quite elegant in its way. The scales suddenly tipped back towards Telford again, so much subtler than Cafferty.

Telford.

Rebus visited Farlowe in his cell. The reporter wasn't asleep.

'How long do I have to stay here?' he asked.

'As long as possible.'

'How's Telford?'

'Minor burns. Don't expect him to press charges. He'll want you on the outside.'

'Then you'll have to let me go.'

'Don't bet on it, Ned. *We* can press charges. We don't need Telford.'

Farlowe looked at him. 'You're going to prosecute me?'

'I saw the whole thing. Unwarranted attack on an innocent man.'

Farlowe snorted, then smiled. 'Ironic, isn't it? Charging me for my own good.' He paused. 'I won't be able to see Sammy, will I?'

Rebus shook his head.

'I didn't think of that. Fact is, I didn't *think*.' He looked up from his ledge. 'I just did. And right up until the moment I did it, it felt … brilliant.'

'And afterwards?'

Farlowe shrugged. 'What does afterwards matter? It's only the rest of my life.'

Rebus didn't go home, knew he wouldn't sleep. And he'd no car, so he couldn't go driving. Instead, he visited the hospital, sat down by Sammy's bedside. He took her hand, rested it against his face.

When a nurse came in and asked if he wanted anything, he asked if she'd any Paracetamol.

'In a hospital?' she said, smiling. 'I'll see what I can do.'

21

Rebus was due for further questioning at St Leonard's at ten o'clock, so when his pager sounded at eight-fifteen, he assumed it was a reminder. But the phone number it wanted him to call was the mortuary down in the Cowgate. He called from the hospital payphone, and was put through to Dr Curt.

'Looks like I've drawn the short straw,' Curt told him.

'You're about to start work on Matsumoto?'

'For my sins. Look, I've heard the stories ... don't suppose there's any truth in them?'

'I didn't kill him.'

'Glad to hear it, John.' Curt seemed to be struggling to say something. 'There are questions of ethics, of course, so I can't suggest that you come down here ...'

'There's something you think I should see?'

'That I can't say.' Curt cleared his throat. 'But if you happened to be here ... and the place is always very quiet this time of the morning ...'

'I'm on my way.'

The Infirmary to the mortuary: a ten-minute walk. Curt himself was waiting to lead Rebus to the body.

The room was all white tile, bright light and stainless steel. Two of the dissecting-tables lay empty. Matsumoto's naked body lay on the third. Rebus walked around it, stunned by what he saw.

Tattoos.

And not just the kilted piper on a sailor's arm. These

were works of art, and they were massive. A scaly green dragon, breathing pink and red fire, covered one shoulder and crept down the arm towards the wrist. Its back legs reached around the body's neck, while its front ones rested on the chest. There were other smaller dragons, and a landscape – Mount Fuji reflected in water. There were Japanese symbols and the visored face of a kendo champion. Curt put on rubber gloves, and had Rebus do the same. Then the two men rolled the body over, displaying a further gallery across Matsumoto's back. A masked actor, something out of a Noh play, and a warrior in full armour. Some delicate flowers. The effect was mesmerising.

'Stunning, aren't they?' Curt said.

'Phenomenal.'

'I've visited Japan a few times, given papers at conferences.'

'So you recognise some of these?'

'A few of the references, yes. Thing is, tattoos – especially on this scale – usually mean you're a gang member.'

'Like the Triads?'

'The Japanese are called Yakuza. Look here.' Curt held up the left hand. The pinkie had been severed at the first joint, the skin healed in a rough crust.

'That's what happens when they screw up, isn't it?' Rebus said, the word 'Yakuza' bouncing around in his head. 'Someone cuts off a finger every time.'

'I think so, yes,' Curt said. 'Just thought you might like to know.'

Rebus nodded, eyes glued to the corpse. 'Anything else?'

'Well, I haven't started on him yet, really. All looks fairly standard: evidence of impact with a moving vehicle. Crushed ribcage, fractures to the arms and legs.' Rebus noticed that a bone was protruding from one calf, obscenely white against the skin. 'There'll be a lot of internal damage.

Shock probably killed him.' Curt was thoughtful. 'I must let Professor Gates know. Doubt he'll have seen anything like it.'

'Can I use your phone?' Rebus asked.

He knew one person who might know about the Yakuza – she'd seemed knowledgeable about every other country's criminal gangs. So he spoke to Miriam Kenworthy in Newcastle.

'Tattoos and missing fingers?' she said.

'Bingo.'

'That's Yakuza.'

'Actually, it's only the top bit missing from one little finger. That's done to them when they step out of line, isn't it?'

'Not quite. They do it to *themselves* as a way of saying they're sorry. I'm not sure I know much more than that.' There was the sound of papers being shifted. 'I'm just looking for my notes.'

'What notes?'

'When I was connecting all these gangs, different cultures, I did some research. Might be something on the Yakuza … Look, can I call you back?'

'How long?'

'Five minutes.'

Rebus gave her Curt's number, then sat and waited. Curt's room wasn't so much an office as a walk-in cupboard. Files were stacked high on his desk, and a dictaphone lay on top of them, along with a fresh pack of tapes. The room reeked of cigarettes and bad ventilation. On the walls: schedules of meetings, postcards, a couple of framed prints. The place was a bolt-hole, a necessity; Curt spent most of his time elsewhere.

Rebus took out Colquhoun's business card, tried home

and office. As far as his secretary was concerned, Dr Colquhoun was still off sick.

Maybe, but he was well enough to visit a casino. One of Telford's casinos. No coincidence surely ...

Kenworthy was good as gold.

'Yakuza,' she said, sounding like she was lifting from her script. 'Ninety thousand members split into something like two and a half thousand groupings. Utterly ruthless, but also highly intelligent and sophisticated. Very hierarchical structure, almost impenetrable to outsiders. Like a secret society. They even have a sort of middle management level, called the Sokaiya.'

Rebus was writing it all down. 'How do you spell that?'

She told him. 'Back in Japan they run *pachinko* parlours – that's a sort of gaming thing – and have fingers in most other illegal pies.'

'Unless they've lopped them off. What about outside Japan?'

'Only thing I've got down here is that they ship expensive designer stuff back home to sell on the black market, also stolen art, ship it back to wealthy buyers ...'

'Wait a minute, you told me Jake Tarawicz started out smuggling icons out of Russia.'

'You're saying Pink Eyes might connect to the Yakuza?'

'Tommy Telford's been chauffeuring them around. There's a warehouse everyone seems interested in, plus a country club.'

'What's in the warehouse?'

'I don't know yet.'

'Maybe you should find out.'

'It's on my list. Something else, these *pachinko* parlours ... would those be like amusement arcades?'

'Pretty much.'

'Another connection with Telford: he puts gaming machines into half the pubs and clubs on the east coast.'

'You think the Yakuza saw someone they could do a deal with?'

'I don't know.' He tried stifling a yawn.

'Too early in the morning for big questions?'

He smiled. 'Something like that. Thanks for your help, Miriam.'

'No problem. Keep me posted.'

'Sure. Anything new on Tarawicz?'

'Nothing I've heard. No sign of Candice either, sorry.'

'Thanks again.'

''Bye.'

Curt was standing in the doorway. He'd stripped off gown and gloves, and his hands smelled of soap.

'Not much I can do till my assistants get in.' He looked at his watch. 'Fancy a spot of breakfast?'

'You have to appreciate how this looks, John. The media could be all over us. I can think of a few journalists who'd give their drinking-arm to nail you.'

Chief Superintendent Watson was in his element. Seated behind his desk, hands folded, he had the serenity of a large stone Buddha. The occasional crises with which John Rebus presented him had hardened the Farmer to life's lesser knocks and taught him calm acceptance.

'You're going to suspend me,' Rebus stated with conviction – he'd been here before. He finished the coffee his boss had given him, but kept his hands locked around the mug. 'Then you're going to open an investigation.'

'Not straight away,' Watson surprised him by saying. 'What I want first of all is your statement – and I mean a full and frank explanation – of your recent movements, your interest in Mr Matsumoto and Thomas Telford. Bring in anything you want about your daughter's accident, any suspicions you've had, and above all the *validity* of those suspicions. Telford already has a lawyer asking awkward questions about our Japanese friend's untimely end. The lawyer ...' Watson looked to Gill Templer, seated by the door, mouth a thin unimpressed line.

'Charles Groal,' she said flatly.

'Groal, yes. He's been asking at the casino. He got a description of a man who came in just after Matsumoto, and left immediately after him. He seems to think it's you.'

'Are you telling him otherwise?' Rebus asked.

'We're telling him nothing, not until our own inquiries have established ... et cetera. But I can't hold him off forever, John.'

'Have you asked anyone what Matsumoto was doing here?'

'He works for a firm of management consultants. He was here at a client's behest, finalising the takeover of a country club.'

'With Tommy Telford in tow.'

'John, let's not lose sight of ...'

'Matsumoto was a member of the Yakuza, sir. The closest I've come to one of those before has been on a TV screen. Now suddenly they're in Edinburgh.' Rebus paused. 'Don't you find that just a *wee* bit curious? I mean, doesn't it worry you at all? I don't know, maybe I'm getting my priorities all wrong, but it seems to me we're splashing about in puddles while a tidal wave's coming in!'

The pressure of his hands around the mug had been increasing by degrees. Now the thing broke, a piece falling to the floor as Rebus winced. He picked one ceramic shard out of his palm. Drops of blood hit the carpet. Gill Templer had come forward, was reaching for his hand.

'Here, let me.'

He spun away from her. 'No!' Way too loud. Fumbling in his pocket for a handkerchief.

'I've got some paper ones in my bag.'

'It's all right.' Blood dripping on to his shoes. Watson

was saying something about the mug having a crack; Templer was staring at him. He wrapped white cotton around the wound.

'I'll go wash it,' he said. 'With your permission, sir?'

'On you go, John. Sure you're all right?'

'I'll be fine.'

It wasn't a bad cut. Cold water helped. He dried off with paper towels, which he flushed down the toilet, waiting to see they'd gone. A first aid box next: half a dozen plasters, cover the nick good and proper. He bunched his fist, saw no sign of leakage. Had to be content with that.

Back at his desk, he started on his memoirs – as ordered by Watson. Gill Templer came past, decided he needed a few soft words.

'None of us thinks you did it, John. But something like this ... questions being asked by the Japanese consul ... it has to be done by the book.'

'It all comes down to politics in the end, eh?' He was thinking of Joseph Lintz.

At lunchtime he dropped in on Ned Farlowe, asked him if he needed anything. Farlowe wanted sandwiches, books, newspapers, company. He looked drawn, weary of imprisonment. Maybe soon he'd think to ask for a lawyer. A lawyer – any lawyer – would get him out.

Rebus handed his report to Watson's secretary and headed out of the station. He'd gone fifty yards when a car pulled up alongside. Range Rover. Pretty-Boy telling him to get in. Rebus looked into the back of the car.

Telford. Ointment on his blistered face. Looking like a scaled-down Jake Tarawicz ...

Rebus hesitated. The cop shop was a short sprint away.

'Get in,' Pretty-Boy repeated. Sucker for a free offer, Rebus got in.

Pretty-Boy turned the car. The giant yellow teddy had been strapped into the passenger seat.

'I don't suppose,' Rebus said, 'it's worth my while asking you to leave Ned Farlowe be?'

Telford's mind was on other things. 'He wants war, he's going to get war.'

'Who?'

'Your boss.'

'I don't work for Cafferty.'

'Don't give me that.'

'I'm the one who put him inside.'

'And you've been snuggling up ever since.'

'I didn't kill Matsumoto.'

Telford looked at him for the first time, and Rebus could see he was itching for violence.

'You know I didn't,' Rebus went on.

'What do you mean?'

'Because you did it, and you want me to –'

Telford's hands were around Rebus's neck. Rebus shrugged them off, tried pinning Telford down. Impossible with the car in motion, cramped in the back seat. Pretty-Boy stopped the car and got out, opened Rebus's door and dragged him on to the pavement. Telford followed, face beetroot-red, eyes bulging.

'You're not going to pin this on me!' he roared. Drivers slowed to watch. Pedestrians crossed the road to safety.

'Who else?' Rebus's voice was shaky.

'Cafferty!' Telford screeched. 'It's you and Cafferty, trying to shut me down!'

'I'm telling you, I didn't do it.'

'Boss,' Pretty-Boy was saying, 'let's screw the head, eh?' He was looking around, nervous of the attention they were attracting. Telford saw his point, let his shoulders relax a little.

'Get in the car,' he said to Rebus. Rebus just stared at

him. 'It's okay. Just get in. I want to show you a couple of things.'

Rebus, world's craziest cop, got back in.

There was silence for a couple of minutes, Telford rearranging the dressings on his fingers, which had come loose during the fight.

'I don't think Cafferty wants war,' Rebus said.

'What makes you so sure?'

Because I've done a deal with him – it's me who's going to shut you down. They were heading west. Rebus tried not to think about possible destinations.

'You were in the Army, weren't you?' Telford asked.

Rebus nodded.

'Paratroops, then the SAS.'

'I didn't get past training.' Rebus thinking: he's well-informed.

'So you decided to become a cop instead.' Telford was completely calm again. He'd brushed down his suit and checked the knot in his tie. 'Thing is, working for structures like those – Army, cops – you need to obey orders. I hear you're not very good at it. You wouldn't last long with me.' He looked out of the window. 'What's Cafferty planning?'

'No idea.'

'Why were you watching Matsumoto?'

'Because he tied into you.'

'Crime Squad pulled their surveillance.' Rebus said nothing. 'But you kept yours going.' Telford turned towards him. 'Why?'

'Because you tried to kill my daughter.'

Telford stared at him, unblinking. 'Is that what this is about?'

'It's why Ned Farlowe tried to blind you. He's her boyfriend.'

Telford choked out a disbelieving laugh, started to shake

his head. 'I'd nothing to do with your daughter. Where's the reason?'

'To get at me. Because she helped me with Candice.'

Telford was thoughtful. 'Okay,' he said, nodding, 'I can see your thinking, and I don't suppose my word's going to count for much, but for what it's worth, I know absolutely nothing about your daughter.' He paused. Rebus could hear sirens nearby. 'Is that what took you to Cafferty?'

Rebus said nothing, which seemed, to Telford's mind, to confirm his suspicions. He smiled again.

'Pull over,' Telford said. Pretty-Boy stopped the car. The road ahead was blocked anyway, police diverting traffic down side-streets. Rebus realised he'd been smelling smoke for some time. The tenements had hidden it from view, but now he could see the fire. It was in the lot where Cafferty kept his taxis. The shed used as an office had been reduced to ash. The garage behind, where the cabs were worked on and cleaned up, was about to lose its corrugated roof. A row of vehicles was burning nicely.

'We could have sold tickets,' Pretty-Boy said. Telford turned from the spectacle to Rebus.

'Fire Brigade's going to be stretched. Two of Cafferty's offices are spontaneously combusting ...' he checked his watch ... 'right about now, as is that beautiful house of his. Don't worry, we waited till his wife was out shopping. Final ultimatums have been delivered to his men – they can shuffle out of town or off this mortal coil.' He shrugged. 'Makes no odds to me. Go tell Cafferty: he's finished in Edinburgh.'

Rebus licked his lips. 'You've just said I'm wrong about you, that you had nothing to do with my daughter. What if *you're* wrong about Cafferty?'

'Wake up, will you? The stabbing at Megan's, then Danny Simpson ... Cafferty's not exactly subtle.'

'Did Danny say it was Cafferty's men?'

'He knows, same as I do.' Telford tapped Pretty-Boy's shoulder. 'Back to base.' To Rebus: 'Another little message for you to take to Barlinnie. Here's what I told Cafferty's men – any of them left in this city after midnight are fair game … and I don't take prisoners.' He sniffed, seemed pleased with himself, settled back in the seat. 'You won't mind if I drop you at Flint Street? Only I've a business meeting in fifteen minutes.'

'With Matsumoto's bosses?'

'If they want Poyntinghame, they'll keep dealing with me.' He looked at Rebus. 'You should deal with me, too. Think about this: who'd want you pissed off with me? It comes back to Cafferty: hitting your daughter, setting up Matsumoto … It *all* comes back to Cafferty. Think it over, then maybe we should talk again.'

After a couple of minutes, Rebus broke the silence.

'You know a man called Joseph Lintz?'

'Bobby Hogan mentioned him.'

'He phoned your office in Flint Street.'

Telford shrugged. 'I'll tell you what I told Hogan. Maybe it was a wrong number. Whatever it was, *I* didn't speak to any old Nazi.'

'You're not the only one uses that office though.' Rebus saw Pretty-Boy watching him in the rearview mirror. 'What about you?'

'Never heard of the cat.'

A car was parked in Flint Street – a huge white limousine with blackened windows. There was a TV aerial on the boot, and the hubcaps were painted pink.

'Christ,' Telford said in amusement, 'look at his latest toy.' He seemed to have forgotten all about Rebus. He was out of the car and loping towards the man who was emerging from the back of the limo. White suit, panama hat, big cigar, and a bright red paisley shirt. None of which stopped you staring at the scarred face and blue-tinted glasses. Telford was commenting on the attire, the car, the audacity, and Mr Pink Eyes was loving it. He put a hand around Telford's shoulder, steering him towards the amusement arcade. But then he stopped, clicked his fingers, turned back to the limo and reached out a hand.

And now a woman was emerging. Short black dress and black tights, fur jacket keeping out the chills. Tarawicz rubbed a hand over her backside; Telford kissed her on the neck. She smiled, eyes slightly glazed. Then Tarawicz and Telford turned towards the Range Rover. They were both staring at Rebus.

'Trip's over, Inspector,' Pretty-Boy said, telling Rebus it was time to get out. He did so, his eyes on Candice. But she wasn't looking at him. She was snuggling into Mr Pink Eyes, head on his chest. He was still rubbing her backside, the dress rising and falling. He was watching Rebus, eyes alight, face pulled into a latex grin. Rebus walked over to them, and now Candice saw him, and looked frightened.

'Inspector,' Tarawicz said, 'good to see you again. Come to whisk the damsel away to safety?'

Rebus ignored him. 'Come on, Candice.' His hand, not quite steady, held out towards her.

She looked at him and shook her head. 'Why would I want that?' she said, and was rewarded with another kiss from Tarawicz.

'You were abducted. You can press charges.'

Tarawicz was laughing, leading her into the café.

'Candice.' Rebus reached for her arm, but she pulled away and followed her master inside.

Two of Telford's men were blocking the door. Pretty-Boy was behind Rebus.

'No cheap heroics?' he asked, making to pass the policeman.

Back at St Leonard's, Rebus took Farlowe his food and

newspapers, then hitched a lift in a patrol car to Torphichen. The man he wanted was DI 'Shug' Davidson, and Davidson was in the CID office, looking frazzled.

'Somebody torched a taxi rank,' he told Rebus.

'Any idea who?'

Davidson's eyes narrowed. 'The rank was owned by Jock Scallow. Is there something you're trying to tell me?'

'Who really owned the outfit, Shug?'

'You know damned well.'

'And who's muscling in on Cafferty's patch?'

'I've heard rumours.'

Rebus rested against Davidson's desk. 'Tommy Telford's going into combat, unless we can stop him.'

' "We"?'

'I want you to take me somewhere,' Rebus said.

Shug Davidson was happily married to an understanding wife, and had kids who didn't see as much of him as they deserved. A year back, he'd won forty grand on the Lottery. Everyone in his station got a drink. The rest of the money had been salted away.

Rebus had worked with him before. He wasn't a bad cop, maybe lacking a little in imagination. They had to work their way around the scene of the fire. A further mile and a half on, Rebus told him to stop.

'What is it?' Davidson asked.

'That's what I want you to tell me.' Rebus was looking towards the brick building, the same one which so interested Tommy Telford.

'It's Maclean's,' Davidson said.

'And what's Maclean's when it's at home?'

Davidson smiled. 'You really don't know?' He opened his car door. 'Come on, I'll show you.'

They had to have their identities checked at the main entrance. Rebus noticed a lot of security, albeit subtle:

cameras trained down from the corners of the building, catching every angle of approach. A phone call was made, and a man in a white coat came down to sign them in. They pinned visitor's badges to their jackets, and the tour began.

'I've been here before,' Davidson confided. 'If you ask me, it's the best kept secret in the city.'

They climbed steps, walked down passageways. Everywhere there was security: guards checked their badges; doors had to be unlocked; cameras charted their progress. Which puzzled Rebus, for it was such an unassuming building, really. And nothing spectacular was happening.

'What is it, Fort Knox?' he asked. But then their guide handed them white coats to put on, before pushing open the door to a laboratory, and Rebus started to understand.

People were working with chemicals, examining test-tubes, writing notes. There were all sorts of weird and wonderful machines, but in essence it was a school chemistry-lab on a slightly grander scale.

'Welcome,' Davidson said, 'to the world's biggest drugs factory.'

Which wasn't quite correct, for Maclean's was only the world's largest *legal* producer of heroin and cocaine, something the guide explained.

'We're licensed by the government. Back in 1961 there was an international agreement: every country in the world was allowed just one producer, and we're it for Britain.'

'So what do you make?' Rebus was staring at the rows of locked fridges.

'All sorts of things: methadone for heroin addicts, pethedine for women in labour. Diamorphine to ease terminal illnesses and cocaine for use in medical procedures. The company started out supplying laudanum to the Victorians.'

'And these days?'

'We produce about seventy tonnes of opiates a year,' the

guide said. 'And around two million pounds' worth of pure cocaine.'

Rebus rubbed his forehead. 'I begin to see the need for security.'

The guide smiled. 'The MoD has asked us for advice – that's how good our security is.'

'No break-ins?'

'A couple of attempts, nothing we couldn't deal with.'

No, Rebus thought, but then you've never had to deal with Tommy Telford and the Yakuza ... not yet.

Rebus walked around the lab, smiled and nodded at a woman who just seemed to be standing there, not doing anything.

'Who's she?' he asked the guide.

'Our nurse. She's on stand-by.'

'What for?'

The guide nodded towards where a man was operating one of the machines. 'Etorphine,' he said. 'Forty thousand pounds a kilo, and extremely potent. The nurse has the antidote, just in case.'

'So what's it used for, this etorphine?'

'Knocking out rhinos,' the guide said, like the answer should have been obvious.

The cocaine was produced from coca leaves flown in from Peru. The opium came from plantations in Tasmania and Australia. The pure heroin and cocaine were kept in a strongroom. Each lab had its share of locked safes. The storage warehouse boasted infrared detectors and movement sensors. Five minutes in the place told Rebus *exactly* why Tommy Telford was interested in Maclean's. And he'd brought the Yakuza in on the plan either because he needed their help – which was unlikely – or to brag about the exploit.

Back at the car, Davidson asked the obvious question. 'What's this all about, John?'

Rebus pinched the bridge of his nose. 'I think Telford's planning to hit this place.'

Davidson snorted. 'He'd never get in. Like you said yourself, it's Fort bloody Knox.'

'It's a prestige thing, Shug. If he can empty the place, it'll make his name. He'll have beaten Cafferty hands down.' It was the same with the fire-bombings: they weren't just a message to Cafferty, but a sort of 'red carpet' for Mr Pink Eyes – welcome to Edinburgh, and look what I can do.

'I'm telling you,' Davidson said, 'there's no way in. Christ, that's cheap!' Davidson's attention had been diverted by signs on the window of the corner shop. Rebus looked, too. Cut-price cigarettes. Cheap sandwiches and hot rolls. Plus five pence off any morning paper.

'Competition around here must be crippling,' Davidson said. 'Fancy a roll?'

Rebus was watching workers leaving the gates of Maclean's. Afternoon break maybe. Saw them cross the road, dodging traffic. Counting small change from their pockets as they pushed open the door to the shop.

'Yes,' Rebus said quietly, 'why not?'

The small shop was packed out. Davidson got in the queue, while Rebus looked at the rack of papers and magazines. The workers were sharing jokes and gossip. Two staff worked behind the counter – young males, mixing banter with less-than-efficient service.

'What do you fancy, John? Bacon?'

'Fine,' Rebus said. Remembered he hadn't had lunch. 'Make it two.'

Two bacon rolls came in at one pound exactly. They sat in the car to eat.

'You know, Shug, the usual ploy with a shop like that is to take a beating on one or two necessities to get the punters in.' Davidson nodded, attacked his roll. 'But that place looked like Bargain City.' Rebus had stopped eating. 'Do us both a favour: find out the shop's history, who owns it, who those two are behind the counter.'

Davidson's chewing slowed. 'You think ... ?'

'Just check it out, all right?'

22

Back at St Leonard's, his telephone was ringing. He sat down and prised the lid from a beaker of coffee. On the drive back he'd been thinking about Candice. Two swigs of coffee and he lifted the receiver.

'DI Rebus,' he said.

'What the fuck is that little shite up to?' The voice of Big Ger Cafferty.

'Where are you?'

'Where do you think I am?'

'Sounds like a mobile.'

'Amazing the things that find their way into Barlinnie. Now tell me, what is happening over there?'

'You've heard then.'

'He torched my house! My *house*! Am I supposed to let him get away with that?'

'Look, I think I may have found a way to get to him.'

Cafferty calmed a little. 'Tell me?'

'Not yet, I want to —'

'And all my taxis,' Cafferty exploded again. 'The little bastard!'

'Look, the point is: what's he expecting you to do? He's waiting for instant retaliation.'

'And he's going to get it.'

'He'll be ready. Wouldn't it be better to catch him off-guard?'

'That little bastard hasn't been off-guard since he was lifted from the cradle.'

'Shall I tell you why he did it?'

Cafferty's anger ebbed again. 'Why?'

'Because he says you killed Matsumoto.'

'Who?'

'A business acquaintance. Whoever did it made it look like I was behind the wheel.'

'It wasn't me.'

'Try telling Telford that. He thinks you ordered me to do it.'

'We know differently.'

'That's right. *We* know someone was setting me up, trying to get me out of the way.'

'What was his name again, the dead one?'

'Matsumoto.'

'Is that Japanese?'

Rebus wished he could see Cafferty's eyes. Even then, it was hard to tell when the man was playing games.

'He was Japanese,' Rebus stated.

'What the hell did he have to do with Telford?'

'Sounds to me like your intelligence has gone to pot.'

There was silence on the line. 'About your daughter ...'

Rebus froze. 'What about her?'

'A secondhand shop in Porty.' Meaning Portobello. 'The owner bought some stuff from a seller. Including opera tapes and Roy Orbison. Stuck in his mind. They don't naturally go together.'

Rebus's hand tightened on the receiver. 'Which shop? What did the seller look like?'

Cold laughter. 'We're working on it, Strawman, just leave everything to us. Now, about this Japanese fellow ...?'

'I said *I'd* put Telford out of the game. That was the agreement.'

'I've yet to see any action.'

'I'm working on it!'

'I want to hear about him anyway.'

Rebus paused.

'How is Samantha anyway?' Cafferty asked. 'That's her name, isn't it?'

'She's ...'

'Because it looks like I'll be fulfilling *my* side of our bargain any day. While you, on the other hand ...'

'Matsumoto was Yakuza: heard of them?'

A moment's silence. 'I've heard of them.'

'Telford's helping them buy a country club.'

'What in God's name do they want with that?'

'I'm not sure.'

Cafferty was silent again. Rebus almost thought his mobile had died. Then: 'He's got big ideas, hasn't he?' Like there was just a touch of respect there, battling the sense of territorial breach.

'We've both seen people overreach themselves.' An idea formed in Rebus's mind, a sudden notion of where everything was headed.

'Looks like Telford's got plenty of stretch left in him though,' Cafferty was saying. 'And me, I'm not even halfway through *my* stretch.'

'Know something, Cafferty? Every time you start to sound beaten, that's when I know you're just coming to the boil.'

'You know I'm going to have to retaliate, whether I want to or not. A little ritual we have to go through, like shaking hands.'

'How many men have you got?'

'More than enough.'

'Listen, one last thing ...' Rebus couldn't believe he was telling his arch-enemy this. 'Jake Tarawicz arrived here today. I think the fireworks were meant to impress him.'

'Telford torched my house just so he'd have something to show that ugly Russian bastard?'

Like a kid showing off to his elders, Rebus was thinking. Overreaching himself …

'That's it, Strawman!' Cafferty was back to being furious. 'All bets are off. Those two want to get dirty with Morris Gerald Cafferty, I'll give them both anthrax. I'll infect the pair of them. They'll think they've caught full-blown fucking AIDS by the time I'm finished!'

Which was about as much as Rebus could take. He put down the phone, drank his cold coffee, checked his messages. Patience wondered if he could make it to supper. Rhona said they'd carried out another scan. Bobby Hogan wanted a word.

He called the hospital first. Rhona said something about a new scan to assess the amount of damage done to the brain.

'Then why the hell didn't they give her *that* scan straight away?'

'I don't know.'

'Did you ask?'

'Why don't *you* come down here? Why don't *you* ask? Seems like when I'm not here, you're happy enough spending time with Samantha, even sleeping in the chair. What is it – do I scare you off?'

'Look, Rhona, I'm sorry. It's been a rough day.'

'For you and everyone else.'

'I know. I'm a selfish bastard.'

The rest of their conversation was predictable. It was a relief to say goodbye. He tried Patience, got her answering machine, and told it he'd be happy to accept the invitation. Then he called Bobby Hogan.

'Hiya, Bobby, what've you got?'

'Not much. I had a word with Telford.'

'I know, he told me.'

'You've been speaking to him?'

'Says he never knew Lintz. Did you talk to The Family?'

'The ones who frequent the office. Same story.'

'Did you mention the five thou'?'

'Think I'm stupid? Listen, I thought you might be able to help me.'

'Fire away.'

'Lintz's address book, I found a couple of addresses for a Dr Colquhoun. Thought at first it must be his GP.'

'He's a Slavic Studies lecturer.'

'Only Lintz seems to have been keeping track of him. Three changes of address, going back twenty years. First two addresses have phone numbers with them, but not the most recent. I checked, and Colquhoun's only been at this latest address three years.'

'So?'

'So Lintz didn't have his home phone number. So if he wanted to speak to him …'

Rebus twigged. 'He'd phone the university.' The call on Lintz's bill: twenty-odd minutes. Rebus was remembering what Colquhoun had said about Lintz.

I met him at a few social functions … our departments weren't that close … As I say, we weren't close …

'They weren't in the same department,' Rebus said. 'Colquhoun told me they'd barely met …'

'So how come Lintz has been keeping up with Colquhoun's various moves around the city?'

'Beats me, Bobby. Have you asked him?'

'No, but I intend to.'

'He's lying low. I've been trying to talk to him for a week.' Last seen at the Morvena: did Colquhoun link Telford to Lintz?

'Well, he's back now.'

'What?'

'I've an appointment with him at his office.'

'Count me in,' Rebus said, getting to his feet.

260

*

As Rebus parked in Buccleuch Place – he was in an unmarked Astra, courtesy of St Leonard's – he saw the car in the neighbouring bay make to leave. He waved, but Kirstin Mede didn't see him, and by the time he'd found the horn, she'd pulled away. He wondered how well she knew Colquhoun. After all, she'd been the one to suggest him as a translator ...

Hogan, standing by the railings, had seen Rebus's attempts at communication.

'Someone you know?'

'Kirstin Mede.'

Hogan placed the name. 'The one who did those translations?'

Rebus looked up at the Slavic Studies building. 'Have you tracked down David Levy?'

'Daughter still hasn't heard from him.'

'How long has that been?'

'Long enough to seem suspicious in itself, only she doesn't seem too bothered.'

'How do you want to play this?' Rebus asked.

'Depends what he's like.'

'You ask your questions. Me, I just want to be there.'

Hogan looked at him, then shrugged and pushed open the door. They started to climb the worn stone steps. 'Hope they haven't put him in the penthouse.'

Colquhoun's name was on a piece of card stuck to a door on the second floor. They pushed it open, and were confronted with a short hallway and another five or six doors. Colquhoun's office was first on the right, and he was already standing in the doorway.

'Thought I heard you. Sound carries in this place. Come in, come in.' He wasn't expecting Hogan to have company. His words dried up when he saw Rebus. He walked back into his office, motioned for both officers to sit, then fussed about moving their chairs around so they'd be facing his desk.

'Terrible muddle,' he said, kicking over a pile of books.

'Know the feeling, sir,' Hogan said.

Colquhoun peered in Rebus's direction. 'My secretary says you used the library.'

'Filling in some of the gaps, sir.' Rebus kept his voice level.

'Yes, Candice ...' Colquhoun was thoughtful. 'Is she ... ? I mean, did she ... ?'

'But today, sir,' Hogan interrupted, 'we want to talk to you about Joseph Lintz.'

Colquhoun sat down heavily in his wooden chair, which creaked under the weight. Then he sprang to his feet again. 'Tea, coffee? You must excuse the mess. Not normally this disorganised ...'

'Not for us, sir,' Hogan said. 'If you'd just take a seat?'

'Of course, of course.' Again, Colquhoun collapsed on to his chair.

'Joseph Lintz, sir,' Hogan prompted.

'Terrible tragedy ... terrible. They think it's murder, you know.'

'Yes, sir, we do know.'

'Of course you do. Apologies.'

The desk in front of Colquhoun was venerable and spotted with woodworm. The shelves were bowed under the weight of textbooks. There were old framed prints on the walls, and a blackboard with the single word CHARACTER on it. University paperwork was piled on the window ledge, all but blacking out the bottom two panes. The smell in the room was that of intellect gone awry.

'It's just that Mr Lintz had your name in his address book, sir,' Hogan continued. 'And we're talking to all his friends.'

'Friends?' Colquhoun looked up. 'I wouldn't call us

"friends" exactly. We were colleagues, but I don't think I met him socially more than three or four times in twenty-odd years.'

'Funny, he seems to have taken an interest in you, sir.' Hogan flipped open his notebook. 'Starting with your address in Warrender Park Terrace.'

'I haven't lived there since the seventies.'

'He also has your telephone number there. After that, it's Currie.'

'I thought I was ready for the rural life …'

'In Currie?' Hogan sounded sceptical.

Colquhoun tipped his head. 'I eventually realised my mistake.'

'And moved to Duddingston.'

'Not at first. I rented a few properties while I was looking for a place to buy.'

'Mr Lintz has your telephone number in Currie, but not for the Duddingston address.'

'Interesting. I went ex-directory when I moved.'

'Any reason for that, sir?'

Colquhoun swayed in his chair. 'Well, I'm sure it sounds awful …'

'Try us.'

'I didn't want students bothering me.'

'Did they do that?'

'Oh, yes, phoning to ask questions, advice. Worried about exams or wanting deadlines extended.'

'Do you remember giving Mr Lintz your address, sir?'

'No, I don't.'

'You're sure of that?'

'Yes, but it wouldn't have been hard for him to find out. I mean, he could just have asked one of the secretaries.'

Colquhoun was beginning to look more agitated than ever. The little chair could barely contain him.

'Sir,' Hogan said, 'is there anything you want to tell us about Mr Lintz, anything at all?'

Colquhoun just shook his head, staring at the surface of his desk.

Rebus decided to use their joker. 'Mr Lintz made a phone call to this office. He was talking for over twenty minutes.'

'That's ... simply not true.' Colquhoun mopped his face with a handkerchief. 'Look, gentlemen, I'd like to help, but the fact is, I barely knew Joseph Lintz.'

'And he didn't phone you?'

'No.'

'And you've no idea why he'd keep note of your Edinburgh addresses for the past three decades?'

'No.'

Hogan sighed theatrically. 'Then we're wasting your time and ours.' He got to his feet. 'Thank you, Dr Colquhoun.'

The look of relief on the old academic's face told both detectives all they needed to know.

They said nothing as they walked back downstairs – like Colquhoun had said, sound could travel. Hogan's car was nearest. They rested against it as they talked.

'He was worried,' Rebus said.

'Hiding something. Think we should go back up?'

Rebus shook his head. 'Let him sweat for a day or so, then hit him.'

'He didn't like the fact you were there.'

'I noticed.'

'That restaurant ... Lintz dining with an elderly gent.'

'We could tell him we've got a description from the restaurant staff.'

'Without going into specifics?'

Rebus nodded. 'See if it flushes him out.'

'What about the other person Lintz took to lunch, the young woman?'

'No idea.'

'Posh restaurant, old man, young woman ...'

'A call girl?'

Hogan smiled. 'Do they still call them that?'

Rebus was thoughtful. 'It might explain the phone call to Telford. Only I doubt Telford's daft enough to discuss business like that from his office. Besides, his escort agency runs from another address.'

'Fact is, he called Telford's office.'

'And nobody's owned up to talking to him.'

'Escort agency stuff, could be very innocent. He doesn't want to eat alone, hires some company. Afterwards, a peck on the cheek and separate taxis.' Hogan exhaled. 'This one's running in circles.'

'I know the feeling, Bobby.'

They looked up at the second-floor windows. Saw Colquhoun staring down, handkerchief to his face.

'Let's leave him to it,' Hogan said, unlocking his car.

'I've been meaning to ask: how did you get on with Abernethy?'

'He didn't give me too much trouble.' Hogan avoided Rebus's eyes.

'So he's gone?'

Hogan had disappeared into the driver's seat. 'He's gone. See you, John.'

Leaving Rebus on the pavement, a frown on his face. He waited till Hogan's car had turned the corner, then went back into the stairwell and climbed the steps again.

Colquhoun's office door was open, the old man fidgeting behind his desk. Rebus sat down opposite him, said nothing.

'I've been ill,' Colquhoun said.

'You've been hiding.' Colquhoun started shaking his

head. 'You told them where to find Candice.' Head still shaking. 'Then you got worried, so they hid you away, maybe in a room at the casino.' Rebus paused. 'How am I doing?'

'I've no comment to make,' Colquhoun snapped.

'What if I just keep talking then?'

'I want you to leave now. If you don't go, I'll have to call my lawyer.'

'Name of Charles Groal?' Rebus smiled. 'They might have spent the last few days tutoring you, but they can't change what you've done.' Rebus stood up. '*You* sent Candice back to them. *You* did that.' He leaned down over the desk. 'You knew all along who she was, didn't you? That's why you were so nervous. How come you knew who she was, Dr Colquhoun? How come you're so chummy with a turd like Tommy Telford?'

Colquhoun picked up the receiver, his hands shaking so badly he kept missing the digits.

'Don't bother,' Rebus said. 'I'm going. But we'll talk again. And you *will* talk. You'll talk because you're a coward, Dr Colquhoun. And cowards always talk eventually ...'

23

The Crime Squad office at Fettes: home of country and western; Claverhouse terminating a phone call. No sign of Ormiston and Clarke.

'They're out on a call,' Claverhouse said.

'Any progress on that stabbing?'

'What do you think?'

'I think there's something you should know.' Rebus seated himself behind Siobhan Clarke's desk, admiring its tidy surface. He opened a drawer: it was tidy, too. Compartments, he thought to himself. Clarke was very good at dividing her life into separate compartments. 'Jake Tarawicz is in town. He's got this outrageous white limo, hard to miss.' Rebus paused. 'And he's brought Candice with him.'

'What's he doing here?'

'I think he's here for the show.'

'What show?'

'Cafferty and Telford, fifteen rounds of bare-knuckle and no referee.' Rebus leaned forward, arms on the desk. 'And I've got an idea where it's headed.'

Rebus went home, called Patience and told her he might be late.

'How late?' she asked.

'How late can I be without us falling out?'

She thought about it. 'Half-nine.'

'I'll be there.'

He checked his answering machine: David Levy, saying he could be reached at home.

'Where the hell have you been?' Rebus asked, when Levy's daughter had put her father on.

'I had business elsewhere.'

'You know your daughter's been worried. You might have phoned her.'

'Does this counselling service come free?'

'My fee cancels out when you answer a few questions. You know Lintz is dead?'

'I've heard.'

'Where were you when you *heard*?'

'I've told you, I had business ... Inspector, am I a suspect?'

'Practically the only one we've got.'

Levy gave a harsh laugh. 'This is preposterous. I'm not a ...' He couldn't say the word. Rebus guessed his daughter was within hearing distance. 'Hold on a moment, please.' The receiver was muffled: Levy ordering his daughter out of the room. He came back on, voice lower than before.

'Inspector, for the record, I feel I must let you know how *angry* I felt when I heard the news. Justice may have been done or not done – I can't argue those points just now – but what is absolutely certain is that history has been cheated here!'

'Of the trial?'

'Of course! And the Rat Line, too. With each suspect who dies, we're that much less likely to prove its existence. Lintz isn't the first, you know. One man, the brakes failed on his car. Another fell from an upstairs window. There've been two apparent suicides, six more cases of what look like natural causes.'

'Am I going to get the full conspiracy theory?'

'This isn't a joke, Inspector.'

'Did you hear me laughing? What about you, Mr Levy? When did you leave Edinburgh?'

'Before Lintz died.'

'Did you see him?' Rebus knowing he had, but seeking a lie.

Levy paused. '*Confronted* would be a more apposite term.'

'Just the once?'

'Three times. He wasn't keen to talk about himself, but I stated my case nonetheless.'

'And the phone call?'

Levy paused. 'What phone call?'

'When he called you at the Roxburghe.'

'I wish I'd recorded it for posterity. Rage, Inspector. Foul-mouthed rage. I'm positive he was mad.'

'Mad?'

'You didn't hear him. He's very good at seeming perfectly normal – he must be, or he wouldn't have gone undetected for so long. But the man is ... was ... mad. Truly mad.'

Rebus was remembering the crooked little man in the cemetery, and how he'd suddenly let fly at a passing dog. Poise, to rage, to poise again.

'The story he told ...' Levy sighed.

'Was this in the restaurant?'

'What restaurant?'

'Sorry, I thought the two of you went out to lunch.'

'I can assure you we didn't.'

'So what story is this then?'

'These men, Inspector, they come to justify their actions by blanking them out, or by transference. Transference is the more common.'

'They tell themselves someone else did it?'

'Yes.'

'And that was Lintz's story?'

'Less believable than most. He said it was all a case of mistaken identity.'

'And who did he think you were mistaking him for?'

'A colleague at the university ... a Dr Colquhoun.'

Rebus called Hogan, gave him the story.

'I told Levy you'd want to speak to him.'

'I'll phone him right now.'

'What do you think?'

'Colquhoun a war criminal?' Hogan snorted.

'Me, too,' Rebus said. 'I asked Levy why he didn't think any of this worth telling us.'

'And?'

'He said as he gave it no credence, it was worthless.'

'All the same, we'd better talk to Colquhoun again. Tonight.'

'I've other plans for tonight, Bobby.'

'Fair enough, John. Look, I really appreciate all your help.'

'You're going to talk to him alone?'

'I'll have someone with me.'

Rebus hated being left out. If he cancelled that late supper ...

'Let me know how you get on.' Rebus put the telephone down. On the hi-fi: Eddie Harris, upbeat and melodic. He went and soaked in a bath, facecloth across his eyes. Everyone, it seemed to him, lived their lives out of little boxes, opening different ones for different occasions. Nobody ever gave their whole self away. Cops were like that, each box a safety mechanism. Most people you met in the course of your life, you never even learned their names. Everybody was boxed off from everybody else. It was called society.

He was wondering about Joseph Lintz, always questioning, turning every conversation into a philosophy lesson. Stuck in his own little box, identity blocked off elsewhere, his past a necessary mystery ... Joseph Lintz, furious when cornered, possibly clinically mad, driven there by … what? Memories? Or the lack of them? Driven there by other people?

The Eddie Harris CD was on its last track by the time he emerged from the bathroom. He put on the clothes he'd be wearing to Patience's. Only he had a couple of stops to make first: check on Sammy at the hospital, and then a meeting at Torphichen.

'The gang's all here,' he said, walking into the CID room.

Shug Davidson, Claverhouse, Ormiston, and Siobhan Clarke, all seated around the one big desk, drinking coffee from identical Rangers mugs. Rebus pulled a chair over.

'Have you filled them in, Shug?'

Davidson nodded.

'What about the shop?'

'I was just getting to that.' Davidson picked up a pen, played with it. 'The last owner went out of business, not enough passing trade. The shop was shut the best part of a year, then suddenly reopened – under new management and with prices that stopped the locals looking elsewhere.'

'And got the workers at Maclean's interested, too,' Rebus added. 'So how long's it been going?'

'Five weeks, selling cut-price everything.'

'No profit motive, you see.' Rebus looked around the table. This was mostly for the benefit of Ormiston and Clarke; he'd given Claverhouse the story already.

'And the owners?' Clarke asked.

'Well, the shop's *run* by a couple of lads called Declan Delaney and Ken Wilkinson. Guess where they come from?'

'Paisley,' Claverhouse said, keen to hurry things on.

'So they're part of Telford's gang?' Ormiston asked.

'Not in so many words, but they're connected to him, no doubt about that.' Davidson blew his nose loudly. 'Of course, Dec and Ken are running the shop, but they don't own it.'

'Telford does,' Rebus stated.

'Okay,' Claverhouse said. 'So we've got Telford owning a loss-making business, in the hope of gathering intelligence.'

'I think it goes further than that,' Rebus said. 'I mean, listening in on gossip is one thing, but I don't suppose any of the workers are standing around talking about the various security systems and how to beat them. Dec and Ken are garrulous, perfect for the job Telford's given them. But it's going to look suspicious if they start asking too many questions.'

'So what's Telford looking for?' Ormiston asked. Siobhan Clarke turned to him.

'A mole,' she said.

'Makes sense,' Davidson went on. 'That place *is* well-protected, but not impregnable. We all know any break-in's going to be a lot easier with someone on the inside.'

'So what do we do?' Clarke asked.

'We fight Telford's sting with our own,' Rebus explained. 'He wants a man on the inside, *we* give him one.'

'I'm seeing the head of Maclean's later on tonight,' Davidson said.

'I'll come with you,' Claverhouse said, keen not to be left out.

'So we put someone of our own inside the factory.' Clarke was working it out for herself. 'And they shoot their mouth off in the shop, making them an attractive proposition. And we sit and pray that Telford approaches *them* rather than anyone else?'

'The less luck we have to rely on the better,' Claverhouse said. 'Got to do this right.'

'Which is why we work it like this.' Rebus said. 'There's a bookie called Marty Jones. He owes me one big favour.

Say our man's just been into Telford's shop. As he's coming out, a car pulls up. Marty and a couple of his men. Marty wants some bets paid off. Big argy-bargy, and a punch in the guts as warning.'

Clarke could see it. 'He stumbles back into the shop, sits down to catch his breath. Dec and Ken ask him what's going on.'

'And he gives them the whole sorry story: gambling debts, broken marriage, whatever.'

'To make him more attractive still,' Davidson said, 'we make him a security guard.'

Ormiston looked at him. 'You think Maclean's will go for it?'

'We'll persuade them,' Claverhouse said quietly.

'More importantly,' Clarke asked, 'will *Telford* go for it?'

'Depends how desperate he is,' Rebus answered.

'A man on the inside …' Ormiston's eyes were alight. 'Working for Telford – it's what we've always wanted.'

Claverhouse nodded. 'Just one thing.' He looked at Rebus and Davidson. 'Who's it going to be? Telford knows us.'

'We get someone from outside,' Rebus said. 'Someone I've worked with before. Telford won't have heard of him. He's a good man.'

'Is he willing?'

There was silence around the table.

'Depends who's asking,' a voice called from the doorway. A stocky man with thick, well-groomed hair and narrow eyes. Rebus got up, shook Jack Morton's hand, made the introductions.

'I'll need a history,' Morton said, all business. 'John's explained the deal, and I like it. But I'll need a flat, something scruffy and local.'

'First thing tomorrow,' Claverhouse said. 'Look, we need to talk to our bosses about this, make sure it's cleared.'

He looked at Morton. 'What did you tell your own boss, Jack?'

'I've got a few days off, didn't think it was worth mentioning.'

Claverhouse nodded. 'I'll talk to him as soon as we get the go-ahead.'

'We need that go-ahead *tonight*,' Rebus said. 'Telford's men may already have lined someone up. If we hang around, we might lose it.'

'Agreed,' Claverhouse said, checking his watch. 'I'll make a few phone calls, interrupt a few post-prandial whiskies.'

'I'll back you up if need be,' Davidson said.

Rebus looked at Jack Morton – his friend – and mouthed the word 'thanks'. Morton shrugged it off. Then Rebus got to his feet.

'I'm going to have to leave you to it,' he told the assembly. 'You've got my pager number and mobile if you need me.'

He was halfway down the hall when Siobhan Clarke caught him.

'I just wanted to say thanks.'

Rebus blinked. 'What for?'

'Ever since you got Claverhouse excited, the tape machine's stayed off.'

24

Supper was fine. He talked to Patience about Sammy, Rhona, his obsession with sixties music, his ignorance of fashion. She talked about work, an experimental cookery class she'd been taking, a trip to Orkney she was thinking of. They ate fresh pasta with a homemade mussel and prawn sauce, and shared a bottle of Highland Spring. Rebus tried his damnedest to forget about the sting operation, Tarawicz, Candice, Lintz ... She could see at least half his mind was elsewhere; tried not to feel betrayed. She asked him if he was going home.

'Is that an invitation?'

'I'm not sure ... I suppose so.'

'Let's pretend it wasn't, then I won't feel like complete scum when I turn it down.'

'That sounds reasonable. Things on your mind?'

'I'm surprised you can't see them leaking out of my ears.'

'Do you want to talk about any of it? I mean, you may not have noticed, but we've talked about practically everything tonight except *us*.'

'I don't think talking would help.'

'But bottling it up does?' She threw out an arm. 'Behold the Scottish male, at his happiest when in denial.'

'What am I denying?'

'For a start, you're denying *me* access to your life.'

'Sorry.'

'Christ, John, get the word put on a t-shirt.'

'Thanks, maybe I will.' He got up from the sofa.

'Oh, hell, I'm sorry.' She smiled. 'Look, you've got me at it now.'

'Yes, it's catching, all right.'

She stood up, touched his arm. 'You're worried about taking the test?'

'Right now, believe it or not, that's the least of my worries.'

'It should be. Everything's going to be fine.'

'Hunky dory.'

'Hunky dory,' she repeated, smiling again. She pecked him on the cheek. 'You know, I've never quite understood what that meant.'

'*Hunky Dory*?'

She nodded.

'It's a David Bowie album.' He kissed her brow.

He would never know what instinct made him decide on the detour, but he was glad he'd made it. For there, parked outside the Morvena casino, stood the white stretch limo. The driver leaned against it, smoking a cigarette, looking bored. From time to time he took out a mobile phone and had a short conversation. Rebus stared at the Morvena, thinking: Tommy Telford has a slice of the place; the hostesses come from Eastern Europe, provided by Mr Pink Eyes. Rebus wondered how closely entwined the two empires – Telford's and Tarawicz's – really were. And add a third strand: the Yakuza. Something refused to add up.

What was Tarawicz getting out of it?

Miriam Kenworthy had suggested muscle: Scottish hardmen trained in Telford's organisation then shipped south. But it wasn't *enough* of a trade. There had to be more. Was Mr Pink Eyes due a share of the Maclean's payout? Was Telford tempting him with some Yakuza action? What about the theory that Telford was Tarawicz's supplier?

At quarter to midnight, another phone call had the driver springing into action. He flicked his cigarette on to the road, started opening doors. Tarawicz and his entourage breezed out of the casino looking like they owned the world. Candice was wearing a black full-length coat over a shimmering pink dress which didn't quite reach her knees. She was carrying a bottle of champagne. Rebus counted three of Tarawicz's men, remembering them from the scrapyard. Two no-shows: the lawyer, and the Crab. Telford was there, too, with a couple of minders, one of them Pretty-Boy. Pretty-Boy was making sure his jacket hung right, trying to decide whether it would look better buttoned. But his eyes raked the darkened street. Rebus had parked away from the street-lights, confident he was invisible. They were piling into the limo. Rebus watched it move off, waited until it had signalled and turned a corner before switching on his own headlamps and starting the engine.

They drove to the same hotel Matsumoto had stayed at. Telford's Range Rover was parked outside. Pedestrians – late-night couples hurrying home from the pub – turned to stare at the limo. Saw the entourage spill out, probably mistook them for pop stars or film people. Rebus as casting director: Candice's starlet being mauled by sleazy producer Tarawicz. Telford a sleek young operator on his way up, looking to learn from the producer before toppling him. The others were bit players, except maybe Pretty-Boy, who was hanging on to his boss's coattails, maybe readying himself for his own big break ...

If Tarawicz had a suite, there might be room for them all. If not, they'd be in the bar. Rebus parked, followed them inside.

The lights hurt his eyes. The reception area was all mirrors and pine, brass and pot-plants. He tried to look like he'd been left behind by the party. They were settling down in the bar, through a double set of swing-doors with glass panels. Rebus hung back. Sitting target in the empty reception; bigger target in the bar. Retreat to the car? Someone was standing up, shrugging off a long black coat. Candice. Smiling now, saying something to Tarawicz, who was nodding. Took her hand and planted a kiss in the palm. Went further: a slow lick across the palm and up her wrist. Everyone laughing, whistling. Candice looking numb. Tarawicz got to the inside of her elbow and took a bite. She squealed, pulled back, rubbed her arm. Tarawicz had his tongue out, playing to the gallery. Give Tommy Telford credit: he wasn't grinning along with everyone else.

Candice stood there, a stooge to her owner's little act. Then he waved her off with a flick of his hand. Permission granted, she started for the doors. Rebus moved back into a recess where the public telephones sat. She turned right out of the doors, disappeared into the ladies'. At the table, they were busy ordering more champagne – and an orange juice for Pretty-Boy.

Rebus looked around, took a deep breath. Walked into the ladies' toilets like it was the most natural thing in the world.

She was splashing her face with water. A little brown bottle sat next to the sink. Three yellow tablets lying ready. Rebus swept them on to the floor.

'Hey!' She turned, saw him, put a hand to her mouth. She tried backing away, but there was nowhere to go.

'Is this what you want, Karina?' Using her real name as a weapon: friendly fire.

She frowned, shook her head: incomprehension on her face. He grabbed her shoulders, squeezed.

'Sammy,' he hissed. 'Sammy's in hospital. Very ill.' He pointed towards the hotel bar. '*They* tried to kill her.'

The gist got through. Candice shook her head. Tears were smudging her mascara.

'Did you tell Sammy anything?'

She frowned again.

'Anything about Telford or Tarawicz? Did you talk to Sammy about them?'

A slow, determined shake of the head. 'Sammy ... hospital?'

He nodded. Turned his hands into a steering-wheel, made engine noises, then slammed a fist into his open palm. Candice turned away, grabbed the sink. She was crying, shoulders jerking. She scrabbled for more tablets. Rebus tore them from her hand.

'You want to blank it all out? Forget it.' He threw them on to the floor, crushed them under his heel. She crouched down, licked a finger and dabbed at the powder. Rebus hauled her to her feet. Her knees wouldn't lock; he had to keep holding her upright. She wouldn't look him in the eyes.

'It's funny, we first met in a toilet, remember? You were scared. You hated your life so much you'd slashed your arms.' He touched her scarred wrists. 'That's how much you hated your life. And now you're straight back in it.'

Her face was against his jacket, tears dropping on to his shirt.

'Remember the Japanese?' he cooed. 'Remember Juniper Green, the golf club?'

She drew back, wiped her nose on her bare wrist. 'Juniper Green,' she said.

'That's right. And a big factory ... the car stopped, and everyone looked at the factory.'

She was nodding.

'Did anyone talk about it? Did they say *anything*?'

She was shaking her head. 'John ...' Her hands on his lapels. She sniffed, swiped at her nose again. She slid down his jacket, his shirt. She was on her knees, looking up at him, blinking tears, while her damp fingers scored white powder from the tiles. Rebus crouched down in front of her.

'Come with me,' he said. 'I'll help you.' He pointed towards the door, towards the world outside, but she was busy in her own world now, fingers going to her mouth. Someone pushed open the door. Rebus looked up.

A woman: young, drunk, hair falling into her eyes. She stopped and studied the two people on the floor, then smiled and headed for a cubicle.

'Save some for me,' she said, sliding the lock.

'Go, John.' There was powder at the corners of Candice's mouth. A tiny piece of tablet had lodged between her front two teeth. 'Please, go now.'

'I don't want you getting hurt.' He sought her hands, squeezed them.

'I do not hurt any more.'

She got to her feet and turned from him. Checked her face in the mirror, wiped away the powder and dabbed at her mascara. Blew her nose and took a deep breath.

Walked out of the toilets.

Rebus waited a moment, time enough for her to reach the table. Then he opened the door and made his exit. Walked back to his car on legs that seemed to belong to someone else.

Drove home, not quite crying.

But not quite not.

25

Four in the morning, the blessed telephone pulled him out of a nightmare.

Prison-camp prostitutes with teeth filed to points were kneeling in front of him. Jake Tarawicz, in full SS regalia, held him from behind, telling him resistance was useless. Through the barred window, Rebus could see black berets – the *maquis*, busy freeing the camp but leaving his billet till last. Alarm bells ringing, everything telling him that salvation was at hand ...

... alarm becoming his telephone ... he staggered from his chair, picked it up.

'Yes.'

'John?' The Chief Super's voice: Aberdonian, instantly recognisable.

'Yes, sir?'

'We've got a spot of bother. Get down here.'

'What kind of bother?'

'I'll tell you when you get here. Now *shift*.'

Night shift, to be precise. The city asleep. St Leonard's was lit up, the tenements around it dark. No sign of the Farmer's 'spot of bother'. The Chief Super's office: the Farmer in conference with Gill Templer.

'Sit down, John. Coffee?'

'No, thanks, sir.'

While Templer and the Chief Super were deciding who should speak, Rebus helped them out.

'Tommy Telford's businesses have been hit.'

Templer blinked. 'Telepathy?'

'Cafferty's offices and taxis got firebombed. So did his house.' Rebus shrugged. 'We knew there'd be payback.'

'Did we?'

What could he say? *I did, because Cafferty told me.* He didn't think they'd like that. 'I just put two and two together.'

The Farmer poured himself a mug of coffee. 'So now we've got open war.'

'What got hit?'

'The arcade on Flint Street,' Templer said. 'Not too much damage: the place has a sprinkler system.' She smiled: an amusement arcade with a sprinkler system ... not that Telford was careful or anything.

'Plus a couple of nightclubs,' the Farmer added. 'And a casino.'

'Which one?'

The Chief Super looked to Templer, who answered: 'The Morvena.'

'Any injuries?'

'The manager and a couple of friends: concussion and bruising.'

'Which they got ...?'

'Falling over each other as they ran down the stairs.'

Rebus nodded. 'Funny how some people have trouble with stairs.' He sat back. 'So what does all this have to do with me? Don't tell me: having disposed of Telford's Japanese partner, I decided to take up fire-raising?'

'John ...' The Farmer got up, rested his backside against the desk. 'The three of us, we know you had nothing to do with that. Tell me, we found an untouched half-bottle of malt under your driver's seat ...'

Rebus nodded. 'It's mine.' Another of his little suicide bombs.

'So why would you be drinking a supermarket blend?'

'Is that what the screw-top was? The cheap bastards.'

'No alcohol in your blood either. Meantime, as you say, Cafferty's in the frame for this. And Cafferty and you ...'

'You want me to talk to him?'

Gill Templer leaned forward in her chair. 'We don't want war.'

'Takes two to make a ceasefire.'

'I'll talk to Telford,' she said.

'He's a sharp little bugger, watch out for him.'

She nodded. 'Will you talk to Cafferty?'

Rebus didn't want a war. It would take Telford's mind off the Maclean's heist. He'd need all the troops he could get; the shop might even have to close. No, Rebus didn't want a war.

'I'll talk to him,' he said.

Breakfast-time at Barlinnie.

Rebus jangling after the drive, knowing a whisky would smooth out his nerve-endings. Cafferty waiting for him, same room as before.

'Top of the morning, Strawman.' Arms folded, looking pleased with himself.

'You've had a busy night.'

'On the contrary, I slept as well as I ever have done in this place. What about you?'

'I was up at four o'clock, checking damage reports. I could have done without driving all the way here. Maybe if you gave me the number of your mobile ...?'

Cafferty grinned. 'I hear the nightclubs were gutted.'

'I think your boys are making themselves look good.' Cafferty's grin tightened. 'Telford's premises seem to have state of the art fire prevention. Smoke sensors, sprinklers, fire-doors. The damage was minimal.'

'This is just the start,' Cafferty said. 'I'll have that little arse-wipe.'

'I thought that was supposed to be *my* job?'

'I've seen precious little from you, Strawman.'

'I've got something in the pipeline. If it comes off, you'll like it.'

Cafferty's eyes narrowed. 'Give me details. Make me believe you.'

But Rebus was shaking his head. 'Sometimes, you just have to have faith.' He paused. 'Deal?'

'I must have missed something.'

Rebus spelled it out. 'Back off. Leave Telford to me.'

'We've been through this. He hits me and I do nothing, I look like something you'd step around on the pavement.'

'We're talking to him, warning him off.'

'And meantime I'm supposed to trust you to get the job done?'

'We shook hands on it.'

Cafferty snorted. 'I've shaken hands with a lot of bastards.'

'And now you've met an exception to the rule.'

'You're an exception to a lot of rules, Strawman.' Cafferty looked thoughtful. 'The casino, the clubs, the arcade ... they weren't badly hit?'

'My guess is the sprinklers will have done as much damage as anything.'

Cafferty's jaw hardened. 'Makes me look even more of a mug.'

Rebus sat in silence, waiting for him to finish whatever chess-game was being played inside his head.

'Okay,' the gangster said at last, 'I'll call off the troops. Maybe it's time to do some recruiting anyway.' He looked up at Rebus. 'Time for some fresh blood.'

Which reminded Rebus of another job he'd been putting off.

*

Danny Simpson lived at home with his mother in a terraced house in Wester Hailes.

This bleak housing-scheme, designed by sadists who'd never had to live anywhere near it, had a heart which had shrivelled but refused to stop pumping. Rebus had a lot of respect for the place. Tommy Smith had grown up here, practising with socks stuffed into the mouth of his sax, so as not to disturb the neighbours through the thin walls of the high-rise. Tommy Smith was one of the best sax players Rebus had ever heard.

In a sense, Wester Hailes existed outside the real world: it wasn't on a route from anywhere to anywhere. Rebus had never had cause to drive *through* it – he only went there if he had business there. The city bypass flew past it, offering many drivers their only encounter with Wester Hailes. They saw: high-rise blocks, terraces, tracts of unused playing field. They didn't see: people. Not so much concrete jungle as concrete vacuum.

Rebus knocked on Danny Simpson's door. He didn't know what he was going to say to the young man. He just wanted to see him again. He wanted to see him without the blood and the pain. Wanted to see him whole and of a piece.

Wanted to see him.

But Danny Simpson wasn't in, and neither was his mother. A neighbour, lacking her top set of dentures, came out and explained the situation.

The situation took Rebus to the Infirmary, where, in a small, gloomy ward not easily found, Danny Simpson lay in bed, head bandaged, sweating like he'd just played a full ninety minutes. He wasn't conscious. His mother sat beside him, stroking his wrist. A nurse explained to Rebus that a hospice would be the best place for Danny, supposing they could find him a bed.

'What happened?'

'We think infection must have set in. When you lose your resistance ... the world's a lethal place.' She shrugged, looked like she'd been through it all once too often. Danny's mother had seen them talking. Maybe she thought Rebus was a doctor. She got up and came towards him, then just stood there, waiting for him to speak.

'I came to see Danny,' he said.

'Yes?'

'The night he ... the night of his accident, I was the one who brought him here. I just wondered how he was doing.'

'See for yourself.' Her voice was breaking.

Rebus thought: a five-minute walk from here, he'd be in Sammy's room. He'd thought her situation unique, because it was unique to *him*. Now he saw that within a short radius of Sammy's bed, other parents were crying, and squeezing their children's hands, and asking why.

'I'm really sorry,' he said. 'I wish ...'

'Me, too,' the woman said. 'You know, he's never been a bad laddie. Cheeky, but never bad. His problem was, he was always itching for something new, something to stop him getting bored. We all know where that can lead.'

Rebus nodded, suddenly not wanting to be here, not wanting to hear Danny Simpson's life story. He had enough ghosts to contend with as it was. He squeezed the woman's arm.

'Look,' he said, 'I'm sorry, but I have to go.'

She nodded distractedly, wandered off in the direction of her son's bed. Rebus wanted to curse Danny Simpson for the mere *possibility* that he'd passed on the virus. He realised now that if they'd met on the doorstep, that's the way their conversation would have gone, and maybe Rebus would have gone further.

He wanted to curse him ... but he couldn't. It would be every bit as efficacious as cursing the Big Man. A waste of time and breath. So instead he went to Sammy's room, to find that she was back on her own. No other patients, no nursing staff, no Rhona. He kissed her forehead. It tasted salty. Sweat: she needed wiping down. There was a smell he hadn't noticed before. Talcum powder. He sat down, took her warm hands in his.

'How are you doing, Sammy? I keep meaning to bring in some Oasis, see if that would bring you round. Your mum sits here listening to classical. I wonder if you can hear it. I don't even know if you like that sort of stuff. Lots of things we've never got round to talking about.'

He saw something. Stood up to be sure. Movement behind her eyelids.

'Sammy? Sammy?'

He hadn't seen her do that before. Pushed the button beside her bed. Waited for a nurse to come. Pushed it again.

'Come on, come on.'

Eyelids fluttering ... then stopping.

'Sammy!'

Door opening, nurse coming in.

'What is it?'

Rebus: 'I thought I saw ... she was moving.'

'Moving?'

'Just her eyes, like she was trying to open them.'

'I'll fetch a doctor.'

'Come on, Sammy, try again. Wakey-wakey, sweetheart.' Patting her wrists, then her cheeks.

The doctor arrived. He was the same one Rebus had shouted at that first day. Lifted her eyelids, shone a thin torch into them, pulling it away, checking her pupils.

'If you saw it, I'm sure it was there.'

'Yes, but does it mean anything?'

'Hard to say.'

'Try anyway.' Eyes boring into the doctor's.

'She's asleep. She has dreams. Sometimes when you dream you experience REM: Rapid Eye Movement.'

'So it could be ...' Rebus sought the word '... involuntary?'

'As I say, it's hard to tell. Latest scans show definite improvement.' He paused. '*Minor* improvement, but certainly there.'

Rebus nodding, trembling. The doctor saw it, asked if he needed anything. Rebus shaking his head. The doctor checking his watch, other places to be. The nurse shuffling her feet. Rebus thanked them both and headed out.

HOGAN: You agree to this interview being taped, Dr Colquhoun?

COLQUHOUN: I've no objections.

HOGAN: It's in your interests as well as ours.

COLQUHOUN: I've nothing to hide, Inspector Hogan. (*Coughs.*)

HOGAN: Fine, sir. Maybe we'll just start then?

COLQUHOUN: Might I ask a question? Just for the record, you want to ask me about Joseph Lintz – nothing else?

HOGAN: What else might there be, sir?

COLQUHOUN: I just wanted to check.

HOGAN: You wish to have a solicitor present?

COLQUHOUN: No.

HOGAN: Right you are, sir. Well, if I can begin ... it's really just a question of your relationship with Professor Joseph Lintz.

COLQUHOUN: Yes.

HOGAN: Only, when we spoke before, you said you didn't know Professor Lintz.

COLQUHOUN: I think I said I didn't know him very well.

HOGAN: Okay, sir. If that's what you said ...

COLQUHOUN: It is, to the best of my recollection.

HOGAN: Only, we've had some new information ...

COLQUHOUN: Yes?

HOGAN: That you knew Professor Lintz a little better than that.

COLQUHOUN: And this is according to …?

HOGAN: New information in our possession. The informant tells us that Joseph Lintz accused you of being a war criminal. Anything to say to that, sir?

COLQUHOUN: Only that it's a lie. An outrageous lie.

HOGAN: He didn't think you were a war criminal?

COLQUHOUN: Oh, he thought it all right! He told me to my face on more than one occasion.

HOGAN: When?

COLQUHOUN: Years back. He got it into his head … the man was mad, Inspector. I could see that. Driven by demons.

HOGAN: What did he say exactly?

COLQUHOUN: Hard to remember. This was a long time ago, the early 1970s, I suppose.

HOGAN: It would help us if you could …

COLQUHOUN: He came out with it in the middle of a party. I believe it was some function to welcome a visiting professor. Anyway, Joseph insisted on taking me to one side. He looked feverish. Then he came out with it: I was some sort of Nazi, and I'd come to this country by some circuitous route. He kept on about it.

HOGAN: What did you do?

COLQUHOUN: Told him he was drunk, babbling.

HOGAN: And?

COLQUHOUN: And he was. Had to be taken home in a taxi. I said no more about it. In academic circles, one becomes used to a certain amount of … eccentric behaviour. We're obsessive people, it can't be helped.

HOGAN: But Lintz persisted?

COLQUHOUN: Not really, no. But every few years … there'd … he'd say something, allege some atrocity …

HOGAN: Did he approach you outside the university?

COLQUHOUN: For a time, he telephoned my home.

HOGAN: You moved?

COLQUHOUN: Yes.

HOGAN: To an unlisted phone number?

COLQUHOUN: Eventually.

HOGAN: To stop him calling you?

COLQUHOUN: I suppose that was part of it.

HOGAN: Did you speak to anyone about Lintz?

COLQUHOUN: You mean the authorities? No, no one. He was a nuisance, nothing more.

HOGAN: And then what happened?

COLQUHOUN: Then these stories started appearing in the papers, saying Joseph might be a Nazi, a war criminal. And suddenly he was on my back again.

HOGAN: He phoned you at your office?

COLQUHOUN: Yes.

HOGAN: You lied to us about that?

COLQUHOUN: I'm sorry. I panicked.

HOGAN: What was there to panic about?

COLQUHOUN: Just ... I don't know.

HOGAN: So you met him? To straighten things out?

COLQUHOUN: We had lunch together. He seemed ... lucid. Only what he was saying, it was the stuff of madness. He had a whole history mapped out, only it wasn't mine. I kept saying to him, 'Joseph, when the war ended I wasn't out of my teens.' Besides, I was born and raised here. It's all on record.

HOGAN: What did he say to that?

COLQUHOUN: He said records could be faked.

HOGAN: Faked records ... one way Josef Linzstek could have gone undetected.

COLQUHOUN: I know.

HOGAN: You think Joseph Lintz was Josef Linzstek?

COLQUHOUN: I don't know. Maybe the stories got to him … he started to believe … I don't know.

HOGAN: Yes, but these accusations, they began before the media circus – decades before.

COLQUHOUN: That's true.

HOGAN: So he was hounding you. Did he say he would go to the media with his version of events?

COLQUHOUN: He may have … I can't remember.

HOGAN: Mmm.

COLQUHOUN: You're looking for a motive, aren't you? You're looking for reasons why I'd want him dead.

HOGAN: Did you kill him, Dr Colquhoun?

COLQUHOUN: Emphatically not.

HOGAN: Any idea who did?

COLQUHOUN: No.

HOGAN: Why didn't you tell us? Why tell lies?

COLQUHOUN: Because I knew this would happen. These suspicions. Stupidly, I thought I could circumvent them.

HOGAN: Circumvent?

COLQUHOUN: Yes.

HOGAN: A young woman was seen dining with Lintz, same restaurant he took you to. Any idea who she might be?

COLQUHOUN: None.

HOGAN: You knew Professor Lintz a long time … what did you think were his sexual proclivities?

COLQUHOUN: Never thought about it.

HOGAN: No?

COLQUHOUN: No.

HOGAN: What about yourself, sir?

COLQUHOUN: I don't see what that … well, for the record, Inspector, I'm monogamous and heterosexual.

HOGAN: Thank you, sir. I appreciate your frankness.

Rebus switched off the tape.

'I'll bet you did.'

'What do you think?' Bobby Hogan asked.

'I think you mistimed the did-you-do-it. Otherwise, not bad.' Rebus tapped the tape machine. 'Is there much more?'

'Not a lot.'

Rebus switched it back on.

HOGAN: When you met in the restaurant, it was the same routine as before?

COLQUHOUN: Oh, yes. Names, dates ... countries I was taken through on my way into Britain from the continent.

HOGAN: He told you how this was achieved?

COLQUHOUN: He called it the Rat Line. Said it was operated by the Vatican, if you can believe that. And all the western governments were in cahoots to get the top Nazis – the scientists and intellectuals – away from the Russians. I mean, really ... it's Ian Fleming meets John Le Carré, isn't it?

HOGAN: But he was very detailed?

COLQUHOUN: Yes, but it can be that way with obsessives.

HOGAN: There have been books written alleging the same thing Professor Lintz was talking about.

COLQUHOUN: Have there?

HOGAN: Nazis smuggled overseas ... war criminals rescued from the gallows.

COLQUHOUN: Well, yes, but those are just stories. You don't seriously think ...?

HOGAN: I'm just collecting information, Dr Colquhoun. In my job, we don't throw anything away.

COLQUHOUN: Yes, I can see that. The problem is, sorting out the wheat from the chaff.

HOGAN: You mean the truths from the lies? Yes, that's one problem.

COLQUHOUN: I mean, the stories you hear about Bosnia

and Croatia ... slaughterhouses, mass torture, the guilty being spirited away ... It's hard to know what's *true*.

HOGAN: Just before we finish ... any idea what happened to the money?

COLQUHOUN: What money?

HOGAN: The withdrawal Lintz made from his bank. Five thousand pounds in cash.

COLQUHOUN: This is the first I've heard of it. Another motive?

HOGAN: Thank you for your time, Dr Colquhoun. It might be necessary for us to talk again. I'm sorry, but you shouldn't have lied to us, it makes our job that much more difficult.

COLQUHOUN: I'm sorry, Inspector Hogan. I quite understand, but I hope you can comprehend why I did it.

HOGAN: My mum always told me never to lie, sir. Thanks again for your time.

Rebus looked at Hogan. 'Your mum?'

Hogan shrugged. 'Maybe it was my granny.'

Rebus drained his coffee. 'So we know one of Lintz's mealtime companions.'

'And we know he was hounding Colquhoun.'

'Is he a suspect?'

'I'm not exactly snowed under with them.'

'Fair point, but all the same ...'

'You think he's on the level?'

'I don't know, Bobby. He sounded like he had it rehearsed. And he was relieved at the end.'

'You don't think I got it all? I could bring him in again.'

Rebus was thinking: *stories you hear ... the guilty being spirited away*. Not stories you *read*, but ones you *hear* ... Who might he have heard them from? Candice? Jake Tarawicz?

Hogan rubbed the bridge of his nose. 'I need a drink.'

Rebus dropped his beaker into a waste-bin. 'Message received and understood. By the way, any word from Abernethy?'

'He's a bloody nuisance,' Hogan said, turning away.

26

'He's in place,' Claverhouse said, when Rebus phoned him to ask about Jack Morton. 'Got him a little one-bedroom shit-hole in Polwarth. Measured him up for his uniform, and he's now officially a member of on-site security.'

'Is anyone else in on it?'

'Just the big boss. His name's Livingstone. We had a long session with him last night.'

'Won't the other security men find it a bit odd, a stranger arriving in their midst?'

'It's down to Jack to put them at ease. He was pretty confident.'

'What's his cover?'

'Secret drinker, open gambler, busted marriage.'

'He doesn't drink.'

'Yes, he told me. Doesn't matter, so long as everyone *thinks* he does.'

'Is he in character?'

'Getting there. He's going to be working double shifts. That way he makes more trips to the shop, some in the evening when the place is quieter. More chance to get to know Ken and Dec. We've no contact with him during the day. Debriefing takes place once he's reached home. Telephone only, can't risk too many meetings.'

'You think they'll watch him?'

'If they're being thorough. And *if* they fall for the plan.'

'Did you talk to Marty Jones?'

'That's set for tomorrow. He'll bring a couple of heavies, but they'll go easy on Jack.'

'Isn't tomorrow a bit soon?'

'Can we afford to wait? They might already have someone in mind.'

'We're asking a lot of him.'

'He was *your* idea.'

'I know.'

'You don't think he's up to it?'

'It's not that … but he's stepping into a war.'

'Then get the ceasefire sorted out.'

'It is.'

'That's not what I hear …'

Rebus heard it too, as soon as he got off the phone. He knocked on the Chief Super's door. The Farmer was in conference with Gill Templer.

'Did you talk to him?' the Farmer asked.

'He agreed to a ceasefire,' Rebus said. He was looking at Templer. 'What about you?'

She took a deep breath. 'I spoke to Mr Telford – his solicitor was present throughout. I kept telling him what we wanted, and the lawyer kept telling me I was blackening his client's name.'

'And Telford?'

'Just sat there, arms folded, smiling at the wall.' Colour was creeping up her face. 'I don't think he looked at me once.'

'But you gave him the message?'

'Yes.'

'You said Cafferty would comply?'

She nodded.

'Then what the hell's happening?'

'We can't let it get out of control,' the Farmer said.

'Looks to me like it already is.'

The latest score-line: two of Cafferty's men, their faces mashed to something resembling fruit-pulp.

'Lucky they're not dead,' the Farmer went on.

'You know what's happening?' Rebus said. 'It's Tarawicz, *he's* the problem. Tommy's playing up to him.'

'It's times like this you yearn for independence,' the Farmer agreed. 'Then we could just extradite the bugger.'

'Why don't we?' Rebus suggested. 'Tell him his presence here is no longer acceptable.'

'And if he stays?'

'We shadow him, make sure everyone knows we're doing it. We make *nuisances* of ourselves.'

'You think that would work?' Gill Templer sounded sceptical.

'Probably not,' Rebus agreed, slumping into a chair.

'We've no real leverage,' the Farmer said, glancing at his watch. 'Which isn't going to please the Chief Constable. He wants me in his office in half an hour.' He got on the phone, ordered a car, rose to his feet.

'Look, see if you can thrash something out between you.'

Rebus and Templer exchanged a look.

'I'll be back in an hour or two.' The Farmer looked around, as if he were suddenly lost. 'Lock the door when you leave.' With that and a wave of his hand, he left. There was silence in the room.

'Has to keep his office locked,' Rebus said, 'to stop people stealing the secret of his terrible coffee.'

'Actually, it's been getting better recently.'

'Maybe your taste buds are being corroded. So, Chief Inspector ...' Rebus turned his chair to face hers. 'What about thrashing it out then, eh?'

She smiled. 'He thinks he's losing it.'

'Is he in for a bollocking?'

'Probably.'

'So it's down to us to come to the rescue?'

'I don't really see us as the Dynamic Duo, do you?'

'No.'

'Then there's always that part of you that says, let them tear each other apart. So long as no civilians get caught in the crossfire.'

Rebus thought of Sammy, of Candice. 'Thing is,' he said, 'they always do.'

She looked at him. 'How are you doing?'

'Same as ever.'

'As bad as that?'

'It's my calling.'

'You're done with Lintz though?'

Rebus shook his head. 'There's half a chance he ties in to Telford.'

'You still think Telford was behind the hit-and-run?'

'Telford or Cafferty.'

'Cafferty?'

'Setting up Telford, the way someone tried to set *me* up for Matsumoto.'

'You know you're not out of the woods?'

He looked at her. 'An internal inquiry? The men with rubber soles?' She nodded. 'Bring them on.' He sat forward in his chair, rubbed his temples. 'No reason they should be left out of the party.'

'What party?'

'The one inside my head. The party that never stops.' Rebus leaned across the desk to answer the phone. 'No, he's not here. Can I take a message? This is DI Rebus.' A pause; he was looking at Gill Templer. 'Yes, I'm working that case.' He found pen and paper, started writing. 'Mmm, I see. Yes, sounds like. I'll let him know when he gets back.' Eyes *boring into* hers. Then the punchline: 'How many did you say were dead?'

Just the one. Another fled the scene, holding his arm, all

but severed from the shoulder. He turned up at a local hospital later, needing surgery and a huge transfusion of blood.

In broad daylight. Not in Edinburgh, but Paisley. Telford's hometown, the town he still ruled. Four men, dressed in council work jackets, like a road team. But in place of picks and shovels, they'd toted machetes and a large-calibre revolver. They'd chased two men into a housing scheme. Kids playing on tricycles; kicking a ball up the street. Women hanging out of their windows. And grown men itching to hurt one another. A machete swung overhead, coming down hard. The wounded man kept running. His friend tried hurdling a fence, wasn't agile enough. Three inches higher and he'd have made it. As it was, his toe caught, and he fell. He was pushing himself back up when the barrel of the gun touched the back of his head. Two shots, a fine drizzle of blood and brain. The children not playing any more, the women screaming for them to run. But something had been satisfied by those two shots. The chase was over. The four men turned and jogged back down the street, towards a waiting van.

A public execution, in Tommy Telford's heartland.

The two victims: known money-lenders. The one in hospital was called 'Wee' Stevie Murray, age twenty-two. The one in the mortuary was Donny Draper – known since childhood as 'Curtains'. They'd be making jokes about that. Curtains was two weeks shy of his twenty-fifth birthday. Rebus hoped he'd made the most of his short time on the planet.

Paisley police knew about Telford's move to Edinburgh, knew there were some problems there. A courtesy call had been placed to Chief Superintendent Watson.

The caller said: the men were two of Telford's brightest and best.

The caller said: descriptions of the attackers were vague.

The caller said: the children weren't talking. They were being shielded by their parents, fearful of reprisals. Well, they might not be talking to the *police*, but Rebus doubted they'd be so reticent when Tommy Telford came calling, armed with his own questions and determined to have answers.

This was bad. This was *escalation*. Fire-bombings and beatings: these could be remedied. But murder ... murder put the grudge-match on to a much higher plane.

'Is it worth talking to them again?' Gill Templer asked. They were in the canteen, sandwiches untouched in front of them.

'What do you think?'

He knew what she thought. She was talking because she thought talking was better than doing nothing. He could have told her to save her breath.

'They used a machete,' he said.

'Same thing they took to Danny Simpson's scalp.' Rebus nodded. 'I've got to ask ...' she said.

'What?'

'About Lintz ... what you said?'

He drained the last inch of his cold coffee. 'Fancy another?'

'John ...'

He looked at her. 'Lintz had some phone calls he was trying to hide. One of them was to Tommy Telford's office in Flint Street. We don't know how it ties in, but we think it *does* tie in.'

'What could Lintz and Telford have had in common?'

'Maybe Lintz went to him for help. Maybe he rented prossies off him. Like I say, we don't *know*. Which is why we're keeping it under the table.'

'You want Telford very badly, don't you?'

Rebus stared at her, thought about it. 'Not as much as I did. He's not enough any more.'

'You want Cafferty, too?'

'And Tarawicz ... and the Yakuza ... and anybody else who's along for the ride.'

She nodded. 'This is the party you were talking about?'

He tapped his head. 'They're all in here, Gill. I've tried kicking them out, but they won't leave.'

'Maybe if you stopped playing their kind of music?'

He smiled tiredly. 'Now there's an idea. What do you reckon: ELP? The Enid? How about a Yes triple album?'

'Your department, not mine, thank God.'

'You don't know what you're missing.'

'Yes, I do: I was there first time round.'

Old Scottish proverb: he who has had knuckles rapped will want to rap someone else's. Which is why Rebus found himself back in Watson's office. The Farmer's cheeks were still red from his meeting with the Chief Constable. When Rebus made to sit, Watson told him to get back on his feet.

'You'll sit when you're told and not before.'

'Thank you, sir.'

'What the bloody hell's going on, John?'

'Pardon, sir?'

The Farmer looked at the note Rebus had left on his desk. 'What's this?'

'One dead, one seriously wounded in Paisley, sir. Telford's men. Cafferty's hitting him where it hurts. Probably reckons that Telford's territory's spun a bit thin. Leaves him open to breaches.'

'Paisley.' The Farmer stuffed the note in his drawer. 'Not our problem.'

'It will be, sir. When Telford hits back, it'll be right here.'

'Never mind that, Inspector. Let's talk about Maclean's Pharmaceuticals.'

Rebus blinked, relaxed his shoulders. 'I was going to tell you, sir.'

'But instead I had to hear it from the Chief Constable?'

'Not really my baby, sir. Crime Squad are pushing the pram.'

'But who put the baby *in* the pram?'

'I was going to tell you, sir.'

'Know how it makes me look? I walk into Fettes and I don't know something one of my junior officers knows? I look like a mug.'

'With respect, sir, I'm sure that's not the case.'

'I look like a *mug*!' The Farmer slammed the desk with both palms. 'And it's not as though this was the first time. I've always tried to do my best for you, you know that.'

'Yes, sir.'

'Always been fair.'

'Absolutely, sir.'

'And you pay me back like this?'

'It won't happen again, sir.'

The Farmer stared at him; Rebus held it, returned it.

'I bloody well hope not.' The Farmer leaned back in his chair. He'd calmed down a little. Bollocking as therapy. 'Nothing else you want to tell me, is there, while I've got you here?'

'No, sir. Except ... well ...'

'Go on.' The Farmer sat forward again.

'It's the man in the flat above me, sir,' Rebus said. 'I think he might be Lord Lucan.'

27

Leonard Cohen: 'There is a War'.

They were waiting for Telford's retaliatory strike. The Chief Constable's idea: 'visible presence as deterrent'. It came as no surprise to Rebus: probably even less so to Telford, who had Charles Groal ready, claiming harassment the minute the patrol cars turned up in Flint Street. How was his client supposed to carry on with his legitimate and substantial business interests, as well as his many community developments, under the pressure of unwarranted and intrusive police surveillance? 'Community developments' meaning the pensioners and their rent-free flats: Telford wouldn't hesitate to use them as pawns. The media would love it.

The patrol cars would be pulled, it was just a matter of time. And afterwards: firework night all over again. That's what everyone was expecting.

Rebus went to the hospital, sat with Rhona. The room, so familiar to him now, was an oasis where calm and order reigned, where each hour of the day brought its comforting rituals.

'They've washed her hair,' he said.

'She's had another scan,' Rhona explained. 'They had to get the gunk off afterwards.' Rebus nodded. 'They said you'd noticed eye movement?'

'I thought I did.'

Rhona touched his arm. 'Jackie says he might manage to come up again at the weekend. Call this fair warning.'

'Received and understood.'

'You look tired.'

He smiled. 'One of these days someone's going to tell me how terrific I'm looking.'

'But not today,' Rhona said.

'Must be all the booze, clubbing and women.'

Thinking: Coke, the Morvena Casino, and Candice.

Thinking: why do I feel like piggy in the middle? Are Cafferty and Telford *both* playing games with me?

Thinking: I hope Jack Morton's okay.

The phone was ringing when he got back to Arden Street. He picked up just as the answering machine was cutting in.

'Hold on till I stop this thing.' Found the right button and hit it.

'Technology, eh, Strawman?'

Cafferty.

'What do you want?'

'I've heard about Paisley.'

'You mean you've been talking to yourself?'

'I had nothing to do with it.'

Rebus laughed out loud.

'I'm telling you.'

Rebus fell into his chair. 'And I'm supposed to believe you?' Games, he was thinking.

'Whether you believe me or not, I wanted you to know.'

'Thanks, I'm sure I'll sleep better for that.'

'I'm being set up, Strawman.'

'Telford doesn't *need* to set you up.' Rebus sighed, stretched his neck to left and right. 'Look, have you considered another possibility?'

'What?'

'Your men have lost it. They're going behind your back.'

'I'd know.'

'You'd know what your own lieutenants tell you. What if

they're lying? I'm not saying it's the whole gang, could be just two or three gone rogue.'

'I'd know.' The emotion had drained from Cafferty's voice. He was thinking it over.

'Fine, okay, you'd know: who'd be the first to tell you? Cafferty, you're on the other side of the country. You're in *prison*. How hard would it be to keep stuff from you?'

'These are men I'd trust with my life.' Cafferty paused. 'They'd tell me.'

'*If* they knew. *If* they hadn't been warned not to tell you. See what I'm saying?'

'Two or three gone rogue ...' Cafferty echoed.

'You must have candidates?'

'Jeffries would know.'

'Jeffries? Is that the Weasel's name?'

'Don't let him hear you call him that.'

'Give me his number. I'll talk to him.'

'No, but I'll get him to call you.'

'And if he's part of the breakaway?'

'We don't know there is one.'

'But you admit it makes sense?'

'I admit Tommy Telford's trying to put me in a box.' Rebus stared from his window. 'You mean literally?'

'I've heard word of a contract.'

'But you've got protection?'

Cafferty chuckled. 'Strawman, you almost sound concerned.'

'You're imagining things.'

'Look, there are only two ways out of this. One, *you* deal with Telford. Two, *I* deal with him. Are we agreed on that? I mean, I'm not the one who went poaching players and territory and putting out frighteners.'

'Maybe he's just more ambitious than you. Maybe he reminds you of the way you used to be.'

'Are you saying I've gone soft?'

'I'm saying it's adapt or die.'

'Have *you* adapted, Strawman?'

'Maybe a little.'

'Aye, a fucking speck, if that.'

'We're not talking about me though.'

'You're as involved as anyone. Remember that, Strawman. And sweet dreams.'

Rebus put down the phone. He felt exhausted, and depressed. The kids across the way were in bed, shutters closed. He looked around the room. Jack Morton had helped him paint it, back when Rebus was thinking of selling. Jack had helped him off the sauce, too ...

He knew he wouldn't be able to sleep. Got back into the car and headed for Young Street. The Oxford Bar was quiet. A couple of philosophers in the corner, and through in the back-room three musicians who'd packed up their fiddles. He drank a couple of cups of black coffee, then drove to Oxford Terrace. Parked the car outside Patience's flat, turned off the ignition and sat there for a while, jazz on the radio. He hit a good streak: Astrid Gilberto, Stan Getz, Art Pepper, Duke Ellington. Told himself he'd wait till a bad record came on, then go knock on Patience's door.

But by then it was too late. He didn't want to turn up unannounced. It would be ... it wouldn't look right. He didn't mind that it smacked of desperation, but he didn't want her to think he was pushing. He started the engine again and moved off, drove around the New Town and down to Granton. Sat by the edge of the Forth, window down, listening to water and the nighttime traffic of HGVs.

Even with eyes closed, he couldn't shut out the world. In fact, in those moments before sleep came, his images were at their most vivid. He wondered what Sammy dreamed about, or even if she dreamed at all. Rhona said that Sammy had come north to be with him. He couldn't think what he'd done to deserve her.

Back into town for an espresso at Gordon's Trattoria, then the hospital: easy to find a parking space this time of night. A taxi was idling outside the entrance. He made his way to Sammy's room, was surprised to see someone there. His first thought: Rhona. The only illumination in the room was that given through the closed curtains. A woman, kneeling by the bed, head resting on the covers. He walked forwards. She heard him, turned, face glistening with tears.

Candice.

Her eyes widened. She stumbled to her feet.

'I wanting see her,' she said quietly.

Rebus nodded. In shadows, she looked even more like Sammy: same build, similar hair and shape to her face. She wore a long red coat, fished in the pocket for a paper hankie.

'I like her,' she said. He nodded again.

'Does Tarawicz know where you are?' he asked.

She shook her head.

'The taxi outside?' he guessed.

She nodded. 'They went casino. I said sore head.' She spoke falteringly, checking each word was right before using it.

'Will he find out you've gone?'

She thought about it, shook her head.

'You sleep in the same room?' Rebus asked.

She shook her head again, smiled. 'Jake not liking women.'

This was news to Rebus. Miriam Kenworthy had said something about him marrying an Englishwoman ... but put that down to immigration. He remembered the way Tarawicz had pawed Candice, realised now it had been for *Telford's* benefit. He'd been showing Telford that he could control his women. While Telford ... well, Telford had let her get arrested, then be taken in by the Crime Squad. A small sign of rivalry between the two partners. Something to be exploited?

'Is she ... will she ...?'

Rebus shrugged. 'We hope so, Candice.'

She looked down at the floor. 'My name is Karina.'

'Karina,' he echoed.

'Sarajevo was ...' She looked up at him. 'You know, like *really*. I was escaping ... lucky. They all said to me: "You lucky, you lucky".' She stabbed at her chest with a finger. 'Lucky. Survivor.' She broke down again, and this time he held her.

The Stones: 'Soul Survivor'. Only sometimes it was the body alone that survived, the soul eaten into, chewed up by experience.

'Karina,' he said, repeating her name, reinforcing her true identity, trying to get through to the one part of her she'd kept hidden since Sarajevo. 'Karina, sshhh. It's going to be all right. Sshhh.' And stroking her hair, her face, his other hand on her back, feeling her tremble. Blinking back his own tears, and watching Sammy's body. The atmosphere in the room crackled like electricity: he wondered if any part of it was reaching Sammy's brain.

'Karina, Karina, Karina ...'

She pulled away, turned her back on him. He wouldn't let her go. Walked up to her and rested his hands on her shoulders.

'Karina,' he said, 'how did Tarawicz find you?' She seemed not to understand. 'In Anstruther, his men found you.'

'Brian,' she said quietly.

Rebus frowned. 'Brian Summers?' Pretty-Boy ...

'He tell Jake.'

'He told Tarawicz where you were?' But why not just take her back to Edinburgh? Rebus thought he knew: she was too dangerous; she'd been too close to the police. Best get her out of the way. Not a killing: that would have implicated all of them. But Tarawicz could control her. Mr Pink Eyes bailing out his friend one more time ...

'He brought you here so he could gloat over Telford.' Rebus was thoughtful. He looked at Candice. What could he do with her? Where would be safe? She seemed to sense his thoughts, squeezed his hand.

'You know I have a ...' She made a cradling motion with her hands.

'A boy,' Rebus said. She nodded. 'And Tarawicz knows where he is?'

She shook her head. 'The lorries ... they took him.'

'Tarawicz's refugee lorries?' She nodded again. 'And you don't know where he is?'

'Jake knows. He says his man ...' she made scuttling motions with her hands '... will kill my boy if ...'

Scuttling motions: the Crab. Something struck Rebus. 'Why isn't the Crab up here with Tarawicz?' She was looking at him. 'Tarawicz here,' he said, 'Crab in Newcastle. Why?'

She shrugged, looked thoughtful. 'He don't come.' She was remembering some snippet of conversation. 'Danger.'

'Dangerous?' Rebus frowned. 'Who for?'

She shrugged again. Rebus took her hands.

'You can't trust him, Karina. You have to leave him.'

She smiled up at him, eyes glinting. 'I tried.'

They looked at one another, held one another for a while. Afterwards, he walked her back out to her taxi.

28

In the morning he called the hospital, found out how Sammy was doing, then asked to be transferred.

'How's Danny Simpson getting on?'

'I'm sorry, are you family?'

Which told him everything. He identified himself, asked when it had happened.

'In the night,' the nurse said.

Body at its lowest ebb: the dying hours. Rebus called the mother, identified himself again.

'Sorry to hear the news,' he said. 'Is the funeral ...?'

'Just family, if you don't mind. No flowers. We're asking for donations to be sent to an ... to a charity. Danny was well thought of, you know.'

'I'm sure.'

Rebus took down details of the charity — an AIDS hospice; the mother couldn't bring herself to say the word. Terminated the call. Got an envelope out and put in ten pounds, plus a note: 'In memory of Danny Simpson'. He wondered about going for that test ... His phone rang and he picked it up.

'Hello?'

Lots of static and engine noise: car-phone, on the move at speed.

'This takes persecution to new levels.' *Telford.*

'What do you mean?' Rebus trying to compose himself.

'Danny Simpson's been dead six hours, and already you're on the phone to his mum.'

'How do you know?'

'I was *there*. Paying my respects.'

'Same reason I phoned then. Know what, Telford? I think *you're* taking persecution complexes to new levels.'

'Yes, and Cafferty's not out to shut me down.'

'He says he didn't have anything to do with Paisley.'

'I bet you believed in the Tooth Fairy when you were a kid.'

'I still do.'

'You'll need more than a good fairy if you side with Cafferty.'

'Is that a threat? Don't tell me: Tarawicz is in the car with you?' Silence. Bingo, Rebus thought. 'You think Tarawicz will respect you because you bad-mouth cops? He's got no respect for you whatsoever – look how he's waving Candice in your face.'

Mixing levity with fury: 'Hey, Rebus, you and Candice in that hotel – what was she like? Jake tells me she's vindaloo.' Background laughter: Mr Pink Eyes, who, according to Candice, had never touched her. For 'laughter' read 'bravado'. Telford and Tarawicz, playing games between themselves, playing games with the world.

Rebus found the tone of voice he wanted. 'I tried to help her. If she's too stupid to know that, she deserves the likes of you and Tarawicz.' Telling them he had no further interest in her. 'Anyway, Tarawicz didn't have any trouble taking her off *your* hands.' Rebus jabbing away, looking for gaps in the armour of the Telford/Tarawicz relationship.

'What if Cafferty wasn't behind Paisley?' he asked into the silence.

'It was his men.'

'Gone rogue.'

'He can't control them, that's his look-out. He's a *joke*, Rebus. He's finished.'

Rebus didn't say anything; listened instead to a muted

conversation. Then Telford again: 'Mr Tarawicz wants a word.' The phone was handed over.

'Rebus? I thought we were civilised men?'

'In what way?'

'When we met in Newcastle ... I thought we came to an understanding?'

The unspoken agreement: leave Telford alone, have nothing more to do with Cafferty, and Candice and her son would be safe. What was Tarawicz getting at?

'I've kept my side.'

A forced chuckle. 'You know what Paisley represents?

'What?'

'The beginning of the end of Morris Gerald Cafferty.'

'And I bet you'd send flowers to the grave.'

Dead flowers at that.

Rebus went into St Leonard's, got settled in front of his computer screen, and took a look at the Crab.

The Crab: William Andrew Colton. Plenty of form. Rebus decided he'd like to read the files. Phoned in and requested them, backed up the request in writing. Buzzed from downstairs: a man to see him, no name supplied. Description: the Weasel.

Rebus went downstairs.

The Weasel was outside, smoking a cigarette. He was wearing a green waxed jacket, torn at both pockets. A lumberjack hat with its flaps down protected his ears from the wind.

'Let's walk,' Rebus said. The Weasel got into step with him. They wandered through an estate of new flats: satellite dishes and windows picked from Lego boxes. Behind the flats sat Salisbury Crags.

'Don't worry,' Rebus said, 'I'm not in the mood for rock-climbing.'

'I'm in the mood for indoors.' The Weasel tucked his chin into the upturned collar of his coat.

'What's the news on my daughter?'

'We're close, I told you.'

'How close?'

The Weasel measured his response. 'We've got the tapes from the car, the guy who sold them. He says he got them from another party.'

'And he is …?'

A sly smile: the Weasel knew he had control over Rebus. He'd play it out as long as possible.

'You're going to be meeting him fairly shortly.'

'Even so … say the tapes got taken from the car after it was abandoned?'

The Weasel was shaking his head. 'That's not how it was.'

'Then how was it?' He wanted to pull his tormentor down on to the ground and start hammering his skull on the pavement.

'Give us a day or two, we'll have everything you need.' The wind gusted some grit towards them. They turned their faces. Rebus saw a heavy-set man loitering sixty yards behind.

'Don't worry,' the Weasel said, 'he's with me.'

'Getting jittery?'

'After Paisley, Telford's out for blood.'

'What do you know about Paisley?'

The Weasel's eyes became slits. 'Nothing.'

'No? Cafferty's beginning to suspect some of his own men might have gone rogue.' Rebus watched the Weasel shake his head.

'I don't know the first thing about it.'

'Who's your boss's main man?'

'Ask Mr Cafferty.' The Weasel was looking around, as if bored by the conversation. He made a signal to the back-marker, who passed it along. Seconds later, a newish Jaguar – arterial-red paint-job – cruised to a stop beside them. Rebus saw: a driver itching for a less sedentary occupation; cream leather interior; the back-marker jogging forwards, opening the door for the Weasel.

'It's you,' Rebus said. The Weasel: Cafferty's eyes and ears on the street; the man with the look and dress-code of a down-and-out. The Weasel was running the show. All the lieutenants in the various outposts … all the tailor-made suits … the collective which, according to police intelligence, ran Cafferty's kingdom in their master's absence … they were a smokescreen. The hunched man pulling off his lumberjack hat, the man with bad teeth and a blunt razor, *he* was in charge.

Rebus actually laughed. The bodyguard got into the car's passenger seat, having made sure his boss was comfortable in the back. Rebus tapped on the window. The Weasel lowered it.

'Tell me,' Rebus asked, 'have you got the bottle to wrest it away from him?'

'Mr Cafferty trusts me. He knows I'll do right by him.'

'What about Telford?'

The Weasel stared at him. 'Telford's not my concern.'

'Then who is?'

But the window was rising again, and the Weasel – Cafferty had called him Jeffries – had turned his face away, dismissing Rebus from his mind.

He stood there, watching the car drive off. Was Cafferty making a big mistake, putting the Weasel in charge? Was it just that his best men had scarpered or gone over to the other side?

Or was the Weasel every bit as sly, clever and vicious as his namesake?

Back at the station, Rebus sought out Bill Pryde. Pryde was

shrugging his shoulders even before Rebus had reached his desk.

'Sorry, John, no news.'

'Nothing at all? What about the stolen tapes?' Pryde shook his head. 'That's funny, I've just been talking to someone who claims to know who sold them on, and who *he* got them from.'

Pryde sat back in his chair. 'I wondered why you hadn't been chasing me up. What've you done, hired a private eye?' Blood was rising to his face. 'I've been working my arse off on this, John, you know I have. Now you don't trust me to do the job?'

'It's not like that, Bill.' Rebus suddenly found himself on the defensive.

'Who've you got working for you, John?'

'Just people on the street.'

'Well-connected people by the sound of it.' He paused. 'Are we talking villains?'

'My daughter's in a coma, Bill.'

'I'm well aware of that. Now answer my question!'

People around them were staring. Rebus lowered his voice. 'Just a few of my grasses.'

'Then give me their names.'

'Come on, Bill ...'

Pryde's hands gripped the table. 'These past days, I've been thinking you'd lost interest. Thinking maybe you didn't *want* an answer.' He was thoughtful. 'You wouldn't go to Telford ... Cafferty?' His eyes widened. 'Is that it, John?'

Rebus turned his head away.

'Christ, John ... what's the deal here? He hands over the driver, what do *you* hand *him*?'

'It's not like that.'

'I can't believe you'd trust Cafferty. You put him away, for Christ's sake!'

'It's not a question of trust.'

But Pryde was shaking his head. 'There's a line we don't cross.'

'Get a grip, Bill. There's no line.' Rebus spread his arms. 'If there is, show me it.'

Pryde tapped his forehead. 'It's up here.'

'Then it's a fiction.'

'You really believe that?'

Rebus sought an answer, slumped against the desk, ran his hands over his head. He remembered something Lintz had once said: *when we stop believing in God, we don't suddenly believe in 'nothing' ... we believe anything.*

'John?' someone called. 'Phone call.'

Rebus stared at Pryde. 'Later,' he said. He walked across to another desk, took the call.

'Rebus here.'

'It's Bobby.' Bobby Hogan.

'What can I do for you, Bobby?'

'For a start, you can help get that Special Branch arsehole off my back.'

'Abernethy?'

'He won't leave me alone.'

'Keeps phoning you?'

'Christ, John, aren't you listening? He's *here*.'

'When did he get in?'

'He never went away.'

'Whoah, hold on.'

'And he's driving me round the twist. He says he knows you from way back, so how about having a word?'

'Are you at Leith?'

'Where else?'

'I'll be there in twenty minutes.'

'I got so pissed off, I went to my boss — and that's something I seldom have to resort to.' Bobby Hogan was

316

drinking coffee like it was something best taken intrave-nously. The top button of his shirt was undone, tie hanging loose.

'Only,' he went on, '*his* boss had a word with my *boss's* boss, and I ended up with a warning: co-operate or else.'

'Meaning?'

'I wasn't to tell anyone he was still around.'

'Thanks, pal. So what's he actually doing?'

'What *isn't* he doing? He wants to be in on any interviews. He wants copies of tapes and transcripts. He wants to see all the paperwork, wants to know what I'm planning to do next, what I had for breakfast ...'

'I don't suppose he's managing to be helpful in any shape or form?'

Hogan's look gave Rebus his answer.

'I don't mind him taking an interest, but this verges on the obstructive. He's slowing the case to a dead stop.'

'Maybe that's his plan.'

Hogan looked up from his cup. 'I don't get it.'

'Neither do I. Look, if he's being obstructive, let's put on a show, see how he reacts.'

'What sort of show?'

'What time will he be in?'

Hogan checked his watch. 'Half an hour or so. That's when my work stops for the day, while I fill him in.'

'Half an hour's enough. Mind if I use your phone?'

29

When Abernethy arrived, he didn't manage not to look surprised. The space put aside for the investigation – Hogan's space – now contained three bodies, and they were working at the devil's own pace.

Hogan was on the telephone to a librarian. He was asking for a run-down of books and articles about the 'Rat Line'. Rebus was sorting through paperwork, putting it in order, cross-referencing, laying aside anything he didn't think useful. And Siobhan Clarke was there, too. She appeared to be on the phone to some Jewish organisation, and was asking them about lists of war criminals. Rebus nodded towards Abernethy, but kept on working.

'What's going on?' Abernethy asked, taking off his raincoat.

'Helping out. Bobby's got so many leads to work on ...' He nodded towards Siobhan. 'And Crime Squad are interested, too.'

'Since when?'

Rebus waved a piece of paper. 'This might be bigger than we think.'

Abernethy looked around. He wanted to speak to Hogan, but Hogan was still on the phone. Rebus was the only one with time to talk.

Which was just the way Rebus had planned it.

He'd only had five minutes in which to brief Siobhan, but she was a born actress, even holding a conversation with the dialling tone. Hogan's fantasy librarian, meantime, was asking him all the right questions. And Abernethy was looking glazed.

'What do you mean?'

'In fact,' Rebus said, putting down a file, 'you might be able to help.'

'How?'

'You're Special Branch, and Special Branch has access to the secret services.' Rebus paused. 'Right?'

Abernethy licked his lips and shrugged.

'See,' Rebus went on, 'we're beginning to wonder something. There could be a dozen reasons why someone would want to kill Joseph Lintz, but the one we've been practically ignoring' (ignoring at Abernethy's suggestion, according to Hogan) 'is the one that just might provide the answer. I'm talking about the Rat Line. What if Lintz's murder had something to do with that?'

'How could it?'

It was Rebus's turn to shrug. 'That's why we need your help. We need any and all information we can get on the Rat Line.'

'But it never existed.'

'Funny, a lot of books seem to say it did.'

'They're wrong.'

'Then there are all these survivors ... except they haven't survived. Suicides, car crashes, a fall from a window. Lintz is just one of a long line of dead men.'

Siobhan Clarke and Bobby Hogan had finished their calls and were listening.

'You're climbing the wrong tree,' Abernethy said.

'Well, you know, if you're in a forest, climbing any tree will give you a better view.'

'There is no Rat Line.'

'You're an expert?'

'I've been collating ...'

'Yes, yes, all the investigations. And how far have you got? Is any one of them going to make it to trial?'

'It's too early to tell.'

'And soon it may be too late. These men aren't getting any younger. I've seen the same thing all around Europe: delay the trial until the defendants are so old they snuff it or go doolally. Result's the same: no trial.'

'Look, this has nothing to do with ...'

'Why are you here, Abernethy? Why did you come up that time to speak to Lintz?'

'Look, Rebus, it's not ...'

'If you can't tell us, talk to your boss. Get *him* to do it. Otherwise, the way we're digging, we're bound to throw up an old bone sooner or later.'

Abernethy stood back a pace. 'I think I get it,' he said. And he began to smile. 'You're trying to stiff me.' He was looking at Hogan. 'That's what this is.'

'Not at all,' Rebus answered. 'What I'm saying is: we'll redouble our efforts. We'll sniff into every little corner. The Rat Line, the Vatican, turning Nazis into cold war spies for the allies ... it could all count as evidence. The other men on your list, the other suspects ... we'll need to talk to all of them, see if they knew Joseph Lintz. Maybe they met him on the trip over.'

Abernethy was shaking his head. 'I'm not going to let you do that.'

'You're going to obstruct the investigation?'

'That's not what I said.'

'No, but it's what you'll *do*.' Rebus paused. 'If you think we're climbing the wrong tree – and, incidentally, that should be *barking up* – go ahead and prove it. Give us everything you've got on Lintz's past.'

Abernethy's eyes were fierce.

'Or we go on digging and sniffing.' Rebus opened another file, lifted out the first sheet. Hogan picked up his telephone, made another call. Siobhan Clarke looked at a list of numbers and chose one.

'Hello, is that the City Synagogue?' Hogan was saying. 'Yes, it's Detective Inspector Hogan here, Leith CID. Do you by any chance have information on a Joseph Lintz?'

Abernethy grabbed his coat, turned on his heels and left. They waited thirty seconds, then Hogan put the receiver down.

'He looked nettled.'

'That's one Christmas wish I can chalk off,' Siobhan Clarke said.

'Thanks for your time, Siobhan,' Rebus said.

'Happy to oblige. But why did it have to be me?'

'Because he knows you're Crime Squad. I wanted him to think interest was escalating. And because the two of you didn't exactly hit it off last time you met. Antagonism always helps.'

'And what did we accomplish?' Bobby Hogan asked, beginning to gather together the files, half of which belonged to other cases.

'We rattled his cage,' Rebus said. 'He's not up here for the good of his health – or yours, come to that. He's here because Special Branch in London want to know all about the investigation. And to me, that means they're scared of something.'

'The Rat Line?'

'That would be my guess. Abernethy's been keeping an eye on all the new cases nationwide. Someone in London is getting a bit sweaty.'

'They're worried this Rat Line will connect to whoever killed Lintz?'

'I'm not sure it goes that far,' Rebus said.

'Meaning?'

He looked at Clarke. 'Meaning I'm not sure it goes that far.'

'Well,' Hogan said, 'looks like he's off my back for a little while at least, for which I'm grateful.' He got to his feet. 'Get anyone a coffee?'

Clarke checked her watch. 'Go on then.'

Rebus waited till Hogan was gone, then thanked Siobhan again. 'I wasn't sure you'd be able to spare the time.'

'We're giving Jack Morton a wide berth,' she explained. 'Nothing to do but bite our fingernails and wait. What about you, what are you up to?'

'Keeping my nose clean.'

She smiled. 'I'll bet.'

Hogan came back with three coffees. 'Powdered milk, sorry.'

Clarke wrinkled her nose. 'Actually, I've got to be getting back.' She stood up and put on her coat.

'That's one I owe you,' Hogan said, shaking her hand.

'I won't let you forget.' She turned to Rebus. 'See you later.'

'Cheers, Siobhan.'

Hogan put her cup beside his own. 'So we got Abernethy off my back, but did we get anything else?'

'Wait and see, Bobby. I didn't exactly have much time to devise a strategy.'

The phone rang, just as Hogan took a mouthful of scalding coffee. Rebus picked up.

'Hello?'

'Is that you, John?' Country and western twanging in the background: Claverhouse.

'You've just missed her,' Rebus told him.

'It's not Clarke I wanted, it's you.'

'Oh?'

'Something I thought you might be interested in. It's just filtered down from NCIS.' Rebus heard Claverhouse pick up a sheet of paper. 'Sakiji Shoda ... I think I've pronounced that right. Flew into Heathrow from Kansai

Airport yesterday. South-East Regional Crime Squad were apprised.'

'Terrific.'

'He didn't hang around, caught a connection to Inverness. Stayed the night in a local hotel, and now I hear he's in Edinburgh.'

Rebus looked out of the window. 'Not exactly golfing weather.'

'I don't think he's up here for the golf. According to the original report, Mr Shoda is a high-ranking member of the ... can't make it out on the fax. Socky-something.'

'Sokaiya?' Rebus sat up.

'That looks about right.'

'Where is he now?'

'I tried a couple of hotels. He's staying at the Caly. What's the Sokaiya?'

'It's the upper echelons of the Yakuza.'

'How does it read to you?'

'I was going to suggest he's Matsumoto's replacement, but it sounds to me like he's a few grades higher.'

'Matsumoto's boss?'

'Which means he's probably here to find out what happened to his boy.' Rebus tapped a pen against his teeth. Hogan was listening, but not getting any of it. 'Why Inverness? Why not direct to Edinburgh?'

'I've been wondering that.' Claverhouse sneezed. 'How pissed off will he be?'

'Somewhere between "mildly" and "very". More importantly, how are Telford and Mr Pink Eyes going to react?'

'You think Telford will drop Maclean's?'

'On the contrary, I think he'll want to show Mr Shoda that he can do *some* things right.' Rebus thought back to something Claverhouse had said. 'South-East Crime Squad?'

'Yes.'

'Rather than Scotland Yard?'

'Maybe the two are the same?'

'Maybe. Do you have a contact number?'

Claverhouse gave it to him.

'You'll speak to Jack Morton tonight?' Rebus asked.

'Yes.'

'Better tell him about this.'

'Talk to you again.'

Rebus put down the receiver, picked it up again, got an outside line and made the call. Explained his reason for calling and asked if there was anyone who could help him.

He was told to hold.

'Is this to do with Telford?' Hogan asked. Rebus nodded.

'Hey, Bobby, did you ever talk to Telford again?'

'I tried a couple of times. He just kept saying: "It must've been a wrong number".'

'And this was echoed by his staff?'

Hogan nodded, smiled. 'Tell you a funny thing. I walked into Telford's office, and someone was at his desk, back to me. I apologised, said I'd come back when he'd finished with the lady. Well, the "lady" turns, face like fury ...'

'Pretty-Boy?'

Hogan nodded. 'And pretty fucking angry the last I saw him.' Hogan laughed.

'Putting you through,' the switchboard told Rebus.

'How can I help you?' The voice sounded Welsh.

'My name's DI Rebus, Scottish Crime Squad.' Rebus winked at Hogan: the lie would give him more clout.

'Yes, Inspector?'

'And you are ...?'

'DI Morgan.'

'We had this message this morning ...'

'Yes?'

'Concerning Sakiji Shoda.'

'That would be my boss has sent you that.'

'What I'm wondering is, what's your interest?'

'Well, Inspector, I'm more of an expert on *vory v zakone*.'

'That clears things up then.'

Morgan chuckled. ' "Thieves within the code". Meaning *mafiya*.'

'Russian mafia?'

'That's it.'

'You'll have to help me here. What's that got to do with …?'

'Why do you want to know?'

Rebus took a sip of coffee. 'We've had a spot of bother with the Yakuza up here. One victim so far. My guess is that Shoda is the victim's boss.'

'And he's up there for a sort of unofficial committal?'

'We don't have the committal stage in Scotland, DI Morgan.'

'Well, pardon me for breathing.'

'Thing is, we've also got a Russian gangster up here. I say he's Russian, word is he's Chechen.'

'Is it Jake Tarawicz?'

'You've heard of him?'

'That's my job, sonny boy.'

'Well, anyway, with the Yakuza and the Chechens in town …'

'You've got a nightmare scenario. Understood. Well, look … What about if you give me your number there, and I'll call back in five minutes? Need to put some facts together first.'

Rebus gave him the number, then waited ten minutes for the call back.

'You were checking me out,' he told the Welshman.

'Got to be careful. Bit naughty of you to say you were Crime Squad.'

'Let's just say I'm the next best thing. So is there anything you can tell me?'

Morgan took a deep breath. 'We've been chasing a lot of dirty money around the world.'

Rebus couldn't find a clean sheet of paper to write on. Hogan gave him a pad.

'See,' Morgan was saying, 'the old Soviet Asia is now the biggest supplier of raw opium in the world. And wherever there's drugs, there's money needs laundering.'

'And this money makes its way to Britain?'

'On its way elsewhere. Companies in London, private banks in Guernsey ... the money gets filtered down, getting cleaner all the time. Everyone wants to do business with the Russians.'

'Why?'

'Because they make everyone money. Russia's one giant bazaar. You want weapons, counterfeit goods, money, fake passports, even plastic surgery? You want any of that, it's in Russia. The place has open borders, airports nobody knows exist ... it's ideal.'

'If you happen to be an international mobster.'

'Exactly. And the *mafiya* have made links with their Sicilian cousins, with the Camorra, the Calabrians ... I could go on forever. British villains go shopping there. They all love the Russians.'

'And now they're here?'

'Oh, they're here all right. Running protection and prossies, dealing drugs ...'

Prostitutes, drugs: Mr Pink Eyes's territory; Telford's territory.

'Any evidence of a hook-up with the Yakuza?'

'Not that I know of.'

'But if they moved into Britain ...?'

'They'd be trying to control drugs and prostitution. They'd be laundering money.'

Ways to launder money: through legitimate businesses such as country clubs and the like; by swopping dirty money for casino chips at an establishment like the Morvena.

Rebus already knew that the Yakuza liked to smuggle artworks back into Japan. Rebus already knew Mr Pink had made his early money smuggling icons out of Russia. Put the two together.

Then add Tommy Telford to the equation.

Did they need the haul from Maclean's? It didn't sound to Rebus like they did. So why was Tommy Telford doing it? Two possible reasons: one, to show off; two, *because they'd told him to*. Some rite of passage ... If he wanted to play with the big boys, he had to prove himself. He had to wipe out Cafferty, and pull off what would be the biggest heist in Scottish history.

Something hit Rebus between the eyes.

Telford wasn't meant to succeed. Telford was meant to fail.

Telford was being set up by Tarawicz and the Yakuza.

Because he had something they wanted: a steady supply of drugs; a kingdom waiting to be plucked from his grasp. Miriam Kenworthy had said as much: rumour was, the drugs were going south from Scotland. Which meant Telford had a supply ... something *nobody* knew about.

With Cafferty out of the way, there'd be no competition. The Yakuza would have their British base – solid, respectable, reliable. The electronics factory would act as perfect cover, maybe even as a laundering operation itself. Every way Rebus looked at it, Telford was unnecessary to the equation, like a zero that could be safely cancelled out.

Which was where Rebus wanted Telford ... only not at the price being asked.

'Thanks for your help,' he said. He noticed that Hogan

had stopped listening and was staring into space. Rebus put the phone down.

'Sorry to have bored you.'

Hogan blinked. 'No, nothing like that. It's just that I thought of something.'

'What?'

'Pretty-Boy. I mistook him for a woman.'

'You're probably not the first.'

'Exactly.'

'I'm not sure I follow you?'

'In the restaurant ... Lintz and a young woman.' Hogan shrugged. 'It's a long shot.'

Rebus saw it. 'Talking business?'

Hogan nodded. 'Pretty-Boy runs Telford's stable.'

'And takes a personal interest in the higher-price models. It's worth a try, Bobby.'

'What do you think – bring him in?'

'Definitely. Beef up the restaurant angle. Say there's a positive ID. See what he says to that.'

'Same gag we pulled with Colquhoun? Pretty-Boy's bound to deny it.'

'Doesn't mean it ain't so.' Rebus patted Hogan on the shoulder.

'What about your call?'

'My call?' Rebus looked at his scrawled notes. Gangsters preparing to carve up Scotland. 'It wasn't the worst news I've ever had.'

'And is that saying much?'

'Afraid not, Bobby,' Rebus said, putting on his jacket. 'Afraid not.'

30

By the end of play, Rebus still hadn't received the files on the Crab, but he had fielded a frank and foul-mouthed call from Abernethy, accusing him of everything from obstruction – which was pretty rich, considering – to racism, which Rebus thought nicely ironic.

They'd given him back his car. Someone had run their finger through the dirt crusted on the boot, creating two messages: TERMINAL CASE, and WASHED BY STEVIE WONDER. The Saab, affronted, started first time and seemed to have shrugged off some of its repertoire of clanks and thunks. On the drive home, Rebus kept the windows open so he wouldn't smell the whisky that had soaked into the upholstery.

The evening had turned out fine, the sky clear, temperature dropping sharply. The low red sun, curse of the city's drivers, had disappeared behind the rooftops. Rebus left his coat unbuttoned as he walked down to the chip shop. He bought a fish supper, two buttered rolls, and a couple of cans of Irn-Bru, then returned to the flat. Nothing on the TV, so he put on a record. Van Morrison: *Astral Weeks*. The record had more scratches than a dog with eczema.

The opening track contained the refrain 'To be born again'. Rebus thought of Father Leary, shored up by a fridge full of medicine. Then he thought of Sammy, crowned with electrodes, machines rising either side of her, like she was being offered to them in sacrifice. Leary often talked of faith, but it was hard to have faith in a human race that never learned, that seemed ready to accept torture, murder, destruction. He opened his newspaper: Kosovo, Zaire, Rwanda. Punishment beatings in Northern Ireland. A young girl found murdered in England, another girl's disappearance termed 'a cause for concern'. The predators were out there, no doubt about it. Strip the veneer, and the world had moved only a couple of steps from the cave.

To be born again ... But sometimes only after a baptism of fire.

Belfast, 1970. A sniper's bullet blew open the skull of a British squaddie. The victim was nineteen, came from Glasgow. Back in the barracks, there'd been little mourning, just an overspill of anger. The assassin would never be caught. He'd slipped back into the shadows of a tower-block, and from there deep into the Catholic housing estate.

Leaving one more newspaper story, one early statistic in the 'Troubles'.

And anger.

The ring-leader went by the nickname of 'Mean Machine'. He was a lance-corporal, came from somewhere in Ayrshire. Cropped blond hair, looked like he'd played rugby, liked to work out, even if it was just press-ups and sit-ups in the barracks. He started the campaign for retribution. It was to be covert – meaning behind the backs of the 'brass'. It was to be a release-valve for the frustration, the pressure that was building in the cramped confines of the barracks. The world outside was enemy terrain, everyone a potential foe. Knowing there was no way to punish the sniper, Mean Machine had decided to hold the entire community to blame: collective responsibility, for which there would be collective justice.

The plan: a raid on a known IRA bar, a place where sympathisers drank and colluded. The pretext: a man with a handgun, chased into the bar, necessitating a search.

Maximum harassment, ending with the beating of the local IRA fundraiser.

And Rebus went along with it ... because it *was* collective. You were either part of the team, or you were dead meat. And Rebus wasn't in the market for pariah status.

But all the same, he knew the line between 'good guys' and 'bad guys' had become blurred. And during the incursion, it disappeared altogether.

Mean Machine went in hardest, teeth bared, eyes ablaze. He swung with his rifle, cracking skulls. Tables flew, pint glasses shattered. Initially the other soldiers seemed shocked by the sudden violence. They looked to each other for guidance. Then one of them lashed out, and the others fell in beside him. A mirror dissolved into glittering stars, stout and lager washed over the wooden floor. Men were shouting, begging, crawling on hands and knees across the glass minefield. Mean Machine had the IRA man pinned to a wall, kneeing him in the groin. He twisted his body, threw him to the floor, then started pummelling him with the rifle-butt. More soldiers were pouring into the drinking-club: armoured cars arriving outside. A chair crashed into the row of optics. The smell of whisky was almost overpowering.

Rebus tried to shut it out, his own teeth bared not in anger but anguish. Then he aimed his rifle at the ceiling and let loose a single shot, and everything froze ... A final kick to the bloodied figure on the floor and Mean Machine turned and walked out of the club. The others hesitated again, then followed. He'd proved something to the other men: for all his lowly rank, he'd become their leader.

They enjoyed themselves that night in the barracks, chiding Rebus for letting his trigger-finger slip. They cracked open cans of beer and told stories, stories which were already being exaggerated, turning the event into a myth, giving it a grandeur it had lacked.

Turning it into a lie.

A few weeks later, the same IRA man was found shot dead in a stolen car south of the city, on a farm road with a view of hills and grazing land. Protestant paramilitaries took the blame, but Mean Machine, though he admitted nothing, would wink and grin when the incident was mentioned. Bravado or confession – Rebus was never sure. All he knew was that he wanted out, away from Mean Machine's newly minted code of ethics. So he did the one thing he could – applied to join the SAS. Nobody would think him a coward or a turncoat for applying to join the elite.

To be born again.

Side one had finished; Rebus turned the record over, switched off the lights and went to sit in his chair. He felt a chill run through him. Because he *knew* how events like Villefranche could come to be. Because he *knew* how the world's continuing horrors could come to be perpetrated at the cusp of the twentieth century. He knew that mankind's instinct was raw, that every act of bravery and kindness was countered by so many acts of savagery.

And he suspected that if his daughter had been that sniper's victim, he'd have run into the bar with his trigger-finger already working.

Telford's gang ran in a pack, too, trusted their leader. But now *he* wanted to run with an even bigger gang ...

The phone rang and he picked up.

'John Rebus,' he said.

'John, it's Jack.' Jack Morton. Rebus put down his can. 'Hello, Jack. Where are you?'

'In the poky one-bedroomed flat our friends at Fettes so graciously provided.'

'It has to fit the image.'

'Aye, I suppose so. Got a phone though. Coin job, but you can't have everything.' He paused. 'You okay, John? You sound ... not all there.'

'That just about sums me up, Jack. What's it like being a security guard?'

'A dawdle, pal. Should have taken it up years ago.'

'Wait till your pension's safe.'

'Aye, right.'

'And it went okay with Marty Jones?'

'Oscars all round. They were just heavy enough. I stumbled back into the shop, said I had to sit down. The Gruesome Twosome were very solicitous, then started asking me all these questions ... Not very subtle.'

'You don't think they twigged?'

'Like you, I was a bit dubious about setting it up so fast, but I think they fell for it. Whether their boss goes along is a different story.'

'Well, he's under a lot of pressure.'

'With the war going on?'

'I don't think that's the whole story, Jack. I think he's under pressure from his partners.'

'The Russian and the Japs?'

'I think they're setting him up for a fall, and Maclean's is the precipice.'

'Evidence?'

'Gut feeling.'

Jack was thoughtful. 'So where do I stand?'

'Just ca' canny, Jack.'

'I never thought of that.'

Rebus laughed. 'When do you think they'll make contact?'

'They followed me home – that's how desperate they are. They're sitting outside right now.'

'They must think you're a good thing.'

Rebus could see the way it was going. Dec and Ken

getting panicky, needing a quick result – feeling vulnerable so far away from Flint Street, not knowing if they'd be Cafferty's next victims. Telford, pressure applied by Tarawicz, and now with the Yakuza boss in town ... needing a result, something to show he was top dog.

'What about you, John? It's been a while.'

'Yes.'

'How are you holding up?'

'I'm on soft drinks only, if that's what you mean.' And a car doused in whisky ... he could taste it in his lungs.

'Hang on,' Jack said. 'Someone's at the door. I'll call you back.'

'Be careful.'

The phone went dead.

Rebus gave it an hour. When Jack hadn't called, he got on the blower to Claverhouse.

'It's okay,' Claverhouse told him from his mobile. 'Tweedledee and Tweedledum came calling, took him off somewhere.'

'You're watching the flat?'

'Decorator's van parked down the street.'

'So you've no idea where they've taken him?'

'I'd guess he's at Flint Street.'

'With no back-up?'

'That's how we all wanted it.'

'Christ, I don't know ...'

'Thanks for the vote of confidence.'

'It's not you in the firing line. And I'm the one who volunteered him.'

'He knows the score, John.'

'So now you wait for him either to come home or end up on a slab?'

'Christ, John, Calvin was Charlie Chester compared to you.' Claverhouse had lost all patience. Rebus tried to think of a comeback, slammed the phone down instead.

Suddenly he couldn't be doing with Van the Man; put on Bowie instead, *Aladdin Sane*: nicely discordant, Mike Garson's piano in key with his thoughts.

Empty juice cans and a dead pack of cigarettes stared up at him. He didn't know Jack's address. The only person who'd give it to him was Claverhouse, and he didn't want to pick up their conversation. He took Bowie off halfway through side one, substituted *Quadrophenia*. Liner notes: 'Schizophrenic? I'm bleeding Quadrophenic'. Which was just about right.

Quarter past midnight, the phone rang. It was Jack Morton.

'Back home safe and sound?' Rebus asked.

'Right as nails.'

'Have you spoken to Claverhouse?'

'He can wait his turn. I said I'd phone you back.'

'So what did you get?'

'The third degree, basically. Some guy with dyed black hair, frizzy ... tight jeans.'

'Pretty-Boy.'

'Wears mascara.'

'Looks like. So what was the gist?'

'Second hurdle passed. Nobody's mentioned what the job is yet. Tonight was a sort of preface. Wanted to know all about me, told me my money worries could be over. If I could help them with a "little problem" – Pretty-Boy's words.'

'You asked what the problem was?'

'He wasn't saying. If you ask me, he goes to Telford, talks it through. Then there's another meeting, and that's where they tell me the plan.'

'And you'll be miked up?'

'Yes.'

'And if they strip you?'

'Claverhouse has access to some miniaturised stuff, cuff-links and the like.'

'And your character would obviously wear cuff-links.'

'True enough. Maybe fit a transmitter into a bookie's pencil.'

'Now you're thinking.'

'I'm thinking I'm wiped out.'

'What was the mood like?'

'Fraught.'

'Any sign of Tarawicz or Shoda?'

'Nope, just Pretty-Boy and the Gruesome Twosome.'

'Claverhouse calls them Tweedledum and Tweedledee.'

'He's obviously classically educated.' Morton paused. 'You've spoken to him?'

'When you didn't call back.'

'I'm touched. Do you think he's up to it?'

'Claverhouse?' Rebus thought about it. 'I'd feel better if *I* was in charge. But that probably puts me in a minority.'

'I didn't say that.'

'You're a pal, Jack.'

'They're running a check on me. But that's all in place. With luck, I'll pass.'

'What did they say to your sudden arrival at Maclean's?'

'I've been transferred from another plant. If they go looking, I'm in the personnel files.' Morton paused again. 'One thing I want to know ...'

'What?'

'Pretty-Boy handed me a hundred quid on account: what do I do with it?'

'That's between you and your conscience, Jack. See you soon.'

'Night, John.'

For the first time in a while, Rebus actually made it as far as his bed. His sleep was deep and dreamless.

31

Doctors in white coats were doing things to Sammy when Rebus arrived at the hospital next morning: taking her pulse, shining lights in her eyes. They were setting up another scanner, a nurse trying to untangle the thin coloured leads. Rhona looked like she'd lost some sleep. She jumped up and ran towards him.

'She woke up!'

It took him a second to take it in. Rhona was holding his arms, shaking him.

'She woke *up*, John!'

He pushed his way to the bedside.

'When?'

'Last night.'

'Why didn't you phone me?'

'I tried three, four times. You were engaged. I tried Patience, but there was no answer there.'

'What happened?' To him, Sammy looked the same as ever.

'She just opened her eyes ... No, first off, it was like she was moving her eyeballs. You know, with her eyelids closed. Then she opened her eyes.'

Rebus could see that the medical personnel were finding their work hampered. Half of him wanted to lash out – *We're her fucking parents!* The other half wanted them to do all they could to bring her round again. He took Rhona by the shoulder and guided her out into the hallway.

'Did she ... Did she look at you? Did she say anything?'

'She was just staring at the ceiling, where the strip-light is. Then I thought she was going to blink, but she closed her eyes again and they stayed shut.' Rhona burst into tears. 'It was like ... I lost her all over again.'

Rebus took her in his arms. She hugged him back.

'She did it once,' he whispered into her ear, 'she'll do it again.'

'That's what one of the doctors said. He said they're "very hopeful". Oh, John, I wanted to tell you! I wanted to tell *everyone!*'

And he'd been busy with work: Claverhouse, Jack Morton. And he'd got Sammy into all this in the first place. Sammy and Candice – pebbles dropped into a pool. And now the ripples had grown so that he'd all but forgotten about the centre, the starting point. Just like when he was married, work consuming him, becoming an end in itself. And Rhona's words: *You've exploited every relationship you ever had.*

To be born again ...

'I'm sorry, Rhona,' he said.

'Can you let Ned know?' She started crying again.

'Come on,' he said, 'let's get some breakfast. Have you been here all night?'

'I couldn't leave.'

'I know.' He kissed her cheek.

'The person in the car ...'

'What?'

She looked at him. 'I don't care any more. I don't care who they were or whether they get caught. All I want is for her to wake up.'

Rebus nodded, told her he understood. Told her breakfast was on him. He kept the talk going, his mind not really on it. Instead, her words bounced around in his head: *I don't care who they were or whether they get caught ...*

Whichever stress he put on it, he couldn't make it sound like surrender.

At St Leonard's, he broke the news to Ned Farlowe. Farlowe wanted to go to the hospital, but Rebus shook his head. Farlowe was crying as Rebus left his cell. Back at his desk, the files on the Crab were waiting.

The Crab: real name, William Andrew Colton. He had form going back to his teens, celebrated his fortieth birthday on Guy Fawkes Day. Rebus hadn't had many dealings with him during his time in Edinburgh. Looked like the Crab had lived in the city for a couple of years in the early-80s, and again in the early-90s. 1982: Rebus gave evidence against him in a conspiracy trial. Charges dropped. 1983: he was in trouble again – a fight in a pub left one man in a coma and his girlfriend needing sixty stitches to her face. Sixty stitches: you could knit a pair of mittens with less.

The Crab had held various jobs: bouncer, bodyguard, general labourer. The Inland Revenue had a go at him in 1986. By '88, he was on the West Coast, which was presumably where Tommy Telford had found him. Knowing good muscle when he saw it, he'd put the Crab on the doors of his club in Paisley. More blood-spilling; more accusations. Nothing came of them. The Crab had lived a charmed life, the sort of life that niggled at cops the world over: witnesses too scared to testify; withdrawing or refusing to give evidence. The Crab didn't often make it to trial. He'd served three adult sentences – a total of twenty-seven months – in a career that was now entering its fourth decade. Rebus went through the paperwork again, picked up the phone and called CID in Paisley. The man he wanted to speak to had been transferred to Motherwell. Rebus made the call, eventually got through to Detective Sergeant Ronnie Hannigan, and explained his interest.

'It's just that reading between the lines, you suspected the Crab of a lot more than ever got put down on paper.'

'You're right.' Hannigan cleared his throat. 'Never got close to proving anything though. You say he's south of the border now?'

'Telford placed him with a gangster in Newcastle.'

'Have criminal tendencies, will travel. Well, let's hope they keep him. He was a one-man reign of terror, and that's no exaggeration. Probably why Telford palmed him off on someone else: the Crab was getting out of control. My theory is, Telford tried him out as a hit-man. Crab wasn't suitable, so Telford needed to jettison him.'

'What was the hit?'

'Down in Ayr. Must've been ... four years ago? Lot of drugs swilling around, most of them inside a dance-club ... can't remember its name. I don't know what happened: maybe a deal went sour, maybe someone was skimming. Whatever, there was a hit outside the club. Guy got his face half torn off with a carving knife.'

'You put the Crab in the frame?'

'He had an alibi, of course, and the eye-witnesses all seemed to have suffered temporary blindness. Could be a plot for the *X-Files* in that.'

A knife attack outside a nightclub ... Rebus tapped his desk with a pen. 'Any idea how the attacker got away?'

'On a motorbike. The Crab likes bikes. Crash helmet makes a good disguise.'

'We had an almost identical attack recently. Guy on a motorbike went for a drug dealer outside one of Tommy Telford's nightclubs. Killed a bouncer instead.'

And Cafferty denied any involvement ...

'Well, like you say, the Crab's in Newcastle.'

Yes, and staying put ... *scared* to come north. Warned off by Tarawicz. Because Edinburgh was too dangerous ... people might *remember* him.

'Do you know how far away Newcastle is?'

'A couple of hours?'

'No distance at all by bike. Anything else I should know?'

'Well, Telford tried the Crab in the van, but he wasn't much good.'

'What van?'

'The ice-cream van.'

Rebus nearly dropped the phone. 'Explain,' he said.

'Easy: Telford's boys were selling dope from an ice-cream van. The "five-pound special", they called it. You handed over a fiver and got back a cone or wafer with a wee plastic bag tucked inside ...'

Rebus thanked Hannigan and terminated the call. Five-pound specials: Mr Taystee with his clients who ate ice-cream in all weathers. His daytime pitches: near schools. His nighttime pitches: outside Telford's clubs. Five-pound specials on the menu, Telford taking his cut ... The new Merc: Mr Taystee's big mistake. Telford's moneymen wouldn't have taken long to work out their boy was skimming. Telford would have decided to turn Mr Taystee into a lesson ...

It was coming together. He spun his pen, caught it, and made another call, this time to Newcastle.

'Nice to hear from you,' Miriam Kenworthy said. 'Any sign of your lady friend?'

'She's turned up here.'

'Great.'

'In tow with Mr Pink Eyes.'

'Not so great. I wondered where he'd gone.'

'And he's not here to see the sights.'

'I'll bet he isn't.'

'Which is really why I'm calling.'

'Mmm?'

'I'm just wondering if he's ever been linked to machete attacks.'

'Machetes? Let me think ...' She was so quiet for so long, he thought the connection had failed. 'You know, that *does* ring a bell. Let me put it up on the screen.' Clackety-clack of her keyboard. Rebus was biting his bottom lip, almost drawing blood.

'God, yes,' she said. 'A year or so back, a battle on an estate. Rival gangs, that was the story, but everyone knew what was behind it: namely, drugs and pitch incursions.'

'And where there's drugs, there's Tarawicz?'

'There was a rumour his men were involved.'

'And they used machetes?'

'One of them did. His name's Patrick Kenneth Moyni-han, known to all and sundry as "PK".'

'Can you give me a description?'

'I can fax you his picture. But meantime: tall, heavy build, curly black hair and a black beard.'

He wasn't part of the Tarawicz retinue. Two of Mr Pink's best muscle-men had been left behind in Newcastle. For safety's sake. Rebus put PK down as one of the Paisley attackers – Cafferty again in the clear.

'Thanks, Miriam. Listen, about that rumour ...'

'Remind me.'

'Telford supplying Tarawicz rather than the other way round: anything to back it up?'

'We tracked Pink Eyes and his men. A couple of jaunts to the continent, only they came back clean.'

'Leading you up the garden path?'

'Which made us start reassessing.'

'Where would Telford be getting the stuff?'

'We didn't reassess that far.'

'Well, thanks again ...'

'Hey, don't leave me hanging: what's the story?'

'Morning Glory. Cheers, Miriam.'

Rebus went and got a coffee, put sugar in it without realising, had finished half the cup before he noticed. Tarawicz was attacking Telford. Telford was blaming Cafferty. The resulting war would destroy Cafferty and weaken Telford. Then Telford would pull off the Maclean's break-in but be grassed up ...

And Tarawicz would fill the vacuum. That had been the plan all along. Bluesbreakers: 'Double-Crossing Time'. Christ, it was beautiful: set the two rivals against one another and wait for the carnage to end ...

The prize: something Rebus didn't yet know. There had to be something big. Tarawicz, the theory went, was sourcing his drugs not from London but from Scotland. From Tommy Telford.

What did Telford know? What was it that made *his* supply so valuable? Did it have something to do with Maclean's? Rebus got another coffee, washed down three Paracetamol with it. His head felt ready to explode. Back at his desk, he tried Claverhouse, couldn't get him. Paged him instead, and got an immediate call back.

'I'm in the van,' Claverhouse said.

'I've something to tell you.'

'What?'

Rebus wanted to know what was happening. Wanted in on the action. 'It's got to be face to face. Where are you parked?'

Claverhouse sounded suspicious. 'Down from the shop.'

'White decorator's van?'

'This definitely isn't a good idea ...'

'You want to hear what I've got?'

'Sell me the idea.'

'It clears everything up,' Rebus lied.

Claverhouse waited for more, but Rebus wasn't obliging. Theatrical sigh: life was hard on Claverhouse.

'I'll be there in half an hour,' Rebus said. He put down

the phone, looked around the office. 'Anyone got a set of overalls?'

'Nice disguise,' Claverhouse said, as Rebus squeezed into the front seat.

Ormiston was in the driver's seat, plastic piece-box open in front of him. A flask of tea had been opened, steaming up the windscreen. The back of the van was full of paint-tins, brushes and other paraphernalia. A ladder was strapped to the roof, and another was leaning against the wall of the tenement beside which the van had been parked. Claverhouse and Ormiston were in white overalls, daubed with swatches of old paint. The best Rebus could come up with was a blue boilersuit, tight at the waist and chest. He pulled the first few studs open as he settled in.

'Anything happening?'

'Jack's been in twice this morning.' Claverhouse looked towards the shop. 'Once for ciggies and a paper, once for a can of juice and a filled roll.'

'He doesn't smoke.'

'He does for this operation: perfect excuse to nip to the shop.'

'He hasn't given you any signal?'

'You expecting him to put the flags out?' Ormiston exhaled fish-paste.

'Just asking.' Rebus checked his watch. 'Either of you want a break?'

'We're fine,' Claverhouse said.

'What's Siobhan up to?'

'Paperwork,' Ormiston said with a smile. 'Ever come across a woman house painter?'

'Done much house painting yourself, Ormie?'

This brought a smile from Claverhouse. 'So, John,' he said, 'what is it you've got for us?'

Rebus filled them in quickly, noting Claverhouse's mounting interest.

'So Tarawicz is planning to double-cross Telford?' Ormiston said at the end.

Rebus shrugged. 'That's my guess.'

'Then why the hell are we bothering to set up a sting? Just let them get on with it.'

'That wouldn't give us Tarawicz,' Claverhouse said, his eyes slitted in concentration. 'If he sets up Telford for a fall, *he's* home and dry. Telford gets put away, and all we've done is replace one villain with another.'

'And an altogether nastier species at that,' Rebus said.

'What? And Telford's Robin Hood?'

'No, but at least with him, we know what we're dealing with.'

'And the old dears in his flats love him,' Claverhouse said.

Rebus thought of Mrs Hetherington, readying herself for her trip to Holland. The only drawback: she had to fly from Inverness ... Sakiji Shoda had flown from London to Inverness ...

Rebus started laughing.

'What's so funny?'

He shook his head, still laughing, wiping his eyes. It wasn't funny, not really.

'We could let Telford know what we know,' Claverhouse said, studying Rebus. 'Set him against Tarawicz, let them eat each other alive.'

Rebus nodded, took a deep breath. 'That's certainly one option.'

'Give me another.'

'Later,' Rebus said. He opened the door.

'Where are you off to?' Claverhouse asked.

'Got to fly.'

32

But in fact he was driving. A long drive, too. North through Perth and from there into the Highlands, taking a route which could be cut off during the worst of the winter. It wasn't a bad road, but traffic was heavy. He'd get past one slow-moving lorry only to catch up with another. He knew he should be thankful for small mercies: in the summer, caravans could end up fronting mile-long tail-backs.

He did pass a couple of caravans outside Pitlochry. They were from the Netherlands. Mrs Hetherington had said it was out of season for a trip to Holland. Most people her age would go in the spring, ready to fill their senses with the bulb-fields. But not Mrs Hetherington. Telford's offer: go when I say. Telford probably provided spending money, too. Told her to have a good time, not worry about a thing ...

As he neared Inverness, Rebus hit dual carriageway again. He'd been on the road well over two hours. Sammy might be coming round again; Rhona had his mobile number. Inverness Airport was signposted from the road into town. Rebus parked and got out, stretched his legs and arched his back, feeling the vertebrae pop. He went into the terminal and asked for security. He got a small balding man with glasses and a limp. Rebus introduced himself. The man offered coffee, but Rebus was jumpy enough after the drive. Hungry though: no lunch. He gave the man his story, and eventually they tracked down a representative of

Her Majesty's Customs. During his tour of the facilities, Rebus got the impression of a low-key operation. The Customs official was in her early thirties, rosy-cheeked and with black curly hair. There was a purple birthmark, the size of a small coin, in the middle of her forehead, looking for all the world like a third eye.

She took Rebus into the Customs area and found a room they could use for their conversation.

'They've just started direct international flights,' she said, in answer to his question. 'It's shocking really.'

'Why?'

'Because at the same time, they've cut back on manpower.'

'You mean in Customs?'

She nodded.

'You're worried about drugs?'

'Of course.' She paused. 'And everything else.'

'Are there flights to Amsterdam?'

'There will be.'

'But as of now ... ?'

She shrugged. 'You can fly to London, make the connection there.'

Rebus was thoughtful. 'There was a guy a few days ago, flew from Japan to Heathrow, then got a flight to Inverness.'

'Did he stop off in London?'

Rebus shook his head. 'Caught the first connection.'

'That counts as an international connection.'

'Meaning?'

'His luggage would be put on the plane in Japan, and he wouldn't see it again until Inverness.'

'So you'd be the first Customs point?'

She nodded.

'And if his flight came in at some horrible hour ...?'

She shrugged again. 'We do what we can, Inspector.'

Yes, Rebus could imagine: a lone, bleary-eyed Customs official, wits not at their sharpest ...

'So the bags change planes at Heathrow, but no one checks them there?'

'That's about it.'

'And if you were flying from Holland to Inverness via London?'

'Same deal.'

Rebus knew now, knew the brilliance of Tommy Telford's thinking. *He* was supplying drugs for Tarawicz, and Christ knew how many others. His little old ladies and men were bringing them in past early-morning or late-night Customs posts. How difficult would it be to slip something into a piece of luggage? Then Telford's men would be on hand to take everyone back to Edinburgh, carry their luggage upstairs ... and surreptitiously remove each package.

Old age pensioners as unwitting drugs couriers. It was stunning.

And Shoda hadn't flown into Inverness so he could check out the local tourist amenities. He'd flown in so he could see how easy it was, what a brilliant route Telford had found, quick and efficient with a minimum of risk. Rebus had to laugh again. The Highlands had its own drugs problem these days: bored teenagers and cash-rich oil-workers. Rebus had smashed one north-east ring back in early summer, only to have Tommy Telford come along ...

Cafferty would never have thought of it. Cafferty would never have been so daring. But Cafferty would have kept it quiet. He wouldn't have sought to expand, wouldn't have brought partners into the scheme.

Telford was still a kid in some respects. The passenger-seat teddy bear was proof of that.

Rebus thanked the Customs official and went in search of food. Parked in the middle of town and grabbed a burger, sat at a window table and thought it all through. There were still aspects that didn't make sense, but he could cope with that.

He made two calls: one to the hospital; one to Bobby Hogan. Sammy hadn't woken up again. Hogan was interviewing Pretty-Boy at seven o'clock. Rebus said he'd be there.

The weather was kind on the trip south, the traffic manageable. The Saab seemed to enjoy long drives, or maybe it was just that at seventy miles an hour the engine noise disguised all the rattles and bumps.

He drove straight to Leith cop-shop, looked at his watch and found he was quarter of an hour late. Which didn't matter, since they were just starting the interview. Pretty-Boy was there with Charles Groal, all-purpose solicitor. Hogan was sitting with another CID officer, DC James Preston. A tape-recorder had been set up. Hogan looked nervous, realising how speculative this whole venture was, especially with a lawyer present. Rebus gave him a reassuring wink and apologised for having been detained. The burger had given him indigestion, and the coffee he'd had with it had done nothing for his frayed nerves. He had to shake his head clear of Inverness and all its implications and concentrate on Pretty-Boy and Joseph Lintz.

Pretty-Boy looked calm. He was wearing a charcoal suit with a yellow t-shirt, black suede winkle-picker boots. He smelt of expensive aftershave. In front of him on the desk: a pair of tortoiseshell Ray-Bans and his car keys. Rebus knew he'd own a Range Rover — it was mandatory for Telford employees — but the key-ring boasted the Porsche marque, and on the street outside Rebus had parked behind a cobalt blue 944. Pretty-Boy showing a touch of individuality …

Groal had his briefcase open on the floor beside him. On the desk in front of him: an A4 pad of ruled paper, and a fat black Mont Blanc pen.

Lawyer and client oozed money easily made and just as easily spent. Pretty-Boy used his money to buy class, but Rebus knew his background: working-class Paisley, a granite-hard introduction to life.

Hogan identified those present for the benefit of the tape-recorder, then looked at his own notes.

'Mr Summers ...' Pretty-Boy's real name: Brian Summers. 'Do you know why you're here?'

Pretty-Boy made an O of his glossy lips and stared ceilingwards.

'Mr Summers,' Charles Groal began, 'has informed me that he is willing to co-operate, Inspector Hogan, but that he'd like some indication of the accusations against him and their validity.'

Hogan stared at Groal, didn't blink. 'Who said he's accused of anything?'

'Inspector, Mr Summers works for Thomas Telford, and your police force's harassment of that individual is on record ...'

'Nothing to do with me, Mr Groal, or this station.' Hogan paused. 'Nothing at all to do with my present inquiries.'

Groal blinked half a dozen times in quick succession. He looked at Pretty-Boy, who was now studying the tips of his boots.

'You want me to say something?' Pretty-Boy asked the lawyer.

'I'm just ... I'm not sure if ...'

Pretty-Boy cut him off with a wave of his hand, then looked at Hogan.

'Ask away.'

Hogan made show of studying his notes again. 'Do you know why you're here, Mr Summers?'

'General vilification as part of your witch-hunt against my employer.' He smiled at the three CID men. 'Bet you didn't think I'd know a word like "vilification".' His gaze rested on Rebus, then he turned to Groal.

'DI Rebus isn't based at this station.'

Groal took the hint. 'That's true, Inspector. Might I ask by what authority you've been allowed to sit in on this interview?'

'That will become clear,' Hogan said, '*if* you'll allow us to begin?'

Groal cleared his throat, but said nothing. Hogan let the silence lie for a few moments, then began.

'Mr Summers, do you know a man called Joseph Lintz?'

'No.'

The silence stretched out. Summers recrossed his feet. He looked up at Hogan, and blinked, the blink deteriorating into a momentary twitch of one eye. He sniffed, rubbed at his nose – trying to make out that the twitch meant nothing.

'You've never met him?'

'No.'

'The name means nothing to you?'

'You've asked me about him before. I'll tell you same as I told you then: I never knew the cat.' Summers sat up a bit straighter in his chair.

'You've never spoken to him by telephone?'

Summers looked at Groal.

'Hasn't my client made himself clear, Inspector?'

'I'd like an answer.'

'I don't know him,' Summers said, forcing himself to relax again, 'I've never spoken to him.' He gave Hogan his stare again, and this time held it. There was nothing behind the eyes but naked self-interest. Rebus wondered how anyone could ever think him 'pretty', when his whole outlook on life was so fundamentally ugly.

'He didn't phone you at your ... business premises?'

'I don't have any business premises.'

'The office you share with your employer.'

Pretty-Boy smiled. He liked those phrases: 'business premises'; 'your employer'. They all knew the truth, yet played this little game ... and he liked playing games.

'I've already said, I never spoke to him.'

'Funny, the phone company says differently.'

'Maybe they made a mistake.'

'I doubt that, Mr Summers.'

'Look, we've been through this before.' Summers sat forward in his chair. 'Maybe it was a wrong number. Maybe he spoke to one of my associates, and they *told* him he had a wrong number.' He opened his arms. 'This is going nowhere.'

'I agree with my client, Inspector,' Charles Groal said, scribbling something down. 'I mean, is this leading anywhere?'

'It's leading, Mr Groal, to an identification of Mr Summers.'

'Where and by whom?'

'In a restaurant with Mr Lintz. The same Mr Lintz he claims never to have met, never to have spoken to.'

Rebus saw hesitation cross Pretty-Boy's face. *Hesitation*, rather than surprise. He made no immediate denial.

'An identification made by a member of staff at the restaurant,' Hogan continued. 'Corroborated by another diner.'

Groal looked to his client, who wasn't saying anything, but the way he was staring at the table, Rebus wondered a smoking hole didn't start appearing in it.

'Well,' Groal went on, 'this is fairly irregular, Inspector.'

Hogan wasn't interested in the lawyer. It was Pretty-Boy and him now.

'What about it, Mr Summers? Care to revise your version of events? What were you talking about with Mr

Lintz? Was he looking for female company? I believe that's your particular area of expertise.'

'Inspector, I must insist ...'

'Insist away, Mr Groal. It won't change the facts. I'm just wondering what Mr Summers will say in court when he's asked about the phone call, the meeting ... when the witnesses identify him. I'm sure he's got a fund of stories, but he'll have to find a bloody good one.'

Summers slapped the desk with both palms, half-rose to his feet. There wasn't an ounce of fat on him. Veins stood out on the backs of his hands.

'I told you, I've never met him, never talked to him. Period, end of story, finito. And if you've got witnesses, they're lying. Maybe *you've* told them to lie. And that's all I've got to say.' He sat back down, put his hands in his pockets.

'I've heard,' Rebus said, as though attempting to liven up a flagging conversation between friends, 'that you run the more upmarket girls, the three-figure jobs rather than the gam-and-bam merchants.'

Summers snorted and shook his head.

'Inspector,' Groal said, 'I can't allow these accusations to continue.'

'Was that what Lintz wanted? Did he have expensive tastes?'

Summers continued shaking his head. He seemed about to say something, but caught himself, laughed instead.

'I would like to remind you,' Groal went on, unheeded by anyone, 'that my client has co-operated fully throughout this outrageous ...'

Rebus caught Pretty-Boy's eyes, held their stare. There was so much he wasn't telling ... so much he very nearly *wanted* to tell. Rebus thought of the length of rope in Lintz's house.

'He liked to tie them up, didn't he?' Rebus asked quietly.

Groal stood up, yanking Summers to his feet.

'Brian?' Rebus asked.

'Thank you, gentlemen,' Groal said. He was stuffing his notepad into his case, closing its brass locks. 'If you should find yourselves with any questions worth my client's time, we'll be pleased to assist. But otherwise, I'd advise you to ...'

'Brian?'

DC Preston had turned off the tape recorder and gone to open the door. Summers picked up his car keys, slipped his sunglasses on.

'Gentlemen,' he said, 'it's been educational.'

'S&M,' Rebus persisted, getting in Pretty-Boy's face. 'Did he tie them up?'

Pretty-Boy snorted, shook his head again. He paused as his lawyer led him past Rebus.

'It was for *him*,' he said in an undertone.

It was for him.

Rebus drove to the hospital. Sat with Sammy for twenty minutes. Twenty minutes of meditation and head-clearing. Twenty reviving minutes, at the end of which he squeezed his daughter's hand.

'Thanks for that,' he said.

Back at the flat, he thought of ignoring the answering-machine until after he'd had a bath. His shoulders and back were aching from the drive to Inverness. But something made him press the button. Jack Morton's voice: 'I'm on for a meeting with TT. Let's meet after. Half-ten at the Ox. I'll aim for that, but can't promise. Wish me luck.'

He walked in at eleven.

There was folk music in the back room. The front would have been quiet if it weren't for two loud-mouths who looked like they'd been at it since their office closed for the night. They still wore work-suits, newspapers rolled in their pockets. They were drinking G&T.

Rebus asked Jack Morton what he wanted.

'A pint of orange and lemonade.'

'So how did it go?' Rebus ordered the drink. In forty minutes, he'd managed to put away two Cokes, and was now on coffee.

'They seem keen.'

'So who was at the meeting?'

'My sponsors from the shop, plus Telford and a couple of his men.'

'The transmitter worked okay?'

'Sound as a pound.'

'Did they search you?'

Morton shook his head. 'They were sloppy, seemed really sweaty about something. Want to hear the plan?' Rebus nodded. 'Middle of the night, truck arrives at the factory, and I let it through the gates. My story is, I had a phone call from the boss okaying the delivery. So I wasn't suspicious.'

'Only your boss never made the call?'

'That's right. So I was duped by a voice. And that's all I need to tell the police.'

'We'd sweat the truth out of you.'

'Like I say, John, the whole plan's half-baked. I'll give them this though – they did check my background. Seemed satisfied.'

'Who's going to be in the truck?'

'Ten men, armed to the teeth. I'm to get a rough plan of the place to Telford tomorrow, let him know how many people will be around, what the alarm system's like ...'

'What's in it for you?'

'Five grand. He's judged that right: five gets my debts repaid and puts a wedge in my pocket.'

Five grand: the amount Joseph Lintz had taken out of his bank ...

'Your story's holding?'

'They've staked out my flat.'

'And they didn't follow you here?'

Morton shook his head, and Rebus filled him in on what he'd learned and what he suspected. While Morton was taking it in, Rebus threw a question at him.

'How does Claverhouse want to play it?'

'The tape evidence is good: Telford talking, me making sure I called him "Mr Telford" and "Tommy" a few times. It's obviously him on the recording. But ... Claverhouse wants Telford's crew caught red-handed.'

' "Got to do it right".'

'That seems to be his catch-phrase.'

'Is there a date?'

'Saturday, all being well.'

'What's the betting we get a tip-off on Friday?'

'If your theory's right.'

'If I'm right,' he agreed.

33

The tip-off didn't come until Saturday lunchtime, but when it did, Rebus knew his hunch had been right.

Claverhouse was the first to congratulate him, which surprised Rebus, because Claverhouse had a lot on his plate and had acted very casually when the call had come. Pinned to the walls of the Crime Squad office were detailed maps of the drugs plant, along with staff rosters. Coloured stickers showed where personnel would be stationed. During the night, it was security only, unless some big order was demanding overtime. Tonight, the usual security staff would be augmented by Lothian & Borders Police. Twenty people inside the plant, with marksmen stationed on roofs and at certain key windows. A dozen cars and vans as back-up. It was the biggest operation of Claverhouse's career; a lot was expected of him. He kept saying 'it has to be done right'. He said he would leave 'nothing to chance'. Those two phrases had become his mantra.

Rebus had listened to a recording of the snitch call: 'Be at Maclean's factory in Slateford tonight. Two in the morning, it's going to be turned over. Ten men, tooled up, driving a lorry. If you're canny, you can catch all of them.'

Scots accent, but sounding long distance. Rebus smiled, looked at the turning spools, and said 'Hello again, Crab' out loud.

No mention of Telford, which was interesting. Telford's men were loyal: they'd go down without saying a word. And Tarawicz wasn't grassing up Telford. He couldn't know the police already had taped evidence of Telford's involvement. Which meant he was planning on letting Telford go ... No, think it through. With the plan dead in the water and ten of his best men in custody, Tarawicz didn't *need* Telford under lock and key. He wanted him out in the open and worried, Yakuza breathing down his neck, all his frailties exposed. He could be picked off at any time, or made to hand over *everything*. No blood-letting required; it would be a simple business proposition.

'It has to be ...'

'Done right,' Rebus said. 'Claverhouse, we *know*, okay?'

Claverhouse lost it. 'You're only here because I tolerate you! So let's get that straight for a start. I snap my fingers and you're out of the game, understood?'

Rebus just stared at him. A line of sweat was running down Claverhouse's left temple. Ormiston was looking up from his desk. Siobhan Clarke, briefing another officer beside a wall-chart, stopped talking.

'I promise I'll be a good boy,' Rebus said quietly, 'if you'll promise to stop with the broken record routine.'

Claverhouse's jaw was working, but eventually he produced a near-smile of apology.

'Let's get on with it then.'

Not that there was much for them to do. Jack Morton was working a double shift, wouldn't start till three o'clock. They'd be watching the place from then on, just in case Telford changed the game-plan. This meant personnel were going to miss the big match: Hibs against Hearts at Easter Road. Rebus had his money on a 3–2 home win.

Ormiston's summing-up: 'Easiest quid you'll ever lose.'

Rebus retired to one of the computers and got back to work. Siobhan Clarke had already come round snooping.

'Writing it up for one of the tabloids?'

'No such luck.'

He tried to keep it simple, and when he was happy with

the finished product he printed off two copies. Then he went out to buy a couple of nice, bright folders ...

He dropped off one of the folders, then returned home, too restless to be much use at Fettes. Three men were waiting in his tenement stairwell. Two more came in behind him, blocking the only escape route. Rebus recognised Jake Tarawicz and one of his muscle-men from the scrapyard. The others were new to him.

'Up the stairs,' Tarawicz ordered. Rebus was a prisoner under escort as they climbed the steps.

'Unlock the door.'

'If I'd known you were coming, I'd have got in some beers,' Rebus said, searching his pockets for keys. He was wondering which was safer: let them in, or keep them out? Tarawicz made the decision for him, nodded some signal. Rebus's arms were grabbed, hands went into his jacket and trousers, found his keys. He kept his face blank, eyes on Tarawicz.

'Big mistake,' he said.

'In,' Tarawicz ordered. They pushed Rebus into the hallway, walked him to the living room.

'Sit.'

Hands pushed Rebus on to the sofa.

'At least let me make a pot of tea,' he said. Inside he was trembling, knowing everything he couldn't afford to give away.

'Nice place,' Mr Pink Eyes was saying. 'Lacks the feminine touch though.' He turned to Rebus. 'Where is she?' Two of the men had peeled off to search the place.

'Who?'

'I mean, who else would she turn to? Not your daughter ... not now she's in a coma.'

Rebus stared at him. 'What do you know about that?' The two men returned, shook their heads.

'I hear things.' Tarawicz pulled out a dining-chair and sat down. There were two men behind the sofa, two in front.

'Make yourselves at home, lads. Where's the Crab, Jake?' Reasoning: a question he might be expected to ask.

'Down south. What's it to you?'

Rebus shrugged.

'Shame about your daughter. Going to make a recovery, is she?' Rebus didn't answer. Tarawicz smiled. 'National Health Service ... I wouldn't trust it myself.' He paused. 'Where is she, Rebus?'

'Using my finely honed detective's skills, I'll assume you mean Candice.' Meaning she'd done a runner. Trusting to herself for once. Rebus was proud of her.

Tarawicz snapped his fingers. Arms grabbed Rebus from behind, pinning back his shoulders. One man stepped forward and punched him solidly on the jaw. Stepped back again. Second man forward: gut punches. A hand tugged his hair, forcing his eyes up to the ceiling. He didn't see the flat-handed chop aiming for his throat. When it came, he thought he was going to cough out his voice-box. They let him go, and he pitched forward, hands going to his throat, retching for breath. A couple of teeth felt loose, and the skin inside his cheek had burst. He got out a handkerchief, spat blood.

'Unfortunately,' Tarawicz was saying, 'I have no sense of humour. So I hope you'll understand I'm not joking when I say that I'll kill you if I have to.'

Rebus shook his head free of all the secrets he knew, all the power he held over Tarawicz. He told himself: *you don't know anything*.

He told himself: *you're not going to die*.

'Even ... if ... I did know ...' Fighting for breath. 'I wouldn't tell you. If the two of us were standing in a minefield, I wouldn't let you know. Want me ... to tell you why?'

'Sticks and stones, Rebus.'

'It's not because of *who* you are, it's *what* you are. You trade in human beings.' Rebus dabbed at his mouth. 'You're no better than the Nazis.'

Tarawicz put a hand to his chest. 'I'm struck to the quick.'

'Chance would be a fine thing.' Rebus coughed again. 'Tell me, why do you want her back?' Rebus knowing the answer: because he was about to head south, leaving Telford in Shit Street. Because to return to Newcastle without her was a small but palpable defeat. Tarawicz wanted it *all*. He wanted every last crumb on the plate.

'My business,' Tarawicz said. Another signal, and the hands grabbed him again, Rebus resisting this time. Packing-tape was being wound around his mouth.

'Everybody tells me how *genteel* Edinburgh is,' Tarawicz was saying. 'Can't have the neighbours complaining about the screams. Put him on a chair.'

Rebus was lifted up. He struggled. A kidney punch buckled his knees. They forced him down on to a dining-chair. Tarawicz was removing his jacket, undoing gold cufflinks so he could roll up the sleeves of his pink and blue striped shirt. His arms were hairless, thick, and the same mottled colour as his face.

'A skin complaint,' he explained, removing his blue-tinted glasses. 'Some distant cousin of leprosy, they tell me.' He loosened his top button. 'I'm not as pretty as Tommy Telford, but I think you'll find me his master in every other respect.' A smile to his troops, a smile Rebus wasn't supposed to understand. 'We can start anywhere you want, Rebus. And *you* get to choose when we stop. Just nod your head, tell me where she is, and I walk out of your life forever.'

He got in close to Rebus, the sheen on his face like a protective seal. His pale blue eyes had tiny black pupils. Rebus thought: consumer as well as pusher. Tarawicz waited for a nod which didn't come, then retreated. Found an anglepoise lamp next to Rebus's chair. Planted both feet on its base and yanked on the mains cable, ripping it free.

'Bring him over here,' he ordered. Two men pulled both Rebus and chair over towards where Tarawicz was checking that the cable was plugged into the wall and that the socket was switched on. Another man closed the curtains: no free show for the kids across the way. Tarawicz was dangling the cable, letting Rebus see the loose wires – the very *live* wires. Two-hundred-and-forty volts just waiting to make his acquaintance.

'Believe me,' Tarawicz said, 'this is nothing. The Serbs had torture down to a fine art. Much of the time, they weren't even looking for a confession. I've helped a few of the more intelligent ones, the ones who knew when it was time to run. There was money to be made in the early days, power for the taking. Now the politicians are moving in, bringing trial-judges with them.' He looked at Rebus. 'The intelligent ones always know when it's time to quit. One last chance, Rebus. Remember, a nod of the head ...' The wires were inches from his cheek. Tarawicz changed his mind, moved them towards his nostrils, then his eyeballs.

'A nod of the head ...'

Rebus was twisting, arms holding him down – his legs, arms, shoulders. Hands holding his head, chest. Wait! The shock would pass straight through Tarawicz's men! Rebus saw it for a bluff. His eyes met Tarawicz's, and they both knew. Tarawicz pulled back.

'Tape him to the chair.' Two-inch-wide runs of tape, fixing him in place.

'This time for real, Rebus.' To his men: 'Hold him till I get close. Pull away when I say.'

Rebus thinking: there'd be a split-second after they let go … A moment in which to break free. The tape wasn't the strongest he'd seen, but there was plenty of it. Maybe too much. He flexed his chest against it, felt no sign that it would break.

'Here we go,' Tarawicz said. 'First the face … then the genitals. You *will* tell me, we both know it. How much bravado you want to show is up to you, but don't think it means anything.'

Rebus said something behind the gag.

'No point talking,' Tarawicz said. 'The only thing I want from you is a nod, understood?'

Rebus nodded.

'Was that a nod?'

Forcing a smile, Rebus shook his head.

Tarawicz didn't look impressed. His mind was on business. That was all Rebus was to him. He aimed the wire at Rebus's cheek.

'Let go!'

The pressure on Rebus fell away. He pushed against his bonds, couldn't budge them. Electricity flashed through his nervous system, and he went rigid. His heart felt like it had doubled in size, his eyeballs bulged, tongue pushing against the gag. Tarawicz lifted the cable away.

'Hold him.'

Arms fell on Rebus again, finding less resistance than before.

'Doesn't even leave a mark,' Tarawicz said. 'And the real beauty is, you end up paying for it from your own electric bill.'

His men laughed. They were beginning to enjoy themselves.

Tarawicz crouched down, face to face. His eyes sought Rebus's.

'For your information, that was a five-second jolt.

363

Things only start to get interesting at the half-minute mark. How's your heart? For your sake, I hope it's in good condition.'

Rebus felt like he'd just mainlined adrenaline. Five seconds: it had seemed much longer. He was changing strategies, trying to think up some new lies Mr Pink might believe, anything to get him out of the flat …

'Undo his trousers,' Tarawicz was saying. 'Let's see what a jolt down there will do.'

Behind the gag, Rebus started screaming. His tormentor was looking around the room again.

'Definitely lacks the feminine touch.'

Hands were loosening his trouser-belt. They stopped when a buzzer sounded. There was someone at the main door.

'Just wait,' Tarawicz said quietly. 'They'll go away.'

The buzzer sounded again. Rebus wrestled with his bonds. Silence. Then the buzzer again, more insistent now. One of the men went for the window.

'Don't!' Tarawicz snapped.

Buzzer again. Rebus hoped it would go on forever. Couldn't think who it might be: Rhona? Patience? A sudden thought … what if they persisted, and Tarawicz decided to allow them inside? Rhona or Patience …

Time stretched. No more buzzing. They'd gone away. Tarawicz was beginning to relax, focusing his mind on his work once more.

Then there was a knock at the flat door. The person had got into the tenement. Now they were on the landing outside. Knocking again. Lifting the flap of the letterbox.

'Rebus!'

A male voice. Tarawicz looked to his men, nodded another signal. Curtains were opened; Rebus's bonds cut; the tape ripped from his face. Tarawicz rolled down his sleeves, put his jacket back on. Left the flex lying on the floor. One last word to Rebus: 'We'll speak again.' Then he marched his men to the door, opened it.

'Excuse us.'

Rebus was left sitting on the chair. He couldn't move, felt too shaky to stand up.

'Hang on a minute, chief!'

Rebus placed the voice: Abernethy. It didn't sound as if Tarawicz was heeding the Special Branch man.

'What's the score?' Now Abernethy was in the living-room, looking around.

'Business meeting,' Rebus croaked.

Abernethy came forward. 'Funny old business where you have to unzip your flies.'

Rebus looked down, started to make repairs.

'Who was that?' Abernethy persisted.

'A Chechen from Newcastle.'

'Likes to travel mob-handed, does he?' Abernethy walked around the room, found the bare flex and tut-tutted, unplugged it at the socket. 'Fun and games,' he said.

'Don't worry,' Rebus told him, 'it's under control.'

Abernethy laughed.

'What do you want anyway?'

'Brought someone to see you.' He nodded towards the doorway. A distinguished-looking man was standing there, dressed in three-quarter-length black woollen coat and white silk scarf. He was completely bald, with a huge dome of a head and cheeks reddened from cold. He had a sniffle, and was wiping his nose with a handkerchief.

'Thought we might pop out somewhere,' the man said, locution impeccable, his eyes everywhere but on Rebus. 'Get a spot to eat, if you're hungry.'

'I'm not,' Rebus said.

'Something to drink then.'

'There's whisky in the kitchen.'

The man looked reluctant.

'Look, pal,' Rebus told him, 'I'm staying right here. You can join me or you can bugger off.'

'I see,' the man said. He put the handkerchief away and stepped forward, stretched out a hand. 'Name's Harris, by the way.'

Rebus took the hand, expecting sparks to leap from his fingertips.

'Mr Harris, let's sit at the dining-table.' Rebus got to his feet. He was shaky, but his knees held till he'd crossed the floor. Abernethy appeared from the kitchen with the bottle and three glasses. Left again, and returned with a milk-jug of water.

Ever the host, Rebus poured, sizing up the trembling in his right arm. He felt disoriented. Adrenaline and electricity coursing through him.

'*Slainte*,' he said, lifting the glass. But he paused with it at his nostrils. Pact with the Big Man: no drinking, and Sammy back. His throat hurt when he swallowed, but he put the glass down untouched. Harris was pouring too much water into his own glass. Even Abernethy looked disapproving.

'So, Mr Harris,' Rebus said, rubbing his throat, 'just who the hell are you?'

Harris affected a smile. He was playing with his glass.

'I'm a member of the intelligence community, Inspector. I know what that probably conjures up in your mind, but I'm afraid the reality is far more prosaic. Intelligence-gathering means just that: lots of paperwork and filing.'

'And you're here because of Joseph Lintz?'

'I'm here because DI Abernethy says you're determined to link the murder of Joseph Lintz with the various accusations which have been made against him.'

'And?'

'And that, of course, is your prerogative. But there are

matters not necessarily germane which might prove ...
embarrassing, if brought into the open.'

'Such as that Lintz really was Linzstek, and was brought
to this country by the Rat Line, probably with help from
the Vatican?'

'As to whether Lintz and Linzstek were the same man ...
I can't tell you. A lot of the documentation was destroyed
just after the war.'

'But "Joseph Lintz" was brought to this country by the
Allies?'

'Yes.'

'And why did we do that?'

'Lintz was useful to this country, Inspector.'

Rebus poured a fresh whisky for Abernethy. Harris
hadn't touched his. 'How useful?'

'He was a reputable academic. As such he was invited to
attend conferences and give guest lectures all round the
world. During this time, he did some work for us.
Translation, intelligence-gathering, recruitment ...'

'He recruited people in other countries?' Rebus stared at
Harris. 'He was a *spy*?'

'He did some dangerous and ... influential work for this
country.'

'And got his reward: the house in Heriot Row?'

'He earned every penny in the early days.'

Harris's tone told Rebus something. 'What happened?'

'He became ... unreliable.' Harris lifted the glass to his
nose, sniffed it, but put it down again untouched.

'Drink it before it evaporates,' Abernethy chided. Harris
looked at him, and the Londoner mumbled an apology.

'Define "unreliable",' Rebus said, pushing aside his own
glass.

'He began to ... fantasise.'

'He thought a colleague at the university had been in the
Rat Line?'

Harris was nodding. 'He became obsessed with the Rat Line, began to imagine that everyone around him had been involved in it, that we were *all* culpable. Paranoia, Inspector. It affected his work and eventually we had to let him go. This was years back. He hasn't worked for us since.'

'So why the interest? What does it matter if any of this comes out?'

Harris sighed. 'You're right, of course. The problem is not the Rat Line *per se*, or the notion of Vatican involvement or any of the other conspiracy theories.'

'Then what is ...?' Rebus broke off, realised the truth. 'The problem is the personnel,' he stated. 'The other people brought in by the Rat Line.' He nodded to himself. 'Who are we talking about? Who might be implicated?'

'Senior figures,' Harris admitted. He'd stopped playing with the glass. His hands were flat on the table. He was telling Rebus: this is *serious*.

'Past or present?'

'Past ... plus people whose children have gone on to achieve positions of power.'

'MPs? Government ministers? Judges?'

Harris was shaking his head. 'I can't tell you, Inspector. I haven't been trusted with that knowledge myself.'

'But you could hazard a guess.'

'I don't deal in guesswork.' He looked at Rebus. There was steel behind the eyes. 'I deal in known quantities. It's a good maxim – one you should try.'

'But whoever killed Lintz did so *because* of his past.'

'Are you sure?'

'It doesn't make sense otherwise.'

'DI Abernethy tells me there's a link with some criminal elements in Edinburgh, perhaps a question of prostitution. It all sounds sordid enough to be believable.'

'And if it's believable, that's good enough for you?'

Harris stood up. 'Thank you for listening.' He blew his nose again, looked to Abernethy. 'Time to go, I believe. DI Hogan is waiting for us.'

'Harris,' Rebus said, 'you said yourself, Lintz had gone loopy, become a liability. Who's to say *you* didn't have him killed?'

Harris shrugged. 'If we'd arranged it, his demise would not have been quite so obvious.'

'Car crash, suicide, falling from a window …?'

'Goodbye, Inspector.'

As Harris walked to the door, Abernethy stood up and locked eyes with Rebus. He didn't say anything, but the message was there.

This is deeper water than either of us wants to be in. So do yourself a favour, swim for shore.

Rebus nodded, reached out a hand. The two men shook.

34

Two in the morning.

Frost on the car windscreens. They couldn't clear them: had to blend in with the other cars on the street. Back-up – four units – parked in a builder's yard just round the corner. Bulbs had been removed from street-lights, leaving the area in almost total darkness. Maclean's was like a Christmas tree: security lights, every window blazing, same as every other night.

No heating in the unmarked cars: heat would melt the frost; exhaust fumes a dead giveaway.

'This all seems very familiar,' Siobhan Clarke said. The surveillance on Flint Street seemed a lifetime ago to Rebus. Clarke was in the driving seat, Rebus in the back. Two to each car. That way, they had space to duck should anyone come snooping. Not that they expected anyone to do that: the whole heist was half-baked. Telford desperate *and* with his mind on other things. Sakiji Shoda was still in town – a quiet word with the hotel manager had revealed a Monday morning check-out. Rebus was betting Tarawicz and his men had already gone.

'You look pretty snug,' Rebus said, referring to her padded ski-jacket. She brought a hand out of her pocket, showed him what it was holding. It looked like a slim lighter. Rebus lifted it from her palm. It was warm.

'What the hell is it?'

Clarke smiled. 'I got it from one of those catalogues. It's a handwarmer.'

'How does it work?'

'Fuel rods. Each one lasts up to twelve hours.'

'So you've got one warm hand?'

She brought her other hand out, showed him an identical rod. 'I bought two,' she said.

'You might have said.' Rebus closed his fingers around the handwarmer, stuck it deep into his pocket.

'That's not fair.'

'Call it a privilege of rank.'

'Lights,' she warned. They dived for cover, surfaced again when the car had sped past: false alarm.

Rebus checked his watch. Jack Morton had been told to expect the truck some time between one-thirty and two-fifteen. Rebus and Clarke had been in the car since just after midnight. The snipers on the roof, poor bastards, had been in position since one o'clock. Rebus hoped they had a good supply of fuel rods. He still felt jittery from the afternoon's events. He didn't like that he owed Abernethy such a huge favour; indeed, maybe owed him his life. He knew he could cancel it out by agreeing – along with Hogan – to soft-pedal on the Lintz inquiry. He didn't like the idea, but all the same ... And the day's silver lining: Candice had made the break from Tarawicz.

Clarke's police radio was silent. They had maintained silence since before midnight. Claverhouse's words: 'The first person to speak will be me, understood? Anyone uses a radio before me, they're in farmyard shit. And I won't utter a sound until the truck's entered the compound. Is that clear?' Nods all around. 'They could be listening in, so this is *important*. We've got to do this *right*.' Averting his eyes from Rebus as he said it. 'I'd wish us all luck, but the less luck's involved the better I'll like it. A few hours from now, if we stick to the plan, we should have broken up Tommy Telford's gang.' He paused. 'Just let that sink in. We'll be heroes.' He swallowed, realising the immensity of the prize.

Rebus couldn't get so excited. The whole enterprise had shown him a simple truth: no vacuum. Where you had society, you had criminals. No belly without an underbelly.

Rebus knew his own criteria came cheaply: his flat, books, music and clapped-out car. And he realised that he had reduced his life to a mere shell in recognition that he had completely failed at the important things: love, relationships, family life. He'd been accused of being in thrall to his career, but that had never been the case. His work sustained him only because it was an easy option. He dealt every day with strangers, with people who didn't mean anything to him in the wider scheme. He could enter their lives, and leave again just as easily. He got to live other people's lives, or at least portions of them, experiencing things at one remove, which wasn't nearly as challenging as the real thing.

Sammy had brought home to him these essential truths: that he was not only a failed father but a failed human being; that police work kept him sane, yet was a substitute for the life he could have had, the kind of life everyone else seemed to lead. And if he became obsessed with his casework, well, that was no different from being obsessed with train numbers or cigarette cards or rock albums. Obsession came easy – especially to men – because it was a cheap way of achieving *control*, albeit control over something practically worthless. What did it matter if you could reel off the track listing to every '60s Stones album? It didn't matter a damn. What did it matter if Tommy Telford got put away? Tarawicz would take his place, and if he didn't, there was always Big Ger Cafferty. And if not Cafferty, then someone else. The disease was endemic, no cure in sight.

'What are you thinking about?' Clarke asked, switching her rod from left hand to right.

'My next cigarette.' Patience's words: *happiest when in denial* ...

They heard the truck before they saw it: changing gears noisily. Slid down into their seats, then up again as it made to pull into Maclean's. A wheeze of air-brakes as it jolted to a stop at the gates. A guard came out to talk to the driver. He carried a clip-board.

'Jack really suits a uniform,' Rebus said.

'Clothes maketh the man.'

'You reckon your boss has got it right?' He meant Claverhouse's plan: when the truck was in the compound, they'd use a megaphone and show the marksmen to whoever was in the driver's cab, tell them to come out. The rest of the men could stay locked in the back of the vehicle. They'd have them toss out any arms and then come out one at a time.

It was either that or wait until they were *all* out of the truck. Merit of this second plan: they'd know what they were dealing with. Merit of the first: most of the gang would be nicely stowed in the truck, and could be dealt with as and when.

Claverhouse had plumped for plan one.

Marked and unmarked cars were to move in as soon as the truck had come to a stop – engine off – in the compound. They would block the exit, then watch from safety while Claverhouse, at a first-floor window with his megaphone, and the marksmen (roof; ground-floor windows) did their stuff. 'Negotiation with force' was how Claverhouse had described it.

'Jack's opening the gates,' Rebus said, peering through the side window.

Engine roar, and the truck jerked forward.

'Driver seems a bit nervous,' Clarke commented.

'Or isn't used to HGVs.'

'Okay, they're in.'

Rebus stared at the radio, willing it to burst into life. Clarke had turned the ignition one click away from starting.

Jack Morton was watching the truck move into the compound. He turned his head towards the line of cars parked across the way.

'Any second ...'

The truck's brake-lights came on, then went off again. Air-brakes sounded.

The radio fizzed a single word: '*Now!*'

Clarke turned the engine, revved hard. Five other cars did the same. Exhaust smoke billowed suddenly into the night air. The noise was like the start of a stock-car race. Rebus wound his window down, the better to hear Claverhouse's megaphone diplomacy. Clarke's car leaped forward, first to the gates. Both she and Rebus jumped out, keeping their heads down, the car a shield between themselves and the truck.

'Engine's still running,' Rebus hissed.

'What?'

'The truck. Its engine's still running!'

Claverhouse's voice, warbling – partly nerves, partly megaphone quality: 'Armed police. Open the cab doors slowly and come out one at a time, hands held high. I repeat: armed police. Discard weapons before coming out. I repeat: discard weapons.'

'Do it!' Rebus hissed. Then: 'Tell them to switch off the bloody engine!'

Claverhouse: 'The gate is blocked, there's no escape, and we don't want anyone getting hurt.'

'Tell them to throw out the keys.' Cursing, Rebus dived back into the car, grabbed the handset. 'Claverhouse, tell them to ditch the bloody keys!'

Windscreen frosted over; he couldn't see a thing. Heard Clarke's yell: '*Get out!*'

Saw: dim white lights. The truck was reversing. At speed. A roar from its engine, veering crazily but heading for the gates.

Heading straight for him.

An explosion: bricks flying from the factory's front wall.

Rebus dropped the handset, got his arm stuck in the seatbelt. Clarke was screaming as he leaped clear.

A second later, truck and car connected in a rending of metal and smashing of glass. Domino effect: Clarke's car hit the one behind, throwing officers off balance. The road was like a skating rink, the truck pushing one car, two cars, then three cars back on to the highway.

Claverhouse was on the megaphone, choking on dust: 'No shooting! Officers too close! Officers too close!'

Yes, all they needed now was to be pinned down by sniper fire. Men and women were slipping, losing their footing, clambering from their cars. Some of them armed, but dazed. The truck's back doors, buckled by the initial collision, flew open, seven or eight men hit the ground running. Two of them had handguns, and loosed off three or four shots apiece.

Shouts, screams, the megaphone. The glass wall of the gatehouse exploded as a bullet hit it. Rebus couldn't see Jack Morton ... couldn't see Siobhan. He was lying on his front on a section of grass verge, hands over his head: classic defence/defeat posture and bloody useless with it. The whole area was picked out by floodlights, and one of the gunmen – Declan from the shop – was now aiming at those. Other members of the gang had headed out into the street and were running for it. They carried shotguns, pickaxe handles. Rebus recognised a few more faces: Ally Cornwell, Deek McGrain. The streetlights were dead, of course, giving them all the cover they could want. Rebus hoped the backup cars from the builder's yard were coming.

Yes: turning the corner now, all lights blazing, sirens howling. Tenement curtains were twitching, palms rubbing at windows. And right in front of Rebus, about an inch from his nose, a thickly rimed blade of grass. He could make out each sliver of frost, and the complex patterns which had formed. But he realised it was melting fast as his breath hit it. And his front was growing cold. And the marksmen were running from the building, lit up like a firing-range.

And Siobhan Clarke was safe: he could see her lying beneath a car. Good girl.

And one policewoman, also lying low, had been wounded in the knee. She kept touching it with her hand, then pulling the hand away to stare at the blood.

And there was still no sign of Jack Morton.

The gunmen were returning fire, scattering shots, smashing windscreens. Uniforms were ordered out of the front back-up car. Four of the gang got in.

Second car: uniforms out, three of the gang got in. No windscreens, but they were rolling. Yelling and whooping, waving their weapons. The two remaining gunmen were cool. They were taking a good look round, assessing the situation. Did they want to be here when the marksmen arrived? Maybe they did. Maybe they fancied their chances in that arena, too. Their luck had held *this* far, after all. Claverhouse: *the less luck's involved, the better I'll like it.*

Rebus got on to his knees, then his feet, staying at a crouch. He felt moderately safe. After all, *his* luck had held today, too.

'You okay, Siobhan?' Voice low, eyes on the gunmen. The two getaway cars added up to seven men. Two still left. Where was number ten?

'Fine,' Clarke said. 'What about you?'

'I'm okay.' Rebus left her, worked his way round to the front of the truck. The driver was unconscious behind his wheel, head bleeding where it had connected after the collision. There was some kind of grenade launcher on the seat beside him. It had left a bloody great hole in the wall of

Maclean's. Rebus checked the driver for firearms, found none. Then checked the pulse: steady. Recognised the face: one of the arcade regulars; looked about nineteen, twenty. Rebus took out his handcuffs, hooked the driver to the steering-wheel, threw the grenade launcher on to the road.

Then headed for the gatehouse. Jack Morton, in uniform but missing his cap, prone on the floor, covered by a glass shroud. The bullet had pierced his right breast-pocket. Pulse was weak.

'Christ, Jack …'

There was a telephone in the booth. Rebus punched 999 and asked for ambulances.

'Police officers down at the Maclean's factory on Slateford Road!' Staring down at his friend.

'Whereabouts on Slateford Road?'

'Believe me, they won't be able to miss it.'

Five marksmen, dressed in black, aimed rifles at Rebus from outside. Saw him on the phone, saw him shake his head, moved on. Saw their targets out on the road, getting into a patrol car. Yelled the order to stop, warning that they would fire.

Response: muzzle-flash. Rebus ducked again. Fire was returned, the noise deafening but momentary.

Shouts from the road: 'Got them!'

A plaintive wail: one of the gunmen wounded. Rebus looked. The other was lying quite still on the road. Marksmen yelling to the wounded man: 'Drop the weapon, turn on to your front, hands behind your back.'

Response: 'I'm shot!'

Rebus to himself: 'Bastard's only wounded. Finish him off.'

Jack Morton unconscious. Rebus knew better than to move him. He could staunch the bleeding, that was all. Removed his jacket, folded it and pressed it to his friend's chest. Must've hurt, but Jack was out of it. Rebus dug the fuel rod out of his own pocket, the tiny canister still warm. Pressed it into Jack's right hand, curled the fingers around it.

'Stick around, pal. Just keep sticking around.'

Siobhan Clarke at the doorway, tears welling in her eyes.

Rebus pushed past her, slid his way across the road to where the Armed Response Team were cuffing the wounded man. Nobody much bothering with his dead partner. A little group of onlookers, keeping their distance. Rebus walked right up to the corpse, prised the handgun from its fingers, walked back around the front of the car. Heard someone call out: 'He's got a gun!'

Rebus bending down until the barrel of the gun touched the back of the wounded man's neck. Declan from the shop: breath coming in short gasps, hair matted with sweat, burrowing his face into the tarmac.

'John …'

Claverhouse. No megaphone needed. Standing right behind him. 'You really want to be like them?'

Like them … Like Mean Machine. Like Telford and Cafferty and Tarawicz. He'd crossed the line before, made several trips forth and back. His foot was on Declan's neck, the gun barrel so hot it was singeing nape-skin.

'Please, no … oh, Christ, please … don't … don't …'

'Shut up,' Rebus hissed. He felt Claverhouse's hand close over his, flick on the safety.

'My responsibility, John. My fuck-up, don't make it yours, too.'

'Jack …'

'I know.'

Rebus's vision blurred. 'They're getting away.'

Claverhouse shook his head. 'Road blocks. Back-up are already on it.'

'And Telford?'

Claverhouse checked his watch. 'Ormie will be picking him up right about now.'

Rebus grabbed Claverhouse's lapels. 'Nail him!'

Sirens nearing. Rebus shouted for the drivers to move their cars, make room for the ambulance. Then he ran back to the gatehouse. Siobhan Clarke was kneeling beside Jack, stroking his forehead. Her face was streaked with tears. She looked up at Rebus and shook her head.

'He's gone,' she said.

'No.' But he knew the truth. Which didn't stop him saying the word over and over again.

35

They divided the gang between two different locations –
Torphichen and Fettes – and took Telford and a few of his
'lieutenants' to St Leonard's. Result: a logistical nightmare.
Claverhouse was washing Pro-Plus down with double-
strength coffee, part of him wanting to do things right, the
other part knowing he was answerable for the blood-bath at
Maclean's. One officer dead, six wounded or otherwise
injured – one of them seriously. One gunman dead, one
wounded – not seriously enough to some people's minds.

The getaway cars had been apprehended and arrests
made – shots exchanged but no bloodshed. None of the
gang was saying anything, not a single damned word.

Rebus was sitting in an empty Interview Room at St
Leonard's, arms on the table, head resting on arms. He'd
been sitting there for a while, just thinking about loss,
about how suddenly it could strike. A life, a friendship, just
snatched away.

Irretrievable.

He hadn't cried, and didn't think he would. Instead, he
felt numb, as if his soul had been spiked with novocaine.
The world seemed to have slowed, like the mechanism was
running down. He wondered if the sun would have the
energy to rise again.

And I got him into it.

He had wallowed before in feelings of guilt and
inadequacy, but nothing to measure up to this. This was
overwhelming. Jack Morton, a copper with a quiet patch in

Falkirk ... murdered in Edinburgh because a friend had asked a favour. Jack Morton, who'd brought himself back to life by swearing off cigarettes and booze, getting into shape, eating right, taking *care* of himself ... Lying in the mortuary, deep-body temperature dropping.

And I put him there.

He jumped up suddenly, threw the chair at the wall. Gill Templer walked into the room.

'All right, John?'

He wiped his mouth with the back of his hand.

'Fine.'

'My office is empty if you want to get your head down.'

'No, I'll be fine. Just ...' He looked around. 'Is this place needed?'

She nodded.

'Right. Okay.' He picked up the chair. 'Who is it?'

'Brian Summers,' she said.

Pretty-Boy. Rebus straightened his back.

'I can make him talk.'

Templer looked sceptical.

'Honest, Gill.' Hands trembling. 'He doesn't know what I've got on him.'

She folded her arms. 'And what's that?'

'I just need ...' He checked his watch. 'An hour or so; two hours tops. Bobby Hogan needs to be here. And I want Colquhoun brought in pronto.'

'Who's he?'

Rebus found the business card and handed it over. 'Pronto,' he repeated. He worked at his tie, making himself presentable. Smoothed back his hair. Said nothing.

'John, I'm not sure you're in any state to ...'

He pointed at her, turned it into a wagging finger. 'Don't presume, Gill. If I say I can break him, I mean it.'

'No one else has said a single word.'

'Summers will be different.' He stared at her. 'Believe me.'

Looking back at him, she believed. 'I'll hold him back till Hogan gets here.'

'Thanks, Gill.'

'And, John?'

'Yes?'

'I'm really sorry about Jack Morton. I didn't know him, but I've heard what everyone's saying.'

Rebus nodded.

'They're saying he'd be the last one to blame you.'

Rebus smiled. 'Right at the back of the queue.'

'There's only one person in the queue, John,' she said quietly. 'And you're it.'

Rebus phoned the night-desk at the Caledonian Hotel, learned that Sakiji Shoda had checked out unexpectedly, less than two hours after Rebus had dropped off the green folder which had cost him fifty-five pence at a stationer's on Raeburn Place. Actually, the folders had come in three-packs at one sixty-five. He had the other two in his car, only one of them empty.

Bobby Hogan was on his way. He lived in Portobello. He said to give him half an hour. Bill Pryde came over to Rebus's desk and said how sorry he was about Jack Morton, how he knew the two of them had been old friends.

'Just don't get too close to me, Bill,' Rebus told him. 'The people closest to me tend to lose their health.'

He got a message from reception: someone there to see him. He headed downstairs, found Patience Aitken.

'Patience?'

She had all her clothes on, but not necessarily in the right order, like she'd dressed in a power-cut.

'I heard on the radio,' she said. 'I couldn't sleep, so I had the radio on, and they said about this police raid and how people were dead … And you weren't in your flat, so I …'

He hugged her. 'I'm okay,' he whispered. 'I should have called you.'

'It's my fault, I …' She looked at him. 'You were there, I can see it on your face.' He nodded. 'What happened?'

'I lost a friend.'

'Oh, Christ, John.' She hugged him again. She was still warm from the bedclothes. He could smell shampoo on her hair, perfume on her neck. *The people closest to me* … He pulled away gently, planted a kiss on her cheek.

'Go get some sleep,' he told her.

'Come for breakfast.'

'I just want to go home and crash.'

'You could sleep at my place. It's Sunday. We could stay in bed.'

'I don't know what time I'll finish here.'

She found his eyes. 'Don't feed on it, John. Don't keep it all inside.'

'Okay, Doc.' He pecked her cheek again. 'Now vamoose.'

He managed a smile and a wink: both felt treacherous. He stood at the door and watched her leave. A lot of times while he'd been married, he'd thought of just walking. There were times when all the responsibilities and the shite at work and the pressure and the *need* would make him dream of escape.

He was tempted again now. Push open the door and head off to somewhere that wasn't here, to do something that wasn't this. But that, too, would be treachery. He had scores to settle, and a reason to settle them. He knew Telford was somewhere in the building, probably consulting with Charles Groal, saying nothing to anyone else. He wondered how the team were playing it. When would they let Telford know about the tape? When would they tell him the security guard had been a plant? When would they tell him that same man was now dead?

He hoped they were being clever. He hoped they were rattling Telford's cage.

He couldn't help wondering – and not for the first time – if it was all worth it. Some cops treated it like a game, others like a crusade, and for most of the rest it was neither, just a way of earning their daily bread. He asked himself why he'd invited Jack Morton in. Answers: because he'd wanted a *friend* involved, someone who'd keep *him* in the game; because he'd thought Jack was bored, and would enjoy the challenge; because tactics had demanded an outsider. There were plenty of reasons. Claverhouse had asked if Morton had any family, anyone who should be informed. Rebus had told him: divorced, four kids.

Did Rebus blame Claverhouse? Easy to be wise after the event, but then Claverhouse's reputation had been built on being wise *before* the event. And he'd failed ... monumentally.

Icy roads: they'd needed the gates closed. The blockade had been too easy to move with the horsepower available to a truck.

Marksmen in the building: fine in the enclosed space of the yard, but they'd failed to keep the truck there, and the marksmen had been ineffectual once the truck had reversed out.

More armed officers *behind* the truck: producing little but a crossfire hazard.

Claverhouse should have got them to turn off the ignition, or – better still – waited for it to be turned off before making his presence known.

Jack Morton should have kept his head down.

And Rebus should have warned him.

Only, a shout would have turned the gunmen's attention towards him. Cowardice: was that what was at the bottom of his feelings? Simple human cowardice. Like in the bar in Belfast, when he hadn't said anything, fearing Mean Machine's wrath, fearing a rifle-butt turned on *him*. Maybe that was why – no, *of course* that was why – Lintz had got beneath Rebus's skin. Because when it came down to it, if Rebus had been in Villefranche ... drunk on failure, the dream of conquest over ... if he'd been under orders, just a lackey with a gun ... if he'd been primed by racism and the loss of comrades ... who was to say what he'd have done?

'Christ, John, how long have you been out here?'

It was Bobby Hogan, touching his face, prising the folder from frozen fingers.

'You're like ice, man, let's get you inside.'

'I'm fine,' Rebus breathed. And it had to be true: how else to explain the sweat on his back and his brow? How else to explain that he only started shivering *after* Bobby led him indoors?

Hogan got two mugs of sweet tea into him. The station was still buzzing: shock, rumour, theories. Rebus filled Hogan in.

'They'll have to let Telford walk, if nobody talks.'

'What about the tape?'

'They'll want to spring that later ... if they're being canny.'

'Who's in with him?'

Rebus shrugged. 'Farmer Watson himself, last time I heard. He was doing a double-act with Bill Pryde, but I saw Bill later, so they've either taken a break or else done a swop.'

Hogan shook his head. 'What a fucking business.'

Rebus stared at his tea. 'I hate sugar.'

'You drank the first mug all right.'

'Did I?' He took a mouthful, squirmed.

'What the hell did you think you were doing out there?'

'Catching a breath.'

'Catching your death more like.' Hogan patted down an unruly clump of hair. 'I had a visit from a man called Harris.'

'What are you going to do?'

Hogan shrugged. 'Let it go, I suppose.'

Rebus stared at him. 'You might not have to.'

36

Colquhoun didn't look happy to be there.

'Thanks for coming in,' Rebus told him.

'I didn't have much choice.' He had a solicitor sitting beside him, a middle-aged man: one of Telford's? Rebus couldn't have cared less.

'You might have to get used to not having choices, Dr Colquhoun. Know who else is in here tonight? Tommy Telford; Brian Summers.'

'Who?'

Rebus shook his head. 'You're getting your script wrong. It's okay for you to know who they are: we talked about them in front of Candice.'

Colquhoun's face flushed.

'You remember Candice, don't you? Her real name's Karina: did I ever tell you that? She's got a son somewhere, only they took him away. Maybe she'll find him one day, maybe not.'

'I don't see what this –'

'Telford and Summers are going to be spending a while behind bars.' Rebus sat back. 'If I want to, I could have a damned good go at putting you in there with them. How would you like that, Dr Colquhoun? Conspiracy to pervert, et cetera.'

Rebus could feel himself relaxing into his work; doing it for Jack.

The solicitor was about to say something, but Colquhoun got in first. 'It was a mistake.'

'A mistake?' Rebus hooted. 'One way of putting it, I suppose.' He sat forward, resting his elbows on the table. 'Time to talk, Dr Colquhoun. You know what they say about confession ...'

Brian 'Pretty-Boy' Summers looked immaculate.

He had a lawyer with him, too, a senior partner who looked like an undertaker and wasn't taking kindly to being kept waiting. As they settled at the table in the Interview Room, and Hogan slotted tapes into cassette machine and video recorder, the lawyer started the protest he'd spent the past hour or two preparing in his head.

'On behalf of my client, Inspector, I feel duty bound to say that this is some of the most appalling behaviour I've –'

'You think you've seen appalling behaviour?' Rebus answered. 'In the words of the song, you ain't seen nothing yet.'

'Look, it's clear to me that you –'

Rebus ignored him, slapped the folder down on to the table, slid it towards Pretty-Boy.

'Take a look.'

Pretty-Boy was wearing a charcoal suit and purple shirt, open at the neck. No sunglasses or car-keys. He'd been brought in from his flat in the New Town. Comment from one of the men who'd gone to fetch him: 'Biggest hi-fi I've seen in my life. Bugger was wide awake, listening to Patsy Cline.'

Rebus started whistling 'Crazy': that got Pretty-Boy's attention and a wry smile, but he kept his arms folded.

'I would if I were you,' Rebus said.

'Ready,' Hogan said, meaning he had the tapes running. They went through the formalities: date and time, location, individuals present. Rebus looked towards the lawyer and smiled. He looked pretty expensive. Telford would have ordered the best, same as always.

'Know any Elton John, Brian?' Rebus asked. 'He's got this song: "Someone Saved My Life Tonight". You'll be singing it to me once you've looked inside.' He tapped the folder. 'Go on, you know it makes sense. I'm not playing some trick, and you don't have to say anything. But you really should do yourself a favour ...'

'I've got nothing to say.'

Rebus shrugged. 'Just open the folder, take a look.'

Pretty-Boy looked to his lawyer, who seemed uncertain.

'Your client won't be incriminating himself,' Rebus explained. 'If you want to read what's in there first, that's fine. It might not mean much to you, but go ahead.'

The lawyer opened the folder, found a dozen sheets of paper.

'Sorry in advance for any mistakes,' Rebus said. 'I typed it in a bit of a rush.'

Pretty-Boy didn't so much as glance towards the material. He kept his eyes on Rebus, while the lawyer sifted through the papers.

'These allegations,' the lawyer finally said, 'you must realise they're worthless?'

'If that's your opinion, fair enough. I'm not asking Mr Summers to admit or deny anything. Like I said, he can do a deaf and dumb routine for all I care, so long as he uses his *eyes*.'

A smile from Pretty-Boy, then a glance towards his lawyer, who shrugged his shoulders, saying there was nothing here to fear. A glance back at Rebus, and Pretty-Boy unfolded his arms, picked up the first sheet, and started reading.

'Just so we have a record for the tape,' Rebus said, 'Mr Summers is now reading a draft report prepared by myself earlier today.' Rebus paused. 'Actually, I mean yesterday, Saturday. He's reading my interpretation of recent events in and around Edinburgh, events concerning his employer,

Thomas Telford, a Japanese business consortium — which is really, in my opinion, a Yakuza front — and a gentleman from Newcastle by the name of Jake Tarawicz.'

He paused. The lawyer said: 'Agreed, thus far.' Rebus nodded and continued.

'My version of events is as follows. Jake Tarawicz became an associate of Thomas Telford only because he wanted something Telford had: namely, a slick operation to bring drugs into Britain without raising suspicion. Either that or it was only later on, once their relationship had become established, that Tarawicz decided he could move in on Telford's turf. To facilitate this, he manufactured a war between Telford and Morris Gerald Cafferty. This was easily accomplished. Telford had moved in aggressively on Cafferty's territory, probably with Tarawicz egging him on. All Tarawicz had to do was make sure things escalated. To this end, he had one of his men attack a drug dealer outside one of Telford's night-clubs, Telford immediately placing the blame on Cafferty. He also had some of his men attack a Telford stronghold in Paisley. Meanwhile, there were attacks on Cafferty's territory and associates, retaliation by Telford for perceived wrongs.'

Rebus cleared his throat, took a sip of tea — a fresh cup, no sugar.

'Does this sound familiar, Mr Summers?' Pretty-Boy said nothing. He was busy reading. 'My guess is that the Japanese were never meant to become involved. In other words, they had no knowledge of what was happening. Telford was showing them around, easing the way for them as they tried to buy a country club. Rest and recreation for their members, plus a good way of laundering money — less suspect than a casino or similar operation, especially when an electronics factory is about to open, so that the Yakuza slip into the country as just a few more Japanese businessmen.

'I think when Tarawicz saw this, he began to worry. He didn't want to get rid of Tommy Telford just to leave the way open for other competitors to muscle in. So he decided they'd have to become part of his plan. He had Matsumoto followed. He had him killed, and in a nice twist made *me* the chief suspect. Why? Two reasons. First, Tommy Telford had me pegged as Cafferty's man, so by fingering me, Tarawicz was fingering Cafferty. Second, he wanted me out of the game, because I'd gone to Newcastle, and had met one of his men, a guy called William 'The Crab' Colton. I knew the Crab of old, and it so happened Tarawicz had used him for the hit on the drug dealer. He didn't want me putting two and two together.'

Rebus paused again. 'How's it sounding, Brian?'

Pretty-Boy had finished reading. His arms were folded again, eyes on Rebus.

'We've yet to see any evidence, Inspector,' the lawyer said.

Rebus shrugged. 'I don't need evidence. See, the same file you've got there, I delivered a copy to a Mr Sakiji Shoda at the Caledonian Hotel.' Rebus watched Pretty-Boy's eyelids flutter. 'Now, the way I see it, Mr Shoda is going to be a bit pissed off. I mean, he's already pissed off, that's why he was here. He'd seen Telford screw up, and wanted to see if he could do anything *right*. I don't suppose the raid on Maclean's will have given him any renewed sense of confidence. But he was also here to find out why one of his men had been killed, and who was responsible. This report tells him Tarawicz was behind it, and if he chooses to believe that, he'll go after Tarawicz. In fact, he checked out of his hotel yesterday evening – seems he was in a bit of a rush. I'm wondering if he was on his way home via Newcastle. Doesn't matter. What matters is that he'll *still* be pissed off at Telford for letting it happen. And meantime Jake Tarawicz is going to be wondering who shopped him to Shoda. The Yakuza are not nice people, Brian. You lot are nursery school by comparison.' Rebus sat back in his chair.

'One last point,' he said. 'Tarawicz's base is Newcastle. I'm betting he had eyes and ears here in Edinburgh. In fact, I know he did. I've just been having a chat with Dr Colquhoun. You remember him, Brian? You'd heard about him from Lintz. Then when Tarawicz offered East Europeans as working girls, you reckoned maybe Tommy should have a few foreign phrases to hand. Colquhoun did the teaching. You told him stories about Tarawicz, about Bosnia. Catch was, he's the only person round these parts who knew the subject, so when we picked up Candice, we ended up using him, too. Colquhoun sussed straight off what was happening. He wasn't sure if he had anything to fear: he'd never met her, and her answers were reassuringly vague – or he kept them that way. All the same, he came to you. Your solution: ship Candice to Fife, then snatch her, and take Colquhoun out of the game till the heat died.'

Rebus smiled. 'He told *you* about Fife. Yet it was *Tarawicz* who got Candice. I think Tommy will find that a bit odd, don't you? So, here we sit. And I can tell you that the minute you walk out of here, you're going to be a marked man. Could be the Yakuza, could be Cafferty, could be your own boss or Tarawicz himself. You haven't got any friends, and nowhere's safe any more.' Rebus paused. 'Unless *we* help you. I've talked to Chief Superintendent Watson, and he's agreeing to witness protection, new identity, whatever you want. There may be a short sentence to serve – just so it looks right – but it'll be a soft option, room of your own, no other prisoners allowed near. And afterwards, you'll be home and dry. That's a big commitment on our part, and we'll need a big commitment from *you*. We'll want everything.' Rebus counted off on his fingers. 'The drug shipments, the war with Cafferty, the

392

Newcastle connection, the Yakuza, the prostitutes.' He paused again, drained his tea. 'Tall order, I know. Your boss had a meteoric rise, Brian, and he nearly made it. But that's all over. Best thing you can do now is talk. It's either that or spend the rest of your days waiting for the bullet or the machete to strike ...'

The lawyer started to protest. Rebus held up a hand.

'We'll need all of it, Brian. Including Lintz.'

'Lintz,' Pretty-Boy said dismissively. 'Lintz is nothing.'

'So where's the harm?'

The look in Pretty-Boy's eyes was a mix of anger, fear and disorientation. Rebus stood up.

'I need something else to drink. What about you gentlemen?'

'Coffee,' the lawyer said, 'black, no sugar.'

Pretty-Boy hesitated, then said, 'Get me a Coke.' And at that point – for the very first time – Rebus knew a deal might be done. He stopped the interview, Hogan switched off the tapes, and both men left the room. Hogan patted him on the back.

Farmer Watson was coming along the corridor towards them. Rebus moved to meet him, leading them away from the door.

'I think we might be in with a shout, sir,' Rebus said. 'He'll try to twist the deal, give us less than we want, but I think there's a chance.'

Watson beamed a smile, as Rebus leaned against the wall, eyes closed. 'I feel about a hundred years old.'

'Experience tells,' Hogan said.

Rebus growled at him, then they went to fetch the drinks.

'Mr Summers,' the lawyer said, as Rebus handed him his cup, 'would like to tell you the story of his relationship with Joseph Lintz. But first we'll need some assurances.'

'What about everything else I mentioned?'

'These can be negotiated.'

Rebus stared at Pretty-Boy. 'You don't trust me?'

Pretty-Boy picked up his can, said 'No', and drank.

'Fine.' Rebus walked over to the far wall. 'In that case, you're free to go.' He checked his watch. 'Soon as you've finished your drinks, I want you out of here. Interview Rooms are at a premium tonight. DI Hogan, mark up the tapes, will you?'

Hogan ejected both cassettes. Rebus sat down beside him and they started discussing work, as though Pretty-Boy had been dismissed from their minds. Hogan examined a sheet of paper, checking who was due to be interviewed next.

From the corner of his eye, Rebus saw Pretty-Boy leaning in towards his lawyer, whispering something. He turned on them.

'Can you do that outside, please? We need to vacate this room.'

Pretty-Boy *knew* Rebus was bluffing ... knew the policeman needed him. But he realised, too, that Rebus was *not* bluffing about giving the file to Shoda, and he was far too intelligent not to be scared. He didn't move from the chair, and held his lawyer's arm so he had to stay and listen. Eventually the lawyer cleared his throat.

'Inspector, Mr Summers is willing to answer your questions.'

'*All* my questions?'

The lawyer nodded. 'But I must insist on hearing more of the "deal" you're proposing.'

Rebus looked at Hogan. 'Go get the Chief Super.'

Rebus left the room, stood in the hallway while Hogan was away. Cadged a cigarette off a passing uniform. He'd just got it lit when Farmer Watson came barrelling towards him, Hogan behind as though attached to Watson by an invisible leash.

'No smoking, John, you know that.'

'Yes, sir,' Rebus said, crimping the tip. 'I was just holding it for Inspector Hogan.'

Watson nodded towards the door. 'What do they want?'

'We've been talking possible immunity from prosecution. At the very least, he'll want a soft sentence, and a safe one, plus new ID afterwards.'

Watson was thoughtful. 'We haven't had a cheep out of any of them. Not that it matters greatly. There's the gang we caught red-handed, plus Telford on the audio tape ...'

'Summers is a real insider, knows Telford's organisation.'

'So how come he's willing to spill?'

'Because he's scared, and his fear is overwhelming his loyalty. I'm not saying we'll get every last detail out of him, but we'll probably get enough to start pressing the other members. Once they know someone's yapping, they'll all want a trade.'

'What's his lawyer like?'

'Expensive.'

'No point shilly-shallying then.'

'I couldn't have put it better myself, sir.'

The Chief Super pinned back his shoulders. 'All right, let's do a deal.'

'When did you first meet Joseph Lintz?'

Pretty-Boy's arms were no longer folded. He was resting them on the desk, head in his hands. His hair flopped forward, making him look younger than ever.

'About six months ago. We'd spoken on the phone before that.'

'He was a punter?'

'Yes.'

'Meaning what exactly?'

Pretty-Boy looked at the turning spools. 'You want me to explain for all our listeners?'

'That's right.'

'Joseph Lintz was a client of the escort service for which I worked.'

'Come on, Brian, you were a bit more than a flunkey. You ran it, didn't you?'

'If you say so.'

'Anytime you want to walk, Brian ...'

Eyes burning. 'Okay, I *ran* it for my employer.'

'And Mr Lintz phoned wanting an escort?'

'He wanted one of our girls to go to his home.'

'And?'

'And that was it. He'd sit there opposite her and just stare for half an hour.'

'Both of them fully clothed?'

'Yes.'

'Nothing else?'

'Not at first.'

'Ah.' Rebus paused. 'You must have been curious.'

Pretty-Boy shrugged. 'Takes all sorts, doesn't it?'

'I suppose it does. So how did your business relationship progress?'

'Well, on a gig like that, there's always a chaperone.'

'Yourself?'

'Yes.'

'You didn't have better things to do?'

Another shrug. 'I was curious.'

'About what?'

'The address: Heriot Row.'

'Mr Lintz had ... class?'

'Coming out his ears. I mean, I've met plenty fat cats, corporate types looking for a shag in their hotel, but Lintz was a long way from that.'

'He just wanted to look at the girls.'

'That's right. And this huge house he had …'

'You went in? You didn't just wait in the car?'

'Told him it was company policy.' A smile. 'Really, all I wanted was to snoop.'

'Did you talk to him?'

'Later, yes.'

'You became friends?'

'Not really … maybe. He knew things, had a real brain on him.'

'You were impressed.'

Pretty-Boy nodded. Yes, Rebus could imagine. His previous role model had always been Tommy Telford, but Pretty-Boy had aspirations. He *wanted* class. He wanted people to acknowledge him for his mind. Rebus knew how seductive Lintz's storytelling could be. How much more seductive would Pretty-Boy have found it?

'Then what happened?'

Pretty-Boy shifted. 'His tastes changed.'

'Or his real tastes started to emerge?'

'That's what I wondered.'

'So what did he want?'

'He wanted the girls … he had this length of rope … he'd made it into a noose.' Pretty-Boy swallowed. His lawyer had stopped writing, was listening intently. 'He wanted the girls to slip it over their heads, then lie down like they were dead.'

'Dressed or naked?'

'Naked.'

'And?'

'And he'd … he'd sit on his chair and get off. Some of the girls wouldn't go along. He wanted the works: bulging eyes, tongue sticking out, neck twisted …' Pretty-Boy rubbed his hands through his hair.

'Did you ever talk about it?'

'With him? No, never.'

'So what did you talk about?'

'All sorts of things.' Pretty-Boy looked up at the ceiling, laughed. 'He told me once, he believed in God. Said the problem was, he wasn't sure God believed in him. That seemed clever at the time ... he always managed to get me thinking. And this was the same guy who tossed himself off over bodies with ropes round their necks.'

'All this personal attention you were giving him,' Rebus said, 'you were sizing him up, weren't you?'

Pretty-Boy looked into his lap, nodded.

'For the tape, please.'

'Tommy always wanted to know if a punter was worth squeezing.'

'And ... ?'

Pretty-Boy shrugged. 'We found out about the Nazi stuff, realised we couldn't hurt him any more than he was already being hurt. Turned into a bit of a joke. There we were, thinking of threatening him with exposure as a perv, and at the same time the papers were saying he was a mass murderer.' He laughed again.

'So you dropped that idea?'

'Yes.'

'But he paid you five grand?' Rebus fishing.

Pretty-Boy licked his lips. 'He'd tried topping himself. He told me that. Tying the rope to the top of his banister and jumping off. Only it didn't work. Banister snapped and he fell half a flight.'

Rebus remembering: the broken stair-rail.

Rebus remembering: Lintz with a scarf around his neck, his voice hoarse. Telling Rebus he had a throat bug.

'He told you this?'

'He phoned the office, said we had to meet. That was unusual. In the past, he'd always used phone boxes and got me on my mobile. Safe old bugger, I'd always thought. Then he calls from home, right to the office.'

'Where did you meet?'

'In a restaurant. He bought me lunch.' The young woman ... 'Told me he'd tried killing himself and couldn't do it. He kept saying he'd proved himself a "moral coward", whatever that means.'

'So what did he want?'

Pretty-Boy stared up at Rebus. 'He needed someone to help him.'

'You?'

Pretty-Boy shrugged.

'And the price was right?'

'No haggling necessary. He wanted it done in Warriston Cemetery.'

'Did you ask him why?'

'I knew he liked the place. We met at his house, really early. I drove him down there. He seemed the same as ever, except he kept thanking me for my "resolve". I wasn't sure what he meant by that. To me, Resolve is something you take after a hard night.'

Rebus smiled, as was expected. 'Go on,' he said.

'Not much more to tell, is there? *He* put the noose over his head. *He* told me to pull on the rope. I had a last go at talking him out of it, but the bugger was determined. It's not murder, is it? Assisted suicide: a lot of places, it's legal.'

'How did the dunt get on his head?'

'He was heavier than I thought. First time I hauled him up, the rope slipped and he fell, thumped himself on the ground.'

Bobby Hogan cleared his throat. 'Brian, did he say anything ... right at the end?'

'Famous last words and all that?' Pretty-Boy shook his head. 'All he said was "thank you". Poor old sod. One thing: he wrote it all down.'

'What?'

'About me helping him. A sort of insurance, in case

anyone ever linked us. Letter says he paid me, begged me to help.'

'Where is this?'

'In a safe. I can get it for you.'

Rebus nodded, stretched his back. 'Did you ever talk about Villefranche?'

'A little bit, mostly about the way the papers and TV were hounding him, how difficult it made it when he wanted … company.'

'But not the massacre itself?'

Pretty-Boy shook his head. 'Know something else? Even if he *had* told me, I wouldn't tell you.'

Rebus tapped his pen against the desk. He knew the Lintz story was as closed as it was ever going to be. Bobby Hogan knew it, too. They had the secret at last, the story of how Lintz had died. They knew he'd been helped by the Rat Line, but they'd never know whether he'd been Josef Linzstek or not. The circumstantial evidence was overwhelming, but so was the evidence that Lintz had been hounded to death. He'd started putting the escorts into nooses only *after* the accusations had been made.

Hogan caught Rebus's eye and shrugged, as if to say: what does it matter? Rebus nodded back. Part of him wanted to take a break, but now that Pretty-Boy was rolling it was important to keep up the steam.

'Thanks for that, Mr Summers. We may come back to Mr Lintz if we think of any more questions. But meantime, let's move on to the relationship between Thomas Telford and Jake Tarawicz.'

Pretty-Boy shifted, as if trying to get comfortable. 'This could take a while,' he said.

'Take as long as you like,' Rebus told him.

37

They got it all, in time.

Pretty-Boy had to rest, and so did they. Other teams came in, worked on different areas. The tapes were filling up, being listened to elsewhere, notes and transcripts made. Back-up questions were forwarded to the Interview Room. Telford wasn't talking. Rebus went and took a look at him, sat across from him. Telford didn't blink once. He sat ramrod-straight, hands on knees. And all the while, Pretty-Boy's confession was being used to squeeze other gang members – without letting slip who was singing.

The ranks broke, slowly at first and then in a cataract of accusation, self-defence and denial. And they got it all.

Telford and Tarawicz: European prostitutes heading north; muscle and dope heading south.

Mr Taystee: taking more than his fair share; dealt with accordingly.

The Japanese: using Telford as their introduction to Scotland, finding it a good base of operations.

Only now Rebus had scuppered that. In his folder to Shoda he'd warned the gangster to leave Poyntinghame alone, or he'd be 'implicated in ongoing criminal investigations'. The Yakuza weren't stupid. He doubted they'd be back ... for a while at least.

His last trip of the night: Rebus went down to the cells, unlocked one of the doors and told Ned Farlowe he was free. Told him he had nothing to fear ...

Unlike Mr Pink Eyes. The Yakuza had a score to settle.

And it didn't stay unsettled long. He was found in his car-crusher, seatbelt welded shut. His men had started running.

Some of them were running still.

Rebus sat in his living-room, staring at the door Jack Morton had stripped and varnished. He was thinking about the funeral, about how the Juice Church would be there in force. He wondered if they'd blame him. Jack's kids would be there, too. Rebus had never met them; didn't think he wanted to see them.

Wednesday morning, he was back in Inverness, meeting Mrs Hetherington off her flight. She'd been delayed in Holland, answering Customs questions. They'd laid a little trap, caught a man called De Gier — a known trafficker — planting the kilo package of heroin in Mrs Hetherington's luggage: a secret compartment in her suitcase, the suitcase itself a gift from her landlord. Several of Telford's other elderly tenants were enjoying short breaks in Belgium. They'd be questioned by local police.

Home again, Rebus telephoned David Levy.

'Lintz committed suicide,' he told him.

'That's your conclusion?'

'It's the truth. No conspiracy, no cover-up.'

A sigh. 'It's of little consequence, Inspector. What matters is that we've lost another one.'

'Villefranche doesn't mean a thing to you, does it? The Rat Line, that's all you care about.'

'There's nothing we can do about Villefranche.'

Rebus took a deep breath. 'A man called Harris came to see me. He works for British Intelligence. They're protecting some big names, high-level people. Rat Line survivors, maybe their children. Tell Mayerlink to keep digging.'

There was silence for a moment. 'Thank you, Inspector.'

Rebus was in a car. It was the Weasel's Jag. The Weasel

was in the back with him. Their driver was missing a big chunk of his left ear. The shape made him resemble a pixie – but only from the side, and you wouldn't want to tell him to his face.

'You did well,' the Weasel was saying. 'Mr Cafferty's pleased.'

'How long have you been holding him?'

The Weasel smiled. 'Nothing gets past you, Rebus.'

'Rangers have offered me a trial in goal. How long have you had him?'

'A few days. Had to be sure we had the right one, didn't we?'

'And now you're sure?'

'Absolutely positive.'

Rebus looked out of the window at the passing parade of shops, pedestrians, buses. The car was heading down towards Newhaven and Granton. 'You wouldn't be setting up some loser to take the blame?'

'He's genuine.'

'You could have spent the past few days making sure he was going to say the right things.'

The Weasel seemed amused. 'Such as?'

'Such as that he was in Telford's pay.'

'Rather than Mr Cafferty's, you mean?' Rebus glared at the Weasel, who laughed. 'I think you'll find him a pretty convincing candidate.'

The way he said it made Rebus shiver. 'He's still alive, isn't he?'

'Oh, yes. How long he remains so is entirely up to you.'

'You think I want him dead?'

'I know you do. You didn't go to Mr Cafferty because you wanted justice. You went out of *revenge*.'

Rebus stared at the Weasel. 'You don't sound like yourself.'

'You mean I don't sound like my persona – different thing entirely.'

'And do many people get behind the persona?' The Who: 'Can You See the Real Me?'

The Weasel smiled again. 'I thought you deserved it, after all the trouble you've gone to.'

'I didn't break Telford just to please your boss.'

'Nevertheless ...' The Weasel slid across his seat towards Rebus. 'How's Sammy, by the way?'

'She's fine.'

'Recuperating?'

'Yes.'

'That's good news. Mr Cafferty will be pleased. He's disappointed you haven't been to see him.'

Rebus took a newspaper from his pocket. It was folded at a story: FATAL STABBING AT JAIL.

'Your boss?' he said, handing the paper over.

The Weasel made show of reading it. ' "Aged twenty-six, from Govan ... stabbed through the heart in his cell ... no witnesses, no weapon recovered despite a thorough search." ' He tutted. 'Bit careless.'

'He'd taken up the contract on Cafferty?'

'Had he?' The Weasel looked amazed.

'Fuck off,' Rebus said, turning back to his window.

'By the way, Rebus, if you decide not to go to trial with the driver ...' The Weasel was holding something out. A homemade screwdriver, filed to a point, grip covered in packing-tape. Rebus looked at it in disgust.

'I washed the blood off,' the Weasel assured him. Then he laughed again. Rebus felt like he was being ferried straight to hell. In front of him he could see the grey expanse of the Firth of Forth, and Fife beyond it. They were coming into an area of docks, gas-plant and ware-houses. It had been earmarked for a development spill-over from Leith. The whole city was changing. Traffic routes and priorities were altered overnight, cranes were kept busy on building-sites, and the council, who always complained about being broke, had all manner of schemes underway to further alter the shape and scope of his chosen home.

'Nearly there,' the Weasel said.

Rebus wondered if there'd be any turning back.

They stopped at the gates to a warehouse complex. The driver undid the padlock, pulled the chain free. The gates swung open. In they went. The Weasel ordered the driver to park around the back. There was a plain white van there, more rust than metal. Its back windows had been painted over, turning it into a suitable hearse should occasion demand.

They got out into a salt wind. The Weasel shuffled over towards a door and banged once. The door was pushed open from within. They stepped inside.

A huge open space, filled with only a few packing cases, a couple of pieces of machinery covered with oil-cloth. And two men: the one who'd let them in, and another at the far end. This man was standing in front of a wooden chair. There was a figure tied to the chair, half-hidden by the man. The Weasel led the procession. Rebus tried to control his breathing, which was growing painfully shallow. His heart was racing, nerves jangling. He pushed back the anger, wasn't sure he could hold it.

When they were eight feet from the chair, the Weasel nodded and the man stood away, revealing to Rebus the terrified figure of a kid.

A boy.

Nine or ten, no older.

One black eye, nose caked with blood, both cheeks bruised and a graze on his chin. Burst lip beginning to heal, trousers torn at the knees, one shoe missing.

And a smell, as if he'd wet himself, maybe even worse.

'What the hell is this?' Rebus asked.

'This,' the Weasel said, 'is the little bastard who stole the car. This is the little bastard who lost his nerve at a red light and gunned through it, losing control of the pedals because he could barely reach them. This ...' The Weasel stepped forward, planted a hand on the kid's shoulder. 'This is the culprit.'

Rebus looked at the faces around him. 'Is this your idea of a joke?'

'No joke, Rebus.'

He looked at the boy. Dried tear-tracks. Eyes bloodshot from crying. Shoulders trembling. They'd tied his arms behind him. Tied his ankles to the chair-legs.

'Puh-please, mister ...' Dry, cracked voice. 'I ... help me, puh-please ...'

'Nicked the car,' the Weasel recited, 'then did the hit and run, got scared, and dumped the car near where he lives. Took the cassette and the tapes. He wanted the car for a race. That's what they do, race cars around the schemes. This little runt can start an engine in ten seconds flat.' He rubbed his hands together. 'So ... here we all are.'

'Help me ...'

Rebus recalling the city's graffiti: Won't Anyone Help? The Weasel nodding towards one of his men, the man producing a pickaxe-handle.

'Or the screwdriver,' the Weasel said. 'Or whatever you like, really. We are at your command.' And he gave a little bow.

Rebus could hardly speak. 'Cut the ropes.'

Silence in the warehouse.

'*Cut those fucking ropes!*'

A sniff from the Weasel. 'You heard the man, Tony.'

Ca-chink of a flick-knife opening. Ropes severed like cutting through butter. Rebus walked to within inches of the boy.

'What's your name?'

'J-Jordan.'

'Is that your first name or your second?'

The boy looked at him. 'First.'

'Okay, Jordan.' Rebus leaned down. The boy flinched, but did not resist as Rebus picked him up. He weighed almost nothing. Rebus started walking with him.

'What now, Rebus?' the Weasel asked. But Rebus didn't answer. He carried the boy to the threshold, kicked open the door, stepped out into sunshine.

'I'm ... I'm really sorry.' The boy had a hand across his eyes, unused to the light. He was starting to cry.

'You know what you did?'

Jordan nodded. 'I've been ... ever since that night. I knew it was bad ...' Now the tears came.

'Did they say who I was?'

'Please don't kill me.'

'I'm not going to kill you, Jordan.'

The boy blinked, trying to clear tears from his eyes, the better to know whether he was being lied to.

'I think you've been through enough, pal,' Rebus said. Then added: 'I think we both have.'

So after everything, it had come to this. Bob Dylan: 'Simple Twist of Fate'. Segue to Leonard Cohen: 'Is This What You Wanted?'

Rebus didn't know the answer to that.

38

Clean and sober, he went to the hospital. An open ward this time, set hours for visitors. No more darkened vigils. No return visit by Candice, though nurses spoke of regular phone calls by someone foreign-sounding. No way of knowing where she was. Maybe out there searching for her son. It didn't matter, so long as she was safe. So long as she was in control.

When he reached the ward's far end, two women rose from their chairs so he could kiss them: Rhona and Patience. He had a carrier-bag with him, magazines and grapes. Sammy was sitting up, supported by three pillows, Pa Broon propped beside her. Her hair had been washed and brushed, and she was smiling at him.

'Women's magazines,' he said, shaking his head. 'They should be on the top-shelf.'

'I need a few fantasies to sustain me in here,' Sammy said. Rebus beamed at her, said hello, then bent down and kissed his daughter.

The sun was shining as they walked through The Meadows – a rare day off for both. They held hands and watched people sunbathing and playing football. He knew Rhona was excited, and thought he knew why. But he wasn't going to spoil things with speculation.

'If you had a daughter, what would you call her?' she asked.

He shrugged. 'Haven't really thought about it.'

'What about a son?'

'I quite like Sam.'

'Sam?'

'When I was a kid, I had a bear called Sam. My mum knitted it for me.'

'Sam …' She tried the name out. 'It would work both ways, wouldn't it?'

He stopped, circled his arms around her waist. 'How do you mean?'

'Well, it could be Samuel or Samantha. You don't get many of those – names that work both ways.'

'I suppose not. Rhona, is there …?'

She put a finger to his lips, then kissed him. They walked on. There didn't seem to be a cloud in the whole damned sky.

Afterword

My fictional French village of Villefranche d'Albarede owes its existence to the real village of Oradour-sur-Glâne, which was the subject of an attack by the 3rd Company of the SS 'Der Führer' regiment.

On the afternoon of Saturday 10 June 1944, 3rd Company – known as 'Das Reich' – entered the village and rounded up everyone. The women and children were herded into the church, while the men were split into groups and marched to various barns and other buildings around the village. Then the slaughter began.

Some 642 victims have been accounted for, but the estimate is that up to a thousand people may have perished that day. Only fifty-three corpses were ever identified. One boy from Lorraine, having first-hand knowledge of SS atrocities, managed to flee when the troops entered the village. Five men escaped the massacre in Laudy's barn. Wounded, they were able to crawl from the burning building and hide until the next day. One woman escaped from the church, climbing out of a window after playing dead beside the corpse of her child.

Soldiers went from house to house, finding villagers too sick or elderly to leave their beds. These people were shot and their houses set alight. Some of the bodies were hidden in mass graves, or dumped down wells and in bread ovens.

General Lammerding was the commanding officer. On 9 June he'd ordered the deaths of ninety-nine hostages in Tulle. He also gave the order for the Oradour massacre.

Later on in the war, Lammerding was captured by the British, who refused his extradition to France. Instead, he was returned to Düsseldorf, where he ran a successful company until his death in 1971.

In the general euphoria of the Normandy landings, the tragedy at Oradour went almost unnoticed. Eventually, in January 1953, the trial opened in Bordeaux of sixty-five men identified as having been involved in the massacre. Of these sixty-five, only twenty-one were present: seven Germans, and fourteen natives of French Alsace. None of the men was of officer rank.

Every individual found guilty at the Bordeaux trial left court a free man. A special Act of Amnesty had been passed, in the interests of national unity. (People in Alsace were disgruntled that their countrymen had been picked out for condemnation.) Meantime, the Germans were said to have already served their terms.

As a result, Oradour broke off all relations with the French state, a rupture which lasted seventeen years.

In May 1983, a man stood trial in East Berlin, charged with having been a lieutenant in 'Das Reich' during the Oradour massacre. He admitted everything, and was sentenced to life imprisonment.

In June 1996, it was reported that around 12,000 foreign volunteers to the Waffen SS are still receiving pensions from the Federal German government. One of these pensioners, a former Obersturmbannführer, was a participant at Oradour ...

Oradour still stands as a shrine. The village has been left just the way it was on that day in June 1944.

Hide & Seek

To Michael Shaw,
not before time

'My devil had long been caged, he came out roaring.'
— *The Strange Case of Dr Jekyll and Mr Hyde*

'Hide!'

He was shrieking now, frantic, his face drained of all colour. She was at the top of the stairs, and he stumbled towards her, grabbing her by the arms, propelling her downstairs with unfocussed force, so that she feared they would both fall. She cried out.

'Ronnie! Hide from who?'

'Hide!' he shrieked again. 'Hide! They're coming! They're coming!'

He had pushed her all the way to the front door now. She'd seen him pretty strung out before, but never this bad. A fix would help him, she knew it would. And she knew, too, that he had the makings upstairs in his bedroom. The sweat trickled from his chilled rat's-tails of hair. Only two minutes ago, the most important decision in her life had been whether or not to dare a trip to the squat's seething lavatory. But now. . . .

'They're coming,' he repeated, his voice a whisper now. 'Hide.'

'Ronnie,' she said, 'you're scaring me.'

He stared at her, his eyes seeming almost to recognise her. Then he looked away again, into a distance all of his own. The word was a snakelike hiss.

'Hide.' And with that he yanked open the door. It was raining outside, and she hesitated. But then fear took her, and she made to cross the threshold. But his hand grabbed at her arm, pulling her back inside. He embraced her, his

1

sweat sea-salty, his body throbbing. His mouth was close to her ear, his breath hot.

'They've murdered me,' he said. Then with sudden ferocity he pushed her again, and this time she was outside, and the door was slamming shut, leaving him alone in the house. Alone with himself. She stood on the garden path, staring at the door, trying to decide whether to knock or not.

It wouldn't make any difference. She knew that. So instead she started to cry. Her head slipped forward in a rare show of self-pity and she wept for a full minute, before, breathing hard three times, she turned and walked quickly down the garden path (such as it was). Someone would take her in. Someone would comfort her and take away the fear and dry her clothes.

Someone always did.

John Rebus stared hard at the dish in front of him, oblivious to the conversation around the table, the background music, the flickering candles. He didn't really care about house prices in Barnton, or the latest delicatessen to be opened in the Grassmarket. He didn't much want to speak to the other guests – a female lecturer to his right, a male bookseller to his left – about ... well, whatever they'd just been discussing. Yes, it was the perfect dinner party, the conversation as tangy as the starter course, and he was glad Rian had invited him. Of course he was. But the more he stared at the half lobster on his plate, the more an unfocussed despair grew within him. What had he in common with these people? Would they laugh if he told the story of the police alsatian and the severed head? No, they would not. They would smile politely, then bow their heads towards their plates, acknowledging that he was ... well, *different* from them.

'Vegetables, John?'

It was Rian's voice, warning him that he was not 'taking part', was not 'conversing' or even looking interested. He accepted the large oval dish with a smile, but avoided her eyes.

She was a nice girl. Quite a stunner in an individual sort of way. Bright red hair, cut short and pageboyish. Eyes deep, striking green. Lips thin but promising. Oh yes, he liked her. He wouldn't have accepted her invitation otherwise. He fished about in the dish for a piece of broccoli that wouldn't break into a thousand pieces as he tried to manoeuvre it onto his plate.

'Gorgeous food, Rian,' said the bookseller, and Rian smiled, accepting the remark, her face reddening slightly. That was all it took, John. That was all you had to say to make this girl happy. But in his mouth he knew it would come out sounding sarcastic. His tone of voice was not something he could suddenly throw off like a piece of clothing. It was a part of him, nurtured over a course of years. So when the lecturer agreed with the bookseller, all John Rebus did was smile and nod, the smile too fixed, the nod going on a second or two too long, so that they were all looking at him again. The piece of broccoli snapped into two neat halves above his plate and splattered onto the tablecloth.

'Shite!' he said, knowing as the word escaped his lips that it was not quite appropriate, not quite the *right* word for the occasion. Well, what was he, a man or a thesaurus?

'Sorry,' he said.

'Couldn't be helped,' said Rian. My God, her voice was cold.

It was the perfect end to a perfect weekend. He'd gone shopping on Saturday, ostensibly for a suit to wear tonight. But had baulked at the prices, and bought some books instead, one of which was intended as a gift to Rian: *Doctor Zhivago*. But then he'd decided he'd like to read it himself first, and so had brought flowers and chocolates instead, forgetting her aversion to lilies (*had he known in*

3

the first place?) and the diet she was in the throes of starting. Damn. And to cap it all, he'd tried a new church this morning, another Church of Scotland offering, not too far from his flat. The last one he'd tried had seemed unbearably cold, promising nothing but sin and repentance, but this latest church had been the oppressive opposite: all love and joy and what was there to forgive anyway? So he'd sung the hymns, then buggered off, leaving the minister with a handshake at the door and a promise of future attendance.

'More wine, John?'

This was the bookseller, proffering the bottle he'd brought himself. It wasn't a bad little wine, actually, but the bookseller had talked about it with such unremitting pride that Rebus felt obliged to decline. The man frowned, but then was cheered to find this refusal left all the more for himself. He replenished his glass with vigour.

'Cheers,' he said.

The conversation returned to how busy Edinburgh seemed these days. Here was something with which Rebus could agree. This being the end of May, the tourists were almost in season. But there was more to it than that. If anyone had told him five years ago that in 1989 people would be emigrating north from the south of England to the Lothians, he'd have laughed out loud. Now it was fact, and a fit topic for the dinner table.

Later, much later, the couple having departed, Rebus helped Rian with the dishes.

'What was wrong with you?' she said, but all he could think about was the minister's handshake, that confident grip which bespoke assurances of an afterlife.

'Nothing,' he said. 'Let's leave these till morning.'

Rian stared at the kitchen, counting the used pots, the half-eaten lobster carcasses, the wine glasses smudged with grease.

'Okay,' she said. 'What did you have in mind instead?'

4

He raised his eyebrows slowly, then brought them down low over his eyes. His lips broadened into a smile which had about it a touch of the leer. She became coy.

'Why, Inspector,' she said. 'Is that supposed to be some kind of a clue?'

'Here's another,' he said, lunging at her, hugging her to him, his face buried in her neck. She squealed, clenched fists beating against his back.

'Police brutality!' she gasped. 'Help! Police, help!'

'Yes, madam?' he inquired, carrying her by the waist out of the kitchen, towards where the bedroom and the end of the weekend waited in shadow.

Late evening at a building site on the outskirts of Edinburgh. The contract was for the construction of an office development. A fifteen-foot-high fence separated the works from the main road. The road, too, was of recent vintage, built to help ease traffic congestion around the city. Built so that commuters could travel easily from their country-side dwellings to jobs in the city centre.

There were no cars on the road tonight. The only sound came from the slow chug-chugging of a cement mixer on the site. A man was feeding it spadefuls of grey sand and remembering the far distant days when he had laboured on a building site. Hard graft it had been, but honest.

Two other men stood above a deep pit, staring down into it.

'Should do it,' one said.

'Yes,' the other agreed. They began walking back to the car, an ageing purple Mercedes.

'He must have some clout. I mean, to get us the keys to this place, to set all this up. Some clout.'

'Ours is not to ask questions, you know that.' The man who spoke was the oldest of the three, and the only Calvinist. He opened the car boot. Inside, the body of a frail teenager lay crumpled, obviously dead. His skin was the colour of pencil shading, darkest where the bruises lay.

'What a waste,' said the Calvinist.

'Aye,' the other agreed. Together they lifted the body from the boot, and carried it gently towards the hole. It dropped softly to the bottom, one leg wedging up against the sticky clay sides, a trouser leg slipping to show a naked ankle.

'All right,' the Calvinist said to the cement man. 'Cover it, and let's get out of here. I'm starving.'

Monday

For close on a generation, no one had appeared to drive away these random visitors or to repair their ravages

What a start to the working week.

The housing estate, what he could see of it through the rain-lashed windscreen, was slowly turning back into the wilderness that had existed here before the builders had moved in many years ago. He had no doubt that in the 1960s it, like its brethren clustered around Edinburgh, had seemed the perfect solution to future housing needs. And he wondered if the planners ever learned through anything other than hindsight. If not, then perhaps today's 'ideal' solutions were going to turn out the same way.

The landscaped areas comprised long grass and an abundance of weeds, while children's tarmacadamed playgrounds had become bombsites, shrapnel glass awaiting a tripped knee or stumbling hand. Most of the terraces boasted boarded-up windows, ruptured drainpipes pouring out teeming rainwater onto the ground, marshy front gardens with broken fences and missing gates. He had the idea that on a sunny day the place would seem even more depressing.

Yet nearby, a matter of a few hundred yards or so, some developer had started building private apartments. The hoarding above the site proclaimed this a LUXURY DEVELOPMENT, and gave its address as MUIR VILLAGE. Rebus wasn't fooled, but wondered how many young buyers would be. This was Pilmuir, and always would be. This was the dumping ground.

There was no mistaking the house he wanted. Two

9

police cars and an ambulance were already there, parked next to a burnt-out Ford Cortina. But even if there hadn't been this sideshow, Rebus would have known the house. Yes, it had its boarded-up windows, like its neighbours on either side, but it also had an open door, opening into the darkness of its interior. And on a day like this, would any house have its door flung wide open were it not for the corpse inside, and the superstitious dread of the living who were incarcerated with it?

Unable to park as close to this door as he would have liked, Rebus cursed under his breath and pushed open the car door, throwing his raincoat over his head as he made to dash through the stiletto shower. Something fell from his pocket onto the verge. Scrap paper, but he picked it up anyway, screwing it into his pocket as he ran. The path to the open door was cracked and slick with weeds, and he almost slipped and fell, but reached the threshold intact, shaking the water from him, awaiting the welcoming committee.

A constable put his head around a doorway, frowning.

'Detective Inspector Rebus,' said Rebus by way of introduction.

'In here, sir.'

'I'll be there in a minute.'

The head disappeared again, and Rebus looked around the hall. Tatters of wallpaper were the only mementoes of what had once been a home. There was an overpowering fragrance of damp plaster, rotting wood. And behind all that, a sense of this being more of a cave than a house, a crude form of shelter, temporary, unloved.

As he moved further into the house, passing the bare stairwell, darkness embraced him. Boards had been hammered into all the window-frames, shutting out light. The intention, he supposed, had been to shut out squatters, but Edinburgh's army of homeless was too great and too wise. They had crept in through the fabric of the place. They had made it their den. And one of their number had died here.

The room he entered was surprisingly large, but with a low ceiling. Two constables held thick rubber torches out to illuminate the scene, casting moving shadows over the plasterboard walls. The effect was of a Caravaggio painting, a centre of light surrounded by degrees of murkiness. Two large candles had burnt down to the shapes of fried eggs against the bare floorboards, and between them lay the body, legs together, arms outstretched. A cross without the nails, naked from the waist up. Near the body stood a glass jar, which had once contained something as innocent as instant coffee, but now held a selection of disposable syringes. Putting the fix into crucifixion, Rebus thought with a guilty smile.

The police doctor, a gaunt and unhappy creature, was kneeling next to the body as though about to offer the last rites. A photographer stood by the far wall, trying to find a reading on his light meter. Rebus moved in towards the corpse, standing over the doctor.

'Give us a torch,' he said, his hand commanding one from the nearest constable. He shone this down across the body, starting at the bare feet, the bedenimed legs, a skinny torso, ribcage showing through the pallid skin. Then up to the neck and face. Mouth open, eyes closed. Sweat looked to have dried on the forehead and in the hair. But wait. . . . Wasn't that moisture around the mouth, on the lips? A drop of water suddenly fell from nowhere into the open mouth. Rebus, startled, expected the man to swallow, to lick his parched lips and return to life. He did not.

'Leak in the roof,' the doctor explained, without looking up from his work. Rebus shone the torch against the ceiling, and saw the damp patch which was the source of the drip. Unnerving all the same.

11

'Sorry I took so long to get here,' he said, trying to keep his voice level. 'So what's the verdict?'

'Overdose,' the doctor said blandly. 'Heroin.' He shook a tiny polythene envelope at Rebus. 'The contents of this sachet, if I'm not mistaken. There's another full one in his right hand.' Rebus shone his torch towards where a lifeless hand was half clutching a small packet of white powder.

'Fair enough,' he said. 'I thought everyone chased the dragon these days instead of injecting.'

The doctor looked up at him at last.

'That's a very naive view, Inspector. Go talk to the Royal Infirmary. They'll tell you how many intravenous abusers there are in Edinburgh. It probably runs into hundreds. That's why we're the AIDS capital of Britain.'

'Aye, we take pride in our records, don't we? Heart disease, false teeth, and now AIDS.'

The doctor smiled. 'Something you might be interested in,' he said. 'There's bruising on the body. Not very distinct in this light, but it's there.'

Rebus squatted down and shone the torch over the torso again. Yes, there was bruising all right. A lot of bruising.

'Mainly to the ribs,' the doctor continued. 'But also some to the face.'

'Maybe he fell,' Rebus suggested.

'Maybe,' said the doctor.

'Sir?' This from one of the constables, his eyes and voice keen. Rebus turned to him.

'Yes, son?'

'Come and look at this.'

Rebus was only too glad of the excuse to move away from the doctor and his patient. The constable was leading him to the far wall, shining his torch against it as he went. Suddenly, Rebus saw why.

On the wall was a drawing. A five-pointed star,

encompassed by two concentric circles, the largest of them some five feet in diameter. The whole had been well drawn, the lines of the star straight, the circles almost exact. The rest of the wall was bare.

'What do you think, sir?' asked the constable.

'Well, it's not just your usual graffiti, that's for sure.'

'Witchcraft?'

'Or astrology. A lot of druggies go in for all sorts of mysticism and hoodoo. It goes with the territory.'

'The candles. . . .'

'Let's not jump to conclusions, son. You'll never make CID that way. Tell me, why are we all carrying torches?'

'Because the electric's been cut off.'

'Right. Ergo, the need for candles.'

'If you say so, sir.'

'I do say so, son. Who found the body?'

'I did, sir. There was a telephone call, female, anonymous, probably one of the other squatters. They seem to have cleared out in a hurry.'

'So there was nobody else here when you arrived?'

'No, sir.'

'Any idea yet who he is?' Rebus nodded the torch towards the corpse.

'No, sir. And the other houses are all squats, too, so I doubt we'll get anything out of them.'

'On the contrary. If anyone knows the identity of the deceased, they're the very people. Take your friend and knock on a few doors. But be casual, make sure they don't think you're about to evict them or anything.'

'Yes, sir.' The constable seemed dubious about the whole venture. For one thing, he was sure to get an amount of hassle. For another, it was still raining hard.

'On you go,' Rebus chided, but gently. The constable shuffled off, collecting his companion on the way.

Rebus approached the photographer.

'You're taking a lot of snaps,' he said.

'I need to in this light, to make sure at least a few come out.'

'Bit quick off the mark in getting here, weren't you?'

'Superintendent Watson's orders. He wants pictures of any drugs-related incidents. Part of his campaign.'

'That's a bit gruesome, isn't it?' Rebus knew the new Chief Superintendent, had met him. Full of social awareness and community involvement. Full of good ideas, and lacking only the manpower to implement them. Rebus had an idea.

'Listen, while you're here, take one or two of that far wall, will you?'

'No problem.'

'Thanks.' Rebus turned to the doctor. 'How soon will we know what's in that full packet?'

'Later on today, maybe tomorrow morning at the latest.'

Rebus nodded to himself. What was his interest? Maybe it was the dreariness of the day, or the atmosphere in this house, or the positioning of the body. All he knew was that he felt something. And if it turned out to be just a damp ache in his bones, well, fair enough. He left the room and made a tour of the rest of the house.

The real horror was in the bathroom.

The toilet must have blocked up weeks before. A plunger lay on the floor, so some cursory attempt had been made to unblock it, but to no avail. Instead, the small, splattered sink had become a urinal, while the bath had become a dumping ground for solids, upon which crawled a dozen large and jet-black flies. The bath had also become a skip, filled with bags of refuse, bits of wood. . . . Rebus didn't stick around, pulling the door tight shut behind him. He didn't envy the council workmen who would eventually have to come and fight the good fight against all this decay.

One bedroom was completely empty, but the other

14

boasted a sleeping bag, damp from the drips coming through the roof. Some kind of identity had been imposed upon the room by the pinning of pictures to its walls. Up close, he noticed that these were original photographs, and that they comprised a sort of portfolio. Certainly they were well taken, even to Rebus's untrained eye. A few were of Edinburgh Castle on damp, misty days. It looked particularly bleak. Others showed it in bright sunshine. It still looked bleak. One or two were of a girl, age indeterminate. She was posing, but grinning broadly, not taking the event seriously.

Next to the sleeping bag was a bin-liner half filled with clothes, and next to this a small pile of dog-eared paperbacks: Harlan Ellison, Clive Barker, Ramsey Campbell. Science fiction and horror. Rebus left the books where they were and went back downstairs.

'All finished,' the photographer said. 'I'll get those photos to you tomorrow.'

'Thanks.'

'I also do portrait work, by the way. A nice family group for the grandparents? Sons and daughters? Here, I'll give you my card.'

Rebus accepted the card and pulled his raincoat back on, heading out to the car. He didn't like photographs, especially of himself. It wasn't just that he photographed badly. No, there was more to it than that.

The sneaking suspicion that photographs really could steal your soul.

On his way back to the station, travelling through the slow midday traffic, Rebus thought about how a group photograph of his wife, his daughter and him might look. But no, he couldn't visualise it. They had grown so far apart, ever since Rhona had taken Samantha to live in London. Sammy still wrote, but Rebus himself was slow at responding, and she seemed to take umbrage at this, writing less and less herself. In her last letter she had hoped Gill and he were happy.

He hadn't the courage to tell her that Gill Templer had left him several months ago. Telling Samantha would have been fine: it was the idea of Rhona's getting to hear of it that he couldn't stand. Another notch in his bow of failed relationships. Gill had taken up with a disc jockey on a local radio station, a man whose enthusing voice Rebus seemed to hear whenever he entered a shop or a filling station, or passed the open window of a tenement block.

He still saw Gill once or twice a week of course, at meetings and in the station-house, as well as at scenes of crimes. Especially now that he had been elevated to her rank.

Detective Inspector John Rebus.

Well, it had taken long enough, hadn't it? And it was a long, hard case, full of personal suffering, which had brought the promotion. He was sure of that.

He was sure, too, that he wouldn't be seeing Rian again. Not after last night's dinner party, not after the fairly unsuccessful bout of lovemaking. *Yet another* unsuccessful bout. It had struck him, lying next to Rian, that her eyes were almost identical to Inspector Gill Templer's. A surrogate? Surely he was too old for that.

'Getting old, John,' he said to himself.

Certainly he was getting hungry, and there was a pub just past the next set of traffic lights. What the hell, he was entitled to a lunch break.

The Sutherland Bar was quiet, Monday lunchtime being one of the lowest points of the week. All money spent, and nothing to look forward to. And of course, as Rebus was quickly reminded by the barman, the Sutherland did not exactly cater for a lunchtime clientele.

'No hot meals,' he said, 'and no sandwiches.'

'A pie then,' begged Rebus, '*any*thing. Just to wash down the beer.'

'If it's food you want, there's plenty of cafes around here. This particular pub happens to sell beers, lagers and spirits. We're not a chippie.'

'What about crisps?'

The barman eyed him for a moment. 'What flavour?'

'Cheese and onion.'

'We've run out.'

'Well, ready salted then.'

'No, they're out too.' The barman had cheered up again.

'Well,' said Rebus in growing frustration, 'what in the name of God *have* you got?'

'Two flavours. Curry, or egg, bacon and tomato.'

'*Egg?*' Rebus sighed. 'All right, give me a packet of each.'

The barman stooped beneath the counter to find the smallest possible bags, past their sell-by dates if possible.

'Any nuts?' It was a last desperate hope. The barman looked up.

'Dry roasted, salt and vinegar, chilli flavour,' he said.

'One of each then,' said Rebus, resigned to an early death. 'And another half of eighty-shillings.'

He was finishing this second drink when the bar door shuddered open and an instantly recognisable figure entered, his hand signalling for refreshment before he was even halfway through the door. He saw Rebus, smiled, and came to join him on one of the high stools.

'Hello, John.'

'Afternoon, Tony.'

Inspector Anthony McCall tried to balance his prodigious bulk on the tiny circumference of the bar stool, thought better of it, and stood instead, one shoe on the foot-rail, and both elbows on the freshly wiped surface of the bar. He stared hungrily at Rebus.

'Give us one of your crisps.'

When the packet was offered, he pulled out a handful and stuffed them into his mouth.

'Where were you this morning then?' said Rebus. 'I'd to take one of your calls.'

'The one at Pilmuir? Ach, sorry about that, John. Heavy night last night. I had a bit of a hangover this morning.' A pint of murky beer was placed in front of him. 'Hair of the dog,' he said, and took four slow gulps, reducing it to a quarter of its former size.

'Well, I'd nothing better to do anyway,' said Rebus, sipping at his own beer. 'Christ, those houses down there are a mess though.'

McCall nodded thoughtfully. 'It wasn't always like that, John. I was born there.'

'Really?'

'Well, to be exact, I was born on the estate that was there before this one. It was so bad, so they said, that they levelled it and built Pilmuir instead. Bloody hell on earth it is now.'

'Funny you should say that,' said Rebus. 'One of the young uniformed kids thought there might be some kind of occult tie-in.' McCall looked up from his drink. 'There was a black-magic painting on the wall,' Rebus explained. 'And candles on the floor.'

'Like a sacrifice?' McCall offered, chuckling. 'My wife's dead keen on all those horror films. Gets them out of the video library. I think she sits watching them all day when I'm out.'

'I suppose it must go on, devil worship, witchcraft. It can't *all* be in the imagination of the Sunday newspaper editors.'

'I know how you might find out.'

'How?'

'The university,' said McCall. Rebus frowned, disbelieving. 'I'm serious. They've got some kind of department

18

that studies ghosts and all that sort of thing. Set up with money from some dead writer.' McCall shook his head. 'Incredible what people will do.'

Rebus was nodding. 'I *did* read about that, now you mention it. Arthur Koestler's money, wasn't it?'

McCall shrugged.

'Arthur Daley's more my style,' he said, emptying his glass.

Rebus was studying the pile of paperwork on his desk when the telephone rang.

'DI Rebus.'

'They said you were the man to talk to.' The voice was young, female, full of unfocussed suspicion.

'They were probably right. What can I do for you, miss . . .?'

'Tracy. . . .' The voice fell to a whisper on the last syllable of the name. She had already been tricked into revealing herself. 'Never mind who I am!' She had become immediately hysterical, but calmed just as quickly. 'I'm phoning about that squat in Pilmuir, the one where they found. . . .' The voice trailed off again.

'Oh yes.' Rebus sat up and began to take notice. 'Was it you who phoned the first time?'

'What?'

'To tell us that someone had died there.'

'Yes, it was me. Poor Ronnie. . . .'

'Ronnie being the deceased?' Rebus scribbled the name onto the back of one of the files from his in-tray. Beside it he wrote 'Tracy – caller'.

'Yes.' Her voice had broken again, near to tears this time.

'Can you give me a surname for Ronnie?'

'No.' She paused. 'I never knew it. I'm not sure Ronnie was even his real name. Hardly anyone uses their real name.'

'Tracy, I'd like to talk to you about Ronnie. We can do it over the telephone, but I'd rather it was face to face. Don't worry, you're not in any trouble –'

'But I *am*. That's why I called. Ronnie told me, you see.'

'Told you what, Tracy?'

'Told me he'd been murdered.'

The room around Rebus seemed suddenly to vanish. There was only this disconnected voice, the telephone, and him.

'He said that to you, Tracy?'

'Yes.' She was crying now, sniffing back the unseen tears. Rebus visualised a frightened little girl, just out of school, standing in a distant callbox. 'I've got to hide,' she said at last. 'Ronnie said over and over that I should hide.'

'Shall I bring my car and fetch you? Just tell me where you are.'

'No!'

'Then tell me how Ronnie was killed. You know how we found him?'

'Lying on the floor by the window. That's where he was.'

'Not quite.'

'Oh yes, that's where he was. By the window. Lying wrapped up into a little ball. I thought he was just sleeping. But when I touched his arm he was cold. . . . I went to find Charlie, but he'd gone. So I just panicked.'

'You say Ronnie was lying in a ball?' Rebus had begun to draw pencilled circles on the back of the file.

'Yes.'

'And this was in the living room?'

She seemed confused. 'What? No, not in the living room. He was upstairs, in his bedroom.'

'I see.' Rebus kept on drawing effortless circles. He was trying to imagine Ronnie dying, but not really dead, crawling downstairs after Tracy had fled, ending up in the living room. That might explain those bruises. But the candles. . . . . He had been so perfectly positioned between them. . . . 'And when was this?'

'Late last night, I don't know exactly when. I panicked. When I calmed down, I phoned for the police.'

'What time was it when you phoned?'

She paused, thinking. 'About seven this morning.'

'Tracy, would you mind telling this to some other people?'

'Why?'

'I'll tell you when I pick you up. Just tell me where you are.'

There was another pause while she considered this. 'I'm back in Pilmuir,' she said finally. 'I've moved into another squat.'

'Well,' said Rebus, 'you don't want me to come down there, do you? But you must be quite close to Shore Road. What about us meeting there?'

'Well. . . . '

'There's a pub called the Dock Leaf,' continued Rebus, giving her no time to debate. 'Do you know it?'

'I've been kicked out of it a few times.'

'Me too. Okay, I'll meet you outside it in an hour. All right?'

'All right.' She didn't sound over-enthusiastic, and Rebus wondered if she would keep the appointment. Well, what of it? She sounded straight enough, but she might just be another casualty, making it up to draw attention to herself, to make her life seem more interesting than it was.

But then he'd had a feeling, hadn't he?

'All right,' she said, and the connection was severed.

Shore Road was a fast road around the north coast of the city. Factories, warehouses, and vast DIY and home furnishing stores were its landmarks, and beyond them lay the Firth of Forth, calm and grey. On most days, the coast of Fife was visible in the distance, but not today, with a cold mist hanging low on the water. On the other side of the road from the warehouses were the tenements, four-storey predecessors of the concrete high-rise. There was a smattering of corner shops, where neighbour met neighbour, and information was passed on, and a few small unmodernised pubs, where strangers did not go unnoticed for long.

The Dock Leaf had shed one generation of low-life drinkers, and discovered another. Its denizens now were young, unemployed, and living six to a three-bedroom rented flat along Shore Road. Petty crime though was not a problem: you didn't mess your own nest. The old community values still held.

Rebus, early for the meeting, just had time for a half in the saloon bar. The beer was cheap but bland, and everyone seemed to know if not who he was then certainly *what* he was, their voices turned down to murmurs, their eyes averted. When, at three thirty, he stepped outside, the sudden daylight made him squint.

'Are you the policeman?'

'That's right, Tracy.'

She had been standing against the pub's exterior wall. He shaded his eyes, trying to make out her face, and was surprised to find himself looking at a woman of between twenty and twenty-five. Her age was transparent in her face, though her style marked her out as the perennial rebel: cropped peroxide hair, two stud earrings in her left ear (but none in the right), tie-dye T-shirt, tight, faded denims, and red basketball boots. She was tall, as tall as Rebus. As his eyes adjusted to the light, he saw the tear-tracks on either cheek, the old acne scars. But there were also crow's-feet around her eyes, evidence of a life used to laughter. There was no laughter in those olive-green eyes though. Somewhere in Tracy's life a wrong turning had been made, and Rebus had the idea that she was still trying to reverse back to that fork in the road.

The last time he had seen her she had been laughing. Laughing as her semblance curled from the wall of Ronnie's bedroom. She was the girl in the photographs.

'Is Tracy your real name?'

'Sort of.' They had begun to walk. She crossed the road at a zebra crossing, not bothering to check whether any cars were approaching, and Rebus followed her to a wall, where she stopped, staring out across the Forth. She wrapped her arms around herself, examining the lifting mist.

'It's my middle name,' she said.

Rebus leaned his forearms against the wall. 'How long have you known Ronnie?'

'Three months. That's how long I've been in Pilmuir.'

'Who else lived in that house?'

She shrugged. 'They came and went. We'd only been in there a few weeks. Sometimes I'd go downstairs in the morning, and there'd be half a dozen strangers sleeping on the floor. Nobody minded. It was like a big family.'

'What makes you think somebody killed Ronnie?'

She turned towards him angrily, but her eyes were liquid. 'I told you on the phone! He *told* me. He'd been off somewhere and come back with some stuff. He didn't look right though. Usually, when he's got a little smack, he's like a kid at Christmas. But he wasn't. He was scared, acting like a robot or something. He kept telling me to hide, telling me they were coming for him.'

'Who were?'

'I don't know.'

'Was this after he'd taken the stuff?'

'No, that's what's really crazy. This was *before*. He had the packet in his hand. He pushed me out of the door.'

'You weren't there while he was fixing?'

'God no. I hated that.' Her eyes drilled into his. 'I'm not

23

a junkie, you know. I mean, I smoke a little, but never. . . .
You know. . . .'

'Was there anything else you noticed about Ronnie?'

'Like what?'

'Well, the state he was in.'

'You mean the bruises?'

'Yes.'

'He often came back looking like that. Never talked about it.'

'Got in a lot of fights, I suppose. Was he short-tempered?'

'Not with me.'

Rebus sunk his hands into his pockets. A chill wind was whipping up off the water, and he wondered whether she was warm enough. He couldn't help noticing that her nipples were very prominent through the cotton of her T-shirt.

'Would you like my jacket?' he asked.

'Only if your wallet's in it,' she said with a quick smile.

He smiled back, and offered a cigarette instead, which she accepted. He didn't take one for himself. There were only three left out of the day's ration, and the evening stretched ahead of him.

'Do you know who Ronnie's dealer was?' he asked casually, helping her to light the cigarette. With her head tucked into his open jacket, the lighter shaking in her hand, she shook her head. Eventually, the windbreak worked, and she sucked hard at the filter.

'I was never really sure,' she said. 'It was something else he didn't talk about.'

'What did he talk about?'

She thought about this, and smiled again. 'Not much, now you mention it. That was what I liked about him. You always felt there was more to him than he was letting on.'

'Such as?'

She shrugged. 'Might have been anything, might have been nothing.'

This was harder work than Rebus had anticipated, and he really was getting cold. It was time to speed things up.

'He was in the bedroom when you found him?'

'Yes.'

'And the squat was empty at the time?'

'Yes. Earlier on, there'd been a few people there, but they'd all gone. One of them was up in Ronnie's room, but I didn't know him. Then there was Charlie.'

'You mentioned him on the telephone.'

'Yes, well, when I found Ronnie, I went looking for him. He's usually around somewhere, in one of the other squats or in town doing a bit of begging. Christ, he's strange.'

'In what way?'

'Didn't you see what was on the living-room wall?'

'You mean the star?'

'Yes, that was Charlie. He painted it.'

'He's keen on the occult then?'

'Mad keen.'

'What about Ronnie?'

'Ronnie? Jesus, no. He couldn't even stand to watch horror films. They scared him.'

'But he had all those horror books in his bedroom.'

'That was Charlie, trying to get Ronnie interested. All they did was give him more nightmares. And all those did was push him into taking more smack.'

'How did he finance his habit?' Rebus watched a small boat come gliding through the mist. Something fell from it into the water, but he couldn't tell what.

'I wasn't his accountant.'

'Who was?' The boat was turning in an arc, slipping further west towards Queensferry.

'Nobody wants to know where the money comes from, that's the truth. It makes you an accessory, doesn't it?'

'That depends.' Rebus shivered.

'Well, *I* didn't want to know. If he tried to tell me, I put my hands over my ears.'

'He's never had a job then?'

'I don't know. He used to talk about being a photographer. That's what he'd set his heart on when he left school. It was the only thing he wouldn't pawn, even to pay for his habit.'

Rebus was lost. 'What was?'

'His camera. It cost him a small fortune, every penny saved out of his social security.'

Social security: now there was a phrase. But Rebus was sure there had been no camera in Ronnie's bedroom. So add robbery to the list.

'Tracy, I'll need a statement.'

She was immediately suspicious. 'What for?'

'Just so I've got it on record, so we can do something about Ronnie's death. Will you help me do that?'

It was a long time before she nodded. The boat had disappeared. There was nothing floating in the water, nothing left in its wake. Rebus put a hand on Tracy's shoulder, but gently.

'Thanks,' he said. 'The car's this way.'

After she had made her statement, Rebus insisted on driving her home, dropping her several streets from her destination but knowing her address now.

'Not that I can swear to be there for the next ten years,' she had said. It didn't matter. He had given her his work and home telephone numbers. He was sure she would keep in touch.

'One last thing,' he said, as she was about to close the car door. She leaned in from the pavement. 'Ronnie kept shouting "They're coming." Who do you think he meant?'

She shrugged. Then froze, remembering the scene. 'He

was strung out, Inspector. Maybe he meant the snakes and spiders.'

Yes, thought Rebus, as she closed the door and he started the car. And then maybe he meant the snakes and spiders who'd supplied him.

Back at Greater London Road station, there was a message that Chief Superintendent Watson wanted to see him. Rebus called his superior's office.

'I'll come along now, if I may.'

The secretary checked, and confirmed that this would be okay.

Rebus had come across Watson on many occasions since the superintendent's posting had brought him from the far north to Edinburgh. He seemed a reasonable man, if just a little, well, agricultural for some tastes. There were a lot of jokes around the station already about his Aberdonian background, and he had earned the whispered nickname of 'Farmer' Watson.

'Come in, John, come in.'

The Superintendent had risen from behind his desk long enough to point Rebus in the vague direction of a chair. Rebus noticed that the desk itself was meticulously arranged, files neatly piled in two trays, nothing in front of Watson but a thick, newish folder and two sharp pencils. There was a photograph of two young children to one side of the folder.

'My two,' Watson explained. 'They're a bit older than that now, but still a handful.'

Watson was a large man, his girth giving truth to the phrase 'barrel-chested'. His face was ruddy, hair thin and silvered at the temples. Yes, Rebus could picture him in galoshes and a trout-fishing hat, stomping his way across a moor, his collie obedient beside him. But what did he want with Rebus? Was he seeking a human collie?

'You were at the scene of a drugs overdose this morning.' It was a statement of fact, so Rebus didn't

27

bother to answer. 'It should have been Inspector McCall's call, but he was . . . well, wherever he was.'

'He's a good copper, sir.'

Watson stared up at him, then smiled. 'Inspector McCall's qualities are not in question. That's not why you're here. But your being on the scene gave me an idea. You probably know that I'm interested in this city's drugs problem. Frankly, the statistics appal me. It's not something I'd encountered in Aberdeen, with the exception of some of the oil workers. But then it was mostly the executives, the ones they flew in from the United States. They brought their habits, if you'll pardon the pun, with them. But here —' He flicked open the folder and began to pick over some of the sheets. 'Here, Inspector, it's Hades. Plain and simple.'

'Yes, sir.'

'Are you a churchgoer?'

'Sir?' Rebus was shifting uncomfortably in his chair.

'It's a simple enough question, isn't it? Do you go to church?'

'Not regularly, sir. But sometimes I do, yes.' Like yesterday, Rebus thought. And here again he felt like fleeing.

'Someone said you did. Then you should know what I'm talking about when I say that this city is turning into Hades.' Watson's face was ruddier than ever. 'The Infirmary has treated addicts as young as eleven and twelve. Your own brother is serving a prison sentence for dealing in drugs.' Watson looked up again, perhaps expecting Rebus to look shamed. But Rebus's eyes were a fiery glare, his cheeks red not with embarrassment.

'With respect, sir,' he said, voice level but as taut as a wire, 'what has this got to do with me?'

'Simply this.' Watson closed the folder and settled back in his chair. 'I'm putting into operation a new anti-drugs campaign. Public awareness and that sort of thing, coupled with funding for discreet information. I've got the backing, and what's more I've got the *money*. A group of the city's businessmen are prepared to put fifty thousand pounds into the campaign.'

'Very public-spirited of them, sir.'

Watson's face became darker. He leaned forward in his chair, filling Rebus's vision. 'You better bloody believe it,' he said.

'But I still don't see where I –'

'John.' The voice was anodyne now. 'You've had . . . experience. Personal experience. I'd like you to help me front our side of the campaign.'

'No, sir, really –'

'Good. That's agreed then.' Watson had already risen. Rebus tried to stand, too, but his legs had lost all power. He pushed against the armrests with his hands and managed to heave himself upright. Was this the price they were demanding? Public atonement for having a rotten brother? Watson was opening the door. 'We'll talk again, go through the details. But for now, try to tie up whatever you're working on, casenotes up to date, that sort of thing. Tell me what you can't finish, and we'll find someone to take it off your hands.'

'Yes, sir.' Rebus clutched at the proffered hand. It was like steel, cool, dry and crushing.

'Goodbye, sir,' Rebus said, standing in the corridor now, to a door that had already closed on him.

That evening, still numb, he grew bored with television and left his flat, planning to drive around a bit, no real destination in mind. Marchmont was quiet, but then it always was. His car sat undisturbed on the cobbles outside his tenement. He started it up and drove, entering the centre of town, crossing to the New Town. At Canonmills he stopped in the forecourt of a petrol station and filled the car, adding a torch, some batteries, and several bars of chocolate to his purchases, paying by credit card.

He ate the chocolate as he drove, trying not to think of the next day's cigarette ration, and listened to the car radio. Gill Templer's lover, Calum McCallum, began his broadcast at eight thirty, and he listened for a few minutes. It was enough. The mock-cheery voice, the jokes so lame they needed wheelchairs, the predictable mix of old records and telephone-linked chatter.... Rebus turned the tuning knob until he found Radio Three. Recognising the music of Mozart, he turned up the volume.

He had always known that it would end here of course. He drove through the ill-lit and winding streets, threading his way further into the maze. A new padlock had been fitted to the door of the house, but Rebus had in his pocket a copy of the key. Switching on his torch, he walked quietly into the living room. The floor was bare. There was no sign that a corpse had lain there only ten hours before. The jar of syringes had gone, too, as had the candlesticks. Ignoring the far wall, Rebus left the room and headed upstairs. He pushed open the door of Ronnie's bedroom and walked in, crossing to the window. This was where Tracy said she had found the body. Rebus squatted, resting on his toes, and shone the torch carefully over the floor. No sign of a camera. Nothing. It wasn't going to be made easy for him, this case. Always supposing there *was* a case.

He only had Tracy's word for it, after all.

He retraced his steps, out of the room and towards the stairwell. Something glinted against the top step, right in at the corner of the stairs. Rebus picked it up and examined it. It was a small piece of metal, like the clasp from a cheap brooch. He pushed it into his pocket anyway and took another look at the staircase, trying to imagine

Ronnie regaining consciousness and making his way to the ground floor.

Possible. Just possible. But to end up positioned like that . . .? Much less feasible.

And why bring the jar of syringes downstairs with him? Rebus nodded to himself, sure that he was wandering the maze in something like the right direction. He went downstairs again and into the living room. It had a smell like the mould on an old jar of jam, earthy and sweet at the same time. The earth sterile, the sweetness sickly. He went over to the far wall and shone his torchlight against it.

Then came up short, blood pounding. The circles were still there, and the five-pointed star within them. But there were fresh additions, zodiac signs and other symbols between the two circles, painted in red. He touched the paint. It was tacky. Bringing his fingers away, he shone the torch further up the wall, and read the dripping message:

HELLO RONNIE

Superstitious to his core, Rebus turned on his heels and fled, not bothering to relock the door behind him. Walking briskly towards his car, his eyes turned back in the direction of the house, he fell into someone, and stumbled. The other figure fell awkwardly, and was slow to rise. Rebus switched on his torch, and confronted a teenager, eyes sparkling, face bruised and cut.

'Jesus, son,' he whispered, 'what happened to you?'

'I got beat up,' the boy said, shuffling away on a painful leg.

Rebus made the car somehow, his nerves as thin as old shoelaces. Inside, he locked the door and sat back, closing his eyes, breathing hard. Relax, John, he told himself. Relax. Soon, he was even able to smile at his momentary lapse of courage. Tomorrow he'd come back. In daylight.

He'd seen enough for now.

Tuesday

I have since had reason to believe the cause to lie much deeper in the nature of man, and to turn on some nobler hinge than the principle of hatred.

Sleep did not come easy, but eventually, slumped in his favourite chair, a book propped open on his lap, he must have dozed off, because it took a nine o'clock call to bring him to life.

His back, legs and arms were stiff and aching as he scrabbled on the floor for his new cordless telephone.

'Yes?'

'Lab here, Inspector Rebus. You wanted to know first thing.'

'What have you got?' Rebus slumped back into the warm chair, pulling at his eyes with his free hand, trying to engage their cooperation in this fresh and waking world. He glanced at his watch and realised just how late he'd slept.

'Well, it's not the purest heroin on the street.'

He nodded to himself, confident that his next question hardly needed asking. 'Would it kill whoever injected it?'

The reply jolted him upright.

'Not at all. In fact, it's very clean, all things considered. A bit watered down from its pure form, but that's not uncommon. In fact, it's mandatory.'

'But it would be okay to use?'

'I imagine it would be very good to use.'

'I see. Well, thank you.' Rebus pressed the disconnect button. He had been so sure. So sure. . . . He reached into his pocket, found the number he needed, and pushed the seven digits quickly, before the thought of morning coffee could overwhelm him.

'Inspector Rebus for Doctor Enfield.' He waited. 'Doctor? Fine thanks. How about you? Good, good. Listen, that body yesterday, the druggie on the Pilmuir Estate, any news?' He listened. 'Yes, I'll hold.'

Pilmuir. What had Tony McCall said? It had been lovely once, a place of innocence, something like that. The old days always were though, weren't they? Memory smoothed the corners, as Rebus himself knew well.

'Hello?' he said to the telephone. 'Yes, that's right.' Paper was rustling in the background, Enfield's voice dispassionate.

'Bruising on the body. Fairly extensive. Result of a heavy fall or some kind of physical confrontation. The stomach was almost completely empty. HIV negative, which is something. As for the cause of death, well. . . .'

'The heroin?' Rebus prompted.

'Mmm. Ninety-five percent impure.'

'Really?' Rebus perked up. 'What had it been diluted with?'

'Still working on that, Inspector. But an educated guess would be anything from ground-up aspirin to rat poison, with the emphasis strictly on rodent control.'

'You're saying it was lethal?'

'Oh, absolutely. Whoever sold the stuff was selling euthanasia. If there's more of it about . . . well, I dread to think.'

More of it about? The thought made Rebus's scalp tingle. What if someone were going around poisoning junkies? But why the one perfect packet? One perfect, one as rotten as could be. It didn't make sense.

'Thanks, Doctor Enfield.'

He rested the telephone on the arm of the chair. Tracy had been right in one respect at least. They *had* murdered Ronnie. Whoever 'they' were. And Ronnie had known, known as soon as he'd used the stuff. . . . No, wait. . . .

36

Known *before* he'd used the stuff? Could that be possible? Rebus had to find the dealer. Had to find out why Ronnie had been chosen to die. Been, indeed, sacrificed. . . .

It was Tony McCall's backyard. All right, so he had moved out of Pilmuir, had eventually bought a crippling mortgage which some people called a house. It was a nice house, too. He knew this because his wife told him it was. Told him continually. She couldn't understand why he spent so little time there. After all, as she told him, it was his home too.

Home. To McCall's wife, it was a palace. 'Home' didn't quite cover it. And the two children, son and daughter, had been brought up to tiptoe through the interior, not leaving crumbs or fingerprints, no mess, no breakages. McCall, who had lived a bruising childhood with his brother Tommy, thought it unnatural. His children had grown up in fear and in a swaddling of love – a bad combination. Now Craig was fourteen, Isabel eleven. Both were shy, introspective, maybe even a bit strange. Bang had gone McCall's dream of a professional footballer for a son, an actress for a daughter. Craig played chess a lot, but no physical sports. (He had won a small plaque at school after one tournament. McCall had tried to learn to play after that, but had failed.) Isabel liked knitting. They sat in the too-perfect living room created by their mother, and were almost silent. The clack-clack of needles; the soft movement of chess pieces.

Christ, was it any wonder he kept away?

So here he was in Pilmuir, not checking on anything exactly, just walking. Taking some air. From his own ultra-modern estate, all detached shoeboxes and Volvos, he had to cross some waste ground, avoid the traffic on a busy arterial road, pass a school playing-field and manoeuvre between some factory units to find himself in

Pilmuir. But it was worth the effort. He knew this place; knew the minds that festered here.

He was one of them, after all.

'Hello, Tony.'

He swirled, not recognising the voice, expecting hassle. John Rebus stood there, smiling at him, hands in pockets.

'John! Christ, you made me jump.'

'Sorry. Stroke of luck bumping into you though.' Rebus checked around them, as though looking for someone. 'I tried phoning, but they said it was your day off.'

'Aye, that's right.'

'So what are you doing here?'

'Just walking. We live over that way.' He jerked his head towards the south-west. 'It's not far. Besides, this is my patch, don't forget. Got to keep an eye on the boys and girls.'

'That's why I wanted to speak to you actually.'

'Oh?'

Rebus had begun to walk along the pavement, and McCall, still rattled by his sudden appearance, followed.

'Yes,' Rebus was saying. 'I wanted to ask if you know someone, a friend of the deceased's. The name is Charlie.'

'That's all? Charlie?' Rebus shrugged. 'What does he look like?'

Rebus shrugged again. 'I've no idea, Tony. It was Ronnie's girlfriend Tracy who told me about him.'

'Ronnie? Tracy?' McCall's eyebrows met. 'Who the hell are they?'

'Ronnie is the deceased. That junkie we found on the estate.'

Everything was suddenly clear in McCall's mind. He nodded slowly. 'You work quickly,' he said.

'The quicker the better. Ronnie's girlfriend told me an interesting story.'

'Oh?'

'She said Ronnie was murdered.' Rebus kept on walking, but McCall had stopped.

'Wait a minute!' He caught Rebus up. 'Murdered? Come on, John, you saw the guy.'

'True. With a needle's worth of rat poison scuppering his veins.'

McCall whistled softly. 'Jesus.'

'Quite,' said Rebus. 'And now I need to talk to Charlie. He's young, could be a bit scared, and interested in the occult.'

McCall sorted through a few mental files. 'I suppose there are one or two places we could try looking,' he said at last. 'But it'd be a slog. The concept of neighbourhood policing hasn't quite stretched this far yet.'

'You're saying we won't be made very welcome?'

'Something like that.'

'Well, just give me the addresses and point me in the right direction. It's your day off after all.'

McCall looked slighted. 'You're forgetting, John. This is my patch. By rights, this should be my case, if there is a case.'

'It would've been your case if you hadn't had that hangover.' They smiled at this, but Rebus was wondering whether, in Tony McCall's hands, there *would* have been anything to investigate. Wouldn't Tony just have let it slip? Should he, Rebus, let it slip, too?

'Anyway,' McCall was saying on cue, 'surely you must have better things to do?'

Rebus shook his head. 'Nothing. All my work's been farmed out, with the emphasis on "farmed".'

'You mean Superintendent Watson?'

'He wants me working on his anti-drugs campaign. Me, for Christ's sake.'

'That could be a bit embarrassing.'

'I know. But the idiot thinks I've got "personal experience".'

'He's got a point, I suppose.' Rebus was about to argue, but McCall got in first. 'So you've nothing to do?'

'Not until summoned by Farmer Watson, no.'

'You jammy bugger. Well, that does change things a bit, but not enough, I'm sorry to say. You're my guest here, and you're going to have to put up with me. Until I get bored, that is.'

Rebus smiled. 'I appreciate it, Tony.' He looked around them. 'So, where to first?'

McCall inclined his head back the way they had just come. They turned around and walked.

'So tell me,' said Rebus, 'what's so awful at home that you'd think of coming here on your day off?'

McCall laughed. 'Is it so obvious then?'

'Only to someone who's been there himself.'

'Ach, I don't know, John. I seem to have everything I've never wanted.'

'And it's still not enough.' It was a simple statement of belief.

'I mean, Sheila's a wonderful mother and all that, and the kids never get into trouble, but. . . .'

'The grass is always greener,' said Rebus, thinking of his own failed marriage, of the way his flat was cold when he came home, the way the door would close with a hollow sound behind him.

'Now Tommy, my brother, I used to think he had it made. Plenty of money, house with a jacuzzi, automatic-opening garage. . . .' McCall saw that Rebus was smiling, and smiled himself.

'Electric blinds,' Rebus continued, 'personalised number plate, car phone. . .'

'Time share in Malaga,' said McCall, close to laughter, 'marble-topped kitchen units.'

It was too ridiculous. They laughed out loud as they walked, adding to the catalogue. But then Rebus saw where they were, and stopped laughing, stopped walking.

This was where he'd been heading all along. He touched the torch in his jacket pocket.

'Come on, Tony,' he said soberly. 'There's something I want to show you.'

'He was found here,' Rebus said, shining the torch over the bare floorboards. 'Legs together, lying on his back, arms outstretched. I don't think he got into that position by accident, do you?'

McCall studied the scene. They were both professionals now, and acting almost like strangers. 'And the girlfriend says she found him upstairs?'

'That's right.'

'You believe her?'

'Why would she lie?'

'There could be a hundred reasons, John. Would I know the girl?'

'She hasn't been in Pilmuir long. Bit older than you'd imagine, midtwenties, maybe more.'

'So this Ronnie's already dead, and he's brought downstairs and laid out with the candles and everything.'

'That's right.'

'I'm beginning to see why you need to find the friend who's into the occult.'

'Right. Now come and look at this.' Rebus led McCall to the far wall and shone the torch onto the pentagram, then further up the wall.

'"Hello Ronnie",' McCall read aloud.

'And this wasn't here yesterday.'

'Really?' McCall sounded surprised. 'Kids, John, that's all.'

'Kids didn't draw that pentagram.'

'No, agreed.'

'Charlie drew that pentagram.'

'Right.' McCall slipped his hands into his pockets and

41

drew himself upright. 'Point taken, Inspector. Let's go squat hunting.'

But the few people they found seemed to know nothing, and to care even less. As McCall pointed out, it was the wrong time of day. Everyone from the squats was in the city centre, stealing purses from handbags, begging, shoplifting, doing deals. Reluctantly, Rebus agreed that they were wasting their time.

Since McCall wanted to listen to the tape Rebus had made of his interview with Tracy, they headed back to Great London Road. McCall had the idea that there might be some clue on the tape that would lead them to Charlie, something that would help him place the guy, something Rebus had missed.

Rebus was a weary step or two ahead of McCall as they climbed the front steps to the station's heavy wooden door. A fresh duty officer was beginning his shift at the desk, still fussing with his shirt collar and his clip-on tie. Simple but clever, Rebus thought to himself. Simple but clever. All uniformed officers wore clip-on ties, so that in a clinch, if the attacker tried to yank the officer's head forwards, the tie would simply come away in his hands. Likewise, the desk sergeant's glasses had special lenses which, if hit, would slip out of their frame without shattering. Simple but clever. Rebus hoped that the case of the crucified junkie would be simple.

He didn't feel very clever.

'Hello, Arthur,' he said, passing the desk, making towards the staircase. 'Any messages for me?'

'Give me a break, John. I've only been on two minutes.'

'Fair enough.' Rebus pushed his hands deep into his pockets, where the fingers of his right hand touched something alien, metal. He brought the brooch-clip out and studied it. Then froze.

McCall looked at him, puzzled.

42

'Go on up,' Rebus told him. 'I'll just be a second.'

'Right you are, John.'

Back at the desk, Rebus held his left hand out to the sergeant. 'Do me a favour, Arthur. Give me your tie.'

'What?'

'You heard me.'

Knowing that he would have a story to tell tonight in the canteen, the desk sergeant pulled at his tie. As it came away from his shirt, the clip made a single snapping sound. Simple but clever, thought Rebus, holding the tie between finger and thumb.

'Thanks, Arthur,' he said.

'Anytime, John,' the sergeant called, watching carefully as Rebus walked back towards the stairs. 'Anytime.'

'Know what this is, Tony?'

McCall had seated himself in Rebus's chair, behind Rebus's desk. He had one fist in a drawer, and looked up, startled. Rebus was holding the necktie out in front of him. McCall nodded, then brought his hand out of the drawer. It was curved around a bottle of whisky.

'It's a tie,' he said. 'Got any cups?'

Rebus placed the tie on the desk. He went to a filing cabinet and searched amongst the many cups which sat unloved and uncleaned on top of it. Finally, one seemed to satisfy him, and he brought it to the desk. McCall was studying the cover of a file lying on the desk.

' "Ronnie," ' he read out, ' "Tracy – caller". I see your casenotes are as precise as ever.'

Rebus handed the cup to McCall.

'Where's yours?' asked McCall, pointing to the cup.

'I don't feel like drinking. To tell you the truth, I hardly touch the stuff now.' Rebus nodded at the bottle. 'That's for visitors.' McCall pursed his lips, his eyes opening wide. 'Besides,' Rebus went on, 'I've got the mother and father of a headache. In-laws, too. Kids, neighbours, town and

43

country.' He noticed a large envelope on the desk: PHOTOGRAPHS – DO NOT BEND.

'You know, Tony, when I was a sergeant, this sort of thing would take days to arrive. It's like royalty being an inspector.' He opened the envelope and took out the set of prints, ten by eights, black and white. He handed one to McCall.

'Look,' Rebus said, 'no writing on the wall. And the pentagram's unfinished. Today it was complete.' McCall nodded, and Rebus took back the picture, handing over another in its place. 'The deceased.'

'Poor little sod,' said McCall. 'It could be one of our kids, eh, John?'

'No,' said Rebus firmly. He rolled the envelope into the shape of a tube, and put it in his jacket pocket.

McCall had picked up the tie. He waved it towards Rebus, demanding an explanation.

'Have you ever worn one of those?' Rebus asked.

'Sure, at my wedding, maybe a funeral or a christening. . . .'

'I mean like this. A clip-on. When I was a kid, I remember my dad decided I'd look good in a kilt. He bought me the whole get-up, including a little tartan bow tie. It was a clip-on.'

'I've worn one,' said McCall. 'Everybody has. We all came through the ranks, didn't we?'

'No,' said Rebus. 'Now get out of my bloody chair.'

McCall found another chair, dragging it over from the wall to the desk. Rebus meantime sat down, picking up the tie.

'Police issue.'

'What is?'

'Clip-on ties,' said Rebus. 'Who else wears them?'

'Christ, I don't know, John.'

Rebus threw the clip across to McCall, who was slow to react. It fell to the floor, from where he retrieved it.

'It's a clip-on,' he said.

'I found it in Ronnie's house,' said Rebus. 'At the top of the stairs.'

'So?'

'So someone's tie broke. Maybe when they were dragging Ronnie downstairs. Maybe a police constable someone.'

'You think one of our lot . . .?'

'Just an idea,' said Rebus. 'Of course, it could belong to one of the lads who found the body.' He held out his hand, and McCall gave him back the clip. 'Maybe I'll talk to them.'

'John, what the hell. . . .' McCall ended with a sort of choking sound, unable to find words for the question he wanted to ask.

'Drink your whisky,' said Rebus solicitously. 'Then you can listen to that tape, see if you think Tracy's telling the truth.'

'What are you going to do?'

'I don't know.' He put the desk sergeant's tie in his pocket. 'Maybe I'll tie up a few loose ends.' McCall was pouring out a measure of whisky as Rebus left, but the parting shot, called from the staircase, was loud enough for him to hear.

'Maybe I'll just go to the devil!'

'Yes, a simple pentangle.'

The psychologist, Dr Poole, who wasn't really a psychologist, but rather, he had explained, a lecturer in psychology, quite a different thing, studied the photographs carefully, bottom lip curling up to cover his top lip in a sign of confident recognition. Rebus played with the empty envelope and stared out of the office window. The day was bright, and some students were lying in George Square Gardens, sharing bottles of wine, their text books forgotten.

Rebus felt uncomfortable. Institutes of higher education, from the simplest college up to the present confines of the University of Edinburgh, made him feel stupid. He felt that his every movement, every utterance, was being judged and interpreted, marking him down as a clever man who could have been cleverer, given the breaks.

'When I returned to the house,' he said, 'someone had drawn some symbols between the two circles. Signs of the zodiac, that sort of thing.'

Rebus watched as the psychologist went over to the bookshelves and began to browse. It had been easy to find this man. Making use of him might be more difficult.

'Probably the usual arcana,' Dr Poole was saying, finding the page he wanted and bringing it back to the desk to show Rebus. 'This sort of thing?'

'Yes, that's it.' Rebus studied the illustration. The pentagram was not identical to the one he had seen, but the differences were slight. 'Tell me, are many people interested in the occult?'

'You mean in Edinburgh?' Poole sat down again, pushing his glasses back up his nose. 'Oh yes. Plenty. Look at how well films about the devil do at the box office.'

Rebus smiled. 'Yes, I used to like horror films myself. But I mean an *active* interest.'

The lecturer smiled. 'I know you do. I was being facetious. So many people think that's what the occult is about – bringing Old Nick back to life. There's much more to it, believe me, Inspector. Or much less to it, depending on your point of view.'

Rebus tried to work out what this meant. 'You know occultists?' he said meantime.

'I know *of* occultists, practising covens of white and black witches.'

'Here? In Edinburgh?'

Poole smiled again. 'Oh yes. Right here. There are six working covens in and around Edinburgh.' He paused, and Rebus could almost see him doing a recount. 'Seven, perhaps. Fortunately, most of these practise white magic.'

'That's using the occult as a supposed force for good, right?'

'Quite correct.'

'And black magic . . .?'

The lecturer sighed. He suddenly became interested in the scene from his window. A summer's day. Rebus was remembering something. A long time ago, he'd bought a book of paintings by H.R. Giger, paintings of Satan flanked by vestal whores. . . . He couldn't say why he'd done it, but it must still be somewhere in the flat. He remembered hiding it from Rhona. . . .

'There is one coven in Edinburgh,' Poole was saying. 'A black coven.'

'Tell me, do they . . . do they make sacrifices?'

Dr Poole shrugged. 'We all make sacrifices.' But, seeing that Rebus was not laughing at his little joke, he straightened in his chair, his face becoming more serious. 'Probably they do, some token. A rat, a mouse, a chicken. It may not even go that far. They could use something symbolic, I really don't know.'

Rebus tapped one of the photographs which were spread across the desk. 'In the house where we found this pentagram, we also found a body. A dead body, in case you were wondering.' He brought these photographs out now. Dr Poole frowned as he glanced at them. 'Dead from a heroin overdose. Laid out with legs together, arms apart. The body was lying between two candles, which had burned down to nothing. Mean anything to you?'

Poole looked horror-struck. 'No,' he said. 'But you think that Satanists. . . .'

'I don't think anything, sir. I'm just trying to piece things together, going through all the possibilities.'

Poole thought for a moment. 'One of our students *might*

be of more use to you than I can. I'd no idea we were talking about a death. . . .'

'A student?'

'Yes. I only know him vaguely. He seems very interested in the occult, wrote rather a long and knowledgeable essay this term. Wants to do some project on demonism. He's a second-year student. They have to do a project over the summer. Yes, maybe he can give you more help than I'm able to.'

'And his name is . . .?'

'Well, his surname escapes me for the moment. He usually just calls himself by his first name. Charles.'

'Charles?'

'Or maybe Charlie. Yes, Charlie, that's it.'

Ronnie's friend's name. The hair on Rebus's neck began to prickle.

'That's right, Charlie,' Poole confirmed to himself, nodding. 'Bit of an eccentric. You can probably find him in one of the student union buildings. I believe he's addicted to these video machines. . . .'

No, not video machines. Pinball machines. The ones with all the extras, all the little tricks and treats that made a game a game. Charlie loved them with a vengeance. It was the kind of love which was all the more fervent for having come to him late in life. He was nineteen after all, life was streaming past, and he wanted to hang on to any piece of driftwood he could. Pinball had played no part in his adolescence. That had belonged to books and music. Besides, there had been no pinball machines at his boarding school.

Now, released into university, he wanted to live. And to play pinball. And do all the other things he had missed out on during the years of prep, sensitive essay-writing, and introspection. Charlie wanted to run faster than anyone had ever run, to live not one life, but two or three

48

or four. As the silver ball made contact with the left flipper, he threw it back up the table with real ferocity. There was a pause while the ball sat in one of the bonus craters, collecting another thousand points. He picked up his lager, took a gulp of it, and then returned his fingers to the buttons. In another ten minutes, he'd have the day's high score.

'Charlie?'

He turned at the sound of his name. A bad mistake, a naive mistake. He turned back to the game again, but too late. The man was striding towards him. The serious man. The unsmiling man.

'I'd like a word, Charlie.'

'Okay, how about carbohydrate. That was always one of my favourites.'

John Rebus's smile lasted less than a second.

'Very clever,' he said. 'Yes, that's what we call a smart answer.'

'We?'

'Lothian CID. My name's Inspector Rebus.'

'Pleased to meet you.'

'Likewise, Charlie.'

'No, you're mistaken. My name's not Charlie. He comes in here sometimes though. I'll tell him you called.'

Charlie was just about to hit the high score, five minutes ahead of schedule, when Rebus gripped his shoulder and spun him around. There were no other students in the games room, so he kept squeezing the shoulder while he spoke.

'You're about as funny as a maggot sandwich, Charlie, and patience isn't my favourite card game. So you'll excuse me if I become irritable, short-tempered, that sort of thing.'

'Hands off.' Charlie's face had taken on a new sheen, but not of fear.

49

'Ronnie,' Rebus said, calmly now, releasing his grip on the young man's shoulder.

The colour drained from Charlie's face. 'What about him?'

'He's dead.'

'Yes.' Charlie's voice was quiet, his eyes unfocussed. 'I heard.'

Rebus nodded. 'Tracy tried to find you.'

'Tracy.' There was venom in the word. 'She's no idea, no idea at all. Have you seen her?' Rebus nodded. 'Yeah, what a loser that woman is. She never understood Ronnie. Never even tried.'

As Charlie spoke, Rebus was learning more about him. His accent was Scottish private school, which was the first surprise. Rebus didn't know what he had expected. He knew he hadn't expected this. Charlie was well built, too, a product of the rugby-playing classes. He had curly dark brown hair, cut not too long, and was dressed in traditional student summer wear: training shoes, denims, and a T-shirt. The T-shirt was black, torn loose at the arms.

'So,' Charlie was saying, 'Ronnie did the big one, eh? Well, it's a good age to die. Live fast, die young.'

'Do you want to die young, Charlie?'

'Me?' Charlie laughed, a high-pitched squeal like a small animal. 'Hell, I want to live to be a hundred. I never want to die.' He looked at Rebus, something sparkling in his eyes. 'Do you?'

Rebus considered the question, but wasn't about to answer. He was here on business, not to discuss the death instinct. The lecturer, Dr Poole, had told him about the death instinct.

'I want to know what you know about Ronnie.'

'Does that mean you're going to take me away for questioning?'

'If you like. We can do it here if you'd prefer. . . .'

'No, no. I *want* to go to the police station. Come on, take me there.' There was a sudden eagerness about Charlie which made him seem much younger than his years. Who the hell wanted to *go* to a police station for questioning?

On the route to the car park and Rebus's car, Charlie insisted on walking a few paces ahead of Rebus, and with his hands behind his back, head slumped. Rebus saw that Charlie was pretending to be handcuffed. He was doing a good impersonation too, drawing attention to Rebus and himself. Someone even called out 'bastard' in Rebus's direction. But the word had lost all meaning over the years. They would have disturbed him more by wishing him a pleasant trip.

'Can I buy a couple of these?' Charlie asked, examining the photographs of his work, his pentagram.

The interview room was bleak. It was its purpose to be bleak. But Charlie had settled in like he was planning to rent it.

'No,' Rebus said, lighting a cigarette. He didn't offer one to Charlie. 'So, why did you paint it?'

'Because it's beautiful.' He still studied the photographs. 'Don't you think? So full of meaning.'

'How long had you known Ronnie?'

Charlie shrugged. For the first time, he looked in the direction of the cassette recorder. Rebus had asked if he minded having the dialogue recorded. He had shrugged. Now he seemed a little pensive. 'Maybe a year,' he said. 'Yes, a year. I met him around the time of my first-year exams. That was when I started to get interested in the *real* Edinburgh.'

'The real Edinburgh?'

'Yes. Not just the piper on the ramparts, or the Royal Mile, or the Scott Monument.' Rebus recalled Ronnie's photographs of the Castle.

'I saw some photos on Ronnie's wall.' Charlie screwed up his face.

'God, those. He had the idea he was going to be a professional photographer. Taking bloody tourist snaps for postcards. That didn't last long. Like most of Ronnie's schemes.'

'Nice camera he had though.'

'What? Oh, yes, his camera. Yes, it was his pride and joy.' Charlie crossed his legs. Rebus continued to stare into the young man's eyes, but Charlie was busily studying the photographs of the pentagram.

'So what was that you were telling me about the "real" Edinburgh?'

'Deacon Brodie,' said Charlie, suddenly interested again, 'Burke and Hare, justified sinners, the lot. But it's all been cleaned up for the tourists, you see. And I thought, hang on, all this Lowland low-life still exists. That was when I started touring the housing estates, Wester Hailes, Oxgangs, Craigmillar, Pilmuir. And sure enough, it's all still here, the past replaying itself in the present.'

'So you started hanging around Pilmuir?'

'Yes.'

'In other words, you became a tourist yourself?' Rebus had seen Charlie's kind before, though usually the older model, the prosperous businessman debasing himself for kicks, visiting sleazy rooms for a dry cough of pleasure. He didn't like the species.

'I wasn't a tourist!' Charlie's anger rose, a trout snapping a hooked worm. 'I was there because I wanted to be there, and they wanted me there.' His voice began to sound sulky. 'I belong there.'

'No you don't, son, you belong in a big house somewhere with parents interested in your university career.'

'Crap.' Charlie pushed back his chair and walked to the wall, resting his head against it. Rebus thought for a moment that he might be about to beat himself senseless, then claim police brutality. But he seemed merely to need something cool against his face.

The interview room was stifling. Rebus had removed his jacket. Now he rolled up his sleeves before stubbing out the cigarette.

'Okay, Charlie.' The young man was soft now, pliable. It was time to ask some questions. 'The night of the overdose, you were in the house with Ronnie, right?'

'That's right. For a little while.'

'Who else was there?'

'Tracy was there. She was there when I left.'

'Anyone else?'

'Some guy visited earlier in the evening. He didn't stay long. I'd seen him with Ronnie before a couple of times. When they were together, they kept to themselves.'

'Was this person his dealer, do you think?'

'No. Ronnie could always get stuff. Well, up until recently. Past couple of weeks, he found it tough. They seemed pretty close, though. Really close, if you get my meaning.'

'Go on.'

'Close as in loving. As in gay.'

'But Tracy . . .?'

'Yeah, yeah, but what's that supposed to prove, huh? You know how most addicts make their money.'

'How? Theft?'

'Yeah, theft, muggings, whatever. And doing a bit of business over by Calton Hill.'

Calton Hill, large, sprawling, lying to the east of Princes Street. Yes, Rebus knew all about Calton Hill, and about the cars which sat much of the night at the foot of it, along Regent Road. He knew about Calton Cemetery, too, about what went on there. . . .

'You're saying Ronnie was a rent boy?' The phrase sounded ridiculous out loud. It was tabloid talk.

'I'm saying he used to hang around there with a load of other guys, and I'm saying he always had money at the end of the night.' Charlie swallowed. 'Money and maybe a few bruises.'

'Jesus.' Rebus added this information to what was becoming a very grubby little dossier in his head. How far would you sink for a fix? The answer was: all the way. And then a little lower. He lit another cigarette.

'Do you know this for a fact?' he asked.

'No.'

'Was Ronnie from Edinburgh, by the way?'

'Stirling.'

'And his surname was –'

'McGrath, I think.'

'What about this guy he was so chummy with? Have you a name for him?'

'He called himself Neil. Ronnie called him Neilly.'

'Neilly? Did you get the impression they'd known one another for a while?'

'Yeah, a goodish while. A nickname like that's a sign of affection, right?' Rebus studied Charlie with new admiration. 'I don't do psychology for nothing, Inspector.'

'Right.' Rebus checked that the small cassette recorder still had some tape left to run. 'Give me a physical description of this Neil character, will you?'

'Tall, skinny, short brown hair. Kind of spotty face, but always clean. Usually wore jeans and a denim jacket. Carried a big black holdall with him.'

'Any idea what was in it?'

'I got the feeling it was just clothes.'

'Okay.'

'Anything else?'

'Let's talk about the pentagram. Someone has been back to the house and added to it since these photographs were taken.'

Charlie said nothing, but did not look surprised.

'It was you, wasn't it?'

Charlie nodded.

'How did you get in?'

'Through the downstairs window. Those wooden slats couldn't keep out an elephant. It's like an extra door. Lots of people used to come into the house that way.'

'Why did you go back?'

'It wasn't finished, was it? I wanted to add the symbols.'

'And the message.'

Charlie smiled to himself. 'Yes, the message.'

'"Hello Ronnie",' Rebus quoted. 'What's that all about?'

'Just what it says. His spirit's still in the house, his soul's still there. I was just saying hello. I had some paint left. Besides, I thought it might give somebody a fright.'

Rebus remembered his own shock at seeing the scrawl. He felt his cheeks redden slightly, but covered the fact with a question.

'Do you remember the candles?'

Charlie nodded, but was becoming restless. Helping police with their inquiries was not as much fun as he had hoped.

'What about your project?' said Rebus, changing tack.

'What about it?'

'It's on demonism, isn't it?'

'Maybe. I haven't decided yet.'

'What aspect of demonism?'

'I don't know. Maybe the popular mythology. How old fears become new fears, that sort of thing.'

'Do you know any of the covens in Edinburgh?'

'I know people who claim to be in some of them.'

'But you've never been along to one?'

'No, worse luck.' Charlie seemed suddenly to come to life. 'Look, what is all this? Ronnie OD'd. He's history. Why all the questions?'

'What can you tell me about the candles?'

Charlie exploded. 'What *about* the candles?'

Rebus was all calmness. He exhaled smoke before responding. 'There were candles in the living room.' He was getting close to telling Charlie something Charlie didn't seem to know. All during the interview, he had been spiralling inwards towards this moment.

'That's right. Big candles. Ronnie got them from some shop that specialises in candles. He *liked* candles. They gave the place *ambience*.'

'Tracy found Ronnie in his bedroom. She thinks he was already dead.' Rebus's voice became lower still, and as flat as the desktop. 'But by the time she'd phoned us, and an officer had turned up at the house, Ronnie's body had been moved downstairs. It was laid out between two candles, which had been burnt down to nothing.'

'There wasn't much left of those candles anyway, not when I left.'

'You left when?'

'Just before midnight. There was supposed to be a party somewhere on the estate. I thought I might get invited in.'

'How long would the candles have burned for?'

'An hour, two hours. God knows.'

'How much smack did Ronnie have?'

'Christ, I don't know.'

'Well, how much would he normally use at any one time?'

'I really don't know. I'm not a user, you know. I hate all that stuff. I've got two friends who were in my sixth form. They're both in private clinics.'

'That's nice for them.'

'Like I said, Ronnie hadn't been able to find any stuff for days. He was a bit whacked out, just about to fall right over the edge. Then he came back with some. End of story.'

'Isn't there much about then?'

'So far as I know, there's plenty, but don't bother asking for names.'

'So if there's plenty, how come Ronnie was finding it so hard?'

'God knows. He didn't know himself. It was like he'd suddenly become bad news. Then he was good news again, and he got that packet.'

It was time. Rebus picked an invisible thread from his shirt.

'He was murdered,' he said. 'Or as good as.'

Charlie's mouth opened. The blood drained from his face, as though a tap had been opened somewhere. 'What?'

'He was murdered. His body was full of rat poison. Self-inflicted, but supplied by someone who probably knew it was lethal. A lot of work was then done to manoeuvre his body into some kind of ritualistic position in the living room. Where your pentagram is.'

'Now wait –'

'How many covens are there in Edinburgh, Charlie?'

'What? Six, seven, I don't know. Look –'

'Do you know them? Any of them? I mean know them personally?'

'Christ, man, you're not going to pin this on me!'

'Why not?' Rebus stubbed out his cigarette.

'Because it's crazy.'

'Seems to me it all fits, Charlie.' String him out, Rebus was thinking. He's already stretched to snapping point. 'Unless you can convince me otherwise.'

Charlie walked to the door purposefully, then paused.

'Go on,' Rebus called, 'it's not locked. Walk out of here if you like. Then I'll *know* you had something to do with it.'

Charlie turned. His eyes seemed moist in the hazy light. A sunbeam from the barred window, penetrating the frosted glass, caught motes of dust and turned them into slow-motion dancers. Charlie moved through them as he returned to the desk.

'I didn't have anything to do with it, honest.'

'Sit down,' said Rebus, a kindly uncle now. 'Let's talk some more.'

But Charlie didn't like uncles. Never had. He placed his hands on the desk and leaned down, looming over Rebus. Something had hardened somewhere within him. His teeth when he spoke glistened with venom.

'Go to hell, Rebus. I see what you're up to, and I'm damned if I'm going to play along. Arrest me if you like, but don't insult me with cheap tricks. I did those in my first term.'

Then he walked, and this time opened the door, and left it open behind him. Rebus got up from the desk, switched off the recorder, took out the tape and, pushing it into his pocket, followed. By the time he reached the entrance hall, Charlie had gone. He approached the desk. The duty sergeant looked up from his paperwork.

'You just missed him,' he said.

Rebus nodded. 'It doesn't matter.'

'He didn't look too happy.'

'Would I be doing my job if they all left here laughing and holding their sides?'

The sergeant smiled. 'I suppose not. So what can I do for you?'

'The Pilmuir overdose. I've got a name for the corpse. Ronnie McGrath. Originally from Stirling. Let's see if we can find his parents, eh?'

The sergeant scribbled the name onto a pad. 'I'm sure they'll be delighted to hear how their son is doing in the big city.'

'Yes,' said Rebus, staring towards the front door of the police station. 'I'm sure they will.'

John Rebus's flat was his castle. Once through the door, he would pull up the drawbridge and let his mind go blank, emptying himself of the world for as long as he could. He would pour himself a drink, put some tenor sax music on the cassette machine, and pick up a book. Many weeks ago, in a crazed state of righteousness, he had put up shelves along one wall of the living room, intending his sprawling collection of books to rest there. But somehow they managed to crawl across the floor, getting under his feet, so that he used them like stepping-stones into the hallway and the bedroom.

He walked across them now, on his way to the bay window where he pulled down the dusty venetian blinds. The slats he left open, so that strawberry slants of evening light came pouring through, reminding him of the interview room. . . .

No, no, no, that wouldn't do. He was being sucked back into work again. He had to clear his mind, find some book which would pull him into its little universe, far away from the sights and smells of Edinburgh. He stepped firmly on the likes of Chekhov, Heller, Rimbaud and Kerouac as he made his way to the kitchen, seeking out a bottle of wine.

There were two cardboard boxes beneath the kitchen worktop, taking up the space where the washing machine had once been. Rhona had taken the washing machine, which was fair enough. He called the resultant space his wine cellar, and now and then would order a mixed case from a good little shop around the corner from his flat. He put a hand into one of the boxes and brought out something called Château Potensac. Yes, he'd had a bottle of this before. It would do.

He poured a third of the bottle into a large glass and returned to the living room, plucking one of the books from the floor as he went. He was seated in his armchair before he looked at its cover: *The Naked Lunch*. No, bad choice. He threw the book down again and groped for another. *Dr Jekyll and Mr Hyde*. Fair enough, he'd been meaning to reread it for ages, and it was blissfully short.

He took a mouthful of wine, sloshed it around before swallowing, and opened the book.

With the timing of a stage-play, there was a rapping at the front door. The noise Rebus made was somewhere between a sigh and a roar. He balanced the book, its covers open, on the arm of the chair, and rose to his feet. Probably it was Mrs Cochrane from downstairs, telling him that it was his turn to wash the communal stairwell. She would have the large, imperative card with her: IT IS YOUR TURN TO WASH THE STAIRS. Why she couldn't just hang it on his door like everyone else seemed to do . . .?

He tried to arrange a neighbourly smile on his face as he opened the door, but the actor in him had left for the evening. So there was something not unlike pain rippling his lips as he stared at the visitor on his doormat.

It was Tracy.

Her face was red, and there were tears in her eyes, but the redness was not from crying. She looked exhausted, her hair cloying with sweat.

'Can I come in?' There was an all too visible effort in her voice. Rebus hadn't the heart to say no. He pushed the door open wide and she stumbled in past him, walking straight through to the living room as though she'd been here a hundred times. Rebus checked that the stairwell was empty of inquisitive neighbours, then closed the door. He was tingling, not a pleasant feeling: he didn't like people visiting him here.

Especially, he didn't like work following him home.

By the time he reached the living room, Tracy had drained the wine and was exhaling with relief, her thirst quenched. Rebus felt the discomfort in him increase until it was almost unbearable.

'How the hell did you find this place?' he asked, standing in the doorway as though waiting for her to leave.

'Not easy,' she said, her voice a little more calm. 'You told me you lived in Marchmont, so I just wandered around looking for your car. Then I found your name on the bell downstairs.'

He had to admit it, she'd have made a good detective. Footwork was what it was all about.

'Somebody's been following me,' she said now. 'I got scared.'

'Following you?' He stepped into the room now, curious, his sense of encroachment easing.

'Yes, two men. I think there were two. They've been following me all afternoon. I was up Princes Street, just walking, and they were always there, a little way behind me. They must've known I could see them.'

'What happened?'

'I lost them. Went into Marks and Spencer, ran like hell for the Rose Street exit, then dived into the ladies' in a pub. Stayed in there for an hour. That seemed to do the trick. Then I headed here.'

'Why didn't you telephone me?'

'No money. That's why I was up Princes Street in the first place.'

She had settled in his chair, her arms hanging over its sides. He nodded towards the empty glass.

'Do you want another?'

'No thanks. I don't really like plonk, but I was thirsty as hell. I could manage a cup of tea though.'

'Tea, right.' Plonk, she had called it! He turned and walked through to the kitchen, his mind half on the idea of tea, half on her story. In one of his sparsely populated cupboards he found an unopened box of teabags. There was no fresh milk in the flat, but an old tin yielded a spoonful or two of powdered substitute. Now, sugar.... Music came suddenly from the living room, a loud rendering of *The White Album*. God, he'd forgotten he still had that old tape. He opened the cutlery drawer, looking for nothing more than a teaspoon, and found several sachets of sugar, stolen from the canteen at some point in his past. Serendipity. The kettle was beginning to boil.

'This flat's huge!'

She startled him, he was so unused to other voices in this place. He turned and watched her lean against the door-jamb, her head angled sideways.

'Is it?' he said, rinsing a mug.

'Christ, yes. Look how high your ceilings are! I could just about touch the ceiling in Ronnie's squat.' She stood on tiptoe and stretched an arm upwards, waving her hand. Rebus feared that she had taken something, some pills or powders, while he'd been on the trail of the furtive teabag. She seemed to sense his thoughts, and smiled.

'I'm just relieved,' she said. 'I feel light-headed from the running. And from being scared, I suppose. But now I feel safe.'

'What did the men look like?'

'I don't know. I think they looked a bit like you.' She smiled again. 'One had a moustache. He was sort of fat, going thin on top, but not old. I can't remember the other one. He wasn't very memorable, I suppose.'

Rebus poured water into the mug and added the teabag. 'Milk?'

'No, just sugar if you've got it.'

He waved one of the sachets at her.

'Great.'

Back in the living room, he went to the stereo and turned it down.

'Sorry,' she said, back in the chair now, sipping tea, her legs tucked under her.

'I keep meaning to find out whether my neighbours can hear the stereo or not,' Rebus said, as if to excuse his action. 'The walls are pretty thick, but the ceiling isn't.'

She nodded, blew onto the surface of the drink, steam covering her face in a veil.

'So,' said Rebus, pulling his director's foldaway chair out from beneath a table and sitting down. 'What can we do about these men who've been following you?'

'I don't know. You're the policeman.'

'It all sounds like something out of a film to me. I mean, *why* should anyone want to follow you?'

'To scare me?' she offered.

'And why should they want to scare you?'

She thought about this, then shrugged her shoulders.

'By the way, I saw Charlie today,' he said.

'Oh?'

'Do you like him?'

'Charlie?' Her laughter was shrill. 'He's horrible. Always hanging around, even when it's obvious nobody wants him anywhere near. Everybody hates him.'

'Everybody?'

'Yes.'

'Did Ronnie hate him?'

She paused. 'No,' she said at last. 'But then Ronnie didn't have much sense that way.'

'What about this other friend of Ronnie's? Neil, or Neilly. What can you tell me about him?'

'Is that the guy who was there last night?'

'Yes.'

She shrugged her shoulders. 'I never saw him before.' She seemed interested in the book on the arm of the chair, picked it up and flipped its pages, pretending to read.

'And Ronnie never mentioned a Neil or a Neilly to you?'

'No.' She waved the book at Rebus. 'But he did talk about someone called Edward. Seemed angry with him about something. Used to shout the name out when he was alone in his room, after a fix.'

Rebus nodded slowly. 'Edward. His dealer maybe?'

'I don't know. Maybe. Ronnie got pretty crazy sometimes after he fixed. He was like a different person. But he was so sweet at times, so gentle. . . .' Her voice died away, eyes glistening.

Rebus checked his watch. 'Okay, what about if I drive you back to the squat now? We can check that there's no one watching.'

'I don't know. . . .' The fear had returned to her face, erasing years from her, turning her into a child again, afraid of shadows and ghosts.

'I'll be there,' Rebus added.

'Well. . . . Can I do something first?'

'What?'

She pulled at her damp clothes. 'Take a bath,' she said. Then she smiled. 'I know it's a bit brassnecked, but I really could use one, and there's no water at all in the squat.'

Rebus smiled too, nodding slowly. 'My bathtub is at your disposal,' he said.

While she was in the bath, he hung her clothes over the radiator in the hall. Turning the central heating on made a sauna of the flat, and Rebus struggled with the sash windows in the living room, trying without success to open them. He made more tea, in a pot this time, and had just carried it into the living room when he heard her call from the bathroom. When he came out into the hall, she had her head around the bathroom door, steam billowing out around her. Her hair, face and neck were gleaming.

'No towels,' she explained.

'Sorry,' said Rebus. He found some in the cupboard in his room, and brought them to her, pushing them through the gap in the door, feeling awkward despite himself.

'Thanks,' she called.

He had swopped *The White Album* for some jazz – barely audible – and was sitting with his tea when she came in. One large red towel was expertly tied around her body, another around her head. He had often wondered how women could be so good at wearing towels. . . . Her arms and legs were pale and thin, but there was no doubting that her shape was pleasing, and the glow from the bath gave her a kind of nimbus. He remembered the photographs of her in Ronnie's room. Then he recalled the missing camera.

'Was Ronnie still keen on photography? I mean, of late.' The choice of words was accidentally unsubtle, and he winced a little, but Tracy appeared not to notice.

'I suppose so. He was quite good, you know. He had a good eye. But he didn't get the breaks.'

'How hard did he try?'

'Bloody hard.' There was resentment in her voice. Perhaps Rebus had allowed too much professional scepticism to creep into his tone.

'Yes, I'm sure. Not an easy profession to get into, I'd imagine.'

'Too true. And there were some who knew how good Ronnie was. They didn't want the competition. Put obstacles in his way whenever and wherever they could.'

'You mean other photographers?'

'That's right. Well, when Ronnie was going through his really keen spell, before disillusionment set in, he didn't know quite how to get the breaks. So he went to a couple of studios, showed some of his work to the guys who worked there. He had some really inspired shots. You know, everyday things seen from weird angles. The Castle, Waverley Monument, Calton Hill.'

'Calton Hill?'

'Yes, the whatsit.'

'The folly?'

'That's it.' The towel was slipping a little from around her shoulders, and as Tracy sat with her legs tucked beneath her, sipping tea, it also fell away to reveal more than enough thigh. Rebus tried to concentrate his eyes on her face. It wasn't easy. 'Well,' she was saying, 'a couple

65

of his ideas got ripped off. He'd see a photo in one of the local rags, and it'd be exactly the angle he'd used, the same time of day, same filters. Those bastards had copied his ideas. He'd see their names beneath the pictures, the same guys he'd shown his portfolio to.'

'What were their names?'

'I don't remember now.' She readjusted the towel. There seemed something defensive in the action. Was it so hard to remember a name? She giggled. 'He tried to get me to pose for him.'

'I saw the results.'

'No, not those ones. You know, nude shots. He said he could sell them for a fortune to some of the magazines. But I wasn't having it. I mean, the money would've been all well and good, but these mags get passed around, don't they? I mean, they never get thrown away. I'd always be wondering if anybody could recognise me on the street.' She waited for Rebus's reaction, and when it was one of thoughtful bemusement, laughed throatily. 'So, it's not true what they say. You *can* embarrass a copper.'

'Sometimes.' Rebus's cheeks were tingling. He put a hand self-consciously to one of them. He had to do something about this. 'So,' he said, 'was Ronnie's camera worth much then?'

She seemed nonplussed by this turn in the conversation, and pulled the towel even tighter around her. 'Depends. I mean, worth and value, they're not the same thing, are they?'

'Aren't they?'

'Well, he might have paid only a tenner for the camera, but that doesn't mean it was only *worth* a tenner to him. Do you see?'

'So he paid a tenner for the camera?'

'No, no, no.' She shook her head, dislodging the towel. 'I thought you had to be brainy to get in the CID? What I mean is . . .' She raised her eyes to the ceiling, and the towel slipped from her head, so that bedraggled rat's-tails of hair strung themselves out across her forehead. 'No, never mind. The camera cost about a hundred and fifty quid. Okay?'

'Fine.'

'Interested in photography are you?'

'Only since recently. More tea?'

He poured from the teapot, then added a sachet of sugar. She liked lots of sugar.

'Thanks,' she said, cradling the mug. 'Listen.' She was bathing her face in the steam from the surface of the tea. 'Can I ask you a favour?'

Here it comes, thought Rebus: money. He had already made a mental note to check whether anything in the flat was missing before letting her leave. 'What?'

Her eyes were on his now. 'Can I stay the night?' Her words came out in a torrent. 'I'll sleep on the couch, on the floor. I don't mind. I just don't want to go back to the squat, not tonight. It's been getting pretty crazy lately, and those men following me. . . .' She shivered, and Rebus had to admit that if this were all an act, she was a top-of-the-form drama student. He shrugged, was about to speak, but rose and went to the window instead, deferring a decision.

The orange street lamps were on, casting a Hollywood film-set glow over the pavement. There was a car outside, directly opposite the flat. Being two floors up, Rebus couldn't quite see into the car, but the driver's side window had been rolled down, and smoke oozed from it.

'Well?' the voice said behind him. It had lost all confidence now.

'What?' Rebus said distractedly.

'Can I?' He turned towards her. 'Can I stay?' she repeated.

'Sure,' Rebus said, making for the door. 'Stay as long as you like.'

*

He was halfway down the curving stairwell before he realised that he was not wearing any shoes. He paused, considering. No, to hell with it. His mother had always warned him about catching chilblains, and he never had. Now was as good a time as any to find out whether his medical luck was holding.

He was passing a door on the first floor when it rattled open and Mrs Cochrane thrust her whole frame out, blocking Rebus's path.

'Mrs Cochrane,' he said after the initial shock had passed.

'Here.' She shoved something towards him, and he could do nothing but take it from her. It was a piece of card, about ten inches by six. Rebus read it: IT IS YOUR TURN TO WASH THE STAIRS. By the time he looked up again, Mrs Cochrane's door was already closing. He could hear her carpet slippers shuffling back towards her TV and her cat. Smelly old thing.

Rebus carried the card downstairs with him, the cold steps penetrating his stockinged soles. The cat didn't smell too good either, he thought maliciously.

The front door was on the latch. He eased it open, trying to keep the aged mechanism as silent as possible. The car was still there. Directly opposite him as he stepped outside. But the driver had already seen him. The cigarette stub was flicked onto the road, and the engine started. Rebus moved forward on his toes. The car's headlamps came on suddenly, their beam as full as a Stalag searchlight. Rebus paused, screwing his eyes, and the car started forward, then swerved to the left, racing downhill to the end of the street. Rebus stared after it, trying to make out the number plate, but his eyes were full of white fuzziness. It had been a Ford Escort. Of that much he was sure.

Looking down the road, he realised that the car had stopped at the junction with the main road, waiting for a space in the traffic. It was less than a hundred yards away. Rebus made up his mind. He had been a handy sprinter in his youth, good enough for the school team when they had been a man short. He ran now with a kind of drunken euphoria, and remembered the wine he had opened. His stomach turned sour at the mere thought, and he slowed. Just then he slipped, skidding on something on the pavement, and, brought up short, he saw the car slip across the junction and roar away.

Never mind. That first glimpse as he'd opened the door had been enough. He'd seen the constabulary uniform. Not the driver's face, but the uniform for sure. A policeman, a constable, driving an Escort. Two young girls were approaching along the pavement. They giggled as they passed Rebus, and he realised that he was standing panting on the pavement, without any shoes but holding a sign telling him it was his turn to WASH THE STAIRS. When he looked down, he saw what it was he had skidded on.

Cursing silently, he removed his socks, tossed them into the gutter, and walked back on bare feet towards the flat.

Dectective Constable Brian Holmes was drinking tea. He had turned this into something of a ritual, holding the cup to his face and blowing on it, then sipping. Blowing then sipping. Swallowing. Then releasing a steamy breath of air. He was chilled tonight, as cold as any tramp on any park bench bed. He didn't even have a newspaper, and the tea tasted revolting. It had come out of one or other of the thermos flasks, piping hot and smelling of plastic. The milk wasn't of the freshest, but at least the brew was warming. Not warming enough to touch his toes, supposing he still had toes.

'Anything happening?' he hissed towards the SSPCA officer, who held binoculars to his eyes as though to hide his embarrassment.

'Nothing,' the officer whispered. It had been an anonymous tip-off. The third this month and, to be fair, the first non-starter. Dog fighting was back in vogue. Several 'arenas' had been found in the past three months, small dirt pits enclosed by lengths of sheet tin. Scrap yards seemed the main source of these arenas, which gave an added meaning to the term 'scrap yard'. But tonight they were watching a piece of waste ground. Goods trains clattered past nearby, heading towards the centre of the city, but apart from that and the low hum of distant traffic, the place was dead. Yes, there was a makeshift pit all right. They'd taken a look at it in daylight, pretending to walk their own alsatian dogs, which were in fact police dogs. Pit bull terriers: that was what they used in the arenas. Brian Holmes had seen a couple of ex-combatants, their eyes maddened with pain and fear. He hadn't stuck around for the vet with his lethal injection.

'Hold on.'

Two men were walking, hands in pockets, across the wilderness, picking their way carefully over the uneven surface, wary of sudden craters. They seemed to know where they were headed: straight towards the shallow pit. Once there, they took a final look around. Brian Holmes stared directly back at them, knowing he could not be seen. Like the SSPCA officer, he was crouching behind thick bracken, behind him one remaining wall of what had been a building of sorts. Though there was some light over towards the pit itself, there was precious little here, and so, as with a two-way mirror, he could see without being seen.

'Got you,' said the SSPCA man as the two men jumped down into the pit.

'Wait . . .' said Holmes, suddenly getting a funny feeling about all of this. The two men had begun to embrace, and their faces merged in a slow, lingering kiss as they sank down towards the ground.

70

'Christ!' exclaimed the SSPCA man.

Holmes sighed, staring down at the damp, rock-hard earth beneath his knees.

'I don't think pit bulls enter the equation,' he said. 'Or if they do, bestiality rather than brutality might be the charge.'

The SSPCA officer still held his binoculars to his eyes, horror-struck and riveted.

'You hear stories,' he said, 'but you never . . . well . . . you know.'

'Get to watch?' Holmes suggested, getting slowly, painfully to his feet.

He was talking with the night duty officer when the message came through. Inspector Rebus wanted a word.

'Rebus? What does he want?' Brian Holmes checked his watch. It was two fifteen a.m. Rebus was at home, and he had been told to phone him there. He used the duty officer's telephone.

'Hello?' He knew John Rebus of course, had worked with him on several cases. Still, middle-of-the-night calls were something else entirely.

'Is that you, Brian?'

'Yes, sir.'

'Have you a sheet of paper? Write this down.' Fumbling with pad and biro, Holmes thought he could hear music playing on the line. Something he recognised. The Beatles' *White Album*. 'Ready?'

'Yes, sir.'

'Right. There was a junkie found dead in Pilmuir yesterday, or a couple of days ago now, strictly speaking. Overdose. Find out who the constables who found him were. Get them to come into my office at ten o'clock. Got that?'

'Yes, sir.'

'Good. Now, when you've got the address where the

body was found, I want you to pick up the keys from whoever's got them and go to the house. Upstairs in one of the bedrooms there's a wall covered in photographs. Some are of Edinburgh Castle. Take them with you and go to the local newspaper's office. They'll have files full of photographs. If you're lucky they might even have a little old man on duty with a memory like an elephant. I want you to look for any photographs that have been published in the newspaper recently and look to have been taken from the same angle as the ones on the bedroom wall. Got that?'

'Yes, sir,' said Holmes, scribbling furiously.

'Good. I want to know who took the newspaper photographs. There'll be a sticker or something on the back of each print giving a name and address.'

'Anything else, sir?' It came out as sarcasm, meant or not.

'Yes.' Rebus seemed to drop his voice a decibel. 'On the bedroom wall you'll also find some photos of a young lady. I'd like to know more about her. She says her middle name is Tracy. That's what she calls herself. Ask around, show the picture to anyone you think might have an inkling.'

'Right, sir. One question.'

'Go ahead.'

'Why me? Why now? What's all this in aid of?'

'That's three questions. I'll answer as many of them as I can when I see you tomorrow afternoon. Be in my office at three.'

And with that, the line went dead on Brian Holmes. He stared at the drunken rows of writing on his pad, his own shorthand of a week's worth of work, delivered to him in a matter of minutes. The duty officer was reading it over his shoulder.

'Rather you than me,' he said with sincerity.

*

John Rebus had chosen Holmes for a whole bundle of reasons, but mostly because Holmes didn't know much about him. He wanted someone who would work efficiently, methodically, without raising too much fuss. Someone who didn't know Rebus well enough to complain about being kept in the dark, about being used as a shunting engine. A message boy and a bloodhound and a dogsbody. Rebus knew that Holmes was gaining a reputation for efficiency and for not being a complaining sod. That was enough to be going on with.

He carried the telephone back from the hall into the living room, placed it on the bookshelves, and went across to the hi-fi, where he switched off the tape machine, then the amplifier. He went to the window and looked out on an empty street whose lamplight was the colour of Red Leicester cheese. The image reminded him of the midnight snack he had promised himself a couple of hours ago, and he decided to make himself something in the kitchen. Tracy wouldn't be wanting anything. He was sure of that. He stared at her as she lay along the settee, her head at an angle towards the floor, one hand across her stomach, the other hanging down to touch the wool carpet. Her eyes were unseeing slits, her mouth open in a pout, revealing a slight gap between her two front teeth. She had slept soundly as he had thrown a blanket over her, and was sleeping still, her breathing regular. Something niggled him, but he couldn't think what it was. Hunger perhaps. He hoped the freezer would yield a pleasant surprise. But first he went to the window and looked out again. The street was absolutely dead, which was just how Rebus himself was feeling: dead but active. He picked *Dr Jekyll and Mr Hyde* from the floor and carried it through to the kitchen.

Wednesday

The more it looks like Queer Street, the less I ask.

Police Constables Harry Todd and Francis O'Rourke were standing outside Rebus's office when he arrived next morning. They had been leaning against the wall, enjoying a lazy conversation, seemingly unconcerned that Rebus was twenty minutes late. He was damned if he was going to apologise. He noted with satisfaction that as he reached the top of the stairs they pulled themselves up straight and shut their mouths.

That was a good start.

He opened the door, walked into the room, and closed the door again. Let them stew for another minute. Now they'd have something really to talk about. He had checked with the desk sergeant, and Brian Holmes wasn't in the station. He took a slip of paper from his pocket and rang Holmes's house. The telephone rang and rang. Holmes must be out working.

The good run was continuing.

There was mail on his desk. He flipped through it, stopping only to extract a note from Superintendent Watson. It was an invitation to lunch. Today. At twelve thirty. Hell. He was meeting Holmes at three. The lunch was with some of the businessmen who were putting up the hard cash for the drugs campaign. Hell. And it was in The Eyrie, which meant wearing a tie and a clean shirt. Rebus looked down at his shirt. It would do. But the tie would not. Hell.

The smile left his soul.

It had been too good to last. Tracy had woken him with breakfast on a tray. Orange juice, toast and honey, strong coffee. She'd gone out early, she explained, taking with her a little money she found on the shelves in the living room. She hoped he didn't mind. She had found a corner shop open, made the purchases, come back to the flat, and made him breakfast.

'I'm surprised the smell of burning toast didn't wake you,' she had said.

'You're looking at the man who slept through *Towering Inferno*,' he had replied. And she had laughed, sitting on the bed taking dainty bites of toast with her exposed teeth, while Rebus chewed his slices slowly, thoughtfully. Luxuriously. How long had it been since he'd been brought breakfast in bed? It frightened him to think. . . .

'Come in!' he roared now, though no one had knocked.

Tracy had left without complaint, too. She felt all right, she said. She couldn't stay cooped up forever, could she? He had driven her back towards Pilmuir, then had done something stupid. Given her ten pounds. It wasn't just money, as he realised a second after handing it over. It was a bond between them, a bond he shouldn't be making. It lay there in her hand, and he felt the temptation to snatch it back. But then she was out of the car and walking away, her body fragile as bone china, her gait determined, full of strength. Sometimes she reminded him of his daughter Sammy, other times. . . .

Other times of Gill Templer, his ex-lover.

'Come in!' he roared again. This time the door opened an inch, then another ten or eleven. A head looked into the room.

'Nobody's been knocking, sir,' the head said nervously.

'Is that so?' said Rebus in his best stage voice. 'Well, in that case I'd better just speak to you two instead. So why don't you *come in*!'

A moment later, they shuffled through the doorway, a

bit less cocky now. Rebus pointed to the two chairs on the other side of his desk. One of them sat immediately, the other stood to attention.

'I'd rather stand, sir,' he said. The other one looked suddenly fearful, terrified that he had broken some rule of protocol.

'This isn't the bloody army,' Rebus said to the standing one, just as the sitting one was rising. 'So sit down!'

They both sat. Rebus rubbed his forehead, pretending a headache. Truth be told, he had almost forgotten who these constables were and why they were here.

'Right,' he said. 'Why do you think I've called you here this morning?' Corny but effective.

'Is it to do with the witches, sir?'

'Witches?' Rebus looked at the constable who had said this, and remembered the keen young man who had shown him the original pentagram. 'That's right, witches. And overdoses.'

They blinked at him. He sought frantically for a route into the interrogation, if interrogation this was to be. He should have thought more about it before coming in.

He should have at least remembered that it had been arranged. He saw a ten-pound note, a smile, could smell burning toast. . . . He looked at the pentagram constable's tie.

'What's your name, son?'

'Todd, sir.'

'Todd? That's German for dead, did you know that, Todd?'

'Yes, sir. I did German at school up to Highers.'

Rebus nodded, pretending to be impressed. Damn, he *was* impressed. They all had Highers these days, it seemed, all these extraordinarily young-looking constables. Some had gone further: college, university. He had the feeling Holmes had been to university. He hoped he hadn't enlisted the aid of a smart arse. . . .

Rebus pointed to the tie.

'That looks a bit squint, Todd.'

Todd immediately looked down towards his tie, his head angled so sharply Rebus feared the neck would snap.

'Sir?'

'That tie. Is it your usual one?'

'Yes, sir.'

'So you haven't broken a tie recently?'

'Broken a tie, sir?'

'Broken the clip,' explained Rebus.

'No, sir.'

'And what's your name, son?' Rebus said quickly, turning to the other constable, who looked completely stunned by proceedings so far.

'O'Rourke, sir.'

'Irish name,' Rebus commented.

'Yes, sir.'

'What about your tie, O'Rourke? Is that a new tie?'

'Not really, sir. I mean, I've got about half a dozen of these things kicking around.'

Rebus nodded. He picked up a pencil, examined it, set it down again. He was wasting his time.

'I'd like to see the reports you made of finding the deceased.'

'Yes, sir,' they said.

'Nothing unusual in the house, was there? I mean, when you first arrived? Nothing out of the ordinary?'

'Only the dead man, sir,' said O'Rourke.

'And the painting on the wall,' said Todd.

'Did either of you bother to check upstairs?'

'No, sir.'

'The body was where, when you arrived?'

'In the downstairs room, sir.'

'And you didn't go upstairs?'

Todd looked towards O'Rourke. 'I think we shouted to see if anyone was up there. But no, we didn't go up.'

So how could the tie clip have got upstairs? Rebus exhaled, then cleared his throat. 'What kind of car do you drive, Todd?'

'Do you mean police car, sir?'

'No I bloody well don't!' Rebus slapped the pencil down against the desk. 'I mean for private use.'

Todd seemed more confused now than ever. 'A Metro, sir.'

'Colour?'

'White.'

Rebus turned his gaze to O'Rourke.

'I don't have a car,' O'Rourke admitted. 'I like motor-bikes. Just now I've got a Honda seven-fifty.'

Rebus nodded. No Ford Escorts then. Nobody hurtling away from his road at midnight.

'Well, that's all right then, isn't it?' And with a smile he dismissed them, picked up the pencil again, examined its point, and very deliberately broke it against the edge of his desk.

Rebus was thinking of Charlie as he stopped his car in front of the tiny old-fashioned men's-wear shop off George Street. He was thinking of Charlie as he grabbed the tie and paid for it. Back in the car, he thought of Charlie as he knotted the tie, started the ignition, and drove off. Heading towards lunch with some of the wealthiest businessmen in the city, all he could think of was Charlie, and how Charlie could probably still choose to be like those businessmen one day. He'd leave university, use his family connections to land a good job, and progress smoothly through to upper management in the space of a year or two. He would forget all about his infatuation with decadence, and would become decadent himself, the way only the rich and successful ever can. . . . True decadence, not the second-hand stuff of witchcraft and demonism, drugs and violence. That bruising on Ronnie's body: could

81

it really have been rough trade? A sadomasochistic game gone wrong? A game played, perhaps, with the mysterious Edward, whose name Ronnie had screamed?

Or a ritual carried too far?

Had he dismissed the Satanism angle too readily? Wasn't a policeman supposed to keep an open mind? Perhaps, but Satanism found him with his mind well and truly closed. He was a Christian, after all. He might not attend church often, detesting all the hymn-singing and the bald sermonising, but that didn't mean he didn't believe in that small, dark personal God of his. Everyone had a God tagging along with them. And the God of the Scots was as ominous as He came.

Midday Edinburgh seemed darker than ever, reflecting his mood perhaps. The Castle appeared to be casting a shadow across the expanse of the New Town, but that shadow did not, could not reach as high as The Eyrie. The Eyrie was the city's most expensive restaurant, and also the most exclusive. Rumour had it that lunchtime was solidly booked twelve months in advance, while dinner entailed the small wait of eight to ten weeks. The restaurant itself was situated on the entire top floor of a Georgian hotel in the heart of the New Town, away from the city centre's human bustle.

Not that the streets here were exactly quiet, a steady amount of through traffic pausing long enough to make parking a problem. But not to a detective. Rebus stopped his car on a double yellow line directly outside the hotel's main door, and, despite the doorman's warnings about wardens and fines, left it there and entered the hotel. He squeezed his stomach as the lift carried him four floors high, and was satisfied that he felt hungry. These businessmen might well bore the pants off him, and the thought of spending two hours with Farmer Watson was almost too much to bear, but he would eat well. Yes, he would eat exceedingly well.

And, given his way with the wine list, he'd bankrupt the buggers to boot.

Brian Holmes left the snack bar carrying a polystyrene cup of grey tea, and studied it, trying to remember when he had last had a cup of good tea, of real tea, of tea he had brewed himself. His life seemed to revolve around polystyrene cups and thermos flasks, unexciting sandwiches and chocolate biscuits. Blow, sip. Blow, sip. Swallow.

For this he had given up an academic career.

Which was to say that he had careered around academia for some eight months, studying History at the University of London. The first month he had spent in awe of the city itself, trying to come to terms with its size, the complexities of actually trying to live and travel and survive with dignity. The second and third months he had spent trying to come to terms with university life, with new friends, the persistent openings for discussion, argument, for inclusion in this or that group. He tested the water each time before joining in, all of them nervous as children learning to swim. By months four and five, he had become a Londoner, commuting to the University every day from his digs in Battersea. Suddenly his life had come to be ruled by numbers, by the times of trains and buses and tube connections, the times, too, of late buses and tubes which would whisk him away from coffee-bar politics towards his noisy single room again. Missing a train connection began to be agony, suffering the rush-hour tube, a season spent in hell. Months six and seven he spent isolated in Battersea, studying from his room, hardly attending lectures at all. And in month eight, May, with the sun warming his back, he left London and returned north, back to old friends and a sudden emptiness in his life that had to be filled by work.

But why in the name of God had he chosen the police?

He screwed up the now empty polystyrene cup and

threw it towards a nearby bin. It missed. So what, he thought. Then caught himself, went to the cup, stooped, picked it up, and deposited it in the bin. You're not in London now, Brian, he told himself. An elderly woman smiled at him.

So shines a good deed in a naughty world.

A naughty world all right. Rebus had landed him in a soup of melted humanity. Pilmuir, Hiroshima of the soul; he couldn't escape quickly enough. Fear of radiation. He had a little list with him, copied down neatly from last night's scrawled telephone conversation, and he took this from his pocket now to examine it. The constables had been easy to locate. Rebus would have seen them by now. Then he had gone to the house in Pilmuir. In his inside pocket he had the photographs. Edinburgh Castle. Good shots, too. Unusual angles. And the girl. She looked quite pretty, he supposed. Hard to tell her age, and her face seemed tempered by hard living, but she was bonny enough in a rough and ready way. He had no idea how he would find out anything about her. All he had to go on was that name, Tracy. True, there were people he could ask. Edinburgh was his home turf, an enormous advantage in this particular line of work. He had contacts all right, old friends, friends of friends. He'd re-established contact after the London fiasco. They'd all told him not to go. They'd all been pleased to see him again so soon after their warnings, pleased because they could boast of their foresight. That had only been five years ago. . . . It seemed longer somehow.

Why had he joined the force? His first choice had been journalism. That went way back, back to his schooldays. Well, childhood dreams could come true, if only momentarily. His next stop would be the offices of the local daily. See if he could find some more unusual angles on the Castle. With any luck, he'd get a decent cup of tea, too.

He was about to walk on when he saw an estate agent's

window across the street. He had always assumed that this particular agency would, because of its name, be expensive. But what the hell: he was a desperate man. He manoeuvred his way through the queue of unmoving traffic and stopped in front of the window of Bowyer Carew. After a minute, his shoulders slightly more hunched than before, he turned away again and stalked towards the Bridges.

'And this is James Carew, of Bowyer Carew.'

James Carew lifted his well-upholstered bottom a millimetre off his well-upholstered chair, shook Rebus's hand, then sat again. Throughout the introduction, his eyes had not left Rebus's tie.

'Finlay Andrews,' continued Superintendent Watson, and Rebus shook another firm masonic hand. He didn't need to know the secret pressure spots to be able to place a freemason. The grip itself told you everything, lasting as it did a little longer than normal, the extra time it took the shaker to work out whether you were of the brotherhood or not.

'You might know Mr Andrews. He has a gaming establishment in Duke Terrace. What's it called again?' Watson was trying too hard: too hard to be the host, too hard to get along with these men, too hard for everyone's comfort.

'It's just called Finlay's,' Finlay Andrews supplied, releasing his grip on Rebus.

'Tommy McCall,' said the final luncheon guest, making his own introduction, and giving Rebus's hand a quick, cool shake. Rebus smiled, and sat down, joining them at the table, thankful to be sitting down at last.

'Not Tony McCall's brother?' he asked conversationally.

'That's right.' McCall smiled. 'You know Tony then?'

'Pretty well,' said Rebus. Watson was looking bemused.

'Inspector McCall,' Rebus explained. Watson nodded vigorously.

'So,' said Carew, shifting in his seat, 'what will you have to drink, Inspector Rebus?'

'Not while on duty, sir,' said Rebus, unfolding his prettily arranged napkin. He saw the look on Carew's face and smiled. 'Just a joke. I'll have a gin and tonic, please.'

They all smiled. A policeman with a sense of humour: it usually surprised people. It would have surprised them even more had they known how seldom Rebus made jokes. But he felt the need to conform here, to 'mix', in that unhappy phrase.

There was a waiter at his shoulder.

'Another gin and tonic, Ronald,' Carew told the waiter, who bowed and moved off. Another waiter replaced him, and started handing out huge leather-bound menus. The thick cloth napkin was heavy on Rebus's lap.

'Where do you live, Inspector?' The question was Carew's. His smile seemed more than a smile, and Rebus was cautious.

'Marchmont,' he said.

'Oh,' Carew enthused, 'that's always been a very good area. Used to be a farming estate back in the old days, you know.'

'Really?'

'Mmm. Lovely neighbourhood.'

'What James means,' interrupted Tommy McCall, 'is that the houses are worth a few bob.'

'So they are,' Carew answered indignantly. 'Handy for the centre of town, close to The Meadows and the University. . . .'

'James,' Finlay Andrews warned, 'you're talking shop.'

'Am I?' Carew seemed genuinely surprised. He gave Rebus that smile again. 'Sorry.'

'I recommend the sirloin,' said Andrews. When the

waiter returned to take their order, Rebus made a point of ordering sole.

He tried to be casual, not to stare at the other diners, not to examine the minutiae of the tablecloth, the implements unknown to him, the finger bowls, the hallmarked cutlery. But then this was one of those once-in-a-lifetime things, wasn't it? So why not stare? He did, and saw fifty or so well-fed, happy faces, mostly male, with the occasional decorative female for the sake of decency, of elegance. Prime fillet. That's what everyone else seemed to be having. And wine.

'Who wants to choose the wine?' said McCall, flourishing the list. Carew looked eager to snatch, and Rebus held back. It wouldn't do, would it? To grab the list, to say me, me, me. To look with hungry eyes at the prices, wishing. . . .

'If I may,' said Finlay Andrews, lifting the wine list from McCall's hand. Rebus studied the hallmark on his fork.

'So,' said McCall, looking at Rebus, 'Superintendent Watson has roped you in on our little mission, eh?'

'I don't know that any rope was needed,' said Rebus. 'I'm glad to help if I can.'

'I'm sure your experience will be invaluable,' Watson said to Rebus, beaming at him. Rebus stared back evenly, but said nothing.

As luck would have it, Andrews seemed to know a bit about wine himself, and ordered a decent '82 claret and a crisp Chablis. Rebus perked up a bit as Andrews did the ordering. What was the name of the gaming club again? Andrews? Finlay's? Yes, that was it. Finlay's. He'd heard of it, a small casino, quiet. There had never been any cause for Rebus to go there, either on business or for pleasure. What pleasure was there in losing money?

'Is your Chinaman still haunting the place, Finlay?' asked McCall now, while two waiters ladled a thin covering of soup into wide-circumferenced Victorian soup plates.

'He won't get in again. Management reserves the right to refuse entry, et cetera.'

McCall chuckled, turned to Rebus.

'Finlay had a bad run back there. The Chinese are terrible for gambling, you know. Well, this one Chinaman was taking Finlay for a ride.'

'I had an inexperienced croupier,' Andrews explained. 'The experienced eye, and I do mean *experienced*, could tell pretty much where the ball was going to land on the roulette wheel, just by watching carefully how this youngster was flicking the ball.'

'Remarkable,' said Watson, before blowing on a spoonful of soup.

'Not really,' said Andrews. 'I've seen it before. It's simply a matter of spotting the type before they manage to lay on a really heavy bet. But then, you have to take the rough with the smooth. This has been a good year so far, a lot of money moving north, finding there's not so much to do up here, so why not simply gamble it away?'

'Money moving north?' Rebus was interested.

'People, jobs. London executives with London salaries and London habits. Haven't you noticed?'

'I can't say I have,' Rebus confessed. 'Not around Pilmuir at any rate.'

There were smiles at this.

'My estate agency has certainly noticed it,' said Carew. 'Larger properties are in great demand. Corporate buyers in some cases. Businesses moving north, opening offices. They know a good thing when they see it, and Edinburgh is a good thing. House prices have gone through the roof. I see no reason for them to stop.' He caught Rebus's eye. 'They're even building new homes in Pilmuir.'

'Finlay,' McCall interrupted, 'tell Inspector Rebus where the Chinese players keep their money.'

'Not while we're eating, please,' said Watson, and when McCall, chuckling to himself, looked down at his soup plate, Rebus saw Andrews flash the man a hateful look.

The wine had arrived, chilled and the colour of honey. Rebus sipped. Carew was asking Andrews about some planning permission to do with an extension to the casino.

'It seems to be all right.' Andrews tried not to sound smug. Tommy McCall laughed.

'I'll bet it does,' he said. 'Would your neighbours find the going as smooth if they tried to stick a big bloody extension on the back of *their* premises?'

Andrews gave a smile as cold as the Chablis. 'Each case is considered individually and scrupulously, Tommy, so far as I know. Maybe you know better?'

'No, no.' McCall had finished his first glass of wine, and was reaching for a second. 'I'm sure it's all totally above board, Finlay.' He looked conspiratorially at Rebus. 'I hope you're not going to tell tales, John.'

'No.' Rebus glanced towards Andrews, who was finishing his soup. 'Over lunch, my ears are closed.'

Watson nodded agreement.

'Hello there, Finlay.' A large man, heavily built but with the accent on muscularity, was standing by the table. He was wearing the most expensive-looking suit Rebus had ever seen. A silken sheen of blue with threads of silver running through it. The man's hair was silvered, too, though his face looked to be fortyish, no more. Beside him, leaning in towards him, stood a delicate Oriental woman, more girl than woman. She was exquisite, and everyone at the table rose in a kind of awe. The man waved an elegant hand, demanding they be seated. The woman hid her pleasure beneath her eyelashes.

'Hello, Malcolm.' Finlay Andrews gestured towards the man. 'This is Malcolm Lanyon, the advocate.' The last two words were unnecessary. Everyone knew Malcolm Lanyon, the gossip column's friend. His very public lifestyle provoked either hatred or envy. He was at the same time all that was most despised about the law profession, and a walking TV mini-series. If his lifestyle occasionally scandalised the prurient, it also satisfied a deep need in the readers of Sunday tabloids. He was also, to Rebus's sure knowledge, an extraordinarily good lawyer. He had to be, otherwise the rest of his image would have been wallpaper, nothing more. It wasn't wallpaper. It was bricks and mortar.

'These,' Andrews said, gesturing now to the occupants of the table, 'are the working members of that committee I was telling you about.'

'Ah.' Lanyon nodded. 'The campaign against drugs. An excellent idea, Superintendent.'

Watson almost blushed at the compliment: the compliment was that Lanyon knew who Watson was.

'Finlay,' Lanyon continued, 'you've not forgotten tomorrow night?'

'Firmly etched in my diary, Malcolm.'

'Excellent.' Lanyon glanced over the table. 'In fact, I'd like you all to come. Just a little gathering at my house. No real reason for it, I just felt like having a party. Eight o'clock. Very casual.' He was already moving off, an arm around the porcelain waist of his companion. Rebus caught his final words: his address. Heriot Row. One of the most exclusive streets in the New Town. This was a new world. Although he couldn't be sure that the invitation was serious, Rebus was tempted to take it up. Once in a lifetime, and all that.

A little later, conversation moved to the anti-drugs campaign itself and the waiter brought more bread.

'Bread,' the nervous young man said, carrying another bound file of newspapers over to the counter where

90

Holmes stood. 'That's what worries me. Everybody's turning into a bread head. You know, nothing matters to them except getting more than anyone else. Guys I went to school with, knew by the age of fourteen that they wanted to be bankers or accountants or economists. Lives were over before they'd begun. These are May.'

'What?' Holmes was shifting his weight from one leg to another. Why couldn't they have chairs in this place? He had been here over an hour, his fingers blackened by old newsprint as he flicked through each day's editions, one daytime, one evening. Now and then, a headline or some football story he'd missed first time around would attract his attention. But soon enough he had tired, and now it was merely routine. What's more, his arms were aching from all that page turning.

'May,' the youth explained. 'These are the May editions.'

'Right, thanks.'

'Finished with June?'

'Yes, thanks.'

The youth nodded, buckled shut two leather straps on the open end of the bound file, and heaved the whole up into his arms, shuffling out of the room. Here we go again, thought Holmes, unbuckling this latest batch of old news and space fillers.

Rebus had been wrong. There had been no old retainer to act as a computer memory, and no computer either. So it was down to hard graft and page turning, looking for photographs of familiar places, made fresh through the use of odd camera angles. Why? He didn't know even that yet, and the thought frustrated him. He'd find out later this afternoon hopefully, when he met with Rebus. There was a shuffling sound again as the youth re-entered, arms dangling now, jaw hanging.

'So why didn't you do the same as your friends?' Holmes said conversationally.

'You mean go in for banking?' The youth wrinkled his nose. 'Wanted something different. I'm learning journalism. Got to start somewhere, haven't you?'

Indeed you have, thought Holmes, turning another page. Indeed you have.

'Well, it's a start,' said McCall, rising. They were crumpling their used napkins, tossing them onto the dishevelled tablecloth. What had once been pristine was now covered with breadcrumbs and splashes of wine, a dark patch of butter, a single dripped coffee stain. Rebus felt woozy as he pulled himself out of the chair. And full. His tongue was furred from too much wine and coffee, and that cognac – Christ! Now these men were about to go back to work, or so they claimed. Rebus, too. He had a meeting at three with Holmes, didn't he? But it was already gone three. Oh well, Holmes wouldn't complain. Couldn't complain, thought Rebus smugly.

'Not a bad spread that,' said Carew, patting his girth. Rebus couldn't be sure whether this, or the food itself, was the spread he meant.

'And we covered a lot of ground,' said Watson, 'let's not forget that.'

'Indeed not,' said McCall. 'A very useful meeting.'

Andrews had insisted on paying the bill. A good three figures' worth by Rebus's hasty calculation. Andrews was studying the bill now, lingering over each item as though checking it against his own mental price list. Not only a businessman, thought Rebus unkindly, but a bloody good Scot. Then Andrews called over the brisk maitre d' and told him quietly about one item for which they had been overcharged. The maitre d' took Andrews' word for it, and altered the bill there and then with his own ballpoint pen, apologising unreservedly.

The restaurant was just beginning to empty. A nice lunch hour over for all the diners. Rebus felt sudden guilt

92

overwhelm him. He had just eaten and drunk his share of about two hundred pounds. Forty quid's worth, in other words. Some had dined better, and were noisily, laughingly making their way out of the dining room. Old stories, cigars, red faces. McCall put an unwelcome arm around Rebus's back, nodding towards the leavetaking.

'If there were only fifty Tory voters left in Scotland, John, they'd all be in this room.'

'I believe it,' said Rebus.

Andrews, turning from the maitre d', had heard them. 'I thought there *were* only fifty Tories left up here,' he said.

There, Rebus noted, were those quiet, confident smiles again. I have eaten ashes for bread, he thought. Ashes for bread. Cigar ash burned red all around him, and for a moment he thought he might be sick. But then McCall stumbled, and Rebus had to hold him up until he found his balance.

'Bit too much to drink, Tommy?' said Carew.

'Just need a breath of air,' said McCall. 'John'll help me, won't you, John?'

'Of course,' said Rebus, glad of this excuse for the very thing he needed.

McCall turned back towards Carew. 'Got your new car with you?'

Carew shook his head. 'I left it in the garage.'

McCall, nodding, turned to Rebus. 'The flash bugger's just bought himself a V-Twelve Jag,' he explained. 'Nearly forty thousand, and I'm not talking about miles on the clock.'

One of the waiters was standing by the lift.

'Nice to have seen you gentlemen again,' he said, his voice as automatic as the lift doors which closed when Rebus and McCall stepped inside.

'I must have arrested him some time,' Rebus said, 'because I've never been here before, so he can't have seen me here before.'

'This place is nothing,' said McCall, screwing up his face. 'Nothing. You want some fun, you should come to the club one night. Just say you're a friend of Finlay's. That'll get you in. Great place it is.'

'I might do that,' said Rebus as the lift doors opened. 'Just as soon as my cummerbund comes back from the dry cleaners.'

McCall laughed all the way out of the building.

Holmes was stiff as he left the building by its staff entrance. The youth, having shown him through the maze of corridors, had already turned back inside, hands in pockets, whistling. Holmes wondered if he really would end up with a career in journalism. Stranger things had happened.

He had found the photographs he wanted, one in each of three consecutive Wednesday daytime's editions. From these, the photographic library had traced the originals, and on the backs of the originals was the same golden rectangular sticker, denoting that the photos were the property of Jimmy Hutton Photographic Studios. The stickers, bless them, even mentioned an address and phone number. So Holmes allowed himself the luxury of a stretch, cracking his spine back into some semblance of shape. He thought about treating himself to a pint, but after leaning over the study table for the best part of two hours the last thing he wanted to do was lean against a bar as he drank. Besides, it was three fifteen. He was already, thanks to a quick-witted but slow-moving photo library, late for his meeting – his *first* – with Inspector Rebus. He didn't know how Rebus stood on the issue of punctuality; he feared the stand would be hard. Well, if the day's work so far didn't cheer him up, he wasn't human.

But then that was the rumour anyway.

Not that Holmes believed rumours. Well, not always.

As it turned out, Rebus was the later of the two for the meeting, though he had phoned ahead to apologise, which was something. Holmes was seated in front of Rebus's desk when Rebus finally arrived, pulling off rather a gaudy tie and dumping it into a drawer. Only then did he turn to Holmes, stare at him, smile, and stretch out a hand, which Holmes accepted.

Well that's something, thought Rebus: he's not a mason either.

'Your first name is Brian, isn't it?' said Rebus sitting down.

'That's right, sir.'

'Good. I'll call you Brian, and you can keep on calling me sir. That seem fair enough?'

Holmes smiled. 'Very fair, sir.'

'Right, any progress?'

So Holmes started at the beginning. As he spoke, he noticed that Rebus, though trying his damnedest to be attentive, was drowsy. His breath across the table was strong-smelling. Whatever he'd had for lunch had agreed with him too well. Finishing his report, he waited for Rebus to speak.

Rebus merely nodded, and was silent for some time. Collecting his thoughts? Holmes felt the need to fill the vacuum.

'What's the problem, sir, if you don't mind my asking?'

'You've every right to ask,' said Rebus at last. But he stopped at that.

'Well, sir?'

'I'm not sure, Brian. That's the truth. Okay, here's what I know – and I stress *know*, because there's plenty I *think*, which isn't quite the same thing in this case.'

'There is a case then?'

'You tell me, as soon as you've listened.' And it was Rebus's turn to make his 'report' of sorts, fixing it again in his mind as he told the story. But it was too fragmented, too speculative. He could see Holmes struggling with the pieces, trying to see the whole picture. Was there a picture there to see?

'So you see,' Rebus ended, 'we've got a junkie full of poison, self-inflicted. Someone who supplied the poison. Bruising on the body, and the hint of a witchcraft connection. We've got a missing camera, a tie clip, some photographs, and a girlfriend being followed. You see my problem?'

'Too much to go on.'

'Exactly.'

'So what do we do now?'

That 'we' caught Rebus's attention. For the first time, he realised that he was no longer in this alone, whatever 'this' was. The thought cheered him a little, though the hangover was starting now, the sleepy slow thumping either side of his forehead.

'I'm going to see a man about a coven,' he said, sure now of the next steps. 'And you're going to visit Hutton's Photographic Studios.'

'That sounds reasonable,' said Holmes.

'So it bloody well should,' said Rebus. 'I'm the one with the brains, Brian. You're the one with the shoeleather. Call me later on to let me know how you get on. Meantime, bugger off.'

Rebus didn't mean to be unkind. But there had been something just too cosy and conspiratorial in the younger man's tone towards the end, and he'd felt the need to re-establish boundaries. His own mistake, he realised as the door closed behind Holmes. His own mistake, for coming on so chattily, for telling all, for confiding, and for using Holmes's first name. That bloody lunch had been to blame. Call me Finlay, call me James, call me Tommy. . . . Never mind, it would all work out. They had begun well, then less well. Things could only get worse, which was fine by Rebus. He enjoyed a measure of antagonism, of competition. They were distinct bonuses in this line of work.

So Rebus was a bastard after all.

Brian Holmes stalked out of the station with hands in pockets tightened to fists. Knuckles red. *You're the one with the shoeleather.* That had really brought him down with a thump, just when he'd thought they were getting on so well. Almost like human beings rather than coppers. Should've known better, Brian. And as for the reason behind all this work. . . . Well, it hardly bore thinking about. It was so flimsy, so personal to Rebus. It wasn't police work at all. It was an inspector with nothing to do for a while, trying to fill the time by playing at being Philip Marlowe. Jesus, they both had better things they could be doing. Well, Holmes did anyway. He wasn't about to head some cushy anti-drugs campaign. And what a choice Rebus was for that! Brother inside Peterhead, doing time for pushing. Biggest dealer in Fife, he'd been. That should have screwed up Rebus's career forever and anon, but instead they'd given him promotion. A naughty world, all right.

He had to visit a photographer. Maybe he could get some passport shots done at the same time. Pack his bags and fly off to Canada, Australia, the States. Sod his flat hunting. Sod the police force. And sod Detective Inspector John Rebus and his witch hunt.

There, it was done.

Rebus found some aspirin in one of his chaotic drawers, and crunched them to a bitter powder as he made his way downstairs. Bad mistake. They removed every fleck of saliva from his mouth, and he couldn't even swallow, couldn't speak. The desk sergeant was sipping a poly-styrene beaker of tea. Rebus grabbed it from him and gulped at the tepid liquid. Then squirmed.

'How much sugar did you put in that, Jack?'

'If I'd known you were coming to tea, John, I'd have made it just the way you like it.'

The desk sergeant always had a smart answer, and Rebus could never think of a smarter rejoinder. He handed back the cup and walked away, feeling the sugar cloy inside him.

I'll never touch another drop, he was thinking as he started his car. Honest to God, only the occasional glass of wine. Allow me that. But no more indulgence, and no more mixing wine and spirits. Okay? So give me a break, God, and lift this hangover. I only drank the one glass of cognac, maybe two glasses of claret, one of Chablis. One gin and tonic. It was hardly the stuff of legend, hardly a case for the detox ward.

The roads were quiet though, which was a break. Not enough of a break, but a break. So he made good time to Pilmuir, and then remembered that he didn't know where Charlie boy lived. Charlie, the person he needed to talk to if he was going to find an address for a coven. A white coven. He wanted to double-check the witchcraft story. He wanted to double-check Charlie, too, come to that. But he didn't want Charlie to know he was being checked.

The witchcraft thing niggled. Rebus believed in good and evil, and believed stupid people could be attracted towards the latter. He understood pagan religions well enough, had read about them in books too thick and intense for their own good. He didn't mind people worshipping the Earth, or whatever. It all came down to the same thing in the end. What he did mind was people worshipping Evil as a force, and as *more* than a force: as an entity. Especially, he disliked the idea of people doing it for 'kicks' without knowing or caring what it was they were involved in.

People like Charlie. He remembered that book of Giger prints again. Satan, poised at the centre of a pair of scales, flanked by a naked woman left and right. The women were being penetrated by huge drills. Satan was a goat's head in a mask. . . .

But where would Charlie be now? He'd find out. Stop and ask. Knock on doors. Hint at retribution should information be withheld. He'd act the big bad policeman if that was what it took.

He didn't need to do anything, as it happened. He just had to find the police constables who were loitering outside one of the boarded-up houses, not too far from where Ronnie had died. One of the constables held a radio to his mouth. The other was writing in a notebook. Rebus stopped his car, stepped out. Then remembered something, leaned back into the car and drew his keys from out of the ignition. You couldn't be too careful around here. A second later, he actually locked his driver's side door, too.

He knew one of the constables. It was Harry Todd, one of the men who had found Ronnie. Todd straightened when he saw Rebus, but Rebus waved this acknowledgment aside, so Todd continued with his radio conversation. Rebus concentrated on the other officer instead.

'What's the score here?' The constable turned from his writing to give Rebus that suspicious, near-hostile look almost unique to the constabulary. 'Inspector Rebus,' Rebus explained. He was wondering where Todd's Irish sidekick O'Rourke was.

'Oh,' said the constable. 'Well . . .' He started to put away his pen. 'We were called to a domestic, sir. In this house. A real screaming match. But by the time we got here, the man had fled. The woman is still inside. She's got herself a black eye, nothing more. Not really your territory, sir.'

'Is that right?' said Rebus. 'Well, thank you for telling me, sonny. It's nice to be told what is and isn't my "territory". Thank you so much. Now, may I have your permission to enter the premises?'

The constable was blushing furiously, his cheeks an almighty red against his bloodless face and neck. No: even his *neck* was blushing now. Rebus enjoyed that. He didn't even mind that behind the constable, but in full view of Rebus himself, Todd was smirking at this encounter.

'Well?' Rebus prompted.

'Sorry, sir,' said the constable.

'Right,' said Rebus, walking towards the door. But before he reached it, it was opened from the inside, and there stood Tracy, both eyes reddened from crying, one eye bruised a deep blue. She didn't seem surprised to see Rebus standing in front of her; she seemed relieved, and threw herself at him, hugging him, her head against his chest, the tears beginning all over again.

Rebus, startled and embarrassed, returned the embrace only lightly, with a patting of his hands on her back: a father's 'there, there' to a frightened child. He turned his head to look at the constables, who were pretending to have noticed nothing. Then a car drew up beside his own, and he saw Tony McCall put on his handbrake before pushing open the driver's door, stepping out and seeing Rebus there, and the girl.

Rebus laid his hands on Tracy's arms and pushed her away from him a little, but still retaining that contact between them. His hands, her arms. She looked at him, and began to fight against the tears. Finally, she pulled one arm away so that she could wipe her eyes. Then the other arm relaxed and Rebus's hand fell from it, the contact broken. For now.

'John?' It was McCall, close behind him.

'Yes, Tony?'

'Why is it my patch has suddenly become your patch?'

'Just passing,' said Rebus.

The interior of the house was surprisingly neat and tidy. There were numerous, if uncoordinated, sticks of furniture – two well-worn settees, a couple of dining chairs, trellis table, half a dozen pouffes, burst at the seams and oozing stuffing – and, most surprising of all, the electricity was connected.

'Wonder if the electric board know about that,' said McCall as Rebus switched on the downstairs lights.

For all its trappings, the place had an air of impermanence. There were sleeping bags laid out on the living-room floor, as though ready for any stray waifs and passers-by. Tracy went to one of the settees and sat down, wrapping her hands around her knees.

'Is this your place, Tracy?' said Rebus, knowing the answer.

'No. It's Charlie's.'

'How long have you known?'

'I only found out today. He moves around all the time. It wasn't easy tracking him down.'

'It didn't take you long.' She shrugged her shoulders. 'What happened?'

'I just wanted to talk to him.'

'About Ronnie?' McCall watched Rebus as he said this. McCall was concentrating now, aware that Rebus was trying to fill him in on the situation while at the same time questioning Tracy. Tracy nodded.

'Stupid, maybe, but I needed to talk to someone.'

'And?'

'And we got into an argument. He started it. Told me I was the cause of Ronnie's death.' She looked up at them; not pleadingly, but just to show that she was sincere. 'It's not true. But Charlie said I should have looked after Ronnie, stopped him taking the stuff, got him away from Pilmuir. How could I have done that? He wouldn't have listened to me. I thought he knew what he was doing. Nobody could tell him otherwise.'

'Is that what you told Charlie?'

She smiled. 'No. I only thought of it just now. That's what always happens, isn't it? You only think of the clever comeback after the argument's finished.'

'I know what you mean, love,' said McCall.

'So you started a slanging match —'

'I never started the slanging match!' she roared at Rebus.

'Okay,' he said quietly, 'Charlie started shouting at you, and you shouted back, then he hit you. Yes?'

'Yes.' She seemed subdued.

'And maybe,' Rebus prompted, 'you hit him back?'

'I gave as good as I got.'

'That's my girl,' said McCall. He was touring the room, turning up cushions on the settees, opening old magazines, crouching to pat each sleeping bag.

'Don't patronise me, you bastard,' said Tracy.

McCall paused, looked up, surprised. Then smiled, and patted the next sleeping bag along. 'Ah-ha,' he said, lifting the sleeping bag and shaking it. A small polythene bag fell out onto the floor. He picked it up, satisfied. 'A little bit of blaw,' he said. 'Makes a house into a home, eh?'

'I don't know anything about that,' said Tracy, looking at the bag.

'We believe you,' said Rebus. 'Charlie did a runner then?'

'Yes. The neighbours must've phoned for the pigs . . . I mean, the police.' She averted her eyes from them.

'We've been called worse,' said McCall, 'haven't we, John?'

'That's for sure. So the constables arrived at one door, and Charlie left by another, right?'

'Out of the back door, yes.'

'Well,' said Rebus, 'while we're here we might as well have a look at his room, if such a thing exists.'

'Good idea,' said McCall, pocketing the polythene bag. 'There's no smoke without fire.'

Charlie had a room all right. It consisted of a single sleeping bag, a desk, anglepoise lamp, and more books than Rebus had ever seen in such an enclosed space. They were piled against the walls, reaching in precarious pillars from floor to ceiling. Many were library books, well overdue.

'Must owe the City Fathers a small fortune,' said McCall.

There were books on economics, politics and history, as well as learned and not so learned tomes on demonism, devil worship and witchcraft. There was little fiction, and most of the books had been read thoroughly, with much underlining and pencilled marginalia. On the desk sat a half-completed essay, part of Charlie's university course work no doubt. It seemed to be trying to link 'magick' to modern society, but was mostly, to Rebus's eye, rambling nonsense.

'Hello!'

This was shouted from downstairs, as the two constables started to climb the staircase.

'Hello yourselves,' McCall called back. Then he shook the contents of a large supermarket carrier bag onto the floor, so that pens, toy cars, cigarette papers, a wooden egg, a spool of cotton, a personal cassette player, a Swiss army knife, and a camera fell out. McCall stooped to pick up the camera between thumb and middle finger. Nice model, thirty-five-millimetre SLR. Good make. He gestured with it towards Rebus, who took it from him, having first produced a handkerchief from his pocket, with which he held it. Rebus turned towards Tracy who was standing against the door with her arms folded. She nodded back at him.

'Yes,' she said. 'That's Ronnie's camera.'

The constables were at the top of the stairs now. Rebus accepted McCall's offer of the supermarket carrier and dropped the camera into it, careful not to mess up any prints.

'Todd,' he said to the constable he knew, 'take this young lady down to Great London Road station.' Tracy's mouth opened. 'It's for your own protection,' Rebus said. 'Go on with them. I'll see you later, soon as I can.'

She still seemed ready to voice a complaint, but thought better of it, nodded and turned, leaving the room. Rebus listened as she went downstairs, accompanied by the officers. McCall was still searching, though without real concern. Two finds were quite enough to be going on with.

'No smoke without fire,' he said.

'I had lunch with Tommy today,' said Rebus.

'My brother Tommy?' McCall looked up. Rebus nodded. 'Then that's one up to you. He's never taken me to lunch these past fifteen years.'

'We were at The Eyrie.' Now McCall whistled. 'To do with Watson's anti-drugs campaign.'

'Yes, Tommy's shelling out for it, isn't he? Ach, I shouldn't be hard on him. He's done me a few favours in his time.'

'He had a few too many.'

McCall laughed gently. 'He hasn't changed then. Still, he can afford it. That transport company of his, it runs itself. He used to be there twenty-four hours a day, fifty-two weeks of the year. Nowadays, he can take off as long as he likes. His accountant once told him to take a *year* off. Can you imagine that? For tax purposes. If only we had those kinds of problem, eh, John?'

'You're right there, Tony.' Rebus was still holding the supermarket bag. McCall nodded towards it.

'Does this tie it up?'

'It makes things a bit clearer,' said Rebus. 'I might get it checked for prints.'

'I can tell you what you'll find,' said McCall. 'The deceased's and this guy Charlie's.'

'You're forgetting someone.'

'Who?'

'You, Tony. You picked the camera up with your fingers, remember?'

'Ah, sorry. I didn't think.'

'Never mind.'

'Anyway, it's something, isn't it? Something to celebrate, I mean. I don't know about you, but I'm starved.'

As they left the room, one pillar of books finally gave way, slewing down across the floor like dominoes waiting to be shuffled. Rebus opened the door again to look in.

'Ghosts,' said McCall. 'That's all. Just ghosts.'

It wasn't much to look at. Not what he'd been expecting. Okay, so there was a potted plant in one corner, and black roller blinds over the windows, and even a word processor gathering dust on a newish plastic desk. But it was still the second floor of a tenement, still designed as somebody's home and never meant to be used as office, studio, workplace. Holmes gave the room – the so-called 'front office' – a tour as the cute little school-leaver went off to fetch 'His Highness'. That was what she'd called him. If your staff didn't hold you in esteem, or at the very least in frightened awe, there was something wrong with you. Certainly, as the door opened and 'His Highness' walked in, it was evident to Holmes that there was something wrong with Jimmy Hutton.

For a start, he was the other side of fifty, yet what hair he still had was long, thin strands covering his forehead almost down to his eyes. He was also wearing denims: a mistake easily made by those aspiring to youth from the wrong side. And he was short. Five foot two or three. Now Holmes began to see the relevance of the secretary's pun. His highness, indeed.

He had a harassed look on his face, but had left the camera through in the back bedroom or box room or whichever room of the smallish flat served as his studio. He stuck out a hand, and Holmes shook it.

'Detective Constable Holmes,' he announced. Hutton nodded, took a cigarette from the packet on his secretary's desk and lit it. She frowned openly at this as she sat down again, smoothing her tight skirt beneath her. Hutton had not yet looked at Holmes. His eyes seemed to be mirroring some distraction in his mind. He went to the window, looked out, arched his neck to blow a plume of smoke towards the high, dark ceiling, then let his head go limp, leaning against the wall.

'Get me a coffee, Christine.' His eyes met Holmes's momentarily. 'Do you want one?' Holmes shook his head.

'Sure?' said Christine kindly, rising out of her seat again.

'Okay then. Thanks.'

With a smile she left the room, off to the kitchen or darkroom to fill a kettle.

'So,' said Hutton. 'What can I do for you?'

That was another thing about the man. His voice was high, not shrill or girlish, just high. And slightly rasping, as though he had damaged his vocal cords at some point in his youth and they had never recovered.

'Mr Hutton?' Holmes needed to be sure. Hutton nodded.

'Jimmy Hutton, professional photographer, at your service. You're getting married and you want me to do you a discount?'

'No, nothing like that.'

'A portrait then. Girlfriend perhaps? Mum and dad?'

'No, this is business, I'm afraid. *My* business, that is.'

'But no new business for me, right?' Hutton smiled, chanced another glance towards Holmes, drew on his cigarette again. 'I *could* do a portrait of you, you know. Nice strong chin, decent cheekbones. With the proper lighting. . . .'

'No, thanks. I hate having my picture taken.'

'I'm not talking about pictures.' Hutton was moving now, circling the desk. 'I'm talking about art.'

'That's why I came here actually.'

'What?'

'Art. I was impressed by some of your photos I saw in a newspaper. I was wondering whether you might be able to help me.'

'Oh?'

'It's a missing person.' Holmes was not a great liar. His ears tingled when he told a real whopper. Not a great liar, but a good one. 'A young man called Ronnie McGrath.'

'Name doesn't mean anything.'

'He wanted to be a photographer, that's why I was wondering.'

'Wondering what?'

'If he'd ever come to you. You know, asking advice, that sort of thing. You're an established name, after all.' It was almost too blatant. Holmes could sense it: could sense Hutton just about realising what the game was. But vanity won in the end.

'Well,' the photographer said, leaning against the desk, folding his arms, crossing his legs, sure of himself. 'What did he look like, this Ronnie?'

'Tallish, short brown hair. Liked to do studies. You know the sort of thing, the Castle, Calton Hill. . . .'

'Are you a photographer yourself, Inspector?'

'I'm only a constable.' Holmes smiled, pleased by the error. Then caught himself: what if Hutton were trying to play the vanity game with *him*? 'And no, I've never really done much photography. Holiday snaps, that sort of thing.'

'Sugar?' Christine put her head around the door, smiling at Holmes again.

'No thanks,' he said. 'Just milk.'

'Put a drop of whisky in mine,' said Hutton. 'There's a love.' He winked towards the door as it closed again. 'Sounds familiar, I have to admit. Ronnie.... Studies of the Castle. Yes, yes. I *do* remember some young guy coming in, bloody pest he was. I was doing a portfolio, some long-term stuff. Mind had to be one hundred percent on the job. He was always coming round, asking to see me, wanting to show me his work.' Hutton raised his hands apologetically. 'I mean, we were all young once. I wish I could have helped him. But I didn't have the time, not right then.'

'You didn't look at his work?'

'No. No time, as I say. He stopped coming by after a few weeks.'

'How long ago was this?'

'Few months. Three or four.'

The secretary appeared with their coffees. Holmes could smell the whisky wafting out of Hutton's mug, and was jealous and repelled in equal measure. Still, the interview was going well enough. Time for a side road.

'Thanks, Christine,' he said, seeming to please her with the familiarity. She sat down, not drinking herself, and lit a cigarette. He thought for a moment of reaching out to light it for her, but held back.

'Look,' said Hutton. 'I'd like to be of assistance, but....'

'You're a busy man.' Holmes nodded agreement. 'I really do appreciate your giving me any time at all. Anyway, that just about wraps it up.' He took a scalding mouthful of coffee, but dared not spit it back into the mug, so swallowed hard instead.

'Right,' said Hutton, rising from the edge of the desk.

'Oh,' said Holmes. 'Just one thing. Curiosity really, but is there any chance I could have a peek at your studio? I've never been in a proper studio before.'

Hutton looked at Christine, who muffled a smile behind her fingers as she pretended to puff on her cigarette.

'Sure,' he said, smiling himself. 'Why not? Come on.'

The room was large, but otherwise pretty much as Holmes had expected, excepting one significant detail. Half a dozen different types of camera stood on half a dozen tripods. There were photographs covering three of the walls, and against the fourth was a large white backcloth, looking suspiciously like a bedsheet. This was all obvious enough. However, in front of the backcloth had been arranged the set for Hutton's present 'portfolio': two large, freestanding sections, painted pink. And in front of these was a chair, against which, arms folded, stood a young, blonde and bored-looking man.

A man who was naked.

'Detective Holmes, this is Arnold,' said Hutton by way of introduction. 'Arnold is a male model. Nothing wrong, is there?'

Holmes, who had been staring, now tried not to. The blood was rising to his face. He turned to Hutton.

'No, no, nothing.'

Hutton went to one camera and bent down to squint through the viewfinder, aiming in Arnold's general direction. Not at head height.

'The male nude can be quite exquisite,' Hutton was saying. 'Nothing photographs quite as well as the human body.' He clicked the shutter, ran the film on, clicked again, then looked up at Holmes, smiling at the policeman's discomfort.

'What will you do with the . . .' Holmes searched for some decorous word. 'I mean, what are they for?'

'My portfolio, I told you. To show to possible future clients.'

'Right.' Holmes nodded, to show he understood.

'I am an artist, you see, as well as a portrait snapper.'

'Right,' Holmes said, nodding again.

'Not against the law, is it?'

'I don't think so.' He went to the heavily draped window and peeked out through a slight opening. 'Not unless it disturbs the neighbours.'

Hutton laughed. Even the sober face of the model opened in a momentary grin.

'They queue up,' said Hutton, coming to the window and peering out. 'That's why I had to put up the curtains. Dirty buggers that they were. Women *and* men, crammed into the width of a window.' He pointed to a top-storey window in the tenement across the way. 'There. I caught them one day, took a couple of quick shots of them with the motor-drive. They didn't like that.' He turned away from the window. Holmes was browsing along the walls, picking out this and that photograph and nodding praise towards Hutton, who lapped it up and began to walk with him, pointing out this or that angle or trick.

'That's good,' said Holmes, gesturing towards one shot of Edinburgh Castle bathed in mist. It was almost identical to the one he had seen in the newspaper, which made it a very near relative to the one in Ronnie's bedroom. Hutton shrugged.

'That's nothing,' he said, resting a hand on Holmes's shoulder. 'Here, have a look at some of my nude work.'

There was a cluster of a dozen black and white ten-by-eights, pinned to the wall in one corner of the room. Men and women, not all of them young or pretty. But well enough taken, artistic even, Holmes supposed.

'These are just the best,' said Hutton.

'The best, or the most tasteful?' Holmes tried not to make the remark sound judgmental, but even so Hutton's good humour vanished. He went to a large chest of drawers and pulled open the bottom one, scooping up an armful of photographs which he threw to the floor.

'Have a look,' he said. 'There's no porn. Nothing sleazy or disgusting or obscene. They're just bodies. Posed bodies.'

Holmes stood over the photographs, not seeming to pay them any attention.

'I'm sorry,' he said, 'if I seemed —'

'Forget it.' Hutton turned away, so that his face was towards the male model. He rubbed at his eyes, shoulders slumped. 'I'm just tired. I didn't mean to snap like that. Just tired.'

Holmes stared at Arnold over Hutton's shoulder, then, because there was no way it could be done stealthily, bent down, picked out a photograph from the selection on the floor, and, coming upright again, stuffed the photo into his jacket. Arnold saw, of course, and Holmes just had time to wink at him conspiratorially before Hutton turned back towards him.

'People imagine it's easy, just taking photos all day,' Hutton said. Holmes risked a look over the man's shoulder and saw Arnold wag an admonitory finger. But he was smiling archly. He wasn't about to tell. 'You're thinking all the time,' Hutton went on. 'Every waking minute of every day, every time you look at something, every time you use your eyes. Everything's material, you see.'

Holmes was at the door now, not about to linger.

'Yes, well, I'd better let you get on,' he said.

'Oh,' said Hutton, as though coming out of a dream. 'Right.'

'Thanks for all your help.'

'Not at all.'

'Bye, Arnold,' Holmes called, then pulled the door shut behind him and was gone.

'Back to work,' said Hutton. He stared at the photographs on the floor. 'Give me a hand with these, Arnold.'

'You're the boss.'

As they began to scoop the photos back into the drawer, Hutton commented, 'Nice enough bloke for a copper.'

'Yes,' said Arnold, standing naked with his hands full of paper. 'He didn't look like one of the dirty raincoat brigade, did he?'

And though Hutton asked him what he meant, Arnold just shrugged. It wasn't his business after all. It was a shame though, the policeman being interested in women. A waste of a good-looking man.

Holmes stood outside for a minute. For some reason, he was trembling, as though a small motor had stuck somewhere inside him. He touched a hand to his chest. Slight heart murmur, nothing more. Everybody got them, didn't they? He felt as though he had just committed some petty crime, which he supposed, really, he had. He had taken someone's property away without their knowledge or consent. Wasn't that theft? As a child, he had stolen from shops, always throwing away whatever he stole. Ach, all kids did it, didn't they? ... Didn't they?

He brought from his pocket the gains from this latest pilfering. The photograph was curled now, but he straightened it between his hands. A woman, pushing a pram past him, glanced at the photograph then hurried on, throwing back a disgusted look towards him. It's all right, madam, I'm a police officer. He smiled at the thought, then studied the nude shot again. It was mildly salacious, nothing more. A young woman, stretched out on what appeared to be silk or satin. Photographed from above, as she lay spreadeagled on this sheet. Her mouth open in an amateur's pout, eyes narrowed to slits of fake

112

ecstasy. All this was common enough. More interesting though was the model's identity.

For Holmes was sure it was the girl Tracy, the one whose photograph he already had from the squat. The one whose background he was trying to ascertain. The girlfriend of the deceased. Posed for the camera, uncovered, not at all shy, and enjoying herself.

What was it that kept bringing him back to this house? Rebus wasn't sure. He turned his torch onto Charlie's wall painting again, trying to make sense of the mind that had created it. But why did he want to try to understand a piece of jetsam like Charlie anyway? Perhaps because of the nagging feeling that he was absolutely integral to the case.

'What case?'

There, he had actually, finally said it aloud. What case? There was no 'case', not in the sense in which any criminal court would understand the term. There were personalities, misdeeds, questions without answers. Illegalities, even. But there was no case. That was the frustrating thing. If there were only a case, only something structured enough, tangible enough for him to hold on to, some casenotes which he could *physically* hold up and say, look, here it is. But there was nothing like that. It was all as insubstantial as candle wax. But candle wax left its mark, didn't it? And nothing ever vanished, not totally. Instead, things altered shape, substance, meaning. A five-pointed star within two concentric circles was nothing in itself. To Rebus it looked like nothing so much as a tin sheriff's badge he'd had as a boy. Lawman of the Texas tin badge state, cap-firing six-gun in his plastic holster.

To others it was evil itself.

He turned his back on it, remembering how proudly he had worn that badge, and went upstairs. Here was where the tie clip had lain. Past it, he entered Ronnie's bedroom and walked over to the window, peering out through a chink in the boards covering the glass. The car had drawn up now, not too far from his own. The car that had followed him from the station. The car he had recognised at once as the Ford Escort which had waited outside his flat, the one which had roared away. Now it was here, parked next to the burnt-out Cortina. It was here. Its driver was here. The car itself was empty.

He heard the floorboard creak just the once, and knew that the man was behind him.

'You must know this place pretty well,' he said. 'You managed to miss most of the noisy ones.'

He turned from the window and shone his torch onto the face of a young man with short dark hair. The man shielded his eyes from the beam, and Rebus angled the light down onto the man's body.

It was dressed in a police constable's uniform.

'You must be Neil,' said Rebus calmly. 'Or do you prefer Neilly?'

He levelled the torch at the floor. There was enough light for him to see and be seen by. The young man nodded.

'Neil's fine. Only my friends call me Neilly.'

'And I'm not your friend,' Rebus said, nodding acquiescence. 'Ronnie was though, wasn't he?'

'He was more than that, Inspector Rebus,' said the constable, moving into the room. 'He was my brother.'

There was nowhere in Ronnie's bedroom for them to sit, but that didn't matter, since neither could have sat still for more than a second or two anyway. They were filled with energy: Neil needing to tell his story, Rebus needing to be told. Rebus chose in front of the window as his territory, and paced backwards and forwards without seeming to, his head down, stopping from time to time to lend more concentration to Neil's words. Neil stayed by the door, swinging the handle to and fro, listening for that moment before the whole door creaked, and then pulling or pushing the door through that slow, rending sound. The torch served the scene well, casting unruly shadows over the walls, making silhouettes of each man's profile, the talker and the listener.

'Sure, I knew what he was up to,' Neil said. 'He may have been older than me, but I always knew him better than he knew me. I mean, I knew how his mind worked.'

'So you knew he was a junkie?'

'I knew he took drugs. He started when we were at school. He was caught once, almost expelled. They let him back in after three months, so he could do his exams. He passed the lot of them. That's more than I did.'

Yes, Rebus thought, admiration could make you turn a blind eye. . . .

'He ran away after the exams. We didn't hear anything from him for months. My mum and dad almost went crazy. Then they just shut him out completely, switched off. It was like he didn't exist. I wasn't supposed to mention him in the house.'

'But he got in touch with you?'

'Yes. Wrote a letter to me care of a pal of mine. Clever move that. So I got the letter without Mum and Dad knowing. He told me he had come to Edinburgh. That he liked it better than Stirling. That he had a job and a girlfriend. That was it, no address or phone number.'

'Did he write often?'

'Now and then. He lied a lot, made things seem better than they were. Said he couldn't come back to Stirling until he had a Porsche and a flat, so he could prove something to Mum and Dad. Then he stopped writing. I left school and joined the police.'

'And came to Edinburgh.'

'Not straight away, but yes, eventually.'

'Specifically to find him?'

Neil smiled.

'Not a bit of it. I was forgetting him, too. I had my own life to think about.'

'So what happened?'

'I caught him one night, out on my regular beat.'

'What beat *is* that exactly?'

'I'm based out at Musselburgh.'

'Musselburgh? Not exactly walking distance of here, is it? So what do you mean "caught him"?'

'Well, not caught, since he wasn't really doing anything. But he was high as a kite, and he'd been bashed up a bit.'

'Did he tell you what he'd been doing?'

'No. I could guess though.'

'What?'

'Acting as a punchbag for some of the rough traders around Calton Hill.'

'Funny, someone else mentioned that.'

'It happens. Quick money for people who don't give a shit.'

'And Ronnie didn't give a shit?'

'Sometimes he did. Other times. . . . I don't know, maybe I didn't know his mind as well as I thought.'

'So you started to visit him?'

'I had to help him home that first night. I came back the next day. He was surprised to see me, didn't even remember that I'd helped him home the previous night.'

'Did you try to get him off drugs?'

Neil was silent. The door creaked on its hinges.

'At the beginning I did,' he said at last. 'But he seemed to be in control. That sounds stupid, I know, after what I've said about finding him in such a state that first night, but it was *his* choice, after all, as he kept reminding me.'

'What did he think of having a brother in the force?'

'He thought it was funny. Mind you, I never came round here with my uniform on.'

116

'Not till tonight.'

'That's right. Anyway, yes, I visited a few times. We stayed up here mostly. He didn't want the others to see me. He was afraid they'd smell pork.'

It was Rebus's turn to smile. 'You didn't happen to follow Tracy, did you?'

'Who's Tracy?'

'Ronnie's girlfriend. She turned up at my flat last night. Some men had been following her.'

Neil shook his head, 'Wasn't me.'

'But you *were* at my flat last night?'

'Yes.'

'And you were here the night Ronnie died.' It was blunt, but necessarily so. Neil stopped playing with the door handle, was silent this time for twenty or thirty seconds, then took a deep breath.

'For a while I was, yes.'

'You left this behind.' Rebus held out the shiny clip, but Neil couldn't quite make it out in the torchlight. Not that he needed to see it to know what it was.

'My tie clip? I wondered about that. My tie had broken that day, it was in my pocket.'

Rebus made no attempt to hand over the clip. Instead, he put it back in his pocket. Neil just nodded, understanding.

'Why did you start following me?'

'I wanted to talk to you. I just couldn't pluck up the courage.'

'You didn't want news of Ronnie's death getting back to your parents?'

'Yes. I thought maybe you wouldn't be able to trace his identity, but you did. I don't know what it'll do to my mum and dad. I think at worst it'll make them happy, because they'll know they were right all along, right not to give him a second's thought.'

'And at best?'

'Best?' Neil stared through the gloom, searching out Rebus's eyes. 'There's no best.'

'I suppose not,' said Rebus. 'But they've still got to be told.'

'I know. I've always known.'

'Then why follow me?'

'Because now you're closer to Ronnie than I am. I don't know why you're so interested in him, but you are. And that interests me. I want you to find whoever sold him that poison.'

'I intend to, son, don't worry.'

'And I want to help.'

'That's the first stupid thing you've said, which isn't bad going for a PC. Truth is, Neil, you'd be the biggest bloody nuisance I could ask for. I've got all the help I need for now.'

'Too many cooks, eh?'

'Something like that.' Rebus decided that the confession was ending, that there was little left to be said. He came away from the window and walked to the door, stopping in front of Neil. 'You've already been a bigger nuisance than I needed. It's not pork I can smell off you, it's fish. Herrings, to be precise. And guess what colour they are.'

'What?'

'Red, son, red.'

There was a noise from downstairs, pressure on floorboards, better than an infra-red alarm anyday. Rebus turned off the torch.

'Stay here,' he whispered. Then he went to the top of the stairs. 'Who's there?' A shadow appeared below him. He switched on the torch, and shone it into Tony McCall's squinting face.

'Christ, Tony.' Rebus started downstairs. 'What a fright.'

'I knew I'd find you here,' said McCall. 'I just knew it.' His voice was nasal, and Rebus reckoned that since the time they'd parted some three hours before, McCall had kept on drinking. He stopped on the staircase, then turned and headed back up.

'Where are you going now?' called McCall.

'Just shutting the door,' said Rebus, closing the bedroom door, leaving Neil inside. 'Don't want the ghosts to catch cold, do we?'

McCall was chuckling as Rebus headed downstairs again.

'Thought we might have a wee snifter,' he said. 'And none of that bloody alcohol-free stuff you were quaffing before.'

'Fair enough,' said Rebus, expertly manoeuvring McCall out of the front door. 'Let's do that.' And he locked the door behind him, figuring that Ronnie's brother would know of the many easy ways in and out of the house. Everybody else seemed to know them, after all.

Everybody.

'Where'll it be?' said Rebus. 'I hope you didn't drive here, Tony.'

'Got a patrol car to drop me off.'

'Fine. We'll take my car then.'

'We could drive down to Leith.'

'No, I fancy something more central. There are a few good pubs in Regent Road.'

'By Calton Hill?' McCall was amazed. 'Christ, John, I can think of better places to go for a drink.'

'I can't,' said Rebus. 'Come on.'

Nell Stapleton was Holmes's girlfriend. Holmes had always preferred tall women, tracing the fixation back to his mother who had been five foot ten. Nell was nearly three quarters of an inch taller than Holmes's mother, but he still loved her.

Nell was more intelligent than Holmes. Or, as he liked to think, they were more intelligent than one another in

119

different ways. Nell could crack the *Guardian* cryptic crossword in under quarter of an hour on a good day. But she had trouble with arithmetic and remembering names: both strengths possessed by Holmes. People said they looked good together in public, looked comfortable with one another, which was probably true. They felt good together, too, living as they did by several simple rules: no talk of marriage, no thoughts of children, no hinting at living together, and definitely no cheating.

Nell worked as a librarian at Edinburgh University, a vocation Holmes found handy. Today, for example, he had asked her to find him some books on the occult. She had done even better, locating a thesis or two which he could read on the premises if he wished. She also had a printed bibliography of relevant materials, which she handed to him in the pub when they met that evening.

The Bridge of Sighs was at a mid-week and mid-evening cusp, as were most of the city centre bars. The just-one-after-work brigade had slung their jackets over their arms and headed off, while the revitalised night-time crowd had yet to catch their buses from the housing estates into the middle of town. Nell and Holmes sat at a corner table, away from the video games, but a bit too close to one of the hi-fi system's loudspeakers. Holmes, at the bar to buy another half for himself, an orange juice and Perrier for Nell, asked if the volume could be turned down.

'Sorry, can't. The customers like it.'

'We *are* the customers,' Holmes persisted.

'You'll have to speak to the manager.'

'Fine.'

'He's not in yet.'

Holmes shot the young barmaid a filthy look before turning towards his table. What he saw made him pause. Nell had opened his briefcase and was examining the photograph of Tracy.

'Who is she?' Nell said, closing the case as he placed her drink on the table.

'Part of a case I'm working on,' he said frostily, sitting down. 'Who said you could open my briefcase?'

'Rule seven, Brian. No secrets.'

'All the same –'

'Pretty, isn't she?'

'What? I haven't really –'

'I've seen her around the university.'

He was interested now. 'You have?'

'Mmm. In the library cafeteria. I remember her because she always seemed a little bit older than the other students she was with.'

'She's a student then?'

'Not necessarily. Anybody can go into the cafe. It's students only in the library itself, but I can't recall having seen her there. Only in the cafe. So what's she done?'

'Nothing, so far as I know.'

'So why is there a nude photo of her in your briefcase?'

'It's part of this thing I'm doing for Inspector Rebus.'

'You're collecting dirty pictures for him.'

She was smiling now, and he smiled too. The smile vanished as Rebus and McCall walked into the pub, laughing at some shared joke as they made for the bar. Holmes didn't want Rebus and Nell to meet. He tried very hard to leave his police life behind him when he was spending the evening with her – favours such as the occult booklist notwithstanding. He was also planning to keep Nell very much up his sleeve, so that he could have a booklist ready to hand should Rebus ever need such a thing.

Now it looked as though Rebus was going to spoil everything. And there was something else, another reason he didn't want Rebus to come sauntering across to their table. He was afraid Rebus would call him 'Shoeleather'.

He kept his eyes to the table as Rebus took in the bar

with a single sweep of his head, and was relieved when the two senior officers, drinks purchased, wandered off towards the distant pool table, where they started another argument about who shouldn't and should provide the two twenty-pence pieces for the game.

'What's wrong?'

Nell was staring at him. To do so, she had brought herself to his level, her head resting against the table.

'Nothing.' He turned towards her, offering the rest of the room a hard profile. 'Are you hungry?'

'I suppose so, yes.'

'Good, me too.'

'I thought you said you'd eaten.'

'Not enough. Come on, I'll treat you to an Indian.'

'Let me finish my drink first.' She did so in three swallows, and they left together, the door swinging shut silently behind them.

'Heads or tails?' Rebus asked McCall, flipping a coin. 'Tails.'

Rebus examined the coin. 'Tails it is. You break.'

As McCall angled his cue down onto the table, closing one eye as he concentrated on the distant triangle of balls, Rebus stared at the door of the bar. Fair enough, he supposed. Holmes was off duty, and had a girl with him, too. He supposed that gave him grounds for ignoring his senior officer. Perhaps there had been no progress, nothing to report. Fair enough again. But Rebus couldn't help thinking that the whole thing was meant to be taken as a snub. He had given Holmes a mouthful earlier on, and now Holmes was sulking.

'You to play, John,' said McCall, who had broken without potting.

'Right you are, Tony,' said Rebus, chalking the tip of his cue. 'Right you are.'

McCall came to Rebus's side as he was making ready to play.

'This must be just about the only straight pub in the whole street,' he said quietly.

'Do you know what homophobia means, Tony?'

'Don't get me wrong, John,' said McCall, straightening up and watching Rebus's chosen ball miss the pocket. 'I mean, each to his own and all that. But some of those pubs and clubs. . . .'

'You seem to know a lot.'

'No, not really. It's just what I hear.'

'Who from?'

McCall potted one striped ball, then another. 'Come on, John. You know Edinburgh as well as I do. Everybody knows the gay scene here.'

'Like you said, Tony, each to his own.' A voice suddenly sounded in Rebus's mind: *you're the brother I never had.* No, no, shut that out. He'd been there too often before. McCall missed on his next shot and Rebus approached the table.

'How come,' he said, completely miscuing, 'you can drink so much and play so well?'

McCall chuckled. 'Alcohol cures the shakes,' he said. 'So finish that pint and I'll buy you another. My treat.'

James Carew felt that he deserved his treat. He had sold a substantial property on the outskirts of Edinburgh to the financial director of a company new to Scotland, and a husband and wife architects' partnership – Scottish in origin, but now relocating from Sevenoaks in Kent – had just made a rather better offer than expected for an estate of seven acres in the Borders. A good day. By no means the best, but nevertheless worthy of celebration.

Carew himself owned a *pied à terre* in one of the loveliest of the New Town's Georgian streets, and a farmhouse with some acreage on the Isle of Skye. These were good days for him. London was shifting north, it seemed, the incomers brimming with cash from properties sold in the south-east, wanting bigger and better and prepared to pay.

He left his George Street offices at six thirty, and returned to his split-level flat. Flat? It seemed an insult to term it such: five bedrooms, living room, dining room, two bathrooms, adequate kitchen, walk-in cupboards the size of a decent Hammersmith bedsit. . . . Carew was in the right place, the only place, and the time was right, too. This was a year to be clutched, embraced, a year unlike any other. He removed his suit in the master bedroom, showered, and changed into something more casual, but without shrugging off the mark of wealth. Though he had walked home, he would need the car for tonight. It was garaged in a mews to the rear of his street. The keys were hanging on their appointed hook in the kitchen. Was the Jaguar an indulgence? He smiled, locking the flat as he left. Perhaps it was. But then his list of indulgences was long, and about to grow longer.

Rebus waited with McCall until the taxi arrived. He gave the driver McCall's address, and watched the cab pull away. Damn, he felt a little groggy himself. He went back into the pub and headed for the toilets. The bar was busier now, the jukebox louder. The bar staff had grown in strength from one to three, and they were working hard to cope. The toilets were a cool tiled haven, free from much of the bar's cigarette smoke. Pine disinfectant caught in Rebus's nostrils as he leaned over into one of the sinks. Two fingers sought out his tonsils, pausing there at the back of his throat until he retched, bringing up half a pint of beer, then another half. He breathed deeply, feeling a little better already, then washed his face thoroughly with cold water, drying himself off with a fistful of paper towels.

'You all right?' The voice lacked real sympathy. Its

owner had just pushed open the door to the gents' and was already seeking the closest urinal.

'Never felt better,' said Rebus.

'That's good.'

Good? He didn't know about that, but at least his head was clearer, the world more in focus. He doubted if he'd fail a breathalyser, which was just as well, since his next port of call was his car, parked on a darkened side road. He was still wondering how Tony McCall, shaky on his pins after half a dozen pints, had managed to play pool with such a steady eye and steady hand. The man was miraculous. He'd beaten Rebus six straight games. And Rebus had been trying. By the end he'd *really* been trying. After all, it didn't look good when a man barely able to stand upright could pot ball after ball, cleaning up and roaring to yet another victory. It didn't look good. It hadn't felt good.

It was eleven o'clock, perhaps a little early yet. He allowed himself one cigarette in the stationary car, window open, picking up the sounds from the world around him. The honest sounds of the late evening: traffic, heightened voices, laughter, the clatter of shoes on cobblestones. One cigarette, that was all. Then he started the car, and slowly drove the half mile or so to his destination. There was still some light in the sky, typical of the Edinburgh summer. Further north he knew it never got truly dark at this time of year.

But the night could be dark in other ways.

He spotted the first one on the pavement outside the Scottish Assembly building. There was no reason for the teenager to be standing there. It was an unlikely time of night to have arranged to meet friends, and the nearest bus stop was a hundred yards further up Waterloo Place. The lad stood there, smoking, one foot up behind him resting against the stone wall. He watched Rebus as the car slowly went past, and even lowered his head forward a little so that he could peer in, as though inspecting the driver. Rebus thought there was a smile there, but couldn't be sure. Further along the road, he turned the car and came back. Another car had stopped beside the boy, and a conversation was taking place. Rebus kept driving. Two young men were talking together outside the Scottish Office building on this side of the road. A little way past them, a line of three cars stood outside Calton Cemetery. Rebus cruised one more circuit, then parked near these cars, and walked.

The night was fresh. No cloud cover. There was a slight breeze, nothing more. The lad outside the Assembly building had gone off in the car. No one stood there now. Rebus crossed the road, stopped by the wall, and waited, biding his time. He watched. One or two cars drove past him slowly, the drivers turning to stare at him. But nobody stopped. He tried memorising the number plates, unsure why.

'Got a light, mister?'

He was young, no more than eighteen or nineteen. Dressed in jeans, training shoes, a shapeless T-shirt and denim jacket. His hair had been razored short, face clean-shaven but scarred with acne. There were two gold studs in his left ear.

'Thanks,' he said as Rebus held out a box of matches. Then: 'What's happening then?', with an amused glance towards Rebus before lighting the cigarette.

'Not much,' Rebus said, taking back the matchbox. The young man blew smoke out through his nostrils. He didn't seem about to go. Rebus wondered if there were any codes he should be using. He felt clammy beneath his thin shirt, despite the gooseflesh.

'Nah, there's never much happens around here. Fancy a drink?'

'At this time? Whereabouts?'

The young man nodded a vague direction. 'Calton Cemetery. You can always get a drink there.'

'No, thanks anyway.' Rebus was appalled to find himself blushing. He hoped the street lighting would disguise it.

'Fair enough. See you around then.' The young man was moving off.

'Yes,' Rebus said, relieved. 'See you.'

'And thanks for the light.'

Rebus watched him go, walking slowly, purposefully, turning from time to time at the sign of an approaching car. A hundred yards or so on, he crossed the road and began walking back, paying Rebus no attention, his mind on other things. It struck Rebus that the boy was sad, lonely, certainly no hustler. But no victim either.

Rebus stared at the wall of Calton Cemetery, broken only by its metal gates. He'd taken his daughter in there once to show her the graves of the famous – David Hume, the publisher Constable, the painter David Allan – and the statue of Abraham Lincoln. She'd asked him about the men who walked briskly from the cemetery, their heads bowed down. One older man, two teenagers. Rebus had wondered about them, too. But not too much.

No, he couldn't do it. Couldn't go in there. It wasn't that he was afraid. Jesus, no, not that, not for one minute. He was just . . . he didn't know what. But he was feeling giddy again, unsteady on his pins. I'll go back to the car, he thought.

He went back to the car.

He had been sitting in the driver's seat, smoking another cigarette thoughtfully for about a minute before he caught sight of the figure out of the corner of his eye. He turned and looked towards where the boy was seated; no, not seated, crouching against a low wall. Rebus turned away and resumed smoking. Only then did the boy rise to his feet and walk towards the car. He tapped on the passenger side window. Rebus took a deep breath before unlocking the door. The boy got in without a word, closing the door solidly behind him. He sat there, staring out through the windscreen, silent. Rebus, unable to think of a single sensible thing to say, stayed silent, too. The boy cracked first.

'Hiya.'

It was a man's voice. Rebus turned to examine the boy. He was maybe sixteen. Dressed in leather jacket, open-necked shirt. Torn jeans.

'Hello,' he said in reply.

'Got a cigarette?'

Rebus handed over the packet. The boy took one and swopped the packet for a box of matches. He inhaled the cigarette smoke deeply, holding it for a long time, then exhaling almost nothing of it back into the atmosphere. Take without give, thought Rebus. The creed of the street.

'So what are you up to tonight then?' The question had been on Rebus's own lips, but the boy had given voice to it.

'Just killing time,' said Rebus. 'I couldn't sleep.'

The boy laughed harshly. 'Yeah, couldn't sleep, so you came for a drive. Got tired driving so you just happened to stop here. This particular street. This time of night. Then you went for a walk, a stretch of the legs, and came back to the car. Right?'

'You've been watching me,' Rebus admitted.

'I didn't *need* to watch you. I've seen it all before.'

'How often?'

'Often enough, James.'

The words were tough, the voice was tough. Rebus had no cause to doubt the teenager. Certainly he was as dissimilar to the first boy as chalk to cheese.

'The name's not James,' he said.

'Of course it is. Everybody's called James. Makes it easier to remember a name, even if you can't recall the face.'

'I see.'

The boy finished the cigarette in silence, then flicked it out of the window.

'So what's it to be?'

'I don't know,' said Rebus sincerely. 'A drive maybe?'

'Fuck that.' He paused, seeming to change his mind. 'Okay, let's drive to the top of Calton Hill. Take a look out over the water, eh?'

'Fine,' said Rebus, starting the car.

They drove up the steep and winding road to the top of the hill, where the observatory and the folly – a copy of one side of Greece's Parthenon – sat silhouetted against the sky. They were not alone at the top. Other darkened cars had parked, facing across the Firth of Forth towards the dimly lit coast of Fife. Rebus, trying not to look too closely at the other cars, decided to park at a discreet distance from them, but the boy had other ideas.

'Stop next to that Jag,' he ordered. 'What a great-looking car.'

Rebus felt his own car take the insult with as much pride as it could muster. The brakes squealed in protest as he pulled to a halt. He turned off the ignition.

'What now?' he asked.

'Whatever you want,' said the boy. 'Cash on delivery, of course.'

'Of course. What if we just talk?'

'Depends on the kind of talk you want. The dirtier it is, the more it'll cost.'

'I was just thinking about a guy I met here once. Not so long ago. Haven't seen him around. I was wondering what happened to him.'

The boy suddenly placed his hand on Rebus's crotch, rubbing hard and fast against the material. Rebus stared at the hand for a full second before calmly, but with a deliberate grip, removing it. The boy grinned, leaning back in his seat.

'What's his name, James?'

Rebus tried to stop himself trembling. His stomach was filling with bile. 'Ronnie,' he said at last, clearing his throat. 'Not too tall. Dark hair, quite short. Used to take a few pictures. You know, keen on photography.'

The boy's eyebrows rose. 'You're a photographer, are you? Like to take a few snaps? I see.' He nodded slowly. Rebus doubted that he did see, but wasn't about to say more than was necessary. And yes, that Jag was nice. New-looking. Paintwork brightly reflective. Someone with a bit of money. And dear God why did he have an erection?

'I think I know which Ronnie you mean now,' said the boy. 'I haven't seen him around much myself.'

'So what can you tell me about him?'

The boy was staring out of the windscreen again. 'Great view from here, isn't it?' he said. 'Even at night. *Especially* at night. Amazing. I hardly ever come here in the daytime. It all looks so ordinary. You're a copper, aren't you?'

Rebus looked towards him, but the boy was still staring out of the windscreen, smiling, unconcerned.

'Thought you were,' he went on. 'Right from the start.'

'So why did you get in the car?'

'Curious, I suppose. Besides,' and now he looked towards Rebus, 'some of my best customers are officers of the law.'

'Well, that's none of my concern.'

'No? It should be. I'm underage, you know.'

'I guessed.'

'Yeah, well. . . .' The boy slumped in his seat, putting his feet up on the dashboard. For a moment, Rebus thought he was about to do something, and jerked himself upright. But the boy just laughed.

'What did you think? Think I was going to *touch* you again? Eh? No such luck, James.'

'So what about Ronnie?' Rebus wasn't sure whether he wanted to punch this rather ugly little kid in the gut, or take him to a good and a caring home. But he knew, above all, that he wanted answers.

'Give me another ciggie.' Rebus obliged. 'Ta. Why are you so interested in him?'

'Because he's dead.'

'Happens all the time.'

'He overdosed.'

'Ditto.'

'The stuff was lethal.'

The boy was silent for a moment.

'Now that *is* bad news.'

'Has there been any poisoned stuff going around recently?'

'No.' He smiled again. 'Only good stuff. Got any on you?' Rebus shook his head, thinking: *I do want to punch him in the gut.* 'Pity,' said the boy.

'What's your name, by the way?'

'No names, James, and no pack drill.' He put out his hand, palm up. 'I need some money.'

'I need some answers first.'

'So give me the questions. But first, a little goodwill, eh?' The hand was still there, expectant as any father-to-be. Rebus found a crumpled tenner in his jacket and handed it over. The boy seemed satisfied. 'This gets you the answers to two questions.'

Rebus's anger ignited. 'It gets me as many answers as I want, or so help me –'

'Rough trade? That your game?' The boy seemed unconcerned. Maybe he'd heard it all before. Rebus wondered.

'Is there much rough stuff goes on?' he asked.

'Not much.' the boy paused. 'But still too much.'

'Ronnie was into it, wasn't he?'

'That's your second question,' stated the boy. 'And the answer is, I don't know.'

'Don't knows don't count,' said Rebus. 'And I've got plenty of questions left.'

'Okay, if that's the way –' The boy was reaching for the door handle, ready to walk away from it all. Rebus grabbed him by the neck and brought his head down against the dashboard, right between where both feet were still resting.

'Jesus Christ!' The boy checked for blood on his forehead. There was none. Rebus was pleased with himself: maximum shock, minimum visible damage. 'You can't –'

'I can do anything I like, son, and that includes tipping you over the edge of the highest point in the city. Now tell me about Ronnie.'

'I can't tell you about Ronnie.' There were tears in his eyes now. He rubbed at his forehead, trying to erase the hurt. 'I didn't know him well enough.'

'So tell me what you *do* know.'

'Okay, okay.' He sniffed, wiping his nose on the sleeve of his jacket. 'All I know is that a few friends of mine have gotten into a scene.'

'What scene?'

'I don't know. Something heavy. They don't talk about it, but the marks are there. Bruises, cuts. One of them ended up in the Infirmary for a week. Said he fell down the stairs. Christ, he looked like he fell down a whole high-rise.'

'But nobody's talking?'

'There must be good money in it somewhere.'

'Anything else?'

'It may not be important. . . .' The kid had broken. Rebus could hear it in his voice. He'd talk from now till judgment day. Good: Rebus didn't have too many ears in this part of the city. A fresh pair might make all the difference.

'What?' he barked, enjoying his role now.

'Photographs. Somebody's putting a whisper around that there's interest in photographs. Not faked ones, either. The real McCoy.'

'Porn shots?'

'I suppose so. The rumours have been a bit vague. Rumours get that way when they've gone past being second-hand.'

'Chinese whispers,' said Rebus. He was thinking: this whole thing is like a game of Chinese whispers, everything at second and third remove, nothing absolutely proof positive.

'What?'

'Never mind. Anything else?'

The boy shook his head. Rebus reached into his pocket and, to his own surprise, found yet another tenner. Then he remembered that he'd visited a cashpoint machine somewhere during the drinking session with McCall. He handed the money over.

'Here. And I'll give you my name and phone number. I'm always open to bits of information, no matter how small. Sorry about your head, by the way.'

The boy took the money. 'That's all right. I've seen worse pay.' Then he smiled.

'Can I give you a lift?'

'The Bridges maybe?'

'No problem. What's your name?'

'James.'

'Really?' Rebus was smiling.

'Yes, really.' The boy was smiling, too. 'Listen, there *is* one other thing.'

'Go ahead, James.'

'It's just a name I've been hearing. Maybe it doesn't mean anything.'

'Yes?'

'Hyde.'

Rebus frowned. 'Hide? Hide what?'

'No, *Hyde*. H-y-d-e.'

'What about Hyde?'

'I don't know. Like I said, it's just a name.'

Rebus gripped the steering wheel. Hyde? *Hyde?* Was that what Ronnie had been telling Tracy? Not just to hide, but to hide from some man called Hyde? Trying to think, he found himself staring at the Jag again. Or rather, staring at the profile of the man in the driver's seat. The man with his hand up around the neck of the much younger occupant of the passenger seat. Stroking, and all the time talking in a low voice. Stroking, talking. All very innocent.

A wonder then that James Carew of Bowyer Carew Estate Agents should look so startled when, being stared at, he returned the stare and found himself eye to eye with Dectective Inspector John Rebus.

Rebus was taking all this in as Carew fumbled with his ignition key, revved up the new V12 engine and reversed out of the car park as though Cutty Sark herself were after him.

'He's in a hurry,' said James.

'Have you seen him before?'

'Didn't really catch his face. Haven't seen the car before though.'

'No, well, it's a new car, isn't it?' said Rebus, lazily starting his own.

The flat was still redolent of Tracy. She lingered in the living room and the bathroom. He saw her with a towel falling down around her head, legs tucked beneath her. . . . Bringing him breakfast: the dirty dishes were still lying beside his unmade bed. She had laughed to find that he slept on a mattress on the floor. 'Just like in a squat,' she had said. The flat seemed emptier now, emptier than it had felt for a while. And Rebus could do with a bath. He returned to the bathroom and turned the hot tap on. He could still feel James's hand on his leg. . . . In the living room, he looked at a bottle of whisky for a full minute, but turned his back on it and fetched a low-alcohol lager from the fridge instead.

The bath was filling slowly. An Archimedean screw would have been more efficient. Still, it gave him time to make another telephone call to the station, to check on how they were treating Tracy. The news was not good. She was becoming irritable, refusing to eat, complaining of pains in her side. Appendicitis? More likely cold turkey. He felt a fair amount of guilt at not having gone to see her before now. Another layer of guilt wouldn't do any harm, so he decided to put off the visit until morning. Just for a few hours he wanted to be away from it all, all the sordid tinkering with other people's lives. His flat didn't feel so secure any more, didn't feel like the castle it had been only a day or two ago. And there was internal damage as well as the structural kind: he was feeling soiled in the pit of his gut, as though the city had scraped away a layer of its surface grime and force-fed him the lot.

To hell with it.

He was caught all right. He was living in the most beautiful, most civilised city in northern Europe, yet every day had to deal with its flipside, with the minor matter of its animus. *Animus?* Now there was a word he hadn't used in a while. He wasn't even sure now what it meant exactly; but it sounded right. He sucked from the beer bottle, holding the foam in his mouth like a child playing with toothpaste. This stuff was all foam. No substance.

All foam. Now there was another idea. He would put some foaming bath oil in the water. Bubblebath. Who the hell had given him this stuff? Oh. Yes. Gill Templer. He remembered now. Remembered the occasion, too. She had been gently chiding him about how he never cleaned the bath. Then had presented him with this bath oil.

'It cleans you *and* your bath,' she had said, reading from the bottle. 'And puts the fun back into bathtime.'

He had suggested that they test this claim together, and they had. . . . Jesus, John, you're getting morbid again. Just because she's gone off with some vacuum-headed disc jockey with the unlikely name of Calum McCallum. It wasn't the end of anybody's world. The bombs weren't falling. There were no sirens in the sky.

Nothing but . . . Ronnie, Tracy, Charlie, James and the rest. And now Hyde. Rebus was beginning to know now the meaning of the term 'dead beat'. He rested his naked limbs in the near-scalding water and closed his eyes.

Thursday

That house of voluntary bondage . . . with its inscrutable recluse.

Dead beat: Holmes yawned again, dead on his feet. For once, he had actually beaten the alarm, so that he was returning to bed with instant coffee when the radio blared into action. What a way to wake up every day. When he had a spare half hour, he'd retune the bloody thing to Radio Three or something. Except he knew Radio Three would send him straight back to sleep, whereas the voice of Calum McCallum and the grating records he played in between hoots and jingles and enthusiastic bad jokes brought him awake with a jolt, ready, teeth gritted, to face another day.

This morning, he had beaten the smug little voice. He switched the radio off.

'Here,' he said. 'Coffee, and time to get up.'

Nell turned her head from the pillow, squinting up at him.

'Has it gone nine?'

'Not quite.'

She turned back into the pillow again, moaning softly.

'Good. Wake me up again when it does.'

'Drink your coffee,' he chided, touching her shoulder. Her shoulder was warm, tempting. He allowed himself a wistful smile, then turned and left the bedroom. He had gone ten paces before he paused, turned, and went back. Nell's arms were long, tanned, and open in welcome.

Despite the breakfast he had brought her in the cell, Tracy

was furious with Rebus, and especially when he explained to her that she could leave whenever she wanted, that she wasn't under arrest.

'This is called *protection*,' he told her. 'Protection from the men who were chasing you. Protection from Charlie.'

'Charlie. . . .' She calmed a little at the sound of his name, and touched her bruised eye. 'But why didn't you come to see me sooner?' she complained. Rebus shrugged.

'Things to do,' he said.

He stared at her photograph now, while Brian Holmes sat on the other side of the desk, warily sipping coffee from a chipped mug. Rebus wasn't sure whether he hated Holmes or loved him for bringing this into the office, for laying it flat on the desktop in front of him. Not saying a word. No good morning, no, hail fellow well met. Just this. This photograph, this nude shot. Of Tracy.

Rebus had stared at it while Holmes made his report. Holmes had worked hard yesterday, and had achieved a result. *So why had he snubbed Rebus in the bar?* If he'd seen this picture last night, it would not now be ruining his morning, not now be eroding the memory of a good night's sleep. Rebus cleared his throat.

'Did you find out anything about her?'

'No, sir,' said Holmes. 'All I got was that.' He nodded towards the photograph, his eyes unblinking: *I've given you that. What more do you want from me?*

'I see,' said Rebus, his voice level. He turned the photo over and read the small label on the back. Hutton Studios. A business telephone number. 'Right. Well, leave this with me, Brian. I'll have to give it some thought.'

'Okay,' said Holmes, thinking: *he called me Brian! He's not thinking straight this morning.*

Rebus sat back, sipping from his own mug. Coffee, milk no sugar. He had been disappointed when Holmes had asked for his coffee the same way. It gave them something in common. A taste in coffee.

'How's the househunting going?' he said conversationally.

'Grim. How did you ...?' Holmes remembered the *Houses for Sale* list, folded in his jacket pocket like a tabloid newspaper. He touched it now. Rebus smiled, nodded.

'I remember buying my flat,' he said. 'I scoured those freesheets for weeks before I found a place I liked.'

'Liked?' Holmes snorted. 'That would be a bonus. The problem for me is just finding somewhere I can afford.'

'That bad, is it?'

'Haven't you noticed?' Holmes was slightly incredulous. So involved was he in the game, it was hard to believe that anyone wasn't. 'Prices are going through the roof. In fact, a roof's about all I can afford near the centre of the city.'

'Yes, I remember someone telling me about it.' Rebus was thoughtful, 'At lunch yesterday. You know I was with the people putting up the money for Farmer Watson's drugs campaign? One of them was James Carew.'

'He wouldn't be anything to do with Carew Bowyers?'

'The head honcho. Do you want me to have a word? See about a discount on your house?'

Holmes smiled. Some of the glacier between them had been chipped away. 'That would be great,' he said. 'Maybe he could arrange for a summertime sale, bargains in all departments.' Holmes started this sentence with a grin, but it trailed away with his words. Rebus wasn't listening, was lost somewhere in thought.

'Yes,' Rebus said quietly. 'I've got to have a word with Mr Carew anyway.'

'Oh?'

'To do with some soliciting.'

'Thinking of moving houses yourself?'

Rebus looked at Holmes, not comprehending. 'Anyway,' he said, 'I suppose we need a plan of attack for today.'

'Ah.' Holmes looked uncomfortable. 'I wanted to ask you about that, sir. I had a phone call this morning. I've been working for some months on a dog-fighting ring, and they're about to arrest the gang.'

'Dog fighting?'

'Yes, you know. Put two dogs in a ring. Let them tear each other to shreds. Place bets on the result.'

'I thought that died with the depression.'

'There's been a revival of late. Vicious it is, too. I could show you some photos –'

'Why the revival?'

'Who knows? People looking for kicks, something less tame than a bet at the bookie's.'

Rebus was nodding now, almost lost to his own thoughts again.

'Would you say it was a yuppie pursuit, Holmes?'

Holmes shrugged: *he's getting better. Stopped calling me by my first name.*

'Well, never mind. So you want to be in on the arrest?'

Holmes nodded. 'If possible, sir.'

'Entirely possible,' said Rebus. 'So where's it all happening?'

'I still have to check that out. Somewhere in Fife though.'

'Fife? Home territory for me.'

'Is it? I didn't know. What's that saying again . . .?'

' "Ye need a lang spoon tae sup wi' a Fifer." '

Holmes smiled. 'Yes, that's it. There's a similar saying about the devil, isn't there?'

'All it means is that we're close, Holmes, tightly knit. We don't suffer fools and strangers gladly. Now off you go to Fife and see what I'm on about.'

'Yes, sir. What about you? I mean, what will you do about . . .?' His eyes were on the photograph again. Rebus picked it up and placed it carefully in the inside pocket of his jacket.

'Don't worry about me, son. I've plenty to keep me busy. Just keeping out of range of Farmer Watson is work enough for a day. Maybe I'll take the car out. Nice day for a drive.'

'Nice day for a drive.'

Tracy was doing her best to ignore him. She stared from her passenger side window, seemingly interested in the passing parade of shops and shoppers, tourists, kids with nothing to do now the schools had broken up for summer.

She'd been keen enough to get out of the station though. He'd held the car door open for her, dissuading her from just walking away. And she'd complied, but silently, sullenly. Okay, she was in the huff with him. He'd get over it. So would she.

'Point taken,' he said. 'You're pissed off. But how many times do I have to tell you? It was for your own safety, while I was doing some checking up.'

'Where are we going?'

'Do you know this part of town?'

She was silent. There was to be no conversation. Only questions and answers: *her* questions.

'We're just driving,' he said. 'You must know this side of town. A lot of dealing used to go on around here.'

'I'm not into that!'

It was Rebus's turn to be silent. He wasn't too old to play a game or two himself. He took a left, then another, then a right.

'We've been here already,' she commented. She'd noticed then, clever girl. Still, that didn't matter. All that mattered was that slowly, by degrees, by left and right then left and right again, he was guiding them towards the destination.

He pulled into the kerb abruptly and yanked on the handbrake.

'Right,' he said. 'We're here.'

'Here?' She looked out of the side window, up at the tenement building. The red stone had been cleaned in the past year, giving it the look of a child's plasticine, pinky ochre and malleable. 'Here?' she repeated, the word choking off as she recognised the exact address, and then tried not to let that recognition show.

The photograph was on her lap when she turned from the window. She flicked it from her with a squeal, as though it were an insect. Rebus plucked the photo from the floor of the car and held it out to her.

'Yours, I believe.'

'Where the hell did you get that?'

'Do you want to tell me about it?'

Her face was as red as the stonework now, her eyes flitting in panic like a bird's. She fumbled with the seatbelt, desperate to be out of the car, but Rebus's hand on the catch was rock hard.

'Let me go!' she yelled, thumping down on his fist. Then she pushed open the door, but the camber of the road pulled it shut again. There was not enough give in the seatbelt anyway. She was securely bound.

'I thought we'd pay Mr Hutton a call,' Rebus was saying, his voice like a blade. 'Ask him about this photo. About how he paid you a few quid to model for him. About how you brought him Ronnie's pictures. Looking for a few bob more maybe, or just to spite Ronnie. Is that how it was, Tracy? I'll bet Ronnie was pissed off when he saw Hutton had stolen his ideas. Couldn't prove it though, could he? And how was he to know how the hell Hutton got them in the first place? I suppose you put the blame on Charlie, and that's why the two of you aren't exactly on speaking terms. Some friend to Ronnie you were, sweetheart. Some friend.'

She broke down at that, and gave up trying to free herself from the seatbelt. Her head angled forward into her hands, and she wept, loudly and at length. While Rebus caught his breath. He wasn't proud of himself, but it had needed saying. She had to stop hiding from the truth. It was all conjecture, of course, but Rebus was sure Hutton could confirm the details if pressed. She had modelled for money, maybe happened to mention that her boyfriend was a photographer. Had taken the photos to Hutton, giving away Ronnie's glimmer of a chance, his creativity, for a few more pound notes. If you couldn't trust your friends, who could you trust?

He had left her overnight in the cells to see if she would crack. She hadn't, so he supposed she must be clean. But that didn't mean she didn't have some kind of habit. If not needles, then something else. Everybody needed a little something, didn't they? And the money was needed, too. So she had ripped off her boyfriend. . . .

'Did you plant that camera in Charlie's squat?'

'No!' It was as though, after all that had gone before, the accusation still hurt. Rebus nodded. So Charlie had taken the camera, or someone else had planted it there. For him to find. No . . . not quite, because *he* hadn't found it: McCall had. And very easily at that, the way he had blithely found the dope in the sleeping bag. A true copper's nose? Or something else? A little information perhaps, *inside* information? If you can't trust your friends. . . .

'Did you see the camera the night Ronnie died?'

'It was in his room, I'm sure it was.' She blinked back the tears and wiped her nose on the handkerchief Rebus gave her. Her voice was cracked still, her throat a little clogged, but she was recovering from the shock of the photo, and the greater shock that Rebus knew now of her betrayal.

'That guy who came to see Ronnie, he was in Ronnie's room after me.'

'You mean Neil?'

'I think that was his name, yes.'

Too many cooks, Rebus was thinking. He was going to have to revise his definition of 'circumstantial'. He had very little so far that *wasn't* circumstantial. It felt like the spiral was widening, taking him further and further away from the central, crucial point, the point where Ronnie lay dead on a damp, bare floor, flanked by candles and dubious friends.

'Neil was Ronnie's brother.'

'Really?' Her voice was disinterested. The safety curtain between her and the world was coming down again. The matinee was over.

'Yes, really.' Rebus felt a sudden chill. If nobody, *nobody* cares what happened to Ronnie except Neil and me, why am I bothering?

'Charlie always thought they had some kind of gay thing going. I never asked Ronnie. I don't suppose he would have told me.' She rested her head against the back of the seat, seeming to relax again. 'Oh God.' She released a whistle of breath from her lungs. 'Do we have to stick around here?'

Her hands were rising slowly, ready to clasp her head, and Rebus was beginning to answer in the negative, when he saw those same hands come swiftly down, curling into tiny fists. There was no room to escape them, and so they hit him full in the groin. A flashgun exploded somewhere behind his eyes, the world turning into nothing but sound and blinding pain. He was roaring, doubled up in agony, head coming to rest on the steering wheel, which was also the car's horn. It was blaring lazily as Tracy undid her seatbelt, opened the door, and swivelled out of the car. She left the door wide open as she ran. Rebus watched through eyes brimming with tears, as if he were in a

146

swimming pool, watching her running along the edge of the pool away from him, chlorine stinging his pupils.

'Jesus Almighty Christ,' he gasped, still hunched over the wheel, and not about to move for some considerable time.

Think like Tarzan, his father had told him once: one of the old man's few pieces of advice. He was talking about fights. About one-to-one scrapes with the lads at school. Four o'clock behind the bike shed, and all that. *Think like Tarzan. You're strong, king of the jungle, and above all else you're going to protect your nuts*. And the old boy had raised a bent knee towards young John's crotch. . . .

'Thanks, Dad,' Rebus hissed now. 'Thanks for reminding me.' Then the reaction hit his stomach.

By lunchtime he could just about walk, so long as he kept his feet close to the ground, moving as though he had wet himself. People stared, of course, and he tried to improvise a limp specially for them. Ever the crowd pleaser.

The thought of the stairs to his office was too much, and driving the car had been excruciating, the foot pedals impossible to operate. So he had taken a taxi to the Sutherland Bar. Three quarter-gill measures of whisky later, he felt the pain replaced by a drowsy numbness.

'"As though of hemlock . . .",' he muttered to himself.

He wasn't worried about Tracy. Anyone with a punch like that could look after herself. There were probably kids on the street harder than half the bloody police force. Not that Tracy was a kid. He still hadn't found out anything about her. That was supposed to be Holmes's department, but Holmes was off on a wild dog chase in Fife. No, Tracy would be all right. Probably there had been no men chasing her. But then why come to him that night? There could be a hundred reasons. After all, she'd conned a bed, the best part of a bottle of wine, a hot bath and breakfast out of him. Not bad going that, and him supposed to be a hardened old copper. Too old maybe. Too much the 'copper', not enough the police officer. Maybe.

Where to next? He already had the answer to that, legs permitting and pray God he could drive.

He parked at a distance from the house, not wanting to scare off anyone who might be there. Then he simply walked up to the door and knocked. Standing there, awaiting a response, he remembered Tracy opening that door and running into his arms, her face bruised, her eyes welling with tears. He didn't think Charlie would be here. He didn't think Tracy would be here. He didn't *want* Tracy to be here.

The door opened. A bleary teenage boy squinted up at Rebus. His hair was lank, lifeless, falling into his eyes.

'What is it?'

'Is Charlie in? I've got a bit of business with him.'

'Naw. Havenae seen him the day.'

'All right if I wait a while?'

'Aye.' The boy was already closing the door on Rebus's face. Rebus stuck a hand up against the door and peered round it.

'I meant, wait indoors.'

The boy shrugged, and slouched back inside, leaving the door ajar. He slipped back into his sleeping bag and pulled it over his head. Just passing through, and catching up on lost sleep. Rebus supposed the boy had nothing to lose by letting a stranger into this way station. He left him to his sleep, and, after a cursory check that there was no one else in the downstairs rooms, climbed the steep staircase.

The books were still slewed like so many felled dominoes, the contents of the bag McCall had emptied still lying in a clutter on the floor. Rebus ignored these and went to the desk, where he sat, studying the pieces of paper in front of him. He had flicked on the light switch beside the door of Charlie's room, and now switched on the desk lamp, too. The walls were miraculously free from posters, postcards and the like. It wasn't like a student's room. Its identity had been left suspended, which was probably exactly the way Charlie wanted it. He didn't want to look like a student to his drop-out friends; he didn't want to look like a drop-out to his student friends. He wanted to be all things to all people. Chameleon, then, as well as tourist.

The essay on Magick was Rebus's main interest, but he gave the rest of the desk a good examination while he was here. Nothing out of the ordinary. Nothing to suggest that Charlie was pushing bad drugs around the city streets. So Rebus picked up the essay, opened it, and began to read.

Nell liked the library when it was quiet like this. During term time, a lot of the students used it as a meeting place, a sort of glorified youth club. Then, the first-floor reading room was filled with noise. Books tended to be left lying everywhere, or to go missing, to be shifted out of their proper sections. All very frustrating. But during the summer months, only the most determined of the students came in: the ones with a thesis to write, or work to catch up on, or those precious few who were passionate about their chosen fields, and who were giving up sunshine and freedom to be here, indoors, in studied silence.

She got to know their faces, and then their names. Conversations could be struck up in the deserted coffee shop, authors' names swopped. And at lunchtime, one could sit in the gardens, or walk behind the library building onto The Meadows, where more books were being read, more faces rapt in thought.

Of course, summer was also the time for the library's most tedious jobs. The check on stock, the rebinding of misused volumes. Reclassification, computer updating, and so on. The atmosphere more than made up for all this. All traces of hurry and haste were gone. No more complaints about there being too few copies of this or that title, desperately needed by a class of two hundred for some overdue essay. But after the summer there would be a new intake, and with every year's fresh intake, she felt that whole year older, and more distanced from the students. They already seemed hopelessly young to her, a glow surrounding them, reminding her of something she could never have.

She was sorting through request forms when the commotion began. The guard on the library entrance had stopped someone who was trying to get in without any identification. Normally, Nell knew, the guard wouldn't have worried, but the girl was so obviously distraught, so obviously not a reader, not even a student. She was loudly argumentative, where a real student would have quietly explained that they had forgotten to bring their matriculation card with them. There was something else, too . . . Nell frowned, trying to place the girl. Catching her profile, she remembered the photograph in Brian's briefcase. Yes, it was the same girl. No girl, really, but a fully grown, if youthful, woman. The lines around the eyes were the giveaway, no matter how slender the body, how fashionably young the clothes. But why was she making this fuss? She'd always gone to the coffee shop, had never, to Nell's knowledge, tried to get into the library proper before now. Nell's curiosity was aroused.

The guard was holding Tracy by the arm, and she was shrieking abuse at him, her eyes frantic. Nell tried to be authoritarian in her walk as she approached the pair of them.

'Is there some problem, Mr Clarke?'

'I can handle it, miss.' His eyes betrayed his words. He was sweating, past retirement age, neither used to this sort of physical struggle nor knowing what to do about it. Nell turned to the girl.

'You can't just barge in here, you know. But if you want a message passed on to one of the students inside, I'll see what I can do.'

The girl struggled again. 'I just want to come in!' All reasoning had gone now. She knew only that if someone was stopping her getting in, then she *had* to get in somehow.

'Well you can't,' Nell said angrily. She should not have interfered. She was used to dealing with quiet, sane, rational people. Okay, some of them might lose their tempers momentarily when frustrated in their search for a book. But they would always remember their place. The girl stared at her, and the stare seemed absolutely malevolent. There was no trace of human kindness in it at all. Nell felt the hairs on her neck bristle. Then the girl gave a banshee wail, throwing herself forward, loosing the guard's grip. Her forehead smashed into Nell's face, sending the librarian flying, feet rooted to the spot, so that she fell like so much timber. Tracy stood there for a moment, seeming to come to herself. The guard made to grab her, but she gave another yell, and he backed off. Then she pushed past him out of the library doors and started running again, head down, arms and legs uncoordinated. The guard watched her, fearful still, then turned his attention to the bloody and unconscious face of Nell Stapleton.

The man who answered the door was blind.

'Yes?' he asked, holding the door, sightless eyes discernible behind the dark green lenses of his glasses. The hallway behind him was in deep shadow. What need had it of light?

'Mr Vanderhyde?'

The man smiled. 'Yes?' he repeated. Rebus couldn't take his own eyes off those of the elderly man. Those green lenses reminded him of claret bottles. Vanderhyde would be sixty-five, maybe seventy. His hair was silvery yellow, thick, well groomed. He was wearing an open-necked shirt, brown waistcoat, a watch chain hanging from one pocket. And he was leaning ever so slightly on a silver-topped stick. For some reason, Rebus had the idea that Vanderhyde would be able to handle that cane swiftly and effectively as a weapon, should anyone unpleasant ever come calling.

'Mr Vanderhyde, I'm a police officer.' Rebus was reaching for his wallet.

'Don't bother with identification, unless it's in braille.' Vanderhyde's words stopped Rebus short, his hand frozen in his inside jacket pocket.

'Of course,' he mumbled, feeling ever so slightly ridiculous. Funny how people with disabilities had that special gift of making you seem so much less able than them.

'You'd better come in, Inspector.'

'Thank you.' Rebus was in the hall before it hit him. 'How did you —?'

Vanderhyde shook his head. 'A lucky guess,' he said, leading the way. 'A shot in the dark, you might say.' His laughter was abrasive. Rebus, studying what he could see of the hall, was wondering how even a blind man could make such a botched job of interior decoration. A stuffed owl stared down from its dusty pedestal, next to an umbrella stand which seemed to consist of a hollowed elephant's foot. An ornately carved occasional table boasted a pile of unread mail and a cordless telephone. Rebus gave this latter item most attention.

'Technology has made such progress, don't you agree?' Vanderhyde was saying. 'Invaluable for those of us who have lost one of the senses.'

'Yes,' Rebus replied, as Vanderhyde opened the door to another room, almost as dark to Rebus's eyes as the hall. 'In here, Inspector.'

'Thank you.' The room was musty, and smelled of old people's medicaments. It was comfortably furnished, with a deep sofa and two robust armchairs. Books lay behind glass along one wall. Some uninspired watercolours stopped the other walls from seeming bare. There were ornaments everywhere. Those on the mantelpiece caught Rebus's eye. There wasn't a spare centimetre of space on the deep wooden mantelpiece, and the ornaments were exotic. Rebus could identify African, Caribbean, Asian and Oriental influences, without being able to pinpoint any one country for any one piece.

Vanderhyde flopped into a chair. It struck Rebus that there were no occasional tables scattered through the room, no extraneous furniture into which the blind man might bump.

'Nick-nacks, Inspector. Gewgaws collected on my travels as a younger man.'

'Evidence of a lot of travel.'

'Evidence of a magpie mind,' Vanderhyde corrected. 'Would you care for some tea?'

'No, thank you, sir.'

'Something a little stronger perhaps?'

'Thank you, but no.' Rebus smiled. 'I'd a bit too much last night.'

'Your smile comes over in your voice.'

'You don't seem curious as to why I'm here, Mr Vanderhyde.'

'Perhaps that's because I *know*, Inspector. Or, perhaps it's because my patience is limitless. Time doesn't mean as much to me as to most people. I'm in no hurry for your explanations. I'm not a clock watcher, you see.' He was smiling again, eyes fixed somewhere just right of Rebus and above him. Rebus stayed silent, inviting further speculation. 'Then again,' Vanderhyde continued, 'since I no longer go out, and have few visitors, and since I have never to my knowledge broken the laws of the land, that certainly narrows the possible reasons for your visit. You're sure you won't have some tea?'

'Don't let me stop you making some for yourself.' Rebus had spotted the near-empty mug sitting on the floor beside the old man's chair. He looked down around his own chair. Another mug sat on the muted pattern of the carpet. He reached a silent arm down towards it. There was a slight warmth on the base of the mug, a warmth on the carpet beneath.

'No,' Vanderhyde said. 'I had one just recently. As did my visitor.'

'Visitor?' Rebus sounded surprised. The old man smiled, giving a slight and indulgent shake of his head. Rebus, feeling caught, decided to push on anyway. 'I thought you said you didn't get many visitors?'

'No, I don't recall *quite* saying that. Still, it happens to be true. Today is the exception that proves the rule. Two visitors.'

'Might I ask who the other visitor was?'

'Might *I* ask, Inspector, why you're here?'

It was Rebus's turn to smile, nodding to himself. The blood was rising in the old man's cheeks. Rebus had succeeded in riling him.

'Well?' There was impatience in Vanderhyde's voice.

'Well, sir.' Rebus deliberately pulled himself out of the chair and began to circuit the room. 'I came across your name in an undergraduate essay on the occult. Does that surprise you?'

The old man considered this. 'It pleases me slightly. I do have an ego that needs feeding, after all.'

'But it doesn't surprise you?' Vanderhyde shrugged. 'This essay mentioned you in connection with the workings of an Edinburgh-based group, a sort of coven, working in the nineteen sixties.'

' "Coven" is an inexact term, but never mind.'

'You were involved in it?'

'I don't deny the fact.'

'Well, while we're dealing in fact, you were, more correctly, its guiding light. "Light" may be an inexact term.'

Vanderhyde laughed, a piping, discomfiting sound. 'Touché, Inspector. Indeed, touché. Do continue.'

'Finding your address wasn't difficult. Not too many Vanderhydes in the phone book.'

'My kin are based in London.'

'The reason for my visit, Mr Vanderhyde, is a murder, or at the very least a case of tampering with evidence at the scene of a death.'

'Intriguing.' Vanderhyde put his hands together, fingertips to his lips. It was hard to believe the man was sightless. Rebus's movements around the room were failing to have any effect on Vanderhyde at all.

'The body was discovered lying with arms stretched wide, legs together –'

'Naked?'

'No, not quite. Shirtless. Candles had been burning either side of the body, and a pentagram had been painted on one wall.'

'Anything else?'

'No. There were some syringes in a jar by the body.'

'The death was caused by an overdose of drugs?'

'Yes.'

'Hmm.' Vanderhyde rose from his chair and walked unerringly to the bookcase. He did not open it, but stood as though staring at the titles. 'If we're dealing with a sacrifice, Inspector – I take it that's your theory?'

'One of many, sir.'

'Well, *if* we are dealing with a sacrifice, then the means of death are quite unusual. No, more than that, are unheard of. To begin with, very few Satanists would ever contemplate a human sacrifice. Plenty of psychopaths have carried out murder and then excused it as ritual, but

155

that's something else again. But in any case, a human sacrifice — a sacrifice of any kind — requires blood. Symbolic in some rites, as in the blood and body of Christ. Real in others. A sacrifice *without* blood? That would be original. And to administer an overdose. . . . No, Inspector, surely the more plausible explanation is that, as you say, someone muddied the water as it were, after the life had expired.'

Vanderhyde turned into the room again, picking out Rebus's position. He raised his arms high, to signal that this was all he had to offer.

Rebus sat down again. The mug when he touched it was no longer warm. The evidence had cooled, dissipated, vanished.

He picked up the mug and looked at it. It was an innocent thing, patterned with flowers. There was a single crack running downwards from its rim. Rebus felt a sudden surge of confidence in his own abilities. He got to his feet again and walked to the door.

'Are you leaving?'

He did not reply to Vanderhyde's question, but walked smartly to the bottom of the dark oak staircase. Halfway up, it twisted in a ninety-degree angle. From the bottom, Rebus's view was of this halfway point, this small landing. A second before, there had been someone there, someone crouching, listening. He hadn't seen the figure so much as *sensed* it. He cleared his throat, a nervous rather than necessary action.

'Come down here, Charlie.' He paused. Silence. But he could still sense the young man, just beyond that turning on the stairs. 'Unless you want me to come up. I don't think you want that, do you? Just the two of us, up there in the dark?' More silence, broken by the shuffling of Vanderhyde's carpet-slippered feet, the walking cane tapping against the floor. When Rebus looked round, the old man's jaw was set defiantly. He still had his pride. Rebus wondered if he felt any shame.

Then the single creak of a floorboard signalled Charlie's presence on the stair landing.

Rebus broke into a smile: of conquest, of relief. He had trusted himself, and had proved worthy of that trust.

'Hello, Charlie,' he said.

'I didn't mean to hit her. She had a go at me first.'

The voice was recognisable, but Charlie seemed rooted to the landing. His body was slightly hunched, his face in silhouette, his arms hanging by his side. The educated voice seemed discorporate, somehow not part of this shadow-puppet.

'Why don't you join us?'

'Are you going to arrest me?'

'What's the charge?' The question was Rebus's, his voice tinged with amusement.

'That should be *your* question, Charles,' Vanderhyde called out, making it sound like an instruction.

Rebus was suddenly bored with these games. 'Come on down,' he commanded. 'Let's have another mug of Earl Grey.'

Rebus had pulled open the crimson velvet curtains in the living room. The interior seemed less cramped in what was left of the daylight, less overpowering, and certainly a lot less gothic. The ornaments on the mantelpiece were revealed as just that: ornaments. The books in the bookcase were revealed as by and large works of popular fiction: Dickens, Hardy, Trollope. Rebus wondered if Trollope *was* still popular.

Charlie had made tea in the narrow kitchen, while Vanderhyde and Rebus sat in silence in the living room, listening to the distant sounds of cups chinking and spoons ringing.

'You have good hearing,' Vanderhyde stated at last.

Rebus shrugged. He was still assessing the room. No, he couldn't live here, but he could at least imagine visiting some aged relative in such a place.

'Ah, tea,' said Vanderhyde as Charlie brought in the unsteady tray. Placing it on the floor between chairs and sofa, his eyes sought Rebus's. They had an imploring look. Rebus ignored it, accepting his cup with a curt nod of the head. He was just about to say something about how well Charlie seemed to know his way around his chosen bolt-hole, when Charlie himself spoke. He was handing a mug to Vanderhyde. The mug itself was only half filled – a wise precaution – and Charlie sought out the old man's hand, guiding it to the large handle.

'There you go, Uncle Matthew,' he said.

'Thank you, Charles,' said Vanderhyde, and if he had been sighted, his slight smile would have been directed straight at Rebus, rather than a few inches over the detective's shoulder.

'Cosy,' Rebus commented, sipping the dry perfume of Earl Grey.

Charlie sat on the sofa, crossing his legs, almost relaxed. Yes, he knew this room well, was slipping into it the way one slipped into an old, comfortable pair of trousers. He might have spoken, but Vanderhyde seemed to want to put his points forward first.

'Charles has told me all about it, Inspector Rebus. Well, when I say that, I mean he has told me as much as he deems it necessary for me to know.' Charlie glared at his uncle, who merely smiled, knowing the frown was there. 'I've already told Charles that he should talk to you again. He seems unwilling. *Seemed* unwilling. Now the choice has been taken away from him.'

'How did you know?' asked Charlie, so much more at home here, Rebus was thinking, than in some ugly squat in Pilmuir.

'Know?' said Rebus.

'Know where to find me? Know about Uncle Matthew?'

'Oh, that.' Rebus picked at invisible threads on his trousers. 'Your essay. It was sitting on your desk. Handy that.'

'What?'

'Doing an essay on the occult, and having a warlock in the family.'

Vanderhyde chuckled. 'Not a warlock, Inspector. Never that. I think I've only ever met one warlock, one *true* warlock, in my whole life. Local he is, mind.'

'Uncle Matthew,' Charlie interrupted, 'I don't think the Inspector wants to hear –'

'On the contrary,' said Rebus. 'It's the reason I'm here.'

'Oh.' Charlie sounded disappointed. 'Not to arrest me then?'

'No, though you deserve a good slap for that bruise you gave Tracy.'

'She deserved it!' Charlie's voice betrayed petulance, his lower lip filling out like a child's.

'You struck a woman?' Vanderhyde sounded aghast. Charlie looked towards him, then away, as if unable to hold a stare that didn't – couldn't – exist.

'Yes,' Charlie hissed. 'But look.' He pulled the polo-necked jumper down from around his neck. There were two huge weals there, the result of prising fingernails.

'Nice scratches,' Rebus commented for the blind man's benefit. 'You got the scratches, she got a bruise on her eye. I suppose that makes it neck and neck in the eye-for-an-eye stakes.'

Vanderhyde chuckled again, leaning forward slightly on his cane.

'Very good, Inspector,' he said. 'Yes, very good. Now –' he lifted the mug to his lips and blew. 'What can we do for you?'

'I saw your name in Charlie's essay. There was a footnote quoting you as an interview source. I reckoned that made you local and reasonably extant, and there aren't too many –'

'– Vanderhydes in the phone book,' finished the old man. 'Yes, you said.'

'But you've already answered most of my questions. Concerning the black magic connection, that is. However, I would just like to clear up a few points with your nephew.'

'Would you like me to –?' Vanderhyde was already rising to his feet. Rebus waved for him to stay, then realised the gesture was in vain. However, Vanderhyde had already paused, as though anticipating the action.

'No, sir,' Rebus said now, as Vanderhyde seated himself again. 'This'll only take a couple of minutes.' He turned to Charlie, who was almost sinking into the deep padded cushions of the sofa. 'So, Charlie,' Rebus began. 'I've got you down this far as thief, and as accessory to murder. Any comments to make?'

Rebus watched with pleasure as the young man's face lost its tea-like colour and became more like uncooked pastry. Vanderhyde twitched, but with pleasure, too, rather than discomfort. Charlie looked from one man to the other, seeking friendly eyes. The eyes he saw were blind to his pleas.

'I – I –'

'Yes?' Rebus prompted.

'I'll just fill my cup,' Charlie said, as though only these five meagre words were left in his vocabulary. Rebus sat back patiently. Let the bugger fill and refill and boil another brew. But he'd have his answers. He'd make Charlie sweat tannin, and he'd have his answers.

'Is Fife always this bleak?'

'Only the more picturesque bits. The rest's no' bad at a'.'

The SSPCA officer was guiding Brian Holmes across a

twilit field, the area around almost completely flat, a dead tree breaking the monotony. A fierce wind was blowing, and it was a cold wind, too. The SSPCA man had called it an 'aist wind'. Holmes assumed that 'aist' translated as 'east', and that the man's sense of geography was somewhat askew, since the wind was clearly blowing from the west.

The landscape proved deceptive. Seeming flat, the land was actually slanting. They were climbing a slope, not steep but perceptible. Holmes was reminded of some hill somewhere in Scotland, the 'electric brae', where a trick of natural perspective made you think you were going uphill when in fact you were travelling *down*. Or was it vice versa? Somehow, he didn't think his companion was the man to ask.

Soon, over the rise, Holmes could see the black, grainy landscape of a disused mineworking, shielded from the field by a line of trees. The mines around here were all worked out, had been since the 1960s. Now, money had appeared from somewhere, and the long-smouldering bings were being levelled, their mass used to fill the chasms left by surface mining. The mine buildings themselves were being dismantled, the landscape reseeded, as though the history of mining in Fife had never existed.

This much Brian Holmes knew. His uncles had been miners. Not here perhaps, but nevertheless they had been great deep workings of information and anecdote. The child Brian had stored away every detail.

'Grim,' he said to himself as he followed the SSPCA officer down a slight slope towards the trees, where a cluster of half a dozen men stood, shuffling, turning at the sound of approach. Holmes introduced himself to the most senior-looking of the plain-clothes men.

'DC Brian Holmes, sir.'

The man smiled, nodded, then jerked his head in the

direction of a much younger man. Everyone, uniformeds, plain-clothes, even the SSPCA Judas, was smiling, enjoying Holmes's mistake. He felt a rush of blood to his face, and was rooted to the spot. The young man saw his discomfort and stuck out a hand.

'I'm DS Hendry, Brian. Sometimes I'm in charge here.' There were more smiles. Holmes joined in this time.

'Sorry, sir.'

'I'm flattered actually. Nice to think I'm so young-looking, and Harry here's so old.' He nodded towards the man Holmes had mistaken for the senior officer. 'Right, Brian. I'll just tell you what I've been telling the lads. We have a good tip that there's going to be a dog fight here tonight. It's secluded, half a mile from the main road, a mile from the nearest house. Perfect, really. There's a track the lorries take from the main road up to the site here. That's the way they'll come in, probably three or four vans carrying the dogs, and then who knows how many cars with the punters. If it gets to Ibrox proportions, we'll call in reinforcements. As it is, we're not bothered so much about nabbing punters as about catching the handlers themselves. The word is that Davy Brightman's the main man. Owns a couple of scrap yards in Kirkcaldy and Methil. We know he keeps a few pit bulls, and we think he fights them.'

There was a blast of static from one of the radios, then a call sign. DS Hendry responded.

'Do you have a Detective Constable Holmes with you?' came the message. Hendry stared at Holmes as he handed him the radio. Holmes could only look apologetic.

'DC Holmes speaking.'

'DC Holmes, we've a message for you.'

'Go ahead,' said Holmes.

'It's to do with a Miss Nell Stapleton.'

Sitting in the hospital waiting room, eating chocolate

from a vending machine, Rebus went over the day's events in his mind. Remembering the incident with Tracy in the car, his scrotum began to rise up into his body in an act of self-protection. Painful still. Like a double hernia, not that he'd ever had one.

But the afternoon had been very interesting indeed. Vanderhyde had been interesting. And Charlie, well, Charlie had sung like a bird.

'What is it you want to ask me?' he had said, bringing more tea into the living room.

'I'm interested in time, Charlie. Your uncle has already told me that *he's* not interested in time. He isn't ruled by it, but policemen are. Especially in a case like this. You see, the chronology of events isn't quite right in my mind. That's what I want to clear up, if possible.'

'All right,' Charlie said. 'How can I help?'

'You were at Ronnie's that night?'

'Yes, for a while.'

'And you left to look for some party or other?'

'That's right.'

'Leaving Neil in the house with Ronnie?'

'No, he'd left by then.'

'You didn't know, of course, that Neil was Ronnie's brother?'

The look of surprise on Charlie's face seemed authentic, but then Rebus knew him for an accomplished actor, and was taking nothing for granted, not any more.

'No, I didn't know that. Shit, his brother. Why didn't he want any of us to meet him?'

'Neil and I are in the same profession,' Rebus explained. Charlie just smiled and shook his head. Vanderhyde was leaning back thoughtfully in his chair, like a meticulous juror at some trial.

'Now,' Rebus continued, 'Neil says he left quite early. Ronnie was being uncommunicative.'

'I can guess why.'

'Why?'

'Easy. He'd just scored, hadn't he? He hadn't seen any stuff for ages, and suddenly he'd scored.' Charlie suddenly remembered that his aged uncle was listening, and stopped short, looking towards the old man. Vanderhyde, shrewd as ever, seemed to sense this, and waved his hand regally before him, as if to say, I've been too long on this planet and can't be shocked any more.

'I think you're right,' Rebus said to Charlie. 'One hundred percent. So, in an empty house, Ronnie shoots up. The stuff's lethal. When Tracy comes in, she finds him in his room –'

'So *she* says,' interrupted Charlie. Rebus nodded, acknowledging his scepticism.

'Let's accept for the moment that's what happened. He's dead, or seems so to her. She panics, and runs off. Right. So far so good. Now it begins to get hazy, and this is where I need your help, Charlie. Thereafter, someone moves Ronnie's body downstairs. I don't know why. Maybe they were just playing silly buggers, or, as Mr Vanderhyde put it so succinctly, trying to muddy the water. Anyway, around this stage in the chronology, a second packet of white powder appears. Tracy only saw one –' Rebus saw that Charlie was about to interrupt again '– so she says. So, Ronnie had one packet and shot up with it. When he died, his body came downstairs and another packet magically appeared. This new packet contains good stuff, not the poison Ronnie used on himself. And, to add a little more to the concoction, Ronnie's camera disappears, to turn up later in your squat, Charlie, in your room, and in your black polythene bag.'

Charlie had stopped looking at Rebus. He was looking at the floor, at his mug, at the teapot. His eyes still weren't on Rebus when he spoke.

'Yes, I took it.'

'You took the camera?'

'I just said I did, didn't I?'

'Okay.' Rebus's voice was neutral. Charlie's smouldering shame might at any moment catch light and ignite into anger. 'When did you take it?'

'Well, I didn't exactly stop to look at my watch.'

'Charles!' Vanderhyde's voice was loud, the word coming from his mouth like a bite. Charlie took notice. He straightened in his chair, reduced to some childhood fear of this imposing creature, his uncle the magician.

Rebus cleared his throat. The taste of Earl Grey was thick on his tongue. 'Was there anyone in the house when you got back?'

'No. Well, yes, if you're counting Ronnie.'

'Was he upstairs or down?'

'He was at the top of the stairs, if you must know. Just lying there, like he'd been trying to come down them. I thought he was crashed out. But he didn't look right. I mean, when someone's sleeping, there's *some* kind of movement. But Ronnie was . . . rigid. His skin was cold, damp.'

'And he was at the top of the stairs?'

'Yes.'

'What did you do then?'

'Well, I knew he was dead. And it was like I was dreaming. That sounds stupid, but it was like that. I know now that I was just trying to shut it out. I went into Ronnie's room.'

'Was the syringe jar there?'

'I can't remember.'

'Never mind. Go on.'

'Well, I knew that when Tracy got back –'

'Yes?'

'God, this is going to make me sound like a monster.'

'What is it?'

'Well, I knew that when she came back, she'd see

Ronnie was dead and grab what she could of his. I *knew* she would, I just felt it. So I took something I thought he'd have wanted me to have.'

'For sentimental reasons then?' asked Rebus archly.

'Not totally,' Charlie admitted. Rebus had a sudden cooling thought: *this is going too easily.* 'It was the only thing Ronnie had that was worth any money.'

Rebus nodded. Yes, that was more like it. Not that Charlie was short of a few bob; he could always rely on Uncle Matthew. But it was the illicit nature of the act that appealed. Something Ronnie would have wanted him to have. Some chance.

'So you lifted the camera?' Rebus said. Charlie nodded. 'Then you left?'

'Went straight back to my squat. Somebody said Tracy had come looking for me. Said she'd been in a right state. So I assumed she already knew about Ronnie.'

'And she hadn't made off with the camera. She'd come looking for you instead.'

'Yes.' Charlie seemed almost contrite. Almost. Rebus wondered what Vanderhyde was making of all this.

'What about the name Hyde, does it mean anything to you?'

'A character in Robert Louis Stevenson.'

'Apart from that.'

Charlie shrugged.

'What about someone called Edward?'

'A character in Robert Louis Stevenson.'

'I don't understand.'

'Sorry, I'm being facetious. Edward is Hyde's first name in *Jekyll and Hyde*. No, I don't know anyone called Edward.'

'Fair enough. Do you want to know something, Charlie?'

'What?'

Rebus looked to Vanderhyde, who sat impassively.

'Actually, I think your uncle already knows what I'm going to say.'

Vanderhyde smiled. 'Indeed. Correct me if I'm wrong, Inspector Rebus, but you were about to say that, the young man's corpse having moved from the bedroom to the stairs, you can only assume that the person who moved the body was actually in the house when Charles arrived.'

Charlie's jaw dropped open. Rebus had never witnessed the effect in real life before.

'Quite right,' he said. 'I'd say you were lucky, Charlie. I'd say that someone was moving the body downstairs and heard you arrive. Then they hid in one of the other rooms, maybe even that stinking bathroom, until you'd left. They were in the house all the time you were.'

Charlie swallowed. Then closed his mouth. Then let his head fall forward and began to weep. Not quite silently, so that his uncle caught the action, and smiled, nodding towards Rebus with satisfaction.

Rebus finished the chocolate. It had tasted of antiseptic, the same strong flavour of the corridor outside, the wards themselves, and this waiting room, where anxious faces buried themselves in old colour supplements and tried to look interested for more than a second or two. The door opened and Holmes came in, looking anxious and exhausted. He'd had the distance of a forty-minute car journey in which to mentally live his worst fears, and the result was carved into his face. Rebus knew that swift treatment was needed.

'She's fine. You can see her whenever you like. They're keeping her in overnight for no good reason at all, and she's got a broken nose.'

'A broken nose?'

'That's all. No concussion, no blurred vision. A good old broken nose, curse of the bare-knuckle fighter.'

Rebus thought for one moment that Holmes was about to take offence at his levity. But then relief flooded the younger man and he smiled, his shoulders relaxing, head dropping a little as though from a sense of anticlimax, albeit a welcome one.

'So,' Rebus said, 'do you want to see her?'

'Yes.'

'Come on, I'll take you.' He placed a hand on Holmes's shoulder and guided him out of the door again.

'But how did you know?' Holmes asked as they walked up the corridor.

'Know what?'

'Know it was Nell? Know about Nell and me?'

'Well now, you're a detective, Brian. Think about it.'

Rebus could see Holmes's mind take on the puzzle. He hoped the process was therapeutic. Finally, Holmes spoke.

'Nell's got no family, so she asked for me.'

'Well, she *wrote* asking for you. The broken nose makes it hard to understand what she's saying.'

Holmes nodded dully. 'But I couldn't be located, and you were asked if you knew where I was.'

'That's close enough. Well done. How was Fife anyway? I only get back there once a year.' *April 28th*, he thought to himself.

'Fife? It was okay. I'd to leave before the bust. That was a shame. And I don't think I exactly impressed the team I was supposed to be part of.'

'Who was in charge?'

'A young DS called Hendry.'

Rebus nodded. 'I know him. I'm surprised you don't, at least by reputation.'

Holmes shrugged. 'I just hope they nab those bastards.'

Rebus had stopped outside the door of a ward.

'This it?' Holmes asked. Rebus nodded.

'Want me to come in with you?'

Holmes stared at his superior with something approaching gratitude, then shook his head.

'No, it's all right. I won't stay if she's asleep. One last thing though.'

'Yes?'

'Who did it?'

Who did it. That was the hardest part to understand. Walking back along the corridor, Rebus saw Nell's puffy face, saw her distress as she tried to talk, and couldn't. She had signalled for some paper. He had taken a notebook from his pocket, and handed her his pen. Then she had written furiously for a full minute. He stopped now and took out the notebook, reading it through for the fourth or fifth time that evening.

'I was working at the library. A woman tried to push her way into the building, past the guard. Talk to him if you want to check. This woman then butted me on the face. I was trying to help, to calm her down. She must have thought I was interfering. But I wasn't. I was trying to help. She was the girl in that photograph, the nude photograph Brian had in his briefcase last night in the pub. You were there, weren't you, in the same pub as us? Not easy not to notice – the place was empty, after all. Where's Brian? Out chasing more salacious pictures for you, Inspector?'

Rebus smiled now, as he had smiled then. She had guts, that one. He rather liked her, her face taped, eyes blackened. She reminded him a lot of Gill.

So, Tracy was leaving a silvery snail's trail of chaos by which to follow her. Little bitch. Had she simply flipped, or was there a real motive for her trip to the University Library? Rebus leaned against the wall of the corridor. God, what a day. He was supposed to be between cases. Supposed to be 'tidying things up' before starting full time on the drugs campaign. He was supposed, for the sake of Christ, to be having things *easy*. That'd be the day.

The ward doors swung shut, alerting him to the figure of Brian Holmes in the corridor. Holmes seemed lacking direction, then spotted his superior and came walking briskly up the hall. Rebus wasn't sure yet whether Holmes was invaluable, or a liability. Could you be both things at once?

'Is she all right?' he asked solicitously.

'Yes. I suppose so. She's awake. Face looks a bit of a mess though.'

'Just bruises. They say the nose will heal. You'll never know it was broken.'

'Yes, that's what Nell said.'

'She talking? That's good.'

'She also told me who did it.' Holmes looked at Rebus, who looked away. 'What's this all about? What's Nell got to do with it?'

'Nothing, so far as I know. She just happened to be in the wrong place, et cetera. Chalk it down to coincidence.'

'Coincidence? That's a nice easy word to say. Put it down to "coincidence" and then we can forget all about it, is that it? I don't know what your game is, Rebus, but I'm not going to play it any longer.'

Holmes turned and stalked off along the hall. Rebus almost warned him that there was no exit at that end of the building, but favours weren't what Holmes wanted. He needed a bit of time, a break. So did Rebus, but he had some thinking to do, and the station was the best place for that.

By taking them slowly, Rebus managed the stairs to his office. He had been at his desk fully ten minutes before a craving for tea had him reaching for the telephone. Then he sat back, holding in front of him a piece of paper on which he had attempted to set out the 'facts' of the 'case'.

He was chilled by the thought that he might be wasting time and effort. A jury would have to work hard to see any crime there at all. There was no suggestion that Ronnie had not injected himself. However, he *had* been starved of his supply, despite there being no shortage of dope in the city, and someone *had* moved his body, and left behind a packet of good heroin, hoping, perhaps, that this would be tested, found clean, and therefore death by misadventure would be recorded: a simple overdose. But the rat poison had been found.

Rebus looked at the paper. Already 'perhapses' and conjecture had entered the picture. Maybe the frame wasn't right. So, turn the picture another way round, John, and start again.

Why had someone gone to the trouble of killing Ronnie? After all, the poor bugger would have topped himself given time. Ronnie had been starved of a fix, then given some, but had known this stuff to be less than pure. So doubtless he had known that the person who supplied it wanted him dead. But he had taken it anyway. . . . No, viewed this way round it was making even less sense. Start again.

Why would someone want Ronnie dead? There were several obvious answers. Because he knew something he shouldn't. Because he possessed something he shouldn't. Because he didn't possess something he should. Which was correct? Rebus didn't know. Nobody seemed to know. The picture still lacked meaning.

There was a knock on the door, and the door itself was pushed open by a constable carrying a mug of tea. The constable was Harry Todd. Rebus recognised him.

'You get around a bit, son.'

'Yes, sir,' said Todd, placing the tea on a corner of the desk, the only three square inches of wood visible from beneath a surface covering of paperwork.

'Is it quiet tonight?'

171

'The usual, sir. A few drunks. Couple of break-ins. Nasty car crash down near the docks.'

Rebus nodded, reaching for the tea. 'Do you know another constable, name of Neil McGrath?' Raising the mug to his lips, Rebus stared up at Todd, who had begun to blush.

'Yes, sir,' he said. 'I know him.'

'Mm-hm.' Rebus tested the tea, seeming to relish the bland flavour of milk and hot water. 'Told you to keep an eye on me, did he?'

'Sir?'

'If you happen to see him, Todd, tell him everything's fine.'

'Yes, sir.' Todd was turning to leave.

'Oh, and Todd?'

'Yes, sir?'

'Don't let me see you near me again, understood?'

'Yes, sir.' Todd was clearly downhearted. At the door, he paused, seeming to have a sudden plan that would ingratiate himself with his superior. Smiling, he turned back to Rebus.

'Did you hear about the action across in Fife, sir?'

'What action?' Rebus sounded uninterested.

'The dog fight, sir.' Rebus tried hard to still look unmoved. 'They broke up some dog fight. Guess who got arrested?'

'Malcolm Rifkind?' guessed Rebus. This deflated Todd totally. The smile left his face.

'No, sir,' he said, turning again to leave. Rebus's patience was short.

'Well who then?' he snapped.

'That disc jockey, Calum McCallum,' Todd said, closing the door after him. Rebus stared at the door for a count of five before it struck home: Calum McCallum ... Gill Templer's lover!

Rebus raised his head and let out a roar which mixed

laughter with a kind of twisted victory cry. And when he had stopped laughing, and was wiping his eyes with a handkerchief, he looked towards the door again and saw that it was open. There was someone standing in the doorway, watching his performance with a look of puzzlement on their face.

It was Gill Templer.

Rebus checked his watch. It was nearly one in the morning.

'Working the late shift, Gill?' he said to cover his confusion.

'I suppose you've heard,' she said, ignoring him.

'Heard what?'

She walked into the room, pushed some papers off the chair onto the floor, and sat down, looking exhausted. Rebus looked at all that paper slewed across the floor.

'The cleaners come in in the morning anyway,' he said. Then: 'I've heard.'

'Is that what all the screaming was about?'

'Oh, that.' Rebus tried to shrug it off, but could feel the blood tingling in his cheeks. 'No,' he said, 'that was just something . . . well, something else. . . .'

'Not very convincing, Rebus, you bastard.' Her words were tired. He wanted to buoy her up, tell her she was looking well or something. But it wouldn't have been true and she would just scowl at him again. So he left it. She *was* looking drawn, not enough sleep and no fun left any more. She'd just had her world locked up in a cell somewhere in Fife. They would be photographing and fingerprinting it perhaps, ready to file it away. Her life, Calum McCallum.

Life was full of surprises.

'So what can I do for you?'

She looked up at him, studying his face as though she wasn't sure who he was or why she was here. Then she shook herself awake with a twitch of the shoulders.

'It sounds corny, but I really was just passing. I dropped into the canteen for a coffee before going home, and then I heard –' She shivered again; the twitch which wasn't quite a twitch. Rebus could see how fragile she was. He hoped she wasn't going to shake apart. 'I heard about Calum. How could he do that to me, John? Keep a secret like that? I mean, where's the fun in watching dogs ripping each other –'

'That's something you'll have to ask him yourself, Gill. Can I get you some more coffee?'

'Christ no, I'm going to find it hard enough getting to sleep as it is. Tell you what I would like though, if it's not too much trouble.'

'Name it.'

'A lift home.' Rebus was already nodding agreement. 'And a hug.'

Rebus got up slowly, donned his jacket, put the pen and piece of paper in his pocket, and met her in the middle of the room. She had already risen from her chair, and, standing on reports to be read, paperwork to be signed, arrest statistics and the rest, they hugged, their arms strong. She buried her head in his shoulder. He rested his chin on her neck, staring at the closed door, rubbing her back with one hand, patting with the other. Eventually, she pulled away, head first, then chest, but still holding him with her arms. Her eyes were moist, but it was over now. She was looking a little better.

'Thanks,' she said.

'I needed it as much as you did,' said Rebus. 'Come on, let's get you home.'

Friday

The inhabitants were all doing well, it seemed, and all emulously hoping to do better still, and laying out the surplus of their grains in coquetry.

Someone was knocking on his door. An authoritarian knock, using the old brass knocker that he never cleaned. Rebus opened his eyes. The sun was streaming into his living room, a record's run-out track crackling. Another night spent in the chair, fully clothed. He'd be as well selling the mattress in the bedroom. Would anyone buy a mattress without a bed-frame?

Knockity knock knock again. Still patient. Still waiting for him to answer. His eyes were gummy, and he pushed his shirt back into his trousers as he walked from the living room to the door. He felt not too bad, considering. Not stiff, no tightness in the neck. A wash and a shave, and he might even feel human.

He opened the door, just as Holmes was about to knock again.

'Brian.' Rebus sounded genuinely pleased.

'Morning. Mind if I come in?'

'Not at all. Is Nell okay?'

'I phoned this morning. They say she had a good night.'

They were walking in the direction of the kitchen, Rebus leading. Holmes had imagined the flat would smell of beer and cigarettes, a typical bachelor pad. In fact, it was tidier than he'd expected, furnished with a modicum of taste. There were a lot of books. Rebus had never struck him as a reader. Mind you, not all the books looked as though they'd been read: bought with a rainy, dead weekend in mind. The weekend that never came.

Rebus pointed vaguely in the direction of kettle and cupboards.

'Make us some coffee, will you? I'll just take a quick shower.'

'Right.' Holmes thought that his news could probably wait. At least until Rebus was fully awake. He sought in vain for instant coffee, but found, in one cupboard, a vacuum pack of ground coffee, several months past its sell-by date. He opened it and spooned some into the teapot while the kettle was boiling. Sounds of running water came from the bathroom, and above these the tinny sound of a transistor radio. Voices. Some talk show, Holmes supposed.

While Rebus was in the bathroom, he took the opportunity to wander through the flat. The living room was huge, with a high corniced ceiling. Holmes felt a pang of jealousy. He'd never be able to buy a place like this. He was looking around Easter Road and Gorgie, near the football grounds of Hibs and Hearts respectively. He could afford a flat in both these parts of the city, a decent-sized flat, too, three bedrooms. But the rooms were small, the areas mean. He was no snob. Hell, yes he was. He wanted to live in the New Town, in Dean Village, here in Marchmont, where students philosophised in pretty coffee shops.

He wasn't overcareful with the stylus when he lifted the arm off the record. The record itself was by some jazz combo. It looked old, and he sought in vain for its sleeve. The noises from the bathroom had stopped. He walked stealthily back to the kitchen and found a tea strainer in the cutlery drawer. So he was able to keep the grounds out of the coffee he now poured into two mugs. Rebus came in, wrapped in a bath-towel, rubbing at his head with another, smaller towel. He needed to lose weight, or to exercise what weight he had. His chest was beginning to hang, pale like a carcass.

He picked up a mug and sipped.

'Mmm. The real McCoy.'

'I found it in the cupboard. No milk though.'

'Never mind. This is fine. You say you found it in the cupboard? We might make a detective of you yet. I'll just put on some togs.' And he was off again, for only two minutes this time. The clothes he came back wearing were clean, but unironed. Holmes noticed that though there was plumbing in the kitchen for a washing machine, there was no machine. Rebus seemed to read his mind.

'My wife took it when she moved out. Took a lot of stuff. That's why the place looks so bare.'

'It doesn't look bare. It looks planned.'

Rebus smiled. 'Let's go into the living room.'

Rebus motioned for Holmes to sit, then sat down himself. The chair was still warm from his night's sleep. 'I see you've already been in here.'

Holmes looked surprised. Caught. He remembered that he'd lifted the stylus off the record.

'Yes,' he said.

'That's what I like to see,' Rebus said. 'Yes, we'll make a detective of you yet, Brian.'

Holmes wasn't sure whether Rebus was being flattering or condescending. He let it go.

'Something I thought you might like to know,' he began.

'I already know,' said Rebus. 'Sorry to spoil the surprise, but I was at the station late last night, and somebody told me.'

'Last night?' Holmes was confused. 'But they only found the body this morning.'

'The body? You mean he's dead?'

'Yes. Suicide.'

'Jesus, poor Gill.'

'Gill?'

'Gill Templer. She was going out with him.'

'Inspector Templer?' Holmes was shocked. 'I thought she was living with that disc jockey?'

Now Rebus was confused. 'Isn't that who we're talking about?'

'No,' said Holmes. The surprise was still intact. He felt real relief.

'So who *are* we talking about?' asked Rebus with a growing sense of dread. 'Who's committed suicide?'

'James Carew.'

'Carew?'

'Yes. Found him in his flat this morning. Overdose apparently.'

'Overdose of what?'

'I don't know. Some kind of pills.'

Rebus was stunned. He recalled the look on Carew's face that night atop Calton Hill.

'Damn,' he said. 'I wanted a word with him.'

'I was wondering . . .' said Holmes.

'What?'

'I don't suppose you ever got round to asking him about getting me a flat?'

'No,' said Rebus. 'I never got the chance.'

'I was only joking,' Holmes said, realising that Rebus had taken his comment literally. 'Was he a friend? I mean, I know you met him for lunch, but I didn't realise –'

'Did he leave a note?'

'I don't know.'

'Well who *would* know?'

Holmes thought for a second. 'I think Inspector McCall was at the scene.'

'Right, come on.' Rebus was up on his feet.

'What about your coffee?'

'Sod the coffee. I want to see Tony McCall.'

'What was all that about Calum McCallum?' said Holmes, rising now.

'You mean you haven't heard?' Holmes shook his head. 'I'll tell you on the way.'

And then Rebus was on the move, grabbing jacket, getting out his keys to lock the front door. Holmes wondered what the secret was. What had Calum McCallum done? God, he hated people who hung on to secrets.

Rebus read the note as he stood in Carew's bedroom. It was elegantly written with a proper nib pen, but in one or two of the words fear could be clearly read, the letters trembling uncontrollably, scribbled out to be tried again. Good-quality writing paper too, thick and watermarked. The V12 was in a garage behind the flat. The flat itself was stunning, a museum for art deco pieces, modern art prints, and valuable first editions, locked behind glass.

This is the flipside of Vanderhyde's home, Rebus had thought as he moved through the flat. Then McCall had handed him the suicide note.

'If I am the chief of sinners, I am the chief of sufferers also.' Was that a quote from somewhere? Certainly, it was a bit prolix for a suicide note. But then Carew would have gone through draft upon draft until satisfied. It had to be exact, had to stand as his monument. 'Some day you may perhaps come to learn the right and wrong of this.' Not that Rebus needed to seek too hard. He had the queasy feeling, reading the note, that Carew's words were directed straight at him, that he was saying things only Rebus could fully understand.

'Funny sort of note to leave behind,' said McCall.

'Yes,' said Rebus.

'You met him recently, didn't you?' said McCall. 'I remember you saying. Did he seem okay then? I mean, he wasn't depressed or anything?'

'I've seen him since then.'

'Oh?'

'I was sniffing around Calton Hill a couple of nights back. He was there in his car.'

'Ah-ha.' McCall nodded. Everything was starting to make a little bit of sense.

Rebus handed back the note and went over to the bed. The sheets were rumpled. Three empty pill bottles stood in a neat line on the bedside table. On the floor lay an empty cognac bottle.

'The man went out in style,' McCall said, pocketing the note. 'He'd gone through a couple of bottles of wine before that.'

'Yes, I saw them in the living room. Lafite sixty-one. The stuff of a very special occasion.'

'They don't come more special, John.'

Both men turned as a third presence became evident in the room. It was Farmer Watson, breathing heavily from the effort of the stairs.

'This is bloody awkward,' he said. 'One of the linchpins of our campaign tops himself, and by taking a bloody overdose. How's that going to look, eh?'

'Awkward, sir,' replied Rebus, 'just as you say.'

'I do say. I do say.' Watson thrust a finger out towards Rebus. 'It's up to you, John, to make sure the media don't make a meal of this, or of us.'

'Yes, sir.'

Watson looked over towards the bed. 'Waste of a bloody decent man. What makes someone do it? I mean, look at this place. And there's an estate somewhere on one of the islands. Own business. Expensive car. Things we can only dream about. Makes you wonder, doesn't it?'

'Yes, sir.'

'Right.' Watson took a last glance towards the bed, then slapped a hand on Rebus's shoulder. 'I'm depending on you, John.'

'Yes, sir.'

McCall and Rebus watched their superior go.

'Bloody hell!' whispered McCall. 'He didn't look at me, not once. I might as well have not been there.'

'You should thank your lucky stars, Tony. I wish I had your gift of invisibility.'

Both men smiled. 'Seen enough?' McCall asked.

'Just one more circuit,' said Rebus. 'Then I'll get out of your hair.'

'Whatever you say, John. Just one thing.'

'What's that?'

'What the hell were you doing up Calton Hill in the middle of the night?'

'Don't ask,' said Rebus, blowing a kiss as he headed for the living area.

It *would* be big news locally, of course. There was no getting away from the fact. The radio stations and newspapers would have trouble deciding which headline deserved most prominence: Disc Jockey Arrested at Illegal Dog Fight or Suicide Shock of Estate Agent Giant. Well, something along those lines. Jim Stevens would have loved it, but then Jim Stevens was in London and married, by all accounts, to some girl half his age.

Rebus admired that kind of dangerous move. He had no admiration for James Carew: none. Watson was right in at least one respect: Carew had everything going for him, and Rebus was finding it difficult to believe that he would commit suicide solely because he had been spotted by a police officer on Calton Hill. No, that might have been the trigger, but there *had* to be something more. Something, perhaps, in the flat, or in the offices of Bowyer Carew on George Street.

James Carew owned a lot of books. A quick examination showed that they were for the most part expensive, impressive titles, but unread, their spines crackling as they were opened by Rebus for the first time. The top right hand section of the bookcase held several titles which interested him more than the others. Books by Genet and Alexander Trocchi, copies of Forster's *Maurice* and even *Last Exit to Brooklyn*. Poems by Walt Whitman, the text of *Torchlight Trilogy*. A mixed bag of predominantly gay reading. Nothing wrong in that. But their positioning in the bookshelves – right at the top and separated from the other titles – suggested to Rebus that here was a man ashamed of himself. There was no reason for this, not these days. . . .

Who was he kidding? AIDS had squeezed homosexuality back into the darker corners of society, and by keeping the truth a secret Carew had laid himself open to feelings of shame, and, therefore, to blackmail of all kinds.

Yes, blackmail. Suicides were occasionally victims of blackmail who could see no way out of their dilemma. Just maybe there would be some evidence, a letter or a note or something. *Anything*. Just so Rebus could prove to himself he wasn't completely paranoid.

Then he found it.

In a drawer. A locked drawer, to be sure, but the keys were in Carew's trousers. He had died in his pyjamas, and his other clothes had not been taken away with the corpse. Rebus got the keys from the bedroom and headed back to the desk in the living room. A gorgeous writing desk, antique for sure: its surface was barely large enough to accommodate a sheet of A4 paper and an elbow. What had been once a useful piece of furniture now found itself an ornament in a rich man's apartment. Rebus opened the drawer carefully and drew out a leather-bound desk diary. A page a day, the pages large. Not a diary for appointments, not locked away in darkness like that. A personal diary then. Eagerly, Rebus flipped it open. His disappointment was immediate. The pages were blank for the most part. A line or two of pencil per page was as much as there was.

Rebus cursed.

All right, John. It's better than nothing. He rested at one of the pages with some writing on it. The pencil marking was faint, neatly written. 'Jerry, 4pm'. A simple appointment. Rebus flipped to the day on which they had all met for lunch at The Eyrie. The page was blank. Good. That meant the appointments weren't of the business lunch variety. There weren't many of them. Rebus felt sure that Carew's diary at his office would be crammed. This was a much more private affair.

'Lindsay, 6.30.'

'Marks, 11am.' An early start that day, and what about that name: two individuals, each named Mark? Or one individual whose surname was Marks? Maybe even the department store . . .? The other names – Jerry, Lindsay – were androgynous, anonymous. He needed a telephone number, a location.

He turned another page. And had to look twice at what was written there. His finger ran along the letters.

'Hyde, 10pm.'

Hyde. What had Ronnie said to Tracy the night he'd died? *Hide, he's after me?* Yes, and James had given him the name, too: not hide but H-y-d-e.

Hyde!

Rebus whooped. Here was a connection, no matter how tenuous. A connection between Ronnie and James Carew. Something more than a fleeting business transaction on Calton Hill. A name. He hurried through the other pages. There were three more mentions of Hyde, always in the late evening (when Calton Hill was starting its trade), always on a Friday. Sometimes the second Friday of the month, sometimes the third. Four mentions in the course of six months.

'Anything?' It was McCall, leaning over Rebus's shoulder for a peek.

'Yes,' Rebus said. Then he changed his mind. 'No, not

really, Tony. Just an old diary, but the bugger wasn't much of a writer.'

McCall nodded and moved away. He was more interested in the hi-fi system.

'The old guy had taste,' McCall said, scrutinising it. 'Linn turntable. Know how much one of those costs, John? Hundreds. They're not showy. They're just bloody good at what they do.'

'A bit like us then,' said Rebus. He was thinking of pushing the diary into his trousers. It wasn't allowed, he knew. And what good would it do him? But with Tony McCall's back turned so conveniently. . . . No, no, he couldn't. He threw it noisily back into its drawer, shut the drawer again and locked it. He handed the key to McCall, who was still squatting in front of the hi-fi.

'Thanks, John. Nice piece of equipment this, you know.'

'I didn't know you were interested in all that stuff.'

'Since I was a kid. Had to get rid of my system when we got married. Too noisy.' He straightened. 'Are we going to find any answers here, do you think?'

Rebus shook his head. 'I think he kept all his secrets in his head. He was a very private man, after all. No, I think he's taken the answers with him to the grave.'

'Oh, well. Makes it nice and clear-cut then, doesn't it?'

'Clear as crystal, Tony,' said Rebus.

What was it the old man, Vanderhyde, had said? Something about muddying the water. Rebus had the gnawing feeling that the solution to these many conundrums was a simple one, as crystal clear as one could wish. The problem was that extraneous stories were being woven into the whole. *Do I mix my metaphors? Very well then, I mix my metaphors.* All that counted was getting to the bottom of the pool, muddied or no, and bringing up that tiny cache of treasure called the truth.

He knew, too, that the problem was one of classification. He had to break the interlinked stories into separate threads, and work from those. At the moment, he was guilty of trying to weave them all into a pattern, a pattern that might not be there. By separating them all, maybe he'd be in with a chance of solving each.

Ronnie committed suicide. So did Carew. That gave them a second thing in common to add to the name of Hyde. Some client of Carew's perhaps? Buying a substantial piece of property with money made through the dealing of hard drugs? That would be a link, for sure. Hyde. The name couldn't be real. How many Hydes were there in the Edinburgh directory? It could always be an assumed name. Male prostitutes seldom used their own names, after all. Hyde. Jekyll and Hyde. Another coincidence: Rebus had been reading Stevenson's book the night Tracy had visited. Maybe he should be looking for someone called Jekyll? Jekyll, the respectable doctor, admired by society; Hyde, his alter ego, small and brutish, a creature of the night. He remembered the shadowy forms he'd encountered by Calton Hill. . . . Could the answer be so obvious?

He parked in the only vacant bay left outside Great London Road station and climbed the familiar steps. They seemed to grow larger with the passing years, and he could swear there were more of them now than there had been when he'd first come to this place, all of – what was it? – six years ago? That wasn't so long in the span of a man's life, was it? So why did it feel so bloody Sisyphean?

'Hello, Jack,' he said to the desk sergeant, who watched him walk past without the usual nod of the head. Strange, Rebus thought. Jack had never been a cheery bugger, but he'd usually had the use of his neck muscles. He was famous for his slight bow of the head, which he could make mean anything from approbation to insult.

But today, for Rebus, nothing.

187

Rebus decided to ignore the slight, and went upstairs. Two constables, in the act of coming down, fell quiet as they passed him. Rebus began to redden, but kept walking, sure now that he had forgotten to zip his fly, or had somehow contrived to get a smudge on his nose. Something like that. He'd check in the privacy of his office.

Holmes was waiting for him, seated in Rebus's chair, at Rebus's desk, some property details spread across the tabletop. He began to rise as Rebus entered, gathering together the sheets of paper like a kid caught with a dirty book.

'Hello, Brian.' Rebus took off his jacket, hanging it on the back of the door. 'Listen, I want you to get me the names and addresses of all Edinburgh inhabitants whose names are Jekyll or Hyde. I know that may sound daft, but just do it. Then –'

'I think you should sit down, sir,' said Holmes tremulously. Rebus stared at him, saw the fear in the young man's eyes, and knew that the worst had happened.

Rebus pushed open the door of the interview room. His face was the colour of pickled beetroot, and Holmes, following, feared that his superior was about to suffer a coronary. There were two CID men in the room, both in their shirtsleeves as though after a hard session. They turned at Rebus's entrance, and the one who was seated rose as if for combat. On the other side of the table, the weasel-faced teenager known to Rebus as 'James' actually squealed, and flew to his feet, knocking the chair with a clatter onto the stone floor.

'Don't let him near me!' he yelled.

'Now, John –' started one detective, a Sergeant Dick. Rebus held up a hand to show that he was not here to cause violence. The detectives eyed one another, not sure whether to believe him. Then Rebus spoke, his eyes on the teenager.

'You're going to get what's coming to you, so help me.' There was calm, lucid anger in Rebus's voice. 'I'm going to have you by your balls for this, son. You better believe that. Really, you better.'

The teenager saw now that the others would restrain Rebus, that the man himself presented an empty physical threat. He sneered.

'Yeah, sure,' he said dismissively. Rebus lurched forward, but Holmes's hand was rigid against his shoulder, pulling him back.

'Leave it be, John,' the other detective, DC Cooper, cautioned. 'Just let the wheels grind round. It won't take long.'

'Too long though,' Rebus hissed, as Holmes pulled him out of the room, closing the door after them. Rebus stood in the shadowy corridor, all rage spent, head bowed. It was so very hard to believe. . . .

'Inspector Rebus!'

Rebus and Holmes both jerked their heads towards the voice. It belonged to a WPC. She looked scared, too.

'Yes?' Rebus managed, swallowing.

'The Super wants to see you in his office. I think it's urgent.'

'I'm sure it is,' said Rebus, walking towards her with such menace that she retreated hurriedly, back towards the reception area and daylight.

'It's a bloody set-up, with all due respect, sir.'

Remember the golden rule, John, Rebus thought to himself: never swear at a superior without adding that 'with all due respect'. It was something he'd learned in the Army. As long as you added that coda, the brass couldn't have you for insubordination.

'John.' Watson interlaced his fingers, studying them as

if they were the latest craze. 'John, we've got to investigate it. That's our duty. *I* know it's daft, and everyone else knows it's daft, but we've got to *show* that it's daft. That's our duty.'

'All the same, sir –'

Watson cut him off with a wave of his hand. Then started twining fingers again.

'God knows, you're already "suspended" from duty as it is, until our little campaign gets into full swing.'

'Yes, sir, but this is just what he wants.'

'He?'

'Some man called Hyde. He wants me to stop poking about in the Ronnie McGrath case. That's what this is all about. That's why it's a set-up job.'

'That's as maybe. The fact remains, a complaint has been made against you –'

'By that little bastard downstairs.'

'He says you gave him money, twenty pounds, I believe.'

'I *did* give him twenty quid, but not for a shag, for Chrissake!'

'For what then?'

Rebus made to answer, but was defeated. Why *had* he handed the teenager called James that money? He'd set himself up, all right. Hyde couldn't have done it better himself. And now James was downstairs, spilling his carefully rehearsed story to CID. And say what you liked, mud stuck. By Christ, it didn't half. No amount of soap and water would clean it off. The little toerag.

'This is playing right into Hyde's hands, sir,' Rebus tried: one last shot. 'If his story's true, why didn't he come in yesterday? Why wait till today?'

But Watson was decided.

'No, John. I want you out of here for a day or two. A week even. Take a break. Do whatever you like, but leave well alone. We'll clear it up, don't worry. We'll break his story down into pieces so small he won't be able to see

190

them any more. One of those pieces will snap, and with it, his whole story. Don't you worry.'

Rebus stared at Watson. What he said made sense; more than that, it was actually fairly subtle and shrewd. Maybe the Farmer wasn't so agricultural in his ways after all. He sighed.

'Whatever you say, sir.'

Watson nodded, smiling.

'By the way,' he said. 'Remember that fellow Andrews, ran a club called Finlay's?'

'We had lunch with him, sir.'

'That's right. He's invited me to apply for membership.'

'Good for you, sir.'

'Apparently the waiting list's about a year long – all these rich Sassenachs coming north – but he said he could do a bit of pruning in my case. I told him not to bother. I seldom drink, and I certainly don't gamble. Still, a nice gesture all the same. Maybe I should ask him to consider you in my place. That'd give you something to do with your time off, eh?'

'Yes, sir.' Rebus seemed to consider the suggestion. Booze and gambling: not a bad combination. His face brightened. 'Yes, sir,' he said. 'That would be very kind of you.'

'I'll see what I can do then. One last thing.'

'Yes, sir?'

'Are you intending to go to Malcolm Lanyon's party tonight? Remember, he invited us at The Eyrie?'

'I'd forgotten all about it, sir. Would it be more . . . proper for me to stay away?'

'Not at all. I may not manage along myself, but I see no reason why you shouldn't attend. But not a word about. . . .' Watson nodded towards the door, and by implication to the interview room beyond.

'Understood, sir. Thank you.'

'Oh, and John?'

'Yes, sir?'

'Don't swear at me. Ever. With respect or otherwise. Okay?'

Rebus felt his cheeks reddening, not in anger but in shame. 'Yes, sir,' he said, making his exit.

Holmes was waiting impatiently in Rebus's office.

'What did he want then?'

'Who?' Rebus was supremely nonchalant. 'Oh, Watson you mean? He wanted to tell me that he's put my name forward for Finlay's.'

'Finlay's Club?' Holmes' face was quizzical; this wasn't what he'd been expecting at all.

'That's right. At my age, I think I deserve a club in town, don't you?'

'I don't know.'

'Oh, and he also wanted to remind me about a party tonight at Malcolm Lanyon's place.'

'The lawyer?'

'That's him.' Rebus had Holmes at a disadvantage, and knew it. 'I hope you've been busy while I've been having a chinwag.'

'Eh?'

'Hydes and Jekylls, Brian. I asked you for addresses.'

'I've got the list here. Not too long, thank the Lord. I suppose I'm going to be Shoeleather on this one?'

Rebus looked flabbergasted. 'Not at all. You've got better things to be doing with your time. No, I think this time the shoeleather ought to be mine.'

'But . . . with respect, shouldn't you be keeping out of things?'

'With respect, Brian, that's none of your bloody business.'

From home, Rebus tried phoning Gill, but she couldn't be reached. Keeping out of things, no doubt. She had been quiet during the drive home last night, and hadn't invited him in. Fair enough, he supposed. He wasn't about to take advantage. . . . So why was he trying to telephone her? Of course he was trying to take advantage! He wanted her back.

He tidied the living room, did some washing up, and took a binbag's-worth of dirty washing to the local laundrette for a service wash. The attendant, Mrs Mackay, was full of outrage about Calum McCallum.

'Yon's a celebrity and a'. They should ken better.'

Rebus smiled and nodded agreement.

Back in the flat, he sat down and picked up a book, knowing he wouldn't be able to keep his mind on it. He didn't want Hyde to win, and, kept away from the case, that's exactly what would happen. He took the slip of paper from his pocket. There were no people with the surname Jekyll in the Lothians, and a scant dozen with the surname Hyde. At least, those were the ones he could be sure about. What if Hyde possessed an unlisted number? He'd get Brian Holmes to check the possibility.

He reached for the telephone and was halfway through the number before he realised he was calling Gill's office. He punched in the rest of the number. What the hell, she wouldn't be there anyway.

'Hello?'

It was Gill Templer's voice, sounding as unflappable as ever. Yes, but that sort of trick was easy by phone. All the oldest tricks were.

'It's John.'

'Hello there. Thanks for the lift home.'

'How are you?'

'I'm fine, honestly. I just feel a bit . . . I don't know, confused doesn't seem to cover it. I feel as though I've been conned. That's as near as I can get to an explanation.'

'Are you going to see him?'

'What? In Fife? No, I don't think so. It's not that I couldn't face *him*. I *want* to see *him*. It's the thought of walking into the station with everyone knowing who I was, why I was there.'

'I'd go with you, Gill, if you wanted.'

'Thanks, John. Maybe in a day or two. But not yet.'

'Understood.' He became aware that he was gripping the receiver too hard, that his fingers were hurting. God, this was hurting him all over. Did she have any inkling of his feelings right this minute? He was sure he couldn't put them into words. The words hadn't been coined. He felt so close to her, and yet so far away, like a schoolkid who'd lost his first girlfriend.

'Thanks for phoning, John. I appreciate it. But I'd better be getting –'

'Oh, right, right you are. Well, you've got my number, Gill. Take care.'

'Bye, J –'

He broke the connection. Don't crowd her, John, he was thinking. That's how you lost her the first time. Don't go making any assumptions. She doesn't like that. Give her space. Maybe he had made a mistake phoning in the first place. Hell and damn.

With respect.

That little weasel called James. That little toerag. He'd rip his head from his shoulders when he got him. He wondered how much Hyde had paid the kid. Considerably more than two ten-pound notes, that was for sure.

The telephone rang.

'Rebus here.'

'John? It's Gill again. I've just heard the news. Why didn't you tell me?'

'Tell you what?' He affected indifference, knowing she'd see through it immediately.

'About this complaint against you.'

194

'Oh, that. Come on, Gill, you know this sort of thing happens from time to time.'

'Yes, but why didn't you *say*? Why did you let me prattle on like that?'

'You weren't prattling.'

'Dammit!' She was almost in tears now. 'Why do you always have to try and hide things from me like that? What's the matter with you?'

He was about to explain, when the line went dead. He stared at the receiver dumbly, wondering just *why* he hadn't told her in the first place. Because she had worries of her own? Because he was embarrassed? Because he hadn't wanted the pity of a vulnerable woman? There were reasons enough.

Weren't there?

Of course there were. It was just that none of them seemed to make him feel any better. *Why do you always have to try and hide things from me?* There was that word again: hide. A verb, an action, and a noun, a place. And a person. Faceless, but Rebus was beginning to know him so well. The adversary was cunning, there was no doubting that. But he couldn't hope to tie up all the loose threads the way he'd tied up Ronnie and Carew, the way he was trying to tie up John Rebus.

The telephone rang again.

'Rebus here.'

'It's Superintendent Watson. I'm glad I caught you at home.'

Because, Rebus added silently, it means I'm not out on the street causing trouble for you.

'Yes, sir. Any problem?'

'Quite the reverse. They're still questioning this male prostitute. Shouldn't be too long now. But meantime, the reason I called is because I've been on to the casino.'

'Casino, sir?'

'You know, Finlay's.'

'Oh, yes.'

'And they say that you'll be welcome there anytime, should you wish to pop in. You've just to mention Finlay Andrews' name, and that's your ticket.'

'Right, sir. Well, thanks for that.'

'My pleasure, John. Shame you're having to take it easy, what with this suicide business and all. The press are all over it, sniffing around for any little piece of dirt they can find. What a job, eh?'

'Yes, sir.'

'McCall's fielding their questions. I just hope he doesn't appear on the box. Not exactly photogenic, is he?'

Watson made this sound like Rebus's fault, and Rebus was on the point of apologising when the Superintendent placed a hand over the mouthpiece at his end, while he had a few words with someone. And when he came on again it was to say a hasty goodbye.

'Press conference apparently,' he said. And that was that.

Rebus stared at the receiver for a full minute. If there were to be any more calls, let them come now. They didn't. He threw the instrument onto the floor, where it landed heavily. Secretly, he was hoping to break it one of these days, so he could go back to an old-style handset. But the blasted thing seemed tougher than it looked.

He was opening the book when the door-knocker sounded. Tappity tap tap. A business call then, and not Mrs Cochrane wondering why he hadn't washed the communal stairwell yet.

It was Brian Holmes.

'Can I come in?'

'I suppose so.' Rebus felt no real enthusiasm, but left the door open for the young detective to follow him through to the living room if he so desired. He so desired, following Rebus with mock heartiness.

'I was just looking at a flat near Tollcross, and thought I'd –'

'Skip the excuses, Brian. You're checking up on me. Sit down and tell me what's been happening in my absence.' Rebus checked his watch while Holmes seated himself. 'An absence, for the record, of just under two hours.'

'Ach, I was concerned, that's all.'

Rebus stared at him. Simple, direct, and to the point. Maybe Rebus could learn something from Holmes after all.

'It's not Farmer's orders then?'

'Not at all. And as it happens, I *did* have a flat to look at.'

'What was it like?'

'Ghastly beyond speech. Cooker in the living room, shower in a wee cupboard. No bath, no kitchen.'

'How much did they want for it? No, on second thoughts don't tell me. It would just depress me.'

'It certainly depressed me.'

'You can always make an offer on this place when they throw me inside for corrupting a minor.'

Holmes looked up, saw that Rebus was smiling, and gave a relieved grin.

'The guy's story's already coming apart at the seams.'

'Did you ever doubt it?'

'Of course not. Anyway, I thought these might cheer you up.' Holmes brandished a large manilla envelope, which had been discreetly tucked inside his cord jacket. Rebus hadn't seen this cord jacket before, and supposed it to be the Detective Constable's flat-buying uniform.

'What are they?' said Rebus, accepting the packet.

'Pics. Last night's raid. Thought you might be interested.'

Rebus opened the envelope and withdrew a set of ten-by-eight black and whites. They showed the more or less blurred shapes of men scrambling across waste ground. What light there was had about it a halogen starkness, sending up huge black shadows and capturing some faces in chalky states of shock and surprise.

'Where did you get these?'

'That DS Hendry sent them across with a note sympathising over Nell. He thought these might cheer me up.'

'I told you he was a good bloke. Any idea which one of these goons is the DJ?'

Holmes leapt from his seat and crouched beside Rebus, who was holding a photograph at the ready.

'No,' Holmes said, 'there's a better shot of him.' He thumbed through the set until he found the picture he was looking for. 'Here we are. That one there. That's McCallum.'

Rebus studied the fuzzy semblance before him. The look of fear, so distinct against the blurred face, could have been drawn by a child. Wide eyes and a mouth puckered into an 'O', arms suspended as though between rapid flight and final surrender.

Rebus smiled a smile that reached all the way up to his eyes.

'You're sure this is him?'

'One of the PCs at the station recognised him. He said he once got McCallum to sign an autograph for him.'

'I'm impressed. Shouldn't think he'll be signing too many more though. Where are they holding him?'

'Everybody they arrested has gone to Dunfermline nick'.

'That's nice for them. By the by, did they nab the ringleaders?'

'Each and every one. Including Brightman. He was the boss.'

'Davy Brightman? The scrappie?'

'That's him.'

'I played against that bugger at football a couple of times when I was at school. He played left back for his team when I was on the wing for ours. He gave me a good studding one match.'

'Revenge is sweet,' said Holmes.

'It is that, Brian.' Rebus was studying the photograph again. 'It is that.'

'Actually, a couple of the punters did scarper apparently, but they're all on film. The camera never lies, eh, sir?'

Rebus began to sift through the other pictures. 'A powerful tool, the camera,' he said. His face suddenly changed.

'Sir? Are you all right?'

Rebus's voice was reduced to a whisper. 'I've just had a revelation, Brian. A whatsit . . .? epiphany, is it?'

'No idea, sir.' Holmes was sure now that something inside his superior had snapped.

'Epiphany, yes. I *know* where this has all been leading, Brian. I'm sure of it. That bastard on Calton Hill said something about pictures, some pictures everybody was interested in. They're *Ronnie's* pictures.'

'What? The ones in his bedroom?'

'No, not those.'

'The ones at Hutton's studio then?'

'Not quite. No, I don't know exactly *where* these particular pictures are, but I've got a bloody good idea. "Hide" can be a noun, Brian. Come on.'

'Where?' Holmes watched as Rebus sprang from his chair, heading for the door. He started to collect the photographs, which Rebus had let fall from his hands.

'Never mind those,' Rebus ordered, slipping on a jacket.

'But where the hell are we going?'

'You just answered your own question,' Rebus said, turning back to grin at Holmes. 'That's exactly where we're going.'

'But *where?*'

'To hell, of course. Come on.'

It was turning cold. The sun had just about tired itself out, and was retiring from the contest. The clouds were sticking-plaster pink. Two great final sunbeams shone down like torchlight upon Pilmuir, and picked out just the one building, leaving the other houses in the street untouched. Rebus sucked in breath. He had to admit, it was quite a sight.

'Like the stable at Bethlehem,' said Holmes.

'A damned queer stable,' Rebus retorted. 'God's got a funny sense of humour if this is His idea of a joke.'

'You did say we were going to hell.'

'I wasn't expecting Cecil B. DeMille to be in on it though. What's going on there?'

Almost hidden by the day's last gasp of sunlight, a van and a hire skip were parked directly in front of Ronnie's house.

'The council?' Holmes suggested. 'Probably cleaning the place up.'

'Why, in God's name?'

'There's plenty that need housing,' Holmes replied. Rebus wasn't listening. As the car pulled to a stop, he was out and walking briskly towards the skip. It was filling up with the detritus of the squat's interior. There were sounds of hammering from within. In the back of the van, a workman supped from a plastic cup, his thermos clutched in his other hand.

'Who's in charge here?' Rebus demanded.

The workman blew on the contents of his cup, then took another swig before replying. 'Me, I suppose.' His eyes were wary. He could smell authority a mile off. 'This is a legitimate tea-break.'

'Never mind that. What's going on?'

'Who wants to know.'

'CID wants to know.'

He looked hard at Rebus's harder face, and made up his mind instantly. 'Well, we got word to come and clean this place up. Make it habitable.'

200

'On whose orders?'

'I don't know. Somebody's. We just take the chitty and go do the job.'

'Right.' Rebus had turned from the man and was walking up the path to the front door. Holmes, having smiled apologetically at the foreman, followed. In the living room, two workmen in overalls and thick red rubber gloves were whitewashing the walls. Charlie's pentagram had already been covered, its outline barely visible through the drying layer of paint. The men looked towards Rebus, then to the wall.

'We'll cover it up next coat,' said one. 'Don't worry yourself about that.'

Rebus stared at the man, then marched past Holmes out of the room. He started to climb the stairs, and turned into Ronnie's bedroom. Another workman, much younger than the two downstairs, was gathering Ronnie's few belongings together into a large black plastic bag. As Rebus entered the room, the boy was caught, frozen, stuffing one of the paperbacks into the pocket of his overalls.

Rebus pointed to the book.

'There's a next of kin, son. Put it in the bag with the rest.'

Something about his tone persuaded the teenager to obey.

'Come across anything else interesting?' Rebus asked now, hands in pockets, approaching the teenager.

'Nothing,' the boy said, guiltily.

'In particular,' Rebus went on, as though the teenager had not spoken, 'photographs. Maybe just a few, maybe a whole packet. Hmm?'

'No. Nothing like that.'

'You're sure?'

'Sure.'

'Right. Get down to the van and bring up a crowbar or something. I want these floorboards up.'

'Eh?'

'You heard me, son. Do it.'

Holmes just stood and watched in silent appreciation. Rebus seemed to have grown in physical stature, becoming broader, taller. Holmes couldn't quite fathom the trick: maybe it had something to do with the hands in the pockets, the way the elbows jarred outwards, lending apparent substance to the frame. Whatever it was, it worked. The young workman stumbled out of the door and down the stairs.

'You're sure they'll be here?' said Holmes quietly. He tried to keep his tone level, not wishing to sound too sceptical. But Rebus was way past that stage. In Rebus's mind, the photographs were already in his hand.

'I'm certain, Brian. I can *smell* them.'

'You're sure that's not just the bathroom?'

Rebus turned and looked at him, as though seeing him for the very first time. 'You might have a point, Brian. You just might.'

Holmes followed Rebus to the bathroom. As Rebus kicked open the door, the stench embraced both men, arching them forward in a convulsive fit of gagging. Rebus brought a handkerchief from his pocket, pushed it to his face, and leaned towards the door handle, pulling the door shut again.

'I'd forgotten about that place,' he said. Then: 'Wait here.'

He returned with the foreman, a plastic dustbin, a shovel, and three small white face-masks, one of which he handed to Holmes. An elasticated band held the cardboard snout in place, and Holmes breathed deeply, testing the apparatus. He was just about to say something about the smell still being noticeable, when Rebus toed open the door again, and, as the foreman angled an industrial lamp into the bathroom, walked over the threshold.

Rebus pulled the dustbin to the rim of the bath and left it there, gesturing for the lamp to be shone into the bath itself. Holmes nearly fell backwards out of the room. A fat rat, caught in the act of feasting upon the rotten contents of the bath, squealed, red eyes burning directly into the light. Rebus swung the shovel down and cut the animal in two neat halves. Holmes spun from the room and, lifting the mask, retched against the damp wall. He tried taking gulps of air, but the smell was overpowering, the nausea returning in quickening floods.

Back inside the room, the foreman and Rebus exchanged a smile which wrinkled their eyes above the face-masks. They had seen worse than this – much worse – in their time. Then, neither man naive enough to want to linger, they set to work, the foreman holding the lamp while Rebus shovelled the contents of the bath slowly into the dustbin. The mess of raw sewage ran slickly from the shovel, spattering Rebus's shirt and trousers. He ignored it, ignored everything but the task at hand. He had done dirtier jobs in the Army, dirtier jobs by far during his failed training in the SAS. This was routine. And at least here there was some purpose to the task, some end in view.

Or so he hoped.

Holmes meantime was wiping his moist eyes with the back of his hand. Through the open door he could see the progress being made, eerie shadows cast across the wall and ceiling by the lamp, as one silhouette shovelled shit into a bin, filling it noisily. It was like a scene from some latter-day *Inferno*, lacking only the devils to goad the damned workers on. But these men looked, if not happy in their work, then at least . . . well, *professional* sprang to mind. Dear God, all he wanted was a flat to call his own, and the occasional holiday, and a decent car. And Nell, of course. This would make a funny story for her one day.

But the last thing he felt like doing was smiling.

Then he heard the cackle of laughter, and, looking around him, it took several moments to realise that it was coming from the bathroom, that it was John Rebus's laugh, and that Rebus was dipping his hand into the mess, drawing it out again with something clinging to it. Holmes didn't even notice the thick rubberised gloves which protected Rebus up to his elbows. He simply turned and walked downstairs on brittle legs.

'Got you!' Rebus cried.

'There's a hose outside,' the foreman said.

'Lead on,' said Rebus, shaking the packet free of some of its clots. 'Lead on, Macduff.'

'The name's MacBeth,' the foreman called back, heading for the stairway.

In the cool, fresh air, they hosed down the package, standing it up against the front wall of the house as they did so. Rebus peered at it closely. A red plastic bag, like the carrier from a record shop, had been wrapped around some cloth, a shirt or the like. The whole had been stuck down with a roll's worth of sellotape, then tied with string, knotted resolutely in the middle.

'Clever little tyke, weren't you, Ronnie?' Rebus said to himself as he picked up the package. 'Cleverer than they could ever have thought.'

At the van, he threw down the rubber gloves, shook the foreman's hand, and exchanged the names of local watering holes with him, making promises of a drink, a nippy sweetie some night in the future. Then he headed for the car, Holmes following sheepishly. All the way back to Rebus's flat, Holmes didn't once dare to suggest that they open a window and let in some fresh air.

Rebus was like a child on a birthday morning who has just found his surprise. He clutched the parcel to him, staining his shirt even more, yet seemed loath to open it.

204

Now that he possessed it, he could forestall the revelation. It would happen; that was all that mattered.

When they arrived at the flat, however, Rebus's mood changed again, and he dashed to the kitchen for some scissors. Holmes meantime made his excuses and went to the bathroom, scrubbing his hands, bared arms, and face thoroughly. His scalp itched, and he wished he could throw himself into the shower and stand beneath it for an hour or two.

As he was coming out of the bathroom, he heard the sound from the kitchen. It was the antithesis of the laughter he had heard earlier, a kind of exasperated wail. He walked quickly to the kitchen, and saw Rebus standing there, head bowed, hands held out against the worktop as though supporting himself. The packet was open in front of him.

'John? What's wrong?'

Rebus's voice was soft, suddenly tired. 'They're just pictures of a bloody boxing match. That's all they are. Just bloody sports photos.'

Holmes came forward slowly, fearing noise and movement might crack Rebus completely.

'Maybe,' he suggested, peering over Rebus's slumped shoulder, 'maybe there's somebody in the crowd. In the audience. This Hyde could be one of the spectators.'

'The spectators are just a blur. Take a look.'

Holmes did. There were twelve or so photographs. Two featherweights, no love lost, were slugging it out. There was nothing subtle about the contest, but nothing unusual about it either.

'Maybe it's Hyde's boxing club.'

'Maybe,' said Rebus, not really caring any more. He had been so sure that he would find the pictures, and so sure that they would prove the final, clinching piece of the puzzle. Why were they hidden away so carefully, so cunningly? And so well protected. There had to be a reason.

'Maybe,' said Holmes, who was becoming irritating again, 'maybe there's something we're missing. The cloth they're wrapped in, the envelope . . .?'

'Don't be so bloody thick, Holmes!' Rebus slammed a hand against the worktop, and immediately calmed. 'Sorry. Jesus, sorry.'

'That's all right,' Holmes said coldly. 'I'll make some coffee or something. Then why don't we take a *good* look at those snaps? Eh?'

'Yes,' Rebus said, pushing himself upright. 'Good idea.' He headed towards the door. 'I'm going to take a shower.' He turned and smiled at Holmes. 'I must stink to high heaven.'

'A very agricultural smell, sir,' Holmes said, smiling also. They laughed at the shared reference to Farmer Watson. Then Rebus went to have his shower, and Holmes made the coffee, jealous of the sounds from the bathroom. He took another look at the photographs, a close look, hoping for something, something he could use to impress Rebus with, to cheer Rebus up just a little.

The boxers were young, photographed from ringside or near as dammit. But the photographer – Ronnie McGrath presumably – hadn't used a flash, depending instead upon the smoky lights above the ring. Consequently, neither boxers nor audience were recognisable as distinct individuals. Their faces were grainy, the outlines of the combatants themselves blurred with sluggish movement. Why hadn't the photographer used a flash?

In one photo, the right-hand side of the frame was dark, cut off at an angle by something getting in the way of the lens. What? A passing spectator? Somebody's jacket?

It struck Holmes with sudden clarity: the *photographer's* jacket had got in the way, and it had done so because the photos were being taken surreptitiously, from beneath a jacket. This would explain the poor quality of the photos, and the uneven angles of most of them. So there *had* to be a reason for them, and they had to be the clue Rebus was seeking. All they had to do now was discover just *what* kind of clue.

The shower became a drip, then died altogether. A few moments later, Rebus appeared clad only in a towel, holding it around his gut as he went to the bedroom to change. He was balancing with one foot poised above a trouser leg when Holmes burst in, waving the photographs.

'I think I've got it!' he exclaimed. Rebus looked up, surprised, then slipped on the trousers.

'Yes,' he said. 'I think I've worked it out, too. It came to me just now in the shower.'

'Oh.'

'So fetch us a coffee,' said Rebus, 'and let's go into the living room and see if we've worked out the same thing. Okay?'

'Right,' said Holmes, wondering again why it was that he'd joined the police when there were so many more rewarding careers out there to be had.

When he arrived in the living room, carrying the two mugs of coffee, Rebus was pacing up and down, his telephone handset wedged against his ear.

'Right,' he was saying. 'I'll wait. No, no, I won't call back. I said I'll *wait*. Thank you.'

Taking the coffee from Holmes, he rolled his eyes, exhibiting disbelief at the stupidity of the person on the other end of the telephone.

'Who is it?' Holmes mouthed silently.

'The council,' said Rebus aloud. 'I got a name and an extension number from Andrew.'

'Who's Andrew?'

'Andrew MacBeth, the foreman. I want to find out who

authorised the cleaning out of the house. A bit of a coincidence that, don't you think? Cleaning it out just as we were about to do a bit of poking around.' He turned his attention to the handset. 'Yes? That's right. Oh, I see.' He looked at Holmes, his eyes betraying nothing. 'How might that have happened?' He listened again. 'Yes, I see. Oh yes, I agree, it does seem a bit curious. Still, these things happen, eh? Roll on computerisation. Thanks for your help anyway.'

He pressed a button, kiling the connection. 'You probably caught the gist of that.'

'They've no record of who authorised the clear-out?'

'Quite so, Brian. The documentation is all in order, but for the little matter of a signature. They can't understand it.'

'Any handwriting to go on?'

'The chitty Andrew showed me was typed.'

'So, what are you saying?'

'That Mr Hyde seems to have friends everywhere. In the council, for starters, but probably in the police, too. Not to mention several less savoury institutions.'

'What now?'

'Those pictures. What else is there to go on?'

They studied each frame closely, taking their time, pointing out this or that blur or detail, trying ideas out on one another. It was a painstaking business. And throughout Rebus was muttering to himself about Ronnie McGrath's final words to Tracy, about how they had been the key throughout. The triple meaning: make yourself scarce, beware a man called Hyde, and I've hidden something away. So clever. So compact. Almost *too* clever for Ronnie. Maybe the meanings had been there without his realising it himself. . . .

At the end of ninety minutes, Rebus threw the final photograph down onto the floor. Holmes was half lying along the settee, rubbing his forehead with one hand as he held up one of the pictures in the other, his eyes refusing to focus any longer.

'It's no use, Brian. No use at all. I can't make sense out of any of them, can you?'

'Not a lot,' Holmes admitted. 'But I take it Hyde wanted – wants – these pictures badly.'

'Meaning?'

'Meaning he knows they exist, but he doesn't know how crude they are. He thinks they show something they don't.'

'Yes, but what? I'll tell you something, Ronnie McGrath had bruises on his body the night he died.'

'Not surprising when you remember that someone dragged his body down the stairs.'

'No, he was already dead then. This was before. His brother noticed, Tracy noticed, but nobody ever asked. Somebody said something to me about rough trade.' He pointed towards the scattering of snapshots. 'Maybe this is what they meant.'

'A boxing match?'

'An illegal bout. Two unmatched kids knocking blue hell out of one another.'

'For what?'

Rebus stared at the wall, looking for the word he lacked. Then he turned to Holmes.

'The same reason men set up dog fights. For kicks.'

'It all sounds incredible.'

'Maybe it *is* incredible. The way my mind is just now, I could believe bombers have been found on the moon.' He stretched. 'What time is it?'

'Nearly eight. Aren't you supposed to be going to Malcolm Lanyon's party?'

'Jesus!' Rebus sprang to his feet. 'I'm late. I forgot all about it.'

'Well, I'll leave you to get ready. There's not much we

can do about this.' Holmes gestured towards the photographs. 'I should visit Nell anyway.'

'Yes, yes, off you go, Brian.' Rebus paused. 'And thanks.'

Holmes smiled and shrugged his shoulders.

'One thing,' Rebus began.

'Yes?'

'I don't have a clean jacket. Can I borrow yours?'

It wasn't a great fit, the sleeves being slightly too long, the chest too small, but it wasn't bad either. Rebus tried to seem casual about it all as he stood on Malcolm Lanyon's doorstep. The door was opened by the same stunning Oriental who had been by Lanyon's side at The Eyrie. She was dressed in a low-cut black dress which barely reached down to her upper thighs. She smiled at Rebus, recognising him, or at least pretending to do so.

'Come in.'

'I hope I'm not late.'

'Not at all. Malcolm's parties aren't run by the clock. People come and go as they please.' Her voice had a cool but not unpleasant edge to it. Looking past her, Rebus was relieved to see several male guests wearing lounge suits, and some wearing sports jackets. Lanyon's personal (Rebus wondered just *how* personal) assistant led him into the dining room, where a barman stood behind a table laden with bottles and glasses.

The doorbell rang again. Fingers touched Rebus's shoulder. 'If you'll excuse me,' she said.

'Of course,' said Rebus. He turned towards the barman. 'Gin and tonic,' he said. Then he turned again to watch her pass through the large hallway towards the main door.

'Hello, John.' A much firmer hand slapped Rebus's shoulder. It belonged to Tommy McCall.

'Hello, Tommy.' Rebus accepted a drink from the

barman, and McCall handed over his own empty glass for a refill.

'Glad you could make it. Of course, it's not quite as lively as usual tonight. Everyone's a bit subdued.'

'Subdued?' It was true, the conversations around them were muted. Then Rebus noticed a few black ties.

'I only came along because I thought James would have wanted it that way.'

'Of course,' Rebus said, nodding. He'd forgotten all about James Carew's suicide. Christ, it had only happened this morning! It seemed like a lifetime ago. And all these people had been Carew's friends or acquaintances. Rebus's nostrils twitched.

'Had he seemed depressed lately?' he asked.

'Not especially. He'd just bought himself that car, remember. Hardly the act of a depressed man!'

'I suppose not. Did you know him well?'

'I don't think any of us knew him well. He kept himself pretty much to himself. And of course he spent a lot of time away from town, sometimes on business, sometimes staying on his estate.'

'He wasn't married, was he?'

Tommy McCall stared at him, then took a large mouthful of whisky. 'No,' he said. 'I don't believe he ever was. It's a blessing in a way.'

'Yes, I see what you mean,' said Rebus, feeling the gin easing itself into his system. 'But I still don't understand why he would do it.'

'It's always the quiet ones though, isn't it? Malcolm was just saying that a few minutes ago.'

Rebus looked around them. 'I haven't seen our host yet.'

'I think he's in the lounge. Shall I give you the tour?'

'Yes, why not?'

'It's quite a place.' McCall turned to Rebus. 'Shall we

start upstairs in the billiards room, or downstairs at the swimming pool?'

Rebus laughed and shook his empty glass. 'I think the first place to visit is the bar, don't you?'

The house was stunning, there was no other word for it. Rebus thought briefly of poor Brian Holmes, and smiled. You and me both, kid. The guests were nice, too. He recognised some of them by face, some by name, a few by reputation, and many by the titles of the companies they headed. But of the host there was no sign, though everyone claimed to have spoken with him 'earlier in the evening'.

Later, as Tommy McCall was becoming noisy and inebriated, Rebus, by no means on his steadiest legs himself, decided on another tour of the house. But alone this time. There was a library on the first floor, which had received cursory attention on the first circuit. But there was a working desk in there, and Rebus was keen to take a closer look. On the landing, he glanced around him, but everyone seemed to be downstairs. A few guests had even donned swimsuits, and were lounging by (or in) the twenty-foot-long heated pool in the basement.

He turned the heavy brass handle and slipped into the dimly lit library. In here there was a smell of old leather, a smell which took Rebus back to past decades – the 'twenties, say, or perhaps the 'thirties. There was a lamp on the desktop, illuminating some papers there. Rebus was at the desk before he realised something: the lamp had not been lit on his first visit here. He turned and saw Lanyon, standing against the far wall with his arms folded, grinning.

'Inspector,' he said, his voice as rich as his tailoring. 'What an interesting jacket that is. Saiko told me you'd arrived.'

Lanyon walked forward slowly and extended a hand, which Rebus took. He returned the firm grip.

'I hope I'm not . . .' he began. 'I mean, it was kind of you. . . .'

'Good lord, not at all. Is the Superintendent coming?'

Rebus shrugged his shoulders, feeling the jacket tight across his back.

'No, well, never mind. I see that like me you are a studious man.' Lanyon surveyed the shelves of books. 'This is my favourite room in the whole house. I don't know why I bother holding parties. It is expected, I suppose, and that's why I do it. Also of course it is interesting to note the various permutations, who's talking with whom, whose hand just happened to squeeze whose arm a touch too tenderly. That sort of thing.'

'You won't see much from here,' Rebus said.

'But Saiko tells me. She's marvellous at catching that sort of thing, no matter how subtle people think they are being. For example, she told me about your jacket. Beige, she said, cord, neither matching the rest of your wardrobe nor quite fitting your figure. Therefore borrowed, am I right?'

Rebus applauded silently. 'Bravo,' he said. 'I suppose that's what makes you such a good lawyer.'

'No, years and years of study are what have made me a good lawyer. But to be a *known* lawyer, well, that demands a few simple party tricks, such as the one I've just shown you.'

Lanyon walked past Rebus and stopped at the writing desk. He sifted through the papers.

'Was there anything special you were interested in?'

'No,' said Rebus. 'Just this room.'

Lanyon glanced towards him, smiling, not quite believing. 'There are more interesting rooms in the house, but I keep those locked.'

'Oh?'

'One doesn't want *everyone* to know just what paintings one has collected for example.'

'Yes, I see.'

Lanyon sat at the desk now, and slipped on a pair of half-moon glasses. He seemed interested in the papers before him.

'I'm James Carew's executor,' he said. 'That's what I've been trying to sort out, who will benefit from his will.'

'A terrible business.'

Lanyon seemed not to understand. Then he nodded. 'Yes, yes, tragic.'

'I take it you were close to him?'

Lanyon smiled again, as though he knew this same question had been asked of several people at the party already. 'I knew him fairly well,' he said at last.

'Did you know he was homosexual?'

Rebus had been hoping for a response. There was none, and he cursed having played his trump card so soon in the game.

'Of course,' Lanyon said in the same level voice. He turned towards Rebus. 'I don't believe it's a crime.'

'That all depends, sir, as you should know.'

'What do you mean?'

'As a lawyer, you must know that there are still certain laws. . . .'

'Yes, yes, of course. But I hope you're not suggesting that James was involved in anything sordid.'

'Why do *you* think he killed himself, Mr Lanyon? I'd appreciate your professional opinion.'

'He was a friend. Professional opinions don't count.' Lanyon stared at the heavy curtains in front of his desk. 'I don't know why he committed suicide. I'm not sure we'll ever know.'

'I wouldn't bet on that, sir,' said Rebus, going to the door. He stopped, hand on the handle. 'I'd be interested to know who *will* benefit from the estate, when you've worked it all out of course.'

Lanyon was silent. Rebus opened the door, closed it behind him, and paused on the landing, breathing deeply. Not a bad performance, he thought to himself. At the very least it was worthy of a drink. And this time he would toast – in silence – the memory of James Carew.

Nursemaid was not his favourite occupation, but he'd known all along that it would come to this.

Tommy McCall was singing a rugby song in the back of the car, while Rebus waved a hasty goodbye to Saiko, who was standing on the doorstep. She even managed a smile. Well, after all he was doing her a favour in quietly removing the loud drunkard from the premises.

'Am I under arrest, John?' McCall yelled, interrupting his song.

'No, now shut up, for Christ's sake!'

Rebus got into the car and started the engine. He glanced back one last time and saw Lanyon join Saiko on the doorstep. She seemed to be filling him in on events, and he was nodding. It was the first Rebus had seen of him since their confrontation in the library. He released the handbrake, pulled out of the parking space, and drove off.

'Left here, then next right.'

Tommy McCall had had too much to drink, but his sense of direction seemed unimpaired. Yet Rebus had a strange feeling. . . .

'Along to the end of this road, and it's the last house on the corner.'

'But this isn't where you live,' Rebus protested.

'Quite correct, Inspector. This is where my brother lives. I thought we'd drop in for a nightcap.'

'Jesus, Tommy, you can't just –'

215

'Rubbish. He'll be delighted to see us.'

As Rebus pulled up in front of the house, he looked out of his side window and was relieved to see that Tony McCall's living room was still illuminated. Suddenly, Tommy's hand thrust past him and pushed down on the horn, sending a loud blare into the silent night. Rebus pushed the hand away, and Tommy fell back into his seat, but he'd done enough. The curtains twitched in the McCall living room, and a moment later a door to the side of the house opened and Tony McCall came out, glancing back nervously. Rebus wound down the window.

'John?' Tony McCall seemed anxious. 'What's the matter?'

But before Rebus could explain, Tommy was out of the car and hugging his brother.

'It's my fault, Tony. All mine. I just wanted to see you, that's all. Sorry though, sorry.'

Tony McCall took the situation in, glanced towards Rebus as if to say *I don't blame you*, then turned to his brother.

'Well, this is very thoughtful of you, Tommy. Long time no see. You'd better come in.'

Tommy McCall turned to Rebus. 'See? I told you there'd be a welcome waiting for us at Tony's house. Always a welcome at Tony's.'

'You'd better come in, too, John,' said Tony.

Rebus nodded unhappily.

Tony directed them through the hall and into the living room. The carpet was thick and yielding underfoot, the furnishings looking like a showroom display. Rebus was afraid to sit, for fear of denting one of the puffed-up cushions. Tommy, however, collapsed immediately into a chair.

'Where's the wee ones?' he said.

'In bed,' Tony answered, keeping his voice low.

'Ach, wake them up then. Tell them their Uncle Tommy's here.'

Tony ignored this. 'I'll put the kettle on,' he said.

Tommy's eyes were already closing, his arms slumped either side of him on the arms of the chair. While Tony was in the kitchen, Rebus studied the room. There were ornaments everywhere: along the length of the mantel-piece, covering the available surfaces of the large wall-unit, arranged on the surface of the coffee table. Small plaster figurines, shimmering glass creations, holiday souvenirs. The arms and backs of chairs and sofa were protected by antimacassars. The whole room was busy and ill at ease. Relaxation would be almost impossible. He began to understand now why Tony McCall had been out walking in Pilmuir on his day off.

A woman's head peered round the door. Its lips were thin and straight, eyes alert but dark. She was staring at the slumbering figure of Tommy McCall, but caught sight of Rebus and prepared a kind of smile. The door opened a little wider, showing that she was wearing a dressing gown. A hand clutched this tight around her throat as she began to speak.

'I'm Sheila, Tony's wife.'

'Yes, hello, John Rebus.' Rebus made to stand, but a nervous hand fluttered him back down.

'Oh yes,' she said, 'Tony's talked about you. You work together, don't you?'

'That's right.'

'Yes.' Her attention was wandering, and she turned her gaze back to Tommy McCall. Her voice became like damp wallpaper. 'Would you look at him. The successful brother. His own business, big house. Just look at him.' She seemed about to launch into a speech on social injustice, but was interrupted by her husband, who was now squeezing past her carrying a tray.

'No need for you to get up, love,' he said.

'I could hardly sleep through that horn blaring, could I?' Her eyes now were on the tray. 'You've forgotten the sugar,' she said critically.

'I don't take sugar,' Rebus said. Tony was pouring tea from the pot into two cups.

'Milk first, Tony, then tea,' she said, ignoring Rebus's remark.

'It doesn't make a blind bit of difference, Sheila,' said Tony. He handed a cup to Rebus.

'Thanks.'

She stood for a second or two watching the two men, then ran a hand down the front of her dressing gown.

'Right then,' she 'said. 'Good night.'

'Good night,' concurred Rebus.

'Try not to be too long, Tony.'

'Right, Sheila.'

They listened, sipping tea, as she climbed the stairs to her bedroom. Then Tony McCall exhaled.

'Sorry about that,' he said.

'What for?' said Rebus. 'If a couple of drunks had walked into *my* home at this time of night, you wouldn't *want* to hear the reception I'd give them! I thought she stayed remarkably calm.'

'Sheila's always remarkably calm. On the outside.'

Rebus nodded towards Tommy. 'What about him?'

'He'll be all right where he is. Let him sleep it off.'

'Are you sure? I can take him home if you —'

'No, no. Christ, he's my brother. I think a chair for the night is called for.' Tony looked across towards Tommy. 'Look at him. You wouldn't believe the tricks we got up to when we were kids. We had the neighbourhood terrified of what we'd do next. Chap-Door-Run, setting bonfires, putting the football through somebody's window. We were wild, I can tell you. Now I never see him unless he's like this.'

'You mean he's pulled this stunt before?'

218

'Once or twice. Turns up in a taxi, crashes out in the chair. When he wakes up the next morning, he can't believe where he is. Has breakfast, slips the kids a few quid, and he's off. Never phones or visits. Then one night we hear the taxi chugging outside, and there he is.'

'I didn't realise.'

'Ach, I don't know why I'm telling you, John. It's not your problem, after all.'

'I don't mind listening.'

But Tony McCall seemed reluctant to go further. 'How do you like this room?' he asked instead.

'It's nice,' Rebus lied. 'A lot of thought's gone into it.'

'Yes.' McCall sounded unconvinced. 'A lot of money, too. See those little glass bauble things? You wouldn't believe how much one of those can cost.'

'Really?'

McCall was examining the room as though he were the visitor. 'Welcome to my life,' he said at last. 'I think I'd rather have one of the cells down the station.' He got up suddenly and walked across to Tommy's chair, then crouched down in front of his brother, one of whose eyes was open but glazed with sleep. 'You bugger,' Tony McCall whispered. 'You bugger, you bugger.' And he bowed his head so as not to show the tears.

It was growing light as Rebus drove the four miles back to Marchmont. He stopped at an all night bakery and bought warm rolls and refrigerated milk. This was the time when he liked the city best, the peaceful camaraderie of early morning. He wondered why people couldn't be happy with their lot. *I've got everything I've never wanted and it isn't enough.* All he wanted now was sleep, and in his bed for a change rather than on the chair. He kept playing the scene over and over: Tommy McCall dead to the world, saliva on his chin, and Tony McCall crouched in front of him, body shaking with emotion. A brother was a terrible thing. He was a lifelong competitor, yet you couldn't hate him without hating yourself. And there were other pictures too: Malcolm Lanyon in his study, Saiko standing at the door, James Carew dead in his bed, Nell Stapleton's bruised face, Ronnie McGrath's battered torso, old Vanderhyde with his unseeing eyes, the fear in Calum McCallum's eyes, Tracy with her tiny fists. . . .

If I am the chief of sinners, I am the chief of sufferers also.

Carew had stolen that line from somewhere . . . but where? Who cares, John, who cares? It would just be another bloody thread, and there were far too many of those already, knotted into an impenetrable tangle. Get home, sleep, forget.

One thing was for sure: he'd have some wild dreams.

Saturday

Or, if you shall so prefer to choose, a new province of knowledge and new avenues to fame and power shall be laid open to you, here, in this room, upon the instant.

In fact, he didn't dream at all. And when he woke up, it was the weekend, the sun was shining, and his telephone was ringing.

'Hello?'

'John? It's Gill.'

'Oh, hello, Gill. How are you?'

'I'm fine. What about you?'

'Great.' This was not a lie. He hadn't slept so well in weeks, and there was not a trace of hangover within him.

'Sorry to ring so early. Any progress on the smear?'

'Smear?'

'The things that kid was saying about you.'

'Oh, that. No, I haven't heard anything yet.' He was thinking about lunch, about a picnic, about a drive in the country. 'Are you in Edinburgh?' he asked.

'No, Fife.'

'Fife? What are you doing there?'

'Calum's here, remember.'

'Of course I remember, but I thought you were steering clear of him?'

'He wanted to see me. Actually, that's why I'm calling.'

'Oh?' Rebus wrinkled his brow, curious.

'Calum wants to talk to you.'

'To *me*? Why?'

'He'll tell you that himself, I suppose. He just asked me to tell you.'

Rebus thought for a moment. 'Do you want me to talk to him?'

'Can't say I'm much bothered either way. I told him I'd pass on the message, and I told him it was the last favour he could expect from me.' Her voice was as slick and cool as a slate roof in the rain. Rebus felt himself sliding down that roof, wanting to please her, wanting to help. 'Oh yes,' she said, 'and he said that if you sounded dubious, I was to tell you it's to do with Hyde's.'

'Hydes?' Rebus stood up sharply.

'H-y-d-e-apostrophe-s.'

'Hyde's what?'

She laughed. 'I don't know, John. But it sounds as if it means *some*thing to you.'

'It does, Gill. Are you in Dunfermline?'

'Calling from the station's front desk.'

'Okay. I'll see you there in an hour.'

'Fine, John.' She sounded unconcerned. 'Bye.'

He cut the connection, put his jacket on, and left the flat. The traffic was busy towards Tollcross, busy all the way down Lothian Road and winding across Princes Street towards Queensferry Road. Since the deregulation of public transport, the centre of the city had become a black farce of buses: double deckers, single deckers, even mini-buses, all vying for custom. Locked behind two claret-coloured LRT double deckers and two green single deckers, Rebus began to lose his tiny cache of patience. He slammed his hand down hard on the horn and pulled out, revving past the line of stalled traffic. A motorcycle messenger, squeezing through between the two directions of slower traffic, had to swerve to avoid the imminent accident, and slewed against a Saab. Rebus knew he should stop. He kept on going.

If only he'd had one of those magnetic flashing sirens, the kind CID used on the roofs of their cars whenever they were late for dinner or an engagement. But all he had were his headlights – full-beam – and the horn. Having cleared the tailback, he eased his hand off the horn, switched off the lamps, and cruised into the outside lane of the widening road.

Despite a pause at the dreaded Barnton roundabout, he made good time to the Forth Road Bridge, paid the toll, and drove across, not too fast, wanting, as ever, to take in the view. Rosyth Naval Dockyard was below him on the left. A lot of his schoolfriends ('lot' being relative: he'd never made that many friends) had slipped easily into jobs at Rosyth, and were probably still there. It seemed to be about the only place in Fife where work was still available. The mines were closing with enforced regularity. Somewhere along the coast in the other direction, men were burrowing beneath the Forth, scooping out coal in a decreasingly profitable curve. . . .

Hyde! Calum McCallum knew something about Hyde! Knew, too, that Rebus was interested, so word must have got around. His foot pressed down further on the accelerator. McCallum would want a trade, of course: charges dropped, or somehow jigged into a shape less damning. Fine, fine, he'd promise him the sun and the moon and the stars.

Just so long as he knew. Knew who Hyde was; knew where Hyde was. Just so long as he knew. . . .

The main police station in Dunfermline was easy to find, situated just off a roundabout on the outskirts of the town. Gill was easy to find, too. She was sitting in her car in the spacious car park outside the station. Rebus parked next to her, got out of his car and into the passenger side of hers.

'Morning,' he said.

'Hello, John.'

'Are you okay?' This was, on reflection, perhaps the most unnecessary question he had ever posed. Her face had lost colour and substance, and her head seemed to be shrinking into her shoulders, while her hands gripped the steering wheel, fingernails rapping softly against the top of the dashboard.

'I'm fine,' she said, and they both smiled at the lie. 'I told them at the desk that you were coming.'

'Anything you want me to tell our friend?'

Her voice was resonant. 'Nothing.'

'Okay.'

Rebus pushed open the car door and closed it again, but softly, then he headed towards the station entrance.

She had wandered the hospital corridors for over an hour. It was visiting time, so no one much minded as she walked into this and that ward, passing the beds, smiling down occasionally on the sick old men and women who stared up at her with lonely eyes. She watched families decide who should and should not take turns at grandpa's bedside, there being two only at a time allowed. She was looking for one woman in particular, though she wasn't sure she would recognise her. All she had to go on was the fact that the librarian would have a broken nose.

Maybe she hadn't been kept in. Maybe she'd already gone home to her husband or boyfriend or whatever. Maybe Tracy would be better off waiting and going to the library again. Except that they'd be watching and waiting for her. The guard would know her. The librarian would know her.

But would *she* know the librarian?

A bell rang out, drilling into her the fact that visiting hours were coming to an end. She hurried to the next ward, wondering: what if the librarian's in a private room? Or in another hospital? Or. . . .

No! There she was! Tracy stopped dead, turned in a half-circle, and walked to the far end of the ward. Visitors were saying their goodbyes and take cares to the patients. Everybody looked relieved, both visitors and visited. She mingled with them as they put chairs back into stacks and donned coats, scarves, gloves. Then she paused and looked back towards the librarian's bed. There were flowers all around it, and the single visitor, a man, was leaning over the librarian to kiss her lingeringly on the forehead. The librarian squeezed the man's hand and. . . . And the man looked familiar to Tracy. She'd seen him before. . . . At the police station! He was some friend of Rebus's, and he was a policeman! She remembered him checking on her while she was being held in the cells.

Oh Jesus, she'd attacked a policeman's wife!

She wasn't sure now, wasn't sure at all. Why had she come? Could she go through with it now? She walked with one family out of the ward, then rested against the wall in the corridor outside. Could she? Yes, if her nerve held. Yes, she could.

She was pretending to examine a drinks vending machine when Holmes sauntered through the swinging ward doors and walked slowly down the corridor away from her. She waited a full two minutes, counting up to one hundred and twenty. He wasn't coming back. He hadn't forgotten anything. Tracy turned from the vending machine and made for the swing doors.

For her, visiting time was just beginning.

She hadn't even reached the bed when a young nurse stopped her.

'Visiting hour's finished now,' the nurse said.

Tracy tried to smile, tried to look normal; it wasn't easy for her, but lying was.

'I just lost my watch. I think I left it at my sister's bed.' She nodded in Nell's direction. Nell, hearing the conversation, had turned towards her. Her eyes opened wide as she recognised Tracy.

'Well, be as quick as you can, eh?' said the nurse, moving away. Tracy smiled at the nurse, and watched her push through the swing doors. Now there were only the patients in their beds, a sudden silence, and her. She approached Nell's bed.

'Hello,' she said. She looked at the chart attached to the end of the iron bedstead. 'Nell Stapleton,' she read.

'What do you want?' Nell's eyes showed no fear. Her voice was thin, coming from the back of her throat, her nose having no part in the process.

'I want to tell you something,' Tracy said. She came close to Nell, and crouched on the floor, so that she would be barely visible from the doors of the ward. She thought this made her look as though she were searching for a lost watch.

'Yes?'

Tracy smiled, finding Nell's imperfect voice amusing. She sounded like a puppet on a children's programme. The smile vanished quickly, and she blushed, remembering that the reason she was here was because *she* was responsible for this woman being here at all. The plasters across the nose, the bruising under the eyes: all her doing.

'I came to say I'm sorry. That's all, really. Just, I'm sorry.'

Nell's eyes were unblinking.

'And,' Tracy continued, 'well . . . nothing.'

'Tell me,' said Nell, but it was too much for her. She'd done most of the talking while Brian Holmes had been in, and her mouth was dry. She turned and reached for the jug of water on the small cupboard beside the bed.

'Here, I'll do that.' Tracy poured water into a plastic beaker, and handed it to Nell, who sipped, coating the inside of her mouth. 'Nice flowers,' said Tracy.

'From my boyfriend,' said Nell, between sips.

'Yes, I saw him leaving. He's a policeman, isn't he? I know he is, because I'm a friend of Inspector Rebus's.'

'Yes, I know.'

'You do?' Tracy seemed shocked. 'So you know who I am?'

228

'I know your name's Tracy, if that's what you mean.'

Tracy bit her bottom lip. Her face reddened again.

'It doesn't matter, does it?' Nell said.

'Oh no.' Tracy tried to sound nonchalant. 'It doesn't matter.'

'I was going to ask . . .'

'Yes?' Tracy seemed keen for a change of subject.

'What were you going to do in the library?'

This wasn't quite to Tracy's liking. She thought about it, shrugged, and said: 'I was going to find Ronnie's photographs.'

'Ronnie's photographs?' Nell perked up. What little Brian had said during visiting hour had been limited to the progress of Ronnie McGrath's case, and especially the discovery of some pictures at the dead boy's house. What was Tracy talking about?

'Yes,' she said. 'Ronnie hid them in the library.'

'What were they exactly? I mean, why did he need to hide them?'

Tracy shrugged. 'All he told me was that they were his life insurance policy. That's exactly what he said, "life insurance policy".'

'And where exactly did he hide them?'

'On the fifth floor, he said. Inside a bound volume of something called the *Edinburgh Review*. I think it's a magazine.'

'That's right,' said Nell, smiling, 'it is.'

Brian Holmes was made light-headed by Nell's telephone call. His first reaction, however, was pure shock, and he chastised her for being out of bed.

'I'm still in bed,' she said, her voice becoming indistinct in her excitement. 'They brought the payphone to my bedside. Now listen. . . .'

Thirty minutes later, he was being shown down an aisle on the fifth floor of Edinburgh University Library. The member of staff checked complicated decimal numbers exhibited at each stack, until, satisfied, she led him down one darkened row of large bound titles. At the end of the aisle, seated at a study desk by a large window, a student stared disinterestedly towards Holmes, a pencil crunching in his mouth. Holmes smiled sympathetically towards the student, who stared right through him.

'Here we are,' said the librarian. '*Edinburgh Review* and *New Edinburgh Review*. It becomes "New" in 1969, as you can see. Of course, we keep the earlier editions in a closed environment. If you want those years specifically, it will take a little time –'

'No, these are fine, really. These are just what I need. Thank you.'

The librarian bowed slightly, accepting his thanks. 'You *will* remember us all to Nell, won't you?' she said.

'I'll be talking to her later today. I won't forget.'

With another bow, the librarian turned and walked back to the end of the stack. She paused there, and pressed a switch. Strip lighting flickered above Holmes, and stayed on. He smiled his thanks, but she was gone, her rubber heels squeaking briskly towards the lift.

Holmes looked at the spines of the bound volumes. The collection was not complete, which meant that someone had borrowed some of the years. A stupid place to hide something. He picked up 1971–72, held its spine by the forefingers of both his right and left hands, and rocked it. No scraps of paper, no photographs were shaken free. He put the volume back on the shelf and selected its neighbour, shook it, then replaced it.

The student at the study desk was no longer looking through him. He was looking *at* him, and doing so as if Holmes were mad. Another volume yielded nothing, then another. Holmes began to fear the worst. He'd been hoping for something with which to surprise Rebus, something to tie up all the loose ends. He'd tried contacting the Inspector, but Rebus wasn't to be found, wasn't anywhere. He had vanished.

The photos made more noise than he'd expected as they slid from the sheaves and hit the polished floor, hit it with their glossy edges, producing a sharp crack. He bent and began to gather them up, while the student looked on in fascination. From what he could see of the images strewn across the floor, Holmes already felt disappointment curdling his elation. They were copies of the boxing match pictures, nothing more. There were no new prints, no revelations, no surprises.

Damn Ronnie McGrath for giving him hope. All they were was life insurance. On a life already forfeit.

He waited for the lift, but it was busy elsewhere, so he took the stairs, winding downwards steeply, and found himself on the ground floor, but in a part of the library he didn't know, a sort of antiquarian bookshop corridor, narrow, with mouldering books stacked up against both walls. He squeezed through, feeling a sudden chill he couldn't place, and found himself opening a door onto the main concourse. The librarian who had shown him around was back behind her desk. She saw him, and waved frantically. He obeyed the command and hurried forward. She picked up a telephone and pressed a button.

'Call for you,' she said, stretching across the desktop to hand him the receiver.

'Hello?' He was quizzical: who the hell knew he was here?

'Brian, where in God's name have you been?' It was Rebus, of course. 'I've been trying to find you everywhere. I'm at the hospital.'

Holmes's heart deflated within his chest. 'Nell?' he said, so dramatically that even the librarian's head shot up.

'What?' growled Rebus. 'No, no, Nell's fine. It's just that she told me where to find you. I'm phoning from the hospital, and it's costing me a fortune.' In confirmation,

231

the pips came, and were followed by the chankling of coins in a slot. The connection was re-established.

'Nell's okay,' Brian told the librarian. She nodded, relieved, and turned back to her work.

'Of course she is,' said Rebus, having caught the words. 'Now listen, there are a few things I want you to do. Have you got a pen and paper?'

Brian found them on the desk. He smiled, remembering the first telephone conversation he'd ever had with John Rebus, so similar to this, a few things to be done. Christ, so much had been done since. . . .

'Got that?'

Holmes started. 'Sorry, sir,' he said. 'My mind was elsewhere. Could you repeat that?'

There was an audible sound of mixed anger and excitement from the receiver. Then Rebus started again, and this time Brian Holmes heard every word.

Tracy couldn't say why it was that she'd visited Nell Stapleton, or why she'd told Nell what she had. She felt some kind of bond, not merely because of what she'd done. There was something about Nell Stapleton, something wise and kind, something Tracy had lacked in her life until now. Maybe that's why she was finding it so hard to leave the hospital. She had walked the corridors, drunk two cups of coffee in a cafe across the road from the main building, wandered in and out of Casualty, X-Ray, even some clinic for diabetics. She'd tried to leave, had walked as far as the city's art college before turning round and retreading the two hundred paces to the hospital.

And she was entering the side gates when the men grabbed her.

'Hey!'

'If you'll just come with us, miss.'

They sounded like security men, policemen even, so she didn't resist. Maybe Nell Stapleton's boyfriend wanted to see her, to give her a good kicking. She didn't care. They were taking her towards the hospital entrance, so she didn't resist. Not until it was too late.

At the last moment, they stopped short, turned her, and pushed her into the back of an ambulance.

'What's –! Hey, come on!' The doors were closing, locking, leaving her alone in the hot, dim interior. She thumped on the doors, but the vehicle was already moving off. As it pulled away, she was thrown against the doors, then back onto the floor. When she had recovered herself, she saw that the ambulance was an old one, no longer used for its original purpose. Its insides had been gutted, making it merely a van. The windows had been boarded over, and a metal panel separated her from the driver. She clawed her way to this panel and began hitting it with her fists, teeth gritted, yelling from time to time as she remembered that the two men who had grabbed her at the gates were the same two men who'd been following her that day on Princes Street, that day she'd run to John Rebus.

'Oh God,' she murmured, 'oh God, oh God.'

They'd found her at last.

The evening was sticky with heat, the streets quiet for a Saturday.

Rebus rang the doorbell and waited. While he waited, he looked to left and right. An immaculate double row of Georgian houses, stone frontages dulled black through time and car fumes. Some of the houses had been turned into offices for Writers to the Signet, chartered accountants, and small, anonymous finance businesses. But a few – a precious few – were still very comfortable and well-appointed homes for the wealthy and the industrious. Rebus had been to this street before, a long time ago now in his earliest CID days, investigating the death of a young girl. He didn't remember much about the case now. He was too busy getting ready for the evening's pleasures.

He tugged at the black bow tie around his throat. The whole outfit, dinner jacket, shirt, bow tie and patent shoes, had been hired earlier in the day from a shop on George Street. He felt like an idiot, but had to admit that, examining himself in his bathroom mirror, he looked pretty sharp. He wouldn't be too out of place in an establishment like Finlay's of Duke Terrace.

The door was opened by a beaming woman, young, dressed exquisitely, and greeting him as though wondering why he didn't come more often.

'Good evening,' she said. 'Will you come in?'

He would, he did. The entrance hall was subtle. Cream paint, deep pile carpeting, a scattering of chairs which might have been designed by Charles Rennie Mackintosh, high backs and looking extraordinarily uncomfortable to sit in.

'I see you're admiring our chairs,' the woman said.

'Yes,' Rebus answered, returning her smile. 'The name's Rebus, by the way. John Rebus.'

'Ah yes. Finlay told me you were expected. Well, as this is your first visit, would you like me to show you around?'

'Thank you.'

'But first, a drink, and the first drink is always on the house.'

Rebus tried not to be nosey, but he was a policeman after all, and not being nosey would have gone against all that he held most dear. So he asked a few questions of his hostess, whose name was Paulette, and pointed to this and that part of the gaming club, being shown the direction of the cellars ('Finlay has their contents insured for quarter of a million'), kitchen ('our chef is worth his weight in Beluga'), and guest bedrooms ('the judges are the worst, there are one or two who always end up sleeping here, too drunk to go home'). The lower ground floor housed the cellars and kitchen, while the ground floor comprised a quiet bar area, and the small restaurant, with cloakrooms and an office. On the first floor, up the carpeted staircase and past the collection of eighteenth- and nineteenth-century Scottish paintings by the likes of Jacob More and David Allan, was the main gaming area: roulette, blackjack, a few other tables for card games, and one table given over to dice. The players were business-men, their bets discreet, nobody losing big or winning big. They held their chips close to them.

Paulette pointed out two closed rooms.

'Private rooms, for private games.'

'Of what?'

'Poker mainly. The serious players book them once a month or so. The games can go on all night.'

'Just like in the movies.'

'Yes,' she laughed. 'Just like the movies.'

The second floor consisted of the three guest bedrooms, again locked, and Finlay Andrews' own private suite.

'Off limits, of course,' Paulette said.

'Of course,' Rebus concurred, as they started downstairs again.

So this was it: Finlay's Club. Tonight was quiet. He had seen only two or three faces he recognised: an advocate, who did not acknowledge him, though they'd clashed before in court, a television presenter, whose dark tan looked fake, and Farmer Watson.

'Hello there, John.' Watson, stuffed into suit and dress shirt, looked like nothing more than a copper out of uniform. He was in the bar when Paulette and Rebus went back in, his hand closed around a glass of orange juice, trying to look comfortable but instead looking distinctly out of place.

'Sir.' Rebus had not for one moment imagined that Watson, despite the threat he had made earlier, would turn up here. He introduced Paulette, who apologised for not being around to greet him at the door.

Watson waved aside her apology, revolving his glass. 'I was well enough taken care of,' he said. They sat at a vacant table. The chairs here were comfortable and well padded, and Rebus felt himself relax. Watson, however, was looking around keenly.

'Finlay not here?' he asked.

'He's somewhere around,' said Paulette. 'Finlay's always around.'

Funny, thought Rebus, that they hadn't bumped into him on their tour.

'What's the place like then, John?' Watson asked.

'Impressive,' Rebus answered, accepting Paulette's smile like praise from a teacher to a doting pupil. 'Very impressive. It's much bigger than you'd think. Wait till you see upstairs.'

'And there's the extension, too,' said Watson.

'Oh yes, I'd forgotten.' Rebus turned to Paulette.

'That's right,' she said. 'We're building out from the back of the premises.'

'Building?' said Watson. 'I thought it was a fait accompli?'

'Oh no.' She smiled again. 'Finlay is very particular. The flooring wasn't quite right, so he had the workmen rip it all up and start again. Now we're waiting on some marble arriving from Italy.'

'That must be costing a few bob,' Watson said, nodding to himself.

Rebus wondered about the extension. Towards the back of the ground floor, past toilets, cloakroom, offices, walk-in cupboards, there must be another door, ostensibly the door to the back garden. But now the door to the extension, perhaps.

'Another drink, John?' Watson was already on his feet, pointing at Rebus's empty glass.

'Gin and fresh orange, please,' he said, handing over the glass.

'And for you, Paulette?'

'No, really.' She was rising from the chair. 'Work to do. Now that you've seen a bit of the club, I'd better get back to door duties. If you want to play upstairs, the office can supply chips. A few of the games accept cash, but not the most interesting ones.'

Another smile, and she was gone in a flurry of silk and a glimpse of black nylon. Watson saw Rebus watching her leave.

'At ease, Inspector,' he said, laughing to himself as he headed for the bar where the barman explained that if he wanted drinks, he only had to signal, and an order would be taken at the gentlemen's table and brought to them directly. Watson slumped back into his chair again.

'This is the life, eh, John?'

'Yes, sir. What's happening back at base?'

'You mean the little sodomite who made the complaint? He's buggered off. Disappeared. Gave us a false address, the works.'

'So I'm off the butcher's hook?'

'Just about.' Rebus was about to remonstrate. 'Give it a few more days, John, that's all I'm asking. Time for it to die a natural death.'

'You mean people are talking?'

'A few of the lads have had a laugh about it. I don't suppose you can blame them. In a day or so, there'll be something else for them to joke about, and it'll all be forgotten.'

'There's nothing *to* forget!'

'I know, I know. It's all some plot to keep you out of action, and this mysterious Mr Hyde's behind it all.'

Rebus stared at Watson, his lips clamped shut. He could yell, could scream and shout. He breathed hard instead, and snatched at the drink when the waiter placed the tray on the table. He'd taken two gulps before the waiter informed him that he was drinking the other gentleman's orange juice. His own gin and orange was the one still on the tray. Rebus reddened as Watson, laughing again, placed a five-pound note on the tray. The waiter coughed in embarrassment.

'Your drinks come to six pounds fifty, sir,' he told Watson.

'Ye gods!' Watson searched in his pocket for some change, found a crumpled pound note and some coins, and placed them on the tray.

'Thank you, sir.' The waiter lifted the tray and turned away before Watson had the chance to ask about any change that might be owing. He looked at Rebus, who was smiling now.

'Well,' Watson said, 'I mean, six pounds fifty! That would feed some families for a week.'

'This is the life,' Rebus said, throwing the Superintendent's words back at him.

'Yes, well said, John. I was in danger of forgetting there can be more to life than personal comfort. Tell me, which church do you attend?'

'Well, well. Come to take us all in, have you?' Both men turned at this new voice. It was Tommy McCall. Rebus checked his watch. Eight thirty. Tommy looked as though he'd been to a few pubs en route to the club. He sat down heavily in what had been Paulette's chair.

'What're you drinking?' He snapped his fingers, and the waiter, a frown on his face, came slowly towards the table.

'Sirs?'

Tommy McCall looked up at him. 'Hello, Simon. Same again for the constabulary, and I'll have the usual.'

Rebus watched the waiter as McCall's words sank in. That's right, son, Rebus thought to himself, we're the police. Now why should that fact frighten you so much?

238

The waiter turned, seeming to read Rebus's mind, and headed stiffly back to the bar.

'So what brings you two here?' McCall was lighting a cigarette, glad to have found some company and ready to make a night of it.

'It was John's idea,' Watson said. 'He wanted to come, so I fixed it with Finlay, then reckoned I might as well come along, too.'

'Quite right.' McCall looked around him. 'Nobody much in tonight though, not yet leastways. The place is usually packed to the gunnels with faces you'd recognise, names you'd know like you know your own. This is tame tonight.'

He had offered round his pack of cigarettes, and Rebus had taken one, which he now lit, inhaling gratefully, regretting it immediately as the smoke mixed with the alcohol fumes in his chest. He needed to think fast and hard. Watson and now McCall: he had planned on dealing with neither.

'By the way, John,' Tommy McCall said, 'thanks for the lift last night.' His tone made the subtext clear to Rebus. 'Sorry if it was any trouble.'

'No trouble, Tommy. Did you sleep well?'

'I never have trouble sleeping.'

'Me neither,' interrupted Farmer Watson. 'The benefits of a clear conscience, eh?'

Tommy turned to Watson. 'Shame you couldn't get to Malcolm Lanyon's party. We had a pretty good time, didn't we, John?'

Tommy smiled across at Rebus, who smiled back. A group at the next table were laughing at some joke, the men drawing on thick cigars, the women playing with their wrist jewellery. McCall leaned across towards them, hoping perhaps to share in the joke, but his shining eyes and uneven smile kept him apart from them.

'Had many tonight, Tommy?' Rebus asked. McCall, hearing his name, turned back to Rebus and Watson.

'One or two,' he said. 'A couple of my trucks didn't deliver on time, drivers on the piss or something. Lost me two big contracts. Drowning my sorrows.'

'I'm sorry to hear that,' Watson said with sincerity. Rebus nodded agreement, but McCall shook his head theatrically.

'It's nothing,' he said. 'I'm thinking of selling the business anyway, retiring while I'm still young. Barbados, Spain, who knows. Buy a little villa.' His eyes narrowed, his voice dropping to a whisper. 'And guess who's interested in buying me out? You'll never guess in a million years. Finlay.'

'Finlay Andrews?'

'The same.' McCall sat back, drew on his cigarette, blinking into the smoke. 'Finlay Andrews.' He leaned forward again confidentially. 'He's got a finger in quite a few pies, you know. It's not just this place. He's got this and that directorship, shares here there and everywhere, you name it.'

'Your drinks.' The waiter's voice had more than a note of disapproval in it. He seemed to want to linger, even after McCall had pitched a ten-pound note onto the tray and waved him away.

'Aye,' McCall continued after the waiter had retreated. 'Fingers in plenty of pies. All strictly above board, mind. You'd have a hellish job proving otherwise.'

'And he wants to buy you out?' Rebus asked.

McCall shrugged. 'He's made a good price. Not a great price, but I won't starve.'

'Your change, sir.' It was the waiter again, his voice cold as a chisel. He held the salver out towards McCall, who stared up at him.

'I didn't want any change,' he explained. 'It was a tip. Still,' he winked at Rebus and Watson, scooping the coins from the tray, 'if you don't want it, son, I suppose I might as well have it back.'

'Thank you, sir.'

Rebus loved this. The waiter was giving McCall every kind of danger signal there was, but McCall was too drunk or too naive to notice. At the same time, Rebus was aware of complications which might be about to result from the presence of Superintendent Watson and Tommy McCall at Finlay's, on the night Finlay's erupted.

There was a sudden commotion from the entrance hall, raised voices, boisterous rather than angry. And Paulette's voice, too, pleading, then remonstrative. Rebus glanced at his watch again. Eight fifty. Right on time.

'What's going on?' Everybody in the bar was interested, and a few had risen from their seats to investigate. The barman pushed a button on the wall beside the optics, then made for the hall. Rebus followed. Just inside the front door Paulette was arguing with several men, dressed in business suits but far the worse for wear. One was telling her that she couldn't refuse him, because he was wearing a tie. Another explained that they were in town for the evening and had heard about the club from someone in a bar.

'Philip, his name was. He told us to say Philip had said it was okay and we could come in.'

'I'm sorry, gentlemen, but this is a *private* club.' The barman was joining in now, but his presence was unwanted.

'Talking to the lady here, pal, okay? All we want is a drink and maybe a wee flutter, isn't that right?'

Rebus watched as two more 'waiters', hard young men with angular faces, came quickly down the stairs from the first floor.

'Now look –'

'Just a wee flutter –'

'In town for the night –'

'I'm sorry –'

'Watch the jacket, pal –'

'Hey! –'

Neil McGrath struck the first blow, catching one of the heavies with a solid right to the gut, doubling the man over. People were gathering in the hallway now, leaving the bar and the restaurant untended. Rebus, still watching the fight, began to move backwards through the crowd, past the door to the bar, past the restaurant, towards the cloakroom, the toilets, the office door, and the door behind that.

'Tony! Is that you?' It had to happen. Tommy McCall had noticed his brother Tony as one of the apparent out-of-town drunks. Tony, his attention diverted, received a blow to the face which sent him flying back against the wall. 'That's my brother you're punching!' Tommy was in there now too, mixing it with the best of them. Constables Neil McGrath and Harry Todd were fit and healthy young men, and they were holding their own. But when they saw Superintendent Watson, they automatically froze, even though he could have no idea who they were. Each was caught with a sickening blow, which woke them to the fact that this was for real. They forgot about Watson and struck out for all they were worth.

Rebus noticed that one of the fighters was hanging back just a little, not really throwing himself into it. He stayed near the door, too, ready to flee when necessary, and he kept glancing towards the back of the hallway, where Rebus stood. Rebus waved an acknowledgment. Detective Constable Brian Holmes did not wave back. Then Rebus turned and faced the door at the end of the hallway, the door to the club's extension. He closed his eyes, screwed up his courage, made a fist of his right hand, and brought it flying up into his own face. Not full strength, some self-protection circuit wouldn't let him do that, but hard. He wondered how people managed to slit their wrists, then

242

opened his watering eyes and checked his nose. There was blood smeared over his top lip, dripping from both nostrils. He let it drip, and hammered on the door.

Nothing. He hammered again. The noise of the fight was at its height now. *Come on, come on.* He pulled a handkerchief from his pocket and held it below his nostrils, catching droplets of brightest crimson. The door was unlocked from within. It opened a couple of inches and eyes peered out at Rebus.

'Yeah?'

Rebus pulled back a little so the man could see the commotion at the front door. The eyes opened wide with surprise, and the man glanced back at Rebus's bloody face before opening the door wider. The man was hefty, not old, but with hair unnaturally thin for his age. As if to compensate for this, he had a copious moustache. Rebus remembered Tracy's description of the man who had followed her the night she'd come to his flat. This man would fit that description.

'We need you out here,' Rebus said. 'Come on.'

The man paused, thinking it over. Rebus thought he was about to close the door again, and was getting ready to kick out with all his might, but the man pulled open the door and stepped out, passing Rebus. Rebus slapped the man's muscular back as he went.

The door was open. Rebus stepped through, sought the key, and locked it behind him. There were bolts top and bottom. He slid the top one across. Let nobody in, he was thinking, and nobody out. Then, and only then, did he look around him. He was at the top of a narrow flight of stairs, concrete, uncarpeted. Maybe Paulette had been right. Maybe the extension wasn't finished after all. It didn't look like it was meant to be part of Finlay's Club though, this staircase. It was too narrow, almost furtive. Slowly, Rebus moved downwards, the heels of his hired shoes making all-too-audible sounds against the steps.

Rebus counted twenty steps, and figured that he was now below the level of the building's lower ground floor, somewhere around cellar level or a bit below that even. Maybe planning restrictions *had* got Finlay Andrews after all. Unable to build up, he had built *down*. The door at the bottom of the stairs looked fairly solid. Again, a utilitarian-looking construction, rather than decorative. It would take a good twenty-pound hammer to break through this door. Rebus tried the handle instead. It turned, and the door opened.

Utter darkness. Rebus shuffled through the door, using what light there was from the top of the stairs to make out what he could. Which was to say, nothing. It looked like he was in some kind of storage area. Some big empty space. Then the lights came on, four rows of strip lights on the ceiling high above him. Their wattage low, they still gave enough illumination to the scene. A small boxing ring stood in the centre of the floor, surrounded by a few dozen stiff-backed chairs. This *was* the place then. The disc jockey had been right.

Calum McCallum had needed all the friends he could get. He had told Rebus all about the rumours he'd heard, rumours of a little club within a club, where the city's increasingly jaded begetters of wealth could place some 'interesting bets'. A bit out of the ordinary, McCallum had said. Yes, like betting on two rent boys, junkies paid handsomely to knock the daylights out of one another and keep quiet about it afterwards. Paid with money and drugs. There was no shortage of either now that the high rollers had spun north.

Hyde's Club. Named after Robert Louis Stevenson's villain, Edward Hyde, the dark side of the human soul. Hyde himself was based on the city's Deacon Brodie, businessman by day, robber by night. Rebus could smell guilt and fear and rank expectation in this large room. Stale cigars and spilt whisky, splashes of sweat. And amongst it all moved Ronnie, and the question which still needed to be answered. Had Ronnie been paid to photograph the influential and the rich – without their knowing they were being snapped, of course? Or had he been freelancing, summoned here only as a punchbag, but stealthy enough to bring a hidden camera with him? The answer was perhaps unimportant. What mattered was that the owner of this place, the puppet-master of all these base desires, had killed Ronnie, had starved him of his fix and then given him some rat poison. Had sent one of his minions along to the squat to make sure it looked like a simple case of an overdose. So they had left the quality powder beside Ronnie. And to muddy the water, they had moved the body downstairs, leaving it in candlelight. Thinking the tableau shockingly effective. But by candlelight they hadn't seen the pentagram on the wall, and they hadn't meant anything by placing the body the way they had.

Rebus had made the mistake of reading too much into the situation, all along. He had blurred the picture himself, seeing connections where there were none, seeing plot and conspiracy where none existed. The real plot was so much bigger, the size of a haystack to his needle.

'Finlay Andrews!' The shout echoed around the room, hanging emptily in air. Rebus hauled himself up into the boxing ring and looked around at the chairs. He could almost see the gleaming, gloating faces of the spectators. The canvas floor of the ring was pockmarked with brown stains, dried blood. It didn't end here, of course. There were also the 'guest bedrooms', the locked doors behind which 'private games' were played. Yes, he could visualise the whole Sodom, held on the third Friday of the month, judging by James Carew's diary. Boys brought back from Calton Hill to service the clients. On a table, in bed, wherever. And Ronnie had perhaps photographed it all. But Andrews had found out that Ronnie had some insurance, some photos stashed away. He couldn't know, of course, that they were next to useless as weapons of blackmail or evidence. All he knew was that they existed.

So Ronnie had died.

Rebus climbed out of the ring and walked past one row of chairs. At the back of the hall, lurking in shadow, were two doors. He listened outside one, then outside the other. No sounds, yet he was sure. . . . He was about to open the door on the left, but something, some instinct, made him choose the right-hand door instead. He paused, turned the handle, pushed.

There was a light switch just inside the door. Rebus found it, and two delicate lamps either side of the bed came on. The bed was against the side wall. There wasn't much else in the room, apart from two large mirrors, one against the wall opposite the bed, and one above the bed. The door clicked shut behind Rebus as he walked over to the bed. Sometimes he had been accused by his superiors of having a vivid imagination. Right now, he shut his imagination out altogether. Stick to the facts, John. The fact of the bed, the fact of the mirrors. The door clicked again. He leapt forwards and yanked at the handle, but it was fast, the door locked tight.

'Shit!' He stood back and kicked out, hitting the belly of the door with the heel of his shoe. The door trembled, but held. His shoe did not, the heel flapping off. Great, bang went his deposit on the dress hire. Hold on though, think it through. Someone had locked the door, therefore someone was down here with him, and the only other place they could have been hiding was the other room, the room next to this. He turned again and studied the mirror opposite the bed.

'Andrews!' he yelled to the mirror. 'Andrews!'

The voice was muffled by the wall, sounding distant, but still lucid.

'Hello, Inspector Rebus. Nice to see you.'

246

Rebus almost smiled, but managed to hide it.

'I wish I could say the same.' He stared into the mirror, visualising Andrews standing directly behind it, watching him. 'A nice idea,' he said, making conversation, needing time to gather his strength and his thoughts. 'People screwing in one room, while everyone else is free to watch through a two-way mirror.'

'Free to watch?' The voice seemed closer. 'No, not free, Inspector. Everything costs.'

'I suppose you set the camera up in there too, did you?'

'Photographed and framed. Framed being quite apt under the circumstances, don't you think?'

'Blackmail.' It was an observation, nothing more.

'Favours merely. Often given without question. But a photograph can be a useful tool when favours are being withheld.'

'That's why James Carew committed suicide?'

'Oh no. That was your doing really, Inspector. James told me you'd recognised him. He thought you might be able to follow your nose from him back to Hyde's.'

'You killed him?'

'*We* killed him, John. Which is a pity. I liked James. He was a good friend.'

'Well, you have lots of friends, don't you?'

There was laughter now, but the voice was level, elegiac almost. 'Yes, I suppose they'd have a job finding a judge to try me, an advocate to prosecute me, fifteen good men and true to stand as jury. They've all been to Hyde's. All of them. Looking for a game with just a little more edge than those played upstairs. I got the idea from a friend in London. He runs a similar establishment, though perhaps with a less sharp edge than Hyde's. There's a lot of new money in Edinburgh, John. Money for all. Would you like money? Would you like a sharper edge to your life? Don't tell me you're happy in your little flat, with your music and your books and your bottles of wine.'

Rebus's face showed surprise. 'Yes, I know quite a bit about you, John. Information is *my* edge.' Andrews' voice fell. 'There's a membership available here if you want it, John. I think maybe you *do* want it. After all, membership has its privileges.'

Rebus leaned his head against the mirror. His voice was a near whisper.

'Your fees are too high.'

'What's that?' Andrews' voice seemed closer than ever, his breathing almost audible. Rebus's voice was still a whisper.

'I said your fees are too high.'

Suddenly, he pulled back an arm, made a fist, and pushed straight through the mirror, shattering it. Another trick from his SAS training. Don't punch *at* something; always punch *through*, even if it's a brick wall you're attacking. Glass splintered around him, digging into the sleeve of his jacket, seeking flesh. His fist uncurled, became a claw. Just through the mirror, he found Andrews' throat, clamped it, and hauled the man forward. Andrews was shrieking. Glass was in his face, flakes of it in his hair, his mouth, prickling his eyes. Rebus held him close, teeth gritted.

'I said,' he hissed, 'your fees are too high.' Then he brought his other hand into a fresh new fist and placed a blow on Andrews' chin, releasing him so that the unconscious figure fell back into the room.

Rebus pulled off the useless shoe and tapped away the shards of glass which still clung around the edges of the frame. Then, carefully, he hauled himself through into the room, went to the door, and opened it.

He saw Tracy immediately. She was standing hesitantly in the middle of the boxing ring, arms hanging by her sides.

'Tracy?' he said.

'She may not hear you, Inspector Rebus. Heroin can do that, you know.'

Rebus watched as Malcolm Lanyon stepped out from the shadows. Behind him were two men. One was tall, well built for a man of his mature years. He had thick black eyebrows and a thick moustache tinged with silver. His eyes were deep-set, his whole face louring. He was the most Calvinist-looking thing Rebus had ever seen. The other man was stouter, less justified in his sinning. His hair was curly but thinning, his face scarred like a knuckle, a labourer's face. He was leering.

Rebus stared at Tracy again. Her eyes were like pinpoints. He went to the ring and climbed in, hugging her to him. Her body was totally compliant, her hair damp with sweat. She might have been a life-sized rag doll for all the impetus in her limbs. But when Rebus held her face so that she had to look back at him, her eyes glimmered, and he felt her body twitch.

'*My* edge,' Lanyon was saying. 'It seems I needed it.' He glanced towards the room where Andrews was lying unconscious. 'Finlay said he could handle you himself. Having seen you last night, I doubted that.' He beckoned to one of the men. 'See if Finlay's going to be all right.' The man headed off. Rebus liked the way the odds were going.

'Would you care to step into my office and talk?' he said.

Lanyon considered this, saw that Rebus was a strong man, but that he had his hands full with the girl. Also, of course, Lanyon had his men, while Rebus was alone. He walked to the ring, grabbed onto a rope, and hauled himself up and in. Now, face to face with Rebus, he saw the cuts on Rebus's arm and hand.

'Nasty,' he said. 'If you don't get those seen to. . . .'

'I might bleed to death?'

'Exactly.'

Rebus looked down at the canvas, where his own blood was making fresh stains beside those of nameless others. 'How many of them died in the ring?' he asked.

'I really don't know. Not many. We're not animals, Inspector Rebus. There may have been the occasional . . . accident. I seldom came to Hyde's. I merely introduced new members into it.'

'So when do they make you a judge?'

Lanyon smiled. 'Not for a considerable time yet. But it *will* happen. I once attended a club similar to Hyde's in London. Actually, that's where I met Saiko.' Rebus's eyes widened. 'Oh yes,' Lanyon said, 'she's a very versatile young woman.'

'I suppose Hyde's has given you and Andrews carte blanche throughout Edinburgh?'

'It has helped with the odd planning application, the odd court case just happening to go the right way, that sort of thing.'

'So what happens now that I know all about it?'

'Ah, well, you needn't worry there. Finlay and I see a long-term future for you in the development of Edinburgh as a great city of commerce and industry.' The guard below chuckled.

'What do you mean?' asked Rebus. He could feel Tracy's body tensing, growing strong again. How long it would last he couldn't know.

'I mean,' Lanyon was saying, 'that you could be preserved in concrete, supporting one of the new orbital roads.'

'You've done that before, have you?' The question was rhetorical; the goon's chuckle had already answered it.

'Once or twice, yes. When there was something that needed clearing away.'

Rebus saw that Tracy's hands were slowly closing into fists. Then the goon who had gone to see Andrews came back.

'Mr Lanyon!' he called. 'I think Mr Andrews is pretty bad!'

Just then, as Lanyon turned from them, Tracy flew from Rebus with a terrifying shriek and swung her fists in a low arc, catching Lanyon with a sickening thump between his legs. He didn't so much fall as deflate, gagging as he went, while Tracy stumbled, the effort having been too great, and fell to the canvas.

Rebus was quick, too. He grabbed Lanyon and pulled him upright, locking his arm behind his back with one hand while the other hand went to his throat. The two heavies made a move towards the ring, but Rebus dug his fingers into Lanyon's flesh just a little deeper, and they hesitated. There was a moment's stalemate before one of them made a dash for the stairs, closely followed by his partner. Rebus was breathing heavily. He released his grip on Lanyon and watched him crumple to the floor. Then, standing in the centre of the ring, he counted softly to ten – referee style – before raising one arm high into the air.

Upstairs, things had quietened down. The staff were tidying themselves up, but held their heads high, having acquitted themselves well. The drunks – Holmes, McCall, McGrath and Todd – had been seen off, and Paulette was smoothing the rumpled atmosphere with offers of free drinks all round. She saw Rebus coming through the door of Hyde's, and froze momentarily, then turned back into the perfect hostess, but with her voice slightly less warm than before, and her smile counterfeit.

'Ah, John.' It was Superintendent Watson, glass still in hand. 'Wasn't that a tussle? Where did you disappear to?'

'Is Tommy McCall around, sir?'

'Somewhere around, yes. Heard the offer of a free drink and headed in the direction of the bar. What have you done to your hand?'

Rebus looked down and saw that his hand was still bleeding in several places.

'Seven years bad luck,' he said. 'Do you have a minute, sir? There's something I'd like to show you. But first I need to phone for an ambulance.'

'But why, for God's sake? The rumpus is over, surely?'

Rebus looked at his superior. 'I wouldn't bet on that, sir,' he said. 'Not even if the chips were on the house.'

Rebus made his way home wearily, not from any real physical tiredness, but because his mind felt abused. The stairwell almost defeated him. He paused on the first floor, outside Mrs Cochrane's door, for what seemed minutes. He tried not to think about Hyde's, about what it meant, what it had been, what emotions it had serviced. But, not consciously thinking of it, bits of it flew around inside his head anyway, little jagged pieces of horror.

Mrs Cochrane's cats wanted out. He could hear them on the other side of the door. A cat-flap would have been the answer, but Mrs Cochrane didn't believe in them. Like leaving your door open to strangers, she had said. Any old moggie could just waltz in.

How true. Somehow, Rebus found that little unwrapped parcel of strength which was necessary to climb the extra flight. He unlocked his door and closed it again behind him. Sanctuary. In the kitchen, he munched on a dry roll while he waited for the kettle to boil.

Watson had listened to his story with mounting unease and disbelief. He had wondered aloud just how many important people were implicated. But then only Andrews and Lanyon could answer that. They'd found some video film as well as an impressive selection of still photographs. Watson's lips had been bloodless, though many of the faces meant nothing to Rebus. Still, a few of them did. Andrews had been right about the judges and the lawyers.

Thankfully, there were no policemen on display. Except one.

Rebus had wanted to clear up a murder, and instead had stumbled into a nest of vipers. He wasn't sure any of it would come to light. Too many reputations would fall. The public's faith in the beliefs and institutions of the city, of the country itself would be shattered. How long would it take to pick up the pieces of *that* broken mirror? Rebus examined his bandaged wrist. How long for the wounds to heal?

He went into the living room, carrying his tea. Tony McCall was seated in a chair, waiting.

'Hello, Tony,' Rebus said.

'Hello, John.'

'Thanks for your help back there.'

'What are friends for?'

Earlier in the day, when Rebus had asked for Tony McCall's help, McCall had broken down.

'I know all about it, John,' he had confessed. 'Tommy took me along there once. It was hideous, and I didn't stick around. But maybe there are pictures of me ... I don't know ... Maybe there are.'

Rebus hadn't needed to ask any more. It had come spilling out like beer from a tap: things bad at home, bit of fun, couldn't tell anyone about it because he didn't know who already knew. Even now he thought it best to keep quiet about it. Rebus had accepted the warning.

'I'm still going ahead,' he had said. 'With you or without. Your choice.'

Tony McCall had agreed to help.

Rebus sat down, placed the tea on the floor, and reached into his pocket for the photograph he had lifted from the files at Hyde's. He threw it in McCall's direction. McCall lifted it, stared at it with fearful eyes.

'You know,' Rebus said, 'Andrews was after Tommy's

haulage company. He'd have had it, too, and at a bargain-basement price.'

'Rotten bastard,' McCall said, tearing the photograph methodically into smaller and smaller pieces.

'Why did you do it, Tony?'

'I told you, John. Tommy took me along. Just a bit of fun –'

'No, I mean why did you break into the squat and plant that powder on Ronnie?'

'Me?' McCall's eyes were wider than ever now, but the look in them was still fear rather than surprise. It was all guesswork, but Rebus knew he was guessing right.

'Come on, Tony. Do you think Finlay Andrews is going to let any names stay secret? He's going down, and he's got no reason to let anyone's head stay above water.'

McCall thought about this. He let the bits of the photograph flutter into the ashtray, then set light to them with a match. They dissolved to blackened ash, and he seemed satisfied.

'Andrews needed a favour. It was always "favours" with him. I think he'd seen *The Godfather* too many times. Pilmuir was my beat, my territory. We'd met through Tommy, so he thought to ask me.'

'And you were happy to oblige.'

'Well, he had the picture, didn't he?'

'There must've been more.'

'Well . . .' McCall paused again, crushed the ash in the ashtray with his forefinger. A fine dust was all that was left. 'Yes, hell, I was happy enough to do it. The guy was a junkie after all, a piece of rubbish. And he was already dead. All I had to do was place a little packet beside him, that's all.'

'You never questioned why?'

'Ask no questions and all that.' He smiled. 'Finlay was offering me membership, you see. Membership of Hyde's. Well, I knew what that meant. I'd be on nodding terms with the big boys, wouldn't I? I even started to dream about career advancement, something I hadn't done in quite some time. Let's face it, John, we're tiny fish in a small pool.'

'And Hyde was offering you the chance to play with the sharks?'

McCall smiled sadly. 'I suppose that was it, yes.'

Rebus sighed. 'Tony, Tony, Tony. Where would it have ended, eh?'

'Probably with you having to call me "sir",' McCall answered, his voice firming up. 'Instead of which, I suppose the trial will see me on the front of the scum sheets. Not quite the kind of fame I was looking for.'

He rose from the chair.

'See you in court,' he said, leaving John Rebus to his flavourless tea and his thoughts.

Rebus slept fitfully, and was awake early. He showered, but without any of his usual vocal accompaniment. He telephoned the hospital, and ascertained that Tracy was fine, and that Finlay Andrews had been patched up with the loss of very little blood. Then he drove to Great London Road, where Malcolm Lanyon was being held for questioning.

Rebus was still officially a non-person, and DS Dick and DC Cooper had been assigned to the interrogation. But Rebus wanted to be close by. He knew the answers to all their questions, knew the sorts of trick Lanyon was capable of pulling. He didn't want the bastard getting away with it because of some technicality.

He went to the canteen first, bought a bacon roll, and, seeing Dick and Cooper seated at a table, went to join them.

'Hello, John,' Dick said, staring into the bottom of a stained coffee mug.

'You lot are early birds,' Rebus noted. 'You must be keen.'

'Farmer Watson wants it out of the way as soon as poss, sooner even.'

'I'll bet he does. Look, I'm going to be around today, if you need me to back up anything.'

'We appreciate that, John,' said Dick, in a voice which told Rebus his offer was as welcome as a dunce's cap.

'Well . . .' Rebus began, but bit off the sentence, and ate his breakfast instead. Dick and Cooper seemed dulled by the enforced early rise. Certainly, they were not the most vivacious of table companions. Rebus finished quickly and rose to his feet.

'Mind if I take a quick look at him?'

'Not at all,' said Dick. 'We'll be there in five minutes.'

Passing through the ground-floor reception area, Rebus almost bumped into Brian Holmes.

'Everyone's after the worm today,' Rebus said. Holmes gave him a puzzled, sleepy look. 'Never mind. I'm off to take a peek at Lanyon-alias-Hyde. Fancy a bit of voyeurism?'

Holmes didn't answer, but fell in stride with Rebus.

'Actually,' Rebus said, 'Lanyon might appreciate that image.' Holmes gave him a more puzzled look yet. Rebus sighed. 'Never mind.'

'Sorry, sir, bit of a late night yesterday.'

'Oh, yes. Thanks for that, by the way.'

'I nearly died when I saw the bloody Farmer staring at the lot of us, him in his undertaker's suit and us pretending to be pissed Dundonians.'

They shared a smile. Okay, the plan had been lame, conceived by Rebus during the course of his fifty-minute drive back from Calum McCallum's cell in Fife. But it had worked. They'd got a result.

'Yes,' Rebus said. 'I thought you looked a bit nervy last night.'

'What do you mean?'

'Well. you were doing your Italian army impression, weren't you? Advancing backwards, and all that.'

Holmes stopped dead, his jaw dropping. 'Is that the thanks I get? We put our careers on the line for you last night, all four of us. You've used me as your gofer – go find this, go check that – as a bit of bloody shoeleather, half the time for jobs that weren't even official, you've had my girlfriend half killed –'

'Now wait just one second –'

'– and all to satisfy your own curiosity. Okay, so there are bad guys behind bars, that's good, but look at the scales. You've got them, the rest of us have got sod all except a few bruises and no bloody soles on our shoes!'

Rebus stared at the floor, almost contrite. The air flew from his nostrils as from a Spanish bull's.

'I forgot,' he said at last. 'I meant to take that bloody suit back this morning. The shoes are ruined. It was you talking about shoeleather that reminded me.'

Then he set off again, along the corridor, towards the cells, leaving Holmes speechless in his wake.

Outside the cell, Lanyon's name had been printed in chalk on a board. Rebus went up to the steel door and pulled aside the shutter, thinking how it reminded him of the shutter on the door of some prohibition club. Give the secret knock and the shutter opened. He peered into the cell, started, and groped for the alarm bell situated beside the door. Holmes, hearing the siren, forgot to be angry and hurt and hurried forward. Rebus was pulling at the edge of the locked door with his fingernails.

'We've got to get in!'

'It's locked, sir.' Holmes was afraid: his superior looked absolutely manic. 'Here they come.'

A uniformed sergeant came at an undignified trot, keys jangling from his chain.

'Quick!'

The lock gave, and Rebus yanked open the door. Inside, Malcolm Lanyon lay slumped on the floor, head resting against the bed. His feet were splayed like a doll's. One hand lay on the floor, some thin nylon wire, like a fishing-line, wrapped around the knuckles, which were blackened. The line was attached to Lanyon's neck in a loop which had embedded itself so far into the flesh that it could hardly be seen. Lanyon's eyes bulged horribly, his swollen tongue obscene against the blood-darkened face. It was like a last macabre gesture, and Rebus watched the tongue protruding towards him, seeming to take it as a personal insult.

He knew it was way too late, but the sergeant loosened the wire anyway and laid the corpse flat on the floor. Holmes was resting his head against the cold metal door, screwing shut his eyes against the parody inside the cell.

'He must've had it hidden on him,' the sergeant said, seeking excuses for the monumental blunder, referring to the wire which he now held in his hands. 'Jesus, what a way to go.'

Rebus was thinking: he's cheated me, he's cheated me. I wouldn't have had the guts to do that, not slowly choke myself. . . . I could never do it, something inside would have stopped me. . . .

'Who's been in here since he was brought in?'

The sergeant stared at Rebus, uncomprehending.

'The usual lot, I suppose. He had a few questions to answer last night when you brought him in.'

'Yes, but *after* that?'

'Well, he had a meal when you lot went. That's about it.'

'Sonofabitch,' growled Rebus, stalking out of the cell and back along the corridor. Holmes, his face white and slick, was a few steps behind, and gaining.

'They're going to bury it, Brian,' Rebus said, his voice an angry vibrato. 'They're going to bury it, I know they are, and there'll be no cross marking the spot, nothing. A junkie died of his own volition. An estate agent committed suicide. Now a lawyer tops himself in a police cell. No connection, no crime committed.'

'But what about Andrews?'

'Where do you think we're headed?'

They arrived at the hospital ward in time to witness the efficiency of the staff in a case of emergency. Rebus hurried forward, pushing his way through. Finlay Andrews, lying on his bed, chest exposed, was being given oxygen while the cardiac apparatus was installed. A doctor held the pads in front of them, then pushed them slowly against Andrews' chest. A moment later, a jolt went through the body. There was no reading from the machine. More oxygen, more electricity. . . . Rebus turned away. He'd seen the script; he knew how the film would end.

'Well?' said Holmes.

'Heart attack.' Rebus's voice was bland. He began to walk away. 'Let's call it that anyway, because that's what the record will say.'

'So what next?' Holmes kept pace with him. He, too, was feeling cheated. Rebus considered the question.

'Probably the photos will disappear. The ones that matter at any rate. And who's left to testify? Testify to what?'

'They've thought of everything.'

'Except one thing, Brian. I know who they are.'

Holmes stopped. 'Will that matter?' he called to his superior's retreating figure. But Rebus just kept walking.

There was a scandal, but it was a small one, soon forgotten. Shuttered rooms in elegant Georgian terraces soon became light again, in a great resurrection of spirit. The deaths of Finlay Andrews and Malcolm Lanyon were reported, and journalists sought what muck and brass they could. Yes, Finlay Andrews had been running a club which was not strictly legitimate in all of its dealings, and yes, Malcolm Lanyon had committed suicide when the authorities had begun to close in on this little empire. No, there were no details of what these 'activities' might have been.

The suicide of local estate agent James Carew was in no way connected to Mr Lanyon's suicide, though it was true the two men were friends. As for Mr Lanyon's connection with Finlay Andrews and his club, well, perhaps we would never know. It was no more than a sad coincidence that Mr Lanyon had been appointed Mr Carew's executor. Still, there were other lawyers, weren't there?

And so it ended, the story petering out, the rumours dying a little less slowly. Rebus was pleased when Tracy announced that Nell Stapleton had found her a job in a cafe/deli near the University Library. One evening, however, having spent some time in the Rutherford Bar, Rebus decided to opt for a takeaway Indian meal before home. In the restaurant, he saw Tracy, Holmes and Nell Stapleton at a corner table, sharing a joke with their meal. He turned and left without ordering.

Back in his flat, he sat at the kitchen table for the umpteenth time, writing a rough draft of his letter of resignation. Somehow, the words failed to put across any of his emotions adequately. He crumpled the paper and tossed it towards the bin. He had been reminded in the restaurant of just how much Hyde's had cost in human terms, and of how little justice there had been. There was a knock at the door. He had hope in his heart as he opened it. Gill Templer stood there, smiling.

In the night, he crept through to the living room, and switched on the desk lamp. It threw light guiltily, like a constable's torch, onto the small filing cabinet beside the stereo. The key was hidden under a corner of the carpet, as secure a hiding place as a granny's mattress. He opened the cabinet and lifted out a slim file, which he carried to his chair, the chair which had for so many months been his bed. There he sat, composed, remembering the day at James Carew's flat. Back then he had been tempted to lift Carew's private diary and keep it for himself. But he had resisted temptation. Not the night at Hyde's though. There, alone in Andrews' office for a moment, he had filched the photograph of Tony McCall. Tony McCall, a friend and colleague with whom, these days, he had nothing in common. Except perhaps a sense of guilt.

He opened the file and took out the photographs. He had taken them along with the one of McCall. Four photographs, lifted at random. He studied the faces again, as he did most nights when he found sleep hard to come by. Faces he recognised. Faces attached to names, and names to handshakes and voices. Important people. Influential people. He'd thought about this a lot. Indeed, he had thought about little else since that night in Hyde's club. He brought out a metal wastepaper bin from beneath the desk, dropped the photographs into it, and lit a match, holding it over the bin, as he had done so many times before.